IR

P9-ELD-989

DISCARD

Westminster Public Library
3705 W 112th Ave
Westminster, CO 80031
www.westminsterlibrary.org

THE
TRUE BASTARDS

THE
TRUE BASTARDS

JONATHAN FRENCH

CROWN
NEW YORK

The True Bastards is a work of fiction. Names, characters, places, and incidents either are the product of the author's imagination or are used fictitiously. Any resemblance to actual persons, living or dead, events, or locales is entirely coincidental.

Copyright © 2019 by Jonathan French

All rights reserved.
Published in the United States by Crown, an imprint of Random House, a division of Penguin Random House LLC, New York.
crownpublishing.com

CROWN and the Crown colophon are registered trademarks of Penguin Random House LLC.

ISBN 978-0-525-57247-3
eISBN 978-0-525-57249-7

Printed in Canada

10 9 8 7 6 5 4 3 2 1

First Edition

Book design by Jen Valero

For Liza, my bride, fearless and fetching.
Thank you for earning a living in your underwear
so I could earn one in mine.

THE
TRUE BASTARDS

ONE

"NYELLOS."

"Nellus."

"No. *Nyellos.*"

". . . Neelus."

"Hard *o* at the end. Like 'open.' *Nyellos.*"

"Neelos."

"Better. But not 'nee.' Quick '*nnn.*' N-yellos."

"Nn . . . nnn . . . n-yell-ose."

"Try not to split the word. The *l*'s roll into the *o*. *Nyellos.*"

". . ."

"Again."

"Nyelos."

"Almost. You need to . . . clip the *l*'s. There is a sound within the sound. *Nyellos.*"

"Nyellos."

"Roll the *l*'s."

"Nyellos."

"But make sure to clip them."

"Nyellos."

"Roll, then clip."

"Nyellos."

"You lost the roll."

"Nyellos."

"You forgot to clip."

"FUCK THIS WITH A HOG'S TWISTED, SHIT-SMEARED COCK!"

Fetching hurled the hunk of rubble with rage-driven arms. The stone smote its fellows resting in the wheelbarrow, upsetting the balance. The load toppled. Mead tried to seize the wheelbarrow handles to prevent it going over, instinctively using both hands. He got hold of the left handle, but the right smashed against his stump as the conveyance tipped. Fetching saw her tutor bite back pain and embarrassment as he floundered away from the small avalanche caused by her anger.

The sounds of labor ceased as all eyes drifted to the disturbance. Fetch barked at the nearest gawkers.

"Bekir, Gosse! Over here and help!" The appointed slopheads sprang at her call, swift and obedient as young hounds. "The rest of you back to it! And be fucking cautious!"

The workers atop the great pile returned their attention to the rubble beneath their feet, shovels tapping gingerly.

Fetch righted the wheelbarrow. As Gosse and Bekir hustled the fallen stone back into its cradle she approached Mead and took a steadying breath. "I'm sorry."

"It's fine, chief," he said without meeting her eyes. His stump was hidden, cradled by his remaining hand. A lie. And she knew it. She also knew it would make the hurt worse if she pressed. He'd told her once that the only thing more painful than losing a hand was forgetting it was gone.

They stood together, silently sweltering. The morning was pale, the sun's heat still abed. It was not the sky above, but the rocks beside, that drew their sweat. Furious at its fall, the ruins of the Kiln still smoldered. Well over a year since the great fortress collapsed and yet the toppled stones continued to weep black smoke into the sky.

The Bastards had tried to harvest usable blocks from the remains of their former home in the first weeks after its demise, but the scorched debris remained hot enough to burn flesh. Months passed before the uppermost layer cooled. Still, gathering the stone remained a dangerous task. The villagers and slops chosen for the day's work detail picked their way along the broken surface of the mound, shifting the occasional stone, slowly loading the wheelbarrows waiting at the base of the rubble. These in turn were taken and emptied into large rope nets to be dragged back to Winsome behind a team of hogs when full.

As she surveyed the crews, Fetch's shoulders and upper back were dripping, itchy beneath her shirt, the linen weighted down by the fall of her braided locks. Cursing, she gathered the plaits in a tighter bundle and retied them higher upon her head. For the hundredth time since becoming chief she considered taking shears to the mass. She wouldn't, unsure why, unsure why she had let it grow in the first place. Perhaps because it marked the days, a living record of her time as hoofmaster. Perhaps she simply liked there being more of her and did not want to willingly return to less.

Either way, in this heat, it was a vanity that was fuck-all irritating.

"Should we continue?" she asked Mead.

"I think we have reached the limit of your patience today, chief."

What Mead really meant was that he had reached his, but Fetch chose not to call him out. Making him give her lessons was abuse enough. In the silence that followed, Mead finally looked up and gave her a pardoning smile.

"Elvish is tricky. But you'll get it."

Fetching nodded, careful not to look away too quickly, but unable to hold Mead's eyes for long.

Shit.

He was still too damned smitten to be a proper taskmaster. The silence was worse than the heat, pointing fingers at the budding discomfort.

Mercifully, Mead shifted first, running his hand through the plumed strip of hair he wore down the center of his otherwise shaved skull. That elvish affectation had once been the source of endless barbs and jibes from the other Bastards, but he had weathered the abuse, wearing the coif of the Tines with the same ease with which he spoke their tongue. Fetching knew how fortunate she was to have him as a sworn brother. He remained as invaluable to his new chief as he had been to the old.

Of course, the Claymaster never had to worry about his men risking a passionate kiss, the poxy cunt.

"Well," Fetch said with a sigh, "I'd best get back to it."

Mead nodded.

Fetch ambled toward the slag, plucking a shovel from the ground on the way.

"Chief?"

She paused, turned back.

"You *are* improving."

She huffed a laugh. "Why? Because I can almost say 'Thank you' to a Tine?"

Mead's face grew hesitant. "*Nyellos* means 'kill.' And only in reference to a male subject."

Fetching scrubbed a dusty hand over her mouth to stifle a scream. "How, exactly, am I improving?"

"This time you managed not to break the wheelbarrow."

The smile he produced was catching.

"Fucking wonderful," Fetching told him, laughing at herself as she approached the hill of debris.

For a long moment, she evaluated the best ascent. All who worked the Kiln's remains had learned to tread the pile as if it were a teeming mass of serpents. Considering the sporadic hisses of steam that issued from between the rocks, it was an easy thing to remember. Not liking any of the immediate approaches, Fetch moved around the edge of the rubble, eventually finding a solid-looking series of larger chunks resting in the sprawl. These she climbed, springing from one to the next until she reached the rough summit of what had once been the outer wall. A stone's throw to her left, a chain of Winsome folk passed pieces of the blasted fortress from hand to hand down the slope. Fetch gave the humans this less-strenuous—and less-perilous—task, leaving her mongrels the duty of searching the ruin, excavating promising pieces, and carrying them to the line.

Deeper into the shattered field, she spotted Abril struggling to shift a large slab with a pry bar. The distance wasn't great, but Fetch took an age to reach him, stepping lightly, using only the toes of her boots.

"You shouldn't be doing that alone, hopeful."

Touro or Petro, or any other senior slop nearing a vote for brotherhood, would have continued to wrestle manfully with the long iron bar, refusing to look weak or incompetent in front of their chief. Not Abril.

"I know," he said, exhaling with relief and ceasing all efforts immediately. "I was working with Sence. We almost had it raised, but then he slipped and . . ." Turning around, he sat on the slab, the shiny arcs of hair hanging in front of his crestfallen face dripping beads of sweat. He rubbed the stone next to his leg reverently. "I guess we can always come here and visit him."

Fetch crossed her arms. "Sence went to get more hands, didn't he?"

Abril continued to fondly stroke the slab. "He did. Left me time to look for the treasure alone."

"There's no treasure, Abril."

He gave her a hopeful look. "My apple rolled under?"

Fetch snorted. That was the least likely tale of all. Setting her shovel down, she gestured for him to stand and hand over the pry bar. For all his buffoonery, Abril was no weakling, possessing the inherent strength and impressive musculature of a half-orc at the threshold of adulthood. Working together, they levered the slab up and slid it to the side, revealing a cache of broken stone of manageable size. Squatting, Fetch splayed a hand and lowered it in stages toward the newly exposed rubble.

"No heat," she said, pleased.

"No apple either," came the disappointed reply from behind.

Rising, she clapped Abril on the shoulder. "Good find, slophead. Let's start moving it to the line."

"Right, chief."

Abril went to set the pry bar aside and a stone slid beneath his heel. He jammed the iron shaft down to keep from falling onto his backside. A reflex.

A rush of escaping air shrieked from where the bar struck.

Fetch was already moving. Diving, she tackled the young mongrel. They both grunted at the impact, and again when they hit the jagged stones. Keeping Abril wrapped tightly in her arms, Fetch rolled as a geyser of jade fire shot upward. They cleared the flames, tumbling apart and scrambling to their knees. Hellish heat forced Fetch's eyes shut and the breath from her lungs. The Al-Unan fire leapt to freedom in a column three times her height. The radiant, emerald blaze had a liquidlike quality, splashing upon the stones and continuing to burn as the column collapsed.

Fetch could hear Abril's strained voice, urging a retreat, but she was unmindful. The fire held her enthralled, this sorcerous substance that had been the downfall of the Kiln and the mad mongrel from whose mind the fortress had sprung. Even as Fetching knelt there, jagged rock digging into her knees, she became aware of sitting upon the Claymaster's tomb, the gout of flame his headstone.

Burn in all the hells, you hateful old fuck.

"Chief! We have to move!"

Rebuking the fire's allure, Fetch began to crab-crawl away, forcing herself to go slowly. It was folly to hurry. Hidden pockets of the dread substance were everywhere, waiting for a rockslide or careless laborer to send it belching forth, eager to consume. The ignition of one made the others restless. The stamp of fleeing feet was likely to rouse them, a lesson that was hard learned.

As Fetch and Abril scuttled away, peals from the warning horns went up. All the workers would be abandoning the pile. Fetch could only hope they remembered not to rush. She could feel her own instinct to run rising, knowing the entire field of rubble could ignite at any moment. At last, they reached the embankment of the fallen wall and made their way down the slope. As soon as their boots touched the dust, Fetch and Abril broke into a sprint, joining the small crowd of anxious faces gathered a thrumshot away from the ruin.

"Anyone hurt?" she enquired, winding her way swiftly through the dozen or so slops and villagers. She was answered with head shakes and muttered assurances. All were pale and drawn from the stress of the ponderous flight, but none were burned.

Mead rode up on his hog, visibly relieved when his eyes fell upon Fetching.

"Any losses?" she demanded.

He shook his head. "Ridden a full circuit. Everyone made it down. No further eruptions, either, far as I can tell."

All good news, but the work for the day, and for weeks to come, was over. The pocket needed to burn itself out. Even if that happened quickly, Fetch would be a fool to order her folk back to this slumbering beast too soon. They needed time, lack of casualties aside. News of the ignition would be carried back to Winsome, where the man who had lost a foot to the fire would be waiting, where the widow of the tanner who had no body left to bury still dwelled with their three children.

"We're done here," Fetch announced. "Mead, tell the others. Let's take what we have."

Mead turned Nyhapsáni's head and spurred the sow away to carry the command.

The mile to Winsome was a long one. They had left for the pile before the sun was up and it was now but midmorning. Of the three teams of hogs brought to haul stone, only one dragged a full net. Fetch walked along with the majority of the work crew, choosing not to ride. The slops needed the time in the saddle.

The village came into view.

Fetch was always struck by how alien Winsome looked enclosed by a stockade. She had grown up here; the vistas of olive groves and vineyards adorning the scrubland on the village borders were the backdrop of all her childhood memories. Now those same vineyards were withered, the groves consumed by locusts, and cut off from the village by a patchwork wall of scavenged timber and salvaged rubble.

The slops serving as sentries saw them coming. The pitiful gate opened. As she entered the confines of the stockade, Fetching rolled her head around atop a stiff neck, soliciting a pop. Hells, she was already tired and the day had just begun.

A scrawny slop came sprinting up the main thoroughfare, bearing a mattock across his shoulders as if it were a yoke. Seeing her, the youth increased his pace.

"Late for digging, Tel?" Fetching called out.

"No, chief," came the response. The little slophead's feet never slowed. "Polecat's pick broke. Sent me for another."

"Faster, then," Fetch encouraged.

The young half-orc obeyed and rushed out the gate.

Fetching turned to her crew. "Slops, go ahead and report to Cat at the ditch. Abril! Don't forget you have patrol."

The older hopefuls, all save Abril, turned and followed after Little Tel. The Winsome men continued on into town. Fetch let them go and sent Mead to oversee the delivery of what stone they gathered to the mason's.

"Get our hogs ready," she ordered Abril.

As the grinning mongrel ran for the stables, she made for the orphanage.

It was quiet inside, but not the exquisite, fragile quiet of sleeping children; this was a silence born from want, from little ones gone too many days without enough to eat. A handful of the younger foundlings were awake, playing numbly together beneath a table. Whatever the game, it had the disturbing look of something done out of habit. There was no laughter, no squeals of delight or even cries of disagreement; it was five morose children, none older than four, simply passing the time. In the surrounding cots, their older companions slept on, keeping the hunger pains at bay with slumber. In Fetch's day, it never would have been this calm. Half-orc children were known for their rowdiness.

Sweeps looked up from some sewing as Fetch entered, putting it aside to rise and meet her at the door.

"Thistle is sleeping," she said in a hush. "One of the babes had her up all night."

Fetching accepted this with a nod, looking the woman over. Sweeps was the walking definition of why mongrels referred to humans as frails. Even in more bountiful times, during the Grey Bastards' days, she was always a willow branch of a girl. Everything about her, from her hair to her limbs, her nose, everything was long and slender.

"And you?" Fetch asked. "Still ailing?"

"No," the woman replied. "Fever broke just before dawn. I'm hale."

That was far from obvious. The fatigue was written beneath Sweeps's eyes in dark smudges.

"I will come back by when Thistle's awake, then."

As Fetching left, the faces of the orphans under the table gazed openly at her, each face a mask of heartbreaking indifference.

She strode to the northern edge of town. Most of the buildings along her way were empty. There had been some chatter of each sworn brother claiming his own house, there were so many left unoccupied. Fetching had squashed that notion before it took root, ordering the Bastards to take up common residence in the vintners' dormitory. She did not need the members of her hoof spread all over town, playing house with their bedwarmers and losing discipline.

Fetch neared what was once the upper outskirts of Winsome. Here, the stockade bulged to encompass a generous patch of flat, open ground. That allotment had stretched their timber to the very limit, but it was vital that their hogs be protected. The sounds and smells of two score barbarians drifted on the breeze. The Bastards' trained mounts were jostling one another at the trough outside the stable, a pair of slops dumping buckets of their namesake over the eager snouts of the noisy animals. These lucky swine knew nothing of rationing and ate more in a day than their minders did in three, but it would be a grave mistake to allow them to weaken. The piglets and twisters were almost as well fed, though they slept rough in the paddock. In the adjacent breaking yard, Dumb Door was astride a strong young sow, hard at the task of accustoming her to a controlling hand on her tusks. It was the greatest challenge in training a barbarian. Hogs hated having their sweeping upper tusks manipulated, especially while on the move.

Leaning against the paddock, Fetch watched Dumb Door lead the animal through a series of turns, slowly increasing the downward pressure on the swine-yankers until the sow was running tight passes along the fence. The former free-rider was a natural at breaking, never losing patience and always knowing just how far to push a hog. Initially, the Bastards took turns training the barbarians, same as they did with the slopheads, but it was soon obvious that none could match Dumb Door's results with the beasts, so Fetching had given him permanent duty over training new mounts.

Seeing his chief waiting, Dumb Door slowed the hog and hopped off, nimble for such a big-boned mongrel. The sow trotted to the far side of the yard, free for the moment.

"That one come from the Tusked Tide?" Fetch inquired, indicating the hog with a lift of her chin.

Dumb Door came up to the fence and nodded.

"She's nearly ready," Fetching commented with no small amount of satisfaction.

Dumb Door held up a pair of calloused fingers.

Fetch hummed in understanding. "Two weeks. Can you make it ten days?" She lowered her voice. "I know you and Mead are itching to put Abril's name up for brotherhood. Be a shame if our new blood didn't have a hog of his own to ride."

Beneath his heavy brow, Dumb Door's eyes shifted upward in contemplation. After a quick weighing of the request, he nodded.

"Good. How are the twisters from the Fangs shaping up? I would love to get more slops on patrol."

A deep sigh issued from Dumb Door, expanding his already prodigious torso. His gaze went to a smaller paddock, where a trio of squealing, bristling terrors was penned separate from the other untrained hogs. Looking back, Dumb Door wrinkled his mouth and his hand came up to rock in the air, palm down.

Fetch let out a frustrated breath of her own. "That's what I thought. Keep at it. But don't get yourself killed. I may try to work one when I get back."

This drew a frown and a shake of the head.

"No need to coddle me, Dumb Door. Have you forgotten what I've been riding?"

As if conjured, Abril approached from the stable, leading a slop mount and Fetch's own saddled hog.

She gave the slophead a nod of approval for his timeliness, and mounted. The barbarian was one of the first gifted to the Bastards by the Fangs of Our Fathers, and the beast remained as savage as his former masters. Chuffing in complaint, the hog bucked, its hind-quarters flailing enough to force Abril a pace or two away. This was an old game, one Fetch always won. Taking hold of both swine-yankers, she wrestled the ornery pig into submission, her legs iron-gripping its belly. There came one final begrudging grunt and the hog settled. Fetching made a point of never naming her mounts, but the Bastards had taken to calling this one Womb Broom: "The only thing keeping the chief's quim free of dust." They thought they were clever. They also thought she didn't know.

She had lived among the hoof too long not to know, and too long not to find the name really damn amusing. Clever imbeciles, her Bastards.

Abril was mounted now too, waiting for her to lead them out.

"Why are you dallying here, slophead?" Fetch demanded. "You have the entire southern run to patrol before dark. That's a good stretch of lot to ride alone. Best get moving."

Abril's face lit with eagerness. "Alone?"

"Try not to die."

"Yes! Chief!"

Abril spurred his hog with gusto, leaving Fetch in an almost disrespectful amount of dust.

Giving Dumb Door a nod and her hog a firm kick, she rode after him.

The slops posted at the gate hauled the doors open. The thin timbers did not look capable of withstanding the force of a charging goat. Winsome had to be further fortified. Dangerous as it was, the Kiln was a resource the Bastards could not afford to ignore.

Shed Snake was just returning from patrol and twisted in the saddle as Abril shot by him with a whoop of pure excitement. Fetch kept a more measured pace and reined up next to Snake in the shadow of the gate.

"Abril's going solo, chief?" he said, pleased.

"You got a report for me, mongrel?" Fetch replied, murdering his smile.

"Clear from here to the Lucia. Of thicks and every other damn thing."

"Still no game?"

Shed Snake scratched idly beneath the half cape he wore over his left arm. The sun irritated the pulpy scars that covered the entirety of that limb, the reminders of a burn he had suffered while working the Kiln's ovens when still a slop. "Not even tracks. Sorry, chief."

The agitation in his voice matched that in Fetch's head.

"Maybe I will have some luck," she told him. "Set up the butts once you're inside. I want the slops on thrum drills."

Snake nodded. "Will do."

As the newest Bastard, sworn only half a year, he was not the best choice to be training the hopefuls, but there were few alternatives.

"And tell Mead he's in charge until I return."

"Chief."

Their hogs parted and Fetch rode a circuit around Winsome, surveying the stockade for signs of weakness. Hells, the whole thing looked made of kindling compared to the former intimidating bulk of the Kiln. Utilizing the blasted stone effectively was slow going. Masonry tools, and men with the knowledge to use them, were in short supply. Most of the town's skilled tradesmen had opted not to return after the downfall of the Claymaster and his fortress. Wood was ever a scarcity in the badlands of Ul-wundulas. Thankfully, free from the need to fuel the ovens of the Kiln, Fetch had managed to secure enough to erect the stockade in her first months as chief. The hoof had lived behind its tenuous protection, sharing space with the people who used to live under their guardianship. Winsome once owed its very existence to the Bastards, its folk able to survive in this pitiless land thanks to the warding presence of the nearby Kiln and its riders. Now, the Kiln was a ruined pile of slag, the Bastards little more than squatters.

But Fetch would be damned if they were going to be idle squatters.

Work on the ditch outside the wall was nearly complete. A rotating crew of slopheads had been slinging dust and unearthing rocks for months. Polecat had agreed to act as overseer. As Fetching rode by, the hatchet-faced brother raised a hand in salute. He was standing above the ditch, filthy from the labor.

"Back to it, you worthless mongrels!" Polecat yelled at the score of slopheads below him. "The chief's watching! You ever want the chance to murder the orc that raped your mother, you'd best impress!"

"Wear them out, Cat!" Fetch replied, playing her part. "I want to see which of them still has strength enough to load a thrum at training. I'll wager not a one!"

Polecat grinned. "My wine ration says you're wrong, chief."

"We'll see," Fetch said, riding on. "I look forward to being drunk tonight!"

As she left the digging behind, Polecat's traditional encouragements could still be heard.

"I have plans for that wine, now! I lose it because you whelps were too weak to dig some long hole in the earth, then I promise tomorrow will be an ass-fucking nightmare! And by that I mean I will bugger each of you with my ungreased c—"

The sound of shovels slicing dirt with renewed vigor drowned out the rest.

Fetching completed her round, noting the spots along the wall that needed Mead's assessment before striking off to the east.

As the badlands of Ul-wundulas spread out before her and the confines of the village receded, Fetch found her breaths coming easier. Some days it was difficult not to shout with relief.

The True Bastards were too few in number to allow any rider exemption from patrolling, but even if they were a hundred strong,

Fetch would take her turn. She would go mad, otherwise. Riding the hoof's lot was the only task that had not changed from rider to chief. Out here, her responsibilities could be counted on one hand with fingers to spare, and a mistake would only cost the lives of her hog and herself. She knew how to spot orc tracks, differentiate the hoofprints of centaurs from those of the cavaleros' horses, how to watch for intruding riders on the horizon, how to remain vigilant for any one of a thousand dangers that Ul-wundulas delighted in summoning. What she did not know was how she was going to keep her hoof safe, fed. She did not know when the Tusked Tide was going to arrive with yet another charitable wagon of supplies, or how she was going to find enough materials to build a proper fortress. Managing Winsome was like trying to hold an egg yolk in one hand. No matter how agile Fetch was, it all just seemed to slide out from between her fingers.

She allowed the patrol to push all other concerns away, Womb's hoofbeats drumming them far from Winsome. Out here the fretting of a hoofmaster was more than useless, it was a detriment. Out here, she needed to be nothing but a rider with two simple pledges.

Live in the saddle. Die on th—

Burning pain lanced through Fetch's gut. Grunting, gnashing her teeth against the sudden agony, she reeled, jerking in the saddle, trying to flee the flaring knife-edge slicing at her insides. She almost kept her seat, but nausea leapt up to dance in her skull. She ate dust, the impact from the hard fall nulled by the whips of fire snapping through her muscles. Throaty moans pushing wetly through her teeth, Fetch curled into a ball atop the spinning earth. But the pain sliced down her spine, settled at the base, and began to chew. Fetch stiffened, convulsed. She needed to cry out, voice a challenge to the pain, but instead of a scream, her lungs filled with a wet weight. Racking coughs joined the uncontrollable jerk of her limbs. Gagging, heaving, tortured chest full of stones, she choked until a warm mass was forced from her throat to land upon her tongue. It was foul-tasting.

And moving.

Fetch lurched to her knees and spit, expelling the wriggling mass.

Through dappled eyes she saw it lying in the dirt, twisting and flopping, surrounded by bright jewels of blood. The size of her thumb and black as jet, the disgorged sludge reflected the bright sun off its oily surface.

Fetch sucked air into her ravaged lungs and croaked out her despair.

"Not again . . ."

TWO

—

IT WAS A MERCY Roundth was dead. He always liked his women with some meat. "Some fun bits I can hold on to and swat with a saddle strap" was the way he used to describe his preference.

Had an orc cutthroat not killed him, seeing Thistle now would have.

The deprivations of the last eight months had been hard on all, but half-orcs weathered hardship with the bestial vitality granted by their thick fathers. Humans were less hardy. Thistle's pleasing plumpness had melted away, stolen by slow hunger, and freely given to the mongrel orphans she allowed to feed at her breast. The woman had served as wet nurse to the foundlings under the Grey Bastards' care for years. If Fetching didn't find a steady supply of food soon, Thistle would not live to serve another season.

Yet even now, poorly as she felt, ghastly as she looked, she gave of herself. There was a mongrel babe on Thistle's depleted tit when Fetch entered her small room.

The woman looked up, half-asleep, but grew alert swiftly, eyes squinting with scrutiny and concern.

"Fetching? You well?"

Damning the keen perceptions of child-raisers, Fetch waved the question away, forcing a smile. "That Cassia?" she whispered, deflecting to the baby.

"Obecco," Thistle corrected with a weak smile.

Fetch's mouth wrinkled. Of course. Not only had she been wrong about the name, she guessed the wrong damn gender. When it came to infants, she was a fool-ass. At least she had managed to divert Thistle's attention.

"This little fellow is easy," the nurse went on. "He can eat and sleep at the same time."

At that moment, Obecco let out a break of wind that would shame a grown hog.

Fetch slapped a hand over her mouth to keep from barking out an earnest laugh.

Unfazed, Thistle gave another languid smile. "He can do that too."

"How are you feeling?" Fetching asked, easing down into a chair beside the bed, mindful that the tulwar hanging from her belt did not clatter.

"I'm well," Thistle answered, lying. As Sweeps had. And Mead.

"The provisions from the Tusked Tide should be here in a day or two," Fetching said, hoping she had not just lied in return.

Thistle only nodded, her head lolling back to rest against the wall. For a moment, Fetching thought she had fallen asleep. She tensed to rise, but Thistle's voice stopped her.

"When they get here, you need to ask them for something. For the next delivery."

"What?"

"Another wet nurse."

Fetch gave an admonishing hiss. "Don't say that. You are—"

"Not going anywhere," Thistle cut in, "but my milk is. I'm drying up, Fetch. Barely have enough for the three sucklings left. We get another babe dropped with us . . ."

"That's not likely," Fetch said. "Winsome is walled off now."

Thistle opened her eyes and managed a dubious squint. "Did that stop this little bag of gas from getting in? Or the other two?"

Fetching gave a conciliatory shrug. Thistle was right. Of the three babes they had now, two of them had been left outside the gate. The other had been foisted onto Polecat while he was on patrol. It was hoof code to take in all half-orc children, but Fetch could only hope Cat had not demanded something selfish from the desperate woman before accepting her unwanted get.

Last spring, the orcs had attempted another Incursion. It had been crushed before it really began, in no small part thanks to the Bastards, but the thicks had made it just north of the Hisparthan border before being repelled. Reports claimed they were all slain, but the crop of half-breeds now appearing contradicted the bravado. There were always orcs in the Lots, which meant there were always women who survived their brutality.

"And what about the ones that the wall does stop?" Thistle continued, her question pained. "The women discouraged because there is no longer a clear path to the orphanage door? What do you think happens to those babes?"

Fetch hardened her jaw. "Nothing that hasn't happened to cast-off mongrel babes since the first orc raped a frail, Thistle."

"It didn't happen to you," the woman said firmly. "Or Mead. Or Cat, or Hood, or any other half-orc that ever survived to be a slop. Foundlings are the future of a hoof. You know that. The babes, the lucky ones, they are going to keep coming. You shouldn't want that to ever stop. I don't want that to ever stop." Thistle's eyes were bright now. "But I'm not going to be able to feed them, Fetching. I will be here to hold them, and change them, and wash them, but not . . . feed them."

The tears never came, the voice did not break, but the sorrow of that admission filled the room.

Fetch took a deep breath. "We have a few goats. I can see if the Tide will—"

"No."

Thistle had said it quietly, yet the force of that denial, the anger in it, disturbed the suckling infant. Obecco whimpered, seemed to wake, but a single touch on the head from his nurse eased him back to sleep.

"No," Thistle repeated, shifting the iron from her voice to the stare she leveled. "Goats can serve in need, if it comes to that. But these children need a wet nurse. Beryl left the orphanage in my care. She would come back in a fury to know I'd stooped to using a nanny. Do you think she ever fed you from a goat?"

Fetching almost missed it, the one small revelation in that challenging question.

"Me?"

Effortlessly, Thistle switched the baby to her other breast without waking him. "You didn't know?"

Fetch felt her own head shaking. It was the same small, uncomfortable motion she did to shake off a punch. "Beryl was never . . . fond of me, when I was here."

"Maybe once you were walking, talking. But as babes, she loved you all. Plain to see, when she talked about it. Impossible not to love the ones you've given suckle."

Fetching stood, feeling the same need to flee she'd felt at the Kiln ruins. "You need to rest."

"A wet nurse," Thistle reminded.

"I'll find one."

Dusk was yielding to night beyond the orphanage door. Fetch's patrol had lasted longer than intended. Womb Broom was not a hog to linger when his rider took a fall. Thankfully, that same wild nature kept him from returning to town and they had been out of sight of the walls. A small mercy. She had been a long time gaining her feet and even longer tracking the unruly pig down. Her late return was met with some anxiousness from Mead. A tale about deer tracks leading her far afield settled his creased brow.

Abril had been more fortunate on the southern patrol. A chance sighting of an actual farrow deer, the first in months, led to a long chase, a chase the slophead was unwilling to give up before putting a thrumbolt in the animal's heart. The smell of the meat had turned out all of Winsome, the folk gathered around a cook pit tended by the five senior slops. A beaming Abril oversaw his comrades, reveling in his role of heroic provider.

It had been a stroke of rare luck, that deer, but, like all fortunes, the weight of it risked breaking the recipients. More than one hundred pairs of eyes were fixed, unblinking, on the preparations. Anticipation of the largesse was palpable, mixing with the aromas of stewed venison and sizzling offal. To guard against a rush, Polecat, Dumb Door, Shed Snake, and the thirteen younger hopefuls surrounded the fire. It was a naked display of distrust between the hoof and Winsome's folk, but better to be rude than foolish.

Fetching approached, winding her way through the crowd. Most of them were blind to her presence, the spell of the impending food unbreakable. Only when she was standing directly in front of the hanging pot, blocking its view from most, did the gazes grudgingly shift.

"The chief's got words!" Polecat announced.

Fetching raised her voice to force the attention of the few still trying to peer through her body. "I know your guts are growling. I know your mouths water. That's about to be satisfied thanks to our bounding friend that ran Abril halfway up Batayat Hill. She's in the pot now, and soon, she will be in your bellies. But let me be clear. The first portions are going in there." Without looking, Fetch extended her arm and pointed at the orphanage door. "After that, your own children. After that, you. That is how it's going to go. No need for it to go any other way. Any harder way."

Fetch let the promise of that last statement hang for a moment.

"Now get your little ones arranged. Youngest to oldest, and line them up."

Parents quickly took to the command, herding their children up front with words and guiding hands. As the crowd shuffled, it was easy to pick out the selfish and petty among the adults; the big man who planted himself behind the children, the old woman who pretended not to see anyone else and used her frailty to bully. Fetch tried to ignore them, but she found her memory marking the faces all the same.

"We are done, chief," Sence's voice informed.

A year ago, Fetching would not have been able to accurately name a single slophead. It was hoof tradition to keep a callous distance from the hopefuls, except when training and then any attention was purposefully harsh. Things had changed a great deal in recent months. The chief of the True Bastards not only knew every slop's name but could recognize their voices without turning.

"Take the orphans their share," Fetching said, still watching the villagers.

Movement behind her signaled the slops jumping to the task. Once they returned, Fetch stepped aside and gestured for the village children to approach. The adults came next, those near the back of the line growing nervy as the wait extended. The children had already hunkered down within steps of the cook fire, slurping at stew that was still too hot to eat, but an empty stomach ignored a scalded tongue. Fetch had ordered the meal be prepared out here in hopes the chance of additional helpings would prevent the villagers from returning to their homes to eat. That seemed to be working, and Fetch relaxed a little. At least she did not have to worry about parents stealing from the mouths of their own children. It may have been an unworthy thought. The people of Winsome had never given her cause to believe them capable of such deeds, but hard times had a way of bringing out the worst instincts.

A shout from the gatehouse snapped Fetch away from her grim thoughts.

"RIDERS APPROACHING!"

Mead's voice.

"Keep this in hand," Fetch told Polecat before running down the main thoroughfare. She sent a wish into the darkening sky that the Tusked Tide had arrived.

Uidal and Bekir were already hauling the gate open when she sprinted up. Hopes of fresh supplies were dashed when Hoodwink rode through the widening gap. Coming in behind him was a small mongrel Fetching knew well. She fixed Hoodwink with a scowl.

Hood shrugged one pale, scar-crossed shoulder. "You said I could not kill him."

"Doesn't mean I won't," Fetching said, glaring at Slivers before motioning for Hood to dismount and follow. He did not move. His dead eyes stared, flashing briefly, alerted by the same clues Thistle had seen. Unlike her, he knew the cause.

Fetch gave him a warning look, resisted looking around. Without breaking that hunter's gaze, the gaze that missed nothing, Hoodwink dismounted and kept his colorless lips tight as he retrieved a sizable sack from his saddlebag. They walked a distance away from the gatehouse, and the nervously grinning nomad, so they would not be overheard. Fetch regarded the cadaverous face of her returned rider and waited.

"No signs of thicks," Hoodwink reported, his voice always reminding Fetch of a tanner's blade scraping a skin. "From our lot to Kalbarca and back. Nothing."

His arm flicked and the sack traversed the small space between them. Fetching caught it, her fingers closing around the bulging canvas, crunchy with coins. She clenched her teeth against the question, but it wriggled free all the same.

"How is he?"

The answer was simple, made her feel simple for asking. "He's Oats."

Fetch nodded, gazing at the bag of coins. "Next time, I'll go." It was a false promise, as always. She looked up and changed the subject. "Any game?"

"Rabbits. None in the last day."

"Horse-cocks?"

Hoodwink shook his hairless head.

"It's happened again," he said.

Fetch gave a disgusted groan. She had hoped he would leave it alone. Instead, he pressed.

"Have you been back?"

Fetch shook her head. "Just happened."

"I will take you."

"Can't spare a five-day ride, Hood."

"Death is longer."

"And you know what to do if it comes to that," she snapped, voice still lowered.

Hoodwink's response was an unblinking stare that somehow reeked of disapproval.

"I will go," she assured him. "Tomorrow. I will go."

"And the draught?"

"Haven't needed it in months."

More pointed silence. Fetch had to look away. Hood's hollow death mask of a face was often harder to endure than the noon sun.

"I have some left," she admitted. "I will take it."

Hood showed his satisfaction by blinking. Once.

Eager to be back in control and to return to the matter at hand, Fetch stepped around him and returned to the gate. The unwelcome arrival had dismounted. Fetch got right in his face.

"You were told not to return here."

Slivers recoiled from her growl, but less than usual. Like most frailings, he was smaller than other half-orcs, and shrank away from Fetch's greater height to hold up placating hands.

"I know, chief—"

"Don't call me that."

Slivers flinched. "Pardon. Just showing respect."

"Don't try to charm me, nomad. Giving respect won't earn you any. Not here. Now mount up and get gone."

"I could be useful, given half a chance," he whined.

"Half a chance?" Fetching could only laugh. "You had your chance during the last Betrayer. But I heard you showed your hog's ass rather than charge the 'taurs. You had another chance when the orcs marched and the Bastards rode to face them. Again, you chose to flee. If you wanted to ride with this hoof, then you should have *ridden* with this hoof."

The nomad's protests were endless. And gratingly familiar. "I spotted the first *ul'usuun*, coming through the Rutters' lot. I rode back with the news. I helped see your folk safely to the Wallow when the Tusked Tide took them in. That should count for something!"

"Being a lookout and an escort counts for shit if you won't fight, Slivers. The True Bastards were born on the day we charged that orc tongue. We found out who we were in that mass of thicks. We found out who could be counted, could be trusted. Dumb Door became one of us. Gripper is counted among our fallen. Your fellow nomads, Slivers. Where the fuck were you?"

He had no answer and she gave him no time to think of one.

"You squandered your chances. Showed who you are. And it is not one of us. You are a stray dog. And I will not take food out of the mouths of my people to feed a stray dog."

Slivers found his voice, high and desperate. "Do you know what they're doing to free-riders out there?"

Fetch knew. She turned, calling to Uidal and Bekir. "Open the gate! This one is riding on." She went to Hoodwink. "Make sure he leaves our lot."

The deep-set serpent's eyes in Hood's skull glinted a question.

"Alive," Fetch told him.

Hoodwink slid past her without further expression to carry out the orders.

Mead took his place, looking troubled. "You sure about this?" His gaze shifted to the departing hogs. "Slivers is a seasoned rider."

"He's a fucking weathervane," Fetch said. "I need mongrels that will not only ride with this hoof, but stand with it too. A mongrel that goes with the fairest wind is worth less than nothing here. There are no fair winds blowing up the Bastards' cracks these days, Mead. I shouldn't have to explain that to you."

"You don't, chief."

They both watched as the gate closed once more.

"I'm riding for Rhecia's in the morning," Fetch said. "Need to find a new wet nurse."

"I'll be ready."

"No. I need you here."

"You shouldn't ride alone."

"No choice. Door's got hogs to break. Shed Snake will have to shoulder my patrols. And you know I can't take Polecat."

"Then wait for Hood to get back or at least take some of the older slops."

"Not about to lose any of our hopefuls to the scent of whores, Mead." She ignored his point about Hoodwink, hoped he'd forget. Fool-ass hope that was.

"Hood will be back—"

"Hoodwink won't be back before I am," she said, and left it at that. Mead's frown deepened, but he knew better than to ask after any task the chief gave Hood. It was the one thing Fetch had inherited from the Claymaster that was worth a damn.

Eager for her bed and an end to the discussion, she walked away.

She had taken the head grover's house for her solar. The smell of olive oil greeted her as she pushed through the door. The cadre of aromas that accompanied a hoof rider could not seem to find a foothold in these rooms. Saddle leather, sweat, weapon oil, none of them kept the field against the entrenched occupation of the long-absent olive grower. Not bothering to light a lamp, Fetch felt her way to the stairs and up. The foreman had built a portico onto the upper story, thrusting out from his bedroom. It had once provided an unobstructed view of Winsome's olive groves. The stockade now interfered with that purpose, but Fetch still found the vantage useful for overlooking the town she had enclosed.

Dropping her sword belt and thrum on the bed, along with the sack of coins, she stepped out onto the balcony. The cook fire had begun to die down, tended only by a trio of slopheads stuck with the clearing up. A few villagers loitered about, those nurturing a desire that another secret cache of food was about to be brought forth. Across the main thoroughfare, Polecat and Dumb Door sat upon the roof of the cooper's shop. Once, they might have passed a bottle between them, but the wine stores had dwindled, were now tightly rationed. Fetch's throat craved a drink, but she refused to keep a private stock. The tanner's widow appeared, briefly joining the riders before she and Polecat slunk off together, no doubt to fuck. The thought caused a low, momentary stirring in Fetching that was quickly chased off by fatigue, the aches of the day, and a rattling in the depths of her lungs.

She hated lying to Mead. He was right, of course. It was foolhardy for anyone to ride alone in the Lots, but she didn't have a choice.

Going to the chest at the foot of her bed, she rummaged around until she unearthed a ceramic bottle, hideously made. She shook the contents, felt them slosh thickly at the bottom. Pulling the stopper, she made a face and tossed back a mouthful. The foul stuff attempted to come right back up. Fetch fought its resurgence. She reckoned hog spend tasted better than this sour shit. Certainly shared a consistency. Slamming the stopper back, banishing the drifting smell of the draught, Fetch sunk onto the bed and lay down beside a scatter of weapons.

She groaned. Her boots were still on.

THREE

—

AT THE WINSOME FORD, Fetch guided Womb Broom halfway across the river and stopped.

"Far as you go," she told her escort.

Mead had insisted the chief be accompanied to the edge of the lot. Himself, of course, plus the three most experienced slops—Touro, Abril, and Petro. They each displayed their own unique expressions of disappointment.

"Get on back. And be careful."

She urged her hog on, but the sounds of following splashes caused her to halt again. Twisting around in the saddle she found Abril on her heels.

"The fuck are you doing, slophead?"

Abril's eyebrows shot up with the same speed that his jaw dropped. "Oh! You meant all of us? I thought you meant only *they* should go home." He cocked a thumb at the others, all glowering. Abril stood in his stirrups and leaned over his saddle horn, his voice dropping to a whisper that could still be heard over the crossing's current. "Remember, chief? You said that since I felled that deer and fed the entire town, you would take me to Rhecia's and pay for my first wet end."

"I never said that, Abril."

The young mongrel gave her a dubious squint. "Are you certain?"

"As certain as I am that if you don't get out of my sight I'm going to put a bolt in you and you can feed the entire town a second time."

Abril took a moment to ponder that with a slow, repetitive nod before rejoining the others. As a group, they turned their hogs south, Mead's parting look lingering the longest. Fetch watched them go, waiting until they were claimed by the heat phantoms on the horizon before she finished the crossing and climbed weak-legged from the saddle.

Shaking hands gripping her knees, stomach muscles heaving in violent spasms, she retched. The sludge was forced out in a sluggish, painful rope. The foulness fell from her mouth, and she stumbled away from it in disgust. Trembling, she reached into her saddlebag for the bottle and downed the last measure of the draught, which stung as it slid down her raw throat.

She used the rage over her own weakness to crawl back atop her hog. There was no time to waste. If she waited to feel hale enough to ride, she would be here forever. Fetch spurred Womb forward. And set her will to being alive when she reached her destination.

Were she headed directly for Rhecia's, as her hoof believed, the quickest route was a narrow stretch of Crown land running almost due north between the Tines' lot to the east and the Amphora Mountains to the west. But it was the mountains for which Fetch was truly bound. They were a low range, not yet intruding on the horizon. Above, the sun slouched in the afternoon sky. Fetch was hard-pressed, but managed to reach the foothills by nightfall. Though far from the Lots' most imposing mountains, the southern slopes of the Amphoras were their most unforgiving face. To enter the range, Fetch would first need to cross through using a pass she knew and come at the slopes from the more traversable north. But that was tomorrow's task.

Putting her back to the darkening peaks, Fetch backtracked until she struck a stream. Dismounting, she allowed Womb to drink while she walked a short distance to a stand of almond trees. A vigorous shake of the lower limbs brought a cascade of hulls, summoning the eagerly snuffling hog. Fetch unsaddled the beast while he ate, and prepared a mean camp. Sitting, she shelled a handful of almonds, but found she had no appetite.

Sleep proved a nervous visitor and was often chased away by the barking of her savage coughs.

Hoodwink was standing nearby at night's end, his sinewy form flanked by the rising sun.

The region was known for wolves and Fetch had kept her stock-bow loaded beneath a resting hand. Only Hood could have intruded upon her camp without taking a bolt.

"Creepy fuck," she greeted him, face scrunched with bleariness and annoyance.

As she sat up, a bundle of cherries fell upon her lap.

"Not hungry."

"Doesn't matter. Eat."

Plucking a cherry with a vengeance and popping it into her disinterested mouth, Fetch got to her feet.

"Time to move."

They rode for the deeper shadows of the pass and were through before the sun rose high enough to find them again. At the other end, they went slower, wary. These lands were just east of the castile and belonged to the Crown, retained due to the sea of olive trees that grew effortlessly in the marches above the Amphora Mountains. The plantations of the old emperors had been so vast, the crops continued to thrive. The villas were long crumbled, the slaves that worked them nothing but the near-forgotten ancestors of Hispartha, the names of their Imperial masters known only to decaying scholars despite all the statues raised to their own vanity. But the olives remained, worth more than any damn monument, to Fetch's thinking. You couldn't eat marble.

Fetch followed Hood through valleys that were leagues-long groves, bitter that these trees were untouched by the blight that destroyed Winsome's. But even the bounty of the Old Imperium had limits. By the time they reached the assailable north-thrusting edge of the Amphoras, the olive trees were bullied away by choking forests of oleander. Only a place as harsh as Ul-wundulas mated prosperity with poison. The thin, twisted trunks of the harmful plants grew upward until they leaned and entwined together, the fingers of a plotting man. Riding within the gnarled tunnels, ducking her head, Fetch kept a careful eye on Womb Broom, making sure he did not attempt to forage while among the oleander. The hoofs called it hogbane with good reason. At least they were safe now from cavalero patrols. The frails had no interest beyond the olives. From here on, the land was a wilderness of thorns and creeping juniper.

The sun beat at them as they ascended the barren slopes of the Amphoras. Hoodwink pulled a cowl over his bald, linen-colored head. They spent the day climbing higher, Hood guiding them along shallowly ascending trails that did not tax the hogs. The air cooled and the wind grew spirited.

Eventually, they crested a long ridgeline and rode westward along its spine. The ground became littered with fragmented rock as they progressed, and soon they traversed a wasteland of broken stone. Slopes and seams molded the rubble until the vistas were lost. They were nestled within a pockmark of the mountain, but not one formed by the slow crawl of time, one burrowed by the suffering labor of many hands. Like the olive groves, this was a vestige of the Imperium. A quarry, worked for centuries and abandoned for far longer. Unlike the olive trees, stone produced nothing when neglected, becoming naught but a calcified wound.

Fetch and Hood dismounted, began leading their hogs over the scrabble of loose stones, picking their way down the side of a crease to a relatively flat stretch. Fetch had come here once before with the same guide and had been confounded then by the bleak, seemingly endless splay of debris. Everything looked the same. This return trip did nothing to help her bearings. But Hood knew his way, then as now, gliding across the tumbles without pause.

At last, they spied a variation in the striated grey.

Ahead, a wooden pole, half again as tall as a man, thrust up from the rocks, its base surrounded by loose stones. Atop was affixed a wheel, the same that would be found on any oxcart, but here, in this place, its appearance was horribly strange. Seated upon the wheel, revolving slowly at the whims of the wind, was a figure. To call it a man was generous to the point of fallacy. Painfully thin and naked, skin both cured by the sun and blanched by rock dust. Hair and beard, vulgarly matted, brittle and dry, blew stiffly in the gusts. Small, desiccated black turds littered the rocks beneath the wheel, waste from a body that had nothing left to rid. A cracked, hollow voice drifted down from the perch, mumblings made unintelligible by thirst, weakness, madness.

Behind this living, totemic scarecrow, a passageway yawned in the side of a rubble hill. A narrow, low lintel of stacked stone, held up by nothing but skilled balance. Or fuck-crazy faith.

The wheel creaked as Fetch and Hood passed beneath, the inhabiting loon issuing his tortured, throaty nothings. They were a child's toss of a stone away from the lintel when the Bone Smiler ducked through.

For the second time in her life, Fetch laid eyes upon the man, and for the second time she was convinced he was the frail that fathered Hoodwink. Parchment skin pulled tight and thin over a bald skull, sockets sunk deep, cheekbones that could cut. Tall and lean, movements fluid and predatory. He was older, though hard to give a number to his years for he was nimble, his eyes clear and clever. Not well-muscled, but then he was a human; the most formidable often wasted down after middle age. Still, picture him getting a mongrel girl with child and the mind's eye conjured Hood, though he possessed one mannerism never seen on Hoodwink's face.

The Bone Smiler smiled. And it was hideous to behold.

His teeth were false, carved. The individual teeth were too large. When exposed beneath his straining lips, they transformed the entire mouth into a chilling rictus. Whatever bones were used, they must have been from multiple remains of various ages, the colors of each tooth forming a patchwork of every shade from white to black, gruesome browns being the most common. Despite the horselike size of the teeth, the entire construction was ill-fitting, sliding and shifting as the man spoke. He had to work his lips in exaggerated patterns to accommodate the unsightly, clicking mass behind them, all the while sucking and slurping to keep it in place.

"Chief of the True *slup* Bastards. Back to visit *sslk*."

Behind, the man on the wheel loosed a protracted moan.

The Bone Smiler's hand drifted behind the lintel and there came the sound of sloshing water. His hand reappeared grasping a thin rod, a dripping rag attached to the end. He walked past Fetch and Hood, stopped a few strides from the perch, and extended the rod, holding the rag up to the wretch's face. It was ignored, but the Bone Smiler stood patiently for a long while, moving the rod to match the motion of the wheel so that it remained hovering before the mad-man's lips. But he never drank.

At last, the Bone Smiler lowered his arms. "Later, perhaps."

Turning, he regarded his visitors for a moment.

"Same complaints? *Ssst*."

Fetch considered. Nodded.

"Liar. They *clik* are worse." He stepped beyond them again. "Come inside. *Schlup*. Weapons remain without."

Ducking through the hole, he vanished. Taking a long breath, Fetch unslung her thrum, unbuckled her sword belt, and handed both to Hood. He pointed down at her boot. Shaking her head, she removed the dagger, handed it over. She tried to bury her trepida-tion, failed, and followed the man into the dark.

The single-chambered grotto was as close and uninviting as be-fore. Worse, even, because it was no longer a fresh mystery. A high, ancient wooden table dominated the center, backed and flanked by dilapidated cupboards. The only light was that which dared enter through the opening, but the Bone Smiler was already touching a taper to numerous tallow candles set about the room. The tepid flames revealed his low cot, single stool, and the plethora of herbs and instruments hanging batlike from the intrusive ceiling.

Fetch stood in front of the table, trying to stay out of the man's way as he moved about the confines. He retrieved a wide-mouthed glass vessel from a cupboard and handed it to Fetch on the move. Last time, this had caused some confusion and no small amount of curse-infused challenges when the explanation came. Now, however, she was less ignorant, though no less discomfited.

Unlacing her breeches one-handed, she worked them down past her knees, squatted slightly, and positioned the vessel. The Bone Smiler went about his preparations, neither ignoring nor heeding Fetch as she pissed. When finished, she set it upon the table and it had barely touched down before being taken up again. The Bone Smiler maneuvered behind the table, squeezed into the space between it and the cupboards. Fetch began to pull her breeches up.

"Leave them."

She stood there, feeling a fool with her bare ass exposed. As the Bone Smiler worked, she avoided looking in his direction, remembering her revulsion upon her first visit when the man tasted her water.

He was busy for some time, and Fetch heard a bubbling hiss, no doubt the result of him mixing one of numerous powders into the urine flask.

"Up on the *hithhht* table."

She hopped up, breeches still sagging at her ankles, and grit her teeth as he opened a vein in her arm with a small blade. He watched her blood flow into a shallow pewter basin with rapt attention, face so close, his nose was in danger of being dipped in crimson. Giving over a linen bandage for her to stanch the bleeding, he returned to his cupboards.

At last, he turned, his eyes fixed somewhere between the edge of the table and the floor.

"Tell me how this began. *Clop*."

"I told you bef—"

"Tell me!" The Bone Smiler raised a forestalling hand. "Again."

Fetch took a breath, delving deep for patience. "The Sludge Man attacked our hoof. He wanted me, for my elven blood. Some kind of sacrifice to heal the Old Maiden Marsh. He was . . . fucking unstoppable." Fetch found herself staring at a scar on her inner forearm. There was another on her shoulder, difficult for her to see, but she reached up and felt along its raised length. Both had been made by

Crafty's hand. Three more adorned her thigh. She could see them now on her exposed leg. Those she had done herself. They were far from her only scars, but they were the only wounds that were also wards.

"There was a wizard with us. He said my blood would protect me from the Sludge Man's touch."

"*Sssp*. His touch?"

"The sludge," Fetch said. "It made you fall unconscious."

The Bone Smiler grunted. "A soporific. Proceed."

"Crafty . . . the wizard, was right. He cut me. I went into the sludge, dragged that fucking bog-sucker out, threw him in a furnace, and now he's dead. Don't know what else I can tell you."

The Bone Smiler pondered in the silence that followed. He peered down at the scars on her thigh, inspected them deftly with his fingers. "The cuts allowed the sludge entry. To take *clop* root. How long ago? Precisely?"

Fetch thought. "Nearly sixteen months."

"How long before you took *clik* ill?"

"Four months . . . I think."

"Think?"

"That was the first fit. First time I hacked up any of that shit."

"*Sssk*. But you felt weak prior?"

Fetch nodded, hating the admission.

"Through what other avenues has it been expulsed?"

"Huh?"

"*Glot*. Have you shit it out? Pissed it? Has it come through the nose?"

Fetch felt a pang of panic. "Hells no! Will that happen?"

The Bone Smiler did not answer, his long fingers coming up to rub at his taut brow. "What about your womb's blood? Last *slup* you were here, you had not had a flow since the attack."

That was true, but not alarming. Unlike their male counterparts, female half-orcs were not sterile, but neither were they overly fertile. Fetch had gone years without bleeding and then, sometimes, it would occur a few months in a row. Beryl had taught her and Cissy that it would remain unpredictable until it vanished entirely.

"I've bled once since I was last here," she said. "Two months back. There was nothing."

The man nodded, thinking. "It comes from your lungs. The stomach *clop*. But worse now. How?"

"I . . . can't breathe. I can feel it lurking, pooling. It's always threatening to come up. When it does, it's suffocating. Feels like I'm going to die before I can choke it out."

"Very well. Lay back."

The Bone Smiler was thorough in his examination, especially in his scrutiny of Fetch's eyes and joints. She suffered the discomforts of his probing hands as she had before, willing herself not to lash out with each pawing. When he was done, he returned to his cupboards. She leaned against the edge of the table, sharing the cramped space with the reclusive apothecary. He faced her, his gaunt face blank.

"The draught I last made for you was a cast of the dice. I was *shup* surprised to see you still living."

Fetch could only bark a grim laugh. "I was about to say the same about your friend outside."

The man smiled, making her regret being amusing.

"He was here long before me. I am merely a tenant of this hermitage now that he forever shuns shelter. *Clut.* He falls, sometimes. But like a bird. Weighs hardly enough for the fall to cause harm. Bones so thin he practically drifts. It will go wrong one day. Broken neck or cracked skull will end his search for whatever truths he seeks. *Sssslk.*"

"And what about my search. Is there a fucking cure?"

The Bone Smiler actually looked regretful. "I am no wizard. Perhaps the one that cut you could help."

"No. He can't."

"Strava, then. It is said the high priest of Belico—"

"No!" She spat the word this time. She had seen the results of bargains struck with Zirko and his god, and wanted no part in such a pact. "Is there nothing your medicines can do?"

The bulging mouth of the apothecary clenched. He looked disturbed as he thought.

"There is something," Fetch declared.

The Bone Smiler went to his cupboards, slowly, gravely. From the very back he withdrew a small bottle, hardly larger than his thumb. The ceramic was stained a pale, unwholesome red. When Fetch was growing up, there had been a Grey Bastard named Creep. Sometimes, when he would visit Winsome, he would entertain the orphans by finding a pair of scorpions and coaxing them to fight. Seeing the way the Bone Smiler held that bottle, she was reminded of how Creep handled the scorpions. Comfortably, yet cautiously.

"Kinnabar," he said, addressing the bottle in his hand, cursing it. "In the mines of Hispartha, men die in droves to dig it from the earth. The Imperium valued it higher than life, just so the wives of emperors could paint their faces. *Sssslk*. Refined to quicksilver, it is prized by alchemists all the way to Tyrkania, believing it can mate with worthless metals and birth gold. Gold. *Clut*. Again, more valuable than man. But in my trade, made into potions, powders, salts, it was *slup* thought to prolong life."

He began to give it over, but as Fetch's hand came up, the Bone Smiler withdrew the bottle.

"Hear me. *Sssslt*. This is poison. Nothing more. It is worthless save in the murder of all that risk its presence. Understand, by taking it you are trying to kill the malignance within you. Orc blood is hardier than man's. Perhaps *ssslt* that will serve you. But know, the kinnabar infusion will likely kill you. Faster even than the invading humors."

The bottle was again proffered.

Fetch reached out with a question first. "So . . . the sludge? It is killing me."

"Yes. I believe so."

She took the vial.

A ripple of disappointment played across the Bone Smiler's skeletal face. "One drop under the tongue. One only."

"Every day?"

"If you can."

Fetch eyed the small vessel. "It won't last very long."

"No," came the somber reply. "One way or another. *Ssslt*. It won't."

FOUR

OUTSIDE, FETCH FOUND a pair of nomads waiting with Hoodwink. She had noted their arrival while on the Bone Smiler's table, hearing the shuffle and snort of the hogs, the brief murmur of introductions. Breechless inside the hut, she had paid it no mind, trusting that any trouble could—and would—be handled by her cadaverous rider. The older of the two gave her a nod as she exited. Orcs were entirely hairless, so any mongrel wearing a beard or locks had their human half to thank. This one possessed flaxen whiskers, a rare color in a half-breed. They grew in bushes above his ears and down his jaw-line, contrasting sharply with his dark skin. Fetch reckoned he had fifteen years on her, perhaps a few more. He wore a stockbow across his back, another oddity. Nomads usually lacked the resources to maintain a thrum. The younger free-rider hardly noticed her presence. He was too busy casting uneasy looks up at the hermit on his pole.

Ignoring them for the moment, Fetch retrieved her weapons from Hood. The Bone Smiler emerged while she was buckling her sword belt.

"Ah, Marrow. *Cluk*. What brings you?"

"Nothing injurious, Smiler," the older nomad replied, and gestured at his companion. "Just showing this youngblood where you dwell. Likely to need you before long. If he lives, that is."

Marrow gave his companion a nudge, breaking him out of his morbid study of the madman.

The apothecary stepped forward and smiled. "*Ssslt*. I am at your service. Though I pray you never need it."

The young nomad was undaunted by that horrid grin. He returned it with a smile of his own, far more comely, and extended his arm.

"I'm called Sluggard," he said, his smile broadening when the Bone Smiler clasped his wrist, a rarely seen greeting in the Lots.

Fetching took in this good-natured mongrel. He wasn't lean, like most underfed nomads, but even with that his name was peculiar. There was not a pinch of indolence in his well-muscled form. On the contrary, there was something of the leopard in this one, his body, even in stillness, appearing on the verge of some sudden, violent action. Unlike his companion, Sluggard's hair grew atop his head, worked into short twists. Fetch's frown deepened as she noticed no scars upon the exposed flesh of his arms. When a rider was cast out, his brothers marred his tattoos with ax blades, marking him an outcast and erasing his connection to the hoof. Marrow and Hoodwink both bore the scars of their ousting, but Sluggard's slate-colored skin was free of injury, old or new. Hells, he did not seem to bear any tattoos at all.

Fetch let their absence go unremarked. She had to. It was hoof code not to question a free-rider about his past.

He wore riding leathers, but unlike Marrow's, they weren't sun-bleached and sweat-eaten. Weathered, certainly, but far from rotten. A stout bow, fashioned in the Unyar way, was in his hand. Both the nomads' hogs were swift-bodied, tough beasts, though Fetch noticed a touch of brush foot in Marrow's spotted sow.

The Bone Smiler saw it too. "There's some *ssslk* swelling in Dead Bride's left hind foot." He moved to squat by the hog. While he and Marrow conferred, Sluggard caught Fetching's eye.

And winked.

"Even your tight-lipped friend there gave his name," he commented playfully. "I hope to hear yours before you ride off. Unless I've just shamed myself by not knowing you were here seeking a cure for dumbness."

Marrow's head jerked up wearing a scowl. "You've just shamed yourself because that there is the leader of the True Bastards, you ignorant!"

That left Sluggard aghast. He looked at the entrance to the hut, as if hoping someone else was about to come out. "I thought . . ."

"I'd be taller?" Fetch finished for him. "Don't worry, my cock is every bit as large as you've heard."

"Pardon him, chief," Marrow said. "Full of nothing but spend and stupid, this one."

"Yes, pardon him," Sluggard recovered well, returning the smirk to his face, "and give him your name."

Tightening Womb's girth strap, she tossed him an answer over her shoulder. "Fetching."

"And I thought all hoof names to be forged in irony." Sluggard's voice was awed.

Fetch wasn't sure what that meant, but from his tone, it wasn't an insult.

Hoodwink drew up on the other side of Womb's saddle. "I need to remain. Hunt a day or two for the Bone Smiler."

Fetch nodded. It was the same as they had done before. The apothecary needed to be compensated, but she couldn't afford the delay. Winsome had been without her too long already.

"I'm for the brothel. Then home."

Hoodwink's brow tightened by a hair.

"If you disagree, Hood, say something."

When he did, his lips hardly moved, voice so low Fetch nearly missed the words. "You should wait."

Fetch snuck a look back to find Sluggard had ambled out of earshot. "Can't."

"You're ill."

"Fucking aware."

"You're chief."

Fetch jerked a stirrup strap. "Again. Aware."

"You can't ride alone."

She slapped the saddle flap back down, causing Womb Broom to grunt and sidle. Seizing his mane, Fetch forced him to stillness as she glared across his back at Hoodwink.

"*Can't?*"

It was a look that would have made a slophead piss his breeches, but Hood was a headstone. And he wasn't wrong. She was ill. Hells, she was dying. The knowledge might have scared her, if it hadn't sounded right. Felt right.

A year ago, it wouldn't have. In truth, all her life it was impossible to fathom. Death, sure, but that was different. Facing thicks in battle on the back of a hog, death was there. It was familiar, expected. Something to be defied with every last screaming, spit-flinging breath. She never felt weak fighting against death. The struggle against dying, however, seemed to be waged in the grip of impotence. Fetch had never understood the complaints of the old and infirm. White hair and wrinkled skin were piss-poor excuses for slower reflexes and dimmed wits. To her mind, best to stop giving power to the ailments of age by refusing to recognize their presence. Weakness could be ignored. So she thought.

Now, she knew the inescapable truth of a body's betrayal. The coughing fits could not be ceased with grit. The lack of breath could not be dismissed by bravery. She could not be strong for the simple, treacherous fact that she was weak. An easy thing to defy death when you weren't dying.

Fucking dying.

But not dead. Not yet. And until she was . . .

"I have a duty, Hood. As chief. Foundlings need a wet nurse. Ain't about to find one sitting here beside that brain-baked vulture up on his wheel. I have to get to Rhecia's. Somewhere you'll be a damn detriment and we both know it."

It was her turn to be right. Hoodwink terrified the whores, and it wasn't just his pale, heavily scarred flesh or the lifeless eyes. Those women dealt with frightening men every waking moment, but one that never took them to bed was a sinister mystery with unknown appetites. There was no controlling a mongrel that possessed no obvious desires. At least, no control for a whore.

"You're staying here," Fetch said. "Make sure we stay square with Smiler. I'll see you back at Winsome. As for me riding alone . . ."

She turned to see Sluggard furtively reaching up to give the hermit's wheel little pushes, spinning him slowly while watching Marrow and the Bone Smiler to avoid getting caught.

"Figure I'll see about these two."

"You don't know them," Hood said.

"Don't need to," Fetch replied. "They know you. Your reputation among the nomads is . . . hells, you're fucking feared. And with good reason. They'd be fool-asses to harm me. Besides, neither is putting a bad taste in my mouth. If they prove solid to Rhecia's, I may invite them to Winsome."

"It's more mouths to feed."

"I know," she sighed. "But we are down to seven riders. With the wall taking so long, we are going to need more strength. It's more mouths, yes, but also more hogs, more blades, more bows. If we don't have a strong fortress, we damn well better have strong arms."

"Six."

"What?"

"We have six brothers. Not seven."

"Fuck," Fetch whispered, shaking her head. She was still counting Oats.

"Something else."

"Hells, get you talking and you don't shut up," Fetch needled.

A pause. "You could end up with a hoof full of cutthroats."

Fetch stopped fussing with her tack, considering. Free-riders were outcasts from the hoofs, voted into exile by their brothers for one slight or another. The Lots were an unforgiving land, meaning much was forgiven in those that dared dwell here. A rider had to be hard, willing to do whatever was needed for the good of his hoof. That commitment bred killers, rustlers. What did a hoofmaster care if his band was full of the worst mongrels ever to sit a hog, as long as they were loyal? Nomads, by their very existence, were not. But second chances were sometimes warranted, worth risking.

Fetch met Hood's pitiless eyes. "We tamed you, didn't we?"

"No," he replied without passion. "I was a spy for Warbler."

"To overthrow the Claymaster," Fetch pointed out.

"To overthrow a *chief*." Suddenly, Hood's voice was no longer without passion. His sudden bout of feeling was unnerving, sobering.

"I hear you," Fetch assured. "But they ain't sitting at our table yet."

"They don't need to be sworn brothers to tell where they met you."

Fetch looked around the quarry, her gaze resting on the door to the Bone Smiler's adopted hermitage. If the Bastards found out she had been here, there would certainly be questions, from Mead especially. And then there would be a choice. Lie or admit to the sickness. What chief would willingly reveal a weakness? It defied everything it was to be a hoofmaster. Fetch had no doubt the Claymaster would have hidden his affliction if he could, but it was the only thing he couldn't conceal. Fetch could tell Hood she would be different, she would keep no secrets, but the words would be lies. And not her first.

"Bone Smiler," she called out, drawing the apothecary's attention. "I expect you'll continue to examine the cause of our crop failure."

The man slipped seamlessly into the mummery. "Indeed. *Clut.* My hope is the vine cuttings you brought will reveal the nature of the blight."

"Good." Fetch shifted to Marrow. "You and the youngblood want to ride with me for a span?"

Sluggard jumped away from the cenobite's pole. "Yes!"

Marrow looked up from his hog's hoof, less enthusiastic. "Where?"

"Rhecia's." Fetch looked at Sluggard. "You been yet?"

"No," he replied. And then came that smile. "But I am finding the prospect undeniably enticing just now."

Fetch turned away from his bald flirtation and looked once more at Marrow. "Not to sully the Smiler's craft, but I'm sure he will tell you, no poultice can do for brush foot what sheltered rest and good fodder will. Your sow will mend quickest in the Bastards' stables. Come with me to the brothel, and after, you can sojourn awhile with us at Winsome."

"Another name well suited, I wager," Sluggard said.

"*Schlup*. She is right," the Bone Smiler put in. "I can provide something to hold you, but this could turn *sssipt* rotten if left."

Marrow's gaze never left Fetching. "You offering me a place in your hoof?"

"I'm offering you the chance to earn a vote. If you want it."

The nomad set his jaw, squinted up at the sky.

"Before you answer," Fetch said, "there are two things you should know. The first is that Winsome is a few hundred furlongs from prosperous. Likely you'll go to sleep hungry most nights."

Marrow shrugged that away. "I do that now. What's the second thing?"

"I demand much from my riders."

"Hhhmm." Marrow's fingers raked his pale whiskers. "Never taken orders from no woman before."

"Sure you have," Fetch said, giving her saddle's girth strap one final, sharp tug. "Had to be at least one that told you to go faster."

Easy laughter burst from Sluggard.

Marrow's hesitation lasted only another moment. "Very well."

Fetch drew Hoodwink farther away while the Bone Smiler went into his hut for the remedy.

"I will take the measure of these two. Should know all I need by the time we reach home."

Hood was looking over her head. "Be vigilant."

"I will."

THE DWINDLING SUN ROASTED UL-WUNDULAS. Once down from the Amphoras, Fetch led Marrow and Sluggard, keeping the hogs at a dust-churning run until they reached the River Cavalero, a tributary of the Guadal-kabir so named because it marked the eastern border of the castile's lot. Ignoring the ford, she eased up on Womb Broom, called a halt. They dismounted and allowed the hogs down to the river's edge to drink. As Marrow squatted to scoop a handful of water to his mouth, Fetch noticed an ax tucked into his belt at the small of his back. The weapon looked suspiciously like the throwing hatchets the hoofs traditionally used to vote against a chief's decisions. All the Bastards' axes had been lost when the Kiln tumbled, and no one was in a hurry to replace them.

"Rumor is, he caught it."

Fetch had not heard Sluggard approach and almost startled at his sudden, soft pronouncement. She turned to find the grinning nomad standing just behind her right shoulder.

"Caught what?" she asked.

"The ax," Sluggard replied, voice lowered to a conspiratorial whisper. "Tried to gain leadership of the Skull Sowers and lost the vote. Marrow stood before the stump for judgment, but when his chief threw, our surly friend down at the bank there? Caught the ax in flight. Walked right out of the Furrow with the damn thing in his hand, cutting across his own tattoos as he went."

Fetch gave him the shit-eye. "I bet you believed it when he told you his cock rivaled a centaur's too."

"Oh, he never said a word," Sluggard said, unaffected. "That's how you know when the stories are true, when they go unsaid from their heroes."

"That some kind of nomad wisdom?"

"I like to think it's the supposition of solid intuition."

"More fancy words," Fetching said, feigning awe. She gave him an appraising look, again noting his lack of hoof tattoos and outcast scars. All half-orcs were well built, but there was something odd about his muscled frame. It was too . . . refined. He looked like one of those headless Imperium statues that remained in the ruins of Kalbarca. Fetching gave voice to her realization with no small amount of disdain, the little clues now forming a clear image. "You're from Hispartha."

Sluggard smiled brightly. "Magerit."

"The fucking king's city?"

"Well, queen's, but yes."

"Hells fuck me! You've never been in a fucking hoof." Sluggard's smug face wilted a bit in the face of her scowl. "Why the fuck are you in the Lots?"

"He's a gritter."

Marrow trod up the embankment, leading his hog by a yanker.

"A what?" Fetching demanded.

Sluggard held up a finger. "It's—"

"A gritter," Marrow repeated. "Mongrels from the kingdom come down to Ul-wundulas to get some dust in their crack, some nomad ink, maybe a few scars. Soft little pieces of fruit looking for the Lots to make them hard men. Most of them die quick. The rest piss themselves after their first glimpse of a thick or a 'taur and run their damp breeches on back home." Marrow leveled a finger at Sluggard. "This one is here so he can go back to the flesh-houses and pass himself off as a blooded orc slayer, up the price the bluebloods will pay for his cod."

Fetch swiveled her head back to look at Sluggard. "This true?"

The accused gritter gave a cocky little shrug. "Noblewomen crave a little danger, a little dirt. I grew tired of riding for the carnavales, plucking pennies from the mud. Once I have experienced the badlands, I will fetch a high price catering to the whims of the most fashionable ladies in Magerit. Comfort. Luxury. These will fill my life."

"While your meat and tongue fill rich frail quim," Marrow muttered, checking his hog's swollen hoof.

Fetching was perplexed and annoyed. "So you came down here, so you can go back up there . . . to be a whore."

"A *cortejo*," Sluggard corrected.

"No, no, no, no," Fetch said, a laugh beginning to bubble. "You said you were going to fuck rich women for coin. I don't know who named you Sluggard, but since you probably picked it yourself and you've never been in a hoof, that can't be your *hoof* name. It's Whore from this moment, if you want to ride with me."

"I—"

"Mount up, Whore," Fetch said, swinging up into her own saddle. Behind her, Marrow made a noise in his throat that might have been a chuckle. "How long have you been in the Lots? Truthfully."

Sluggard lifted his chin. "Nearly half a year. And I'm not dead yet."

"Can he fight?" Fetch asked, craning around to Marrow. "Shoot?"

The nomad scratched at one of his bushy cheek whiskers and produced an uncaring shrug.

Sluggard's jaw tensed with defiance. "Do you think it's only a hardship being a mongrel in the Lot Lands? Think coming up a half-breed in Hispartha is free from scorn? Every frail ruffian with something to prove sees you as a challenge. Bragging rights for besting the half-orc. And winning doesn't save you from the retribution of the challenger's friends. I can fight. I can also read. Think anyone wanted to teach me? I can speak orcish. Try finding a tutor for that in a bastion of culture. You ridicule me for coming to Ul-wundulas, for wanting to see if I can survive here. Tell me, the both of you, have you ever tried to live in Hispartha? Have you tried to thrive in the callous, casual wickedness of civilization? I learned to ride a hog in the carnavales because it was the only way to avoid the arenas. Because, fortunately, it is fashionable among the nobles to witness dramatic enactments of the Great Orc Incursion. Merchants' wives would come to me with coin for their pleasure after seeing the spectacle. But the ladies of court want only genuine badlanders. So I have come."

Fetch decided she wanted to see him squirm some more. "I only asked if you could shoot."

Sluggard snatched an arrow from his quiver, nocked, raised, and loosed in one motion. The arrow sped across the Cavalero, squarely striking a mossy rock protruding from the current midstream.

Considering the distance, Fetch gave a slow, approving nod. "But can you use a thrum?"

"Stockbows are forbidden to Hisparthan citizens," Sluggard said. "I was only ever allowed to carry a mock one during a performance for the Queen Madre's birthday where I played the Clay Monster."

It took Fetching a moment to understand what had just been said. "You mean . . . the Claymaster?"

Sluggard's brow creased. "The leader of the Grey Bastards? The Clay Monster."

Now Marrow really was laughing.

"There are . . . playacts of him?" Fetch found her stomach pushing something up toward her throat. Sludge or simple disgust, she didn't know, but fought it down regardless.

"Dramatic enactments," Sluggard insisted. "Yes. He is quite the romantic figure among—"

"Fucking hells, Whore, stop speaking!"

Silence was the order for the rest of the day's ride. They pushed their hogs into the night for as long as was wise; there was a limit to even the endurance of a Lot-born barbarian. The moon and stars were stewed in a murky broth of clouds, making a night ride foolhardy besides. They made camp upon the plain. Risky, but the time it would take to find something more defensible could not be spared. Fetching allowed a fire. Their meal consisted of a few pulls from a waterskin. Neither nomad complained.

"You two sleep," Fetching told them. "I will watch. We'll give the hogs a proper rest, but if this sky clears after midnight, we ride."

There were noises of agreement. Sluggard bedded down, reclining against the belly of his sow. The mongrel hoofs called such a position "skull-suckling," and not every hog would tolerate it, especially the males. Hearth used to allow Jackal, one of the many behaviors that made that hog so special. The thought caused Fetching a moment of pain. She shook it away. Womb Broom snuffled at the edge of the firelight. There was no way in all the hells that pig would suffer to be a cushion. None of the Fangs' mounts would, not even the females.

Across the fire, Marrow worked diligently, cleaning his stockbow.

"You should sleep," Fetching said.

"Thrum will turn to shit, 'less I tend it."

"How long have you managed to keep it up? Most free-riders can't."

Marrow paused his chore for a moment, thinking. "This one, near five years."

There was a long silence, and Fetch resolved to leave him to his task, when he spoke again.

"Lost my first. I did good keeping the rust off the prods, the string waxed. Failed to notice the leather on the backstrap was wearing. Was crossing the Guadal-kabir in the spring when the river was flush. Current almost did it for me and my hog. We managed the crossing, but the thrum was gone. Spent the rest of the season holed up in Kalbarca practicing with a cunting bow. Just not the same."

"No," Fetch agreed.

Marrow's attention flicked between her and the stockbow for a moment, clearly chewing on whether to say something.

"What is it?" she asked.

"The tongue-waggle among the nomads says you have some hulk of a thrice-blood in the hoof. Acts as your right hand. But I didn't see such a brute at Smiler's. Just Hoodwink."

Fetch found herself growing wary. "Why ask after the thrice?"

Marrow shrugged, still focused on the catch of his stockbow. "I stood with a thrice from the Grey Bastards during the Betrayer. Years ago. He was freshly sworn. Just wondered if it were the same mongrel."

"Oats," Fetch offered.

"That was him. He die? Hard to imagine, really, but I know your hoof got hit hard when the thicks came last spring."

"I had to send him away. Due to rationing."

Marrow barked a humorless laugh. "Monster ate too much, eh? Well, that's a thrice to the bone."

"Other way around," Fetch said. "He didn't eat enough. Or at all, most times. Figured he could endure an empty belly better than the rest of us. But he does fool-ass shit like that."

"So you cast him out?"

Marrow looked more concerned with the give in the thrum's tickler than in an answer, but Fetch gave it anyway. "No. He still serves the hoof. Just somewhere he won't starve himself."

"Lucky him, then. Away from the privation, the danger."

"He's at the Pit of Homage."

Marrow's head snapped up. He stared intently at Fetching, the stockbow forgotten. When he saw she did not jest, he blew a hard breath from his whiskered cheeks.

"How long?" he asked.

Fetch pointed at the sleeping Sluggard with her chin. "Longer than our boy-whore's been in the Lots."

Marrow grunted in renewed wonder and redoubled his efforts on the stockbow. "That's why no gods can be found in the Lots. They're all watching over your friend."

"Then they know which way to bet."

No further words passed between them. Soon, Marrow set the thrum aside and settled down upon his thin bedroll. The fire crackled as half-orcs and hogs snored.

Fetch made sure both nomads were fully given to their dreams before removing the Bone Smiler's poison. She considered the vial for a moment before pulling the stopper. Carefully, she tilted it above her open mouth, righting it as soon as she felt a drop land beneath her tongue. It burned the soft flesh, turned it gritty. A foul metallic taste took up residence in her mouth. Fetch ran her tongue around, spat, but the caustic tang had penetrated her teeth and refused to be expelled.

The clouds never parted. Fetch passed the night sweating and shivering, eyes seeping feverish tears, biting down upon her arm to keep from whimpering, hoping her companions would not awaken.

FIVE

"SPIES. FEED. FLIES." Sluggard recited the words carved into the corpse's torso with dull criticism. "You'd think they would be more clever."

Marrow spit. "Lies got no need to be clever."

Fetch said nothing, allowing the buzzing of those feasting on the poor mongrel nailed to the tree to voice her agreement. His naked body had swelled in the heat, the old scars that marked him as a nomad stretched over the remnants of hoof tattoos all but erased by the mottled purple of rot. They'd seen his hog several miles back hosting a half dozen vultures. The cavaleros must have enjoyed the chase to allow him to make it this far on foot.

"Certain it's a lie?" Sluggard rubbed the back of his neck. "I heard the orcs almost made it into Hispartha last year. Folks say they couldn't have pressed so far without help."

Marrow cast the gritter a hard look for the half-wit remark. "Free-riders don't scout for thicks, boy. Hearken? Not ever. That's a truth you can take back north with you."

"The orcs would do far worse than this to any half-breed they caught," Fetch added.

Sluggard peered at the ghastly carcass. "Worse?"

"Another truth," Marrow agreed.

"Why the falsehood?" Sluggard asked. "Frails never needed a reason to murder mongrels far as I know. So why bother with the hogshit about spies?"

"Captain of the castile's gone mad," Marrow replied. "Lost a leg and got blood fever. Seeing foes everywhere now."

Again, Fetch stayed silent. Bermudo had lost a leg, and possibly his mind, but it was only one foe he hunted among the nomads. One mongrel Fetch knew to be far from the Lots.

Marrow sent another dart of spit into the dirt. "Let's get him down."

"Leave him."

Fetch's words froze the nomad in his saddle. "Like hells I will!"

"You will if you don't want more nomads to suffer the same." Fetch nodded at the tree and its ornament of meat. "That there is the best warning other free-riders have that the cavaleros are in the area. We put it in the ground, we take that warning away."

Marrow chewed on her wisdom, displeased but unable to discount good sense.

"Not far now to the brothel," he said. "Strong chance the frails that did this are there."

Fetch had thought the same. "You looking for a reckoning? Or a reason not to go?"

Marrow gestured at the churned earth surrounding the tree. "This was a score of horses. Maybe more."

Fetch nodded. "I saw."

"Seven to one if we find them," Sluggard said.

"Whore's right," Fetch told Marrow.

The nomad grunted. "Those odds don't support much of a reckoning."

"And we'd have to get them all. Every last one so that none report to the castile."

"Say we do. Nothing to stop Rhecia's girls from saying who done it. Unless you plan on killing them all in the bargain?"

"I don't," Fetch said.

"What then?"

"The hardest task." Fetch swept both mongrels with a look. "We leave it alone."

Marrow liked that less than leaving the murdered mongrel unburied. His jaw bulged.

"You can't do that, best ride away now," Fetch told him. "I got business at Rhecia's. Can't have bloodshed getting in the way."

Marrow glowered at the body on the tree. "And when *they* can't leave it alone? When those frail fucks see two free-riders and a mongrel woman and choose to push it? What then?"

Fetch could feel Sluggard's eyes on her, awaiting the answer.

"It's a risk," she said. "One you don't have to take. Ride on. I sure as shit won't think less of you for it. Truth is, out there you're still a nomad, Marrow. You still risk ending your days nailed to a tree or buried up to your chin in the dirt. You may be fortunate and never cross paths with the cavaleros. But if you do, would you rather be alone, like this unfortunate fuck? Or would you rather be with the chief of the True Bastards, a hopeful to the hoof? Bermudo's men may be killing nomads, but they need a lie to do it. That means they're afraid of something. The Crown? Fucking doubtful. More likely it's us, the mongrel hoofs. Twenty men hunting one speaks to their cowardice. I'm willing to wager that off their horses, with us standing before them, they won't have the grit to look us squarely."

"And if you're wrong?" Sluggard asked, more curious than concerned.

Fetch shrugged. "We're dead before the sun sets. No different than any day in the Lots. Least you'll die in a brothel. Sounds close to what you want anyway, Whore."

The young mongrel grinned. "It does, at that. I'm with you. What do you say, Marrow?"

"I say I've got a pair of silver maravedís that no passel of backy frails is going to keep me from spending at Rhecia's."

Fetch snorted. "Quim. The source of all mongrel bravery."

"To hells with quim," Marrow declared. "It's a hot meal I want. A full belly is worth a ransom more than an empty spend sack."

"Here lies Marrow," Sluggard recited in the same dull tone he used when reading the knife cuts. "He died for stew."

Fetch gave that the smirk it was due and turned her hog, leaving the tree behind and two nests of maggots staring at her back.

SANCHO'S.

Easy to refer to the place by a different name when away from its presence, but seeing the compound of low buildings hunkered on the ugly plain, promising a respite from the badlands and a glut of uncomfortable memories, Fetch could not help but think of it as it was.

Flanked by the free-riders, she rode into the enclosure of the dusty yard. None were about, save a lone figure at the well. A mongrel woman, filling buckets. Fetch led her riders to the stables. Sancho had employed a boy, Olivar, to tend his guests' mounts, but, like many of the fat pedant's servants, the lad had run off after his master was killed. It was a crook-backed man of middle years who offered to take their hogs.

Fetch waved him off as she and Marrow dismounted. Sluggard stayed ahog to keep watch as planned. Leaving Womb and Dead Bride in Marrow's hands, Fetch strode past the now-anxious stable hand into the pungent confines of the stalls. She made a swift count.

Marrow's frown deepened at the look on her face when she came out. "They're here."

"Seven horses," Fetch confirmed. "All castile cavalry steeds."

"Just seven." Sluggard gave a small grunt. "There's some luck."

Fetch didn't like the grin growing between Marrow's whiskers. She shot a look at the stable hand. "Why are they still saddled?"

The crookback's tongue dragged along a plump, recently split lower lip. "Cavaleros insisted on it."

"Like they insisted our brother nomad wed that tree," Marrow said.

"There's a barbarian too," Fetch said, aiming to distract him. "A nomad hog."

"You know it?" Marrow asked.

Fetch nodded. "I know it."

She swung a leg over her hog and spurred across the yard. The half-orc woman at the well looked up as she passed, revealing a face puckered by a multitude of crisscrossing scars. Small wonder she was dressed as a common laborer, the poor cloth of her tunic and breeches blanched by sun and dust. Revealing silks would be wasted on this one. Hells, in his day Sancho would never have allowed such a face to remain. Rhecia must be a more tolerant whoremonger.

There were no mounts tethered to the hitching post outside the brothel proper. Hopping from the saddle, Fetch began securing her hog, gesturing for Sluggard and Marrow to tie up at the opposite end, leaving Womb Broom space to be the foul-tempered swine he was. As she put a final, hard tug on the knot, the bucket-laden shadow of the scarred woman stretched across the dirt beneath the post.

"You're—"

"Not tarrying," Fetch said, and pushed through the door.

The occupants of the brothel's pitiful taproom startled at her entrance. A stool scraped, banged on the floor as one man shot to his feet. His companion bumped their table in his hurry to rise, upsetting the cups. Wine dribbled upon the floor as both men squinted against the glare Fetch let in behind her. The brightness dulled as Marrow and Sluggard filled the doorway. Stepping in, they returned the mercy of gloom to the nervy faces.

Fetch counted three cavaleros. The two who'd leapt up, and another keeping his own company—as well as his seat—at a table deeper into the gloom. They all stared for a moment, hands on the grips of their swords, but none drew steel. The arrival of a woman bearing fresh cups to the table of the duo severed their tension. With a final, hard look, they resettled. The loner remained still and watchful, but his scrutiny was quickly blocked as the woman, weaving back through the tables, came to stand before Fetching.

"Welcome, hoofmaster," she said, her Hisparthan accented with the lilt of Anville. She offered the three remaining cups on her serving tray. "I am honored to have you take your ease here."

Fetch had only a vague recollection of this milk-skinned trollop with the dark tresses. She'd been sitting on Jackal's knee, the perfect demure young plaything for him and Delia to share. Fetch recalled waiting for the older whore to grow jealous and run Rhecia off, but it never happened. The new girl knew her trade, enticing Jack without supplanting Delia. A delicate balance. Fetch had been repulsed and impressed. Now, the comely girl with the practiced pout ran the brothel frequented by cavaleros and half-orcs. Fetching hoped to remain impressed by her ability to balance.

"Where are the other four?" she asked, taking a cup and keeping her voice low.

Rhecia kept her smile steady and did not so much as cock an eye in the direction of the cavaleros. "Three are keeping company with women in their rooms. The last is bathing."

Fetch brought the wine to her lips, using the cup to block her mouth. "And where is Slivers hiding?"

"On the roof of the bathhouse," Rhecia replied evenly.

Fetch bit back a curse. "We need a room. And don't dare ask me for any damn coin."

Rhecia weathered the rudeness with ease and motioned her to follow.

They went down the low, dismal corridor off the rear of the taproom. One of the doors opened just as Fetch was passing and a man's exit stomped short upon seeing the passage blocked. Fetch's own steps came to a sudden halt, as well, but not because of the flushed cavalero still adjusting his damp shirt. It was the naked mongrel woman on the bed behind him, ludicrously posed to offer a farewell intended to solicit a swift return. Cissy's eyes widened when they met Fetch's, surprise and shame quickly hardening into a resentful challenge.

"It's this way," Rhecia urged.

Fetching moved on.

At the corridor's end, Rhecia opened a door like all the rest. Stepping in, Fetch took in the decrepit furnishings, the musty smell, remembering the nights she'd spent in this damn place. Sluggard and Marrow drifted in after, making the already-close space cramped. Rhecia, too, entered and closed the door.

"You need to get that frail out of the baths," Fetch told her.

"He is already being enticed to do so," the whore mistress said.

"Have the men asked about the hog?"

"They have. I told them it arrived here without a rider."

"They believe you?"

"Of course."

"Were they part of a larger troop?"

Rhecia shook her head.

"Likely broke off from the main body," Marrow said, sitting on the edge of the bed. "The rest are back at the castile by now, I'd say. These are the lucky few get to sit guard here for a span. Lucky *few*."

"Jumpy bunch," Sluggard said. "You notice?"

Marrow huffed. "Murderin' cowards usually are."

Fetch shot him a warning look. "Best not be getting ideas. I said we were leaving it alone."

"That was when it was twenty," the nomad said.

"It was when I fucking said it!" Fetch felt a cold tickle building to a cough in her throat. She shuddered, swallowed, forced it down. "My orders don't change based on numbers. They change when I tell you they change."

"Very well. Seems a waste, though." Marrow fished beneath his brigand. Producing a coin, he handed it up to Rhecia. "Food. Much as that will get. I expect it will be substantial."

The woman dipped her chin and looked to Fetching. "And you? Why have you come?"

"Any of your girls with child? Or got one on the tit? Hoof's foundlings need a wet nurse."

Rhecia's face was placid.

"Don't dare dissemble with me," Fetch warned. "I'll ask each of your girls myself if I have to."

Rhecia took a long breath through the nose. "Hilde's time is near. I shall ask her."

"I'll ask her. Send her here."

"She is a Guabian and her Hisparthan is poor. Best if I—"

"I speak Guabic," Sluggard announced.

Rhecia's carefully held countenance cracked with annoyance.

Fetch smiled at her. "There. I'll have my Whore talk to yours. Send her."

Resettling her composure, Rhecia slipped out.

Marrow began loading his stockbow, drawing quizzical looks from Fetch and Sluggard. The older nomad lifted his chin at the door.

"She decides to send those cavaleros in here rather than lose a coin slot, I'd rather greet them with something more than wounded feelings."

"Fair point," Fetch said, and put a bolt in her own thrum.

Sluggard, glancing about the room and realizing there was no space to draw back a bowstring, pulled his knife and looked perturbed.

When the door again opened, it wasn't the cavaleros or a pregnant frail from Guabia. It was Cissy, bearing a tray of bread, half a wheel of cheese, a leg of mutton, and a bowl of something steaming. The aromas turned Fetch's stomach into an angry dog. Marrow set his stockbow aside, stretched up from the bed, and took the tray with a sigh of deep satisfaction.

Fetch hadn't seen Cissy in nearly half a year and she wasn't too keen on looking at her now. Cissy, the flirtatious girl with the ample ass who could make men hard with a look, or so the hoof brothers used to say. She had never wanted anything other than to be a bedwarmer, reside in the Kiln, had dreamed of it even when an orphan living in Beryl's care. Fetch could still remember all the giggly, whispered confessions, all of Cissy's breathless wonderings over which of the Bastards would favor her. It had turned Fetch's stomach even then, though she stayed a loyal confidant for years.

Marrow tucked into his food with noisy relish. Cissy lingered. Fetch tried to send her off with a glare, but received an insistent motion toward the door. Inwardly cursing, Fetch followed her into the corridor. When the door was closed fast, Cissy affixed her bold eyes.

"Hilde won't be coming," she said. "Not to this room. Not to Winsome."

"If that Anvillese hussy thinks she can keep her from me . . ."

Fetch turned to set off down the hall, but Cissy seized her arm.

"It's not Rhecia."

Spinning back around, freeing herself from the grip in the same motion, Fetching seethed. "I won't play games here. Fucking explain."

"It was me," Cissy declared, refusing to be cowed. "I told Hilde not to go. Told her what awaited her if she took up with the Bastards."

"An end to taking unwashed cock for coin?"

"An end to eating more than once every three days!"

"She'd have more than that—"

"How?" Cissy demanded, her voice beginning to quiver. "Thistle didn't! Is that why you've come? Is she dead? Did you finally leech the last of her? Hells, I begged her to come with me and—"

"Turning whore's not the answer for all—"

"Now you've fucking killed her. How many more will you lead to death before you—"

"She's alive—"

"Give up this sick jest of being chief?"

It was all Fetching could do to stop herself from seizing the little slattern by the throat. The impulse sent her darting forward, teeth bared.

"Be careful, Cissy," she snarled, nearly nose to nose with the smaller woman, but the aggression only fueled her defiance.

"Why? You don't rule here. You can't command me. This isn't your lot. Nor your hoof. You're not master of anything inside these walls, *Isabet*."

Lungs crackling, threatening, Fetching hid her discomfort, and her fury, behind a grin.

"You should know," she nearly whispered, "Polecat's been begging me leave to come here since the day you left. I've refused. Not certain if he intends to haul you back to Winsome over his saddle horn . . . or skin you alive for abandoning him. I didn't want to have to live with either outcome, being honest. But you disrespect me again, you callow cunt, I'll allow him to ride this way and we'll both take our chances."

Cissy's eyes widened. She was now holding her breath.

Fetch flicked her eyes down the corridor. "You can return to your back."

Once the whore had fled, Fetch pushed open the door to find Marrow sopping his bowl with a wedge of bread, Sluggard watching him with a sickened expression. "You already put all that down?"

"I eat fast."

"*So* fast," Sluggard said, appalled.

Fetch cocked her head toward the hall. "We're riding out."

Marrow jammed the bread into his already-stuffed mouth and stood, taking up his thrum. They hadn't gone three steps when a commotion punched through the brothel's thin walls. Men's raised voices. The scrapes and thumps of a struggle. All coming from the direction of the bathhouse.

Fetch halted.

Slivers.

Shit.

Leave it alone. That's what she'd said to do. They could go straight for their hogs, *should* go straight for their hogs. But leaving a corpse on a tree and his killers unchallenged was one course. Allowing those same men to murder another mongrel, no matter how much a worthless craven, was another path entirely.

Fetch ran for the opposite end of the corridor, Marrow and Sluggard right behind. There was no door to the bathhouse, just an arch opening onto the fenced court that hugged the tubs, and their ramshackle shelter, to the brothel. Rushing through the arch, Fetch found Slivers, knife in hand, keeping two cavaleros at bay. One of the men was naked, sopping, and bleeding from a cut along his ribs. The other was the lonely drinker from the taproom, fully dressed in his scale coat, thrusting at Slivers with his sword across a tub. Four of the great oaken things comprised the baths, each able to hold three people with ease. Slivers danced around the edge of one, keeping it between him and the cavaleros.

The swordsman whirled at Fetch's arrival. Next to her, Marrow's thrum came up, but she pushed it down, kept her own lowered.

"Not here for that," she told the room just as three more armed cavaleros bulled through the arch. Sluggard had to scurry out of their path, knocking over—and nearly tripping on—a bench in his haste to get away from the reach of their blades. Fetch couldn't prevent Marrow from spinning and training his stockbow on the newcomers, but looking directly into the prods of the loaded weapon kept the men from pressing further. It was the skittish pair from the taproom along with the man who had fucked Cissy.

Rhecia appeared in the arch behind them.

"I will not allow this!" she shouted into the court. "Put away your weapons!"

The naked cavalero clutched his leaking side and yelled back, keeping an eye cocked at Slivers. "You lied to us, Rhecia!"

"I spoke true! This mongrel must have come sneaking to reclaim his mount. I did not know he was here!"

The little nomad didn't appreciate the mistress's quick thinking. "Forked-tongued she-devil!"

"Put a cock in it, Slivers!" Fetch snapped.

The naked man jabbed a finger at her. "She knows him!"

"I know him. He's no—"

"A scout for the rest!" This accusation came from over her shoulder. One of the three men near the archway. "They're here for us!"

"We're not!" Fetch insisted. "Here on a hoof matter, nothing else!"

A wildness took over the naked man's face. His head made rapid twists, birdlike, trying to address his fellows while keeping an eye on Slivers. "We can't trust that! You lads want half-breed trackers on our ass? Never reach the Smelteds—"

"Shut your fucking mouth, Cino!" the swordsman nearest him growled through clenched teeth, cuffing his nude companion on the shoulder. His glare darted to Fetching, but she kept her expression blank, trying to pretend she hadn't heard . . . yet her flesh crawled as the clues congealed. The saddled horses. The jumpy men. Talk of the hills. These weren't cavaleros. Not anymore. And that was far more dangerous. She'd heard. She knew. If these frails realized she knew . . .

Fetch thrust a finger at Slivers. "I'm here for him. Fucking skulker sheltered with us for a time. Repaid the kindness by raping one of our bedwarmers and making off with a sack of beans."

Slivers's face went slack with disbelief. "The fuck I did!"

Fetch ignored him, kept her gaze on the naked frail. He was injured and vulnerable. If she could convince him, perhaps his cut would be the end of it. "I got every intention of taking him back to Winsome, letting the woman he harmed geld him and then have my slopheads feather him for target practice. But"—Fetch flicked her eyes to the man's bleeding ribs—"he did slice you, so I'd be satisfied if you wanted to take him back to the castile. I know your captain would see justice done."

It was a bald ploy, like throwing a snake into a crowded room, but it had the desired effect. Now faced with the thing they most feared, these men could focus only on getting away from it.

"No," the swordsman said, leaning a bit closer to the dripping Cino. "She can have him, eh? Let these soot-skins handle their own."

Cino's jaw bulged. "He fucking cut me. . . ."

Slivers threatened with his knife. "Teach you to haul me off a roof in nothing but your skin, fool-ass frail!"

The swordsman snickered. "Was fucking unwise, Cino."

Fetch seized upon the break in the tension. "Takes a brave man to fight with his cod swinging in the wind. The kind of man Rhecia's girls would be happy to tend, I'd wager."

"Most happy," the whoremonger agreed.

The other three cavaleros' determined frowns were softening.

Fetch again looked to the lone swordsman. "What say we mongrels ride on so you men can get back to better company?"

He was heeding her words, liked the sound of them. His gaze shifted beyond her as his sword arm lowered.

"I say we put steel away, boys. This isn't—"

Slivers darted around the tub and plunged his knife into the man's ear. His whole body went stiff for a heartbeat, began to convulse.

And the bathhouse erupted.

Fetch heard the three cavaleros curse, followed by the thrum of a loosed stockbow. Snapping her head around, she saw Marrow's bolt fly clear through the throat of one man and punch into the archway, sending shards of plaster flying and Rhecia fleeing. As the dead cavalero dropped, his flanking comrades sprang. One chopped at Sluggard, but his sword struck the low beams of the bathhouse roof and lodged. Sluggard closed the gap, knife driving for the exposed belly. It was an inexpert blow, directly into the cavalero's scale coat, yet the strength of the half-orc sent the blade through the armor to pierce guts. The stricken man gurgled, blood blooming behind his clenched teeth.

The other had more sense in the close confines, using his sword to thrust. Marrow sidestepped, snatched the hatchet from his belt, and buried it in his assailant's skull.

Fetch wanted to scream at them to stop, but it was too late. Nothing now but to complete the butchery.

She'd been right about Cino. It was a brave man that fought naked. He struggled with Slivers, wrestling for control of the knife. A struggle that ended when the nomad smashed a knee into his fruits, bashed his head into the edge of the tub, and slit his throat.

All went still. The puddles of the bathhouse were inked with blood. Fetch stood, numb to the carnage, her thrum still loaded, eyes sweeping across the five dead men sprawled on the moist boards.

Two more. There should have been two more. They couldn't have failed to hear. What manner of men didn't come when their comrades were in need?

Fetch's skull boiled.

"The stable! The last two! They're running!"

Sluggard bolted out the archway and was gone before Marrow could react.

Fetch had another route in mind. Springing, she caught the edge of the bathhouse roof with one hand and hauled herself up. Two running steps and a jump brought her across the gap to the roof of the brothel. She sprinted over the flat-topped structure and reached the front just as the two cavaleros emerged from the shadows of the stable across the yard, spurring their horses with a fury. She could let them go. They weren't bound for the castile, the cowards. The killers. The frails!

Fetch snatched her stockbow to her shoulder and pulled the tickler. Unseen, her chosen man rode full tilt into his death. The bolt took him in the chest, knocking him backward to fall beneath the eaves of the stables.

The other cavalero kept going. Cursing, Fetch pulled another bolt. She felt the tightness in her chest, knew the coughing fit was coming, tried to hold it at bay for another few moments. Lungs fluttering in complaint, hands shaking with the effort, she fumbled the reload, the wet hacks bursting forth as her thrumbolt clattered to the roof.

The last cavalero passed beyond the brothel's low wall, his horse surging into a full gallop. Fetch succumbed to the fit, knowing to fight it was hopeless. Movement drew her eye below. Sluggard, freeing his hog from the hitching post, vaulting into the saddle. Bow in hand, he pursued. He couldn't hope to catch up. Horses were swifter than barbarians. But he didn't need to catch the rider. Only close the gap.

His hog still on the run, Sluggard stood in his stirrups. His arm snapped and returned to the bow three times in rapid succession. His arrows were invisible at this distance, but Fetch saw the rider jerk from the saddle at the gritter's first pull. The next two brought down the horse.

Fetch would have exhaled with relief, were she able to breathe.

By the time Sluggard returned to the yard, the fit had subsided. Fetch went back to the bathhouse, once again over the roof. Dropping down, she found Marrow gone and Slivers pawing at the dead men.

Seeing Fetch, he straightened, sour-faced. "Not a coin among them."

"You expected the purses of deserters to be bulging?"

The frailing dismissed that with a grunt, produced a grin, and swept the bathhouse with splayed arms. "How's that for standing with the Bastards, eh?"

Fetch planted a boot in his gut and pushed him to the ground.

"You rabid fucking dog!"

From the damp, Slivers crab-crawled, gaining some distance. One hand made a desperate gesture at the collection of new-made corpses. "I helped! Fought!"

"You want a reward?" Fetching snarled, ripping her tulwar free. At the sight of the drawn sword, Slivers shot to his feet in a backward stumble, kicking up gory water and panic. The bathhouse wall thumped him in the back, unexpected. He made a move to the left and Fetching threw, windmilling the curved blade into the timber next to Slivers's head. The steel smote wood, sending chunks flying as it buried deep. The frailing cried out in alarm and careened away in the opposite direction. Fetch intercepted, grabbing him by the front of his rotting brigand. Pressing her other hand into Slivers's cheek, she shoved his head toward the tulwar, still quivering in the wall. She forced his face up against the flat of the blade.

"You think me mad?" Fetching hissed. "You think me foolish?"

"Th-thought you wanted them . . . ah! Wanted them dead!"

She kept the pressure on Slivers's head with one hand, the other now seizing the grip of her tulwar. Slowly, she levered the blade downward, toward the pinned nomad's collarbone.

"You have no notion what I want. You're nothing but a louse trying to cling to a hog's back."

The edge of the tulwar slid down. Slivers struggled, but Fetch held him fast. The frailing's hands were free, no doubt there was a dagger within reach at his belt. Fetch ignored the danger. Hells, she courted it. Let this coward try to put steel in her gut, give her a reason to end him. In an attempt to escape the oncoming blade, Slivers let his knees go slack, but Fetch hooked a thumb under his jaw and lifted, arresting his collapse. Wood crunched as the sword hinged, approaching flesh and bone.

"Why us, Slivers? You want to be a sworn brother again, why not go to one of the other hoofs? I'll tell you. You're afraid of them. But not of the True Bastards. Not of me! You think I got some motherly instinct that will warm at the pitiful sight of you. It's not there,

Slivers. What should I do to make you understand that? What should I do to make you afraid of *me*?"

Decayed leather parted as the tulwar bit down, tasting flesh beneath. Slivers grunted with the pain, a higher note rising in his throat as fear took hold.

Fetching ceased pulling on the sword. "I've told you there's no place in my hoof. I've yelled, threatened, kicked. And still you try to cozen me with your whining, begging. Your backstabbing! Don't force me to put a thrumbolt in you, Slivers. I see you again, that's what I'll do."

Releasing the now-quaking frailing, Fetch let him fall, tearing her sword from the wall as she stepped away. She found Marrow and Sluggard standing in the enclosure. The older nomad wore a grimace.

"You see something disagreeable?" Fetch asked.

"Try and treat me like that," he said, pointing his nose at Slivers, "you will find out I am the disagreeable sort."

"Why would I treat you like that? You done something to make me angry?"

"Seems killing cavaleros is enough."

"Don't let nomad pride make you stupid, Marrow." Fetch pointed down at Slivers with her sword. "This useless fuck put us all in needless danger."

Marrow shrugged. "He's a frailing. Got more human blood than orc. Can't expect too much."

Fetch took a step toward the nomad. "I can't? I got a human woman tending our foundlings worth ten of the best riders in the Lots. Not a drop of orc blood in her. Every day, she shows me what I can expect, and it's a great deal. She's the reason I came to this damned place. You want to preach some shit about the strength of orc blood, go sniff around the Orc Stains. You don't look like a thrice, so they wouldn't have you. Maybe the Fangs of Our Fathers. How's your orcish?"

Stepping around the free-riders, she left the bathhouse.

Rhecia was in the taproom, her fair face flecked with small

scrapes. Several of the whores, including Cissy, were gathered nearby, tending their mistress. Their whispered voices hushed as Fetching came in. Reaching into the gaggle she grabbed Rhecia's arm.

"The rest of you stay put," she said, and pulled the woman out into the yard, half-dragging her to the well to be far from earshot. Rhecia was sullen as Fetch faced her. "They were penniless. Deserters heading for the Smelted Mounts. Don't know what they intended to do once you discovered they couldn't pay."

"Slap us. Laugh. Leave. You think this has not happened before?"

Fetch had no need to answer that. "Send your stable hand to the castile with word. If Bermudo needs me to vouch for what happened, he can send a rider to Winsome. Understand?"

"Yes."

Fetch strode to the hitching post. Marrow and Sluggard were already mounted.

"His orcish is terrible," Sluggard explained.

Fetch only grunted.

The brothel door jerked open while she was mounting. A slim human woman with a headscarf rushed out, her fresh, pretty face a sharp contrast to that of the scarred half-orc woman with her, the same one Fetch had seen earlier at the well. The mongrel hung back as the pretty frail approached.

"Please, hoofmaster," she said, the words delivered with deliberate deference and a trace of an accent Fetch could not place. "There are some here that would ask to come with you. To offer service to the True Bastards."

Fetch looked down. "Any of you a wet nurse?"

"No, but—"

"Then I got no place for you."

Fetch put heel to hog and left Sancho's, vowing for the last time.

SIX

"HAS THE TIDE ARRIVED?"

Fetch voiced the question before she was down from her hog.

Mead motioned for a slop to take Womb Broom in hand, shook his head.

"Damn . . ." She was home without a wet nurse and had hoped that, at the least, she would return to find fresh supplies waiting.

"But this did."

Mead produced a small hollowed bone and handed it over.

"Which of our birds?" Fetch asked as she removed the tiny coil of parchment from within.

"Strava."

Fetch felt her heart catch at the prospect of the Betrayer Moon, for the danger it posed. And for the mongrel it would force to return. Her fingers were suddenly clumsy, but she managed to roll out the sliver of parchment and reveal the message penned in a meticulous scrawl.

ZIRKO, HERO FATHER, HIGH PRIEST OF BELICO SUMMONS
THE CHIEFTAINS OF THE MONGREL HOOFS TO STRAVA ON
THE NOUMENIA GORPERETOS.

Frowning, she read it again.

"How long do we have?" Mead asked.

"It's not . . . I don't think it's the Betrayer. Zirko wants the chiefs to gather. He's fucking *summoning* us." She thrust the scroll back at Mead. "When is this? Never was good with Hispartha's fucking calendar."

His eyes moved quickly, his mind quicker. "It's the last new moon of summer. You have . . . a little less than a fortnight."

Mead handed the parchment back and Fetch crumpled it with a growl. Her people were starving and now she was being bidden to ride to halfling lands on the mysterious whim of their meddling holy man.

Marrow and Sluggard were off their hogs, the nomad reluctant to turn his over to the waiting slops while the gritter reveled in the help with an amused smile. Hood must have told the hoof about the possibility their chief was bringing free-riders back, for the newcomers were met without reluctance.

Fetch held fast to her own reservations.

"You two have earned yourselves somewhere to sleep tonight. Come the morning, you have to start convincing me you belong here."

Marrow frowned, taking in the twilit town. "Have we also earned dinner?"

"You want to be a Bastard, you eat what we eat," Fetch replied.

"And that is?"

"Tonight? Nothing." Fetching beckoned the slopheads to lead the nomads to the stables. As the young mongrels stepped to it, Fetch grabbed Abril's arm. "The fuck is wrong with your head, hopeful?"

The entire right half of his scalp was shaved from the center over.

"Orcs are bald," was all the explanation he gave.

Fetch gawked at him.

"I'm a half-orc," Abril told her. He pointed at the bisected hair and moved his finger slowly across the shaved side. "Half. Orc."

"Hells overburdened. You've just crowned yourself king of the fool-asses."

"What?" Abril lifted his chin at Mead. "He wears his hair like a Tine! Thinks it makes him immortal like them."

Mead expelled a laugh. "That's a widow's tale. Elves age and die same as us and the frails."

"Just see to the hogs, slop," Fetch said, releasing Abril with a slight shove.

They could still hear him muttering to Sence as they walked away. "Half. Orc. How's that fool-ass? What we are. He ain't an elf. . . ."

Following the hopefuls, Sluggard flashed a smile at Fetch as he passed. "Reminds me of the carnavales. I like it here already!"

Marrow stayed silent behind a frown.

Once they were out of earshot, Fetch turned to Mead. "Bunk them with the hoof. I want the boys to start taking their measure."

"I'll keep an eye on them," Mead said, tracking their progress into town. "Especially the dour one."

"It's the other that needs minding. Sluggard. Any mongrel that smiles so much needs to be watched closely."

"Jackal was always smiling," Mead observed.

Fetch began to walk away. "Exactly."

"Chief . . . where are you going?"

"My solar," she replied. "Need some damn rest."

"What about Zirko's message?"

"Fuck Zirko!"

Fetching needed to check in on the orphanage, but without a new wet nurse, the prospect of facing Thistle was not a welcome one. Besides, she'd been truthful with Mead. She was tired. The Bone Smiler's potion was to blame. Even the lone drop was difficult to endure. He wasn't wrong to call it poison. It left her feeling wobbly, with aches in her head and joints, and a dryness ever upon her tongue.

Once in her solar, she took a dose, lay back on her bed, and waited for the shivers to take root. It made her nights fitful, but far better than to suffer the effects during the day. She dozed. And awoke to full darkness beyond the balcony. A man stood before the opening.

Harelipped and sullen-eyed. Well, *eye*. The other had a thrumbolt embedded in the socket. Cavalero Garcia. Fetch had killed him at the brothel. Not today. The man today took the bolt in the chest and she'd not gotten a good look at his face. Perhaps that meant she would be spared a visit from him later.

Fetching cursed under her breath. The Bone Smiler had warned that the potion might cause her to see things. Why couldn't it have been a nicer vision? Jackal with his head at work between her legs, perhaps. She lay back down.

A cry from the wall sawed through a dreamless void.

Fetching snapped up, hand slapping down on her stockbow. It was still dark. The room had cooled. Instinct said she'd been asleep most of the night.

The shout came again, followed by another, this one answering, questioning. Fetch slung her stockbow and snatched up her sword belt. She descended the steps two at a time, buckling the tulwar to her hips as she went. Outside, slopheads and Bastards were making for the gate, where the sentries continued to yell, pointing with big gestures over the wall.

"Touro!" Fetching called out to the nearest rushing mongrel. The older slophead skidded to a stop. "Get two others and run the palisade. Make sure we aren't getting hit from all sides."

Touro nodded an affirmation and sprinted away, gathering up assistance on the run.

Fetch bolted for the gate, outpacing Dumb Door and several slops. Polecat had already gained the wall and joined the sentries that raised the alarm.

"What we got? Thicks?" Fetch demanded, her boot striking the third rung as she leapt onto the ladder and began to climb.

"It's . . . runners, chief," Polecat answered, his gaze fixed beyond the sharpened timbers of the stockade.

Clambering onto the walk, Fetch straightened and joined her men, following their uncertain eyes out into the night-shrouded expanse of the lot.

Revealed in the light of moon and stars, and the savage perceptions of her orc blood, Fetch saw a pair of figures making for the fort on foot, fast as their legs would allow. One was much larger than the other, bearing something across its shoulders. Another person.

"Open the gate!" Fetch cried.

She jumped from the walk to help. The timbers of the gate creaked as they pulled one-half open. The pair of sprinters rushed through the gap as soon as it was wide enough, the smaller entering and spilling face-first into the dust, legs given out. The opening barely permitted the bulk of the second arrival. It was a mongrel female, clearly a thrice-blood from her size. It was rare for a thrice to have hair, but this one's face was all but hidden behind a wild black curtain, as dry and coarse as a hog's bristles. Unlike her companion, she kept her feet as she trundled to a halt, jostling the limp form draped across her broad shoulders.

"Get that gate closed!" Fetch ordered, going to the prone figure. Squatting, she found the half-orc woman from Rhecia's raising her scarred face from the ground. "The hells? What's chasing you? Orcs?"

The mongrel shook her head, tried to answer, but was foiled by a dry tongue and heaving ribs.

"Chief!" Polecat hollered from above. "We got a rider!"

"Sss . . . Slivers," the scarred woman managed.

Fetch gnashed teeth. "He was fucking hunting you?"

"N-no. Kept . . . them off. Off . . . us."

"Them *who*?"

"The beasts."

It was the thrice-blood that answered.

Fetch jumped to her feet. "I need every thrum on the wall now! We got centaurs coming!"

She ran for the ladder, but as she passed the thrice, the hand of the figure slung over her shoulder darted out and grabbed Fetch's arm. It was the pretty frail who spoke to her at the brothel, barely conscious. Her voice leaked out, hardly a sigh.

"They're not . . . natural."

The girl's eyes rolled drunkenly and her hand fell away.

Fetch climbed the ladder. Polecat and Shed Snake made room at the edge of the stockade. Looking, she saw the hog, farther out than the women had been. Its gait was labored, flagging. The slight rider, unmistakably Slivers, twisted around in the saddle, loosing arrows over the barbarian's rump. Panic had seized his aim and the arrows flew impotently, never striking his pursuers.

"The fuck?" Fetch breathed, leaning forward and squinting at the loping shapes harrowing the fleeing hog.

Shed Snake affirmed her confusion. "Those . . . aren't 'taurs."

He was right. Fetch counted nearly a score of the creatures. From a distance, they could have been wolves, but each step closer betrayed them for something else. Something Fetch had never seen.

They were larger than wolves. Not longer or even taller, but more robust, especially in the chest and shoulders. The necks were thick and elongated, protruding from hunchbacked withers, and ending in broad heads with squat muzzles and rounded ears. Working as a pack, they harried Slivers's hog in relays, four of them rushing in to bite the barbarian's flanks, the remainder forming a wide, pursuing arc, blocking routes of escape.

"Take aim!" Fetch yelled, bringing her own weapon to her eye.

Slivers was trying to ride for the gate, but the strange beasts were herding him toward the neglected vineyards, where the ground was sloped and choked with withered vines.

Whatever these animals were, they were cunning hunters.

Slivers spent his last, fruitless, arrow. He faced forward and began an attempt to adjust his course. His hog fought him, fought against going nearer the snapping fangs of the encircling pack. The nomad was forced to toss his bow and seize the swine-yankers, muscling the hog's head away from the slopes. The pack punished the hog for its rebellion, surging forward to tear at its hocks. The barbarian squealed.

The beasts . . . laughed.

It was a queer, pulsing cackle, a high-pitched chorus of chilling giggles punctuated with throbbing whoops. The sound caused Fetch's hair to stand up, her scalp tingling with gooseflesh. She could feel her brothers on the wall shift uneasily at the sound, casting sidelong glances to see if anyone else was unnerved. She chose to answer that laughter by squeezing the tickler of her stockbow.

The string snapped forward, the prods thrummed, and the bolt flew. Her aim was true. The bolt took one of the beasts just above the foreleg, between the chest and shoulder. A heart-shot. The impact knocked the animal off its feet, its forward momentum causing it to hover in the air for a moment before spilling heavily into the dust, tumbling and sliding until it came to rest in a heap.

"Put these dogs down!" Fetch yelled, yanking back her bow-string until it locked and drawing another bolt from her quiver. The hoof began to loose, the thrums creating their own chorus. The ground around the chase erupted with striking shafts. Slivers flinched and ducked against the deadly, closely falling volley, but the sure aim of the hoof left him unstruck, a feat that also spared most of the surrounding, slavering beasts. They lurched and reeled against the onslaught of thrumbolts, but refused to give up their prey.

Four more fell. Not nearly enough

Slivers's hog was barely maintaining a trot now, blood trailing its slowing steps and staining the maws of its attackers. Through that terrible, undulating laughter, the nomad's voice rose.

"Open the gate! Please!"

Fetching felt the eyes of her hoof upon her. She said nothing. She could not risk those cackling curs getting inside.

Slivers's shouts were strident with fear. "OPEN! PLEASE!"

"Chief?" Snake prodded.

Without acknowledging he had spoken, Fetching reloaded her thrum and sighted along the shaft. She had told Slivers if he returned, he would die. Better by her promised hand, than the jaws of some vicious hounds.

An idea caused Fetch's fingers to jerk away from the tickler.

"Slivers!" she cried out, waving her arm repeatedly to the right. "The ditch! Ride in the ditch!"

For a heartbeat, it did not appear that the nomad understood, but at the last moment he pulled hard on his hog's left swine-yanker, forcing her head toward the fort's dry moat. The barbarian trundled down into the ditch, kicking up a storm of dust. The beasts followed, but were now hindered by the close confines of the rough trench, al-lowing only a pair to reach the hog at a time.

"Move!" Fetch commanded, rushing to her left, shoving past Shed Snake, and waving the rest of the hoof out of her way. She began sprinting along the palisade, in the opposite direction taken by Slivers. "Rope! Someone toss me some damn rope!"

"Chief!" a voice alerted her from below as a coil was thrown up from the yard. She caught it on the move, slung her stockbow, and began knotting a loop in one end of the stout hempen cord. Her boots pounding the boards of the walk, Fetch kept her gaze fixed beyond the wall, looking ahead and down, watching for Slivers. The ditch remained unfinished along the stretch below. She had to meet the nomad before he reached the end of the digging.

The laughter of the pack had not dwindled and seemed to roof Winsome with its bloodthirsty cadence. Farther down the walk, Fetch spied Touro and a pair of younger slops, those she had ordered away from the gate to check the perimeter.

"They coming?!" she called.

Touro did not allow his confusion to slow his wits. He leaned far out over the wall and looked. "They are!"

Without breaking stride, Fetch threw the loop of the rope around one stake in the stockade, wrapped the other end around her left wrist, and vaulted over the wall. Stomach lurching, she dropped until the rope arrested her fall with a vicious jerk that tore at her shoulder. She was now dangling only a few handspans above where the base of the wall met the earthworks. Planting her boots against the timbers, Fetching leaned out over the ditch, extending both her arms to their limits, one gripping the rope, the other thrust out and waiting.

Slivers appeared a heartbeat later, his hog coming around the bend in the ditch. Two of the beasts were now running along the outer edge of the moat, keeping pace, forcing him to bend doubled over his hog's neck to keep out of reach of their snapping jaws.

Fetch sent a strident whistle through her teeth. It lanced through the cackling of the pack and Slivers's gaze snapped up, fixing on Fetch's outstretched hand. The pack must have seen it too, for they stopped laughing. Somehow, the sudden silence was worse. Slivers spurred his barbarian onward, and like all good hogs, she had a little more to give at the very end. The sow surged away from the pack, bringing Slivers charging toward Fetch's arm. Just as he stood in the saddle, his own arms reaching, Fetch kicked away from the wall. The nomad's hands slapped around her forearm, his forward momentum causing Fetch to swing backward. The extra weight forced the rope around her wrist to tighten, biting flesh.

"Hold tight, you scrawny fuck!" Fetch growled through her teeth.

Swinging forward again, she twisted her body so her boots again smote the wall. Using the nomad as a pendulum, she began to run along the surface of the stockade. The pack was below, jostling one another as they struggled to maneuver in the confines of the ditch. Slivers began to shout, kicking his dangling legs as the animals jumped up, jaws snapping wetly. Powered by her legs and the swinging weight of the frailing, Fetch reached the upmost swell of the arc. There was a moment of weightlessness and in that moment Fetch swiftly rotated her wrist, wrapping more of the rope around her arm. As she and Slivers began to swing down once more, they were a handbreadth closer to the top of the palisade.

The nomad gave a wordless cry as his legs again baited the beasts. They were yowling and snarling, trying to use the embankment to scramble toward their prey.

Touro appeared above, leaning out to grasp the swaying rope.

"Leave it!" Fetch shouted, and the slop obeyed. He wouldn't be able to haul them up on his own and the two hopefuls with him were little more than boys. All they would accomplish was to cease the rope's swing, and Fetch would be damned if she was going to dangle motionless. She just needed to keep free from the fangs long enough for the hoof to pull them up.

The pack had other designs.

Looking down into those leering faces, Fetch realized that not one had pursued the injured hog. Too late, she remembered the pair that left the trench.

She looked up in time to see the first pounce, leaping over the ditch to barrel into Slivers just as their backward swing began to angle upward. The rope threatened to sever Fetch's wrist as the added weight struck. Slivers howled as the beast's jaws clamped down on his arm. Unable to let go of Fetch, unable to fight back, the little nomad could do nothing as the beast savaged him, hanging from its teeth, shaking its head and body furiously until flesh and muscle tore free. The demon-dog dropped into the ditch, a crimson hunk of Slivers clenched between its gory teeth. Tormented wails gushed from the frailing's lips. His ravaged arm could no longer sustain a grip. Now grasping one-handed, Slivers slipped closer to the ditch and its ravenous occupants.

Shouts from above signaled the hoof's arrival. Immediately, Fetch felt her pendulous course arrested as the rope was hauled upward. Pain and dread had fully possessed Slivers, causing him to struggle. His frantic kicks only served to loosen his hold, and Fetch felt him slipping.

"Slivers! Stop! We have you!" she cried.

Her voice reached him and he stilled, feeling the rising of the rope. He looked up then, his face molded into a wide mask of relief.

And then the other beast struck.

A moment more and they would have been too high to reach, but the devil shot across the expanse, mouth agape, until it closed around the nomad's ankle. Fetch steeled her fingers around Slivers's arm, yet he slipped from her as easily as water. The nomad plunged into the waiting mouths. He vanished beneath a roiling mass of filthy, spotted fur, his shrieks all that remained until they too were swallowed.

Strong hands helped lift Fetching over the stockade, a dozen exclamations of relief issuing from her hoofmates before her feet even touched the boards. She was deaf to their concern, hearing only the sound of the feasting pack, and when that ended, the mocking laughter as it slunk away, dragging a horrid tangle of moist bones.

SEVEN

THE ENTIRE HOOF STOOD WATCH for the rest of the night, slops alongside sworn brothers and nomads, every spear, javelin, and thrumbolt brought up from the sad stores of the armory. Fetching walked a steady patrol, never stopping, avoiding the questions she could not answer. What, in all the hells, were those dogs? What if they returned? Fetch had no answers, no matter if the questions came from her brethren or from her own uneasy mind.

Dawn found the slopheads still manning the wall, and the True Bastards riding out in loaded kit. At full strength they were only six riders, and Fetch was tempted to bring Marrow and Sluggard along. But this was not their problem, so Fetching gave them a reprieve. And a meager meal.

The gate creaked open. Fetch rode point, Mead and Dumb Door on her left flank, Polecat and Shed Snake on her right. Hoodwink took the rear guard. They ran a tight circuit around Winsome, making sure the pack was truly gone. They saw nothing, heard nothing. Returning to the gate, they set off to get a look at the beasts they had slain.

And found nothing.

"I put one down right here!" Polecat declared from astride his hog at the edge of a neglected vineyard. "Right. Fucking! HERE!"

He stabbed furiously with a finger, pointing at empty ground.

"Fan out," Fetching ordered, meeting Cat's ire with calm. "See if they slunk off before dying."

She knew it would be a wasted effort. Her own stockbow had dropped two of the animals, putting a bolt through the heart of the first and the eye of the second. Nothing crawled away with such injuries.

The hoof came back with only a few recovered thrumbolts.

"It's possible they came back for their dead," Mead offered. "Easy meat."

"Anybody see them come back?" Shed Snake asked. "We were all on the walls."

Head shakes answered.

Beneath Fetching, Womb Broom stamped and snorted, displaying the frustration she kept locked behind her jaw. She looked at Hoodwink. "Any sign of that? Drag trails? Blood?"

"No."

"Then we keep looking."

In the ditch, it was a gruesome, simple matter to find where Slivers died, the blood obvious and accusing.

"We got sign, chief," Shed Snake said.

Paw prints and drag marks decorated the dust above the ditch, leading away from Winsome. Slivers's hog was also visible, the body lying at the end of the trench where the digging had not been completed. Fetch was about to lead her hoof away, follow the pack's trail, when Dumb Door broke formation, yanking his hog around and riding hard until he was above the pitiful lump of Slivers's barbarian. The big mongrel dismounted and half climbed, half slid down the dusty slope into the ditch. When Fetch and the hoof caught up, Dumb Door was squatting beside the sow's body, hands and eyes at work.

"Door?" Fetch asked.

The mute mongrel looked up and held his fist in front of his chest, fingers splaying and clenching in repetition.

Fetch was amazed. "She's still alive?"

Dumb Door nodded.

"Can you save her?"

A pause. Another nod, this one less sure, but the face was hopeful.

The slopheads along the wall had been watching. Fetch ordered five of them to come out and lend aid.

"Move her inside if you can," Fetch told Dumb Door. "But if she's still out here come sundown, we will have to end her."

Another nod, this one grave.

Fetch signaled Hood and he led the rest of the hoof along the pack's trail. After a straight path away from the walls it began to meander, running for less than a mile before entering a stretch of scrub. The mean vegetation was not enough to conceal even one of the devil-dogs, much less a pack. The Bastards rode slowly through the sharp bushes and pale grass, searching for spoor. When that yielded nothing, Fetch again ordered them to fan out. Every mongrel came back shaking his head.

The trail had vanished.

Polecat raged. "This is fucking hogshit!"

"Rein it in," Fetch told him. "You're bordering on useless."

He calmed and nodded, joining his brothers in silence as they gave their chief a moment to think.

A grouped patrol of the entire lot was impossible before nightfall, and Fetch would not split the hoof. The pack had proven it was capable of taking a lone rider. There was no other course but to scout the more inaccessible places, the myriad slot canyons, gulches, and boulder-choked hills, the most likely spots for the pack to have gone to ground. She gave the order and the True Bastards rode, mongrels and hogs searching tirelessly.

The day bequeathed one clue on its deathbed, revealed by a flight of circling vultures to the west. The hoof was just south of the Alhundra River, picking through the marshy lowlands that spilled away from the confluence with the River Lucia. By the time they arrived, the carrion birds cavorted upon a sunbaked causeway of cracked mud.

Fetch had expected to find Slivers's remains. The truth was far worse.

The stench struck them before the sight. It was the throat-choking, unmistakable smell of Ul-wundulas's heat at work upon dead flesh, forcing every rider to tie a kerchief around their lower face. Every rider except Hoodwink. Five dead hogs littered the bleached ground, surrounding an overturned wagon. Casks and crates lay shattered, their contents rotting in the heat along with the mongrels tasked with delivering them. There would be six bodies, though it was difficult to discern individuals among the bestrewn rib cages and viscera. Six half-orc riders reduced to table scraps.

"Hells fuck my mouth," Polecat groaned through his kerchief.

Mead's eyes were unblinking. "It's our supplies. From the Tusked Tide."

Any other day such an obvious remark would have earned him a cuff across the back of the head, but today the Bastards' shit luck had to be voiced to be believed.

"See if anything can be salvaged," Fetch said.

They chased off the vultures with whoops and rushing hogs, dismounting to pick through the debris. It was a useless effort. There was nothing but corpse flies.

"No spent bolts," Hoodwink remarked, returning from a scout of the area. His breeches were wet to the thigh, showing he had gone wading in the marsh.

"Their quivers were empty long before they got here," Fetch agreed. "This was a last stand after a long chase. They were herded here."

Polecat squatted by the yoke of the overturned cart. "One of the draft pigs broke harness. That's what flipped them." He pointed out to the body of the farthest hog, half-submerged in bog water. "Bolted that far before they drug him down. The three mongrels riding wain were probably torn apart before they even picked themselves up."

"And the patrol riders made a stand of it," Mead finished, picking up a fallen tulwar. "With nothing but slicers."

The ground was ravaged, but a few discernible paw prints were stamped in the mud. And again, the trail vanished without trace.

Hoodwink mounted up next to Fetching, his pale eyes flicking up at the darkening sky. "We need to go."

Fetching could only nod in agreement and turn her hog's head to home.

The sun had kerchiefed its own face with the horizon by the time they returned to Winsome. Fetch dismounted and sent a slop to find Dumb Door, ordering that the sworn brethren meet. Before that, there were others she wanted words with.

Mead went with her to the cordwainer's house. The man and his wife were long gone, lost to the Tide after the Kiln fell, but the woven awning extending from the front remained. Where once the trades-man sat in the shade working leather into shoes, now waited the trio of unwelcome guests, guarded by Abril and Petro. The scarred one was much recovered, standing firm with sinewy arms crossed as if offended by the presence of the armed slopheads. She had at least a dozen years on Fetching, though the damage to her face may have weighted the estimation. The human was seated, still feeble, but conscious. She once again wore the headscarf of undyed linen draped loosely over her head and shoulders. Between mongrel and frail, the thrice-blood leaned against the doorjamb to keep her head from brushing against the awning's crucks.

"What can you tell me?" Fetch demanded, striding up.

"Name's Dacia," the scarred one said, stepping out into the fad-ing sun. "We came with a mind to—"

"I don't care a fuck about your names or what was on your minds. The beasts. Tell me about the hells-damned dogs! Where did they set upon you?"

Fetch's harshness washed over the haggard mongrel. "Didn't see them until we were almost in sight of these walls. Heard them a ways before that, though."

"That queer laughing?"

A single nod.

Fetch stepped around her, went beneath the awning to lean down in the human's face. "You said they weren't natural."

This one didn't quail at Fetch's anger either. No surprise. Whores were inured to hostility. The memory, however, turned the woman's already-wide eyes into lustrous, disturbed seas.

"They would not die. Slivers put arrows in them, but they stood once more. Kept chasing."

Fetch shot Mead a look over her shoulder. He'd gone a bit ashen.

"There are similar beasts in my homeland," the frail went numbly on. "Smaller. *Dibà*, we call them. They are mere animals. Vile scavengers, but animals."

"*Dibà?*" Mead repeated, his gift for tongues able to match the girl's accent.

Her eyes shifted to him, managed to focus. "It would come to your tongue from the name given by the Old Imperium. Hyenas. The creatures that attacked us, however, were larger than any I have ever seen. Surely, they were *djinn*. Devils in animal guise."

Fetch didn't have Mead's talents, but she knew swaddlehead when she heard it. And she didn't like the sound.

"Where's your home?" she asked.

"Sardiz."

Fetch gave an affirming grunt, narrowed her eyes. "In Tyrkania."

"The Empire may have claimed my city," the frail replied with some fire. "That does not mean I must claim the Empire."

Fetch straightened, uncaring, and walked out to Mead. "Time to talk to the brethren."

"What about us?" the scarred mongrel called after them.

"What about you?" Fetch replied, only half turning.

"We got a purpose here."

"It was better served where you were. Soon as it's safe, my riders will escort you back to the brothel."

Again, she turned to go.

"We're no whores."

Fetch didn't begin this day with patience and had no desire to go digging deep for an untapped vein. She spun.

"No, I reckon not. You cleaned. The thrice there, what, cracked skulls when the men got rowdy? Did Rhecia cast her out when she failed to even show her face against those deserters? Because I don't recall seeing her." Fetch threw a dismissive hand at the small, seated woman. "As for the frail, fresh as she looks, I'll wager she just lost nerve. I'm sure Rhecia will help her with that before long. Nothing here for you—any of you—but hunger, believe me. You walked here for nothing."

The scarred mongrel's gaze was steady. "We walked so we could ride."

It took Fetch a moment to realize what she had just heard. Even with understanding, she hesitated.

"You want to join the hoof?"

Another nod. "We do."

Fetch cast dagger-eyes at Mead, her ire causing him confusion. Hells, she didn't know why she was angry. Sparing him the injustice, she returned to the stranger. "What was your name?"

"Dacia," the mongrel woman answered. She gestured back beneath the canopy. "The big one is Incus and the slip is—"

"No frails in a mongrel hoof," Fetch cut in.

Dacia gave a thin smile. "Best come out, Ahlamra. Let the chief get a better look."

The slender woman moved from beneath the awning, her gait fluid. Like Dacia, she wore breeches and shirt, though far less tattered. She reached up and lowered the scarf to reveal golden curls that fell just past her ears, far from the black hair possessed by most Easterners. She kept her chin lowered as she approached, raising those limpid eyes once she stood before Fetch. Her honey skin matched her hair, though here the gold was infused with a flawless flush of olive. It was this subtle hue that spoke of orc blood, but only a vestige. The girl did not have even a hint of lower fangs. Fetch had been called beautiful and received lustful stares from men in her life, but the creature before her possessed something unrivaled.

"My grandmother was a frailing," she offered in response to Fetch's dubious squint. Her tone was modest yet not meek.

"It's a *half*-orc hoof, waif," Fetch told her. "My tulwar weighs more than you."

"Let this one make up the difference," Dacia said, and motioned for the thrice-blood to come forward.

Skin the color of iron emerged from the shadows, encasing

gnarled muscles and swollen veins on the exposed flesh of the thrice's arms. Had Oats been standing here, they would be of equal height.

"And you're called Incus?" Fetch asked.

"Yes."

The voice that emerged from the black mane was thick and dull-sounding.

"She simple?" Fetch asked Dacia.

"No," Incus replied. "But I am deaf."

Fetch rewarded the jest with a laugh, holding up a contrite hand. "Very well. Pardons for being a cunt."

"She's telling you true," Dacia said. "Incus can't hear thunder."

Fetch found herself with a slack jaw. "Fucking deaf? How is she answering me?"

"Your lips shape the words," came the hollow reply.

"Dumb Door's mute, chief," Mead pointed out.

"Then you best pretend you're him right now!" Fetch snapped. She looked at the thrice-blood. "You can't be in a hoof if you can't hear."

Dacia scratched at her close-cropped hair. "My understanding is hogs are loud on the run. Pounding hooves and all. Reason the hoofs use hand signals."

"Hand signals don't do much good standing watch on our walls," Fetch said. "Need to be able to hear if a cry is raised to warn of thicks or centaurs."

"Hope that mute mongrel you got ain't the one needing to raise the cry, then," Dacia returned.

Fetching punched the woman in her clever, cut-up face and knocked her flat.

She expected Incus to retaliate, but the thrice remained motionless. Ahlamra merely lowered her eyes. Dacia sat up from her back and spit blood in the dust. Fetching paced in front of them, clenched fists itching for further defiance. When none came, she called over her shoulder to Mead.

"Get these three outside my walls."

"Chief?"

"You fucking heard!"

Dacia jumped back to her feet, split lip wrinkled with confused alarm.

"This a jest? Some fucking trial?"

Fetch shook her head. "No. You've no place in my hoof. Any of you."

"Why cast us out?" Ahlamra asked. "What offense have we given?"

"Got my reasons. And the offense is pretending you all don't know them. Run off and tell your master you failed."

"I have no master," Incus said. The voice was toneless, yet still Fetch detected offense.

Dacia cast searching looks at the other two. These three didn't know each other well, Fetch now saw.

"Sounds like you got enemies," Dacia said. "We ain't them. Not serving anyone but ourselves. And you, if you'll let us."

"Can't risk that," Fetch replied. "Three mongrels I don't know, brought by another I didn't much like, all chased by some queer beasts." She stepped to Ahlamra and leaned down close. "And one of you has all manner of names for them. Names that are damn tough to say. What were they again?"

The girl took a breath to answer, but Fetch cut her off.

"Uhad Ul-badir Taruk Ultani."

Ahlamra was unaffected. "You think me something I am not. That name is not known to me."

Fetch sneered. "I suspect he's got more than one."

"I do not serve any."

"And I've a second cunt!" Fetch stepped away. "Mead. We'll be escorting these strangers out of town. *Now.*"

"Please. I can prove myself. I can be useful, given a chance—"

The girl's words trailed off at the sight of Fetch unslinging her stockbow.

"No chance, Tyrkanian." Fetch loaded a bolt. "Just a choice."

"Chief," Mead cautioned.

Refusing to heed, Fetch pointed her weapon. Ahlamra quailed, retreating a step from the thrumbolt now trained upon her chest.

"Choice is this," Fetch said. "Leave my walls and live. Or stay.

And I put this bolt through your heart here and now. Your traveling companions can make their choice after they see I'm not bluffing."

Dacia took a step, placed herself between Ahlamra and the thrum.

"I don't think you're bluffing," she said. "But I am starting to think you're fucking mad."

"Neither quality bodes well for you, does it?"

"No. Means I'm likely to die today. Either from you or those cackling curs lurking outside. Also means I was wrong to come. Wrong to leave Hispartha, to wait in that fuckhouse until a rider came along to lead us here. And one did. Not some nomad, neither, but Fetching, the chief herself. The one we all came here to find, the three of us, from different roads. But she thought us whores and refused to listen and left us standing. We had a choice then too. To give up or press the fuck on! Well . . ." Dacia gave a bitter shrug. "Slivers wasn't welcome at the brothel no more, so we offered him what coin Incus had left and were picking your dust out of our teeth before it could settle. He was to get us close and ride on, seeing as he believed you'd kill him, same as I believe you'll kill us now. But then those dogs attacked and it was his turn to make a choice. He could have left us. Didn't. If you could ask him now, reckon he'd say it was the wrong one. That's the way I'm feeling about mine this very heartbeat, in all earnest. So pull that tickler, chief, if you think me a liar. Swore when I left for the Lot Lands it was to ride with the Bastards or die trying. Rather take a swift bolt than be torn apart by them monsters, given that's the choice."

"Warming speech," Fetch said. "But the Bastards have experience with a strange mongrel showing up unexpected. He was good with words too. And running his minions in here while making it appear they're in danger is just the manner of scheme he'd use. Your story changes nothing."

"Then do what you must," Ahlamra said. Slowly, with fluid grace, she stepped around Dacia's shielding form and knelt. "I do not serve this man you named. If I did, I would not fear the *djinn* shaped as *dibà*. I do. So I shall die here, swiftly, cleanly, and under the command of none since you will not take me."

Dacia swallowed hard and knelt beside her.

The thrice's face was obscured by her hair, but she too, lowered herself to the dust.

"Enough of this shit," Fetch said. "Get the fuck on your feet."

None moved.

"I said on your damn feet, slopheads! Being deaf, scarred, or a waif shouldn't mean I must repeat myself! UP!"

Dacia was the first to comprehend, and she bounced up with a smile growing on her busted lips. Incus followed to tower on her left. Last came Ahlamra, eyes downcast.

Fetch swept an arm at Petro and Abril. "Get them installed in the slop barracks."

"Yes, chief." Petro gestured for the women to follow.

Abril placed himself in front of Incus, walking backward. "Fortunate you can't hear. Most of the boys snore. I'm Abril. I'll help you find a lower bunk. Or maybe an upper if it's above Uidal. He snores loudest. That way, if you break the bunk and fall, you'll crush him and we'll all sleep better . . . after we get back to sleep from the crash . . ."

Fetch caught Ahlamra's arm as she passed, hauled her close and hissed. "I catch you fucking the boys for favors or easy treatment, you're back out in the badlands, devil-dogs or no. Understand?"

"I do."

"It's 'Yes, chief.'"

"Yes, chief."

Fetch released her, choking on a rising cough to keep it quiet.

Mead came up beside her. "Thought you were going to feather them there for a moment. Damn good ruse, chief."

"No ruse. Would have killed them, but . . ."

"Your gut said otherwise."

Fetch nodded. "They're either telling the truth or are damn good mummers. Perhaps I should ask Sluggard to evaluate their performance."

"You trust him already, then?"

He tried to bury it, but she caught the chide in Mead's voice. It forced her to consider.

"Do I trust him with my life? No. That's reserved for sworn

brothers. But I don't think he means us any harm. He didn't show up unexpected with a stiff cod for joining the hoof. Reckon that will make me suspicious to my dying day."

Mead nodded slowly with agreement. The way his eyes twitched and mouth drew tight betrayed he was holding something back.

"What?"

"Well . . ." Mead ran a hand through his Tine plume. "He didn't show up with a stiff cod for the *hoof*."

Fetch regretted goading him, and made him regret being goaded with the look she gave. "I'm getting the urge to put a thrumbolt in someone again."

Mead began to sidle off. "I'll just go gather the boys."

"It's like you're fucking smart or something."

THE BASTARDS ASSEMBLED IN THE abandoned cooper's shop, the place where they once voted to make Fetch chief. It had since become their new meeting hall. Mead sat at the cooper's old workbench, Polecat and Shed Snake on either side of him. Dumb Door settled his big frame on a stack of boards behind them. Hoodwink stood in his usual place, leaning against the wall next to the unfinished coffins. No one spoke. Gone was the typical crassness and levity that customarily began a hoof meet, even in the hardest of times.

Fetch usually stood, but she allowed the weight of the past night and day to sink her onto the edge of an old barrel, running a hand through her tightly braided locks and untying the leather thong that held them all together. She shook the dust out of her hair with aggravated fingers and glanced at Dumb Door.

"How's that sow?"

Dumb Door picked up a stray nail from among his seat of lumber and held it up.

Fetch found a grin. "Tough. Good work. Hope she pulls through. Anyone remember what Slivers called her?"

There was a small silence before Hoodwink's thin voice answered. "Little Orphan Girl."

Fetch saw Polecat's eyes brighten and the corners of his mouth draw up.

"Don't," she said, just as he drew breath to make the jest.

Polecat's teeth clacked shut.

Mead blew out a long breath. "Well. Now we know why we are starving. These . . . hyenas have picked our lot clean. First they kill all the game, then stop our resupply."

"You don't really believe that," Shed Snake said. "No pack of animals is that cunning."

Snake was trying to convince himself, trying to find any other explanation. But he had seen what they all saw, beasts that left no dead. Beasts that dogged seasoned mongrel riders into inescapable terrain to be slaughtered in a place patrols rarely penetrated.

"Crafty is."

Every eye fixed on Fetching. Her face must have been carved in certainty, for none challenged her statement. And she *was* certain. She could smell that tubby, turbaned wizard in this new devilry.

"Then," Mead began slowly, "that means Jackal hasn't found him."

"Or did find him," Hoodwink said.

"So . . ." Polecat ventured, "if Crafty is back in the Lots, does that mean Jackal is—"

"I don't know." Fetch cut him off, trying not to snap, and failing. "I just know that for the first months we were getting through. Then the vines withered, the groves were consumed by pests, and now that we are weak from hunger these mocking demons show themselves, and all of it reeks of that fat, swaddleheaded Tyrkanian FUCK!"

Jumping up, Fetching stomped a kick into the barrel behind, staving it in.

Silence followed. Eventually, Mead cleared his throat.

"We need to inform the Tusked Tide."

Fetch had already considered that. "I'll send a bird."

"We certain it will arrive? If Crafty is trying to cut us off, he won't allow—"

"I know. But I can't risk one of you to make the ride. Those creatures are clearly stalking the route between here and the Wallow. If they intend to cut us off, no rider from either hoof is making that journey unmolested. Six mongrels weren't safe, let alone one. We can't go. Right now I'm more concerned with feeding our folk. How long can we hold out with what food we have?"

Mead sighed. "At current ration? A fortnight. But barely. After that we're eating our hogs' rations. And then, we're eating . . ."

The Bastards let silence reign, chewing on that bitter root.

Slaughtering a barbarian for meat was nearly unthinkable. A hoof that resorted to that may as well starve. But such ideals would be meaningless to the villagers once their children started dying.

"There's something hitched to that same yoke. We got five new mouths to feed. Two nomads and three female hopefuls. We will see what they're worth beginning tomorrow. But so long as those women are slopheads, they are to be treated like slopheads. That means you can't bed them."

Polecat grinned and elbowed Mead. "Hells, I've been known to shag a slop ass a time or two. Sometimes they even like it."

Fetch sighed. "I hope you're jesting, Cat. Trouble is, I can't tell."

Polecat winked across the table at Shed Snake. "You can ask our newest blood."

There came the sound of splintering wood. "Do anything to those women, Polecat, and I'll make you one! You better hope your cock is as big as you claim because it will be the only thing you'll eat for a fucking month!"

Fetch found the end of one table board broken beneath the knuckles of her right hand. Her lungs felt solid and she could not fight the fit of coughing. When she recovered, the hoof was still, all eyes staring. Most were wide, but Hood was frowning.

"Fucking sawdust," Fetch said, clearing her clogged throat. Blinking the water from her eyes, she sat back down and regarded her brothers. "The free-riders need your attention more than the new slops. Focus on them."

There were mumbled assents and reserved nods.

"We need to kill the dogs," Hood hissed, drawing the focus away from Fetch's rasping.

Dumb Door rapped a knuckle on the lumber to gain attention. He shook his head, made a slicing motion across his throat with a finger, shook his head again, and placed a hand over his eyes.

"You're right," Fetching said. "We can't kill what we can't find."

Shed Snake clicked his tongue with annoyance. "So . . . what? We're stuck waiting on them to strike again?"

"What says they will?" Polecat asked. "If the wizard is trying to starve us out, he doesn't need to do anything more. Just wait."

"Then why attack Slivers and those women?" Shed Snake countered.

"Maybe he wanted us to see his hand in this," Mead said. "Spook us. Fear eats away at a foe same as hunger. Crafty would know that."

"And the dogs will not be his only trick," Hoodwink said.

Fetch heard the implication in his spare voice. Was Crafty to blame for her sickness? It was likely.

Crafty had said her elf blood would protect her from the Sludge Man's touch. The wizard had been right, and the Sludge Man was now dead, one of the few beings Crafty seemed to fear. But had the wizard gained more than one dead rival? Had he also manipulated the poisoning of another? The same blood that aided in the defeat of the Sludge Man also thwarted Crafty's own magic. She could still recall the shocked look on his puffy face when his flung powder failed to stop her on the Kiln's gantry.

Fetching stood, revelation making the movement swift and abrupt. She walked a tight circle, popping a few knuckles before facing her hoof once more.

"He fears me," she declared. "Us! He can no longer come at us with guile, so he's become a besieger, strangling our ability to survive. His laughing dogs killed six Tuskers. What was to prevent them from doing the same to the six of us today?"

Polecat rubbed at his jaw. "Hoodwink? Certainly wasn't Shed Snake. Unless them dogs are scared of nasty burn scars."

That earned a few smiles.

Mead remained pensive. "If your elf blood is holding him back from a direct assault, perhaps we should turn to Dog Fall. The Tines might know the best way to fight him."

"The only folk that go into Dog Fall without an invitation are those the Tines have taken prisoner. And they are never seen again." Fetch shook her head. "No. If we were welcome in those mountains, Warbler would have sent word. Besides, you've heard my elvish."

Mead's raised eyebrows conceded the point. "You'd start a war."

Fetch gave him a withering look.

"We don't know Crafty's limits, but he has them, and we need to stop allowing him to decide ours. If he wanted us dead, he could have set his dogs upon our patrol riders, picked us off one at a time. No, he wants us weak, not to be rid of us."

The thought made Polecat anxious. "Weak for what?"

Fetch's silence was an admission. She didn't damn know.

EIGHT

THE HOOF HUNTED THE DOGS by day. When that proved fruitless they began hunting at night. They rode eleven strong, every sworn brother plus the two nomads and three senior slops, every saddle bristling with full quivers and javelin braces. It sent a surge through Fetching, having that many riders in formation behind her. Yet every excursion saw them return to Winsome with nothing. If not for her brothers' rage at their elusiveness, Fetch would have thought the pack to be another addled vision caused by the Bone Smiler's medicine.

They searched with dogged determination for nearly a week, the rationing tightened with every day their quarry remained hidden.

Despite the furious patrols, life within the walls remained a succession of tedious chores. Fetch had to survey the small gardens and orchards the villagers maintained, and listen to the predictions of their increasingly nervous tenders.

"My broad bean patches do well, but I fear a fungus before harvest."

"This last medlar tree barely yields enough for my children."

"Someone's been pilfering my quinces. You need to put a stop to it!"

All were met with empty promises and hollow encouragement.

She could not summon even that meager generosity when training the slops.

"Worthless! Do I need to light these butts afire for you to be able to hit them?"

The Bastards had returned from their fifth night hunt and Fetching, refusing to rest, ordered the hopefuls roused before the sun for stockbow drills. The straw targets set up beneath the western curve of the wall were winning the engagement.

"If those were charging thicks, you'd all be butchered by now!" She swatted one slop on the back of the head. "I expect better from you, Graviel. Touro, have you been struck blind?"

"No, chief."

"Sorry, chief."

She'd commanded the three women to join the drill. Traditionally, it was far too soon to give a fresh slop a stockbow, but every one of the trio was older than the other hopefuls and Fetch needed to see their skill. Needed to see if they were worth feeding.

She was not pleased.

"That was three flights, Dacia. You strike true even once?"

"Yes, chief. Once," the mongrel answered, never taking her eyes off the butt.

"Where?"

"Center. Near the ground."

"Unless he was dangling a cock the size of an elephant trunk, that bolt would have passed between his legs. That's a miss. Didn't even slow him. You were the first to die."

Incus had struck center with two bolts, but the third was not to be found.

"Those all you loosed?"

The deaf thrice-blood nodded. She had tied her dense hair away from her broad face to reveal jutting cheekbones and a single fang protruding from her wide lower lip.

"You're a steady shot," Fetch commended, "but take too damn

long to aim. Anyone can strike center if they have all the time it takes. Get faster."

"I will."

Fetching hissed with displeasure when she reached Ahlamra. The barely mongrel girl had not loosed a single bolt and was still struggling to pull back the string on her weapon.

"Enough," Fetch said, snatching the stockbow from her shaking grip. "You ain't got the strength. Hells, doubtful you could do it with a crank to help you like the damn frails. Dacia may be dead, but you? You're alive right now. Sprawled in the dirt, an entire *ulyud* having its way with you. That's six orcs with their blood and cocks up. Best hope they get overzealous and kill you quick. Otherwise, you're bringing a get into the world with more thick blood than you got."

Ahlamra weathered that prognostication with her customary dipped chin.

Fetch dismissed the waif with a tilt of her head. "Go find Dumb Door at the stables. Tell him you're to shovel hogshit until you're strong enough to yank a thrumcord." The lithe mongrel hurried away, the admonishment removing none of the grace from her steps. "The rest of you, another volley! Whoever misses is going to be deepening the gong pit. I'm wagering Dacia will be up to her elbows in my nightsoil before the dew has dried. Wonder who else is going to join her? Load! Aim . . . LOOSE!"

By the time Hoodwink arrived to drill the slops in hand-fighting, Fetch's prediction had proved true. Dacia had been sent away, along with Lopo and Graviel. Both hopefuls had long since proven to be keen aims, but their skills had faded. Lack of food was the cause. The solution was as evasive as the laughing dogs.

"Prop your stockbows against the wall and circle up!" Fetch said. "Who's going to test themselves against Hood today?"

The hopefuls were tired, listless, most keeping their noses pointed at the dust.

"I will," came a toneless reply.

Incus's arms were crossed in front of her chest, two fingers of her right hand raised.

The ring of slops came awake.

Hoodwink was already shedding his sword belt, plucking knives from everywhere and tossing them point first into the ground. Stepping forward, his movements struck Fetch as weirdly reminiscent of Ahlamra's, silent and smooth. Incus's approach was akin to a sullen ox. Slowly, she removed the leather thong from atop her head, allowing her hair to once again smother her face. Fetch didn't know how the thrice could even see through that wiry drape.

Her first jab was so swift, propelling such a large mass of fist, that the rush of air barreling out of its path was audible. The only thing faster was Hood. Twisting, he slipped the blow and danced back, out of his opponent's greater reach. There had been an opening there for him to punish her ribs, but he'd chosen to ignore it, Fetch saw. Incus saw too, for her hair billowed slightly from a perturbed breath and she did not press the attack. Instead, she lowered her hands, abandoned her stance, and just stood.

Waiting.

Hoodwink paced around her. The slops widened the circle at his approach as if he were made of snake venom. All of them had faced him in training. None had ever landed a blow.

He darted, a viper with four limbs, quick enough to flank Incus, though she'd been revolving to track him. His fist came for her kidney, but she hunched, caught his knuckles on her elbow. Several slops winced at the sound. Hood had no time for pain. His other fist came for Incus's face and, to whoops of approval, she leaned into the blow. Another thud resounded as the thrice head-butted Hood's hand, bending his wrist. It was a small miracle the bones did not snap. Fetch thought she might actually have seen Hoodwink's lip turn down in a grimace. This time, he didn't retreat, and threw a knee at Incus's gut. She slapped it down, answered with a cutting elbow. Hood ducked, refusing to leave the eye of the storm. The two fighters struck and blocked, slipped and countered, neither able to breach the other's skill. It became entrancing to watch as this large, dark-cliff-face of a woman battled the pale serpent of a smaller man.

The slopheads' cheering had grown so loud at the spectacle that half of Winsome drifted over to see the cause. Within moments, another two score voices were lifted by the unexpected entertainment, reaching such a furious pitch that Fetch was having a difficult time concentrating on the fight. It must have rattled Hoodwink, too, for his strikes were growing sloppy, the seamless web of violence he normally spun fraying. Incus, by contrast, remained as unshakable as a castle wall. A wall that could punch.

"You may want to consider pulling your albino out of there."

Looking to her right, Fetch found Sluggard giving her a grin. She'd been so intent on the fight, she hadn't noticed his arrival. That made twice he had come up on her unawares. Her slops weren't the only ones whose skills were withering.

"It's just training," she told him.

The gritter gave a careless shrug. "Even still. You could end up with one less brother if the Anvil's Bride gets a temper on."

"The Anvil's . . . ? You mean Incus?"

"Saw her fight one bout in Magerit," Sluggard said, his eyes returning to the match. "Her head was shaved then, but seeing her fight now, it's certainly her."

Within the growing circle of onlookers, Hood and Incus continued to scrap. Blows were landing now, though most of the meaty slaps came from blocked punches. Both fighters had abandoned dodging altogether.

Fetch frowned. "So she's some famed brawler in Hispartha?"

"Earned her name in Traedria," Sluggard replied, shouting a bit to be heard. "Bested everyone of note on that narrow peninsula, so she came to our expansive one. Fought at court for the pleasure of the king and queen before her master took her on a circuit of all the great cities. One of the carnavales I rode for hosted her as the principal entertainment. That night I saw the Anvil's Bride drop eight of Magerit's most celebrated pugilists."

"Thought you only saw her fight one bout?"

Sluggard cocked an eye at Fetching and winked. "I did. She fought all eight at once."

A bursting cheer drew both their attentions back to the ring. Hood had gotten hold of Incus's left arm, likely taking advantage of an overextended punch. Keeping the arm pinned between his own, he spun, hammered an elbow into Incus's back, and stomped a foot behind her knee, collapsing the leg. A sweep of the planted foot brought her down.

The crowd erupted.

Hoodwink did not bask in the victory, but immediately stalked over to Fetching. He leaned close and whispered in her ear.

"She's holding back." There was a tone to his voice Fetch had never heard before. He sounded . . . intrigued.

"Oh, she is, is she?"

Fetching removed her sword belt, slapped it into Sluggard's un-prepared hands, and walked into the ring.

Incus was already on her feet, unmindful of the dust now whiten-ing her hair. Fetch strode up until the toes of their boots were nearly touching and stretched up toward the thrice's concealed face. The crowd had gone silent, so she merely mouthed the words: *You fight me now. Hold back, and you're done here. Understand?*

The hair nodded.

The next instant, Fetch had to dive backward to keep from losing her head. Off-balance, she gave herself to the fall, kicking back when her rump struck the ground and rolling over herself into a crouch. Incus was still coming. Fetch launched forward. The thrice's arm tensed to strike. Fetch jumped, placing her foot on Incus's surging leg and using it to vault upward. She caught the arm, used her mo-mentum to arrest the punch, and swung atop the thrice's shoulders. One leg was hooked beside her neck, the other beneath the arm. Fetch grasped Incus under the jaw and hauled backward. It should have sent them both toppling, but the thrice thrust a leg out behind, rooted, and spun, seizing Fetch's wrist and throwing her bodily. She struck the crowd, cries of alarm going up from the slops who broke her fall. Disentangling herself, she rushed back into the now-broken circle. She didn't give Incus a chance to strike, hopping forward and launching a kick as soon as she had the distance. The thrice batted her foot away with little effort and unleashed a hailstorm of punches, crisscrossing the space between them, the space Fetch had to strug-gle to stay out of.

Hells damn, she was fast!

Faster than Oats to be sure and just as powerful. One mistake and Fetch would be spitting teeth. Or fragments of skull.

So focused on those deadly fists, Fetch never saw the foot coming. It was an inelegant thing, more a stamping push than a kick, but it rammed Fetch's midsection all the same. The air left her faster even than she flew backward. By the time she struck the ground, she was already choking. Having the wind knocked out was never pleasant, but the presence of the sludge made it terrifying. Writhing, struggling to breathe, wanting to vomit, Fetch realized she was about to die because of a sparring match. She might have laughed if anything were possible besides wheezing. Fingers clutching the dirt in spasms, she waited for the next failed breath to be her last.

A large hand seized the back of her neck, lifted her until she was sitting, and forced her head down until it almost kissed the dirt between her legs. A few more agonizing moments passed. Her torso was moving, heaving, the hand at her neck giving to the motion. Her vision cleared before her lungs, but all she saw was dust and her own crotch. The crowd was dead silent. Fetch heard nothing but labored inhalations. The hand left her neck and a sizable presence settled in front of her. Fetch looked up to find Incus kneeling there. One of her large hands parted the hair to reveal a face both contrite and resolved. The question came without inflection.

"Can I stay?"

Fetch reached up and placed a hand on the thrice's cheek. Her voice had not yet returned, but what matter?

Are you ever going to hold back again?

She felt the head shake. "No, chief."

Good. You can stay.

Incus helped Fetching to her feet and the spectators issued a collective sigh. Whether it was relief or disappointment, Fetch could not discern. She tried to keep her boots from dragging as she walked back to where Hoodwink stood.

"Get a sword in her hand," she managed with a raw voice. "Don't pair her with other slops. Just you."

Hood nodded as Fetch took her trappings back from Sluggard.

"My arm makes a fine support, if you require," the gritter offered.

"I don't," Fetch rasped, and walked away alone.

That night, she gave the hoof a much-needed respite and retired early to her solar. Sleep beckoned. And withdrew. She coughed into the cushions, sweated into the linens. The night, the bed, became a prison, keeping her trapped on the verge of sleep. Shivering with fever, hammers at work within her skull, she could find neither the peace of slumber nor the strength to rise. A burning weight crept from her chest into her throat, undeterred by her painful hacking. These torments became a living thing, insidious and insistent, cunning enough to come only when she was alone, making her weakness an intimate, isolated turmoil.

This night, another intruded.

Fetch's lethargy lifted, the brutal ache in her head dulled, the cough abated. All the familiar pains fled as if offended she would allow a witness to their workings. She wrestled herself upright and there he was, his bulk lounging on the stool, back to the wall.

"Crafty."

His smile glimmered in the poor light, gold teeth tarnishing the pure moonbeams.

"I knew you were here to fuck us," she snarled.

The wizard scratched idly at his great belly. "Truly, it was not my first intent. I would have rather made allies of you all."

"Save your lies. I'll not listen."

"Pity. For I fear if you do not heed me, your hoof is doomed."

A breeze from the balcony cooled the sweat on Fetch's skin and chilled her more than was warranted. Crafty had hardly stirred. He was a nearly featureless lump of shadow filling the corner of the room, topped by the outline of a turban. It was his stillness that was frightening, as if he were holding himself back. Fetch tried to recall where she had laid her tulwar, but the location of the sword slipped her mind as easily as a wriggling eel through the fingers. Her hands, then. Get a grip around his fat neck and squeeze. Now was the time to strike. Now! But she could not make her body move. A fresh fit of coughing seized her.

"I'll kill you," she croaked.

The wizard actually laughed. "It is a path you may attempt. Though I think your steps will falter. I do not yearn for any to die, but neither will I dally in the murder of all your brothers should you force it. That choice will be yours."

"Choice? I'm not playing your games!"

"You must cast your vote against Jackal."

"My vote? What are you . . . against Jackal? You're mad."

"No." Rings glinted as Crafty's fingers moved to rub at the side of his nose. "Indeed, it is the only sane solution. You will cast against him and give him no warning of your betrayal. That should see the end of his ambitions."

The realization did not strike Fetch so much as caress her, a hand that was on hers all along, unnoticed until the gentlest stroking of the thumb.

This infuriating palaver had already taken place.

"It hurts me to do this," Crafty went on, his words now remembered and predictable. "I am fond of him. Truly. But now is not the time for Jackal to become master, I am thinking."

Fetch's jaw worked and she heard her words from that day echo in the dark bedchamber. "He *is* going to sit the chief's chair, Tyrkanian. I'm going to help put him there and together we are going to cast you out on your blubbery ass."

Crafty produced a weary sigh. "There is no time for such fencing. Jackal has made his challenge. Soon you must all gather and fling your little axes. Yours will be cast for the Claymaster. Do otherwise and I will destroy the Grey Bastards. The riders, the youths in training, the hogs. I will bring this fortress down atop your heads." The wizard swirled a finger languidly at the ceiling. Unlike now, they had been inside the Kiln. Like now, Crafty had appeared in her chamber uninvited. "And I shall not stop there. Your quaint Winsome town will also burn. Your hoof, your lot, everything laid waste. Why? For loyalty. For love? I wonder, dread Fetching, what you love more? The mongrel? Or the Bastards?"

She had hesitated then. Should have opened his guts.

Crafty leaned forward and his voice oozed sympathy. "Jackal

will not be harmed. The Claymaster knows his death will . . . sour things within the brotherhood. You have my word, as I have your chief's. Jackal will be allowed to become a free-rider. Betray him and you save him. You save all of them. It is your choice. But I must ask that you make it now."

She had, her ax blade striking for the Claymaster. Yet, the vote was a draw, demanding a bout between chosen champions. Again, Crafty had the answer. And again, she complied. Oats fought for Jack, she for the chief, and toppled the two mongrels she cared about above all else.

All else, it seemed, save the hoof.

"You didn't know . . ." Fetching said, shattering the words of memory. "What I was. You didn't know. *I* didn't know. Had I, I would have feasted on your organs!"

She lunged from the bed, barked her knee on the foot board, and crashed into the wall, tripping on the empty stool.

"Show yourself."

It would have been a challenge screamed into the night, but the fury was throttled by a retching cough.

Dreading the delirious hell of the bed, she refused to return, and passed the night slumped on the floor, brooding on dead days, waiting for them to be conjured from the shadows.

NINE

"AL-UNAN FIRE!"

Fetch strode triumphantly into the mason's hall. In yet another of Winsome's abandoned buildings, Mead had taken over the place for use in planning the town's fortifications. She was not expecting to see Sluggard look up as soon as she came through the doorway, but didn't let the surprise slow her steps.

"To kill the dogs," Fetch continued. "We'll use Al-Unan fire."

The words seemed to freeze Mead as he leaned over the chart on the table before him, though his concentration was clearly broken. His words and eye contact were both slow to come.

"Chief. That is not—"

"Whore, out." Fetch jerked a thumb over her shoulder at the door.

Sluggard cleared his throat, stood, and left.

"It will kill them," Fetch told Mead when they were alone. "No more of this vanishing shit."

"They have to reappear first."

"They will. And then we'll be ready with something they can't recover from."

"You don't know that."

"It killed the Sludge Man, it can kill anything."

"Yes. It also destroyed a fortress of stone. We are living behind wooden walls, Fetch."

It was not often that her brothers used her name these days. The familiarity was both comforting and infuriating. She pushed both reactions down.

"You have another way? I'm listening."

She waited. Mead's stare drifted back to his table.

"Neither do I," Fetch said. "No one does. That awful demon's spend is our only chance."

"It's not. We don't have any."

"It's still burning at the Kiln. We get it from there."

Mead laughed. It was a bitter sound. "No. It can only be handled when inert. Once it's burning . . . Fetch—"

She slapped the table. "*Chief!*"

That brought him up short. He took a breath. "Chief. It can't be contained once loose. That's why it's so dangerous."

"Don't explain things to me like I'm a damn slop, Mead. I understand! But if anyone can find a way it's you."

The bench flew back and fell noisily to the floor as the young mongrel jumped to his feet. He held his stump in front of Fetch's face, his own quivering with rage.

"And how many other parts do I need to lose for that miracle?! I'm not a wizard, Fetching! Crafty was the one that finally got that shit under control, not me!"

Fetch allowed him his anger, waited as its expulsion snuffed it as quick as a candle flame. Mead lowered his arm, stood straight, and ran his good hand through his Tine plume. He shook his head at the ceiling, spoke to it, the words crawling from a cranny of bitter recollection.

"The Claymaster had me on that insanity almost from the instant I put a brigand on. I don't know where he got it, I didn't know how I was going to make it work without bringing the entire Kiln down. And what happened?"

Fetch watched Mead's haunted stillness, saying nothing. At last, he paced back a step, met her eyes. "The old mongrel wanted a way to secure the Kiln without using wood. Even then, we were in short supply. Did you know he even worked on it himself? I found him, several times, late at night . . . just staring into the ovens, a small amount of that green hell burning within. I kept hoping he would figure it out. Or realize it was impossible and give up. But he kept at it. Kept me at it. Had me recruit slops to help. I convinced Salik . . . I convinced Shed Snake to help. I thought it would get him a vote faster if we solved the puzzle. He was damn lucky that day. We all were."

"I remember," Fetching said.

It was early experimentation with the unnatural fire that had caused Snake's burns when he was still a slophead. He was fortunate to have kept the arm, the flesh sloughing off as it healed. Grocer had tended him, the miserly old fuck even keeping one of the peels that had come away in a single, unbroken tube.

"That slop's arm looks like a freshly shed snake," the ornery quartermaster had remarked, unknowingly providing Salik with his future hoof name.

Grocer had died on the same day as the Kiln, along with the Claymaster and the Grey Bastards. Seemed only fitting when Salik rose to the brotherhood that Grocer make one final contribution. That had been Mead's idea. Mead, who looked at her now with something very near disgust.

"You remember the aftermath, but you weren't there. You were out on patrol with Oats and Jackal. Like always. I was the only sworn brother in the furnace chamber when the slops were mucking about with that shit. I was the one who saw the fire knock the furnace doors open and lick outward, like it was alive and hungry. It barely touched Salik, and his flesh ignited like a brush fire."

The memory tortured Mead, his stare directed at Fetch, but seeing something else.

"How did you put it out?" she asked, ashamed she did not know. Like he said, she hadn't been there, just heard the report in a hoof meet, sitting around that fucking coffin-shaped table where she always did her best to remain small and quiet.

Mead's unblinking eyes refocused. For a moment he looked confused, as if he didn't recall. He expelled a short, darkly amused breath. "Urine. I'd read somewhere that stale urine would extinguish it. I had the slops pissing in buckets from the first day, leaving them around. Didn't even know if it would work until I tossed one on Snake. Too afraid to test it, in case it made it worse. But in that moment . . ."

"There was nothing to lose."

Mead nodded, his quick mind seizing on the fact that he had just lost his argument. Wearing a gloomy little grin, he righted the bench and sat back down. Fetch joined him and placed an arm around his shoulders, to hells with how he might respond.

Mead only sighed. "Guess I have to tell the boys to start saving their piss."

"I'd do it," Fetch told him, "but I'm not going to."

They both laughed. Fetching withdrew the embrace and slid a little ways down the bench, tapping the fortification plans on the table with a finger.

"We can't wall off our entire lot. We need a way to attack as well as defend."

"I know. But . . . chief. It won't sit well with Snake. We do this, we need to be prepared to lose him. He might go nomad rather than risk the fire again."

Fetching stood. "I understand. There's no need to tell him anything yet. Like everything I need to keep this hoof alive, the stuff is not in our possession. I was hoping you knew where it came from."

Mead looked down, stifling a laugh.

"What?"

"Well . . . it is called *Al-Unan* fire."

Fetch made a mock lunge at her grinning rider. "Keen-ass! Just keep working on your damn chart and I will work on the thousand and one other miracles." Remembering, she pointed at the door. "And what the fuck was Whore doing in here?"

"Helping me," Mead replied, perturbed at her question. "*Sluggard's* spent his life in walled cities. Knows a thing or two. He even suggested one day we build an aqueduct."

"An ack-wa-what?"

"It's a way to bring water into the town."

"That's called a well, Mead."

"No, this would be *from* the Alhundra itself—" He was growing excited, but Fetch killed his enthusiasm with her dubious sneer. "Never mind."

Guilt made her take a breath, preparing to encourage him to explain further.

They both startled as the door was rammed open by Dumb Door's cumbersome form, killing the chance. He was sweating and winded, jaw slack.

Fetch sprang from the bench. "What is it?"

Dumb Door put the sides of his meaty hands together and fanned them open.

Mead was standing now too. "The gate."

"The dogs?" Fetch asked, moving around the table.

Two extended fingers on one hand held below a single finger on the other.

Worse.

The stockade was filled with backs when Fetch arrived. None on the wall looked around when she began climbing the ladder. Mead was on her ass, his ascent hardly slowed by his lack of a hand.

"Make a gap!" Fetch commanded.

A pair of backs parted and she looked over the stakes, thrum leading.

A line of horsemen were assembled beneath the morning sun. Cavaleros.

Had to be a hundred. Four score, at least. Too many.

One man was ahead of the others, less than a stone's throw from the gate. His head was craned upward and his voice raised a moment after Fetch reached the wall.

"Hoofmaster of the Grey Bastards, I am Cavalero Ramon. You're to come with me to the castile by order of Captain Bermudo."

"It's True Bastards, you foal-fucking frail!" Polecat yelled down.

Ramon ignored the laughter along the stockade. His face was as humorless as Fetch's.

She kept her stockbow trained, eyes darting. The sun reflected dully off steel helms, armor scales, the heads of demi-lances, the edges of shields. Hundreds of little blazes accompanied by the occasional thud of a hoof, the clink of a harness as a horse shifted. There *were* a hundred men, she saw now. Some seventy cavaleros along with thirty scouts dressed in canvas jerkins and brimmed hats, each bearing a loaded stockbow.

She looked again to Ramon.

They both knew she had a choice.

"I'm coming down!" The tension that settled over the mongrels atop the stockade at her pronouncement was palpable. "Bastards with me."

The brothers converged on her at the bottom of the wall. Fetch kept a steady stride as she made for the stables, forcing them to trail along. Away from the slops, their concerns spilled forth.

"You're not serious about going?" Shed Snake asked.

"I am. Figured this might happen."

"Chief." Mead sounded on the verge of pleading. "The dogs are still out there."

"I suspect so."

"And if they come for you?"

"They didn't attack the eleven of us. Doubt they'll risk a hundred men."

"Hundred frails ain't worth the eleven of us, chief," Polecat said.

"No. And Crafty's curs can feast on every last one of them before they reach me. Be the most damn use any cavalero has ever been in the history of Ul-wundulas."

"Still shouldn't go alone," Mead said, quickening his pace to pull ahead.

"Where do you think you're going?" Fetch demanded.

"To saddle my hog!"

"STAY FUCKING PUT!"

The savagery in her voice rooted Mead in place.

Fetch stopped, the others along with her. She revolved in a slow circle, daring them not to heed her words.

"This is a hogshit errand. Put Bermudo's mind at ease, convince him that his men would actually desert. Fucker can't sit a horse any-more, so he's bringing me to him."

Polecat grunted in agreement. "Let's show him that was a mis-take."

Fetch let that hang in the air a moment before shaking her head, letting loose a small, biting laugh. "Is that what you all want? To fight? To make a fucking stand? We could. We'd feather some frails, wet our blades with cavalero blood." Her sweeping gaze settled on Polecat. "We could open the gate, ride out as a hoof, and hit them with a tusker they don't see coming. With the slops on the walls, we stand a chance of killing every last one. Today. But next time? They won't just ask for me. Hells, they won't say a damn word. They'll raze Winsome and put everyone behind this wall of driftwood to the sword. Everyone. Do I need to call a vote to see who wants that?"

"We can't just give over our chief because the castile whistled," Polecat said. "What does that makes us? What does that make you?"

"It makes you loyal to my command," Fetch told her brothers. "It makes me less of a prideful fuck than Bermudo, and more sane than the Claymaster. Boys, we ain't the Grey Bastards anymore. There's no Kiln to protect us, no Captain Ignacio to come when *we* whistle. And no vengeful old pus sack of a chief to bring us all down with him."

"You're not him," Mead said, voice going thick. "Never were. You're one of us. One of ours."

Fetch wanted to embrace him for that, wanted to embrace them all for the proud set of their faces, showing her they agreed. Instead, she thrust a finger at the gate.

"Get back up on that wall and tell those backy frails your chief will join them directly."

With parting, resilient nods they did as told.

Save one.

"I know what you're thinking, Hood."

"They won't see me. Neither will you."

Fetch took a step closer to the serpent's mask.

"No. You won't shadow us. That's your chief telling you. You won't. You're needed here."

"You're getting worse."

Fetch took in the scarred, bald, wax-skinned, corpse-eyed mongrel. "Yes. And not even you can do anything about it."

She left Winsome in full kit, riding alone beneath the gate under the conflicted eyes of the hoof. Cavalero Ramon turned his horse as she drew close, riding alongside as they passed through the line of waiting cavalry. He was a heavy-jawed, ill-shaven man. His troop fell into formation around them and set a quick pace. Though cavaleros in name, it was clear from the quality of their mounts and arms that all save Ramon were lowborn. There wasn't a pennant or banner among them. While all bore demi-lances, it was a rare belt that held a sword. Axes and maces—cheaper to make and easier to maintain—outnumbered the good blades. Not a helm or coat of plates was free from tarnish. Fetch put no stock in the so-called quality of a man's blood the way frails did, but most of these men were just a small step removed from brigands and, if their fortunes changed but a little, would likely become deserters.

"Bermudo must be desperate to avoid idleness in his ranks," Fetch said, unwilling to let the farce go unremarked. "This is an abundance of men to ride escort for one mongrel. Even a hoofmaster."

Ramon gave no response.

At the Winsome Ford, the farce increased. In truth, it doubled. An identical troop of cavaleros waited just over the river. A further one hundred mounted men, equipped as the rest. Ramon produced a smirk that crowned him king of the gloating shiteaters. Fetch's teeth began to grind. She'd been wrong. There'd been no chance of victory if the Bastards chose to fight. The hunting horn dangling from Ramon's tack along with at least a dozen more among his troop would have signaled the reserves. Bringing the entire force to the gates would have quelled any notion of defiance from the first moment.

"Fuckers," Fetch hissed.

A greasy, grinning ferret of a scout broke away from the reserves and crossed the ford.

"Blas," Ramon droned at the repulsive man, "you have charge of the half-breed's . . . safety."

"Aye, Cavalero." Blas stuck finger and thumb between his lips to emit an impressive shriek of a whistle, summoning a detachment of his fellow outriders.

Fetch nudged Womb forward to meet them. Thirty men snapped stockbows to their shoulders. Their weapons had a rack and pinion to aid the frails with the reload, making them slow. Still, at this distance they wouldn't need a second volley. Half these cunts could have shit aim and Fetch would still be more feathered than a goose. She masked the puzzlement and alarm with a yawn. This was more than the disdainful distrust frails held for half-orcs. They feared her. Two hundred to one, yet they feared her.

Womb Broom snorted with aggravation as the horsemen began to encircle him. This Blas was foolish, surrounding a barbarian. A hog was easily capable of barreling through the horses, crippling and killing as it went if Fetch risked a break. Her face must have betrayed the thought, for Blas, peering at her, grew concerned.

"If your mongrel brain tells you to become disagreeable at any moment"—the lead scout crafted a threatening smile—"I'd welcome it."

Fetch showed her own teeth. "You certain? Because if I become disagreeable, you'll be the first to die."

Blas tried to hide it, but he grew visibly less sure. He called to Ramon.

"Suggest we shackle the hussy and throw her over the back of a horse, Cavalero!"

"You're not putting me in chains," Fetch promised Ramon as he rode through the scouts. His eyes flicked to her hand, resting upon the grip of her tulwar. The man's tongue pushed at his tightly closed lips, bulging the flesh of his mouth as he considered.

"Leave her be, Blas," he said, at last, urging his horse onward.

The scout squirmed in his saddle. "What if she turns savage?"

Ramon did not slow or turn as he replied. "Have your men kill the hog from under her. Surely they won't miss as they'll have her surrounded."

Sour-faced, Blas jerked his head and gave another whistle, signaling his men to move. Fetch allowed them to herd her across the ford. There was little else she could do. Even if she won free from the scouts, there was a troop of cavaleros riding ahead as well as behind. The numbers of the men, to say nothing of their actions, pointed to Bermudo wanting her for something more than a palaver regarding dead deserters.

The badlands spread out before the column, sunbaked and endless, the expanse broken only by scrub, heat phantoms, and the occasional low hill. Fetch supped on dust, malicious glances, and the dark suspicions of Bermudo's true aims for leagues. By day's end she had a dry throat, a renewed hatred for frails on foals, and no fucking notion what the captain intended.

The sky was beaten purple after its bout with dusk, so the smoke remained hidden until it reached Fetch's nostrils. The column slowed. Blas's men spread out, revealing Ramon sitting his horse before the blackened, gutted, smoking remnants of what had been Rhecia's brothel.

"I think we will have those shackles now," the cavalero said.

Fetch shook her head. "I did not do this."

"Tell the captain," Ramon replied without feeling.

As Blas rode forward with the chains, Fetch considered being true to her word and putting a bolt in the man. What would it come to if she did? There was small chance of escape, and should fortune kiss her ass, Ramon would certainly order his men back to Winsome. Even if she went nomad and never again returned to the hoof, they would pay for her rebellion.

And so she remained carefully still as the manacles were fastened about her wrists.

TEN

FETCHING BEAT THE STABLEMASTER until her knuckles were shredded by his broken teeth. Bloody spittle greased every blow. The man's nose shattered, next his jaw. Just when she thought he was growing senseless, numb to the pain, she hooked a thumb into his eye and gouged it from the socket. The scream that followed lanced Fetch's ears in the high pitch of agonized panic—

"Ay."

Blas's voice jerked her out of the black reverie.

She blinked, nearly blind from the sun. A few strides away, within the shadows of the stable, the man was still on his feet, still whole, still drumming the simple-minded boy upon the head with harsh words and lazy cuffs. The stablemaster's callousness was practiced, familiar, as was Muro's response. The boy did nothing, merely continued to sit upon his little stool and attempt to practice shoeing, his clumsy efforts made more futile by the steady rain of slaps and insults. Juggling the hammer, shoe, and the wooden dummy hoof, he kept his head bowed, face turned away, as comfortable weathering the abuse as the stablemaster was in its delivery.

Fetch began to move forward, feeling her imagined vengeance crawling to existence.

A sword barred her way, the flat of the blade slapped across her stomach.

"Ay!"

Seething, she settled. Blas withdrew his blade, though his vigilant stare remained. Fetch could feel it upon her temple. Gritting her teeth, she watched the cruel display until the stablemaster was called away to attend another matter back in the stalls, leaving Muro to his task. The boy abandoned it as soon as his master was out of sight and came plodding up to Fetch.

"Grey Bastrin?" Muro asked, pointing a finger.

"Yes," Fetch told him. "I'm a Bastard."

"Like Oads. Bears and Moundtans!"

Fetch smiled. "Like Oats."

"He here?"

"No. I'm sorry, but I'll tell him you—"

"Get back to your work, mush head!" Blas yelled, raising a threatening hand.

Muro flinched, though he did not have the speed of mind or body to get out of reach. Blas did not strike him. Instead, he gave the boy a hard shove.

"Get!"

Crestfallen, Muro turned and went back to his stool.

Fetch turned a disgusted eye on Blas. Had Oats been here, the cruel fuck's head would be pulp. Maybe not, since the stablemaster would already have been broken in half and none would dare touch Muro after seeing that. Oats had long wished to remove the boy from the castile. But the hard truth was, callous treatment aside, Muro was better off here. The castile had strong walls and plenty of food. Winsome had neither.

Glancing over her shoulder, Fetch was gratified to see her guards squinting and sweating in the oppressive heat of the yard. Their horses had long since been taken into the stables, but such shelter was forbidden them as long as they minded Fetching, for it would never enter the frails' minds to allow a half-breed any comfort. No, mongrels could stand for hours without shade. That was their place.

As they stood, waiting, scorching, the castile bustled around them. Grooms moved in and out of the stables, some leading horses, others bearing fodder or water. Garrison patrols passed regularly, the eyes of each man regarding Fetch with a stew of curiosity and loathing. Page boys and serving girls hurried to and fro, careful to ignore the half-orc entirely.

Ramon and his men had announced themselves at the gate before dawn. The cavaleros had sought the barracks, leaving Blas and his scouts to keep the prisoner. Now the sun was at its height with not so much as an offer of water. It would be infuriating if it weren't so damn obvious. Bermudo was trying to soften her with fatigue and thirst. There was no need. She'd allowed her weapons to be confiscated, suffered the placing of the shackles upon her wrists. Her hog had been taken hells-knew-where, though he'd put up more of a fight and knocked over three of the men tasked with leading him away, breaking the wrist of one.

Behind her, one of the scouts uttered an exasperated oath at the heat, the wait. Blas shot a warning scowl, but failed to squash the complaint.

"When's this gash going to be taken off our backs?"

There were mutters of agreement, but Blas remained silent.

The answer arrived with a cavalero approaching on foot. Bandy-legged and bearded, he stopped in front of the scouts and surveyed them a moment before laughing, amused by some private jest. His loutish appearance was common to the quality of cavaleros now inhabiting the castile. What was not common was the chain-mace he carried thrust through his belt. It was not a weapon usually employed by the king's cavalry, requiring a marriage of brute strength and cold cunning to wield. Sizing this man up, Fetch determined he reflected his choice of arms.

Removing his helmet, the cavalero made a show of arranging his sweat-soaked hair before producing a wide smile and low bow, the latter made awkward by his rust-stained breastplate. One upper front tooth was missing, the black hole contrasting sharply with the pearl white of its surviving fellows.

"I am Cavalero Maneto," he announced with amusement. "The captain bids me bring you to his presence."

Tucking his helmet into the crook of his arm, the man gestured back the way he had come with exaggerated grace.

Chains clattering against her knees, Fetch walked past the cavalero and his outstretched arm. Maneto caught up, falling into step on her left as he replaced his helmet. Despite his bowed legs, he was of equal height to Fetch, something most men could not claim. Leaning back as they walked, he leered for a long moment at her backside.

"Blessed fuckin' Magritta, but aren't ye a pert mongrel cunny!" he exclaimed with appreciation. All affected gentility was gone from his voice, replaced with a wet growl. "I'd proclaim ye the comeliest soot-skinned bitch in the kingdom, but such would make a liar a'me, for you're no ashy mongrel are ye? No, by the sticky linens of all the chaste priests of Galiza, that ripe flesh is green as old mint, yet I would wager it defies appearance and is spicy to the tongue."

"Poisonous, in fact," Fetch replied. "Like a serpent. Men attached to grasping hands don't live very long."

Maneto chuckled with genuine humor. Winking, he drew a hand up close to his face and pointed at her mouth. "Look'it there! Even them lower fangs is hardly pronounced. I'd say your papi was a man, but no frailing I ever sired was so sage-colored, no! You're no damn thrice-blood, elsewise. They usually blacker than a negro. Confession, girl. I'd pay a quarter year's coin in the king's service to have you suck the spend out my cock. Never had that from a mongrel gal before, too afraid of them teeth."

"Fear is a good thing to have in the Lots. Especially around mongrels."

The chuckles kept coming. "No mistake, it's not my first turn here, not by a furlong. But I'll gamble whatever is left in my purse— after paying for your mouth—that it will be my last."

"I'd say that's a sure wager." Fetch grinned. "I was just thinking you were going to die soon."

Maneto guffawed, more than was warranted, mocking her assertion with his jovial acceptance of the threat. "Half a year's coin, then."

Fetch looked over again. Maneto brightened, showing his gap-toothed smile.

She had long ago grown accustomed to lusty men. Hells, she had lived her entire life amidst them. She knew their minds, reckoned she even understood them. This was different. This vulgar villain on display was another mask, like the guise of courteousness from only moments ago. And just like with that guise, Maneto wanted her to see through it. Offering to pay while knowing she was in chains—he was baiting her, as much with his insults as with the baldness of his mummery.

Looking into that grinning face she found not a man who wanted to fuck her, but a man who wanted to cause harm. Not just to her, but to everything. His cock didn't stiffen at the thought of ass or quim, but the sowing of mayhem. She'd known far fewer of his type. Fetch kept her eyes fixed upon Maneto's, but her mind went to the chain-mace in his belt.

Brutal. Unpredictable. A weapon that need always be in motion to remain dangerous.

"I'll remember the offer, cavalero."

Paying no more mind to his dark glee, Fetch turned toward the keep, but was halted by the clicking of Maneto's tongue.

"We are for the battlements, pretty missy."

She gave him a dubious squint. "Captain Bermudo is atop the walls?"

The cavalero winked. "There's all manner of shiny things upon the wall today that weren't the day before."

With that he turned his back and sauntered down a narrow lane between two storehouses without waiting to see if she followed.

Finding herself ignored and unguarded was oddly unnerving. Another mummer's act. Fetch gathered the slack out of her chains and went after Maneto.

The sounds of industrious labor echoed through the alley, increasing as they went. Emerging near the eastern swell of the curtain wall, Fetch discovered a great scaffold had taken the place of a shattered tower. Men and mules pulled at ropes wound through block and tackle, slowly hauling columns of cast bronze up to the battlements. These brazen cumbrances were of various sizes, but most were slightly longer than the height of an average man. All had a hole at one end big enough for the same man to thrust his arm through.

"Beauties," Maneto declared, raising his voice above the shouted exchanges between the workers above and below. He made for the scaffolding and scuttled into the shadows beneath. Stepping through the same space between two of the beams, Fetch found the cavalero barking at two laborers in the midst of loading heavy black spheres onto a small platform set within a narrow shaft surrounded by planking.

"You sweatbacks fuck off for a tarry. Chief-cock of a mongrel hoof wants to go up same way as the captain."

The men ceased their task as Maneto gestured for Fetch to step onto the platform. Ducking her head, she entered the shaft. The stack of leaden spheres left little room for her feet, and the slat ceiling prevented her from standing fully upright, making her feel as if she hunkered in a vertical coffin. Her discomfort only increased when Maneto squeezed himself in front of her, close enough to smell the rust upon his armor.

"Perhaps I should have said 'chief-quim,' eh?"

Grinning, he reached up and yanked twice on a cord dangling through the slats. After a moment, the platform lurched and began to rise. Fetch could hear the groan and scrape of ropes through the thin boards that served as walls.

As they ascended, Maneto stared dully at her, unblinking, and Fetch caught a glimpse of his true face. Sullen. Unfeeling. A pit in the shape of a man. Hoodwink didn't possess such emptiness.

Light began to intrude upon the shadows of the box as it crept toward the sun. Behind Maneto, the battlements lowered into view. He took a single, ducking step backward, providing Fetch a path to escape the wretched cupboard. Stepping from beneath the scaffolding once more, they began traversing the rampart. Maneto made for a square tower straddling the wall, sidestepping laborers with practiced ease. All along the way teams of men reached out to receive the brass cylinders hoisted up from the yard. Farther on, Fetch saw them being affixed to wooden, wheeled cradles.

She stopped at the first one unattended by workers, peered at it with a growing sense of disquiet. The cylinder's open end was thrust between the crenellations, slightly raised, pointing out defiantly at the surrounding badlands of Ul-wundulas.

"First sight of guns, eh girl?" Maneto asked. "Don't right know what they are, I see, but a warrior knows a weapon at a glance, don't she?"

"Guns," Fetch repeated, not liking the taste of the word. "Sounds fucking orcish."

Maneto spat over the wall. "Nah. Call them cannons if you find that less offensive. Invention of the swaddleheads, I hear, along with the powder they need to spit death. Come now, the captain don't like to be kept waiting."

"Neither do chief-quims."

Maneto scratched at his beard. "Well, I'll be in for some entertainments, seeing you take that up with him."

They continued on until they reached the tower. An arched doorway led into the gloom of the structure, but Maneto eschewed it for a flight of stone steps set into the exterior tower wall, leading to its top. Fetch followed his quick boots, slowing when she spied blood droplets on the steps and smears low on the wall.

The hot wind played freely atop the tower.

The castile was built upon an escarpment, its formidable walls adding to the imposing height of the natural rock, affording an untrammeled view to every horizon. Bulbous clouds sailed across the blue, gifting Fetch with a moment's dizziness. Leveling her gaze, she waited for the sensation to pass.

Teams of half a dozen men fussed over a pair of guns installed atop the tower. These were larger than the others, at least twice as wide and half again as long. They were set at the southeast and southwest corners. A lone figure stood near the battlements between them, ignoring the guns entirely to stare over the dun land. Maneto escorted Fetch over and the fawning courtliness returned to his words.

"Fetching, chief of the True Bastards, as you requested, my lord Captain Bermudo."

"Thank you, cavalero."

"My pleasure and honor, my lord."

Bowing crisply, Maneto turned on his heel and removed himself several strides.

Bermudo lurched slightly as he pivoted, thumping sounds coming up from the stones as he maneuvered the long crutch beneath his right arm. His once hale complexion was sallow, sharp features blunted by a year of constant pain. Sweat sheened his face, the stubborn moisture of a fever that would not yield, even to the wind. He wore no armor, his wasted muscles and remaining leg unable to bear the weight. Fetch knew Bermudo had led his cavalry against an encroaching *ul'usuun*, an advance force of marauding thicks, during the last attempted Incursion. He was victorious, but lost nearly all of his men, over three hundred cavaleros of noble stock cut down by orc scimitars. One of those blades had lopped off the captain's leg below the knee, killing his horse with the same stroke if the rumors were true. The beast had fallen atop him, crushing his opposing hip. And though he survived, his torment had not ended. What was left of his leg refused to heal, plagued by infection. The barbers had been forced to cut twice more, finally taking the knee.

Fetch saw that the pinned leg of his breeches, buffeted by the wind, was darkly stained.

That accounted for the blood on the stairs. Also for her long wait in the sun. No doubt it had taken the crippled captain hours to reach the tower, the stage where he wanted to receive his prisoner. She could only hope such foolish exertion would finally put this arrogant fuck in the grave.

"There is a pair of wagons in the yard," the captain said. He faced her, but did not deign to look her in the eye. Instead, his eyes cocked sideways, to the guns and their crews. "One is loaded with . . . ?"

"Wheat, beans, cured meat, Captain!" Maneto barked.

Bermudo looked unimpressed. "*Food*. The other wagon, cut stone. They are part of a caravan arriving from Hispartha every...?"

"Six weeks, Captain!"

"The stone is for maintenance of the castile. The food is—*was*—for Sancho's filthy establishment. My castellan informs me our walls are sound and the stone will need to be stored. As for the food? Well..."

Fetch was losing her patience and did not bother to hide it. "Why am I here, Bermudo?"

The captain neglected to answer, instead raising his chin toward the crew to his left and calling over the wind.

"Are you ready?"

One of the men shouted an assent.

Bermudo raised a hand over his head, the motion challenging his balance, and let it fall.

Thunder blasted the tower.

Fetch's shoulders jumped and she flinched against the sudden, explosive bark. An invisible fist punched her in the chest, causing a swift pressure to batter her heart. The mouth of the southeast gun spewed a torrent of smoke, the entire weapon pushed backward on its wheeled cradle by the violence of its own power. The top of the tower was briefly lost in smoke before the wind carried away the afterbirth of the gun's aggressive declaration.

Surprise and instinct had caused Fetch to duck, and she was just beginning to straighten when the second gun roared. Her ears were ringing, yet she could still hear more distant booms discharging from atop the castile's other towers. Coughing against the singed air, feeling the sludge encouraged to stir, Fetch waved the smoke from her eyes and looked out to see fountains of dust erupting erratically across the badlands.

When the angry echoes dwindled and the ground around the castile ceased to shake, Bermudo regarded her with a sickly gloat.

"With the Kiln gone, this fortress is now undeniably the strongest in the Lot Lands. I intend for it to remain so. However, your hoof need not continue to live behind a fence."

Fetch clenched her jaw, not knowing where this hog was trotting.

"One wagon will not build a fortress," Bermudo went on. "A start on a proper gatehouse, perhaps, but with regular resupply it is only a matter of time before the Bastards once again have a stronghold." The crutch thumped forward. "I will offer trade. You can ride out with your wagons full of bricks and beans the moment you tell me where he is."

Fetch clutched the chains. There it was.

Bermudo did not appreciate her silence.

"I want to know where you are hiding him! Where is Jackal?!"

"Don't know. Not in the Lots. He's no longer sworn to my hoof."

Three answers. And only the last was a lie.

Unconvinced, Bermudo gave a sneer of loathing.

"Make ready!" he called over his shoulder at the gun crews. The soot-stained men jumped to the order. Fetch watched the process of the reload. And started a count in her head.

Bermudo went back to working the shovel full of hogshit that was his mouth. "So you see, Maneto? I tried to be charitable, but, as ever, these mongrels are too mulish. So now, the rod. Your crime at the whorehouse is enough to condemn you, mongrel. I could execute you here and now. And I will. Mark me, half-orc, I will! But I would rather have Jackal. I would rather return you to leading your band of ash-coloreds and place those chains on him. Far better to send him back to Hispartha to answer for his far greater offenses than to have you die here for him, and for little gain."

"I committed no crime."

Bermudo's nose crinkled. "You slew a cavalero in the king's service and conspired to cover the deed."

"That man was a fucking deserter! And I covered nothing. The brothel was still standing when I put heel to hog."

"Of course it was," Bermudo said, speaking to her as one would a simpleton. "It was I that ordered that vile den razed."

That took Fetch aback.

"Hells overburdened," she swore. "You *have* lost your mind."

The captain's eyes flashed. "Letting it stand for so long was the true madness. Nothing but a haven for rogues and outlaws. A bolt-hole for deserters and nomads. Ul-wundulas will no longer suffer such places."

"Rhecia didn't know those men had deserted, you fuck."

"Yes. That was her claim. All the whores said the same . . . right up until the moment their warren was put to the torch. Then they said much more, did they not, Maneto?"

"A chorus of eager birds, my lord."

Bermudo's mouth turned downward. "Yes. And so you find yourself here, bound for killing a cavalero."

"They can lie," Fetch said. "You and your gap-toothed eunuch back there can lie. False ain't made true by the number of wagging tongues."

"And yet it takes only one tongue to sweep away a lie." Bermudo held up a single, victorious finger. "One whore in desperation to name you as Cavalero Garcia's killer."

Fetch's mouth suddenly tasted of stale piss.

Fuck.

Bermudo leaned forward quizzically, aping as if she'd spoken and he hadn't heard. "What? No claim that it was Jackal who did the deed? Should that not be your response? He is not here. He remains free and elusive. No reason to avoid placing the blame on his head where it has rested comfortably for near two years. Yet you are silent. Because pride will not allow you to give him credit for a killing you committed. I can see it in the set of your jaw! It is one matter to *allow* me to believe it was Jackal, but you will not *name* him the slayer. No! That would be cowardice. More than that, it would be denying an act for which you are proud!"

"You're hells-damned right."

And he was. Fetch never wanted to hide behind Jackal for the death of the harelip. She'd been in the man's presence for all of a dozen heartbeats and it was more than enough to know for a certainty she'd done the Lots a kindness by planting a bolt in his brain.

Her confession curdled the captain's face into an ugly mixture of triumph and repugnance. The bead of sweat nestled in the divot beneath his nose quivered. His indrawn breaths grew audible.

"The Marquesa Punela has long waited to see justice done to the mongrel that slew her son."

"Careful, Bermudo. Doesn't look like you have blood to spare for an erect cod."

The man was so enraptured with the thought of justice, the disrespect did not faze him. "The wagons or death. Choose."

"The fuck you on about?"

"My charity stands. You may leave here, free, with supplies for your hoof. Just give me Jackal."

Fetch could only marvel.

"You need not die for your crime!" Bermudo pressed.

Fetch scratched her nose with joined hands. "You won't talk to me of crimes, frail. You, who gave command to run down free-riders and stake them to whatever was nearest."

Bermudo's eyes were wide above dark, unhealthy stains, his face incensed. "It is no crime to protect the kingdom of Hispartha, a duty to which I am sworn."

"Protect it? By killing nomads? Placing hoofmasters in chains? Your hatred weakens all of Ul-wundulas!"

"Weakens? We have no need of your kind." Bermudo scoffed. "You useless swine-straddlers failed to keep the thicks from crossing our borders. No more!" The agitated cripple nearly toppled as he flung an impassioned arm behind him. "These guns will ensure the orcs never again stain civilized land."

"What do you think you have here?" Fetch demanded. "Orcs won't assault this place, not when they can go around it! Keeping them contained requires we see them coming and to see them coming we have to keep an eye on every stretch of scrub and length of bleached canyon. That means mounts, warriors in the saddle. You're a cavalero, you know this! This is a land of the horse and the hog, it is vast, and only strong hooves can traverse it. Only strong hoofs can protect it!"

Bermudo bristled. "The hoofs are no longer necessary! You are nothing but watchmen. And your time is ending."

It was Fetch's turn to take a step forward. In her periphery, Maneto tensed, but she drew nose to nose with the captain, undeterred.

"Watchmen? We rode out, Bermudo. We. Rode. Out. And bled and died to stop another Incursion, same as you. And we will again. Yet you repay us with persecution. Leave the nomads be, give up this crazed hunt for Jackal. Return to your fucking senses!"

Bermudo was affronted, bewildered. "You think it is I that so desperately wants him? You think I do not wish to turn my attentions to broader concerns? It is the Crown that demands him. The queen herself! She was most distressed when I wrote to her of the rogue half-orc, ousted from his hoof, left to wander without restraint or master. How he conspired with another outcast to be taken prisoner here, escaped with the help of Ignacio, all so he could seek out the wizard tasked with protecting this castile and slay him. I was, at first, blind to why he would wish to do this. It was only upon surviving the orc raid that understanding came to me, lying on the surgeon's cot. He was aiding them. The orcs! Abzul was a filthy dotard, but his sorcery had yet to wither and the orcs were right to fear it. When his tower burst with smoke and fire, flinging the wizard to his death, that fear was removed. By *Jackal*! A half-breed acting as the orcs' cat's-paw! To what other lengths would this dog go to help his new masters? Would he not also engineer the destruction of the Kiln, his former home, to sow further discord and ease the orc march?"

Fetching's guts soured. Bermudo didn't know the real truth, not yet, but he could smell it, a bit of rotten meat that lay between them as they circled each other atop this tower. She feared what would happen to the Bastards if Bermudo learned the truth of the Claymaster's role in Crafty's scheme to usurp the throne.

Her fear must have shown, and been misread, for a thin, triumphant grin grew on the man's face.

"Would Jackal have wrought such treachery had he not been banished? I posed to Her Majesty, outcasts from so rough a society as the mongrel hoofs can only bring further peril. Were we ever wise to allow them such freedom? Difficult enough convincing loyal subjects to settle here without the danger of begrudged nomads. Though I think it was the knowledge that these same nomads were now spying for the orcs that finally swayed the queen. I was most clear that last year's encroachment would never have occurred if the thicks had not been guided by Jackal and other vengeful free-riders."

Petty. Lying. Fuck.

The words gathered on Fetch's tongue, but they went unuttered, for she saw that Bermudo wasn't lying. He believed everything he said. But belief makes men blind. If Jackal betrayed the Bastards, why would she hide him? Why would she die for him? Again, she said nothing. Fingering the holes in this man's sanity would only provoke him to look deeper, harder, and that wouldn't save the hoof. Better to let him float in his own delusions and hope they drowned his weakened mind.

Bermudo was enjoying himself now. "And so, Her Majesty acted. All Crown lands in Ul-wundulas are hers by rights, through her father. Her husband, while king of Hispartha, has no claims in the Lots, yet only he is bound by the terms of the charters which formed them. In essence, the hoofs are not obliged to recognize the king's sovereignty, but can do nothing to dispute that the lands upon which you reside fall under the queen's inherited holdings." Bermudo made a hum of amusement. "Forgive me. I forget that all of this is no doubt impossible for a mongrel to understand."

"I know useless cruelty disguised as law when I hear it," Fetch said. "Changes nothing. You frails have mistreated us without cause from the beginning."

"Yes, but it was unlawful. Distasteful. A thing best done by a malfeasant like Captain Ignacio. With him gone—and I am glad of it—I was left with none of low enough repute to stain their hands such."

Fetch tilted her head back toward Maneto. "A rare breed, I'm sure."

Bermudo's thin smile curdled. "Oh, the cavaleros left to me are lowborn curs to a man. Villains, pillagers, rapers every last one. The very reason they must be leashed by decree. Ignacio had rank if not title. He kept his cavaleros well-heeled, and he was from the same stock. I don't carry the stain of peasantry nor can I ride among the men, keep them accustomed to the commands of their betters. Rather than attempt to rein in yet another raucous band of killers in the

Lots, I took steps to ensure that all they do falls under royal sufferance. There is a difference between a wild dog and one whose master allows it to bite. The threat of the rod still looms, a ward against notions of sole reliance. That's where we erred with you mongrels, allowing the belief that you were no longer ruled."

"We aren't ruled," Fetch declared through her teeth.

The captain smiled. "You will soon discover how wrong you are. If you choose to live."

"You won't get Jackal from me, frail. Stop wasting what little strength you've got. Go ahead and condemn me, send me to this Marquesa cunt. I'll use my last breath to tell her what a pleasure it was to turn the spoiled fruit she squeezed out into rancid meat."

Bermudo gave an earnest smile. "You think I would send you north? I am not such a fool as to admit I was wrong to one such as the Marquesa. Not when the truth is so odious. She expects to make the execution of Garcia's killer a spectacle for the common folk. Maneto, can you imagine the lady's shame if she were to put forth some mongrel hussy as the hand that snuffed her noble line?"

"An untenable disgrace, my lord."

Bermudo leaned closer to Fetch, his voice dropping to just above a whisper. "You will die here. Today. The hunt for Jackal will continue. And with all free-riders now deemed in defiance of the king no matter where they are found, sanctuary among the hoofs no longer protects them. Jackal may indeed be gone from the Lots, but should he ever return there is nowhere he can safely rest. I will have him, and it is he who will die on a scaffold in Hispartha before a raucous mob. Your choice . . . Fetching . . . is whether you will greet him in whatever foul hell is put aside for mongrels."

"The Bastards will seek your blood for this," Fetch said. It was no empty boast, though she wished it were. Her brothers' need for vengeance would be the death of them.

Bermudo knew it, too, for his face brightened with relish at the thought.

Fetch tried one more truth. "You'll set all the hoofs against you, Bermudo. None of the mongrel chiefs will let this go unanswered for long."

The captain backed away, crutch tapping, eyes dancing above a grin. "They can come. The voices of these guns shall be my envoys. Their reach secures the castile. All that falls within their range is Hispartha. Not the Lots, not even Crown land, but Hispartha. Reclaimed! Only the short-sighted see limits to that reclamation. Look beyond where the cannonballs fall if you can, half-orc, and you will discover not the end of my reach, but the beginning."

Taking a pompous breath, Bermudo winced, pivoting on his crutch to look out over the battlements once more. He raised his voice over the wind.

"I give you one last chance to tell me where he is."

"I don't know. Fucking hang me!"

That same damn hum. "Oh, I'm not going to *hang* you."

ELEVEN

———

LITTLE MURO WAS CURLED on his side next to the upset stool, hands pressed to his ears. He was rocking and issuing a steady series of moans, his simple mind overwhelmed by the continued roar of the guns. Fetch could not hear Maneto's chuckling at the boy's plight as they stood waiting for the horses to be readied, only saw the gaptoothed mirth stretching his face. The reports were worse in the yard, trapped and rendered sharp by the encircling stone buildings. A second salvo, and a third, was completed by the time Cavalero Ramon and a troop of ten men were mounted in full gear. A horse was brought out for Maneto as well, and the big man pulled himself astride.

He made one of his courtly gestures. "After you, Chief Cunny."

Fetch started walking. Horseshoes clacked on the cobbles behind. She was shepherded to the gatehouse. Twenty men from the garrison were assembled in its shadow, surrounding a group of prisoners, halberds leveled.

Fetch knew the faces of the guarded, and was surprised to see them still living.

Eva and Red Ynes. Violante and Black Ynes. Rhecia and the stooped stable hand.

Cissy.

The terrified denizens of the brothel numbered nearly two dozen and Fetch was brought into their whimpering, trembling company. All were filthy, hard-used. There was no time for talk. They were shoved toward the gate, given no choice but to walk for the sunlight.

The guns were quiet now.

As the shadow of the tunnel seized them, Fetch suppressed a shudder, glancing up at the large murder hole set into the arched stone. She wasn't going to hang. Didn't mean a cauldron of boiling pitch wasn't about to come vomiting out that insidious trap. Yet all passed beneath unharmed. Emerging from the barbican, they reached the sun-smote trail and, at the prodding insistence of their escort, began descending the escarpment. The switchbacks made the journey a long one.

Fetch could feel the nerves of her fellow captives buzzing, almost hearing them as clearly as a passing bee. Her chest tightened, the grip cold. Fear was never something lightly admitted to in the Lots, but she found herself wishing that it was only the growing dread of approaching death. If the sludge induced another fit now she'd die weak and feeble. Unable to fulfill her oath, she at least wanted to meet the hells on her feet.

They reached the bottom.

Thin plumes of smoke sprouted from the plain ahead, the blossoms of implanted cannonballs.

"Keep moving!" came a shout.

The halberdiers kept pushing, but Maneto, Ramon, and the other mounted men reined up at the base of the cliff. The brutal lean of their minds was clear. Lead the prisoners far out onto the plain, send them scurrying, and make sport of the hunt.

Cunts.

Fetch kept a steady pace and pulled ahead of the shuffling gaggle of condemned. Swift movement and panting breaths to her right heralded someone catching up.

"It wasn't me," Cissy said. "I told them nothing. It was Hilde that squawked."

Fetch had to laugh, short and bitter. "Guess she knew enough Hisparthan after all."

Cissy was less forgiving. "Spineless Guabian."

Fetch didn't bother with a response. Pregnant women had a heap to lose. Hilde had saved more than herself, as long as Bermudo's men left her alone. Far from certain. Maneto seemed just the sort of evil fuck to prey on one so vulnerable.

Cissy was still gnawing on useless regret. "If she'd just gone with you . . . if I hadn't warned her off."

"Don't go thinking you're that important, Cissy. Wouldn't be here if Slivers hadn't killed that cavalero. Wouldn't if those men hadn't deserted. Or *had* and just gone straight to the hills. Leagues of links in this chain and you're far from the weakest."

"You pardoning me because we're about to die, Isabet?"

"Afraid so."

Silent now, they trudged on.

Soon, Fetch could see the blackened, pitted border that charted the limits of the castile's guns. When the broad strip of churned earth was beneath her boots, the guards yelled for her to stop.

Understanding brought a strange calm.

Fetching turned, saw the others bullied to keep moving by men not willing to take another step. With a few final coaxing thrusts of their halberds and threatening shouts, the guards began withdrawing, walking backward, demanding the prisoners not move. The cavaleros at the base of the trail were rendered invisible by distance. As the footmen, too, dwindled away, one of the clustered whores spoke, voice strangled with worry and confusion, yet loosed by hope.

"Are we being let go?"

"No," Fetch said, firm and clear. "We're not." Nostrils filled with the rough edge of smoke, she looked down, kicking at the gun-tilled dirt. Three volleys, yet still there were broad patches untouched. What were the chances of that? The guns didn't strike her as all that accurate, but there might be gaps in where the balls fell. Fetch began snatching at the brothel folk, pulling them to huddle in one such wishful island.

"You'll all want to run," she said. "*Don't*. Stand firm. Stand still. No matter the dread, do not move."

Cissy remained beside her.

Fetch reached, took hold of her wrist. "What happens if you run through hornets?"

Cissy's brow creased. "You get stung."

"And if you stay still?"

"You . . . might not."

Fetch nodded, insistent. "Do *not* run. None of you! No matter what. Until I say."

Cissy's arm twisted, broke Fetch's hold. And took her hand, fingers intertwining.

Fetching raised her eyes to the castile and glared at the tower where she knew Bermudo stood, unable to see him, but over the gulf of air she could feel his fucking smile.

The walls thundered.

The prisoners gasped, flinched. A heartbeat. An unnerving hollow shriek.

And the ground became a living, enraged beast.

Unseen giant fists smote the plain, shook it, transformed it into a deafening hell. Roaring, thrashing waves of earth crested before Fetch's horrified eyes, crashed over her, blinding, stinging, choking. Screams filled the space between the booming impacts. Acrid, pelting dirt rained down. A blast to Fetch's left. A hunkering woman on the edge of the group ruptured, head and torso jerked backward, an arm snapping free to spin in the air. A piece of someone struck Fetch in the shoulder, the face. Heavy and meaty, it nearly knocked her over, slapping her with blood and pain. The guns no longer drowned out the screams as people were torn apart. The knot of prisoners, frayed by the reaping, began to come apart.

Someone ran. Another.

Through the onslaught, Fetch saw the stable hand fleeing, terror lending speed to his crooked body. A gun blast struck a bow shot away, the ground slowing the ball enough to make it visible, skipping across the ground as a rock would on water. Barreling into the stableman, it took his feet out from under him, throwing him head over heels, his body a floppy windmill. His leg broke off at the knee in flight.

Hazy phantoms fled in all directions, many changing course as the guns' fury cut them off.

Fetch was pulled to join them, by instinct and by Cissy. She quashed the one and hauled back on the other, forcing them both to remain planted within the tumult of ravaged earth, smoke, and the tossed body parts of the unfortunate. Ears pummeled to empty caverns where sound was unwelcome, she barely knew when the barrage ended, barely heard her own lung-busting cry.

"NOW!"

She and Cissy dashed directly away from the castile, their steps hindered by smoke, shattered ground, and shattered bodies. They weaved around singed scrub and splintered rock, jumping charred depressions, stumbling, crawling back to their feet.

The cavalry would be coming.

Breaching the smoke, they surged onto unspoiled plain. The land surrounding the castile was rippled with the lesser kindred of the great escarpment upon which it sat. Legs pumping, Fetch made for the nearest ridge, still a taunting distance across the flats. Impossible to outrun the horses, but if she could reach rougher terrain, something to impede the cavaleros, her stand would fare better. She might be able to kill that twisted fuck Maneto before they took her down. Ramon too. Hells, she would try for them all.

Cissy had fallen behind. Fetch bolted back, seized the smaller mongrel's hand, and dragged her to greater speed.

Reaching the ridge, they found a gulch notched into its base by a strangled stream.

A choice. Up the slope or down the cleft?

Liking the narrow confines and the bed of leg-breaking rocks, Fetch scurried for lower ground. She and Cissy were soon swallowed by the embankment. Screened from view, they hustled through the gulch until the sides began to grow shallow, the depression becoming level with the land once more. The ridge rose sheer to their right. A sprawl of boulders and scrub bordered the lip to their left. Fetch scrambled up, using the cover to gain a look at their back-trail.

"Shit," she hissed, ducking back down almost as soon as she peeked out.

Six cavaleros were on the ridge above. In their pursuit they'd seen the same choice and must have split up. The others were either risking their horses within the gulch or were riding along the lip. She guessed the latter.

Skidding down the scree to Cissy, she whispered, pointing the way they'd come.

"Head back. If you run into horses, run back here, but don't leave the gulch. If the cavaleros are above, stop, surrender. Keep their eyes on you."

Fearful but resolved, Cissy nodded.

"Go."

Fetch waited until the meander of the gulch hid Cissy from sight before making her gamble. She climbed out on the side opposite the ridge, moved at a crouch through the scrub. The cavaleros searching from the high ground would notice her eventually, but the slope above this end of the gulch was too steep for them to ride down. They'd be forced to double back. She'd have to be swift.

And hells-damned lucky.

Shouts of men's voices ahead. The lower party had seen Cissy, and it sounded like they weren't inside the gully, but above on Fetch's side.

There was the luck.

Shouts from the ridge. She'd been spotted herself.

Time for the swift.

Gathering the slack of her chains on the run, Fetch sprinted across the scrabble. Rounding a curve caused by a thrust of the ridge, she reached the cavaleros. They'd been riding single file, but were now turned side-facing, every man with his attention focused on a pleading Cissy below.

The lead cavalero never saw Fetch coming.

Springing, she seized his shield and yanked him from the saddle. He tumbled to the stones with a yelp, helm falling from his head. He tried to rise, but Fetch stomped his face with her bootheel, cracking the back of his skull against a rock. Blood sprayed.

One.

Nickering with agitation, his horse shied and stamped, but did not spook. It was hemmed on three sides by Fetching to its left, the gulch in front, and to its right by the next cavalero in the line. Alerted by the scuffle, the man turned, swearing at the empty saddle next to him and the escaped half-orc just beyond. Fetch ducked, scrambling for a weapon, but the lance of the man she'd brained had slid into the gulch. Before she could free the sword from his belt, the other cavalero rode around the impeding horse.

Fetch whipped the loop of her chain up into the oncoming animal's face, causing it to rear in pain and alarm, dumping its rider into the scrub. The other cavaleros were shouting, their voices raw with anger and confusion. The struck horse continued to buck, beating at Fetch with its front hooves. Recoiling, she made another attempt for the sword and filled her hand with steel. The unhorsed cavalero was struggling in the embrace of the scrub, unable to find enough leverage to rise. Splayed out, tangled in his cloak, he could only scream as Fetch rushed in, thrusting the blade through his open mouth. The crossguard broke his teeth as the blade buried to the hilt.

Two.

She was in full view of the others now. The remaining three cavaleros had turned their mounts and were now fanning out from the edge of the gulch, getting into position to ride her down. Leaving the sword, she snatched the lance from Two's dead hand and vaulted onto One's horse, got her ass in the saddle. Her seat felt too tall, too precarious, the uncooperative animal beneath her legs powerful but ungainly. No hope getting her feet in the stirrups, and her bound wrists made it impossible to wield the lance and use the reins.

The cavaleros spurred forward.

"Fuck this."

Fetch slapped a hand down on the saddle horn, bracing as she hopped up, her boots perching atop the saddle. She jumped high off the animal's back, launching herself at the oncoming men. The lance in both hands, she drove it down, taking the center cavalero in the chest. The long, keen point of the lance pierced his armor, ripping through the scales to find his heart.

Three.

She kept hold of the lance as the man toppled over the rump of his horse. His back struck the dust, the lance driving deeper as Fetch landed on her feet, straddling the impaled carcass. Turning, she saw the last cavaleros were riding away, gaining distance to turn for another charge.

"Isa!"

Fetch whirled at Cissy's warning, just in time to see Maneto bearing down, chain-mace swinging. Throwing her arms up in front of her face, Fetch caught the flanged head on her shackled wrists. The force of the blow knocked the iron cuffs into her nose. Reeling, she groped for the lance planted in Three's body. Bright smears of color announced the mace striking the back of her head. A numbing weightlessness took hold.

Her sight returned, a bleary, nauseating thing. She was lying on stones, Maneto and Ramon atop towering horses above. Cissy was kneeling beside her, clutching a lance. But she'd been . . . at the bottom of the gulch. So was Fetching.

Maneto said something, the words muddled as they swam through the pulsing, sickening weight of Fetch's skull.

"—better that than going down there after them."

"Heathen way to kill." Ramon. Not pleased.

"You can wear a hair shirt after," Maneto needled. "You men start gathering those bigger rocks! We'll kill these soot-skins and bury them with the same effort."

With a groan, Fetch pushed herself up, pawed at the lance in Cissy's hands. Wide-eyed, the woman relinquished the weapon. Shoving the butt end of the shaft into the dry bed, Fetch began climbing to her feet. The first effort made her vomit on her boots, much to Maneto's amusement.

"Oh, ho-ho! Look here! This one don't take to the notion a' dying, lads! Martyred Madre, if that's not the fighting spirit to separate a chief from the common mongrel. Bear witness, boys, and count yer-selves better men!"

Fetch made it upright. The number of Manetos wavered from one lout to four and back again.

He leaned across his saddle horn to better leer down at her. "What do you expect to render, Chief Cunny, skull-broke and barely able to stand in your half-dug grave?"

"Add one . . . more to my . . . grand tally of cunt cavaleros killed," Fetch said, slurring. "Promised you'd die soon, frail."

Maneto only guffawed.

It hurt to smile, but Fetch managed.

Maneto turned to Ramon. "Make certain—"

Fetch threw the lance. Would have been fucking awkward with shackled hands, but Maneto's mace had broken one of the cuffs. She'd hidden it until time to make the cast. Her bashed head sought immediate vengeance for the effort, pouring on the dizzying pain, enough to send her sprawling back to the stones.

Ramon was cursing, a horse was whinnying. Clacking rocks and crunching bootfalls as the dismounted cavaleros abandoned their stone gathering to see what had happened.

Fetch forced her squinted eyes open and up. From his own mount, Ramon was snatching at the bridle of Maneto's furious horse. Its saddle was vacant.

"Four."

She looked at Cissy, sorry she couldn't get them all.

And then they heard the chuckling.

It grew in intensity as Maneto stomped into view, dusty, helm-less, holding the side of his head. Still chortling, he moved his hand, splayed the glistening red palm.

"Add an ear to your tally, quim. Add an ear!" Maneto burst into fresh peals of laughter. He climbed atop his horse. "Stone 'em, lads!"

With that command, he rode away, still trumpeting his mirth.

Ramon watched him go. His men ambled back to the rocks piled at the edge of the gulch, each bending to lift one.

Cissy rose to stand beside Fetch as the men lifted the boulders over their heads.

"Wait!"

The command came from Ramon. The men heeded.

Ramon dismounted. He gestured the men away. Putting the rocks down, they gathered, lost from sight. The occasional pulse of Ramon's lowered voice reached the gully, but only as deep hums.

Fetch met Cissy's questioning eye, saw the uncertainty birth fresh fear.

They waited.

The cavaleros came back to stand at the lip and gaze down, but said nothing. They did not take up the stones. Ramon kept looking in the direction Maneto had gone. Nothing happened for a long while.

So long, Fetch gave up on the foolery of standing.

At last, the sounds of approaching horses roused her back to her feet.

It wasn't Maneto. It was that rodent Blas, along with a dozen of his men.

"Come up out of there," Ramon told Fetch and Cissy as soon as the scouts' stockbows were trained. The climb up the slope nearly caused Fetch to vomit again, but she reached the top.

Blas and his troop weren't the only new arrivals. There were also five fresh cavaleros, a string of pack mules.

And Womb Broom.

Fetch puzzled at the sight of her hog alive, saddled. The brace of javelins was full, and her stockbow and tulwar hung from the harness.

All hopes of being given inexplicable freedom were dashed when Blas brought forth more chains.

Fetch looked around at the twenty-six men. And held her wrists out.

"What's happening?" she asked Ramon.

"We're taking you to Vallisoletum," came the terse reply.

Hispartha. Fetch gave Ramon as hard a stare as her busted skull would allow. He was angry, anxious.

"You're all deserting," Fetch said.

Ramon grimaced. "We are taking Garcia's killer to the marquesa. Bermudo can choose to squander his chance of getting away from here. Not us."

The reply wasn't for her, Fetch realized. Ramon was trying to keep his conspirators from losing their courage.

As Blas secured the chains, Ramon fixed Fetching with flinty eyes from atop his horse. "The journey is long. You will be tempted to escape. For every disobedience, every one of my men you harm, try to harm, for every attempt at flight, I will punish her." The hard stare flicked to Cissy, also being chained. "Get them on a mule, Blas. If they even drag their feet, notch the whore's ear."

Fetch went to the mule, focused on walking steadily. The nausea had faded during the wait in the gulch, but the pain matured, grew roots. The first plodding steps of the mule were a fresh hell. Wasn't long before the rolling, rough ride summoned the queasiness back from whatever crack in her skull it had slithered into to sleep. She did not know the distribution of her captors, could not perceive the direction they traveled, though she guessed northward. The journey was the spearing glare of the sun encouraging her discomfort to become a thing near unbearable.

She had no notion where Vallisoletum lay within the kingdom. Didn't really matter. She did know Ramon wanted her to get there alive. This marquesa cunt would feel slighted otherwise. Bermudo said her vengeance required an audience. That's how these noble fucks thought. Sluggard and Incus were proof of that. Carnavales. Arenas. Half-orcs were a thing to witness. To fear. To desire. To master. It was the damn reason Blas had brought Fetch's hog. A lone half-orc woman would make a poor parade to the gallows. The gathered frails would likely complain, think they'd been cheated. No, you needed the feral hog, the well-used weapons. Trappings necessary to complete the picture of the bloodthirsty, tattooed, filthy mongrel savage who killed one of their blue-blood betters.

Your time is ending.

Bermudo's words kept slithering through the muddled morass of Fetch's mind.

This was more than the persecution of the nomads. Jackal's head could appear on a platter at the captain's next meal and he would continue to make the badlands bleed. Hells, the man had declared it from his own lips. Hispartha was moving to reclaim Ul-wundulas.

Your time is ending.

Sure as shit wasn't ended yet.

The other chiefs needed to be told, warned.

Fuck Ramon's threats. Fetch and Cissy had to escape. Night was their only chance, when the frails would be trammeled by their piss-poor vision in the darkness. To save the Bastards, the Lots, from Bermudo's madness, they had to escape.

And they had to do it before the border.

TWELVE

RAMON CALLED A HALT well after dusk. He'd ordered a brutal pace, clearly intent on getting as far from the castile as possible. For their camp, he chose the lee of a rocky rise, his men placing a fire and their captives close to its sheltering face. A pair of almond trees stood removed from the rise, the only other residents of the place. The cavaleros hobbled their mounts and corralled them a short distance from the rocks, out in the plain. The scouts kept their animals separate, likely because the watch duties fell to them. Womb Broom was tied beneath the nearer of the almond trees, where he immediately began to root around. It wasn't a kindness. A contented hog, focused on finding fallen morsels, would be more difficult to liberate.

Cavalero Ramon was clever and careful. Had she a choice, Fetch would have preferred him to be a drunken, witless coward. Sitting next to Cissy, she watched him and his men closely, vigilant for any advantage. It didn't help that Cissy's manacles had been removed and used to adjoin Fetch's ankles.

The men spent twilight building up and loitering around their fire. The dice soon came out and Fetch waited for the bottle to follow, but it did not appear until after the men had supped on salted meat and hard biscuit. Fetch and Cissy were given nothing.

"Courteous of them not to feed the women," Fetch muttered in orcish.

"Lucky thing," Cissy replied. "I remember how you get when hungry. Now you'll be able to bite through the chains."

Fetch snorted from her sore nose, the vibration making her head buzz with pain. "Hog's ass."

A pause. "We'll have a chance tonight. They'll remove the chains when they come to rape us."

The chilling truth of that statement was made worse by the blunt certainty in Cissy's voice. There was no sense denying it. Two dozen pieces of human shit who believed they held power over two women. Their actions were as fixed as the rising of the sun. But Cissy was also right about it being their chance. Men were never more vulnerable, in body and mind, than when their cods were stiff in the wind.

Cissy read her thoughts. "I'll make them stupid. You make them corpses."

Fetch nodded.

It happened when the dice grew tiresome.

Two of the boldest sauntered over, sharing a bottle. They merely stood for a while, staring down, features turned to blackness by the fire behind them. Their presence drew three others, the sort of men too afraid to begin the evil, but all too eager to latch on once it's started.

"Leave off," Ramon droned at them from his bedroll by the fire, but there was no weight in his words. Clever men know a pointless task when faced with one. Fetch was surprised he said anything at all. The cavaleros before her did not acknowledge that he spoke.

"What do you reckon?" one asked the rest. "Four enough to hold the Bastard?"

"You mad? Gonna need at least twice that. That mongrel's savage as a lynx."

"Not with that knock Maneto gave her, she ain't."

"Best stick with the tame one, Alvaro," another cautioned.

"Already had her."

A growling laugh. "All of us have."

"I haven't."

"You're a cunting liar, Luys."

"Not! I ain't never."

"He lying, Cissy?" Alvaro asked, casual and kind.

"He's lying," she replied, voice tinged with good humor.

"Don't recall, though," Luys said, put off. "Drunk, most like."

"Take her, then. I want that hoof-inked flesh." Alvaro turned toward the fire, giving Fetch a glimpse of his mustachioed, wine-flushed face. "Some'a you, off your asses, help us here!"

"Fuck you, 'Varo!" came the reply, its speaker all but hidden behind the flames. "Ain't your damn servant."

"What you are is a backy fuck afraid of quim, Guillen!" Alvaro turned back, muttering under his breath. "Man-shafting pederast."

"And take it elsewhere," Ramon barked with far more heat than before. "I don't have a powerful need to watch your bare asses at work."

This was good. Less than half of Ramon's men were indulging their monstrous appetites. Fetch could kill five on foot. All they needed was to get to Womb while unbound, and they could be gone.

Alvaro took another drink, swatted one of the other men on the chest with the back of his hand. "Get some of Blas's boys. They'll help."

The man made a disgusted noise, taking the bottle. "Then we got to share with 'em. Filthy buggers all got the drips."

"They'll go last or not at all," Alvaro declared. "Go on."

Shit. Eight of the scouts were on watch. The remaining four were asleep, resting before their turn at sentry. If they all roused themselves for the promise of forced flesh, that would make nine. Far different odds.

"Wait," Cissy purred. The five silhouettes standing over them stilled.

"You're doing this wrong," she told them, keeping her voice low. "You want us spoiled by poxy cocks the first night? Leave those others out of it, and I'll show you something never for sale at Rhecia's."

"And what's that?" Luys asked, intrigued but suspicious.

Cissy made a breathy noise as if the answer should be obvious. "This is the Bastards' chief. You boys ain't wrong. She's gonna fight. Die before she'll let herself be dishonored. Won't be able to barter her to the noblewoman then and your new lives are over before they start. But"—Cissy directed the proposal at Fetching—"this one loves quim more than you all put together. Reckon she'd rather have me service her in front of you than fight you off. What say, chief?"

Before Fetch could answer, the men approved of the idea with grunted laughter.

Cissy continued to weave her web. "And after, I'll take care of you lot, docile as a lamb. Have what you will." The anticipation of that promise danced through the men. Their silhouettes seemed to bristle.

Alvaro's voice crawled from his obscured face. "That's the way it'll be."

"Let's take them behind the rocks," Luys said, voice now high as a boy's. "Ramon told us to, besides."

He was already heading off.

"Wait," Alvaro said. Fetch could feel his stare. "Get the mongrel bitch's stockbow."

"What?" Luys whined. "Why?"

"You want to wake those scabby outriders for one? I want a way to put a bolt in this Bastard bitch if she decides to go berserk. And bring your knives. Hear that, half-breed?"

"I heard," Fetch told him with forced disinterest. "Cissy said it. Rather spend than die tonight."

Luys stumped off, returning with Fetch's thrum, quiver, and a fresh bottle. Surrounded by their drunken drovers, Fetch and Cissy were made to walk the length of the ridge's base, until at last shuffling behind its shoulder.

"Shit," one of them complained, tripping. "Can't see much."

"Go get a torch, then," Alvaro told him.

The man jumped to it. "Don't have 'em do nothing yet!"

Luys was swearing, trying to pull the string of the heavy stockbow. Another man helped and together they managed to lock it back.

"Why'd we send Gaspar for that torch?" Alvaro groused, swilling the last of the first bottle and tossing it. "Never was a man slower with a task."

He wasn't wrong. It was a long span before the man returned. He had the torch in his hand. And Blas at his heels.

Fuck. Six to slaughter, now. And this new one sober.

The cavaleros, faces now revealed in choppy light, were as unhappy with the lead scout's arrival as Fetch was. Every man gave a curse or a groan upon seeing him.

"Gaspar, you stupid shit," the one with the pug nose said.

Blas was indifferent to their scorn. He grinned widely, displaying a mass of crooked teeth. "This looks diverting. Yes."

"Not for you it's not," Alvaro said. "Get gone."

Blas removed his filthy hat, revealing a balding head shiny with sweat. "No, no. Cavalero Ramon said I was to watch these doings. Make certain you did not kill either of the prisoners."

Alvaro took a threatening step toward the smaller man. "I should thrash you all the way back to the castile."

"Leave him," Luys said. He was having difficulty juggling the bottle and the stockbow, not wanting to relinquish either. "Let's get to it."

Cissy pounced on their impatience. Taking Fetch's hands, she guided her to the ground. Her every movement became fluid yet overwrought, provocative. Back turned toward the men, Cissy knelt before Fetching, crawled to her lap. It would have been ludicrous were it not holding the frails entranced. Back arched, Cissy hiked her skirt up past her hips. The cavaleros gawked.

She gave Fetching the look that said to be ready before casting her eyes over her shoulder. "Not going to be able to get her breeches off with these shackles."

Alvaro seethed a moment. "I ain't got th——"

A rattle of metal interrupted. Grinning, Blas dangled the key. "Glad I'm here now?"

He tossed it to the stocky man next to him, but the unready oaf missed the catch.

"Hells, pick it up and free 'em," Alvaro said. "And train that bow, Luys, or give it over!"

Luys handed the bottle to Alvaro and pointed the thrum at Fetching, the head of the bolt wavering.

"May I?" Cissy asked, holding a hand up for the bottle.

Alvaro eyed her and didn't move.

"Be an ungenerous fuck, then, 'Varo," she pouted, her skirt falling at the same moment to again cover her backside.

Stocky had fished the key from the dust and, as he straightened, Alvaro shoved the bottle at him, gesturing at Cissy. The man walked over and squatted. He handed the bottle to Cissy and shifted to unlock Fetch's ankles. Soon as they were open he picked up the chains and stood.

Fetch seized the dragging links and jerked. Stocky should have let go, but the instinct of strong men is always to hang on, to pull back. Not a contest to have with a half-orc. Jumping to her feet, Fetch snatched the man toward her, grabbed his jerkin, broke his nose with her forehead and spun him around.

She heard her thrum release. Stocky made a gargling sound as Fetch felt a sting in her ribs. The bolt had come out the back of her now-dying shield, penetrated her brigand, and pierced the flesh beneath. It did not slow her.

Reaching around, she jerked the dagger from Stocky's belt and booted him away, sending the heavier man tumbling into Alvaro. They spilled to the ground in a struggling lump. Next to them, Blas's hand went to his lips to unleash one of his damn whistles. Cissy sprang, smashed the bottle over his skull and jammed the jagged remnants into his neck. The scout staggered a few steps backward, blood fountaining up to coat his cheek in crimson. He crumpled to his knees before falling on his face. Luys was struggling to reload the stockbow, but Pug Nose had abandoned him to perform the task alone and rushed Cissy, dagger drawn. Fetch darted into his path, rammed her blade into his ear. Using the weapon in his skull as a handle, she held him upright, and plucked the dagger from his twitching hand, tossing it to Cissy. She caught it deftly, bent to retrieve the fallen key, and quickly freed Fetch's hands.

Gaspar had taken off running, the torchlight fleeing with him.

Luys still wrestled with the stockbow, making high-pitched

whines with every fruitless tug on the string. Fetch rushed over and took the thrum from his grasp. The man gave a startled whimper, but did nothing save shiver as she removed a bolt from the quiver on his belt. Loading quickly, she raised the thrum and pulled the tickler. Gaspar jerked as the bolt took him in the back before he rounded the rocks. She'd made sure to pierce his lung to prevent him crying out. His body spilled atop the dropped torch and smothered the flame.

A few steps away, Alvaro had disentangled himself from Stocky's weighty corpse and stood, but the sudden departure of the light had left him blind. Yet Fetch could still see him, crouched and trying to make out shapes in the dark, brandishing his knife. The fool might have called for aid, but must not have wanted to reveal himself, wrongly believing he was concealed by the night. Fetch took three strides, rammed the heel of her hand upon the pommel of Alvaro's dagger, and forced the man's own blade up beneath his jaw. Gurgling, choking on the blood, he fell once more, this time upon his dead companion. By the time Fetch turned around, Cissy had ended Luys's whimpers by slitting his throat. She removed the quiver from his belt, offering it up.

"We need to move," Fetch hissed, taking the bolts. "We'll circle out beyond the sentries and come at the hog from the darkness. With luck, most of the men will be sleeping."

The eight scouts screened the camp. They weren't riding patrol paths, just sitting their horses, facing away from the ridge, peering into the night. Fetch and Cissy hunkered among some scrub nearest the man on the far right of the picket. The almond tree where Womb was tethered stood a stone's throw behind him. The campfire had died down a bit, but the tree was still within its glow. If any of the scouts glanced back while Fetch and Cissy were freeing the hog they would be plainly visible. A look at the camp revealed prone forms scattered around the fire, a few men propped up against the rock face. It was too far to tell if any were still awake. If just one opened his eyes they would be discovered.

Fetch's gut whispered the right moment and she took it. She stayed low, Cissy dogging her steps. They snuck past the flank scout and padded swiftly for the tree. Womb Broom snorted and stamped when Fetch came up, and she inwardly cursed him for an ornery villain. Crouched, she froze, using the hog to shield her from the camp, craning around to see if the scout had turned.

The man remained oblivious.

Cissy knelt at the tree, working the tethers free while Fetch covered the scout with her thrum, ready to feather him should the need arise. A sharp intake of breath from Cissy drew her attention.

Blas came stumbling into the light, the hand clasped to his throat soaked red. He was leaning on the rock face, barely able to remain upright. His jaw was working, trying in vain to push a sound out of his gushing mouth. Fetch stood and raised her stockbow to her shoulder, but the life went out of Blas before she could take the shot. He fell atop one of the sleeping men. That man awakened screaming.

The camp came alive.

Spinning about, Fetch put her bolt through the sentry rider. He fell from the saddle, his horse emitting a screech. Men scrambled from their blankets, taking up arms, most immediately rushing for their horses.

"You three, check around the ridge!" Ramon, yelling commands. "Find them, go!"

"There! The hog—!"

Fetch had already reloaded and put the observant man down. But not quick enough.

Cissy had the lines undone.

"Get astride!" Fetching shouted, loosing another bolt, trying to keep the cavaleros hiding behind their shields.

Cissy mounted. Fetch moved to join her. Womb Broom screamed, a thrumbolt seeming to sprout from his flank. He twisted, trying to flee the pain, and slammed into Fetching. Blobs of light, pain. Her injured head had smacked something. The tree? She didn't know, tried to stand, but was sickened by the bobbing world. She felt a tugging at her brigand, saw Cissy's swimming outline above. Hoofbeats and hog squeals. Horse nickers and men shouting. They all converged on the pain in Fetch's skull, drummed it deeper. Cissy cried out and the tugging ceased.

It was replaced by hard blows. Boots and fists and the hafts of lances. She was pummeled until the agony in her head spread to her gut and chest, back and limbs. More tugging. Stronger. Dragging her. She drooled blood until the dust clogged her mouth. The hands released, dumping the burden of her. Face slapped something hard and rough. She clawed forward, felt bark. Back at the tree? No. The other. Farther from the light.

"Get a damn rope!"

"Pfft. Easier to put a lance through her, have done."

"I say she hangs."

"Tree ain't tall enough for that, Ramon."

"Will be after we cut her legs off."

Fetch managed to roll over. Men stood over her, around her. Behind them loomed horsemen, one reloading his stockbow.

"Fucking frails," she mumbled, spitting blood at them.

She tried to look around, could barely control her lolling head. Couldn't see Cissy. She pushed up, slid back. Ramon stomped her chest and the tree hammered her spine. Propped by the trunk, she waited for the rope.

It arrived around Cissy's neck.

"Isa?"

"No!" Fetch tried to rise again.

Ramon kicked her, kept kicking her.

"I told you!" he bellowed, panting from the exertion. "Told you what would happen!"

"Isabet!" The plea was panicked. "FETC—"

A horse ran forward, rope sawed across a tree limb, and the cry was throttled.

A cavalero gave a small grunt. "Tree's tall enough, after all."

"No . . ." The word dribbled from Fetch's swollen lips, a weak and useless utterance she could not cease. "No . . . no . . ."

An arm's length and a finger's breadth away, Cissy dangled, her kicking feet less than a handspan from the ground.

Rage boiled within Fetching, promising to put her on her feet, to suffer the blunt blows until the cavaleros were forced to wield sharp steel. She let it rise. And was betrayed. The sludge choked her, banished her breath with its wet weight. Ramon took the fit for a trick and booted her again. It would have been a mercy to succumb right then, strangle beside Cissy. But the sludge was cruel. Fetch did not die with her. All she could do was hold Cissy's eyes until they rolled to white. The girl she'd known from her first memory was dead long before the twitching of her suspended limbs subsided.

Fetch tried to curse the frails, promise them death by her hand, but she spewed nothing but racking coughs.

"I want her wrapped in chains!" Ramon screamed. "And none will touch her unless it's to throw her over the back of a mule! You and you, get Blas and the rest of those curs and drag them far away from camp. Come sunrise, I don't want to break my fast with vultures."

"We're not burying them?"

Ramon growled a dissent. "Let those raping fools rot in the sun."

"And the whore?"

"Take her too."

Cissy's body barely made a sound when it crumpled to the ground. Her slumped form covered the distance between them, and Fetch placed a hand on her head, briefly caressing the hair she'd braided so many times in the orphanage. Cissy slid from beneath her fingers, dragged away by the cavaleros. Through the dust.

"That was *your* doing," Ramon said. He turned away.

A chorus of screams split the night, snatching the man's attention.

Fetch had heard horses in panic, but these were the cries of animals beyond terror, animals whose minds had become unhinged. The cavaleros turned as one to the camp's rope paddock. Their mounts were rearing, bucking, so frightened they began to snap their hobbles.

"Watch her!" Ramon commanded the scouts, and led the rest of his men rushing to their crazed animals.

So intent on trying to wrangle the screeching horses, they failed to see the pack of dogs lining the top of the ridge. Then that damn cackling warbled across the night and all eyes went upward.

Fetch joined the hyenas in laughter. She'd managed to kill every cavalero after all.

Come and get me, Crafty, you jowly fuck.

A figure appeared on the ridge, striding to its edge at the center of the dogs. It wasn't a fat, turbaned wizard.

It was a towering, brutish shadow of long limbs and wide shoulders limned in moonlight and menace. The rise was nearly ten times the height of a man and the figure stepped off as one would a footstool. Its massive frame smote the ground, corded legs bending against the shock. Straightening in the cowering glow of the campfire was a monstrous orc, the largest Fetch had ever seen, a specimen of barbarous thews. Savagery and bloodlust seemed to pulse off its slate-dark flesh even as it simply stood there, breathing. It was unarmed and naked, save for adornments of bone and tusk pierced through its skin, especially across the chest and down the arms.

The scouts were the first to react, each letting a bolt fly at the huge orc that had landed in the center of their camp. Only two found their mark. One struck it in the chest, the other in the meat of its thigh. Both bolts snapped against its bone-pierced flesh.

The cavaleros now fumbled in the dirt for their shields and lances, discarded to tend the horses. Slowly, the orc's hairless pate revolved to look at them.

The men ran.

At least, they tried.

The orc moved with a speed impossible for Fetch's fuddled eyes to track. In an instant he was upon them, seizing legs, dashing heads against the rock face, splattering blood and brains. Ramon spun, tried to make a manful stand. He raised his shield, thrust with his lance. The steel struck. And bent. The nightmarish thick swatted Ramon's shield aside and pulped the man's skull between clapping hands, the crunching squelch audible even over the cries of the horses.

The swiftest cavaleros had gained some distance, their pumping limbs carrying them away from the slaughter fast as they could manage. The orc remained where it was, standing before the maddened horses. The animals could endure his presence no more. Ropes snapped and they bolted, but the orc seized one before it could escape, fingers gouging into its neck and belly. The brute lifted the kicking animal over its head and hurled it at the fleeing men. The shrieking mass slammed into them. Men were tossed, crushed, as the horse impacted, the sound of snapping bones preceding a final, grisly thud. The beast's body slid to a stop, broken men pinned beneath.

The scouts cursed and turned their mounts, spurring them away. The orc gave the smallest upward motion of its head. The dogs left the ridge, their laughter rising as their loping forms descended the slopes to either side.

The horsemen would not get far.

The orc's gaze shifted.

He walked through the camp, toward the almond tree. Toward Fetching.

She tried to stand. To flee. The effort demanded more breath. Breath she did not have. The indrawn air hit a wall. She hit the dust. Her lungs were flooded, nothing but a coin's width at the top unclogged. Fetch used the thin allowance, felt it shrink with every labored gasp. A bare foot slid beneath her, flipped her over. Bending, the orc grabbed her neck, lifted her one-handed into the air. She dangled, as Cissy had dangled. Strangled, as Cissy had strangled. Strangled by the sludge, by the thick's constricting fingers. She was drawn eye to eye. Amber irises shone in the firelight, studying her face with contempt.

Through dancing black spots, Fetch saw the orc's mouth open, felt the warm, wet tongue slide up her cheek.

"*Ul ulma'huuq.*"

The voice was distant thunder rolling from the depths of Dhar'gest.

The black spots melded into a seamless darkness as Fetch died with those words.

You taste weak.

THIRTEEN

—

THE HELLS WERE HOT. And bright as midday.

Fetch's eyes had fluttered open and been abused for their daring. Clenched tight now, the gates of her lids did little to brunt the battering light. Cowed and blinded, she felt dust scratching her cheek, between her fingers. There was also a sound. Wet. Ebbing and flowing, but harsh. Jagged pebbles sliding in a drenched sack. It was her breath, tortured and clogged, hardly strong enough to push against the dry earth beneath her chest.

Keeping her eyes shut, she pushed up. Too soon. Trembling and dizzy, she ate dirt again, cheekbone slapping the hard-packed pebbles beneath the grit. Twice chastened, she waited. Waited to grow accustomed to the light's assault, for her lungs to clear, for her limbs to steady. Patience did for the light and for her limbs, but her breath remained ragged and shallow. Still, she made a second, slower attempt to sit up and fared better.

Fetch opened her eyes to slits and recalled something Thistle had said once.

I imagine the worst of all the hells is the one that looks just like living.

Looking about, Fetch beheld the face of a ridge. *The* ridge. There were no dogs along its crest, but dead men were strewn at its feet. Sprawled and bloody and still. The remnants of their campfire was a sooty stain, black to contrast the smears of red. Out on the plain, the vultures were feasting on the humps that were once horses.

Gathering her legs, Fetch stood, hissing at a sudden pain in her ribs. Inspecting the source revealed an angry-looking puncture wound. Probing it gingerly she remembered the bolt from her own thrum that transfixed the cavalero. Her hand moved to the back of her head. The hair was crusted, mud and blood impossible to differentiate, but the soreness in her skull, the welt from Maneto's mace, couldn't hide from her searching fingers.

Fetch again looked around, the injuries forcing her to wonder.

Was she still fucking alive?

Plodding steps brought her closer to the ridge. She inspected the corpses, too weak and stiff to use anything but her eyes. Death and its trappings rendered most of the cavaleros identical. Few had discernible wounds, straddling that queer line between the sleeping and the dead. Only the small, gruesome details betrayed them. The poses only a corpse can attain. The half-lidded, sightless eyes. Plus, the flies of Ul-wundulas were never lazy. Scanning the slaughtered, Fetch wondered why her own meat wasn't among them. A massive orc, impervious to steel, had jumped from the ridge's deadly height and . . . broken these men. With nothing but bare, brute savagery. It had commanded the dogs, set them upon the fleeing. The shimmering blobs of buzzards supping within the heat phantoms out on the plain showed the success of their hunt.

She had gone mad. Grief and sickness had shattered her mind, serving up a host of visions. She'd died and her hell was crafted from the delusions of her final moments.

Yet . . . she knew the dogs to be real. Her brothers had seen them. And their tracks were evident among the carnage. As were the orc's. Fetch followed them back to where she had lain, the path the orc had taken before he seized her, named her weak. A judgment. A condemnation. Why had he allowed her to live? An orc of his size and strength was unknown. An orc that would show mercy to a half-breed was impossible.

Fetch shambled about, following the tracks for answers. She found Cissy first.

The cavaleros had only dragged her a few dozen strides from the tree before the orc appeared. She'd been abandoned, the noose still around her stretched and discolored neck. Fetch's legs threatened to give out. She let them carry her down, but only long enough to get her arms beneath Cissy. Cradling her close, Fetch stood once more. She would not leave Cissy here for the vultures, nor would she bury her beside her murderers. No. She would carry her away from here. If this was her hell, she'd choose how to suffer.

She began walking.

THE SUN WAS A FIERY MALLET. Cissy's back took the brunt from above. The reflected glare and heat from the parched ground was Fetch's to bear, along with the yoke of her dead companion. She had stopped only once, to remove her brigand and shift Cissy up across her shoulders. Free from the vest's weight, she continued onward, trying to keep south and west, but the fully ascended sun did not help her muzzy brain stay confident of a true course. South and west. To the one place that may provide refuge. The castile was closer, but that was just another way to die.

Cissy's deadweight pressed down upon her. Fetch kept meaning to halt, to put her down and build a cairn. But she kept walking.

She had no notion how far they'd gone. Her knowledge of distance in the badlands was gained from the back of a hog, measured by their long, familiar paces. Only orcs walked through Ul-wundulas and lived. Anyone else was a future bounty for the vultures.

Sweating, aching, Fetch squinted at the landscape. She needed to climb a ridge, gain a vantage. Hauling Cissy up a rocky slope would tax her legs, but she could not leave her.

With no choice, they climbed.

The first few upward steps brought Fetch confidence. The sliding dirt and treacherous rocks soon robbed her of that. A quarter way to the top and her thighs were afire, her shoulders knotting from holding Cissy steady. Each exhalation birthed a small sound of exertion.

Every foot forward was watered by a hundred droplets from her chin and nose. Halfway up she considered putting Cissy down, just for a moment to ease her spine. The thought of picking her up again scattered that idea to the woefully scant breeze. At last, they crested the ridge.

Ul-wundulas rewarded her effort by gifting a barren view to every horizon.

Fuck you.

She started back down.

The afternoon was spent keeping to flat earth. Doing so destroyed a direct course. Dry gulches, boulder scrabbles, hills, all forced Fetch's path to meander. Her mind was seduced into the hope that a lemon or pear tree would be waiting around the next obstacle, something to provide moisture to their mouths and a break from the unchanging terrain. The badlands mocked such hopes. It gave her nothing but heat and the toil of her own steps. The sun was lower, taunting her with the secret of west, but direction no longer had meaning. She was a slave to level ground.

At some point, the boulders and ridgelines ceased diverting her path and crept in to enclose it. The shade solicited a sob of relief. Forward, ever forward. Fetch convinced herself she was walking deeper into a box canyon and would have to turn around and walk back out again. To think otherwise would only summon the dead end. Holm oaks began to appear. Had Fetch been ahog, the fallen acorns would have been a welcome sight for her barbarian. They did nothing to tempt her sandy tongue. As the trees increased, becoming a proper grove, she dared to become vigilant for water.

She found the shrine first.

Nestled among the oaks, she came upon it without knowing. It was a broken column of carved marble, its jagged top chest high. The white of the stone was besmirched with the accumulated dirt of long years, embraced by generations of vines both withered and lush. Its round, fluted body was wide as a rain barrel and rose from a square base. A slaughtered goat lay beneath, exposed entrails a lurid pink dotted black with roaming flies. Dozens of dead snakes were scattered around the goat, some freshly killed, some desiccated; most had rotted to nothing but strands of delicate rib cages still affixed to spines and fanged skulls. The sickly sweet smell of old decay spiced the air.

Silently, Fetch cursed herself. Though she had never laid eyes on such a shrine, she knew what it portended.

Her errant steps had caused her to wander into centaur lands.

Backing away, as if the pillar were as dangerous as the sacrificed serpents surrounding it had been in life, Fetch turned and retraced her steps, going quicker now. She almost made it to the edge of the grove. Voices and the plod of hooves heralded an end to any chance of surviving her trespass. There were the trees for cover, but she couldn't move swiftly or silently enough to properly hide. The thought of fighting was laughable and tiresome. This was her mistake, raging against it was fruitless.

Fetch stayed where she was, waiting as the centaurs came into view.

There were three of them, two females and a male. They were moving carelessly, talking carelessly. They even laughed. Why not? A fool-ass half-orc had just blundered into their grove, weak, tired, unmounted and unarmed. It was worthy of laughter. Their voices died when they saw Fetching, their steps came up short. She expected cruel sneers, merciless grins that bespoke the anticipation of bloodshed. What she saw was wide-eyed surprise. The females clutched baskets, the male bore nothing but a long-handled spade. They had no weapons. The trio cast uncertain looks at one another, their front hooves shifting nervously.

They had not known she was here. Her presence had taken them as unexpectedly as the shrine did her.

The female in the center spoke to the other two in a taut whisper, her eyes never leaving Fetch. The male answered in low tones. Their words were a mystery. The other female pointed at her, or maybe Cissy, and gave voice to something with great concern. They conferred in their tongue for some time, wary and tense. Arguing over who was going to go summon the warriors to come put a few spears in the intruder, most likely. Fetch wondered if it would be that quick. Likely not.

A decision was reached and the females passed their baskets to the male. Their empty hands came up, palms spread toward Fetch. The older spoke to her, unintelligible. Slowly, the females approached, arms still extended. The gesture was calming, peaceful yet warding, as if they feared she would bolt or attack. Hells, it was identical in tone and appearance to what Fetch would have done to an agitated hog.

She stayed motionless, watched the male as the females began to spread out a bit, moving to either side. The older female kept up a stream of words, soothing at their core, but frightened at the edges. They stopped within spitting distance. The speaker repeated the same phrase several times. Slower than before, they moved in, reaching . . .

For Cissy!

Fetch jerked, tried to keep them away, but the sudden motion made her stumble, undermined what little endurance she had left. She was falling.

The centaurs darted in, took hold of Cissy's feet, her shoulders, caught her. The relief of the weight made Fetch lightheaded and she allowed the earth to greet her rump. The centaur women laid Cissy on her back, their front legs forced to kneel in order to lower her gently.

Now that Fetch was sitting, the proud notion of dying on her feet no longer seemed so important. She'd be right here on her ass when the spears came and think no less of herself. The older female spoke, made an urgent clicking noise with her tongue, sending the younger to reclaim the baskets and trot deeper into the grove. Off to get the killers. The male was also given some instruction, but his face darkened at whatever he was told and he seemed to protest. The female countered with sterner words and shooing gestures that defeated any further defiance. He clomped away.

The remaining centaur carefully lowered the bulk of her horse body down, folding the legs beneath. She gestured to Cissy and said a few words, her face piteous. Hells, she thinks . . .

"I know she's dead," Fetch croaked. "I'm not mad."

Not mad. Not dead.

The centaur reached and slowly, *slowly*, lifted Fetch's shirt. Fetch made no move to stop her. Now that she was seated, all she seemed capable of was staring, numb and dumb.

The centaur hissed at the puncture wound. She let the shirt fall.

The male returned, bearing a load of sticks. Lowering himself in the same fashion as the other, he worked setting a fire. When the wood was laid, he unslung a horn hanging from a strap across his body and produced something that smoked weakly. Cupping it in his hands, he blew gently until the smoldering bundle rekindled and flames arose. Gently, he set the burning bundle beneath the wood. Soon, the fire was strong and the male fed it with sticks, building it up. The younger female returned with her basket full of acorns, which she handed down before going away once more. Using a rock and a flat stone, the older female began breaking the hulls and grinding the freed nuts.

Watching all of this, Fetch's exhausted mind began to understand. They were helping her.

It was another trick of the hell. It must have been. Horse-cocks were blood-crazed slayers, lurking in their scattered and shunned lands until the Betrayer Moon when they rode forth in search of murder and rapine.

Not mad. Not dead.

Then the sun must have boiled her brain and this was some delirium born of thirst. Knowing her thoughts, the illusion of the younger woman came back with a skin of water and proffered it with a tremulous hand.

Fetch snatched it, causing the filly to flinch and shy away. Upending the skin, she directed the stream into her eager mouth. The water was warm and silty and glorious. She waited for it to turn to dust, to choke her, for the skin to vanish. But the liquid continued to splash upon her tongue and she guzzled. Tearing her mouth away from the flow, she collapsed next to Cissy, giving herself up to the blissful mirage.

HER EYES OPENED TO STARS and the song of crickets. Firelight pulsed upon the surrounding oaks. Sitting up provided a throbbing skull and proof she was still in the grove. Cissy was still nearby, still dead, but she now rested upon a well-constructed, unkindled pyre. Her body had also been cleaned. Fetch rose and felt something sticky beneath her shirt. Looking, she found her wound covered with some glistening paste.

If the centaurs had been visions, Fetch was now asleep, and they had journeyed into her dreams. There were seven of them now, gathered just beyond the edge of the trees. Another, larger fire had been built and they encircled the blaze, each holding a ring of woven reeds. These they held up above their heads, chanting in their strange tongue. Fetch followed their eyes skyward and felt a pang of foreboding seeing the moon. It appeared normal, but the horse-cocks were directing their voices to its quarter-full face. Fetch despaired that it would wax before her very eyes and turn her would-be saviors to ravening beasts. But the moon held true.

Lowering the reed circles, the centaurs held them to the flames. Once they were alight, they were again thrust toward the heavens until the flames threatened the hands of their bearers. Each centaur threw their ring skyward in a way that set it wheeling, catching it and throwing it again. They touched the burning wreaths only long enough to toss them again, repeating the action until they came apart, scattering embers and smoldering stalks to drift into the night. The chanting ceased and the group held for only a moment more. They drifted away with somber faces, all except the female who first knelt and crushed the acorns. She turned, saw Fetch regarding her, and approached, bringing a brand from the bonfire. Speaking, she indicated a basket nearby covered with a piece of hide. Fetch removed it to reveal persimmons, goat meat, figs, and the power of her own hunger. The centaur unslung another waterskin from her body and passed it down.

"Thank you," Fetch told her.

The centaur's eyebrows narrowed, as if trying to remember the answer to a riddle. Without another word or sign, she handed the brand to Fetch before turning to tread deeper into the grove, where the firelight could not follow.

Fetch rested the brand in the small campfire.

She ate.

It was difficult not to devour the entire contents of the basket, though plenty had been provided. She kept some over, for tomorrow. There was going to be a day following this night, she became more certain of that the more she chewed. This was no dream, no vision, no hell. The horrors, the mysteries, were real. Fetch wasn't mad, though she'd felt its grip out there in the badlands. Why else had she saddled herself with a body rather than weapons, provisions?

Why else . . .

Taking the waterskin, Fetch approached the pyre. The centaurs had washed the morass of blood and dirt from Cissy's face, but there was no erasing the mark of the noose. Fetch spared a little of the water, placed it on the dead mongrel's lips. She had comforted her like this once before, when they were children.

A sickness had scourged the orphanage. She and Oats had been spared, but Jackal was laid low. So was Cissy. They'd all been seven or eight. One of the younger children had died, Fetch remembered, a little frailing girl. She was terrified it was going to happen to Jack and Cissy, refused to leave them. Beryl had shown her what to do, how to soothe their fevers. That night she had remained awake until her friends were out of danger. Tonight, however, no vigil would help.

Fetch returned to the fire, took up the brand.

"Seek peace, sister," she whispered.

Keeping her eyes on Cissy's face, she lit the pyre.

SHE JERKED AWAKE in the morning to the sound of approaching hooves. Strengthened by rest and food, Fetch shot to her feet to find the male centaur returning.

"Fuck. My. Ass . . ."

She stood, flooded by disbelief, by utter relief at the sight of the centaur leading Womb Broom. As the hog trotted closer, intent on something affixed to the centaur's pronged pole, Fetch's jaw hung slack. The barbarian was still saddled, though her tulwar was gone. She went to the barbarian with a joyful exhalation. Womb Broom did not care a shit. He was fixed on what had been used to bait him. The centaur removed the black wad from the end of the pole and tossed it to Fetch. It proved to be a pungent, shapeless black fungus.

"A damn truffle," she mused, tossing it down for Womb to devour with grunting relish.

They were a rarity that the hoof never fed to the hogs, but after coming this far with the succulence in his nostrils, it would be cruel to deny the beast. She inspected him while he ate. The thrumbolt had been removed from his flank, the wound patched with the same acorn paste used on her. It wouldn't be wise to push him, but she could certainly ride.

The centaur wasn't interested in Fetch's assessment. He had shouldered the pole and now dipped his chin at the hog, saying something before pointing away from the grove.

"Seems our welcome is at an end," Fetch told Womb.

He was still mystified by the truffle—though it was long gone—and gave an ungrateful grunt in reply. Taking advantage of his distraction, Fetch stowed what she'd saved of the centaur provisions in the hog's saddlebag. There was nothing else to take. The pyre had been reduced to ash.

Fetch swung up into the saddle and urged Womb Broom to carry them away from the watchful centaur, the trees, and the canyon of inexplicable charity. She rode for the only place that might help her now, the last place she wished to go.

South and west.

FOURTEEN

—

IT WAS OFTEN SAID there were no gods in Ul-wundulas. Often said, and far from true.

The frails worshiped their gaggle of drunken, lustful immortals and imperious virgins, so it was a rare settler who didn't bring some small icon down from Hispartha, lighting candles at night while whispering pleas for protection. Fetch did not hold with any of that nonsense, few half-orcs did. No one was ever spared from an orc's scimitar by praying to a statue.

But there was one god dwelling in Ul-wundulas whose power she found difficult to deny, for she had witnessed it with her own eyes. One god that had been here since before Hispartha abandoned the land to irreverent mongrels.

Belico, the Master Slave.

Two days after departing the centaur canyon, Fetch crossed into his lands.

Belief in the ancient human warlord who won divinity was central to halfling life, as well as the lives of the Unyars, a tribe of frails descended from Belico's soldiers and pledged to protect his temple at Strava. Consisting of an ancient tower perched atop a hideous man-made hill, Strava's true sanctuary lay beneath the earth. Once, in bed, Jackal had tried to describe the maze of low tunnels that connected the subterranean tombs of Belico and his host, but the thought had clearly disturbed him. He and Fetching had decided they would rather fuck again than discuss the place further.

Fetch had not returned here since she, Oats, Jackal, and Crafty came with a Tine girl rescued from the Sludge Man. Jackal had suffered a grievous injury fighting the bog trotter and sought help from Belico's high priest. None of them had known it at the time, but that visit changed everything. Jackal was healed, but Zirko made him swear vows that would prove to be unbreakable. The ritual had also left Jackal with a vitality that could only be described as unnatural. Without those strange gifts, he might never have been able to save the Bastards from Crafty and the Claymaster. Without those gifts he would not now be away from the Lots, hunting a wizard until yanked back by puppet strings held firmly by a god and his stunted earthly servant.

Unyar horsemen met Fetch even before the hill and tower came into view. She was accustomed to the tribe's stalwart vigilance, but something was different. The slanted eyes of the Unyar riders were suspicious as well as watchful, the powerful recurve bows in their hands already fitted with arrows. Even the motions of their hardy and spirited steeds seemed more fractious.

"I am Fetching, chief of the True Bastards," she told them. "I need to speak with the Hero Father."

One Unyar gave the barest hint of a nod, but said nothing.

With a surrounding escort, she was brought to Strava and its supplicant village. The Unyars were industrious as ever. The ride through their huts was a spectacle of herding, fletching, weaving, and cooking. The tribesmen guided their mounts with confidence through the confusing sprawl, at last reining up before a hut identical to hundreds already passed. An ancient Unyar couple stood waiting outside the door, small and wrinkled as old fruit. It was clear Fetch was to dismount, so she slid from the saddle. The troop turned their mounts as soon as her boots touched the ground.

"I must speak with Zirko!" Fetch called after them. Clods of dirt kicked up by the retreating hooves were her only answer.

"You'll have to wait like the rest of us, woman."

The deep voice rolled out of the hut across the way. A big half-orc ducked through the hide flaps covering the entrance. His size and lack of hair or beard were the obvious traits of a thrice-blood, though he carried a layer of well-fed flesh over his muscles. The pair of mongrels who followed him into the sun were also thrices. Their hoof tattoos marked them all as sworn to the Orc Stains. The speaker looked her up and down with a sneer before sauntering off in the opposite direction of the Unyar riders, his brothers in tow.

Taken off guard by the appearance of the mongrels, Fetch had said nothing, but after a moment she followed, leading Womb Broom and ignoring the incomprehensible words of the elderly Unyars still standing in welcome. She meant to catch up to the three Stains and demand what that big fuck meant, but she caught sight of other mongrels along the way, slowing her steps. They were milling outside huts, some drinking from clay jars. Others she saw tending hogs in rope paddocks set back from the dwellings. There were brethren from the Shards, the Cauldron Brotherhood, and the Sons of Perdition. Fetch's hands went to her hair.

The centaurs *had* been summoning it.

The Betrayer Moon.

"Fetch?"

The voice was familiar, strained with shock. And relief.

She spun and pulled Mead's rush to reach her into an embrace. They stepped back, still clutching each other.

Mead's eyes were agog as he took in her bedraggled appearance. "Where . . . ? Chief, we thought—"

"I know. Listen, Mead, I must talk to Zirko. Before the 'taurs come. It can't wait."

Mead's brow creased. "It's not the Betrayer."

"What? Why the fuck are all these mongrels here, then?"

"The *Noumenia Gorperetos.*"

It was Fetch's turn to be confused.

"Zirko's summons," Mead said. "He asked all the chiefs to come."

"Shit." Fetch sagged. She hadn't remembered. Hells, she hadn't cared a shit. "What's the reason?"

"We don't know. The Tide, the Skull Sowers, and the Fangs haven't arrived yet. They're late. It's already a day past the *Noumenia*, so whatever Zirko wants, it was never about the day. I figure he just wanted to give us all time to arrive and tried to make it happen at the same time. No one has been allowed to see him, though we've all asked, some louder than others."

Fetch shot a look down the track between the huts where the thrice-bloods had been swallowed by the teeming life of the village.

"Reckon I just saw the Orc Stains chief."

Mead nodded. "Knob."

"Wager that lumbering cock's been grousing."

"He and Pulp Ear, mostly. Though Notch is starting to get restless too."

"Notch. That's the Shards' hoofmaster?"

"Right. And Pulp Ear leads the Cauldron Brotherhood."

Fetch knew some of the chiefs by name or reputation, yet none by sight. Communication between the hoofs was limited. Hells, the Claymaster never met with all his fellow leaders at any time in Fetch's memory.

She smirked at Mead. "And what's the chief of the Bastards feeling?"

"Figured someone had to come," he said, mortified. "But there's been no vote."

Fetch patted his cheek with rough affection. "You did right. Which of the brothers did you bring?"

"None. Just Sluggard and Marrow." Mead held up his stump. "That way if whatever Zirko wanted had a chance of getting us killed, the hoof would only lose a one-handed rider and a couple of nomads. Plus, after this we planned to ride to the castile. Look for you."

Fetch wanted to tell him how invaluable he was to the hoof, that the Bastards would likely crumble without him, but the words seemed feeble. So she smiled, tousled his Tine plume, and called him a fool-ass instead.

He suffered the playful indignity with a smile, but when she was done, his face fell.

"Chief. What happened to you?"

Fetch took a breath. "They got you bunked with the nomads?"

"Yes."

"This way, then. I think I got my own hut with two Unyars that look like walnuts."

Sitting upon the floor with the fire pit between them, they spoke. The ancient husband and wife fussed over them, pressed them with tea and bowls of curdled cheese while Fetch told Mead what had transpired since her departure from Winsome. About Bermudo and the guns, the destruction of Rhecia's and the execution of all her folk, about the attempt to take Fetch to Hispartha, the murder of Cissy. She told him about the centaurs, but it was the giant orc that truly puzzled him.

Mead rubbed at the back of his head. "Saved you from cavaleros and left you alive? Not like any thick I've ever heard of, to say nothing of the hyenas."

Fetch allowed her silence to voice her agreement. But the fingers on Mead's hand were tapping his thumb in sequence, forefinger to small and back again. He only did that when his mind had come to grips with an idea and was wrestling it into submission.

"What?" she asked.

"The night we saw the dogs. They killed Slivers. But not . . ." Mead grew hesitant. Fetch leaned in, insisting he continue. "Not the women. Slivers was protecting them, but that pack was big enough to split. Why leave them alone? Why leave you alive?"

You taste weak. "You're saying this fucker doesn't think women are worth killing?"

Mead shook his head. "I don't know. Might be your worth is . . . what you can provide alive."

Fetch saw the fear he had to master to put that forward. "He didn't rape me, Mead."

His relief was quickly chased away by a further perplexing thought. "Sounding less and less like an orc."

He hadn't meant it to be funny, but Fetch had to laugh. "Speaking of women. How are our three new slopheads?"

"Incus and Dacia are shaping up fast. Ahlamra . . . ?" Mead's mouth wrinkled.

Fetch raised her eyebrows in agreement. "Figured that."

Mead did not allow the following silence to linger long. "So what are we doing, chief? About all this?"

"I have to talk to Zirko. He's the only one who might know anything about this fucking thick. I just don't want to start a war with Strava to get it done, but they're not giving me much choice. You speak Unyar?"

"Not enough. Marrow seems to have a grasp, though."

"Get him."

Mead jumped up from the floor and left the hut.

The Unyar man placed a bowl of dumplings in Fetch's lap. She was on her second portion when Mead returned without Marrow and looking troubled.

"Problem?" Fetch sucked another dumpling down.

"He's leaving."

"The fuck he is!"

Fetch followed Mead out and into the lane. Hurrying through the crowd he led her to one of the hog paddocks. Marrow was within, making last adjustments to his tack. He glanced over his saddle as Fetch approached, but did not pause.

"Sorry, chief," he said, tying a bag down. "Glad to see you breathing, but I can't stay."

"Need to hear a reason."

"Just heard the Sowers arrived."

"You don't care to see your former brothers," Fetch realized.

Marrow grunted in affirmation. He kept glancing toward the entrance of the paddock as if he expected his old hoof to come charging in at any moment. "There's bad blood 'twixt me and Tomb. Bad blood."

"Strava is neutral ground," Fetch told him. "He can't do anything to you here."

Marrow's flaxen whiskers bowed outward as he gave a grim chuckle. "You don't know Tomb. A colder mongrel was never born." He shot a glare at Mead. "Had I known there was going to be a meet like this, I sure as shit would not have come. I've tarried long as I dare."

"You don't strike me as a coward, Marrow."

He bristled. "It's never been said in my hearing."

"Good. Because I need you here. You speak the Unyar tongue?"

"How do you think I got warning about who was coming? Had every slant-eye in here on the lookout."

Marrow's gaze shifted, arms tensing to climb into the saddle, as a trio of mongrels rode into the paddock. Seeing they weren't Skull Sowers, he relaxed. A little.

"I need to get in front of Zirko," Fetch pressed. "The Unyars think I'm here at his bidding and just squawking like all these other impatient mongrels, but I've come on another matter. Zirko will want to hear me. Marrow, I've got to have someone that can speak to them, make them understand. You wanted a chance to be with the Bastards, and far as I can see you're a worthy rider. But if you ride off now to flee your old hoof you're fleeing all chances of the new one too. The places a nomad can go are vanishing. You need a home and the Bastards need good mongrels. Fuck Tomb! Fuck the Sowers. Show them, show me, you're a True Bastard."

Marrow set his whiskered jaw. He thought a moment and met her eyes. "Very well. I will try to get you an audience with the waddler priest." He pointed at Mead. "*You're* untacking Dead Bride."

"And Marrow," Fetch said when he came around the hog. "Go faster."

With a laugh, the nomad departed.

Mead set to unsaddling Dead Bride.

"Once you're done there, can you see to Womb Broom?" Fetch asked. "He got feathered and I don't want it to fester."

"Sure, chief." After a moment, Mead's look brightened. He tried to hide it, but she saw.

"What?"

"Polecat owes me a month's wine ration." Mead let the smile loose. "I bet him you knew what we were calling that hog."

"Funny fucks, every last thumb-cocked one of you," Fetch said. "I'm going back to my hut to be fed to death."

The trio of riders were seeing to their barbarians. As Fetch drew near, she recognized one as Red Nail, the older mongrel who'd helped Jackal during the Claymaster's betrayal and escorted the Winsome folk to the Wallow.

A cold stone dropped into Fetch's gut.

That meant these riders were from the Tusked Tide.

Red Nail saw her coming and said something to a mongrel even more grizzled than himself.

"Fetching," the Tide's master said, stepping around his barbarian. "We meet at last. I am Boar Lip."

It was simple to see where the name came from. His lower fangs protruded greatly before sweeping back toward his nose. Most half-breeds developed such teeth, but none Fetch had ever seen boasted a pair that immense.

Fetching clasped the offered arm. "I'm sorry for the riders you lost trying to aid us."

He took that with the hardened resolve of an experienced chief. "They were good brothers. I only wish you could have brought back their remains, so they could be mourned at the Wallow."

Fetch gave a regretful nod. "I am sorry. I also want to thank you for all you've done for the True Bastards."

"Not much need for that," Boar Lip told her. "You've paid enough shine for it."

"You took our people in when the Kiln fell with no promise of coin, and kept them safe while we recovered. The Bastards owe the Tide. And we will make good."

"You can make good by telling me why that god's-cock-sucking waddler made us all ride out here." Fetch opened her mouth to answer and then realized Boar Lip was only grousing. He took a deep breath. "You should hear it from me. I regret having to withdraw our help. But the Tide is down to seventeen sworn brothers. I could not afford to lose any more to the troubles of another hoof."

He didn't want to lose any more to a lost cause is what he meant.

To the hoof that had a leader go mad and bring about the fall of their stronghold. To the hoof that was beset by sorcery, starvation, whose numbers had fallen to the point that they could hardly patrol their own lot. Boar Lip did not want to lose any more men to the hoof whose beggar chief stood before him without thrum or brigand.

Yet the decision still set her brain afire. She wanted to scream, proclaim that he and the rest of his hoof were cunts and cowards, that with seventeen riders they should be afraid of nothing. With seventeen riders, the Bastards could take the world! That same fire raged with flames of another sort, the sort that pushed her to beg forgiveness of the Tide for getting their boys killed, for needing their help at all. Boar Lip's own barely concealed pity only helped fuel both blazes.

It was hogshit that they would blame her. But they did, should. She was chief. It was deeper hogshit that she blamed herself, but she did. The deepest was that she blamed Jackal. She often wondered what he would do in her position. Not as a means of inspiration, but a genuine question, edged with spite. *What* would *you do, pretty Jackal? You wanted this so badly. Only you didn't, you wouldn't, not this. Building walls, training slops, feeding frails, begging from other hoofs. This wasn't what you wanted. It's what you handed off!*

Fetch gave Boar Lip the only reply she could.

"I understand."

FETCH GOT DRUNK.

She hadn't meant for it to happen, but the kinnabar infusion was still in her saddlebags and she'd taken her first dose in days, once Marrow came back after nightfall shaking his head. The Unyars wouldn't budge. Zirko would not meet with any mongrel chief until all had arrived. Forced to languish, hating the delay, she made sure Mead was keeping a tight rein on the nomad lest he run afoul of the Skull Sowers while she holed up in her hut, eating all offered by the old couple. If she were to be stuck here, she would use the time to get stronger. After the stew of mutton, the bread, there came the fermented mare's milk. Fetch almost gagged on the first sip, but the sour drink took the edge off the Bone Smiler's medicine. By the second saucer, the stuff was going down easy enough.

The milk, foul-tasting as it was, also proved a remedy to the growing guilt of feasting while her folk were wanting. Not remembering the last time there was enough wine to allow for such abandon, she soon found herself swimming in a fuddled, boot-toppling current.

The mare's milk sloshed.

She wandered around the Unyar village, jug dangling in her hand. Beneath the moon, the tribesfolk sang and danced in clusters, rewarding themselves for another day endured. Children darted across Fetch's shuffling path, laughing and calling after one another. Every throng she passed beckoned in welcome. The words were lost, but the offers were clear. Offers to dance, to sing, offers of skewered meat and more mare's milk. Offers to join. The Unyars were an insular people, but their hospitality was bound to their honor. Their broad, tanned faces with their narrow, friendly eyes smiled openly at Fetching, but she kept walking, allowing her drunkenness to provide excuse for her self-seclusion. She pretended not to notice the food, the drink, the well-meaning calls. Pretended not to hear the name Attukhan rise up out of their mostly nonsensical words.

Jackal was beloved here. He was, the Unyars believed, a vessel of one of their cherished ancestors. And it wasn't simple superstition that drove such a belief, but Jackal's own actions. He had stood against the centaurs in one of the most hellish Betrayer Moons in memory, saving Strava itself from being overrun. Hells, they fucking loved him. Is that why they smiled at her so? Did they know? That she loved him too, more than they? Did they know she fucked him? Was there some awed title for that?

"The Arm of Attukhan's Quim. Cunt of Attukhan. Attukhunt."

She chuckled, hearing the bitter sound. Drunk, perhaps, but she knew what she was saying, aware that she was glaring at every man and woman that spoke to her. Fuck. She was looking for a fight. Her reason was still there, but it was a rider clinging to the back of a berserk hog, able to do little but shout uselessly and watch. Fetch had a sudden urge to punch the next smiling face.

Nearing the limits of the village, she stumbled on. Out here, the festivities were more raucous. Fewer children, the clan structure un-raveling to reveal its frayed edges. This was the boasting ground of unwed men, dishonored women, inebriates, and *ghan* addicts. Here, the faces were less welcoming, more likely to sneer, to give offense. More likely to deserve a thrashing.

A cheering ring had formed around two wrestling men. Whether this was arranged sport or the clashing of tempers, Fetch did not know or care. She pushed her way to the front to watch, courting complaints from those she shoved aside, but none protested. It turned out to be nothing but a bout between two drunks, and she quickly tired of the feeble display of sluggish grapples and sloppy punches. She nearly waded in, added a third drunk to the brawl, one that would actually prove effective, but she was stopped short by a face spied across the ring.

A face that did not regard the fight but looked directly at Fetch-ing, a mask of intense calm within a flood of teeming abandon. It was akin to the Unyars that surrounded it, yet the small differences screamed across the distance.

Almond eyes, though wider, limpid. Tanned skin, but lacking the harsh swarthiness, rather a flawless flush of chestnut.

They were elven features, those of a Tine, and not just any rust-skin.

"Starling?"

Fetch mumbled the name, slurred it, knew she sounded a besot-ted fool. Looked like one, too, when she jostled forward into the ring in her hurry to reach the elf. Something collided into her side. She nearly lost her feet, did lose her jar. It broke upon the ground. Angry now, she broke the nose, and the senses, of the wrestler who'd caused the damage. His opponent, seeing him fall, changed loyalties with the speed and backward thinking only the drunk can conjure. Shout-ing an Unyar curse, he rushed Fetch. She sidestepped, though it was more of a stumble, snatched the back of his head with an outflung hand, pivoted, and pushed downward. The spinning motion and the pressure demolished what little balance remained to the man and he flopped into the dirt, face-first. She wasn't sure if the noises coming from the onlookers were cheers or jeers. The spilled drunkard certainly wasn't pleased. He tried to rise, making furious noises. Fetch kicked him in the face. He ate dirt again, remained silent and unmoving.

Fetch raised an arm, pointed down at her own head with a sloppy wrist. *"Va Gara Attukhunt!"*

She was the only one amused. The now scowling faces made it difficult to find Starling again. But there she was, still watching. Fetch moved toward her, made it almost to the edge of the ring when the elf turned. She wore Unyar garments, but the baggy breeches, voluminous shirt, and sheepskin vest could not hide her bulging middle. She was greatly pregnant, though it did not prevent her from disappearing nimbly into the crowd.

Frowning with confusion, Fetch made a clumsy pursuit. The sullen crowd parted to let her pass, but the elf was gone.

Had she remained in Strava all this time? They'd brought her; Fetch and Jackal and Oats and Crafty, brought her here from the Old Maiden. No, she hadn't remained—Fetch's memory was beginning to work—she'd come to the Kiln. Hells, she'd slept in Fetch's room!

Last time she saw her, was, was . . . on Hearth's back, the day Jackal was ousted from the Grey Bastards. Fetch had watched them leave from the wall, careful not to be seen.

The rest she knew only from accounts, Jackal's and Warbler's. Starling had been orc-raped while the Sludge Man's captive, was carrying a half-breed. She set the Sludge Man after Fetch, telling him of her elf blood. Telling everyone, really. It was all to save the child in her belly from the bog trotter's insane need to sacrifice an elf-orc mongrel to the marsh. Jackal had rushed to the Kiln with a warning and had not seen Starling again. Warbler traveled with her to the border of Tine land, where he claimed she convinced the point-ears to come to the Bastards' aid against the invading thicks. After that, none knew what became of her. Fetch certainly never cared a fuck.

So, why was she careening around a bunch of Unyar tents looking for her?

Fetch shook her head, belched, and shook her head further in protest of the stink. She needed to sit. And did. Sank right down where she was. Through the ragged wall of hides next to her came the unmistakable sounds of fucking. The exclamations were foreign, but lustful moans sound the same in any tongue. They were mostly male. That usually meant a whore at work. Or a wife.

Now that she had stopped moving, the tide of spirits in Fetch's skull rose, flooding the beach of her resolve. Unable to stand back up, unable even to sit up any longer, she lay back with a groan of defeat. Her head lolled to the side and she found she could see beneath the edge of the tent. An Unyar man was thrusting into a woman on all fours. Her head was hanging down, so was her hair, her breasts, her pregnant belly.

Starling. Fetch blinked hard and the woman focused into a wearied Unyar.

Fetch stopped watching, navigated her storm-tossed head to look up at the stars.

Shit. Fucking mare's milk. Fucking medicine-poison.

Starling could not have been pregnant. Been enough time for her to have delivered twice over. A thought drifted into Fetch's muzzy brain. What had the elf done with her child? Dumped it with a hoof? Fucking half-wit notion. Starling would never want another thing to do with the half-orcs. Killed it? Few other fates awaited mongrel babes. Had she done that?

The thought was sobering, intruding even upon the most desperate of escapes. Fetch blew a spattering breath through her lips. Damn.

She rolled to her front, pushed up.

And fell right back down.

FIFTEEN

___

SHE AWOKE TO PICKAXES fucking her skull. A hand shaking her.

Mead's face rested at the center of a throbbing world.

"It's time, chief. The Fangs just rode in. Zirko's called us to meet at the Hill."

Fetch was lying on sheepskins in the old couple's hut with no notion how she got there.

"Right," she croaked.

Seeing that she was now roused, Mead withdrew. Fetch nearly went back to sleep, but then the wizened faces of her hosts came into focus, both smiling with encouragement, he holding tea, she a steaming bowl.

Her head managed to leave the blankets. "That dumplings?"

Outside, the sun was an assault of hells' cocks in her eye sockets. Mead was already astride Nyhapsáni. Sluggard stood nearby, holding his barbarian by a yanker.

"Up you get," he said.

"Where's my hog?"

"Being tended by the Unyar," Mead told her. "He's not making it easy."

Sluggard gave his easy grin. "That pig's ill-tempered enough when he's not injured. So you'll take mine to this meeting of the hoofmasters. Unless you want to be the only bootmaster?"

The bad jest made Fetch wince; the gritter knowing it was bad and saying it anyway made her smile.

"What will you ride?"

"I think it's best if only sworn riders accompany you, chief," Mead said.

Giving Sluggard a grateful squeeze on the shoulder, Fetch mounted. Her good mood lasted until they got moving and her head became a drum for the pounding hoofbeats.

The ride to the hill passed in an aching mirage of morning sun.

All of the other chiefs were waiting. They had brought retinues of various sizes. Some had more in an escort than the True Bastards could boast in the entire hoof. It was the most half-orc riders Fetch had seen gathered at one time. Still fighting not to see double, she did not bother with a count.

But the assembled Unyar warriors certainly outnumbered them.

A horn blared, causing Fetch to flinch.

"Fucking mare's milk," she muttered.

The tribesmen began to move off, surrounding the hogs on the move and sweeping them forward.

"You catch sight of Zirko?" Fetch asked Mead.

"No."

Without another choice, the half-orcs rode among the Unyars and struck out to the northeast, moving slowly within the bounds of the village.

Fetch felt a pair of eyes on her.

Looking to her left she found a hairless mongrel riding alongside, staring with wolfish eyes and wearing little but bone fetishes and a feral grin.

"*Ul'shuum tashruuk, t'huruuk.*"

"Kul'huun?" Fetch realized. Hells, that milk had slowed her wits. She had not even noticed the familiar Fang in the group, a mongrel she had fought beside against an orc *ul'usuun*. This savage had been responsible for the gift of new barbarians after nearly all the Bastards' mounts had been killed during the battle.

"The drink of these frails is strong," Kul'huun told her in orcish, her discomfort clearly the cause of his smirk.

Fetch responded in the same language, respecting the Fangs of Our Fathers' belief that human tongues weakened them. "Drink the horse's milk and feel like it kicked you . . . after you gave birth to it."

Kul'huun reached into a hide sack hanging from his saddle and produced a black, twisted hunk of something dried. He offered it over.

"Looks like a turd," Fetch observed blandly, taking the stuff.

Kul'huun pulled his lower lip away from his teeth and gestured at the space between.

Following along, Fetch put the plug in her mouth. The juices her spit coaxed from the thing were worse than the milk. She wrinkled her mouth.

"Great . . . doesn't just *look* like a turd." Yet, she felt the throbbing in her skull ease, and her guts lost their sour fluttering. "Well, damn."

Kul'huun looked pleased. "Our fathers are strong. So is their medicine."

The thicks had no words for gratitude, so Fetch made do with a nod.

"How fare the Fangs?"

"We continue to match our strength against the full-bloods," Kul'huun answered. "They die. We die. More of them die."

Fetch had never been to the Fangs of Our Fathers' lot. From what she'd heard, there was little to see. Of all the hoofs, their lands were the farthest south, placing them very near the Gut, the narrow strait separating Ul-wundulas from Dhar'gest. So close to the orcs' only means of crossing the Deluged Sea, the Fangs found it prudent not to raise a fortress or permanent settlement. Instead, they traveled in constant patrol, sleeping rough, eating only what could be hunted. You had to be half-mad to enter such a life, one with more hardship than that endured by most free-riders. Yet, half-mad wasn't enough, in truth. For the Fangs also held to staunch beliefs inconceivable to most mongrels. They revered the orcs, emulating them in manner and appearance, shaving all hair, using only their guttural speech. It was widely whispered they also knew something of the thicks' blood-magic. Chewing on Kul'huun's evil-tasting but effective cure, Fetch was becoming certain there was truth in that.

Now was not the time to ask. They had reached the flats, the Unyars increasing their pace.

Encircled by horses, it was difficult to judge the distance they rode. Several leagues, at the least, keeping to the dusty plains beyond Strava for the meat of the journey before riding up a ridge, skirting the edge until the plains below were hemmed into a canyon. The column reined up and the horsemen parted, allowing the half-orcs vantage of a wide valley. Awaiting them at the edge, framed by the lurid sky, was Zirko.

The halfling's linen robes billowed above his sandaled feet, his hand resting on the pommel of the stout sword at his side.

His resonant voice ignored the fierce wind.

"I thank you for coming, hoofmasters."

It was the Orc Stains' chief who blurted the question they all wanted answered. "Why did you send for us, priest?"

Zirko was unfazed by the thrice-blood's rudeness.

"I thought it prudent that your eyes, not my words, deliver this news, since you will trust one and not the other. Approach, chiefs, and you will know."

Fetch, Boar Lip, Knob, and five other mongrels dismounted to get closer to the edge. Fetch again found Kul'huun on her left.

"Hells overburdened," she said in a low tone as the nearly naked mongrel strode beside her. "You never said you led the Fangs of Our Fathers."

Kul'huun merely gave her a bright look and scratched idly at his chest.

"What you see below is the former lot of your brother hoof, the Rutters," Zirko proclaimed.

Curses and oaths peppered the wind as the chiefs beheld the valley.

Fetch could only stare.

Years ago, the Rutters had been all but wiped out by centaurs during a particularly vicious Betrayer Moon. They tried to recover, but Ul-wundulas had other designs. In the end, they disbanded, their few remaining brothers scattering. Some, like Polecat, found places within new hoofs. Fetch had never cared to ride through the vacant valley that had once housed the Rutters' stronghold, but it was not the ruins of the fortress or the nearby town that caused her amazement.

Below, countless tents formed a sprawling camp. Cook fires sent up enough columns of smoke to support an army. And it *was* an army. Men moved through the makeshift settlement, many ahorse, retrieving their mounts from no fewer than thirty sizable paddocks. Fetch could no longer keep her teeth from grinding when her eyes at last reconciled the elephants. She had seen one years ago in a caravan of entertainers. Now she beheld ten of the great beasts below, lumbering and laboring, dragging sleds of timber and cut stone. Already, there were signs of construction, the half-orc fortress being pillaged to raise a new.

An angry noise rumbled past Boar Lip's massive teeth. "Hispartha has taken back the hells-damned lot."

Fetch's jaw bulged. Damn Bermudo. He had known. It was all in that self-satisfied smile. A snarl ground up her throat and through her teeth. Her ire was not lonely. All along the ridge there was an audible rustle of agitation.

"I suggest we ride back to Strava," Zirko said. "There we may hold council and decide how best to proceed."

The little priest had a way of making his suggestions sound like commands.

"No!" Knob burst out. "I will not languish any longer at your insistence, you stunted negroid. Not while Hisparthan eunuchs raise a damn banner in the Lots!"

"Settle, Knob," Boar Lip growled.

The thrice-blood chief turned on him. "Why? Do I offend you, Tusker? Worried I offend *him*?" Knob cast a huge, contemptuous arm in Zirko's direction. "So long as I send a rider to risk himself every Betrayer, he can do nothing to me. That is the pact. The Stains have honored it. Nothing says I must stoop to lick his asshole. And if I have affronted him? What then? You fail to send a little bird to me, little priest? No warning of the Betrayer because I insult your child-high pride? Very well. The centaurs may catch us unawares, wipe us out. That's what happened to the Rutters. Left you short one mongrel rider every time that cursed moon shows its face. And left a hole in the Lots. One which Hispartha is now claiming. This is your fault, dwarf! So fuck your pride and your birds and your god."

"It's not Hispartha," another of the chiefs said evenly.

"Fuck it's not!" Knob exclaimed.

The Shards chief shrugged with an absence of concern. He was picking beneath a fingernail with a small piece of bent iron. The kerchief tied about his head was a faded crimson, as was the embroidered sash about his waist, more color than was boasted by anyone else on the ridge. His scraper flicked at the valley. "Hispartha doesn't arrange their camps that way."

"And you know how?" Knob demanded.

"Because Notch used to be a scout in the king's army," a sour-faced, swaybacked mongrel answered, curling his lip. This could only be Pulp Ear of the Cauldron Brotherhood, though in truth it was both ears that looked to have been smashed so many times they resembled the curds served by Fetch's Unyar hosts. His hair was greying, worn long, though it was thinning along the top.

"That's right," Notch said, looking up from his grooming. "I did. And that isn't them. The thrice-blood mentioned banners. That's another sign. None down there. Tents are wrong too."

"Then who is it?" Boar Lip asked.

"Elephants point eas—" Fetch began.

"Doesn't matter," Knob said, anger unabated. "It's frails on foals. They need to be shown they do not belong here."

"That is rash," Zirko said.

Knob made an airy noise in his throat, jaw clenching. "If you had no intention of defying them, why bring us here?"

"Intention," Zirko echoed. "Perhaps that is something we should learn from the new arrivals, their intention, before going to war."

Pulp Ear was dubious. "You trying to sell us that you don't already know?"

"Meaning?" Zirko inquired.

"Meaning you waddlers are known to grub for whatever you can get," Knob said. "What tribute have you haggled out of these intruders for your warning of the Betrayer?"

"I have not spoken with them," Zirko replied.

"Why?" Fetch asked. "What good was wai—"

"He wants us to fight the battle, so his people don't have to," Pulp Ear rolled over her. "He's looking to squeeze more blood from us to save his damn followers."

"Battle?" Notch asked, smirking. "Can you not count? There are at least eight hundred men down there."

"Afraid, are you, Shard?" Knob needled.

Notch tipped him a wink. "Not of you, big'un."

"Settle, lads," a paunchy, white-haired half-orc put in, watching the younger mongrels with a sharp eye. This could only be Father, chief to the Sons of Perdition. "Not the time."

"And this isn't the Sons, old cod," Knob said. "I don't worship your every word like the backy boys in your hoof."

Father only laughed and shook his head.

"Even eight hundred could be dealt with," Boar Lip considered, "if taken by surprise. They get that fortress finished, it will be too late. Most are likely builders. As long as they never reach their horses, it can be done."

Knob gave a big nod. "Then let's get it done."

"Luck to you," Notch said.

Pulp Ear pointed a finger at the Shard. "Best watch this one. He'll be skulking off to his old masters, tell them we are coming."

Notch shrugged again. "If the coin was right. But whoever is down there won't need to be warned. Not against your fool-ass plan. The Stains brought three riders. Oh, apologies, they're thrice-bloods, so in their minds they count for three each. Call it nine. I saw eleven from the Brotherhood. Three Tuskers. Nine for the Sowers. The Fang showed up fucking alone. Though Father seems to have brought half his hoof, so that's another score. And I rode with two. So, less than three score, if you agree with Knob's swollen idea of his brood's worth."

Fetch did not fail to notice the omission in Notch's tally. She found herself embracing old habits, slipping into the silences that had been the only way to endure the hoof meets of the Grey Bastards. The Claymaster had never wanted her sworn to the brethren, but none could deny her skill in the saddle or her prowess with weapons. Out on patrol, fighting thicks, she was useful and tolerated, but her voice at the table was never welcome. In that room she was ever the aberration. Speaking up only called the Claymaster's attention. It was simpler, safer, to become a mute observer, barely moving lest she earn further ire.

It was the same now.

She was the outsider. Only, she did not need to work to be ignored. These mongrels had ruled for years longer. Becoming chief had taught her nothing about this kind of fight. Her brothers voted and from that moment they obeyed. Her voice, formerly gagged, was now law.

And these cocksure mongrels were stuffing the rag back down her throat.

The bickering had begun to boil. Knob was hungry for a fight, and Notch was amusing himself baiting the thrice. Father and Boar Lip were trying to bring peace, while Pulp Ear continued to demand answers from Zirko. At her side, Kul'huun watched the growing turmoil with a hunter's gaze, waiting. The Skull Sowers' chief had remained silent. He was a wan mongrel, for the Sowers' stronghold was underground. His pale skin and laconic demeanor reminded Fetching of Hoodwink, but where the Bastard was lithe and sinewy, the Skull was slabbed in muscle. Coarse hair, black as pitch, stood out sharply against the blanched grey flesh of his chest and arms. A peasant's brimmed felt hat darkened his face.

Now he moved, striding steadily toward his hog.

Father called after him. "Tomb. Where are you going?"

"Back to the Furrow," the Skull answered, his voice as hollow and remorseless as his name. "Priest, my thanks for allowing me to see this."

"You would run?" Knob demanded.

Tomb paused, leaning his hat against the assaulting sun. "Ul-wundulas is not generous. No lot can support eight hundred men for long. The Skull Sowers need do nothing. Only wait."

The pallid hoofmaster mounted, turned his hog, and rode off with his brethren.

"Coward," Pulp Ear spat.

"You think so?" Notch mused. "You may be more of an idiot than the Stain."

Knob bristled. "We can count your brains in a moment."

Father held up a weary hand. "Enough. Hells, enough. Questions of wits and bravery mean little here. Boar Lip says the camp can be taken. I agree. What then? We've shown we have heavy balls and stiff cods. We've also declared war on Hispartha. Notch and the Hero Father say it's not them, but I ask all of you, what are the odds whoever is in that valley is there without the Crown's leave? We make corpses of them and our days will be filled with chances to prove just how brave we are. And how foolish we have been."

Boar Lip agreed with a pensive nod.

"It will come to war anyway," Fetch tossed in, seeing an opening. "Those down there are just the beginning. If we—"

"We?" Knob said, looking at her for the first time. "*We?* We did not come to Strava without a thrum, astride a bleeding barbarian. We did not come to this ridge on a lent nomad's hog, accompanied by a single, crippled rider. We are not bedwarmers that cozened the pitiful remainder of a fallen hoof into following us with a wet mouth and tight quim. We are not the chosen slut of an outcast rider fled the Lots out of shame for destroying his brothers. Oh yes, Stone Gut told me about him. About Jackal. Cur, more like." A scoffing huff came out of the thrice's thick neck. "*We.* We are the Orc Stains, and the Tusked Tide. The Shards, and the Cauldron Brotherhood. You are not even the remnants of the Grey Bastards. Just some comely mongrel girl paying for loyalty with her holes."

Notch shook with a soundless laugh. Next to him, Pulp Ear's gaze crept over Fetching.

Ignoring them, she narrowed her eyes at Knob. Zirko was right to be deaf to this blustering cock sack.

Fetch shifted her attention to Father. "You worry about war. It's been declared. By Hispartha. We're all looking at it down there. I've seen it in dead nomads, burned buildings. Seen it in the terrible weapons atop the walls of the castile."

"Weapons?" Boar Lip's attention hardened. "What weapons?"

"Ride there and find out," Fetch replied. "Bermudo will be more than happy to let you hear their thunder."

That pulled Notch away from his fingernails. "Cannons?"

Fetch nodded.

"You know them?" Father asked the Shard.

"In the east, fighting swaddleheads for the Crown. Big fucking things, though. Could put holes in castle walls, not fit atop them."

"These are smaller, then," Fetch said. "And they can still put holes in anything I could imagine."

Pulp Ear grew suspicious. "How did you see these weapons?"

"Bermudo gave me a close look before trying to execute me with them."

"Then they're nothing to fear," Knob snorted. "You live."

"I'm not going to waste my breath convincing you, thrice. Any of you. The cavaleros came for me on my own lot, put me in chains, would have killed me. Bermudo dared do this to a hoofmaster. You think he won't do it to you? 'Cause he fucking intends to. I got that from his own lips."

"A frail's words are nothing," Knob said. "Bermudo is a worm. What has he done? Moved into the Rutters' empty lot. Empty! He dares to reclaim undefended land. What does it say of the Bastards that he came for their hoofmaster? You and yours are finished, woman. You fell with the Kiln. The humans can have your lands, I say. Let them build their walls and put these weapons upon them. Let them finally help fight the orcs. It's time they bled a little. We're not endangered by their strength." Knob stepped close, leaned down in Fetch's face. "We are by your weakness."

Fetch did not budge a hair. "Sounds like a challenge to my leadership."

Knob's eyes flashed, seeing the violence he craved in reach.

"Foolish posturing," Pulp Ear said, disgusted. "Cunt's unarmed."

"Don't need weapons for him or you, you fuck-ugly spend stain," Fetch hissed.

Knob showed his teeth. "I'm beginning to see why your riders like you, woman."

"Yours are going to love me for giving them a chance to vote a new chief."

"I won't allow this," Zirko said.

"Stay out of it, waddler, or I'll use you to ass-fuck her corpse."

"Dammit, Knob, leave off," Father urged.

"Let them at it." Notch. "Wager my hog's weight in silver she gouges out one of Knob's eyes before he puts her down."

Fetching heard the voices, but her vision had shrunk to the smiling thrice-blood. Her lips drew back.

A hand touched her arm. Not a grip, just a touch, one that remained. She moved her head slowly, keeping one eye on Knob, and found Kul'huun behind her, arm extended. Their eyes met and the Fang gave a small shake of his head.

"Don't."

He said it in Hisparthan.

Fetching breathed out and took a step back. Zirko looked up at her with a condemning stare, though his eyes betrayed relief as well.

Turning her back on him, and the valley below, Fetch walked away. Tomb had the right of it. There was nothing to be gained here.

"Let's go," she told Mead as she swung into the saddle.

When they were away from the Unyars and down from the ridge, she rode hard.

Directly for the newcomers' camp.

SIXTEEN

——

THE FIRST MAN WHO SAW them ride by merely stood and stared, pausing in his efforts to clear a stone with the help of a mule. He was unarmed, a swarthy-skinned laborer with a black beard, and a scarf wrapped about his head. Fetch made sure to keep their pace slow but purposeful. They were still a fair distance from the edge of the camps, passing mule trains laden with rock dragged from the dust. One of the elephants she saw from the ridge also pulled a loaded sled, bearing a boulder twice the size of a hog. The day was hot, making a hell of such work. Men and beasts were all bent to their tasks. Most did not notice the half-orcs on hogs until they passed. The few tired exclamations the men emitted were in a language Fetching did not understand. Still, the head-wraps, the elephants, it all pointed east.

Tyrkania.

Land of deserts. Land of slaves. Land of Crafty.

It wasn't long before their presence was noted by more than the fools hauling rock. They were a bowshot away from the tents when a troop of cavalry appeared ahead. They were coming quickly, almost at a full gallop, hooves drumming. Fetch kept one hand up, the other gripping her hog's mane.

"Shit, chief," Mead said as the troop thundered closer.

Sun glinted off metal. The horses were armored. A shaped steel mask protected the face, while a drape of segmented plates blanketed the animals to the saddle. It seemed a cruelty in such heat, but no doubt these mounts were used to far more searing climes. The armor lent a metallic song to their movements, adding weight to an already rumbling gait. The men bore lean lances and large, round shields. Helmets bulged from beneath their head wrappings, and a vest of splinted mail protected them to the knee. She pulled her hog to a stop, Mead settling on her right.

"You speak Tyrkanian, right?" Fetch asked.

"My elvish is better."

"Meaning?"

"Meaning I actually *speak* elvish, chief."

"Shit."

Their greeters reined up a stone's throw away, fanning out to block their path, yet not surrounding them. It was hard to charge if your troop formed up in a circle. Whoever these men were, they were no strangers to war in the saddle.

Time to announce herself and hope one of these swaddleheads spoke Hisparthan.

"I am Fetching, leader of the half-orc hoof known as the True Bastards. I need to know who you cocksuckers are and what you are doing in the fucking Lots."

"Aw, hells," Mead said under his breath.

In response, one of the riders hissed and waved his lance at her, as if he were trying to scare off a stray dog.

"Listen you dune-humping frail, I'm not riding away from here without speaking to someone."

The lance waved again and the hiss was replaced by a shouted command.

"We don't speak sand-eater!"

More shouts urged them to depart.

Fetching blew out a breath of frustration. "Let's go."

They turned their hogs and rode the way they had come. The

valley, while not exactly lush, was home to more vegetation than was typical in Ul-wundulas. A sight caught Fetch's eye off to her right, one she had not noticed before: a grove of trees heavy with spheres of bright-ochre fruit. There were no laborers about. She cocked her head toward the grove and Mead followed her in.

"Keep an eye out," Fetch said. Reaching up from the saddle, she seized one of the orbs, pulling until it snapped free. It was the color of an apricot, but its rind was akin to a lemon's. "Lend me a knife."

Mead handed a blade over and Fetch sliced the fruit in half, drawing forth a torrent of sticky, fragrant juice. Again she was reminded of a lemon with its segmented innards, though the smell was less sharp.

She held it up so Mead could get a look. "Any idea?"

He shook his head. "I can tell you it doesn't speak Tyrkanian either."

"Tine-haired cock."

Digging out a hunk of the shiny, pulpy flesh, she tossed it down in front of Sluggard's hog. The animal devoured it with a snuffle.

Fetch curled her lip. "Bet you'd eat anything."

She slid the second wedge into her own mouth. The flavor was strong and sweet, almost overwhelming, but Fetch did not let that stop her. She tore the rind away from each half, tossed one to Mead, and ate the other with increasing relish. The hogs were already rooting for fallen fruit.

"Another?"

Mead shot a look around. "Hells yes."

Fetch peeled another, more expertly this time. She tossed it to Mead along with his knife, dismounted, and began making room in her saddlebags while tallying the number of Winsome's children in her head.

"You think some of the olive grovers could cultivate these trees from the fruit's seeds?"

Mead thought about it while pulling sections off the fruit with his teeth. He nodded at the ground.

"Look at the roots. Those trees are freshly planted."

Fetch could see a broad swath of trampled ground showing where the elephants had come through, likely bringing the trees in on the same sleds with which they now hauled boulders.

"Must have brought them here fully grown. Still, it's worth a try."

Mead smiled. "Well, at least this wasn't a fruitless errand."

"Fucking hells! You're starting to sound like Sluggard."

Soon, both hogs were loaded with purloined fruit. Fetch was about to mount when a thought stopped her.

"We weren't a threat."

"Chief?"

"The swaddleheads. They didn't see us as a threat. Just some dust-stained mongrels spewing nonsense in an unknown tongue."

Mead looked uncomfortable.

Fetch ducked into his eye line. "What?"

"An unarmed woman and a one-handed man. That's what they saw."

"Yes, but would that have stopped any cavaleros you've ever known?"

"No. What are you thinking?"

Fetch hauled herself onto the hog's back. "I'm thinking you need to ride back to Strava. Get Marrow to tell the Unyars that I *will* be speaking with Zirko. And find Kul'huun. I need to talk to him, too, when I return."

"When you return?" Mead rolled his eyes as he figured it out. "You're going back in there."

"They've either got some form of honor or else they've been ordered not to harm us."

"Fetch, you're guessing!"

"Well, if I'm wrong, keep being a good chief."

She kicked her hog out of the grove.

And—not long after—rode straight into the heart of the human camp. The troop of horsemen was not far behind, shouting chastisements, but none used violence to stop her. Fetching made straight for the biggest tent. The damn thing was a pavilion, in truth, a monster of billowing silk. A pair of men guarded the entrance. They were black-skinned, like Zirko, but weren't limited by his stature. Tall, bald, and heavyset, they stepped forward as she reined up, raising massive, two-handed scimitars.

Fetching held up both hands, heard the yelling horsemen rein up behind. "I just want to speak with the master of this place!"

A man ducked out of the pavilion's shadow, stepping between the large blacks to take in the disturbance with sharp, perturbed eyes. His skin bore the same tawny shade as the riders, his features aquiline, punctuated with a small, sharp beard at the chin. He wore a vest and loose breeches, the sash at his waist the same green as the scarf about his head. Beneath the vest, he was well formed, especially for a frail, muscles bespeaking a life preserved by prowess. His keen stare settled upon Fetching.

"You may speak with me," he said, his Hisparthan accented but confident. He looked beyond her and called out orders to the cavalry in his own tongue before giving quieter instruction to the tent guards. Fetch was glad to see them lower their huge, curved swords. "Come within."

Dismounting, Fetch hobbled Sluggard's hog and walked into the tent.

It was pleasantly cool within. Incense and oil lamps burned from hanging brass vessels, tickling Fetch's throat and eyes. An eagle spread its wings in greeting from a perch near the center of the space, where a thick arrangement of carpets formed around a low table of darkly lacquered wood. The head Tyrkanian sat there in a nest of cushions, attended by a woman in flowing garments of blue, white, and gold.

He gestured to the cushions opposite the table. "Please. Sit."

Fetching complied and the woman offered a small cup containing a steaming drink. Her kohl-rimmed eyes did not meet Fetch's, but her movements were calm, assured. The man was given an identical cup and he spoke a word before sipping. Fetch kept the cup in her hand, but did not drink. The man noticed this with a flick of his eyes, said nothing. He regarded her for a moment before setting his drink lightly upon the table. Leaning forward, he stretched out his hand for Fetch's cup. She gave it over and he took a swallow, offering it back.

"I am Tarif Abu Nusar. And I do not poison my guests."

Fetch left the cup hanging between them. "And what about your enemies?"

The man's arm remained steady. "Are we already enemies?"

"If you are hosting Crafty in this camp, we've been enemies since before you awoke this morning."

Tarif set the cup down upon the table and leaned back once more, his face betraying nothing. "Forgive me. I speak your tongue, but some of the expressions are strange. Hosting crafty?"

"Don't play the ignorant foreigner with me, frail. Uhad Ul-badir Taruk Ultani."

"I do not know this name."

"Whatever he's calling himself, he's a lard-ass half-orc wizard, so let's quit pawing at each other's cleverness and bring him the fuck in here!"

Tarif studied her for a moment. He nodded slowly. "He is not here."

The earnestness in the man's pronouncement was undeniable.

Fetching tensed. "But you do know him."

"Yes. I was never given a name, but it was such a half-orc that encouraged me to bring my people here."

"Hells. I fucking knew it."

"It pains me to know he is your enemy. He was a great friend to my tribe. I owe him a debt."

Fetching had to laugh. "I bet he was. And I bet you do."

"Please," Tarif said, lifting the cup once more. "Drink some tea and tell me your name."

"Fetching. Chief of the True Bastards." She left the tea where it was.

"These True Bastards, they are one of the much-spoke-of hooves of Ul-wundulas?"

"Hoofs," Fetch corrected, "but yes. You going to sell me the wizard never mentioned us."

"I sell nothing. I can, however, give you the truth. Our meeting was brief and he said nothing of you or your True Bastards. Why would he?"

Fetch could not quite tell if she was being mocked. The man's face may as well have been carved from wood. "Because we were at the center of his schemes once. But we know his face now, know all that leaks from his mouth are lies. Reckon it's not a leap that he'll now come at us through his Tyrkanian minions."

"We are not Tyrkanian," Tarif told her.

"You sure as shit look it, swaddlehead."

She actually managed to get a wrinkle to form in his brow. "Tell me, how many riders do you command as chief of the Shards?"

"Bastards, you mean."

Tarif's eyebrows rose. "Do I? A hog-mounted half-orc with flesh sullied by patterns of vulgar ink. This I understood was the appearance of a mongrel hoof and the only hoof I have heard tell of is the Shards. You . . . sure as shit . . . look like one."

"Very well," Fetching said, smiling with appreciation as she caught the point. "If you're not Tyrkanian, what are you?"

Tarif stood, retrieving a tray from the serving woman. "We are the Zahracenes."

"Still means shit to me, frail."

Tarif walked over to the perched eagle and began hand-feeding it morsels from the tray.

"Ours was a land of mountain tribes," he explained, "long before Tyrkania rose. As with every land in the world in those ancient days, we found ourselves standing against the conquering steps of the Imperium. My ancestors fought their legions and bravely failed. But the Imperium was never wasteful. Recognizing the fighting spirit of the Zahracene tribes, they used them to help conquer other lands. Generations later, the Imperium was no more, but my tribe endured, molded by time and war into formidable horsemen. This is the reason the wizard said we should petition Hispartha to settle here, for he told me the hoof is what truly reigns in Ul-wundulas. Only now do I come to understand the meaning of this."

Not liking the man standing while she was not, Fetching got to her feet. "What Crafty wants to truly reign here is him. He likes using the hoofs to make that happen. Know that. And why would you want to come? Surely your mountains would be better."

Tarif turned away from the eagle. "Ul-wundulas is not the only harsh land in the world. We come from rocky places rising from the desert. And still would we dwell there if our home was not now lost to Tyrkania."

Understanding settled over Fetching. "You're nomads."

"No longer," Tarif proclaimed, giving the tray over to the waiting hands of the serving woman. "After the wizard told us of this vacant parcel, we fled those who would rule us and took ship at Al-Unan, crossing the Deluged Sea to arrive at Valentia on the eastern shores of Hispartha, where we were met and welcomed by envoys of your queen—"

"I don't have a damn queen."

Tarif looked embarrassed. "Yes, of course. Apologies. Perhaps it should be enough to say that it has been a long journey, and not without loss. But we are here at last in our new home and grateful for that."

"Give it a year," Fetch told him. "After your first thick raid, your first Betrayer, if you survive, you might find yourself wishing you were back in the desert."

"The Zahracenes will endure," Tarif claimed, returning to his cushions.

Fetch remained standing. "Hear me, frail. Nothing is certain in the Lots, survival least of all. Crafty is using you because he knew Hispartha would use you. Up north, the blue-bloods are shitting their silks because the orcs just tried to launch another Incursion that he fucking arranged. We mongrels repelled them because that's what we are here to do, but as you said, not without loss. Hispartha sees the defenses here thinning and they are shoving you in to fill the gap. Take it from one who inherited this heap of hogshit."

"If our presence aids with the defense, why would you have us leave?"

"Because up to now the Lots haven't played host to a hoof with both Hispartha's and Crafty's bejeweled hands up its ass."

"He has asked nothing of us, and the Hisparthans have only been generous."

"Give it time. You'll see Crafty again, and he'll still smile, but he'll name a price for his help. Don't think Hispartha won't, either."

"They have. We are to help defend Ul-wundulas. They ask this of their own people. They maintain garrisons here, yes?"

"Hardly," Fetch scoffed. "Crown lands are few and all in the upper lots or along the coast. The last fortress they keep here is formidable, but its warden is a madman, hanging on by a hair, and the men left to him are animals. Seems to me, you are the next grand idea to shield the kingdom from the thicks. But other than your new neighbors, the Unyars, frails have never fared well in Ul-wundulas, and they have a god on their side."

"How do you know we do not?"

Fetch held out a hand. "Spare me any preaching. If you've come here with a mind to convert the backward mongrels to some twisted, haughty beliefs, save your breath. It's been tried. Half-orcs don't suffer gods, yours or any others. We also won't suffer you being the tip of some conquering spear. Hispartha has plans to retake the Lots. They come asking for you to lead the charge, best refuse. You don't want to put yourself between the hoofs and our land."

It was a damn bluff. From what she'd just seen on the ridge, the other chiefs would certainly fight hard to protect their own patches of ground, but working together in defense of the Lots entire, that was a fucking child's jest.

Tarif was perplexed. "We are putting ourselves between the orcs and the Hisparthan monarchy. Just as you are."

Fetch had to concentrate to keep her fists from clenching. "We are not here for any damn monarchy. Or king, caliph, emir, or any other fucking inbred with a crown. We are here because we carved this land out of the fists of the orcs and continue to keep their fingers from closing around it with the swords of our living and the bodies of our dead. You want to fight because you need a home. I understand. But you're feeling grateful to Hispartha for allowing you to settle here, feel like you owe them. Wait until you've survived a famine or two, had your homes razed by centaurs, watched your men be slaughtered by a few marauding *ulyud*. Then you will feel like it's Hispartha that owes you." Fetch raised her chin at the serving girl. "You'll find gratitude tough to conjure when you've endured your women being ravaged by thicks, the unfortunate survivors left to bear a half-breed. But you'll see. If this is to be your new home, you'll have to."

Tarif's wooden stare had calcified. "My wife would never live with such indignity. Nor would any Zahracene woman."

A mocking breath blew from Fetch's nostrils. "That's what the Tines say. I'm living proof such vows don't hold."

Confusion brought Tarif's eyebrows a little closer together, but he masked it quickly.

"Just remember what I've said," Fetch told him, moving for the flaps.

"Wait."

Fetch turned to find Tarif whispering in his wife's ear. She replied with a single, soft word, and moved behind a partitioning drape. Curious, Fetch waited. It only took a moment for the woman to return, holding a long, thin case. Tarif rose and took this from her before approaching.

"I have a gift for you," he said.

Fetching grew wary and it must have showed.

"From none but me," Tarif assured her.

The case was made from a light wood, heavily carved with intricate depictions of strange animals. Balancing it on one forearm, Tarif opened the lid. Inside was a sheathed weapon. The blade was wide and triangular, tapering away from a strange hilt comprised of a pair of parallel arms running back from the blade. Between them were forged another set of metal bars forming a handle. Tarif gave an inviting nod. Fetch lifted the weapon out, finding a twin beneath. Gripping the handle, she drew the odd dagger, a smile forming at the weight and balance. The composition of the weapon when gripped caused the blade to extend directly away from the wielder's knuckles, the flanking arms running along the forearm. Both sides of the blade were edged, effectively turning Fetch's arm into a spear.

"Do you know of the Kingdom of Narasinga?" Tarif asked.

Fetching tore her eyes away from the weapon long enough to shake her head.

"It was once a grand empire, farther east even than Tyrkania. The weapon you hold, in their tongue, was called *katara*. Among the warriors of Narasinga, the truest test of skill and bravery was to slay a tiger with only a pair of these blades."

"Was?"

Tarif nodded, a look of regret affecting his immutable face. "After the fall of the Imperium, my people continued to fight the wars of other masters. When the sultans that would one day form Tyrkania began to subjugate all lands east of the Deluged Sea, the Zahracenes joined their armies. Soon, their invasion eastward brought them to the Kingdom of Narasinga. The war between them was long, ebbing and flowing over generations. Narasinga was destroyed, though that was the last time the Zahracenes would ever serve Tyrkania."

"Why give this to me?" Fetch asked, sheathing the katara.

"Because you came hunting the tiger, unarmed and alone. It seems only fitting that you have claws of your own."

"Are you saying I am going to fight you one day?"

"I wish to make a gift of friendship," Tarif replied. "But I will tell you truly, if Hispartha asks us to be enemies, I will not rebuke them. And if it comes to conflict between us, I will take the katara from you just as I did from the last warrior of Narasinga."

The earnest stare of the Zahracene was difficult to stand, but Fetch did not look away. Instead, she smiled and placed the dagger back into the case, snapping the lid closed.

"You should not worry over Hispartha asking us to be enemies," she said. "You should consider what your answer will be when the wizard returns and demands your people make war on Hispartha. Because he will, Tarif Abu Nusar, certain as sunrise. Where will your loyalty lie then? With the frails that offered you land on which to live? Or the mongrel that told you where to find it?"

"The wizard saved my life," Tarif answered without pause. "Honor forbids me to deny him."

"Then the Zahracenes will serve Tyrkania once again, for Crafty is their instrument."

"Then I can only pray you are wrong."

"Luck with that," Fetch said. She pushed the case toward him. "I already took about two bushels of that fucking good fruit from your trees. Rather have that if you're in a giving mood."

"Have both," Tarif said, managing a slight smile himself and placing the case in her arms. "The kataras as a gift, the bounty of the *nāranj* as payment for the wise advice of one who knows these lands."

Fetching took the gift with a surrendering smile, and Tarif returned to his place on the carpets. Instead of leaving, Fetch stepped forward and retrieved her cup from the table, drinking the contents down. The tea was now cold, but sweet. She raised the empty cup in salute.

"Welcome to the Lot Lands, Tarif Abu Nusar of the Zahracenes."

The man nodded in acceptance. The woman was clearing the table and Tarif gently caught her hand, placing a kiss upon it as he tenderly pulled her down to sit with him upon the cushions.

Fetch stopped once more at the flap, turned.

"Oh, and if I find out you were lying to me—if Crafty is here and you're protecting him—I will come back to return these fancy daggers to you. Blade first."

SEVENTEEN

AN ACOLYTE CAME to the hut and spoke with Fetching's wrinkled hosts. The Unyar tongue passed between them in an incomprehensible report before the halfling told Fetching directly that the Hero Father would soon arrive. The Unyars returned to their serene preparations as soon as the acolyte was gone.

"I don't know that Zirko will stoop to speaking orcish," Fetch told Kul'huun.

Squatting across the fire pit, the Fangs' chief ignored the old man offering him tea until he went away. "He has always respected our ways. He knows our hatred of Dhar'gest matches his own."

Mead shifted, his curiosity taking hold. "Why do you emulate the orcs if you hate them so much?"

Fetch, like Mead, had a bemused understanding of the beliefs that drove the Fangs of Our Fathers, but it was obvious he could not pass up the chance to delve a little deeper. Kul'huun was so silent, so still, for so long Fetch thought he was treating the question like the tea. An annoyance not to be humored. At last, the guttural language of the orcs passed through the woodsmoke.

"You wear your hair as an elf."

It wasn't a question or an accusation. Fetch wasn't certain it was an answer either. Neither was Mead.

"I respect them," he said.

"You love them," Kul'huun grunted, forced to speak Hisparthan because orcs had no word for love.

Mead cleared his throat. "I don't know that I understand them enough for that."

"It is the ignorance that allows your love. You fill the holes in your understanding with this affection."

"There's much about the orcs I don't know, but I have no love for them," Mead countered.

Kul'huun leaned forward. He spoke orcish once more. "Do you hate the orc that took your hand, Elf Hair?"

Mead's good hand slid to cradle his stump. "Yes."

"Do you hate him so much that if you could replace your lost hand with his, you would refuse?"

It was Mead who took a long time to answer now. "No. I would not refuse."

Kul'huun's eyelids flared. "The Fangs of Our Fathers seek to understand the orc. We use his ways in place of our own to strengthen us and we do not fill the holes in our knowledge. We leave them empty. To fill them as you have with the elves breeds respect; that is the foolish way of the Orc Stains. The Fangs do not hold the orc above us, we keep him close beside us so that we may continue to see the vicious beast he is. Close, so that we can put that beast down."

Mead held Kul'huun's gaze and answered the best way he could in a tongue with no expressions of gratitude. "Your words are strong."

The hut brightened as the flaps were pulled wide by the old couple, bowing deeply as they invited sunlight and Zirko into their home. The Hero Father spoke to the overjoyed, genuflecting ancients. He took one of the wife's hands between his own and whatever he said sent tears running through the wrinkles of her face. Zirko was shown to their fire and, once he was seated on their best sheepskin, the Unyars placed a small feast before him then humbly absented the hut.

Fetch had been well fed by the old couple, but compared to what they served Zirko, her portions had been lacking.

"Please, help me with this repast," the halfling said, encompassing the food and the three half-orcs sharing the fire with a circular sweep of his hand. "They forget that Belico's High Priest is also a small man, but they will be deeply dejected if all is not eaten."

"Should have brought Marrow," Fetch muttered to Mead, taking a dumpling and tossing it to him. Kul'huun seized an entire lamb shank and the jug of mare's milk.

"The other chiefs have all left to return to their lots," Zirko said, using a piece of bread to pluck a hunk of roast mutton from the piled platter. "I am curious why the pair of you have remained."

Fetch knew from speaking to Kul'huun while they waited that nothing more had been accomplished upon the ridge. Knob continued to press the idea of charging the frails and wiping them out. Pulp Ear was swayed, but Notch and Father refused. Boar Lip was torn. Kul'huun told them he would ride to battle himself if they chose to attack, but that the Fangs would not abandon their lot to fight frails. Knob's wind lost all strength when Zirko decreed the Unyars would not support such an action. In the end, it went how Fetch knew it would. Limp as a severed cock. She'd told Kul'huun all she learned in the Zahracene camp with Mead listening. She wasn't going to bother informing Zirko. He would speak to Tarif before long and reach his own conclusions.

As for the other matter . . .

"What do you two know of orc sorcerers?"

Both priest and chief stopped eating at the weight of her words.

Zirko frowned. "What makes you ask?"

"A giant thick that killed a troop of cavaleros with his bare hands," Fetch told him.

"This orc has craft?"

"If you call having skin tough as iron, the strength of all the hells, and a pack of devil-dogs at his command that are nearly as impossible to kill as he is, craft."

Zirko grew more troubled. "Among their own kind they are called *uq'huul*."

Fetch sighed at the simplicity of it, the honesty. "The strongest."

"Yet it is the elves' name for them that I believe provides the most truth," the little priest said. "*Asily'a kaga arkhu.*"

Fetch looked to Mead.

"Ruin Made Flesh," he said, growing very still.

He deserved the name. Fetch had never seen a larger orc, never fought one so strong. Fought, hells, that was generous. She'd crawled away. In his grip, she had been less than a child's doll.

Kul'huun brooded into the fire. "For as close as the Fangs dwell to the Gut, I have never seen one. It is said they can summon dust storms, boil the blood of their foes, even raise corpses to fight for them. But the domination of beasts? This *uq'huul* must be truly powerful, for all animals fear and shun the orc. To take his head would be a deadly, worthy task."

The Fangs' chief looked hungrier for the chance than the meat in his hands.

"Their powers are great, varied, and fortunately rare," the priest said. "Even during the Great Incursion, they were few."

"And they were defeated by the Tines. In the Old Maiden," Mead said.

"They suffered much to achieve that victory," Zirko said. "The battle in the marsh was a calamity."

"Wasn't aware Strava fought there," Mead said.

Fetch put some bread in her mouth to keep from laughing. Wasn't everyone that could call hogshit on the High Priest of Belico and manage it politely.

"No, but we saw the aftermath. The elves were the only survivors, and they but few. The Hisparthan wizards, the army that supported them, and the orcs that fought there were all utterly destroyed." Zirko looked to Fetching with grave concern. "But now you say an *uq'huul* has returned."

"The Fangs will hunt this orc and his dogs," Kul'huun declared, staring at the fire as if all the willing quim in the world was spread before his eyes.

Fetch brightened. "You know a way to kill him?"

Kul'huun stood. "I will tell you when I have done it."

"Dammit, you cod-swinging savage!" Fetch rose to look him in the eager eyes. "Kul'huun, this thick isn't a trophy, he's a hells-damned nightmare."

"Then he cannot be allowed to roam Ul-wundulas."

Fetch took a breath. "And the Fangs can't ride the entire badlands hunting him. You'll be leaving your lot unprotected! You refused to do that to fight these new frails. Why risk it for this orc? Don't be foolish. I asked you here because none know the orcs better, not so you could ride off and get your entire hoof killed."

Kul'huun sniffed once, smiled. "Live in the battle."

Fetch would never change his mind. Like all of them. "Die in a fury."

The feral mongrel slipped out of the hut, lithe and quiet as a lynx.

Zirko let loose a deep sigh. "I have never known if the Claymaster erred in dividing the half-orcs into tribes or if he simply saw the futility in trying to unite them."

"Who cares a fuck," Fetch said, staring at the hut flaps. "He's dead."

"Our greatest triumphs and fallacies often linger."

"I didn't come for wisdom, priest. I came with a hope you would know how to slay this . . . Ruin."

"I regret I cannot help with that task. Sorcery is an art best shunned and my knowledge is limited to the few unwelcome occasions it has intruded and stained the lives of my faithful. But perhaps there is something I can provide."

"What?"

"Ul-wundulas is an unforgiving land," Zirko intoned. "I have heard of your hoof's troubles. I am certain my people can spare enough to help yours. Might I offer such aid in place of what you sought?"

Fetching hesitated. She had never been fond of this pious waddler, and the halflings were not known for their charity. There was usually a price. She waited for it to be named.

The fire was all that spoke for several long moments.

Eventually, Zirko cocked his head. "Shall I have the supplies arranged?"

"Yes," Fetch agreed, a little off-balance.

Zirko looked at Mead. "Tell my acolytes waiting outside what you require. They will know it to be my will."

After receiving a nod from Fetch, Mead went out.

Zirko's brows lowered, concerned and, Fetch saw, contrite. The little man folded his hands in his lap. "I must ask your forgiveness. When you arrived and asked to speak with me, you were purposefully ignored. All the hoofmasters made such requests and I feared meeting with one over the others would cause turmoil. The hoof founders were not so mistrustful of one another, but they fought a war together. These newer chiefs are . . ."

"Useful as a slophead milking his own cod?" Fetch offered.

Zirko gave a thin, tired smile. "Not as individuals. Together, yes, it is as you say. I hoped for a better outcome. Had I known what you wished to tell me, I would not have protected their pride so. I confess, I thought you wanted to speak on another, more personal, matter."

Fetch found her throat closing, her teeth clenching. "Do you have news of him?"

"I do not," Zirko replied. "All signs point to the Betrayer Moon remaining dormant for some time. I do not expect the Arm of Attukhan will need to return to Strava for months yet. Until then, Jackal is wherever he journeyed in your service."

Fetch took a steadying breath. *Summon him back.* The words nearly left her mouth. She choked them down along with fury at the very impulse to speak them. She refused to be a conspirator in the bondage Jackal had so willingly placed himself in. She would not be the reason his freedom was taken from him.

"There is something more," Zirko said. Fetch looked up to find his unblinking gaze fixed. "You have brought something within you to Strava. Something that should not be."

Shit.

She knew he might sense it.

Fetch's body stiffened, her face hardened. "It is not a danger to your people. It will depart with me."

"It is not my people that I fear for, Fetching, chief of the True Bastards. It is you."

Fetch stood, looked down at the halfling. "Don't."

"You fear my help."

"I refuse your help! What I fear is being made a slave!"

Her outburst brought a sad, pensive look to the priest's face. He dipped a small nod of acceptance. "I understand. You, however, do not."

"I understand your aid demands a price."

"Belico is rarely generous."

Fetch gave a warning shake of her head. "You won't cozen me, Zirko. Jackal told me all about your bargain. How there were two payments. To serve Belico should he return. That was what you told him your god demanded. But it was you, *you*, that said he must stand at Strava for every Betrayer."

"My powers are not limitless. I am bound by the blessings of Belico and his relics. Were it not so I could, would, save every sick child brought to me by a desperate mother. Yet miracles, I am afraid, have no pity. They are hard, immutable. They cannot be shaped like metal nor nurtured like a vine. They wait, inert and heartless, until tragedy and chance align to suit them. Only then will they stir and only then for those with the courage to risk their touch. Should that chance, that daring soul, never appear, they do not weep, they have no pity for the countless souls that suffered absent their intercession. Had Jackal not claimed the Arm of Attukhan it would have slumbered to the burning of the world with no regret. Yet Jackal's injury, his audacity, his very nature shaped him into the perfect vessel."

"A weapon, you mean," Fetch said. "One you're happy to have to hand."

Zirko's normally placid countenance darkened. It was anger, but born from hurt. He quenched the fire quickly, averting his eyes and closing them tight as he took a breath. When next he spoke, his voice was filled with forced patience.

"Unlike miracles, I am not heartless. Va Gara Attukhan was too great a power to return to this world without placing it in service to my people. Far fewer of the Unyars will die during the centaurs' frenzies with Jackal defending Strava. Far fewer children will be pulled from their parents' arms and slain. Yes, I demanded a price from him, but it was not to make him a slave. It was to save his life as he desired. In the doing, I made him a shield for my faithful."

"And what would you make me, priest?" Fetch asked, hating herself for wondering. Hating him for the temptation.

"Yourself," Zirko said.

Caution leaked into Fetch's gut. "Explain."

"The evil that dwelled in the Old Maiden Marsh has existed since the battle fought there during the Incursion. I have grown familiar with its presence in the decades since. It resides within you now." Zirko's stare became grave. "You know it is killing you."

Fetch felt the sludge stir, cold and constricting. "Yes."

"I need give you nothing to save you, Fetching. Only remove what does not belong. You would not be accepting anything from me nor Belico. No great power that must be harnessed. All my help grants you is your own strength returned."

Fetch could still feel the dread orc's tongue sliding up her cheek, his words a cinder in her mind.

You taste weak.

She looked at Zirko squarely. "Get this shit out of me."

His face softened with relief. "Come."

Outside, there was no sign of Mead. Fetch was relieved she would be spared an explanation, a lie. Trailed by two halfling acolytes and a half dozen mounted Unyars, she followed Zirko to the hill and climbed toward the tower. The tribesmen remained at the base.

"Please remain," Zirko said when they reached the summit. "I will return."

Fetch watched the halflings vanish into the darkness beyond the tower's single, arched portal. Again, relief. She had no desire to ever enter the catacombs housed within the hill.

She stood in the wind, Strava spread out before her in every direction. There was a great deal to defend, easily twenty times the area of Winsome with hells-knew-how-many more inhabitants.

Knowing all she would do—had done—for her own people, Fetch was forced to allow a bit more understanding for the Hero Father.

She did not turn when he emerged from the tower, but could sense he was now alone.

"Why do the centaurs attack?" she asked, thinking of the grove and its inhabitants beseeching the moon. "Do you know?"

Zirko's response was leaden. "They earned the enmity of a god and were cursed."

"Belico?"

"No. Another. Older. Yet many are drawn here when the Betrayer incites their bloodlust. I have yet to discover the reason."

Fetch faced him, saw he bore something in his hands.

"My faithful have unearthed many curiosities in their search for the true relics of Belico's mortal life, some arcane and perilous. Though they bear no connection to the Master Slave or his brethren they are brought here and stored." Zirko walked steadily forward as he spoke, arms extending to hold the object forth. It was an earthenware oil lamp the color of old blood. The body was crudely fashioned into a man's head, mouth agape in a rictus. The twin nozzles of the lamp were his protruding forked tongue, the handle a bulb of some strange headdress or hair. There was no lid to cover the oil receptacle, just the open nostrils of the skyward-pointing nose. A hideous and ancient piece of pottery shaped by a demented mind. "This will contain the marsh creature."

"Not big enough," Fetch said, eyeing the lamp with distaste. "I've coughed out more than that would hold."

"Such things are not beholden to size," Zirko replied. "Nor the brittleness of their appearance. Once you take hold of it, the power of this lamp will draw the evil from you and keep it imprisoned. The ordeal will be unpleasant, but swift."

A life spent with a mongrel hoof brought a dozen jests to the tip of Fetch's tongue. She left them unsaid. Instead, she reached out, her hand hovering over the proffered lamp for a moment before descending to grasp the barren clay.

The sludge rose, faster than she anticipated. Eager.

A mass pushed up through her throat, cutting off her coughs, her screams. Fetch lurched, all breath gone. Gagging, she hit her knees. The sludge crawled past her stretched lips in a lump. Pressure released from her eyes, weight played down her strained cheeks, and Fetch knew she shed black tears. Had the lamp been made of clay absent sinister magic, it would have shattered beneath her seizing fingers. At the very edge of what she could endure, the sludge fully emerged, as long as her arm and near twice as thick.

The sudden intake of air knocked her back on her rump.

She could feel the fuliginous mass flowing down her neck, watched it creep down her arm, coating her flesh. As it neared the lamp the sludge shrank from the imprisoning vessel, sensing the trap. It rippled, peeled back at the congealing edge. Fetch craned her neck away, stretched her arm out as the sludge tried to prevent itself from being sucked into the nostrils of the lamp's molded face.

"Ah, fuck you!" she growled.

The sludge detached from her arm with frightening speed, softening as it leapt to her face. Stumbling backward, blind, she tried to tear it away, but it clung to her hands, sucked them in to aid in smothering her. It flowed into her nostrils, leaked between her clenched lips. She choked on its vileness, gagged as it lodged in her throat, began to drown as it flooded her lungs. The darkness slid away from her eyes as the last of the living tar crawled into her nose. There was no air. It would not humor any attempts to cough, to vomit it out. This was punishment for an unforgivable denial.

She had slain the Sludge Man, but he repaid the debt, poisoned her with his evil. Remnants of his loathsome pets had nestled within, made her ill, made her body capricious, her mind uncertain. His patient vengeance was finally at hand. Convulsing with panic, clawing at her neck, she fell. The lamp was gone, dropped.

A hand seized Fetch's hair, snatched her head back. Her tongue tasted barren clay as Zirko forced the twin nozzles of the lamp into her mouth. In a rush, the black muck was ripped from her body. The violence of its flight was torturous, the speed blissful.

Fetch lay upon the ground, panting. Swirls of windswept dust played around Zirko's sandaled feet, the lamp clutched in his hands. It appeared unchanged, betraying no sign of what it now contained.

The priest came to her side, deceptively strong as he helped her to rise.

"Are you hale?" he asked.

Fetch was breathing heavy from the exertion. Heavy, but easy. Her chest felt weightless, her lungs clear and deep. She answered the priest with grateful laughter, so joyous and protracted she had to rest her hands on knees.

"I'm hale," she said at last, breath still punctuated by giggles. Fetch straightened and met the priest's studying eye. "Thank you, Hero Father."

THE PROMISED SUPPLIES WERE READY before noon. Marrow and Mead sat their hogs beside the laden wagon. Womb Broom was tied at the rear, still too injured to be ridden at the pace required. Sluggard was up on the driver's bench, holding the mule team's leads. He gave Fetch an easy grin.

"Take good care of my hog."

It was a rare rider who would be so generous, entrusting his barbarian to another. Sluggard was certainly rare, but Fetch wasn't a fool. Generosity was not the gritter's sole motivation.

"Treat him like my own" was the only promise she would offer. "Might be good to know his name."

"Palla."

"*Palla?*"

Sluggard wore a perfectly artless expression. "After the great troubadour from Galiza."

Fetch cocked an eye at Mead. "Did you know that?"

"No, chief," he responded with a laugh.

"I did," Marrow grumbled. "But only because I had the misfortune of fucking asking."

Sluggard was affronted. "That hog is worthy of song!"

Fetch held up a forestalling hand. "Easy, Whore. Don't go frothing at the mouth." She smiled and placed a hand on the edge of the wagon's bench. "In earnest. Thank you."

Sluggard bowed his head once. "You are welcome."

"You'll need this too," Mead said, offering his stockbow. "And don't try to deny it. We both know I carry it mostly out of habit these days."

He had fashioned a brace of leather with an iron hook affixed to the bottom to wear over his stump so that he could pull back his thrum string, but he was still slow on the reload.

Fetch took the stockbow and, a moment later, Mead's full quiver. "You get killed on the way back to Winsome because you didn't have these, I'm coming down to the hells to skin you."

Mead glanced at the eight Unyar horsemen waiting to escort the wagon. "Think there will be plenty of arrows flying if we run into trouble."

"I should only be a day or two behind you."

"We'll be watching. Be good to have you both back."

"Yes it will." Fetch pushed the heel of her fist into his thigh. "Now get going."

Her unease grew as she watched the wagon depart. Those supplies were Winsome's salvation, but the orc and his dogs were still out there. Fetch would have felt better going with them, but there was one more place she must go first.

She eyed Sluggard's hog. "Palla, eh? Fair warning, pig, this ain't going to be a damn carnavale."

Mounting up, she rode to the north, leaving Strava behind. And the sludge with it. Zirko had taken the lamp back into the bowels of the hill, where it could rest with all the other entombed horrors.

Urging Palla to a trot, Fetch gave herself to the cleansing rush of the wind.

She was a hoof rider once more. A half-orc strong. She had a slicer, a thrum, the katara daggers, a barbarian. What more did she need? Only her hoof. Only her brothers. One more than all the others. Fetch kicked the hog into a gallop, eager to bring him home.

Oats had been gone far too long.

EIGHTEEN

—

A YEAR AGO Kalbarca was a ruin inhabited only by broken glory, squatting free-riders, and bone-picking zealots, little but a haunting landmark, a crossroads for those on lonely journeys.

No more.

Fetch sat her hog on a rise east of the city, ancient sentinel of the great Guadal-kabir. Lines of barges were tied to both banks of the broad river, laden with timber, enough languishing wood to rebuild Winsome's stockade ten times over. More vessels plied the currents, navigating the crowded approach to newly constructed docks. Even from her distant vantage, Fetch detected steady movement on the Old Imperial Bridge, men and mules traversing the water to enter the city. A staccato of falling hammers echoed behind walls barnacled with fresh scaffolding. And everywhere was the black bull of the Crown, arrogant upon a red and gold field. It lazed on banners draped from the bridge, snapped on pennants atop the towers where guns were being raised on ropes. Though she could not see it so far removed, Fetch knew the same sigil decorated the chests of the soldiers posted along the wharf, the bridge, the walls, and the reconstructed gatehouse.

"Well, fuck, Palla."

Hispartha had reclaimed more than the Rutters' lot.

The city had stood since Imperial times, inherited by fledgling Hispartha after all the emperors finally lost hold of the last threads of their sanity and the world. Hells knew how old the place was, what-all it had seen and survived. What it had not withstood was the Great Orc Incursion. The thicks crushed the place as easily as an egg, then squatted in the wreckage to glut on the yolk. The Crown left it abandoned after the war was won, but they were finally back, sweeping away the rotten shell so they could squat their plump ass down and lay a fresh, shining prize.

Fetch had to spit. This was going to slow her down.

She couldn't risk entering the city. It was doubtful Bermudo knew the fate of Ramon and his men, but it was certain he knew his men had deserted without killing their prisoner. If the men down there had been ordered to keep an eye out, Fetch would be back in chains before she was halfway across the bridge. Hells, even if she weren't wanted there was slim chance she'd be allowed to pass unmolested. They were executing nomads. What would they attempt on a lone female half-orc on a hog?

Cursing, Fetch set off south.

She was a solid two leagues from Kalbarca before she risked turning Palla toward the banks of the river. The dark expanse of the Guadal-kabir grew closer, unchallenged as the great river of Ul-wundulas. No hog could swim its span. The nearest ford was days downriver near the Old Maiden Marsh. Fetch was forced to tarry along the shore for the meat of a day, waiting for a barge heading downstream. A hail to the men poling it, and a few coins taken from Mead created a ferry.

The eight frails aboard all had the cropped breeches and bug-bitten flesh of swampers. There were long knives at their belts, and frog-gigging spears close at hand, but the men menaced her with nothing but a few wary looks. They seemed more leery of the hog than the half-orc. Fetch held Palla firm at the barge's center next to the pile of crates, baskets, nets, and barrels that would be used to bring back whatever the swampers could trap, hunt, or gather in the Maiden. Sluggard's pig stood docile and cooperative the entire crossing, and Fetch was suddenly glad she did not have Womb Broom along. Shit-tempered swine would likely have tried to knock them all into the drink.

Fetch disembarked, leaving the swampers with the promised coin, a word of thanks, and an inward plea that they would have forgotten about her by the time they returned to Kalbarca with their snails and leeches to sell.

On the other side of the river, dark, sullen humps covered the north and western horizons.

The Smelted Mounts.

Likely the Imperium once had another name for the mountains, but Fetch was fucked if she knew what it was. The range formed the northwestern border between Hispartha and Ul-wundulas. Kalbarca and the southern foothills, while still part of the Lots, were Crown land. Like most of the parcels they held, the nobles were content to leave the area abandoned, yet forbade trespass. It was typical royal folly. During the allotment of the badlands, the frails made sure not one spit of land that touched Hispartha was held by the mongrel hoofs, creating a wide swath of country ignored by the Crown yet denied all others. But a decree cannot uphold itself, only soldiers can, and they were never sent. Until now.

The half-orcs of Ul-wundulas, especially the nomads, had a long tradition of flagrantly disregarding any ban to their travels, and Fetch was happy to keep it alive.

So too were brigands and cutthroats from the other side of the border. Ancient Imperial mining tunnels provided a labyrinth of hideaways for those frails fleeing Hisparthan justice, but too craven to risk the Lots. Murderers, highwaymen, disgraced cavaleros, and escaped prisoners were drawn to the Smelteds, forming a deterrent along the border that the Crown never intended.

Fetching pushed Palla toward the mountains, but she had lost time and did not reach the foothills before the sun set. She passed the night in a grove of stone pine. Unable to resist, Fetch ate another of the Zahracene fruit she'd kept back from the supply wagon before bedding down. She slept under the stars and was back in the saddle before they yielded to the sunrise.

She had come this way only once before, more than half a year ago, and kept her eyes sharp for familiar signs. But this was Ul-wundulas. Everything looked dry, thirsty, and miserable. The Mounts were replete with passes. The wrong choice could cost days, if not worse. Trusting to instinct, Fetch pressed on. There had been the barest trace of an old Hisparthan fortress on a peak above the pass, she remembered, just a wink of white stone. She kept an eye out as the foothills fully claimed her journey.

By midday she had scouted the mouths of four passes, but the correct one remained elusive. Cursing, Fetch began riding swiftly back and forth between the gaps, looking for something to guide a choice. The recalled white stone was not to be found.

"Twice-damned mountain goat likely mistook it for a nanny and fucked it off the ridge!" she screamed into the hills. As the echoes faded, her anger grew. She was wasting the day and Palla's strength. There was nothing for it but to make a decision.

"You, then," she told the gap currently frustrating her memory, and rode into the clutches of the Smelteds.

The pass soon widened into a broad saddle between boulder-crowned peaks. Though this range rolled across the breadth of Ul-wundulas, eventually joining the imposing Umber Mountains in Tine territory, the Smelteds were the runt of the litter. Few of the slopes were steep enough to deter a skilled hog rider. However, picking a way up and over the grades was a tedious business. That's why the passes were so vital, providing a winding, though more or less level, path. Fetching remained uncertain of her choice until she spotted an abandoned castile upon a nearby summit.

This was it. This was as far as she had come last time. Oats had insisted on going the rest of the way alone. The parting had not been easy. The chief of the True Bastards was nowhere to be seen that morning. Hells, Fetching and Oats hardly existed in that last, hard embrace. They were Isabet and Idris again, holding each other in comfort as they had done so many times as children.

Sitting her hog now, she stared ahead at the path Oats and Ug-fuck had taken. That day, she had watched until they were lost to the rocky folds of the earth.

"Our turn," Fetching told Palla and kicked him forward.

There was nothing to do now but wander and wait to be noticed.

She knew Oats had been taken in by the mountain-dwellers. Hoodwink made the journey here each month since the thrice-blood left, always bringing back a heavy bag of silver. For the Bastards, those bulging sacks of coin meant the Tusked Tide could be paid for another load of supplies. For Fetching, it meant Oats was still alive. She could only hope that when she reached the infamous place of his exile, there would be another bag of coins waiting. And a big, fool-ass thrice handing it to her.

Nightfall found Fetching still riding among the mountains. Only with the darkness did the denizens of the Smelteds reveal themselves. Six men came down from outcroppings in the slopes to block her path. An equal number slipped down behind. Fetch loaded her stock-bow. Not waiting for the bandits to make a move, she rode to the group ahead.

"I'm looking for the Pit of Homage."

One of the men detached from his fellows. He was lanky, the rot in his clothes reaching Fetch's nostrils before the moonlight etched out his features. Long hair, thin yet pendulous with grime, swung from beneath a pitiful wad of a hat. His belts were heavy with knives.

"We could take you," the man said. "Or we can take you."

This drew rough laughter from his group. The gang to Fetch's rear was still closing in. She could feel their approach.

She leveled her stockbow at the speaker. "I'm not going to do this with you, frail. Take me to the Pit or I will loose this bolt into your mouth."

"You do and my men will kill you."

Fetch gave a perplexed hum. "Strange threat. You'll be dead. Do you expect revenge will bring you back to life? Think. This hogshit goes on a moment longer, I'm going to kill you. And you won't be the last. Your men might manage to drag me off this hog before I win free, but he's a mean son of a sow. He'll likely get more of you than I will. Either way, I'm the one who will see how this ends. Not you."

Palla was no Womb Broom, so she wasn't certain how mean he really was, but a barbarian was still a barbarian, and Fetch meant every damn word. There was no bluff for these cunts to sniff out.

A few heartbeats of silence passed before the man raised an arm. The footsteps of the bandits behind ceased.

"Naturally, I was merely jesting," the man proclaimed with a jovial sincerity that was difficult to deny. "Allow us to be your guides."

"I don't need a dozen frails to do anything in this world. Much less show me the way someplace."

"Of course!"

A whistle lanced from the spokesman's lips as he made a whirling gesture over his head. The brigands shuffled off, melting into the shadows of the pass.

"Allow I alone, Jacintho, to act as escort."

Without waiting for a reply, the lanky figure began walking.

Ready to keep her promise and put a bolt between the man's shoulder blades if his cohorts reappeared, Fetching followed. They did not remain in the pass long. Jacintho began edging toward the slopes and soon had them traversing a switchback trail. Eventually, the trail ran along a ridgeline, encircling the slope as it snuck upward. Reaching the summit, Jacintho crossed the rocks and picked his way down the other side. They traveled in the dark. The heavens provided some illumination, but Fetch wasn't sure how the man was making his way so assuredly.

Humans did not see as well in the dark as half-orcs. Hells, other half-orcs did not see as well in the dark as Fetching. It used to rankle Jackal and Oats when they were younger, never sure why she could spot things they could not when playing after sundown. Later, her brother Bastards learned to trust her sight beyond all others. Now she knew she had her elf mother to thank. This loathsome Jacintho sure as shit didn't possess any point-ear blood, so he must have been making his way on instinct and familiarity.

Fetching tried to mark their course, but it was impossible. They went scrambling up and down the shoulders of half a dozen peaks, traversed long ridgelines and short saddle-gaps, until Fetch began to wonder if they were going in circles. She was certain they were staying in the heights, for she could see valleys and passes below, rivers and lagoons of shadow among the starlit lumps of the mountains. At last, they began to descend, but only as far as a bowl between two slopes, little more than a pockmark eaten into the mountainside.

Here, a cave mouth gaped with predatory invitation.

"From here, you must lead your hog," Jacintho said.

Fetching dismounted and took hold of Palla by a yanker tusk. Her stockbow remained in her other hand.

The brigand made a clucking sound. "You had best sling that. I care for my life. Those within will not. Nor yours. A loaded arbalest will only get us both killed."

After quick consideration, Fetching removed the bolt and released the string. Stockbow now hanging at her back, she followed Jacintho into the cave. Palla fought her a little at the threshold, grunting and digging his hooves in, trying to shake her hold, but Fetch hauled him within. A sloshing sound was followed by a few clicks, both echoing in the cave mouth as Jacintho drew a torch from a barrel and struck flint with one of his daggers, throwing sparks into the oil-drenched head until it ignited. In the glow, the cave proved to be a mine.

The shaft was low but wide, the walls and ceiling striated from the blows of uncountable picks. The ground sloped downward, a gullet in the mountain. The entrance was a memory by the time they reached a branch in the passage. Jacintho went left. The tunnel became less regular, bending snakelike around sharp juts. Downward, ever downward.

Sounds began to drift up from the unseen deep, beginning as faint whispers residing in the space between hearing and madness, growing into dull echoes swimming along the rock. The brigand's torch became unnecessary as fat lamps began to appear, affixed to the tunnel walls. The passage leveled out and widened, dug-out chambers blistered along its length. Haggard women lingered in the entrance to one. Their years made them girls, but their eyes were those of bitter crones. One of them made a dispassionate invitation for Jacintho to enter and join the throng of other men within the chamber noisily having their way with half as many whores. Promising to return, the bandit passed by. Farther on, he thrust his torch into another chamber, soliciting ornery squeals from within.

"You may leave your pig here."

Fetch led Palla inside. Three other barbarians, big and well fed, were tethered in the cramped, subterranean stable. Fetch thought she recognized one of them, but she did not dwell on it for long. She tied Palla to an iron ring on the opposite wall before turning back to her guide.

"Let's go."

The tunnel lasted only a few dozen more steps before turning. Around the bend a sizable chamber had been chiseled from the guts of the mountain. The air this deep should have been cool and thin, but Fetch was assaulted with a heady reek of unwashed bodies, excrement of men and animals, and something else she could not identify—a sharp, vaguely sour odor. The noise within was deafening, generated by a pressed mob of bedraggled forms. Men shouted through savage throats, cackled with unbridled glee. Harsh whistles and violent cheers rose to a deafening pitch. And under it all, something else, like the smell, something nameless. It was akin to the sound of surf along the seashore, but not low or lulling. This had an edge, a thousand edges, as if voiced from an avalanche of hissing serpents.

Jacintho turned to face her, his spreading smile made of mossy gravestones. "Welcome to the Pit of Homage."

Fetching could barely hear him over the din. Leaning close, she yelled into his ear.

"I'm looking for a thrice! Been here half a year!"

The brigand merely preserved his horrible smile and gestured grandly at the chamber.

Gritting her teeth against the wall of sound and stink, she stepped through.

The size of the place could hardly be discerned. The ceiling was out of reach, though Fetch could have touched it if she jumped. The rest of its proportions were blocked by teeming walls of filthy men.

Most had their backs turned, forming large rough circles. Finding the sliver of an avenue between the edges of two of these circles, Fetch pushed her way forward, jostled and bumped from both sides as the men at the rear of the press struggled to get a better view of whatever the fuck they were cheering about.

Something splashed across Fetch's shoulder and she grimaced against the smell of wine so vile it insulted vinegar. Spying the culprit by the jug raised high in his fist as he screamed and cavorted, Fetch snatched the back of his tunic and jerked him to the ground. The wine jug shattered and the man's wrathful snarl only burned up from the floor for an instant before Fetch stomped her boot in his face. Nose going the way of the crockery, the fool went limp.

A small circle widened around the scene, momentarily drawing attention. In the lurid light men with yellowed eyes peered at Fetching, but quickly lost interest in the face of her challenging glower. Wisely choosing to ignore the unconscious man, they turned back to their entertainments. The only stare that remained was Jacintho's, gleaming with approval. He made another of his theatrical gestures, pointing through the press. Fetch forced her way through. Some of these wretches were taller, but none were stronger. Any angry resistance she encountered was quickly banished. The mere sight of a half-orc caused most to make room.

Emerging from the crowd, Fetching discovered the source of the strange smell and the rasping sound. Her toes were a handspan away from a deep pit, basin-shaped, with no rail to guard against falling down the steeply angled sides. Fetch would have been hard-pressed to throw a rock and clear the depression. Coins filled its bottom, a tide pool of tarnished, reeking coins, so many they sloshed up the incline. The sour reek of mildewed metal, familiar from the scent of a single coin, was made horribly unknowable when birthed from this uncountable mass.

Three men occupied the treasure-carpeted arena, wading ankle-deep to come to grips with one another. Two were bearded, wearing unbelted roughspun tunics. The third seemed younger because he was smooth-faced, and naked to the skin. The bearded men were converging on him, trying to keep their quarry from darting away.

The coins made the footing difficult, but as Fetch watched, the naked youth darted between his opponents, his run turning into a dive that set the coins hissing.

Jacintho's voice leaked into Fetch's ear.

"It is said the hole was once bare. Then the emperor came to tour his mines and grew bored. He commanded slaves fight for him. Not the trained warriors of the city arenas, but merely miners, they knew less of battle than they did the sun. They pummeled each other like children, but were not killers. Pleased with their baseness, the emperor threw coins down, proclaiming the man to slay his opponent could leave the pit with all the money he could carry. Soon, the richest families of the Imperium came to see this new spectacle, throwing coins to ape the emperor. Enslaved men fought and died, but none could carry out all the shine that was thrown. The Imperium is a thousand years dead. No more coins are tossed, but men still fight and die, the victor filling his hands, and still the pit does not empty."

Fetch found bitter bile settling in her throat, born from Jacintho's closeness, his breath. Born from the tale he told. Born from the distaste of knowing she sent a brother to take part in this perverse invention of decadent madmen.

Below, one of the bearded men managed to catch hold of the nude youth, dragging him through the coins by the ankle until close enough to be pounced upon. Thin, pale limbs flailed. The man pushed the youth's face into the coins, smothering the fight out of him. Hooking an arm up beneath his half-dead prey's chin, the man lifted. The naked man's face rose from the pile, coins clinging to his forehead for a moment before falling in tinny tears. Fetch waited for the end, for the snapped neck that would not be heard over the raucous screeching of the crowd. But the bearded man began fumbling beneath the hem of his tunic. His fist emerged, coaxing his cock to harden.

Fetch threw a look at Jacintho.

The brigand was amused by her revolted confusion. "*This* contest is won by the first man to bugger the fop."

A cheer went up as the other bearded combatant came rushing across the trilling arena to tackle his competition, knocking him off the youth. The two men began to beat and gnash at each other, rolling and wrestling, as the dazed youth crawled away, eyes glazed, with all the speed of a half-crushed slug.

Fetch seized Jacintho by his greasy neck. "I said I was looking for a damn thrice!"

"Ah, but he would not be here," the bandit rasped, still amused despite his constricted windpipe. "This is the Pit of Flesh. You want the Pit of Greatness."

"The Pit of Homage!" Fetch growled, tightening her grip.

"You're in it," Jacintho coughed out. "The whole mine."

Hells, why hadn't she known? Inwardly cursing Hoodwink for the taciturn fuck he was, Fetch released Jacintho.

"I'll find it myself."

As she shoved back through the crowd, wails of violation rose up from the pit at her back.

The search revealed more arenas, all equally filled with coins and nightmare. Fetch was a child of the Lots, but the cruelty of those pits was difficult to stare full in the face.

At last, the insanity of the mine working its way into her skull, she found what she sought.

It was the largest arena yet. Nearly twice the width of the Pit of Flesh and half again as deep, it was oblong, dug at the back of the cave, so that the crowd could only gather at the short ends and the long side opposite the cavern wall. The other pits had been nothing but craters, but this one contained a pair of tunnels, each set into the long slope beneath the wall. They were separated by only a few arm spans, the left barred by a thick metal grate. Other than the coins, the floor was vacant, but the mass of men bordering the edges was tense with anticipation.

"Should prove a good fight," a deep voice tolled at Fetch's right.

She looked up to find the scowling profile of Knob staring into the arena. It was no surprise. She had seen his hog on the way in.

"Won't be," Fetching told the Orc Stains' chief. "Soon as my boy enters, I'm stopping it."

Knob smiled. "Do that, and these frails will chew you to pieces. They put great importance on this pathetic ritual."

In these confines, with this many men, Fetch knew he was right, and that got her venom flowing.

"What are you doing here, Stain?"

"I'm here to offer a brother-thrice a place in my hoof."

Before Fetching could respond, the crowd erupted. A tall figure emerged from the open tunnel, bare-chested and hulking, bald head wrapped in a kerchief, a fierce beard thrusting from a shovel-jaw.

Oats.

Fetch's breath caught.

His bulging torso hosted a colony of new scars. Some of the wounds were still adorned with stitches. But it was not the cuts, healed or fresh, that hurt to look upon. It was the empty eyes, the dull stare that would not rise toward the roaring men above.

Fetch had to bite her cheek to keep from calling out. It would not have done any good. She would never have been heard. The men were shaking the cave with a chant.

"BIG! BASTARD! BIG! BASTARD!"

With bare feet, Oats moved across the coins. He went slowly down the length of the pit, ignoring the adoration. The audience began to howl as the grate of the remaining passage began to rise.

Fetch went cold.

The only reason for such a grate was to prevent something from escaping, something kept caged. Oats had walked out freely, and he would not be matched with some underfed prisoner. No, in a place this horrible, this inured to death, few things would be feared enough to keep under lock. In the other pits, Fetch had caught glimpses of feral boars, wolves, bulls, and mountain lions. Whatever was about to be released was a much more dangerous beast.

The creature that stepped forth made the men burst with jeering calls.

"Hells!" Fetch exclaimed. "A fucking cyclops?!"

She'd never seen one in the flesh, only a skeleton that had once been a prized possession of Grocer and Creep before they lost it in a fire that claimed the Kiln's original supply hall. Fetch had hated that damn thing, but sneaking to look at it was a favorite game of Jackal's when they were children. Adding meat to those ponderous bones only made it worse.

The cyclops in the pit was a big-bellied, umber-skinned brute. Shaggy black hair, streaked with grey and twisted with filth, hung in ropes beside its wide, chinless face, framing the great, yellowed single eye set deep beneath the slab of a sloping brow. The cyclops stood stooped even after leaving the confines of the tunnel for the open space of the arena.

"The flesh merchants will sometimes risk raiding Aetynia," Knob said without feeling. "They can subdue the older one-eyes. Bring them alive to the Pit."

The sight turned Fetch's stomach. "Gaggle of fucking slavers."

Hunched back aside, the cyclops was well over half the height of the arena hole. A looming savage clad only in a soiled hide clout. Slowly, the eye revolved upward to stare at the men. Contempt for the frails was imbued in the brute's stillness.

Quick as a panther, it struck, darting for the nearest slope and reaching. Men recoiled from the edge, but one unfortunate had his leg seized by the grasping cyclops and he was dragged squealing down the slope. Monster and man slid back onto the jingling floor. The cyclops barely lost its footing on the friable surface of coins, but the panicking brigand was sprawled on his back. The cyclops took a single step, stomped upon the man's chest. Blood burst from his mouth, followed by nothing but a rattling wheeze.

Wine jugs and refuse began to be flung down upon the creature, not in any attempt to save the fallen fool, but to deter it from attempting another leap. Several of the jugs struck, breaking against the swarthy body, but it remained heedless of the bombardment. It watched the man beneath its foot die before turning to face its opponent.

From the other side of the pit, Oats had witnessed the killing with a detached stare.

He began to move now, slowly at first. He quickened his pace once his feet found purchase on the treacherous floor, becoming a steady, aggressive advance. The cyclops strode to meet him.

Oats was a large mongrel, even for a thrice-blood. His father must have been a truly monstrous thick, and it was a miracle Beryl survived the ravaging that left her carrying the orc's get. As Fetch watched the cyclops draw closer, she saw something dwarf her friend for the first time. Hells, the damn thing was at least two heads taller.

Fists still clenched at his sides, Oats barreled forward. The cyclops lunged for him. He twisted and delivered a crushing punch to the ribs. The old one-eye barely twitched. Spinning, it bent low and rushed in, weathering an elbow to the skull and slamming into Oats's midsection. Before he could adjust, the brute's powerful legs straightened, heaving Oats into the air and tossing him bodily over its shoulder. He hit the ground hard, coins crunching, but rolled as soon as he struck, avoiding a stamping foot.

The brigands bellowed as Oats quickly gained his feet. The cyclops was already upon him. Oats's arm dashed out, throwing a fistful of coins hard into its face. The large eye was pelted with metal and clenched shut. Stalled, the cyclops swung with a millstone fist.

Oats wasn't there.

He had pivoted to its exposed back, seized it about the waist, tried to wrestle it down.

"Get out, Oats," Fetch whispered.

But he committed. Briefly releasing the beast, he jumped to wrap his legs around its hips and caught hold beneath its shoulders, wrapping its armpits and trying to lock his hands behind its head. The cyclops fought the hold, pressing down with its own powerful arms.

Oats moved his right arm around its neck and hauled backward. The cyclops thrust one leg back to remain standing, but its foot slipped in the coins, forcing it to a knee. Oats's left arm now encircled the neck. Any other opponent would have died of a snapped spine, but this brute merely tucked forward, reached back, seized Oats by the head, and threw him off.

Fetching flinched.

The biggest hells-damned thrice alive and he had just been tossed as if no more than a child.

Twice.

The cyclops left its crouch in a charge and was upon Oats before he even landed, ramming him into the slope. Feet over head, Oats began to slide, but the cyclops planted a foot on his chest to hold him in place before hammering at his guts and groin with its fists. Grunting against the horrendous blows, Oats paid the old one-eye back by reaching up under its clout to seize it by the fruits. Howling, the monster scuttled backward, away from the pain, trying to dislodge the hand tearing at its cod.

Oats hung on until he was dragged off the slope. Soon as he touched the ground, he let go, allowing the cyclops to retreat. As the thrice got to his feet, movements labored, the cyclops kept stalking backward, lowing in pained anger. Fetch realized its intention only a moment before.

"Dammit, Oats, rush him!"

But her voice was one in hundreds of bloodthirsty encouragements.

The cyclops reached down and seized the man it had killed by both ankles, one-handed. Grinning, it began advancing, dragging the corpse. Oats waited, brow furrowed. He didn't see it. Could not conceive of it until it was too late.

Taking one mighty step forward, twisting its great torso, the cyclops swung the body forward, sending a torrent of coins flying as the dead man was hauled through them before lifting off the ground. Oats jumped back, barely avoiding the reaping swing. Still held in the cyclops's fist, the corpse slapped back down, eliciting groans of amused disgust from the crowd. But there was hardly a pause and the cyclops again struck, bringing its arm back around, launching its grisly flail once more into the air. With the slope now at his back, there was nowhere for Oats to go. He tried to duck, but was clipped by the corpse's head. Skulls collided with a wooden noise heard over the brigands' astonished adulation. Dazed, Oats tried to recover, but managed only a few stumbling steps before the corpse came careening into him once more, sending him flying into the slope.

The broken body in the monster's hand was flinging blood now as well as coins. With Oats pinned, unable to escape the reach of the awful weapon, the cyclops merely stood in place, preparing the next—the final—swing. Adjusting its grip, the brute held an ankle in each hand now, taking a few sidelong steps until the corpse trailed out behind. Battered and bleary, Oats could only lean against the side of the pit and watch as the cyclops tensed, hauling the corpse into the air for a vicious hammering chop.

Fetch's bolt sunk to the fletching in the single eye, punching through the jelly to the skull beyond. Brain pierced, the cyclops went limp, the man's body leaving its nerveless fingers to hang for a moment before falling atop its former wielder. A dead frail fell atop a dead one-eye, the meaty sound of their mating clearly heard in the stunned silence.

All eyes turned to her, but Fetch returned only one wide stare.

"Time to go home, Big Bastard!" she called down.

Oats's jaw was slack.

The crowd shook off the stupefying interruption as resentful murmurings grew into shouted protestations.

"No homage!"

The first cry went up right next to Fetching, voiced by Knob. It was quickly taken up by the rabble.

"No homage! NO homage! NO HOMAGE!"

They were screaming down at Oats, accusatory fists pumping.

The grate blocking the tunnel again began to rise. Something else was being set loose.

Cursing, Fetch began to reload her stockbow, but Knob's meaty hand slapped down over the runnel. The thrice-blood chief jerked the weapon from her hands just as the men at her back surged, pushing her over the edge of the pit. She slid down into the coins, landing in a crouch.

Across the width of the pit, Oats had gained his feet, eyes moving slowly between her and the grate. Out of the shadowed tunnel, ducking under the teeth of the grate before it was fully raised, walked a centaur.

Agitated horse hooves stamped the coins. The man's torso atop the beast legs was thickly muscled, the face beneath the matted hair full of malevolence for being caged.

"Fucking hells," Fetch hissed, and drew her Unyar sword.

In response, jeers and wine jugs were flung in objection. The barrage left her no choice but to let the weapon fall. She made to rise, but saw Oats holding a staying hand in her direction. Their eyes met, his no longer dull.

He winked.

Screeching a war-cry the centaur charged, coins spraying from beneath pounding hooves. The thrice-blood bent low, spread his bulging arms, and surged forward. Half-orc and horse-cock met in the center of the pit, the impact of their bodies concussive. Fetch narrowed her eyes, waiting for her brother to be trampled, but Oats wrapped his arms about the waist of the man-half, stiffening his legs out behind him. Pushed backward, metal hissed as Oats's feet dug furrows in the coins. With a lung-busting bellow he dug his toes in and hauled backward, lifting an impossible weight of man and horse flesh into the air, the creature's own speed serving to carry it over his head. Oats extended his arms, fell flat on his back, and drove the centaur into the ground, bringing all of its weight crashing down upon its own head. Bones snapped, the spine loudest of all.

As six limbs twitched in death-throes, Oats rose. He walked over to Fetch as the crowd burst with cheers, freeing itself from fresh amazement.

"Let's go home, then," Oats grunted, and bent to scoop a pile of coins into his huge hands.

NINETEEN

OATS SAT UPON an overturned bucket, listening, while a halfling woman tended his injuries. Even with the thrice on so low a perch, she still had to stand on a stool to reach his face.

Once Fetching had told him all, he nodded slowly, probing one of his lower fangs with a finger. The halfling slapped at his hand and gave him an admonishing look. She had only one eye, the other covered by a leather patch, but she managed to place double the reproach in half the stare. Oats lowered his hand.

"When I saw you had come for me, I hoped it was because things were better, being earnest. But this . . ."

Fetch let her silence agree.

"Ruin Made Flesh," the thrice grunted. "Shit. And we thought Crafty was an ass pain."

"We're not free of him either."

"But you don't think these Sar . . . Zayra . . . what was it?"

"Zahracenes."

"You don't think he's with them?"

"I don't know," Fetch admitted, seated upon the rickety cot that served as Oats's bed. The damp cave he'd been living in since coming to the Pit was cramped and cheerless. "It didn't appear so, but that's what the fat fuck was best at. Appearances."

Oats began to nod again, but the motion upset the halfling's ministrations to a large welt. Clicking her tongue sharply, she swatted him expertly on the back of the head.

"Damn, Xhreka!" Oats complained, flinching away.

"Stop moving," the small woman commanded, pointing a finger at him.

Fetch had to stifle a smile. It was a good thing Beryl was not here. She might have murdered this Xhreka out of jealousy. Oats stilled, suffering the attentions with a petulant grimace.

The coins he had won sat in large bags against the moist wall at the head of the cot. The quantity hurt to look upon. The little cave had no door. Fetch could not fathom how the money remained safe, but neither did she understand why all the wealth had not been pilfered from the Pit ages ago. There was so much she did not know about this wicked place, so much she did not want to know, then or now. The choice was in the past, the money won, and Oats survived. He was damn lucky to be alive. Fetch was damn lucky he was alive.

"Once we're back," she said, "we'll decide what to do. As a hoof."

Oats's bearded jaw kept clenching, and not because of the sting of the halfling's rag. He hadn't quite been able to look Fetch in the eye.

"What is it?" she asked, knowing.

"How long?" Irritation edged the question.

Fetch paused, weighing how to answer. Oats wasn't having it.

"How long were you going to let those coughing fits go on without telling me? How long were you going to be sick, spitting up sludge, thinking it was killing you, before telling *me*?"

She met his pained eyes. It was better to just admit it.

"I wasn't."

Oats blew out a furious breath. "Damn, Isa . . ."

There was more. And she needed to say it.

"It was one of the reasons I sent you away. Feared you'd see it."

Oats's jaw hardened and he pulled his head away from the halfling's care with such slow intensity that the little woman did not attempt to prevent him. "One of the reasons? Wager it was the only reason."

"You were starving yourself, Oats."

"We were all starving."

"The rest of us weren't doing it on fucking purpose."

"'Least I wasn't doing it in secret!"

"I was trying to protect the hoof!"

"So was I!"

"By dying of hunger?"

"By drowning in sludge? Fool-ass!"

"What could you have done? If you'd known?"

"I don't know. I wasn't there. Because you sent me here!"

"It was for your own good!"

"It was for yours!"

"Hogshit!"

"You just admitted it!"

"Exactly! I'm hells-damned sorry!"

"Sorry? You're fucking sorry?!"

"You want a tit to suck on too? Fuck! I don't know what else to say!"

"How about y—"

"AY!" the halfling woman screamed, going still as a statue.

Fetch and Oats stopped yelling. There was a long silence where they simply sat, steaming at each other.

"Done?" Xhreka demanded. "I've lost half my sight. Not about to lose half my hearing suffering this. Belico's Cock, half-orcs can bellow! I'd say just thrash each other, get this out, but I don't want more work than I got already. So, I'll ask again. Are. You. Done? Otherwise, I got more rags here that I can shove in your loud, fangy mouths."

"We're done," Oats mumbled. He took a slow breath. "The brothers know?"

"Do they know what?" Fetch asked.

"About the sludge."

"Only Hood. He smelled the weakness on me like a damn carrion bird. But I'm going to tell them all. Everything. If you want to challenge me for leadership I'll understand."

"Xhreka, hand me one of those rags. Feel like stuffing one all the way down my chief's throat."

The halfling didn't move for the rag, but she did shift her eye to Fetching.

"Self-pity's not worth a dung heap down here, girl."

Fetch let go of a humorless laugh. "Very well. But the others may feel differently. It's not self-pity to prepare to lose the seat. Secrets like these buried the Claymaster."

Oats said nothing. She didn't blame him. Only thing worth less than self-pity was pity from others.

"Oats, however it goes with the brethren, you should know . . . this may be the end for us. For the Bastards. Fuck, I don't even know that we will find Winsome still standing when we get back. That's the cold shit truth of it. This orc and his beasts, the famine, fucking Bermudo, I might not . . . we might not find a way to best them. I want you to know, straight from me, that's why I came for you. Figured you would want to be there with all of us. Figured . . . you would never forgive me if the Bastards went to the dust without you."

Oats was very still. "Then we go back. We struggle on. And if all this proves to be too much then there's only one thing we can do."

"We live in the saddle."

The apple of Oats's throat bobbed at the center of his thick neck. "We die on the hog."

He stood less than a heartbeat before she did. A step brought them to each other's arms.

"Hells overburdened," Fetch said from the depths of his torso. "I forgot how hard you squeeze."

Oats only increased the constriction. "Take it and like it, sister mine."

After separating, they allowed silence to reign and Xhreka to return to her work. The way the halfling cleaned and dressed Oats's battered bulk reminded Fetch of a rider grooming a hog. There was affection, but also a detachment. A necessary, though not hated, chore. She was certainly a curiosity. Not just the eye patch, and the fact that she was the only halfling Fetch had seen down here, it was her entire manner. Most of her kind were serene, patient to the point of aloof. But Xhreka's movements, though deft and competent, were edged with a productive vexation. Fetch found the age of halflings difficult to figure. They did not wear the care of their years as obviously as the fairer frails. There was no grey in the tight rows of Xhreka's twistlocked hair, no lines upon her ebony face. Yet her few words and actions, both filled with an easy courage, bespoke a woman long-accustomed to spitting at the harshness of the world.

"You take care of all the fighters?" Fetch found herself asking.

Xhreka made a noise in her throat that was either amusement or disgust. Or both. "No."

When no other explanation followed, Oats spoke up. "Xhreka used to enter the Pit of Bait." Something disturbed the thrice's face and he grew hesitant. "She used to . . ."

The halfling came to his rescue. "I entered a pit with several other fools and a pack of wolves or starved dogs, maybe a bear. Whoever was last alive was hauled out."

"She helped me find my feet in this place," Oats added.

Fetch nodded. "I understand."

And she did. Xhreka found a way to survive the pit without needing to compete. No doubt Oats was paying her from his winnings. It might have been irritating if Fetch didn't know the big fool-ass so well. He always needed someone to care for, to look after. Even in the orphanage, that was his way. More than half the reason Fetching was a sworn rider was due to that very nature. She wondered if Xhreka knew how much she was truly aiding the thrice, beyond stitching cuts and massaging muscles. Fetch was willing to wager she did.

"Was that the first cyclops they've made you fight?" she asked.

It was Xhreka who answered, attention never leaving her charge. "Third. But the others were older, crippled."

Oats could only raise his eyebrows in confirmation.

I never should have sent you here. Fetch's heart wanted to say it, but best not to dredge it up again.

She stood. "Tell me where Ugfuck is and I'll get him saddled."

"No," Xhreka said, her single eye snapping where her voice did not. "He cannot ride. Not until morning."

"I can," Oats groused.

His head was smacked again. "You cannot."

Oats gave Fetch an apologetic look.

"It's fine," she told him. It wasn't. Every moment away brought the ax closer to the hoof's neck, if it hadn't fallen already. But Oats looked hard-used. "Get some sleep. We can leave at first light."

"No sleeping either," Xhreka said.

Oats threw up a hand. "Not that again."

The halfling put up her own hands, abandoning her task of bandaging the thrice's head. "Very well. Do not listen. Lay down." She flicked the bandage at the cot. "Sleep." She flicked the bandage at the cave entrance. "Ride. But if I were asked, I would say a man who wants to die in the saddle should do it in battle, not because he grew dizzy, fell off his hideous farting hog, and dashed his brains on a rock."

Oats exhaled in compliance, but his caregiver was not ready to accept surrender and the reprimand kept coming.

"*If* asked, I would say a man who wants to die in bed should do it while pleasing his woman, not because he was a lazy lout who chose slumber after having his head cracked by an Aetynian giant and never woke again, pissing himself as he passed from the mortal world."

Again Fetch found herself biting back amusement. She did not much like having her orders countermanded by this stunted woman, but could not help liking her.

"We will leave at dawn," Fetch repeated, stepping toward the entranceway.

Oats gave her a confused frown. "Where are you going?"

"To get my thrum back."

The mining tunnels were narrower in this section than those leading into the Pit. When Oats and Fetch had left the arena, using the same tunnel he had to enter, she made sure to track the route as they navigated the suffocating shafts. Though Oats's feet were a bit unsteady from the fight, his familiarity with the mines was obvious, disheartening. His chamber had not been far from the arena, though it did feel they had climbed a bit higher. Xhreka had been waiting, ready to wash, stitch, and splint.

Fetching did not retrace the route back to the arena, but followed her gut through what was clearly the dormitory for the fighters. In one of the small caves, she saw the unfortunate youth from the Pit of Flesh, curled up on a cot, unmoving. A little farther on, she found Jacintho, loitering in the tunnel. It was obvious he was waiting for her, a fact that made her skin crawl. Still, at this moment, she was in need of a guide.

"Take me to the Orc Stains."

Jacintho rubbed at his throat, the marks from her throttling visible on his oily skin. "Mayhaps you are not grateful enough of my help, eh?"

"You're right," Fetch replied, passing him by. "I'll find them without you."

The ruffian did a crablike caper to catch up. "But! I am a forgiving man, so I shall be beneficent. Come."

Jacintho moved to the lead, taking her down a steadily curving tunnel to the right.

The mines were a veritable hive. Cut-outs and caverns were regular, most occupied. Many were filled with nothing but drunken, stinking men, sleeping upon the stone. One held a meeting of hush-voiced cutthroats, plotting over a table, its lone candle casting no light upon their dark schemes.

The Orc Stains were taking their ease in a cave furnished with rough benches. The three thrice-bloods had either bartered or bullied for a supply of wine and women. When Fetching entered, she found Knob lounging upon a bench, his back against the wall and a woman kneeling between his legs, head bobbing. The chief grinned over the girl's knotted hair, his eyes narrowed with pleasure. He made no move to stop the service, but his two riders ceased their own carousing when Fetch stepped into their midst.

She spied her stockbow leaning against the wall. "You like trying to take what's mine, don't you, Knob?"

"I'm not taking it," the Stains' chief replied. "You should thank me for saving your hide from the mob."

"So, you're not stealing my thrum, but you were going to try and steal my rider."

Knob chuckled. "Rider? Oats hasn't ridden anywhere since you dumped him here. Did you think word of that would not blow through the Lots? A hoof-rider languishing in the Pit of Homage? When I saw he wasn't with you at Strava, I knew it was true. Reckoned I'd offer him a better home."

Fetch took a step closer, ignoring the slurping sounds. "It's against hoof code to poach brothers."

"You don't have a hoof, quim. I told you before."

"And you think you decide?"

"I do. Who else? We aren't frails. We are the mongrel hoofs. There is no court or council to govern what we do, to approach for permission. Ul-wundulas is our only judge and she respects strength. I say you are no chief. I say your rider belongs in a proud hoof among his brother thrice-bloods. I say! You cannot stop that if you cannot stop it with strength. And you. Have. None."

Fetch made a show of consideration. "You're right. At least about the hoofs. There is no council. Hells, we could not reach an accord on some damn frails squatting in the Rutters' lands. What did you decide there, Knob? I know! None of the others agreed to go to war, so you skulked off. The Orc Stains can't ride against the newcomers alone? Sounds like strength to me."

Knob's eyes flashed and he sat up. The girl had to adjust her head, but did not stop.

"Those frails cross the Stains and they will see how strong we are."

"You're not adding to that strength with my brethren."

"Had you not arrived, I would already have made Oats the offer."

"Then you should be thanking me for saving your life. Oats is a Bastard to the blood. He would not have taken kindly to you trying to pull him away from his brothers."

"Brothers?" Knob grinned, leaning back once more with a satisfied sigh. "Or is it the sister he can't refuse? The tight gash that gives command as well as favors."

Fetching looked down at the busy whore for the first time. She smiled and shifted her gaze up to Knob.

"You're right," she said, slowly moving to stand just behind the girl. "You can't offer what I can. And wouldn't it be easier to find out for yourself why I inspire such loyalty? Why take one of my riders, when there is so much more you could get from me?"

Fetch languidly entwined her fingers in the whore's tangled tresses, and pulled her head back until there was a wet pop. "I see where you got your hoof name," she remarked, looking down. The whore's expression was full of venom for the interference, but she was expert enough to know Knob was enjoying himself. The chief's face was flushed with eager curiosity. He inhaled sharply when Fetch guided the woman's head back down, his eyes closing.

Throwing her weight forward, Fetching wedged her knee behind the whore's neck and drew one of the katara, the weapon transforming her fist into a blade. Knob's eyes flew open and bulged when the steel kissed his throat.

"Move and I open him!" Fetch shouted at the other Stains without taking her eyes off their master. Beneath the weight of her leg, the woman tried to free herself, but was held fast.

"You ever sucked a cock, Knob?" Fetch demanded. "I wager you have. In your slophead days. In some hoofs, I hear they're not given that name just because they feed the hogs. Did you forget that when a cod is this deep down your throat, you can't breathe?"

The whore's squirms intensified. Muffled, choking protests filled the cave.

Fetch leaned closer to Knob's enraged face. "I wonder how long she'll hold out before biting it off?"

The thrice paled.

"Or will you scare first," Fetch taunted, "and try to throw me off? Give me a reason to wash in your glorious. Thrice. Blood."

Bucking against the restraining leg, the woman began to gag.

"Now! You ever think to meddle in the ranks of the True Bastards—MY FUCKING HOOF—again, and there won't be a whore's breath standing in the way of you being made a fucking eunuch! Where's the strength here now?"

Fetch removed her knee, allowing the woman to pull away, retching. The katara stayed at Knob's throat.

"Jacintho!" Fetch called over her shoulder.

"How can I be of use?" came the bandit's unctuous reply from outside the cave.

"Get my stockbow and load it. Should be plenty of bolts around."

There was a pause. "Truly . . . the half-orcs within are quite large. And they look as if they very much wish to kill someone."

"So do I," Fetch proclaimed. "And he's under my knife. Reckon we will see who has the stronger desire."

The unseen cavern at her back filled with small, tense sounds. Fetch made sure to keep her blade and gaze firmly on Knob, both an unwavering promise should he act on the burning ire smoldering across his countenance.

Some frantic little noises were followed by Jacintho issuing a few whispered curses.

"Problem?" Fetch asked.

"I . . . cannot pull the string back."

Fucking frails. Fetch had forgotten that few could ready a thrum without the help of a crank. Her mind began racing for a solution. The moment Knob was out of danger, the Stains would attack.

"I got it," a familiar voice rumbled.

"There is another very large half-orc now," Jacintho dutifully informed.

Fetch smiled. "Yeah, that one is with me."

"We have trouble in here?" Oats asked. Ride with a mongrel long enough, you can tell when he is holding a weapon just from the way he sounds.

"No," Fetch answered, slowly withdrawing from Knob. "Just a small dispute between chiefs."

She backed up until Oats and Jacintho were on either side, both with loaded, leveled thrums.

Once in the tunnel, only two could stand abreast, so Fetch moved to the rear, leaving the others to cover their asses.

Oats eyed the katara as she passed. "The hells is that?"

"Had a pair sheathed to my hips this entire time, fool-ass."

"See if you notice what I got strapped after you've been bludgeoned by a corpse!"

"Fair point."

"Perhaps the bickering could wait until after we are safe," Jacintho suggested.

One of the Orc Stains stepped out into the tunnel, stockbow in hand.

Letting out a surprised chirp, Jacintho startled and his thrum let loose, sending a bolt shattering into the tunnel ceiling not far from the Stain's head. The mongrel ducked back into the safety of the cave.

Sheathing the foreign blade, Fetch snatched her stockbow from the brigand's hands, pushed him behind her and reloaded.

"We may be ignoring your little wet nurse's orders," she told Oats, the pair of them walking backward shoulder to shoulder.

"Already sent her to get my hog."

"That halfling can handle Ugfuck?" Fetch asked.

"He really likes her."

"Don't tell me she also hauled those coin sacks."

Oats grunted a laugh. "No. Those we will have to get."

"Jacintho," Fetch said. "Care to earn some silver?"

"You will find that I am faster and stronger when burdened with wealth," the wretch declared with pride.

A thought came to Fetch. "Oats? How did you know to come looking for me?"

"I saw that look you get when you're about to piss into a viper pit. Could have been beat with a hundred corpse-clubs and still seen *that* look."

They made their way back to Oats's cave with no further signs of pursuit. While Fetch watched the tunnel, Oats tied the money sacks together and helped Jacintho hoist the jingling yoke across his bony shoulders.

"We need to move fast," Fetch told them. "The Stains have their barbarians stabled in the same place as mine. If they get there first—"

"Say no more," Jacintho said, scampering past her. "I know these mines better than any. There are byways. Follow!"

The lanky bandit sped away.

"He really is faster loaded down with shine," Oats observed.

Jacintho made good on his word, leading them to the cave where Palla waited. The Orc Stains were nowhere to be found, though their hogs remained tethered.

Fetching slung her stockbow, motioned for Oats to cover the tunnel, and lifted the sacks off of Jacintho, slinging them across Palla's back. The hog snorted in complaint.

"Take off your hat," Fetch told Jacintho. The man merely stood, puzzled. "Hurry!"

She went to the bag and scooped out a fistful of coins. Realization sent Jacintho skipping to her side. Fetch filled the hat.

"Get gone," she said. "You don't want Knob and his boys to ever see you again."

"Best to stay with you, then."

Fetch snorted and untied Palla. "You don't want to go where we're bound, frail. And we don't have a mount to carry you."

Jacintho cocked an uncertain eye at the Orc Stains' barbarians.

"That's one way to die," Fetch told him.

"I could get a mule."

Oats let loose a chuckle from the cave entrance.

"Luck to you, Jacintho," Fetch said.

She led Palla into the tunnel and began heading out of the mine. Oats watched their backtrail.

Night still reigned when they emerged from the shaft, but morning was snapping at its heels.

Xhreka and Ugfuck were waiting. Oats's massive and incomprehensibly hideous hog stood quietly next to the halfling, her hand resting on one of his swine-yankers.

"Farewell, Idris," was all Xhreka said when Oats approached.

Fetching mounted and found the thrice looking up at her.

"She's owed some coin, chief."

"Of course. She can have it." Fetch looked at the halfling. "Or you can come with us."

Xhreka said nothing, but Oats let out a pleased, airy laugh.

"There could be a place for you in Winsome," Fetch told the little woman. "It won't be eas—"

Xhreka threw up a hand. "Yes, yes, life is difficult. I know. I'm coming. I was just trying to decide how to tell Idris I would rather ride with you. Ugfuck's smell is an insult to the earth."

TWENTY

WINSOME WAS WHOLE.

The breath of relief Fetching released upon seeing the walls still standing, the gate intact, the slopheads along the wall, was nearly an ecstasy. The ride back had been punishing, for hogs and riders, especially for Xhreka, whose legs cramped miserably after the first day, though she never complained. The pace Fetching set during the last leg, after crossing the River Lucia, bordered on madness. Now, after five days of hard riding, they were home. The slops on the wall called out a greeting and the gates opened.

The True Bastards rode out to meet them.

Polecat and Mead went straight to Oats, leaning over in their saddles to welcome him back. The meaty arm-clasps and violent embraces nearly knocked Xhreka off her place in front of Oats.

"Bring yourself back a pet, Oats?" Polecat asked, eyeing the halfling with an arch grin. "Must have been nice, having her at the perfect height to lick your ass while you fucked your hog these past months."

"Actually," Xhreka spoke up, "we just spit in my empty socket and he pokes that." She looked at Polecat and made to lift her eye patch. "Your cod's probably small enough. Want a go?"

Cat's grin grew. "Maybe."

Oats's hard, affectionate shove ended the exchange, everyone laughing and nodding appreciatively at the halfling.

"Well, you all aren't bones," Fetching observed. "I gather the Unyar supplies are helping."

"They are, chief," Mead answered. "We were able to relax the rationing a little. Still, without our own crops—"

"The crops will be dealt with," Fetching told him. "Let's be glad we're better than we were. Any further sign of the dogs?"

"None."

More good fortune. So much that Fetch could not trust it.

"There's a heap to discuss, and I need to hear all that happened while I was away. Soon as these hogs are seen to, we will meet."

"That may have to wait, chief," Mead said.

"Why?"

"We have guests," Shed Snake answered, but said nothing more.

Fetch swept her hoof with a hard look. "Someone want to fucking speak up?"

"Tell her, Dumb Door," Polecat said with a tilt of his head.

The mute mongrel frowned at him.

"It's the Sons of Perdition," Mead said, seeing Fetch was not amused. "Ten of them showed up just before dusk yesterday, their chief among them."

"And you let them in?" Fetch demanded.

"A hoofmaster rode up to our gates. Figured it was better to let him in than risk giving offense and souring an alliance."

"Except that's ten more mongrels we're feeding, Mead!"

The young rider looked momentarily sheepish, but he soon set his jaw, lifted his chin. "I made a decision."

Shit. He'd had to, hadn't he? And for more than this. He'd been chief in all but name and may get that if she kept acting the snapping dog, testing his patience. She was soon to test his trust.

Fetch let out a breath and squeezed Mead on the shoulder. "Tell me they are honoring the rationing."

"They are."

"We're watching them close, chief," Polecat added.

"Not out here, we're not," Fetch said. "I'll go see what Father wants and get these mouths off our lot. You all show Oats to his bunk. He may have forgotten where it is."

They rode through the gates, a whole hoof once again. Almost.

Fetch hopped off Palla and turned him over to Sence.

"Welcome home, chief," the waiting slop said.

"Did you just look your chief in the eye, hopeful?" Polecat barked, making Sence jump. Ducking his head, he set to his duty.

"Sure you don't want me to come with you?" Oats asked, lowering Xhreka down from the saddle with one arm.

"Or me?" Mead offered, a bit too quickly.

"No," Fetch answered them both. "I'll handle it. Just tell me where they are."

THE SONS OF PERDITION had been placed in an old storehouse. Big enough to house them and their hogs, but far from comfortable, discouraging them from staying long. Clever Mead. It was near noon, so Father and his boys milled inside, out of the sun. The old mongrel was sitting on a milking stool, showing two of his riders how to make a complicated plait out of leather thongs.

"You ever need to make a repair to your tack, boys, this is how you do it. Take the time. Make it right and sound."

Father looked up from his instruction when Fetch's shadow intruded upon the lesson. His face was composed of wrinkles and scars, and the wisdom bought with them.

"Keep at it," he told the riders sitting at his feet, and stood. He was short for a half-orc, though likely age had shrunk him somewhat. Fetch stayed where she was while Father trudged to meet her in the wide doorway.

"Didn't expect to ride here ahead of you," he said in greeting, though there was a kernel of chide buried in the tone.

"Didn't expect any but my hoof to be waiting."

"Well, the ride to Strava isn't a short one from my lot. Figured it best to stop here on the way back. Save me an ass-tanning, later."

Fetch clenched her jaw. What was this shit? The Bastards' lot was not on the way back for the Sons. Their lands were almost due south from Strava. The old coffin-dodger either thought the sun now rose in the south, or believed she was a complete fool and didn't know the arrangement of the damn Lots. Still, she swallowed the building ire. Having already made an enemy of one hoofmaster, she wasn't in a hurry to piss this one off as well.

"Can we walk a span?" Father suggested, before lowering his voice. "Get stiff now if I laze too long."

Fetch nodded and began ambling for the far end of the compound.

Father took an appraising look around. "You've done good here. It isn't the Kiln—that was a hard loss for the Lots—but it isn't nothing."

There was silence between them almost all the way to the hog pens. Finally, Father spoke again.

"You talked with the new frails." It was not a question.

Fetch looked at the old mongrel's wrinkled profile. "I did."

"Clever of you to ride down there while the rest of us were jawing on the ridge." A disapproving gurgle rose from Father's throat. "Fucking Knob! That hairless ape doesn't see anything beyond the reach of his sword or his cock. Not me. I heard you that morning, trying to tell us what's brewing."

"And?"

"Do you think these frails are a danger?"

They reached the pens. Dumb Door was working one of the twisters, but was out of earshot. Not that he could repeat anything he heard.

Fetch rested a foot upon the lowest fence rail and watched the young boar being broken to the saddle. Taking a deep breath she gave Father her opinion.

"Eight hundred men, most of them trained warriors born to the saddle, on horses half-covered in steel, led by a man proven not only in war, but conquest. Yes. That's dangerous. But to who? Right now, not us. The Unyars are closest and still outnumber them."

Father rested his elbows on the fence. "But will Zirko send his followers to war against them?"

"Surely you can decide that on your own."

"He's never been afraid to fight. But he won't do it for the mongrel hoofs. Or even the Lots. No . . . Zirko will only go to war to protect his own folk. I don't think he would ally with the swaddle-heads against us, but you can damn well count on him letting them ride right by so long as his people are left untouched."

Fetching was not overly fond of the priest, but she found herself defending him. "He marshaled the Unyars last year when the orcs made their move. Fought during the Great Incursion too."

Father chuckled. "I know that last part better than you, girl. I was there. But their aid was slow in coming, and even when committed, they were looking out for Strava beyond all else."

"We're no different. We place our lots over all else. Think you all made that clear. Hells, right now all I'm thinking about is getting you and your brood off Bastard land before you eat what little we can spare, which is nothing."

Father nodded slowly, and when he spoke next, it was as if he spoke only to himself. "The Bastards are not in a good way. And the Sons aren't here to make it tougher on you."

"You're not making it easier."

"But perhaps we could."

Fetch stared at the old mongrel, waiting on that to be explained, making it clear she had little patience left. Father was unaffected. He met her glower and smiled, reflection softening his crags.

"When the Incursion was done, I never thought what it might be like this many years later. Never conceived I would live this long. I don't know if there was ever a plan for the Lots beyond the next sunrise. I do know the chiefs collaborated more back then. The first master of the Sons—called him Dark Hog—he rode regular to the Shards, the Tuskers, Bastards. Likely most of it was about the poor wretches bearing that damn plague."

Fetch imagined the old mongrel had the right there. The plague-bearers, each a living weapon, were what really kept the orcs and Hispartha from making any more earnest attempts on Ul-wundulas. By the time Fetch became a Grey Bastard, the Claymaster was the only one remaining, and only his descent into madness, hastened by

Crafty's influence, brought that truth back to the Lots. A few old-timers had kept the secret; Warbler, Father obviously, their knowledge all but useless. The truth of the past mattered little when the truth of the present was a daily fight to stay alive.

But hells, now that history had been laid straight, these fossils loved to wallow in it.

"I was the slop-wrangler in those days," Father droned on, "rearing the new blood, so I didn't leave our lands much, but there was hardly a moon's turn that we didn't open our gates to Coffin Moth or the Claymaster. I weren't privy to all those talks between the founders, what was being hatched, if anything. It didn't matter. We had tusk-fucked the thicks back across the Deluged and told Hispartha we were to be counted. Yes, we were left stuck between the steaming asshole of Dhar'gest and Hispartha's sweaty seed skin, but we were still proud. Proud and belligerent."

Father grew silent. Fetch hoped he was finished and was about to reach a point, but a deep breath signaled more to come.

"I want to say something fool-ass like 'And then it all suddenly went wrong,' but the truth is not so simple and memory is a tricky thing. Seasons came and went, Betrayers waxed and waned, orc raids, poor harvests, unworthy slopheads. Thinking back it all just makes me tired. Dark Hog had been dead for years and the Sons found themselves being led by a drunkard. We refer to our fellow riders as brothers, but after so long whipping young mongrels into something with grit, there was not a sworn member of my hoof that I didn't see as a son. The name our founder gave us took on new meaning . . . possessed me. Not even a word I once knew, 'possessed.' But it did. We weren't just the Sons, they were *my* Sons. I challenged the chief, won, took his place, and changed my hoof name. But leadership didn't come with allies. Like all the other hoofs, the Sons of Perdition had gone from a band of proud and belligerent half-breeds to something . . . shrunk. We were all just guarding our little parcels of badland, rarely sharing news and never meeting. A patrol rider would arrive from another hoof, maybe, but never another chief."

Fetch could not hold her tongue any longer. "Am I going to be as old as you by the time you tell me what you are about?"

If Father was offended, he gave no sign. He really did look damn tired.

"The mongrel hoofs are divided, girl. And not just by the distance between our lands. You saw that at Strava. As you said, we are all just looking out for our own, scraping in the dust for what little Ul-wundulas has to give. For all Knob's boasting, not one of us is as strong now as the day we were founded. Hells, I have more boys than some of you combined and it's still an old mongrel's weak piss stream compared to what it was.

"We should not be meeting to worry over eight hundred frails! In the beginning, twice that many would never have dared come. Ul-wundulas may always be stuck between a hammer and an anvil, but the half-orcs have a choice of letting that break them or harden them. If we are in pieces, we are already broken."

At last, Fetch understood. "You want to unite the hoofs."

Father gave her a look both shocked and relieved, as if he dared not say it, feared she would not see it, but now that it was voiced, worried about the consequences. He gave a wet grunt and shook his coarse, white head.

"Not me. Too fucking old. Never see it through. Hells, it will take years, if it's even possible."

Again the old mongrel's lips drew tight, but he had more to say, and this time, Fetch waited without agitation until his words again began to flow.

"Some would say we were simply fortunate last year. But if even half the rumors are true about the Claymaster, what he planned . . . that doesn't get foiled by luck alone. Repelling the thicks took more than that. We all fought, but only because we were all warned. If the Lots have a hope of enduring *any* coming threat, we need the one who did that. We need the leader of the Grey Bastards."

Fetching's throat constricted. "You mean Jackal."

Father nodded. "That's why I've come. To find out where he is, when he will return."

"I don't know," Fetch said, her voice coming out a whisper. It didn't matter. Father was too busy talking to hear.

"I had hoped to see him at Strava. It's said Zirko favors him.

Duster—that's one of my boys—fought with Jackal during the Betrayer. Says he saved his life and that the Unyars damn near worship him. Claims he's the keenest fighter he has ever seen, and I always take what my Sons tell me as truth. I need to know when he will come back, so he can start knitting us together."

Fetching pushed away from the fence and began walking away.

"You refuse to tell me?"

"I can't tell you what I don't know," Fetch declared, spinning around. "He may never come back, old man. Understand? That's why he is not chief of the Bastards, the *True* Bastards. I am! I was voted to the seat."

Father's face soured. "Would you have been? Can you tell me I would not be speaking to Jackal now had he not gone fuck-knows-where?"

"Take your boys and get off my fucking lot."

She made to leave again, but Father reached out, stalling her with a firm but unaggressive hand upon the wrist.

"My boys follow me out of love. I've striven to make that true, so I know of what I say. Your riders love you, girl. It's the root of their loyalty. For some hoofmasters it's strength or cunning or fear. Not us. But the love for a father, something no mongrels know, is a vastly different thing from the stirring in their breeches they feel when looking at you, something all mongrels know."

Fetch snatched her arm free. "That's not why they follow me."

"Maybe not all," Father conceded, "but tell me that hatchet-faced lech and the lackhand don't want to bed you. Could smell it on them the moment I asked after you."

"Doesn't matter," Fetch seethed.

"It does matter! Lust won't keep a hoof together. What I've built with the Sons won't last past my death, but what you have here won't last another season. Jackal needs to return if the Bastards have any chance. He needs to return if the Lots have any chance."

"He is *not* coming back."

She didn't know if that was a lie, and did not care. The conviction in her words made it true for Father.

The old mongrel slumped. "Then show your brethren their love isn't wasted. Don't let them rot here for a lost cause. Disband the Bastards. I will take them all into the Sons. Your townsfolk too. We can all ride out of here together, stronger than we were. Once you've seen them safely installed at Mongrel's Cradle, you can go nomad, perhaps find Jackal and bring him home."

Fetch felt her brows draw together. "Nomad? You would take my brothers and not allow me to stay with them?"

"Girl," Father huffed, "I am old, but not yet mad. Not like the Claymaster. Ain't blind either. You think I didn't see those two training with your slops? We half-breed men may be sterile, but I swear to you the day will come when I sire children before the Sons of Perdition allow daughters within its ranks."

Fetch leaned close, spoke through clenched teeth. "I hope you can still straddle a razor and ride hard with your creaking joints, because if you and your boys are even a dust smudge on my horizon by the time I come back from taking a piss, there will be one less hoof in the Lots and *I swear* it won't be mine."

Leaving the incensed old mongrel, she pushed through the paddock gate to make sure the slops on stable duty turned the Sons' hogs out quick as they could. Little Tel was in the main pen, pushing a heaping wheelbarrow to the gong pile. The ten additional hogs were spewing almost as much shit as Father.

"Tel!" Fetch called as she stalked across the pen. "The Sons are leaving. Who else is with you?"

The small mongrel halted, jaw falling at the sight of the chief.

"Yes, I'm fucking back. Now, where's the other hand? I'll help. The three of us are getting this done. Who else has this duty?"

"A-Ahlamra. Chief."

"Why isn't she with you, then?"

Little Tel pointed to the stable. "She's, uh, she's in there."

"She not helping you? Did the pretty frailing not deign to soil herself with hogshit?"

Without waiting for an answer Fetch made her way over. Entering the stable, she didn't immediately see Ahlamra, but even the low walls separating the stalls could have hidden her if she was bent behind a shovel. The piles of manure outside the first few stalls gave testament that the girl had not shirked the labor, unless all this was Tel's doing. As Fetch made her way down the aisle she was startled when a figure stood up within the last stall on the left, issuing a satisfied sigh as it stretched.

It was one of the Sons. The tattoos on his bare back made that plain.

Fetch's steps quickened, cold fingers kneading her gut. Her hand went to the grip of her sword as she reached the open stall door.

The Son turned at her arrival. He was surprised to find her standing there, but masked it quickly with a small grin. His breeches were around his knees, his erect cock only just beginning to soften.

"Chief," the mongrel said, drawing the word out. "Just came to check on my hog, found I could be of some use here."

He was blocking most of her view, but Fetch could see someone behind him. She could also see his weapons propped in the corner, well out of his reach. She shoved him aside to reveal Ahlamra just beginning to stand, naked to the skin.

But unharmed.

Fetch's eyes searched desperately for the signs. The blemishes left by rough hands. The tears and snot running down a begrimed face. The blood.

They weren't there.

Ahlamra had smudges on her knees, a piece of straw in her hair. Nothing more.

But it was her stare that proved it. There was no fear, no pain, just the surprise of being discovered, and even that was scant.

"Get out," Fetch commanded the Son.

He pulled his breeches up, still smiling, retrieved the rest of his kit, and withdrew.

Ahlamra made no move to dress. She stood, making no apologies, seeking no pardons. It was the first time her traditionally demure stare did not seek the ground.

Fetch grit her teeth and stared back.

The beauty of this woman's face had been undeniable from the first, but Fetch had not suspected her to have a figure, save that of a boy. Standing there now, Ahlamra was revealed as no waif. Small, yes, but far from delicate. There was nothing fragile in the flatness of her stomach, the hard set of her shoulders. The curve of hips and breasts, so easy to miss when clothed, were a soft complement to the compact strength of her form. The blood of the orc had not diluted within Ahlamra, it had distilled, producing a veneer of human softness over flawless steel.

"You're not raped," Fetch said.

"No. He was comely. I sought comfort."

"Comfort," Fetch scoffed. "Life in a hoof contains little comfort, girl. Hells certain not for a damn slop! Was that the ploy? Convince him to finish these last stalls for you?"

"Earnest labor is not in his nature. Likely he would have been slow and careless. I did not need him for the mucking. I got from him what I wished."

"In defiance of my command!"

Ahlamra's calm demeanor faltered slightly. "He was not of this hoof. I did not think it was a defiance."

"I told you no whoring!"

"There was no coin involved. I desired him. Forgive me. I did not know this was a trespass."

"A trespass? You were assigned to mucking the stables. You had a fucking task. And that task wasn't fucking!"

"You are right, of course. This life is new. I am finding habits of the old difficult to shed, it appears."

Fetch sneered at her. She could just imagine what the old life had been for this woman who spoke more confidently naked than clothed, whose idea of comfort was muddy knees and a mouthful of spend.

"The Sons are riding on. Put your damn clothes on and leave with them."

To her credit, Ahlamra did not panic. She did not plead. "May I ask a question?"

Fetch gave no reply, waited.

"Do you recall I come from Sardiz?"

Fetch could only shake her head.

"It was swallowed by Tyrkania long before I was born, yet we kept some of our ways. Those we were allowed to keep. The sultans certainly kept the House of Lustrous Gaze. Hearing the name of this house, what do you think it was?"

"A brothel," Fetch admitted.

Ahlamra's words did not waver, her stare remained even. "Nothing so vulgar. To begin, it is an orphanage, though only for girls. It is also a school. From childhood I learned to dance, sing, read and write in more languages than you can name, compose poetry in those same languages, play instruments with perfection. All this and more was my daily tutelage in a rich house of flowing fountains and shaded gardens and screened balconies that overlooked a street crawling with lice-ridden beggar children of similar age to myself. And yes, age brought training in seduction and men's pleasure. This was no source of shame, for the women of my house were celebrated and I knew little else. I know much more of the world beyond that house now and still I am not ashamed. The skills I attained with time and training and dedication provided advantage. Tell me, chief, are you shamed by your skill with a blade, your accuracy with a stock-bow, your prowess astride a hog? Are you ashamed of the advantages you strived for to survive in your homeland?"

The answer was simple, yet the question caused Fetch to hesitate. "No."

"No. Here you would die swiftly without them. You would die swiftly in my city even with them. Sardiz is prosperous and peaceful and you would starve because your skills would mean little, and where they could be used is the province of men. I could have lived my days in comfort and splendor, yet I came here, to Ul-wundulas to find the mongrel woman who spat at the provinces of men. I wished to master new skills. Your skills. I found you. Yet you are casting me out. Not for defying you, nor for the dalliance while I should have been at work, which I regret. No. You are casting me out because you judge me to be nothing but a useless whore."

Slowly, Ahlamra recovered her garments. Fetch found the calm fury in the movements of this delicate, smaller, weaker woman difficult to look upon. Soon she was dressed and made to leave the stall.

Fetch caught her arm, rougher than she'd intended. "You'll never be a rider."

Ahlamra's chin dipped as her gaze sought the ground. "I know you think so."

"No . . ." Fetch released her. "That was what I was told. By a girl I was raised with. A friend. We never could understand the other's desires. Turned us hateful in the end. Because I proved her wrong. And she . . . proved me right. She wanted nothing but to be a bed-warmer and ended up without the grit for even that."

"And you think me the same."

Fetch took a breath. "Perhaps you're stronger than she was. I'm seeing that. But you'll never ride a hog, Ahlamra. Never rack a thrum. There's not enough mongrel muscle in you. Just too damn small. With time maybe we could make you passable with a tulwar, but the Bastards ain't in a place to coddle you. So we won't. Instead, I reckon it best to wager on the skills you already have. The ones we don't."

Ahlamra's eyes raised. "Meaning?"

"Meaning there's a way you can serve this hoof. Just not here. And it's going to require a thrice-blood's weight in grit."

"Tell me."

TWENTY-ONE

—

AS SOON AS THE GATE CLOSED on the Sons of Perdition, the Bastards gathered. Within the cooper's shop, six faces regarded Fetching from around the big rectangular table that dominated the center of the room. Oats was opposite her at the foot, Mead at her right.

No more secrets.

"There is a heap to discuss," Fetch began. "Mead's told you most, but there's more you need to hear from me. But I hate repeating myself, so first let's see if there is going to be another brother to sit in on this meet."

Pleased smiles grew on the faces of Polecat, Mead, and Dumb Door.

"Some of you believe Abril is ready to leave the slops," Fetch continued. "Who is putting his name forward?"

"Me," Mead said.

Across from him, Dumb Door knocked twice on the table.

"There's the required two," Fetch said. "So let's ride this pig and see where we are. Abril came up at the orphanage here in Winsome, began as a slophead at the Kiln, endured Grocer . . ." The name of the Grey Bastards' fallen quartermaster added some grim reflection to most of the faces around the table. "... returned to Winsome after fostering with the Tusked Tide—it should be said not all the slops did—and has worked hard for this hoof since. But it takes more than being a strong worker to become a sworn brother. So, since I did not put his name forward, I want to hear from you. Mead?"

"His orcish is good, chief. He's never shirked a duty that I know of, and he's tireless on watch."

Fetch nodded and turned to Polecat.

"Abril is solid on patrol," he said. "Doesn't get distracted, despite his antics. Keeps his bearings. And digs a ditch like I lick quim, with vigor and very little wandering."

"That ditch is also dry and resistant," Shed Snake muttered, coaxing a snort from Oats.

Fetch moved on. "Dumb Door? How is he with the hogs?"

A meaty thumb went up.

"His hand-fighting needs work," Hoodwink said without waiting for a prompt. "Passable with the tulwar, but with a knife he's weak."

Mead came to the hopeful's defense. "Weak compared to whom, Hood? You? That's like saying he's not as good a shot as the chief. Some walls can't be scaled."

"How *is* he with a thrum?" Fetching asked. She had her own opinion, but wanted to see the hoof's response.

"Better than me now," Mead said with a forced laugh.

"Good enough," Polecat said.

Shed Snake was less certain. "He hasn't had much chance with targets on the move."

Hoodwink dipped his chin in agreement.

"I also have some concerns there," Fetch said.

Mead scrubbed at his Tine mane in frustration. "He brought that deer down and I'm sure it didn't stand still to let him. Fed the town too."

"Oats?" Fetch prodded.

The thrice had been quiet, but that was understandable, having been away. He took a deep breath. "He wasn't ready when I left. Bit of a jester from what I recall, not that it discounts him. But I trust what I've heard and can weigh it. I can vote."

"Hood, Warbler left you his vote, yes?"

A nod.

"I have Jackal's," Oats said.

"All right, brothers," Fetch said. "Raise your hand if you believe Abril is ready to join the True Bastards."

Mead, Dumb Door, and Polecat gave their votes readily. Neither Oats nor Hoodwink raised a hand. Shed Snake was reluctant. This was his first vote, clearly torn between his friendship with Mead, his own doubts, and a desire to please his chief. He was eyeing Fetch, trying to discern which way she was leaning, scratching at his scarred arm. Fetch kept her face blank, her palms on the table. Snake needed to become confident with his place at this table, vote his own mind. It was common for fresh-sworns to behave with deference to their chief, but the heart of a hoof should not be made up of bootlickers.

No one pressured him, honoring the tradition.

At last, with only a small, rueful glance at Mead, Shed Snake shook his head.

Fetch looked to Oats.

"Jack would like him," the thrice decided. "Yes."

"Warbler is a no," Hood said.

That left Fetching the deciding vote. The hoof watched her, waiting.

Any other day, she would have made her mind in a heartbeat. Abril needed more time. But Father's words were nibbling at her mind, damn him. The Bastards—hells, all the hoofs—were dwindling. They needed sworn brothers. Slopheads were not bound to a hoof. They could leave at any moment. Several had not returned after the Kiln fell, solid hopefuls, and still more in the time since. Fetch did not think Abril was about to abandon Winsome, but the days ahead were likely to reap fresh crops of hardship, enough to test the loyalty of even the staunchest among them. Admitting him into the ranks would solidify not only his loyalty, but that of the other hopefuls as well. It was important the other slops saw that it was possible to earn a place among the brethren, give them a reason to keep toiling and training.

Burying her reservations, Fetch put up her hand.

There was back-slapping and table-thumping from Abril's supporters, immediately taken up by those who did not cast votes in his favor. This was a mongrel hoof, they did not waste time sulking over a difference in opinion. A new brother was a cause to celebrate. There was a second vote that needed to be called for Marrow, but it would have to wait for another day. Abril deserved to have his own initiation.

"Who is going to get him?" Fetch asked, smiling.

"Should be Hood," Polecat offered. "He'll suspect if it's me or Mead."

Hoodwink's taut-skinned face peered at Polecat, unblinking.

"Ooooorrrr," Polecat amended, "maybe Oats."

Oats shrugged. "What am I telling him?"

The mirth in the room became palpable.

Polecat's mischievous smile was nearly cracking his face in half. "Tell him the chief got drunk and has stripped down to dance for all of us."

It was Fetch's turn to give him an unblinking stare.

"Ooooorrrr you could say it's me."

Shed Snake curled his lip. "No one wants to see that, Cat."

Dumb Door banged on the wall to get the room's attention. Beaming, he stood up, bent over, and made quick gestures away from his rump, flicking his fingers outward.

The hoof began to howl.

"You oafs get any louder and all of Winsome will know what you're cooking," Fetch warned, trying to keep her own laughter from spilling over.

Mead was wiping away a tear. "That's it! We tell him Dumb Door has the galloping trots and has shit-sprayed everywhere. . . ."

Polecat was grabbing his sides, unable to breathe.

Shed Snake looked at Oats. "Make sure he brings a bucket."

"There is a water ration," Hoodwink put in. "He can't use a bucket."

Unable to tell if the cadaverous mongrel was adding to the jest or being earnest, the room erupted in fresh, barely stifled hilarity.

Trying to shake his own face into something straight, Oats went for the door.

"Wait," Fetch said. "Still needs a hoof name."

The room stilled.

Shed Snake gave a solemn nod. "I got it."

Shortly, Oats returned, holding the door open and gesturing inside with gruff apathy. "The mess is in here."

A very determined-looking Abril entered, carrying a bundle of dry rags. He stopped short, seeing the hoof standing around the table, his confused stare taking them in before settling on the objects resting upon the table. A saddle, draped with a brigand.

Abril threw his arms into the air, sending the rags sailing, and let loose a whoop.

The True Bastards began laughing again, cheering for their newest rider.

Fetching picked the brigand up and approached Abril. The room quieted. Abril attempted to relax, but was still trembling when Fetch helped him into the armored vest.

Stepping back, she looked him in the eyes. "What are you?"

Abril's voice nearly broke. "I'm a True Bastard, chief."

"Brothers?" Fetching asked the room, still looking at her newest rider. "What do we know he is going to do?"

"LIVE IN THE SADDLE! DIE ON THE HOG!"

Abril was nodding fiercely, eyes welling, throat and jaw clenched.

Fetching stepped back and Shed Snake came around the table. He motioned at Abril with mock disdain.

"This fuck and I grew up together. Even before the slops, we were foundlings together. I was quiet, too afraid of Beryl to step out of line. Not this one. Anything got broken, any food went missing, any of the girls came crying, Beryl always knew who it was. We all did. But she had a word for it." Shed Snake stepped forward, held his arm out to Abril, fingers spread. "Welcome to the True Bastards. Culprit."

Abril let go of his birth name and seized the offered hand, allowed himself to be pulled into a hard embrace.

Fetching caught Oats's eye. He winked at her and she smiled, both remembering their own days in the orphanage and who it was that used to get the pair of them in trouble.

One by one, the rest of the hoof welcomed their new brother in his own way; a bearlike shake from Oats, a flick in the cods from Polecat, completely ignored by Hoodwink.

"I'm getting my first hoof tattoo right here!" Culprit announced, slapping the shaved half of his head. "Cat, will you do it tonight?"

"Somewhere you can't see what I'm doing? Absolutely! What do you think, brothers? A cock and fruits?"

Abril pointed a stern finger at Polecat. "It's got to be a Bastards sign."

"*My* cock and fruits?"

Traditionally, there would be wine, and plenty of it, but rationing made drunken revelry impossible. Instead, Fetch gave out the pieces of Zahracene fruit she had Mead set aside for the hoof. There were some dubious squints, but Oats had sampled a piece on the ride back from the Smelteds and cut into his with gusto, encouraging the rest to do the same. Soon the room was filled with surprised sighs of pleasure and the sounds of errant juice being sucked off fingers. Mead made sure to collect all the seeds.

When it was all done, she motioned for them to gather around the table once more. "We got business."

Chairs and stools scraped along the rough flooring as the brethren mustered around the table.

One brother was still standing, looking lost.

"Culprit?" Fetch said. "You want to move your fucking saddle and sit down so we can get to this?"

Blinking hard, Culprit jumped to the task, surrounded by good-natured chuckles.

Fetching looked at her seven riders. "No more secrets."

And she made good on that.

At last, weary with the sound of her own voice, she had revealed all about her illness and the sludge.

A pensive silence settled within the cooper's shop, every mongrel chewing on what was said. Fetch waited for the challenge to her leadership, tried not to consider who would back her and failed. Oats, with Jackal's vote, was two. Hoodwink would remain loyal, but she wasn't sure what he'd say for Warbler. Culprit had just reached the table. He wouldn't be able to conceive going against her. The rest, however, she could not guess.

Dumb Door was the first to respond, signing a question to Fetch. The simple generosity of it nearly made her step down as chief. She didn't deserve these mongrels.

"Yes," she answered, "I'm hale now. No longer sick."

"Glad to hear it, chief," Polecat said. "Though I will say, you would have made a far better-looking Sludge Man." He leaned left and nudged Mead. "Remember that fucking frail? Hells, what an inbred!"

Mead humored him with a grin, but it melted back to a brood. He was wooden, staring at the table. Polecat didn't notice, his attention turned to the rest of the brethren.

"Me and the chief were the only ones here that fought him. Oats was out cold and Mead was nursemaiding him. Hood was . . . where were you? Ah, who cares a shit! The rest of you weren't sworn yet. Fucking fortunate, too. Me and Hobnail were running to help the chief and that slack-mouthed bog dweller—"

"Nearly killed you," Fetch cut him off. "He was a madman and a horror. And, thankfully, all that's left of him is sitting trapped beneath Strava."

Mead's silence was the only sign of ill feeling in the hoof. There was a calm in the room that took Fetch a moment to grasp. Relief when there should have been anger, obedience where there should have been rebellion. Her brothers accepted what she'd told them, accepted her solution. Yet she knew what they would *not* accept. An offer to step down. And she understood.

The True Bastards had their chief back.

She had been taken from them, and had returned. It was a victory against Hispartha, against the devil-dogs. It was a victory against Ul-wundulas.

Once again, Fetch was forced to face her predecessor. By taking the chief's seat she was more akin to him than she ever thought possible to stomach. From all accounts, the Claymaster had been canny, powerful, and feared in the beginning. That's what made him the warlord who won the Lots. Perhaps the bitter, hateful, mad fuck was always there, eating away at the rest. Certainly that was all that was left at the end, but Fetch had to accept she'd known a chief diminished by age, pain, and the harshness of hoof life. Why then had he lasted? Why had Warbler's challenge failed? Why had there not been a dozen more before Jackal threw his ax in defiance? Now she looked upon the answer.

A hoof rallies around power, strength, but that's not what holds them. Their loyalty is bound to a conviction that the one leading them has the grit to stand longest in the storm, the one who will bear the hardest tasks so they don't have to. Father was wrong about her. And about himself. This had nothing to do with lust or love or fear. This was about backing the mongrel who had the appetite to eat punishment and come back for more. Hard as living in the badlands could be, it was nothing compared to living it in the hoofmaster's chair. Why would any want to issue challenge and take that on when there was another willing to stand between them and the flying bolts? What wouldn't they forgive to keep that protection?

"What's the move now, chief?"

Fetch wasn't certain which of them had asked the question. Wasn't sure it was even a voice in the room and not one inside her head. No, not her head. It was the sound made by her heart every time it beat.

"Hispartha will be outside our gates again one day soon," she said. "Either looking for me, or Jackal, or just because their reclamation of Ul-wundulas puts us in their path. We'll all die on that day. And that's if this fucking Ruin thick hasn't beat them to the slaughter. The only way to survive is not be here when they come."

The comfortable calm in the room vanished.

"What are you saying, chief?" Shed Snake asked.

"That it's time to abandon Winsome."

"You jesting right now?" Oats asked, his confusion bordering on hostile.

Fetch knew she'd hurt him with this. That's why she avoided telling him on the journey back.

"Home is the hoof, Oats," she said, wishing now she hadn't waited.

"Not for the townsfolk," Shed Snake said.

Dumb Door knocked on the table in agreement.

Fetch nodded. "They will have to leave."

"Where?" Culprit asked, spooked.

"The Tusked Tide?" Snake offered. "They took them in once before."

Fetch would only give the truth. "Boar Lip won't have anything else to do with us."

Polecat leaned back in his chair, spread his hands, and gave a mocking, searching look about the cooper's shop. "Then where?"

"The Sons."

"That shriveled seed sack that leads them thinks we're a lost cause!" Polecat was close to spitting with anger. "You think I didn't talk to some of his boys? Hells, half the Lots already believe we're dead. The other half has simply forgotten us. We go to the Sons or any other mongrel hoof and beg them to take our folk, word will spread across Ul-wundulas that we are done."

"But we won't be."

The entire table looked at Mead.

"Think on it," he said. "A hoof is riders. Half-orcs on hogs. Our creed doesn't say anything about fortresses and farms. The Fangs of Our Fathers don't bother with such things and none are saying they should disband."

"Mead"—Polecat could not keep the chastisement from his voice—"listen to yourself. You're encouraging us to give up on the people we are supposed to protect."

"I am. If it saves them *and* the hoof, then yes, I am. Chief's right. We are barely feeding them now. They will start abandoning Winsome before long as it is. Maybe one day this hoof will be a power in the Lots again, maybe build a fortress to rival the Kiln. But that's not where we are now! We are on the edge of starvation and assailed by shit we can't fight. We are trying to hold on to something that died with the Claymaster. I say we take these people somewhere they can at least feel safe and then we can focus on making this hoof strong again."

"And what about our slops?" Oats challenged, clearly not happy with Mead's reasoning. "We just cast them all aside too?"

Mead's answer was calm, cold. Correct. "Half of them will desert wherever we take the townsfolk. We saw that last year when most of our hopefuls decided they had more hope with the Tide. Let them. It's less mouths. We will figure out which ones just want to wear a brigand and which ones are True Bastards."

Oats growled in his throat. "And what about the True Bastards? Where are we going to go?"

"Dog Fall," Mead replied.

Culprit gawked at Fetch as if she'd been the one to answer. "The Tines?"

Polecat was the next to entreat her. "We're really going to go hide behind the elves?"

"They're the only ones who know how to fight the *asily'a kaga arkhu*," Mead said.

The foreign words only increased Cat's agitation. "We're going to abandon our land for *that*? Let the orcs walk right through because one of their hoodoo cunts is skulking around? We haven't seen hide nor hair of those dogs since the first night they came."

"*You* haven't," Fetch said.

"It's a fair point, though," Oats said, jumping on the chance for the discussion to turn. "Fetch, you said yourself he let you live. Mead got through with the Unyar supplies. Nothing bothered us the entire ride from the Smelteds. Don't think any of us would pretend to know what that orc was doing, but looks like he's moved on."

Mead leaned forward, pressed a finger into the table. "That orc will keep coming at us. Wager on it. Even *if* he leaves us alone, Hispartha won't. Kalbarca won't be the end of it. Are none of you hearing the chief?"

"I'm hearing the chief say we're fleeing our lot and just handing it to the orcs," Polecat said. "You're riding that crazed hog with her because you think it's galloping for Tine land."

Mead threw up his hand. "Not hearing me either, then."

"I heard you when you came back from Strava and told me there are now some dune-humping frails on the Rutters' lot, and now the chief's telling me they're going to have this one!"

Dumb Door cut off the growing argument between the two by snapping his fingers. He pointed at Hoodwink before splaying a hand in the semblance of antlers on his head.

"There's an idea," Shed Snake said. "Chief, why can't Hood go to the Tines? He knows Warbler best. Then we can stay and—"

Fetch smacked the table. "Enough! None of us can stay. None. We do, we die. Now this is happening. I don't know where just yet, but we *are* going. Winsome can't sustain us, can't protect us. We will never be better provisioned to leave than we are now. But it's still going to require time. The people will be resistant to leave, so we—"

"No."

Polecat's hand jerked up, came down, and slammed a knife into the table.

The quivering steel was all that moved for an eternity.

Fetch took a breath. "Cat, listen—"

"I am! I did. Pardons, chief, but no. Bastards are going to die, I say we die here, on our land. Nowhere else. We proved we were willing to do it once. How is this different from that?" His hatchet face swept the table. "Brothers, it's not. So, I say no. We stay. If you all disagree then the chief can put this dagger through my fucking eye. That's the code. But I'll die before I take leave of another lot. Today, if I must."

Fetch rested her hands on the table, the slight movement commanding the attention of all. "He's right. True Bastards, the decision to leave Winsome has been challenged. Stick a knife if you think we should remain."

Dumb Door stood, drew his knife and pushed it into the table without rancor.

"I am with the chief," Hoodwink said. Yet even as his thin voice declared his support, he slid a knife between the slats of the table, smooth and silent. "This is for Warbler."

The pale mongrel did not fear to look at Fetching after he'd done it, and there was no remorse in the unblinking eyes. She gave him a nod. Warbler had been ousted from the hoof, spent nearly two decades away before being able to return only to leave again, willingly, to help a plague-stricken child. But his heart was ever in Winsome. Hood was right, the old thrice would never agree that the hoof should leave.

Shed Snake's knife was now in his hand, but he peered at the blade for a long time, almost puzzled at its presence. At last, as if the feel of it were burning him worse than the Al-Unan fire, he buried it in the wood.

Four votes against. Fetch only had herself and Hood.

Mead looked ready to flip the entire table as he chewed on growing consternation. "I'm with the chief."

Three with her.

None could believe when Culprit's knife struck. Fetch struggled not to glare. Not that the youngblood had the stones to look at her. So much for her faith in the loyalty of fresh-sworns.

Oats remained seated at the foot, trunk-arms crossed. Slowly, he pulled the kerchief off his head and scratched at his pate.

"Jackal told me when he left to stay right with you, so I know what he'd do."

Four. Fetch held Oats's gaze.

"But he doesn't control my vote."

Oats smote the table with his knife without standing, splitting one of the boards and hammering home the decision for the hoof to stay.

Fetch did not allow anything to control the next instant, not silence, not hesitance, not remorse. Only her steady voice followed that final vote.

"We're staying, then. That means duties as normal. Mead, I want an inventory of our supplies and a rationing plan. Door, keep on those hogs. We need them all broken to the saddle. Polecat, get that ditch finished. Culprit, Snake, Hood, I want you riding patrols. The rest of us will join you when able, but the slack is on you. Oats, slop training. Get them used to seeing you again. Fucking *work* them. I'll be leading a crew to the Kiln ruin. Still need stone, especially since we're making a stand. You have your tasks. Get to them."

The brothers stood, began shuffling out the door. Polecat lingered a moment.

"Chief . . ."

"Vote's decided, Cat," Fetch said. "You won. Only thing worse than gloating is sulking. We're still in this together and, unless you want to try your luck with a different challenge, I'm still chief. Now go."

Once he was gone, Mead and Oats still loitered, both sitting.

Annoyed, Fetch gave them a look. "You two need something?"

"Just seeing if there was anything more I needed to know," Mead replied, voice as stiff as his body. "About the Sons, or anything else?"

"What did I just say about sulking? I didn't tell you about being sick, Mead. I didn't tell anyone. Hood figured it out. You didn't. Be angry, but find a way past it. And quickly."

"I'm not angry, chief. I know why you didn't tell anyone, just like I know why Oats voted against you just now. It would have brought the vote to a tie if he backed you, force the sides to a fight to decide the challenge. With Oats and Hood with you, there was no one Polecat could put forward that could win. We had this won. The two of you think no one can see the looks that pass between you. Sure, you've known each other so long they're all but invisible, but they are still there. I saw it. Oats asked what you wanted him to do and you answered. You gave the vote to Cat."

"Hoof doesn't need the strife caused by a fight like that," Fetch said. "I didn't see Abri—I didn't see Culprit siding against me. I can win him over. Snake, too. A few days and I can bring it back to the table. Might need to feel Marrow out about it before offering his name for brotherhood."

Mead stood. "I know, Fetch. I understand all that. I understand you didn't tell us about the sickness because you were afraid of looking weak. What I don't understand is why you thought you were alone in that fear. Why you didn't talk to . . . someone who might know a little bit about surviving in a hoof that sees them as weak."

"Because I never saw you as weak, Mead. None of us do."

That took him off guard, scattered some of his anger.

"Still. I could have helped."

Mead lingered for another uncomfortable moment, trying not to look at Oats and failing. At last, he turned and left the shop.

"I think he liked me being gone," the thrice said. He was attempting to make her smile, Fetch knew.

Instead, she shot him a warning look.

Taking the hint, Oats stood.

"You did the right thing here."

Fetch did laugh now, but it was a humorless thing. "I was just thinking they would never challenge me. What a fool-ass."

"Wish you'd told me what you were thinking beforehand. Couldn't get to grips with it at first. Probably didn't help."

Fetch could only nod. She opted to change the subject. "Xhreka settled?"

Oats grunted an affirmative. "Still surprised you offered her a place, being earnest."

Fetching shrugged. "She may wish she had declined before it's all done."

"Not what I meant."

"I know. Go on. Get to the slops. And take stock of Marrow and Sluggard too. I'll want to know what you think."

Oats nodded and stood up. "We'll turn it around, Fetch."

The door to the cooper's shop opened and closed once more, leaving Fetch alone to figure out how she was going to save this hoof, the hoof she had just increased, the hoof that had just openly defied her for the first time and not for the reasons she suspected.

The shadows lengthened across half-finished barrels and coffins, and still she found no answer.

TWENTY-TWO

FETCH, AND THE RAIN, PRESIDED over slop training for the second day. Skirmish drills, tack repair, and practice falls from a tethered hog were all made slick and muddy. Fetch took over the regimen so Oats could lend his strong back at the ditch. The runoff had opposed the dig crew and was now gaining ground by dumping it into the ditch.

By noon the slops were advancing between abandoned houses with aimed, if unloaded, stockbows.

"Watch the angle of that thrum, Tel," Fetch advised. "You get spooked and pull the tickler, Touro is getting a bolt in the back. Bekir, fan out more. Don't overtake the hub, Incus, you're rearguard. *Incus.* Shit."

Fetch was trailing the formation, putting her behind the deaf thrice.

"That's going to be a problem," Marrow said from Fetch's right.

"Only for training," she replied. "In the field, the goal would be silence. Gosse, face front! What are you looking back here for? You, too, Dacia. None of what I'm saying concerns you! Touro, give the sign to halt."

The lead slop planted the toes of his trailing foot in the ground.

The rest seamlessly stopped the advance. Fetch stepped around to face Incus.

"Keep all your brothers in sight at all times," she instructed, motioning to show the thrice that she had outpaced the flanks. "Your height is an advantage here, so this will always be your position. Tonight, I want you to talk with Oats. He'll have better guidance. Learn everything he can tell you."

"Yes, chief."

As Fetch went back to her place, she heard an exasperated breath. She spun on her heel.

"Is there a fucking problem, Gosse?"

The slop's guilty face went blank, his eyes wide with the surprise of being identified. He was in the middle years of training, old enough to know a few things, just enough to make him cocky, but young enough to still be a fool-ass.

"You got something to say, let's hear it."

"N-nothing, chief."

Fetch gave him an iron eyeball. With shit on it.

"Touro," she said, and the formation was once again moving.

Fetch waited until they reached the cordwainer's shop and called another halt. She walked up next to one of the beams supporting the awning and addressed the slops.

"You've just been set upon by two *ulyud*. Dacia, how many orcs is that?"

"A dozen, chief."

"A dozen orcs. And one just broke through to your middle." Fetch slapped the beam with an open palm. "You all have to resist the urge to feather him. He's in your hub. You loose bolts and miss, you risk striking each other. And you cease holding back the other eleven thicks. This shit situation falls to one mongrel. Gosse, kill this thick before his cleaver starts taking your brothers' heads."

The slop raised his unloaded stockbow.

"Looks like you're out of bolts, hopeful," Fetch observed blandly. "Gonna have to fight him."

Allowing his stockbow to fall to the end of its strap, Gosse drew his tulwar. He took a swift step and hacked into the beam. His blade bit the width of a finger into the wood and held. After a couple of tugs, he pulled it free.

"Your foe is still standing," Fetch said, taking in the height of the beam, half again as tall as she. "And you're dead." She took a long step to her right. "Incus."

Gosse had to dive away as the thrice charged. She had no weapon drawn, and smote the beam with both grasping hands, bunched tight to her body. As soon as she struck, she shoved, putting all the weight of body and motion behind the blow. The beam snapped a handspan from the ground and toppled, scattering the slops nearest the awning as it buckled.

All stared dumbfounded, including Marrow. Fetch was looking hard at Gosse.

"Incus has just given your patrol a few more moments to live," she said with a raised voice. "If you use them well, with a little luck, you're going home with only one dead brother. But with two *ulyud*, that's far from certain. Would be for the most seasoned riders. So, I'd rather have a thrice at my back as not. You all can hear. She can't." Fetch kicked at the debris. "She can do that. You can't. She bolsters your weaknesses. See you do the same for hers. Understood?"

Every slop gave an eager and earnest "Yes, chief."

"Very good. Return to formation."

Incus strode back to her place, but Fetch stopped Gosse by clearing her throat. She peered at the fallen beam.

"The sight of this dead orc pleases me," she said. "I'd like to keep it as a trophy."

The slophead nodded and hauled the sundered wood around for the rest of the drill without complaint. After, she sent all the hopefuls to the ditch and trudged through the morass of Winsome's thoroughfare to the stables.

She found Dumb Door in the makeshift farrowing shed tending to Slivers's hog. The big mongrel looked up from the animal as Fetch stooped into the confines of the low structure. Little Orphan Girl stood calmly as Dumb Door re-dressed the wounds suffered from the dogs. They didn't look to have festered, a testament to the mute rider's skill.

"Would have wagered we were going to need to put her down," Fetch said.

Dumb Door shook his head, looking pleased. He raised three fingers and waved them back and forth. Next, he extended one finger on the opposite hand, reduced the three on the other to two, and used them to straddle the first.

"Ready to ride in a few days?"

Door kept his hands in the figure of a rider and moved them slowly up and down.

"Easy to start. Of course."

Dumb Door dipped his chin in that slow way. Fetch resisted the urge to broach the subject of leaving Winsome. Swaying this former nomad to her side would be difficult. He well knew the hardships of a homeless wanderer, and she was asking him to take up that life once more. The shadow of orcs and cavaleros was nothing compared to the years he'd spent in the badlands, vulnerable and isolated. Hells, the other brothers said he had yet to take a bunk and continued to sleep on the floor. How could she convince him to return to something that in many ways he'd never left? He still went to sleep hungry most nights. Winsome's walls, this stable, were what marked the difference between the old life and the new, tethered him to the hoof. Fetch had no counter to that, not yet, so she was left with little choice but to leave him alone and accept that he and Polecat were the staunchest of the opposition.

Shed Snake and Culprit, however, could be won over. Mead was working on Snake. Once they had him, Fetch was hopeful their newest blood would fall into line.

The rain thinned by twilight, just enough to make the air muggy. Hoodwink was leading Touro and Petro through knife drills near the gate. The eldest and most seasoned hopefuls worked hard, the news of Culprit's rise clearly giving them some added gumption, enough to overcome their innate fear of Hood. Almost.

Fetching watched the training until full darkness brought Polecat and his ditch diggers back within the walls, all begrimed and weary. Dacia and Incus were among the crew, walking side by side. Sluggard and Marrow had also been recruited, no doubt at Oats's insistence. The thrice came to stand beside her caked with earth.

"Nearly done," he told her.

Hells, it was good to have him back.

Fetching resolved to spend some time at the dig herself on the morrow. It would feel good to hit something hard with a piece of metal, even if it was only dirt and stones.

"Good work," she told the grimy crew as they passed. She thumped Oats on the arm. "Come to my solar when you're cleaned up."

"I will be happy to."

It was Sluggard who responded. He'd been passing by and was now walking backward, displaying a bright smile.

"Keep moving, Whore," Fetching told him.

The nomad did as he was told, letting loose a laugh. Something about that sound, birthed with such sincere amusement after the drudgery of the ditch, caused Fetch to have a thought that needed to be quickly snuffed. Needed to be, but wasn't. Fetch found she watched Sluggard until he'd vanished into the vintners' dormitory.

That night, a meager measure of wine passed between Fetch and Oats. It was all she could do not to guzzle the entirety of the paltry ration in one pull.

"Think the Unyar supplies contain any of that vile, glorious milk?" Fetch mused, leaning forward from the edge of the bed, elbows resting on knees.

Oats watched her with poorly hidden concern from his stool.

"I know," she said. "Not the time to get drunk." She wondered if the Pit of Homage had provided Oats with much in the way of spirits, but let the question die in her head. It didn't seem like something he would want to discuss much. "You gain any ground with Polecat today?"

Oats gave a frustrated shrug. "I ribbed him a bit about the challenge. He's uneasy for doing it."

"Enough to change his vote?"

"Maybe. With enough bullying. You want to take that path?"

Fetch handed the bottle back, shook her head. "No. But am I wrong for that? Was I wrong in not fighting to win the vote?"

"You know there's no answer to that."

There wasn't. She did know there was no way to be certain Hood wouldn't have killed whoever Polecat chose as champion. And she couldn't choose Oats for the same reason, not after the Pit.

"Claymaster would've fought." She took the wine back, swigged.

"Yes. But he wouldn't have allowed women slops."

The bitter laugh made her dribble a little wine. She wiped her chin. "The truth? It never occurred to me. Shit. What the fuck does that say? I spent years fighting the Claymaster's scorn only to discover I'm no different. I took them for whores, Oats."

"You weren't fully wrong. One of 'em was, right? You sent her outta here with the Sons so fast, I barely got a look at her. Them other two will think twice about ever disobeying an order."

He was trying to make her feel better. She didn't want to feel better. And she didn't want to dwell on Ahlamra. She'd done her no favors with the task she'd placed on the girl. A task she did not dare speak about, even to Oats.

Fetch took another pull, relinquished the bottle. "What's worse. Even when I realized their aim . . . fuck, all I could think was that there was no chance any of them would succeed."

Oats grunted. "Well, one of them did the work of ten today in the ditch."

"Says one thrice about another."

"Not her. The one with the scars . . . Dacia."

Fetch credited that with a nod. "She's got grit. But enough? Looks like she's used to hard work, but digging ain't riding. It's not fighting thicks and keeping formation while straddling a razor, loosing a thrum on the gallop and killing your mark."

"And it's likely neither of them will be able to do that, even with training."

Fetch shot him a look. "Seems I'm not the only one that thinks like the Claymaster."

"You were never a slop."

"I fucking know that!"

Oats held up a hand, wordlessly asking for patience. "When Jackal and I were coming up, there was this other slophead." He paused a moment, concentrating until he fished the name from his memory. "Joam. Good rider. Tough fighter. Steadiest aim with a thrum among us. And one night . . . we found him dangling from the rafters in the barracks. Hung himself. No signs it was coming. Another pair a bit older than us—can't even remember their names— they failed to get the votes for brotherhood, so they left on foot to try their chances with the Skull Sowers. Never made it to the Furrow. There's a reason Winsome . . . hells, *all* the lots, don't contain more mongrels that ain't hoof brothers or nomads. Most don't survive training or don't survive the shame of failing. The odds weren't against those three from the very beginning because of what's between their legs, Isa. Swinging cods have been failing and dying for years because it's just damn hard."

"Never thought about it, really," Fetch admitted.

"We don't talk about it. Slops are no one until they prove themselves. Those that die, or desert, may as well have never lived. But that's not something you know. You taught yourself to shoot, to fight. By the time me and Jack were Bastards and got you in the saddle, you took to that swift too. None of it was a hardship for you, Fetch, except the old puss pot himself."

Fearing where that hog would carry them, Fetch deflected. "Wasn't a hardship for you. Or Jackal either."

"Shit!" Oats blurted, laughing. "The chief was easy on me. Wanted a thrice so badly he overlooked that I was barely passable with a stockbow. And Jackal? He nearly never wore a brigand."

Fetch couldn't help but smile. "Always rebelling."

"Wasn't that at all." Oats took a drink. "He couldn't keep the signals in his head. Never seen a better mongrel on hogback, but Jack was useless as soon as the lead rider gave commands. Tusker. Shank shot. Snails. He couldn't remember any of them. And that's saying nothing of the patrol paces!"

Fetch was enthralled. She didn't think there were any secrets left between the three of them. "So what did he do?"

"*Him?* Me! I stayed awake with him every night drilling them. Took weeks! You'd never know it now, thank all the hells."

"No," Fetch said, sobering. "No, he can do no wrong now. Small wonder Father has such a stiff cod for him."

Oats scratched at his beard when she was done. "So . . . what's got you bothered?"

"That Father was right. *Is* right. If Jackal had stayed, he'd be chief right now, instead of me."

Oats dismissed that with a belch. "But he couldn't stay. He's the Charm of Azhulthickhan . . . or whatever the fuck."

"I know!" Fetch said, springing up from the bed to get some distance from her own foolishness. "That's not . . . it's not that I'm angry it might have been him and not me. It's that had it been him, the Bastards would not be in this pile of hogshit. If he were chief, the Orc Stains would not dismiss us, the Sons would want to help us. Hells, Father looked ready to turn his entire hoof over if only . . . it were Jackal. It would all be so different if it were him and, most days, I wish it were."

That admission made her want to smash something.

"You're right," Oats said after a moment's consideration. "We would not be in this hogshit if Jackal were chief. We'd be dead."

That caused Fetch to turn and look at her oldest friend.

Oats leaned forward on his stool. "I love that mongrel beyond a brother. It might be a bit backy, if I'm honest. But he never could have led this hoof through the shit we are in. Jackal never saw the . . . daily struggle. He was blind to it. Jack's idea of the Bastards was the Kiln, and hunting *ulyud*, and having whores on their knees worshipping his orc-slaying cod. You know that. He has this fucking way of just living that and little else. Made me want to hit him, some days." Oats took a long drink. Swallowing, he looked hard at Fetch, suddenly reminding her of the face Beryl made when she wanted to be heard. "He loved the Lots and this hoof and he loved us. I hope, wherever he is, he still does. But listen to me when I tell you, in earnest, he could not have led us through that first year. We weren't at war, Fetch. What would he have seen? He may have handed this hoof to you, but it was because he knew you could do what he couldn't. Not ever. None of us wrestle the daily struggle to the ground like you. Because you've never been allowed to ignore it. So, best start coming to grips with what the rest of us already know. Only you can see us through this."

He offered the bottle back.

Fetch smiled. And let him finish the wine.

MORNING ARRIVED WITH ANOTHER RAIN, this one heavy enough to darken the sky. It was uncommon to have so much, but at least Winsome's cistern was getting much-needed replenishment.

Culprit, Shed Snake, and Hoodwink returned from a dawn run to the river as Fetch and Oats were coming in from the dig. The work continued, but would be done before the day was out. Fetch needed to get a crew to the Kiln. Oats had volunteered to help conscript the townsmen.

"Any luck?" Fetch asked the returning riders as they passed through the gate.

Culprit shook his freshly tattooed head. Fortunately, Polecat had given him the traditional hoof wreathed in broken chains. "It seems me and Snake are shit fishermen."

"Would have wagered that," Fetch needled.

"Thankfully," Shed Snake pronounced, and cocked an eye at Hoodwink, "this one has some hoodoo over other cold-fleshed creatures that don't blink."

Ignoring the jibe, Hood handed a basket down from the saddle. Inside, Fetching was pleased to see four fat barbels.

"Not enough to feed the town," Hoodwink whispered.

From any other mongrel such a statement may have been taken as one of regret. From Hood, it was a calculated suggestion.

"Then the slops will eat well tonight," Fetching decided. She hated dictating what food would go where. It was especially difficult not to send everything to the orphanage, but there was a grim balance to rationing. Hells, even the sworn brethren had to eat at least once a week, though her instincts had them bear the brunt of the hunger pains. The Unyar supplies would not last forever, especially if they were careless.

Graviel and Lopo were standing nearby, ready to take the barbarians from the patrol riders. Both were trying to pretend they had not heard what their chief said, but the excitement over their unexpected reward was dancing across their faces. Fetching waved them over and relinquished the basket.

"Wait until late to eat," she instructed. "Keep the smell down. Boil them or eat them fucking raw if you have to, but if you cause a stir in town, torturing us all with savory smells, the next thing that gets cooked is you. Understood?"

A pair of hopeful heads nodded vigorously. "Yes, chief."

Oats leaned down over the slops, beard dripping. "And no gifting the village girls with a fish feast to get your cods wetted by more than rain. Keep this to yourselves."

More nods.

Fetch dismissed them with a tilt of her head. "Get gone. Hide that basket. We'll take the hogs." As the slopheads ran off, the riders began walking their mounts toward the pens. Snake and Hoodwink were ahead. Culprit drifted into step beside Oats.

Fetch bumped the thrice on the arm and raised her chin at the retreating slops. "Hungry as they all are, they would still trade food for sex?"

The thrice grunted. "That young? They're more full of spend than brains."

Culprit was thoughtful. "Plus . . ."

"What?" Fetch asked, leaning so she could see him around Oats's bulk.

Culprit gave a little shrug. "Being the hero, I dunno, providing for the girl with the sweet smile, giving her your ration. Likely that feels better than the short rut they might get."

"Hells," Fetch said with a laugh, "you may have something there. For a whole fish spitted over a fire? I might let some shivering hopeful climb atop me for the six heartbeats it would take him to spurt."

"No, you wouldn't," Oats said.

Culprit gave an exaggerated shiver and stuck his tongue out. "Hells, chief! *Yelch*."

Fetch didn't know whether to be offended or amused. "The thought of fucking me disgusts you, mongrel?"

Culprit shuddered again. "Be like bedding my mother, except I know who *you* are. Right, Oats?"

Oats's nose wrinkled. "More like my sister, but yes. Let's stop talking about this right damn now."

It felt good to walk in the rain, especially after grubbing in the ditch. Fetch was overdue for a bath and the steady drops invading the air, shrinking the world, would serve well enough. She'd have to tend her weapons carefully tonight, but that was a small chore.

Fetch found her mood lifting. Ul-wundulas was a land of mostly unchanging clime, each day looking much like the next, just another of its slow tactics to wear thin the sanity of its inhabitants. The change, the break from the sun, the heat, it had an enlivening effect. Plus, the rain had sent the villagers inside, removing many of a chief's cares from immediate sight. It was a fleeting, illusory relief, but Fetch would take it while it lasted. An amusing thought occurred. She gave Oats's shoulder a goading punch.

"Is that what you and Jackal did as slops? Bribed Winsome girls to—"

She stopped short.

A dozen strides ahead, Hoodwink and Shed Snake had halted. Hood's hand was raised in a warning sign, water running from his elbow. He and Snake were already bringing their stockbows around. Instinctively, Fetch and Oats did the same. Culprit was a moment behind. The three of them approached quick and quiet until drawing even with their brothers. All eyes fixed on the hog pens, a stone's throw away, grey in the rain.

Something was very wrong.

In the main pen, the hogs were clustered in and around the stables, most trying to crowd the western side of the building, farthest from the breaking yard. Within, a lone hog stood, still and quiet. Its wet hide shone, slick with water and sticky blood, covering it from tusks to hocks. Lying just outside the fence, the rails smeared with crimson where he'd crawled over, was Dumb Door.

"Shit," Shed Snake breathed, and made to rush the fallen mongrel, but Hoodwink shot out a hand, stopping him.

The pens sat beneath the northern bend of the stockade. Keeping her stockbow tight to her shoulder, Fetching swept the palisade walkway. The slopheads on sentry for this section of the wall were still on patrol. They kept watch on the land beyond as they walked, but Sence was just now circling back to the pens and noticed the turmoil in the breaking yard. Fetch shot a pointed whistle at the sentry, and when he looked down, she raised a splayed hand, then put her fingers together and made a sharp dipping motion.

Hold. Look for scalers.

Obeying the commands, Sence readied his spear and began cautiously craning over the wall, searching for signs of intruders. The other three sentries in sight, alerted by the whistle, did the same, trusting the Bastards on the ground to deal with whatever had occurred at the pens.

"Oats, Snake," Fetch hissed.

That was all they needed. While she, Culprit, and Hood covered their approach, Oats and Shed Snake hustled forward. When they reached Dumb Door, they knelt to check him.

Without warning, the hog in the yard charged the fence, causing Oats and Snake to recoil as the beast's tusks impacted the wood. The rails buckled.

"Get out of there!" Fetch yelled.

Grabbing fistfuls of Dumb Door's brigand, Oats and Snake dragged him away from the enclosure. The hog had launched another charge upon the fence. It was not going to hold.

"Keep going," Fetch commanded when her retreating brothers reached her position. "Get Door to safety. Culprit, bring the others! But tell Mead to secure the gate!" She did not take her eyes from sighting down the runnel of her thrum, not daring to relinquish her aim on the crazed hog, not wanting to see if Dumb Door was still alive.

The next charge splintered the upper rail. As it collapsed, the gory hog leapt what was left of the fence, barreling straight for Hood and Fetching.

They loosed at the same moment.

Dull impacts sounded. Bolts striking meat. The hog never slowed.

Fetch rolled away from death. Not quite quick enough. She took a savage blow to the hip and ribs, turning her roll into a graceless tumble, the wet ground giggling with each impact until she came to a stop. Wincing, she looked at her side, finding only mud. The curve of the hog's tusk must have struck her, but fortune spared her a goring.

Looking up through eyes bedimmed by pain and rainwater, she saw the beast coming again. There was no time to reload. Fetch tensed, readying herself to spring. A spear came hurtling down from above, striking just to her right.

A gift.

Wishing Sence a cock-sucking every day for the rest of his life, Fetching snatched the spear from the mud and charged the oncoming hog.

Leaping, she struck, stabbing down into the shoulder, twisting in the air and throwing herself away. Landing on her feet with a squelch she saw the hog's momentum continue to carry it forward. Barbarians were a damn hardy animal, bred to take punishment. By rights, it should have at least stumbled, but it remained solidly on its hooves.

Fetch could not muster much surprise. Fuck all if she wasn't growing used to ensorcelled animals.

The hog made a slow turn, bristling with the spear shaft and a trio of thrumbolts. Hood must have put another bolt in its flank during its last attempt to trample Fetching. He came running to her side now, quickly handing over a bolt. Her own quiver was empty, contents scattered. The hog had stopped just beneath the wall, facing them, watching. It afforded Fetch a long look.

"It's Little Orphan Girl," she said grimly, reloading her stockbow.

"Slivers's mount," Hoodwink agreed.

"Damn."

They never should have brought the beast inside, should have put her down when they had the chance. It had been too much of a blessing that the sow survived the ravaging by the dogs, even for all Dumb Door's skill. Barbarians were tough, but they still gave voice to pain. Orphan Girl had just suffered grievous wounds and not uttered a single squeal.

Culprit, Oats, and Shed Snake returned with Polecat, Marrow, and Sluggard in tow. Fetch and Hoodwink stood near the pens, their brothers far to their right, Orphan Girl forming the apex of the triangle. The sow had again adopted the unnerving stillness that she displayed in the breaking yard.

"Feather her!" Fetching cried out, and the Bastards responded.

Bowstrings snapped, fletched shafts thudded into the hog. They may as well have been pulling their ticklers at a practice butt. A chill went down Fetch's spine at the horrendous sight of the animal, struck with shots that should have slain, rocking slightly with each impact, only to stand firm when the volley ceased.

"Enough of this," Fetch hissed, and threw her thrum down. She drew the kataras from her hips and quickly ran each blade across her shoulders.

"Chief?" Hoodwink said, seeing her cut herself, his voice taking on not the barest edge of alarm.

"Stay here."

Fetch strode away from the pen, getting no closer to Orphan Girl, but putting herself squarely between Hood and the other Bastards. Oats took a step forward.

"Don't move!" Fetch declared, stopping him.

"Fetching . . . the fuck you doing?"

"Killing this damn thing. All of you stay put!"

If Ruin was going to continue to assault her people within their own damn home, she was going to ram his sorcery back down his throat. Nothing had seemed capable of stopping the Sludge Man until Crafty had slashed Fetching's flesh, exposing her blood, equal parts orc and elf. It had worked then, it might work now.

Warm rain and hot blood ran down her arms, dripped from the

ends of the kataras. Little Orphan Girl, or whatever resided in the sow's skin, watched her deliberate approach with the dauntingly intelligent eyes possessed by all barbarians. Fetching swiped the flat of her blades across her seeping wounds, inwardly cursing the rain for diluting the flow.

Displaying none of the natural, agitated signs of aggression, the hog charged, transforming from perfect stillness into a barreling mass of muscle. Droplets sprayed from her hide in a swarm, the multitude of protruding shafts quivering with each hoofbeat. Fetching matched the beast step for step, boots stomping the sodden ground. At the last moment, she dove, feet leading, plowing waves of mud. Her course was just a handbreadth to the right of the oncoming beast and Orphan Girl's head jerked downward, trying to catch Fetching with a tusk, but struck only the ground.

Punching upward with her left hand, Fetch drove her blade, her blood, deep into the hog's belly. Its own forward momentum caused the blade to tear along the gut, eviscerating the beast. But no blood fell, no guts spilled. Ripping the katara free, Fetch flipped up, going from her back to her feet in one snapping motion. Spinning, she rushed Orphan Girl before the sow could turn, and leapt astride her back. Hammering down with both fists, she drove the kataras hilt-deep into the barbarian's back. The pig bucked and spun, trying to dislodge its murderous rider, but Fetch twisted the vicious daggers and held firm. Gripping with her legs, she removed one weapon, again swiped it across her bleeding shoulder before driving it back down, pulling the other hand free and repeating the attack.

Again and again.

But the hog was not flagging. Nothing could extinguish its dread vitality.

Ignoring the barrage of puncturing blows, it ran for the pens, straight for an intact section of fence enclosing the main paddock.

Fetch heard her brothers yelling for her to jump clear.

If they struck and the fence held, she would likely be thrown. If it broke, Orphan Girl would be rampant among the hoof's hogs. She could maim all their mounts and they would be powerless to stop it.

Leaving the daggers embedded in the beast, Fetch gripped the spear still in its shoulder. Using the shaft for balance, she jumped up to stand on the hog's back. Screaming as she bent every muscle to the task, she thrust downward on the spear. There was a heartbeat of resistance before the blade plunged the rest of the way. Fetch felt it punch through the animal and sink into the ground, sending her flying as the hog's charge was arrested, turned into a violent, headlong collapse.

Fetch landed hard inside the paddock, tumbling through a quagmire of mud and hogshit. Rolling, she saw Orphan Girl sprawled on her side, kicking hooves battering the fence.

The Bastards rushed the fallen creature, Polecat, Marrow, and Shed Snake bearing spears thrown to them by the sentries on the wall. They thrust at the hog, trying to pin it before it could again gain its feet.

Scrambling, Fetch ran into the stables and retrieved the heavy knacker's maul from its hook. This morose instrument was sometimes needed to put a hog out of its misery, the heavy tapered head delivering a killing blow between the eyes. Fighting not to slip in the muck, she crossed the paddock and yelled for Oats, tossing the hammer over the fence. The thrice snatched it from the air and the other Bastards danced away to give him room. Stepping to get at Orphan Girl's head, Oats brought the maul up and swung with all the force in his brutish arms. There was a sickening, dull crack.

Fetch had seen half a dozen hogs so dispatched. Done correctly, they went limp and dropped. Oats's blow had been precise, strong, enough to fell a fucking elephant.

Little Orphan Girl fell, but only from the impact. No sooner was she down but her legs again began to scrape for purchase.

Even Hoodwink's eyes went wide with disturbed disbelief.

"Ropes!" Sluggard cried out. "Lasso her to our hogs and drag her outside the walls!"

"Good!" Fetch replied. "Oats, we're going to need Ug!"

Oats nodded. "Keep it pinned if you can!"

As the thrice ran for the stables, Hood rushed back toward the village proper, Culprit following. Shed Snake tossed his spear to Sluggard and went after them. Their mounts were still saddled, left on Winsome's thoroughfare.

Polecat and the two nomads tried to keep the hog down with their spears, but it was fruitless. The beast felt no pain and was undaunted by the thrusting steel. She pushed against the blades, uncaring that they sank deeper into her hide. The mongrels strained with every sinew, but not even the considerable might of three half-orcs could keep her down. The sow stood, twisting savagely, tusks swinging at her attackers. Sluggard was nearest her head and tried to maintain hold of his spear, but the haft snapped under the pressure. The gritter stumbled forward just as the tusk whipped around, catching him across the chest and neck. Blood spurted into the rain as Sluggard was tossed aside.

"Get back!" Fetching yelled at the others. "Get to the walls!"

Marrow and Polecat abandoned their spears, leaving them in the beast, to make a run for the palisade stairs.

Orphan Girl made to pursue, but Fetch jumped onto the top rail of the fence, using it to vault onto the hog's back once more. Grabbing the swine-yankers, she wrestled the sow away from the mongrels' heels.

"Fetch!" Oats cried, riding out of the paddock on Ugfuck, a rope whirling over his head. "Get clear!"

She jumped just as Oats tossed, snagged the pig around the neck. Lassos from Hoodwink, Culprit, and Shed Snake followed close behind. Culprit's failed to catch, but the other two looped around Orphan Girl's head. The eerily silent hog attempted to charge Oats, but Hood rode a quick wheel around behind, holding her back with the rope looped around his saddle horn. When she turned on Hood, Snake stalled her. This dance continued while Culprit attempted to snare her back legs, but he again missed the toss.

"She's not tiring!" Oats declared. "We can stop her, but can't move her!"

Ugfuck was the strongest barbarian in the Bastards' stable, and he was going to fatigue long before the foul craft that had its claws sunk in Orphan Girl.

"Get your mounts saddled!" Fetch yelled to her hoof. "It will take all of us!"

She ran to Culprit's side, took the lasso from him, tossed, and trapped Orphan Girl's back hooves. Culprit took the rope back and quickly wound it around his saddle horn, urging his hog to back up. The rope went taut, pulling the sow's legs back. She resisted, but with Oats, Snake, and Hood now pulling at her head in the opposite direction, she was forced onto her belly.

Fetching ran for the stables, passing the fallen Sluggard. There was no time to check him. If they didn't get more ropes on that devil-beast, the entire hoof would end up facedown and bleeding in the mud. Marrow and Polecat ran along the palisade until they were above the pens, jumping directly onto the roof of the stable to clamber down.

A bellow of alarm from Oats and a yelled curse from Snake caused Fetch to whirl.

Little Orphan Girl had begun to roll, winding the ropes around her neck. Oats, Snake, and Hoodwink tried to restrain her, but their hogs were being drawn in, planted hooves skidding.

Marrow and Polecat were struggling to get their spooked hogs rounded up and saddled. They weren't going to be quick enough to help.

"Cut the ropes!" Fetch shouted.

"We won't get another chance!" Oats replied.

"Cut them!"

The riders drew their tulwars.

A sonorous boom impregnated the air. Reeling against the sound, Fetch saw the rain explode, forced outward by a spherical void centered on Orphan Girl. The resonant cry had no end, a never-ending blast from a thousand war horns. Head swimming, legs liquid, Fetching lost her balance, ate mud. The low-pitched, thunderous assault roared in her ears, clenched her eyes. She may have screamed in a feeble reply devoured by the greater fury. The ropes holding Orphan Girl frayed, soundlessly snapped. The hog stood, protruding thrumbolts and spear-shafts shattering an instant before the beast's tusks. Fetching put up an arm, warding herself against fragments of wood and ivory. The hide reverberated and split. A rush of blood, unshed from the hog's many wounds, dumped to the ground as its entire body ruptured.

The rain returned, reclaiming the air. It was a moment before Fetching realized she could again hear the drops falling. All around, hogs and half-orcs were picking themselves from the mud, movements dazed, faces slack, shaken but unharmed.

Nothing remained of Little Orphan Girl but a sodden heap of burst skin lying atop scattered guts and fractured bones.

TWENTY-THREE

FETCHING SAT BESIDE DUMB DOOR until he died.

She could not have said how long it took. When the last shuddering inhale rattled in his broken body, the mud upon Fetch's skin was caked, her boots dry, the cuts on her shoulders clotted. The candle in the apothecary's back room had been replaced several times, once by Bekir, another time by Sweeps. There might have been a third.

When Dumb Door was first brought inside, they had washed him as best they could, the blood and filth making it impossible to see his wounds. Each mopping cloth revealed another gash, another exposed bone. Whatever had happened, it happened swiftly, brutally. The sentries on the wall had seen him lead a hog into the breaking yard. By the time they came back around, mere minutes later, he was down.

"He could not cry out for help," Fetch had muttered to one of the candle deliverers.

At some point during her helpless vigil, Mead had come in, told her Sluggard was alive and awake. His injuries would heal.

"Good" was all she had managed in reply.

The Guabic woman that served as Winsome's apothecary had

returned to the town after the downfall of the Kiln, but the famine had not been easy on her aging body. She died last winter, taking all hope of mending Dumb Door with her. The shelves in her rooms were mostly bare anyway. What good were a few herbs and liniments for a bashed-in skull? That was the moment they knew it was hopeless. Sweeps's laving rag had revealed the horror, mud and blood cleared away to expose the poor mongrel's brains. On the other side of the table, the tanner's widow had continued to stitch up the ragged rend beneath Dumb Door's ribs, but all alacrity fled her hands.

Fetch had Xhreka sent for. The halfling woman had merely narrowed her one eye.

"I know how to pull teeth, set bones. Things learned from necessity in the Pit. This . . . I ain't a healer. Don't think it would matter if I were."

She hadn't remained long after her words were spoken.

Dumb Door flew into fits a few times before the end. The first startled Fetching from her slumped torpor on the stool beside his cot. For a moment she thought perhaps he had come to. That was the worst, fearing he might have awoken to terrible agony, not knowing what could be done, wondering if she should end his suffering only to realize she had no weapon. No doubt some of the herbs hanging from the rafters were poison, but she had no idea which ones. She would have to smother him, hold his nose and mouth closed. All this went through her mind in a single, damnable instant. Alongside those black notions came the hope that he might wake long enough to tell her something about what happened.

It was a laughable hope. This mute mongrel, who uttered no sound even as he convulsed with seizures, telling her through gesture a tale she already knew.

The first fit ended. Others followed, weaker, further apart each time. Fetch did not bother to count. Why were none of the other Bastards in here with her to be with their brother at the last?

Right. She had commanded them to leave her alone. Commanded with a shout and a flung stool. This stool? No, the other had broken against the wall. Sweeps had brought the one she now sat on, along with the new candle. The one that was now a guttering nub. Dumb Door's flesh and the wax were akin in color and texture. She could see that in the dwindling light.

And then came that final indrawn breath, the air that went in and never came out, trapped in the moment of death. Dumb Door did not look peaceful. His face was still pained, drawn. Fetching continued to sit there, staring at that tortured mask until the candle went out.

Standing on stiff legs, feet full of stinging ants, she reached out in the darkness and touched her fallen rider's arm. She nearly said the words, but they were somehow too vulgar, so she let them wilt in her throat.

Saying nothing was better. It's what Dumb Door would have done.

Out in the main room, Fetching found Sweeps waiting with a hunk of cheese and half a cup of wine on a tray. Taking the wine, Fetch downed it in one swallow, set the cup down, and pointed wearily at the cheese.

"You have that."

"Mead told me you would say that," Sweeps replied, eyes and voice lowered. "He said I was to insist."

"You're just now recovered from illness, Sweeps. Eat."

There was a pause. Slowly, Sweeps set the tray down on a counter once used to grind herbs. She picked up the cheese and tore it in two.

"I'll eat half," she said, holding out one of the pieces.

"Hells." Fetch breathed, taking it.

They chewed together in silence, both making their morsels last.

"He's gone?" Sweeps asked at last.

Fetching sighed. "He is."

"I'll . . . clean him up better. Before you have to . . . before."

"No need. The hoof will do it."

Sweeps made a small sound of assent before picking up the tray. She stood there a moment, just holding it, looking down at it, before walking out the door.

Fetch lingered, wishing for all the world she did not have to face whatever awaited outside the confines of the apothecary's low rooms.

But she had hid here long enough, her reason for staying growing cold.

It was full night outside. The rain had ceased, leaving the air chill. Uidal stood by the door. Fetch sent him to find Mead and Oats, with orders to meet up on the walls. The seclusion of her solar beckoned, but Winsome was under siege. The duties were never-ending, for everyone. And now they were down a man, a good one. May as well stand a post while hearing reports.

Climbing the stairs, Fetch reached the top of the palisade and walked until coming to the south-facing wall. There she stopped, for no real reason other than it was farthest from the hog pens.

Oats was the first to arrive, bearing Fetch's weapons. Without a word, he handed them over.

Fetching's eyebrows went up when she saw the kataras. "Surprised these survived. They were still in Orphan Girl when . . ."

"Fished them out of the mess," Oats said. "Thought you were loon-fucking-crazy, cutting yourself and all, but hells if it didn't work."

"I don't think that was me, Oats. That sound, that . . . scream. No. Not anything I did."

The thrice grimaced. "Then what?"

"No one saw anything?"

"Not me, not the others. Whatever popped that pig left no sign. If it wasn't you, maybe whatever had it bewitched . . . time ran out."

"Maybe," Fetch said, but she wasn't convinced.

Mead joined them.

"You tell her?" he asked, speaking past Fetch to Oats, who only shook his head.

"Tell me?"

"Marrow's gone," Mead said. "Said this hoof was cursed. He said—"

Fetch held up a hand. She didn't need to hear any more.

"He won't be the last," she declared, staring into the shadow-veiled badlands.

"None of us are going anywhere," Oats rumbled. "Unless you order it."

"You're damn right I'm ordering it. We're fucking leaving. Nothing anyone can do about it now." It was a cold truth and she felt a cunt for saying it, but with Door dead, Polecat no longer had the votes. Fetch lifted her chin beyond the stockade. "We're better off out there. In here, Marrow's right, we're cursed."

They stood for a while, the three of them.

Mead broke the silence. "How did Sweeps take it?"

Fetch looked over and squinted at him.

"Dumb Door," Mead prompted with a little hesitance.

And then Fetch saw it. She made a disgusted noise, aimed at herself. "Fuck . . . I'm a cunt."

"You didn't know," Oats said, trying to sound comforting and failing.

Leaning her elbows between the palisade stakes, Fetch let her forehead rest on the rough wood and shook her head.

She *hadn't* known. Because she ignored it.

Back in the Kiln, riders had their own quarters, private rooms off a common hall. For years she had seen women come up from the town to keep company with the hoof, often awoken by the ruckus of vigorous fucking, especially from behind Roundth's and Polecat's doors, when they bothered to close them. But all the Bastards, with the exception of Hoodwink, had noisily entertained a town girl or two in their bed. Just like in the orphanage, where you learned who was getting up in the night from the sound of their footfalls alone, Fetch became an expert on which groans belonged to which Bastard.

Of course, she had no such comfort. None of the village men would dare come up to the Kiln, even if she had invited them, which she never did. The Claymaster had made sure she understood her limitations. Prior to her being chief, most of the slopheads would gleefully have come to her room, but that was also forbidden, not to mention unthinkable to Fetch. Slops were supposed to fear sworn riders, respect them, not lust after them. The Lots were filled with nomads ousted from the hoofs for using slopheads for base needs, if the rumors could be believed, and she was not about to hand the Claymaster a reason to vote her from the ranks.

To survive, she learned to blend in. She became like her hoofmates in all things, including their appetites. It was a ploy, one which the Bastards eventually fell for. But she never did. The first girl at Sancho's that she took to bed was almost less interested than Fetch was herself. The next was more vigorous, more generous, but it hardly made a difference. Soon, all the whores were eager for Fetching's coin and company. What other poke paid to sit on the bed and clean their weapons while the girl took a nap?

She confined her ruse to the whorehouse and never brought anyone to her room at the Kiln.

Cissy, Thistle, Sweeps, and all the other women who came down the hall and were ushered into the adjacent chambers became something she ignored. They were an annoyance, a source of sleepless nights. After a time, however, if Fetch was honest, they became something she hated. Perhaps because they were something she refused to be, perhaps because they had something denied her, perhaps both.

Whatever the reasons, they were carried over when she became chief.

Relations between riders and townsfolk had changed since the Kiln. There were no more private rooms for the riders, they were all bunked together in the vintners' dormitory. For most, that necessitated a change in how they conducted time with women. Before Cissy left, she and Polecat continued on as normal, heedless of the lack of walls, a source of much complaining from the others. Fetching had told them to handle it among themselves, refusing to get involved. She had her solar, and need no longer be party to where her brethren stuck their cods.

And so, she had not known about Sweeps and Dumb Door. Along with Cissy, Sweeps had been a frequent visitor to Polecat's room in the Kiln, most times as a pair. Fetch had just assumed that continued, if she thought about it at all.

That assumption, that willful ignorance, had just caused her to be very, unknowingly, heartless.

"How long?" she asked.

"Since before I left," Oats replied.

Fetch lifted her head away from the stake. "Mead. Go find Sweeps. Tell her the hoof would like her to prepare Door's body. Tell her . . . forget it. I will tell her. You two tell the boys to pack up. We're leaving soon as we're able."

She made her way to the orphanage. Late as it was, Fetch slipped in quietly, something long practiced from her girlhood. Each of the caretakers had their own rooms in the back, near the bunk room for the older children, nearer still the room for the babes. Thistle never closed her door, keeping to Beryl's old practice, but her ears were not as keen. Fetching could still remember the first time she had managed to sneak back to bed without being noticed. Jackal and Oats were already living as slopheads at the Kiln and had made the near-impossible task part of her training. She still wasn't certain she had actually accomplished it. Beryl may very well have simply given up chastising her for staying out.

Tonight, no amount of successful prowling was going to go unnoticed, for the common room held a waking occupant.

Xhreka was pacing the floor in front of the fireplace, gently humming to an infant in her arms. Half-orc babes weren't small and halfling women weren't large, but Xhreka's hold was firm and sure. She looked past the baby's swaddled head at Fetching, her brow creasing with a silent question.

Stepping lightly across the room, Fetch approached.

"Sweeps in her room?" she whispered.

"That the willowy girl or the blond woman with the saggy teats?" Xhreka asked in the same low tone.

"The willowy one."

Xhreka nodded.

Fetch thanked her with the same gesture and began to move toward the rear corridor, but the halfling touched her wrist.

"She was quite upset."

Fetching had learned to ride a barbarian, joined a mongrel hoof, fought rokhs, demons, a wizard, and an orc horde. But that one light touch, those four words, drained her courage. She sat down on one of the tables by the hearth, one of the little ones where the orphans ate, slowly so her weapons did not clatter.

Xhreka stood between her and the unlit fireplace, bouncing a bit to keep the baby calm.

Fetching was not sure the halfling woman cared a shit, but she found herself talking anyway.

"I denied her the chance to be with her dying man at the end. Denied everyone."

Xhreka shrugged, more with a downturn of her mouth than with a rise of her shoulders. "I've seen a lot of men die. Not always the best memory to have. From what I saw of that mongrel, you did the girl a kindness."

"She won't see it the same way."

"No. Why would she? Her man just died. The world contains no kindness right now. But the bad of the past is quickly forgotten. There is no time for it, the bad of the present sees to that. Good memories remain. That girl will remember the things she liked most, whatever those were. The smell of him, fucking him, sound of his voice."

"He was mute."

Xhreka rolled her eye. "Well, not that then. My point, she won't have his final breath haunting her head during this first, worst bit."

"But she's hating me."

"You were friends before today?"

"No," Fetching admitted.

"So, you've lost nothing."

"I lost a rider. A brother."

"And she a lover. Maybe more. It's not ours to know. Seeking her pardon makes you feel less guilt, nothing else. You were selfish, keeping others from his deathbed. Don't be more selfish by marching into that girl's tears and bandying for forgiveness."

Fetch snorted a small, bitter laugh. "Hells. Is it mad that I just enjoyed being told what to do?"

"How long you been leading this bunch?"

Fetch had to think before answering. "A year and . . . about half another."

"Then, no. It's not mad. It's relief. And you could use some, especially since you ain't had a cock in all that time."

Fetch was taken aback. "How did you . . . ?"

"Please. I'm only half blind. Look at the way you walk." Xhreka let Fetch's mouth hang open for a moment before producing a mischievous grin. "I'm flicking your clitty, girl. Idris told me."

"Fucking big-mouthed thrice."

Xhreka cocked her eye down at the now-still infant. She held a finger up to Fetch before padding into the corridor, coming back a short time later, arms unburdened. The halfling came and sat down on the bench below the table, leaning back on the edge, her head now beside Fetch's knee.

She let out a weary breath. "Hard to get those little ones down without a tit ofttimes."

"I need to bring in a new wet nurse," Fetch said, feeling the weight of leadership settle back onto her shoulders. "Another thing I've failed to do."

"Well, don't ask me to help you there," Xhreka said with a chuckle, talking a little above a whisper now that the infant was tucked away. "Can't much stand a man to lip-tug my tits, much less a babe. Make a damn meager meal for them besides." The halfling's neck craned around and her eye surveyed Fetching with exaggerated objection. "Unlike you, all legs and breasts, muscles and ass. Belico's Balls, I hate you and you ain't even kept me away from my dying man. Fetching don't really do justice, being honest."

Fetch tried to hold her smile, but it was forced. "Not how I got the name."

"I know," Xhreka said more soberly. "Idris told me that too."

"You really should use his hoof name."

Xhreka blew a rude noise from between her lips and waved a dismissive hand. "I do what I like."

"You do, don't you?" Fetching replied, peering down and giving the halfling an appraising look. "So why do this? When I offered you a place here, I did not expect to find you rocking babies to sleep."

"Well, if you expected me to suck cock to earn my keep you will be disappointed." Xhreka's head tilted with a show of consideration. "Though if that hairless, pale mongrel asked . . ."

"Hoodwink?" Fetching asked, finding her smile returning.

Xhreka just gave a low whistle.

Finding the thought disturbing, and not because of the halfling,

Fetch steered the conversation back to her original interest. "I just meant there is more work in Winsome than this place."

Xhreka gave her a hard stare. "You think caring for children is weak."

It was not a question.

Fetch shook her head firmly. "No, but coming from the Pit—"

Xhreka held up both hands, stopping her. She then turned her splayed palms upward and made a weighing motion. "Fighting animals in a hole while degenerates scream with enjoyment. Or. Holding, cleaning, and feeding adorable little creatures whose biggest offense is occasionally pissing on you. If that's a hard choice for you to fathom, you have strange notions, my girl."

Fetch gave no reply. The truth had stolen her voice.

Xhreka slapped her shin. "Oh, don't brood. My teeth, you half-orcs are a grim bunch. There's nothing wrong with you. Youth, perhaps, but life or death will rid you of that. Give it time. Enough years of fighting and you will find the prospect of wiping tiny asses much less demeaning. You may even wish for it. And not because you've a quim! Hells, it's all Idris wants, though his dense head doesn't really know it yet."

That truth gave Fetch her voice back. "You're right. There is this simple-minded boy—"

"Muro."

Fetch marveled. "He really did tell you everything."

"He did. And don't think I don't realize that's why you offered me a place. You wanted to make it easier for him to return, not because I was needed."

"That reason makes you needed, Xhreka."

"Well, I'll earn my keep. Going to help repair a roof tomorrow."

"What happened to caring for cute little creatures?"

The halfling gave a careless shrug. "I get bored."

Fetching took a breath, started to speak, but Xhreka stopped her with a hand.

"Don't. I know what's coming. You want to ask why I'm not out walking the broad back of the world, digging for Belico's relics like the rest of my kind."

"I was."

"Don't," Xhreka repeated. "Not now. Or ever. Idris did and got the same answer. I don't speak about that."

"Good enough," Fetch said, and stood up. "When you see Sweeps, tell her the True Bastards got permission from their chief for her to clean and dress Dumb Door. Can you do that?"

"I can."

"Thank you."

She went for the door.

"And, Fetching," Xhreka called her attention back. "I know why you keep the name. It's about spitting in the eye of the man that gave it to you."

Again, the halfling spoke the truth.

TWENTY-FOUR

—

"WHAT IF WE DO NOT wish to leave?"

Glaucio had once been nothing but a chandler's apprentice. Now he stood, hands resting on the table before him, speaking for the people of Winsome. He was a small, unimposing man, even for a frail, his cheeks hollow, his curly hair thinning, but he had no trouble meeting Fetching's eyes, and there was steel in his question.

Fetching remained seated. "You don't have a choice. None of us do."

"I would still like an answer."

"As would I," Thistle said from her chair across the table to Glaucio's right. She was the only other villager Fetch had invited to the cooper's shop. Both her voice and gaze were frigid.

"What if you do not wish to leave," Fetch echoed dully. "Then the two of you will have Winsome all to yourselves."

"That's a foolish answer," Thistle said.

"It was a fool-ass question," Fetch returned, looking at both humans. "The True Bastards will be escorting all those who want to live away from here. The *entire* hoof, slops and riders. None will remain to secure this place. Why would you want to stay, knowing that?"

Glaucio answered her question with another. "And once we are . . . delivered? What will you do?"

"That's a hoof concern."

"They will return here," Thistle told Glaucio. "Quick as they can."

"One day, perhaps. It's our lot, Thistle. We have to return. It's our home."

The woman's eyes flashed. "And it's not ours?"

"Not one you need die for, no."

"That should be our decision," Glaucio declared.

"But it's not," Fetch said, letting the man hear she could put steel in words too. "The Lots belong to the mongrel hoofs. Mongrel. All frails that live here do so because we allow it."

"To the mutual benefit of both." Glaucio met her metal with heat.

"In the past. Not now. The Bastards cannot endure as a hoof on this land. We can no longer protect you. You must make a fresh start, somewhere safer, with less want. You get to live."

Glaucio made a scoffing sound and paced away from the table. "If we survive the journey to wherever you intend to take us."

"The where is why you are in this room," Fetch said, swallowing her agitation. "As for the journey, the hoof will protect you. In absence of walls, we will put ourselves between you and whatever may happen along the way. I want to ensure no one dies."

"You can't be certain none will," Thistle said.

"I can be certain all will if you stay."

"It's not right, Fetching."

"It's as right as I can make it."

Thistle's eyes, permanently darkened with weariness, were unblinking. "I have children to worry about. Infants! And you are ousting them into the badlands."

"I don't want them to starve, Thistle."

"Then! Fucking! Feed them!"

Thistle shot to her feet, nostrils flared, fair hair disturbed by the speed of motion. Glaucio's head snapped around at the outburst, concern crinkling his own careworn features.

Fetch's teeth were clenched so tight they ached.

Glaucio came over to Thistle and placed a gentle hand upon her arm. She startled, anger causing her to forget his presence. For an instant, the baleful glare shifted to him.

"Let's sit," Glaucio suggested.

Slowly, Thistle sat back down, her expression filled with pain. Glaucio settled on the stool next to her and regarded Fetching.

"You said we would have some say in where we are to go."

"Some," Fetching said, clearing her throat. "You should know that returning to the Tusked Tide is not a choice, though the Sons of Perdition might be."

"Might?" Thistle turned the single word into an accusation.

Fetch ignored her. "If you would rather not live under another hoof's protection, Kalbarca is being rebuilt, refortified."

Glaucio made a disgusted noise. "So we men can be conscripted into the army? Our women made into barracks whores?"

"You would not have to remain there," Fetch offered. "Surely, the cavaleros would escort you up the Old Imperial Road into Hispartha."

The man across from her produced a small, morose smile. He gazed down at the table, picked idly at an imaginary splinter. "Forgive me, chief," he said, not looking up and not sounding at all contrite, despite his words, "but do you believe that all humans are given land and coin, justice and protection, simply by returning north? Because I must tell you, half-orcs are not the only beings that scrape out a life in Ul-wundulas for the love of freedom. Hispartha is a kingdom of plenty for only a few, and that plenty is reaped from the masses. Men like my father. I was not born here in the Lots. I remember enough of Hispartha to tell you, Winsome is far from the only place a child faces death from an empty, distended belly."

"And what of orcs?" Fetch asked, refusing to be sold her own ignorance. "What of centaurs and demon dogs that laugh when they kill? Does Hispartha have such things?"

"No," Thistle answered. "Worse. It has pimps and child-rapers, as many among the nobles as in the gutter. It has slave markets and arenas. And the men that profit from them laugh very loudly over the misery they cause. Hispartha delights in its cruelty to the poor and the weak. Its pleasure only swells if you fight back, because there is no hope you will succeed. The Lots are cruel. But at least here the fight is welcomed. Possible."

Thistle never spoke of her life before coming to live at Winsome. She had arrived shortly after Fetch was sworn to the Bastards, a comely, curvy woman with breasts full of milk, yet no babe on her hip. Beryl had immediately taken her on as wet nurse. She'd been serving for months before coming up to the Kiln, finally convinced by Roundth to visit his chamber. Fetch wondered if the wide-dicked mongrel had ever gotten his bedwarmer to tell her tale. If so, he kept the secret until the night an orc put a blade in his neck. Thistle was no longer plump, her lover and her milk turned to dust. But that hard-earned resolve from a life before Winsome, which had ever kept her back straight, was still firmly in place.

Fetch had come to respect her. That was the reason she had invited her to these talks, the reason she was now weathering the passionate, fierce stare of defiance and disappointment.

"Then not Kalbarca," Fetch conceded. "If Ul-wundulas is where you want to stay, your only choice is another hoof."

It was doubtful the Skull Sowers would welcome new arrivals. Tomb, their chief, had expressed strong notions at Strava about the scarcity of resources in the Lots. The Orc Stains' lands were nearest, but Fetch would not willingly offer her people up to Knob's control. He would likely abuse them for his own amusement, if he did not flat refuse them out of spite. That left only three choices.

"The Shards, Sons, or the Cauldron Brotherhood," Fetch informed the humans. "I would encourage the Sons. Their fortress sits near the coast. So long as there are fish in the Deluged, they won't go hungry."

Such an endorsement would not come without a price. Father would likely use the acceptance of Winsome's people to make another attempt at absorbing the Bastards. On his own lot, in his own stronghold, he would be bolder. Fetch would have to get her hoof away quickly if she did not want to lose every slop to the Sons. Possibly a few sworn brothers. Still, it remained the best choice, and she would take the risk. The people here deserved nothing less.

Glaucio rose. "I must speak with some of the others. When do you need an answer?"

"Yesterday," Fetch told him, hating the necessity of such callousness. "If you do not decide on a different destination by tonight, then we leave for Mongrel's Cradle. Either way, all should make preparations now. They have today to gather what they own."

There was no point in expressing a need to travel light. This was the second time Winsome's folk had been forced to flee, and the span between had not been kind. They owned little.

Glaucio took his leave, but Thistle lingered a moment longer.

"You should have left us with the Tusked Tide," she said, head shaking with resignation. Standing, the woman left the room.

Fetch remained still. It had not been her decision alone back then, she had not yet been chief. The Grey Bastards voted in common that day. Oats wanted Beryl to come home, Polecat wanted Cissy and Sweeps. They were all in a rush to return to the way things were, blind to the fact that those days would never return. All in a rush, save Jackal and Warbler, both reluctant for their own reasons. And that was the reason Fetch herself had pressed the issue, been the first to vote in favor of the people coming back. She had thought Jackal was to become chief, with her and Oats and Warbler in his ear, at his side. A driving need to give him something to lead had raised her voice and her hand. Would she still have done so if she knew the truth? That Jackal had no intention of leading? That he and Warbler both were planning on leaving, handing her mastery of a broken hoof, newly saddled with bedraggled villagers? There were none among Winsome's folk she needed. No mother. No lover. What she cared about was the hoof, her brothers, and the mongrel she betrayed to save. The one who abandoned them, abandoned her, to chase down the mistakes he made in his bid for leadership. The leadership that was now hers!

Crying out with a fury, Fetching stood and flipped the table over.

She did not bother to right it before leaving the workshop.

The Bastards were already deep in their own preparations for the journey. This time, none had voted against the decision. She checked in with each of her riders, making sure all efforts would guarantee their readiness to depart. Every hog was to have a rider, the older slops being given mounts to aid with the scouting. There were four wagons in town, but only draft oxen to pull one. The rest would need to be hitched to mules. One of the wagons was reserved for the orphans, the rest for what food remained in town. All else would have to be borne by the walking.

Closeted away in her solar, Fetch obsessed over the one crude map the Bastards possessed of Ul-wundulas. Glaucio had come to her chambers hours ago, confirming the Sons' lot as the villagers' preference. If they were fortunate, the trek there could be completed inside a fortnight.

The food would hold. The frequent rains would have swollen the rivers and ephemeral streams, but they would be crossing the Skull Sowers' lot, which was the driest in all the badlands. Hogs, riders, children, villagers, all told it was nearly two hundred tongues that would need to be wetted daily. Thankfully, they had one of the most talented water sniffers in the Lots sworn to the hoof, though it also meant Hoodwink would be away from the main body most of the time. In her planning, Fetch kept relying on Dumb Door to act as return runner, gnashing her teeth when her weary brain remembered he was gone. None knew the Lots like seasoned nomads, and Door, like Hood, had spent years as a free-rider before joining the Bastards. Fuck Marrow for showing his hog's tail just when he would have been most useful.

The biggest hardship would come near journey's end. Most of the southern coast of Ul-wundulas was bulwarked with mountains, and Mongrel's Cradle lay behind the Hoar Tops, a confined, yet towering range that was named for the visible caps of snow ever upon the peaks. Of course, half-orc crudity demanded they were referred to as simply the Whores. Even Hoodwink wasn't familiar with the safest passes. The most forgiving would be impossible for the wagons and grueling for the frails. Fetch had sent a bird to Father, but if the coot was holding a grudge and didn't have riders on the lookout for their arrival, the Whores could prove a lethal obstacle.

Fetch found she could barely see the map.

Standing, she went out on her balcony. Night had claimed the village while she obsessed over the scrawls of mountains and rivers. Winsome was already a graveyard, its people spending their last night in their homes. They would not be sleeping indoors again for some time. It was a damnably pleasant night, with a breeze that chased the heat without bringing chill to the air. The moon was little more than a sliver, leaving the stars dominion over the sky. Hells, it was just enough calm and beauty to make Fetch want to annul the order to leave.

She stood for a long while, watching the slops walk the palisade. Mead came and oversaw the watch change on his way to the gate. Culprit emerged from the dormitory and headed for the stables, likely to check his tack for the fourth time. Polecat crept down the street, but the tanner's widow must have denied him, for he returned much too soon wearing a scowl. It was only when Oats's bulk appeared on the palisade to manage another watch rotation that Fetch realized she had been standing there half the night. The prospect of sleep was made into a gnawing dread by the task looming in the coming morning.

Another figure came out from the hoof's quarters.

Sluggard.

The vintner's dormitory sat beside her solar, but thrust farther out, making her vantage above and behind the nomad's left shoulder. He simply stood for a while, though something in the set of his shoulders bespoke discomfort. The small, circular steps, the deep, weary breaths, all the signs of one beset by sleeplessness. Fetch waited and watched, wondering if he would go back inside with her vigilance unnoticed.

When he paced away from the building, stretching one shoulder gingerly as he turned, his eyes came up. Seeing her, he stopped. Fetching cocked her head back toward the bedchamber and, without waiting to see his response, went back inside.

The door opened below, followed by Sluggard's measured boot-falls sounding on the stairs. He walked slowly into the room. Fetch lit the lamp. He was bare-chested save for a bandage that wrapped from his right shoulder to beneath his left arm. Bruising from Little Orphan Girl's tusk crept from beneath the linen and stood out upon his jaw.

"Pain keeping you awake?" she asked.

"A bit," Sluggard admitted. "Mostly, I am tired of lying in a cot."

Fetching nodded with understanding. Retrieving a bottle, she poured him a healthy measure of wine. There was no more cause to save it.

Sluggard nearly jumped at the proffered cup. "Oh! You are a savior."

He downed the contents in two long swallows and groaned with appreciation when Fetch immediately refilled his cup. "None for you?"

She shook her head. "Long ride ahead."

"But not for me," Sluggard realized aloud, grinning before sipping his wine. "Is that why you invited me up? To tell me I will no longer be riding with the hoof."

Fetch cocked a dubious eye at his bandages. "Can you?"

"Given enough of this," Sluggard replied, holding up and swirling the wine, "I can do anything."

"Well, that's about the last of it. So . . ."

"That's unfortunate."

Crossing the room, Sluggard passed Fetching and approached the bed, straddling a corner at the foot and sitting without the barest hint of hesitance.

"How are your injuries?" Fetch asked.

The gritter blew out a sighing breath, reaching up to gently touch his bandaged shoulder and chest. "My yoke bone is broken. So that hurts. The tusk only split me a little just beneath that. Nothing a few stitches and a one-eyed halfling could not mend." Sluggard's cheek bulged as he probed the inside of his mouth with his tongue. "Lost a damn tooth. Probably the worst of it really since that won't come back. Luckily, it wasn't in the front. Women don't favor gap-toothed smiles."

"You'll get a scar out of it," Fetch pointed out. "On the chest, too. Hisparthan blue-bloods will flood their skirts over that."

"We can hope."

Sluggard's cup was again empty. Fetch handed over the bottle.

"Are you certain you won't partake?" he asked. "I'm likely to have finished this by the time you change your mind."

"I'm certain."

Shrugging, Sluggard set the cup between his feet and pulled straight from the bottle. He sucked his teeth after swallowing and looked up at her. "Well, if you won't drink, at least sit."

Fetch stayed where she was. "What will you do now? Go back to the cities? Start your whoring? Whore."

"So you *are* ousting me. Not even being given a chance to slow you down tomorrow. Let me hook Palla to one of the wagons. He'll take to the yoke better than any of your barbarians. You know I can damn well drive a team."

Hells, no. Don't be sensible.

Unable to outright deny his reasoning, and not wanting to agree, Fetch laughed and hung her head. "Palla. That's why you are not coming tomorrow."

"What? My hog?"

"Named after the great troubadour from Galiza," she repeated, mocking his voice. "Hells, I did not know what a gritter was until you, but you must be the king of them all. Hoof riders don't talk like that. They don't know shit like that."

"Fine! I will change his name to Cunt Fart and fit right in." The wine and his own jest caused Sluggard to chuckle. It was a childish sound, though a charming one. It was also infectious.

"You will never fit in," Fetch told him, her own voice quivering with laughter. "Scars. Missing teeth. Awful names. It's not a life for you." She took a breath, grew serious. "Sluggard, you could be useful tomorrow, for months even, all the hells know we could use another good rider, but soon—if we survive—I would have to offer you a place within the hoof. You can't accept, not if you want to be a whore—"

"A *cortejo*."

"And if you refuse the brotherhood you will have to leave. Better that you go now and live long enough to return to Hispartha."

Sluggard regarded the floor for a moment. When he looked up, the laughter was gone from his face, replaced by an earnestness that Fetch had never seen. And did not care for.

"What if I don't refuse?" he asked. "What if I stay, earn my place, and become a True—"

Fetch took a step forward, halving the distance between them. "No. You should be balls deep in noblewomen and neck deep in their coin. So. How much?"

Sluggard looked confused.

Going to the chest against the wall, Fetch withdrew a bag of coins, just a fraction of Oats's winnings, yet still heavy in her hand. With a flick of her wrist she tossed the bag at Sluggard. He was taken aback, but managed to catch it, wincing slightly at the sudden motion.

"I want to pay you. I want you to please me. And then I want you to go."

Sluggard dangled the bag in his fingers, carefully aimed, and dropped it into the cup between his feet. The size prevented it from sinking into the vessel. Instead it perched atop, an offering upon a pedestal.

Tossing the empty bottle aside, Sluggard met her eyes. "Come over here."

Another step brought Fetch the rest of the way, standing between his knees.

Sluggard seized her, quick and hard, one arm wrapping beneath her buttocks and pulling her body into his. Her thighs pressed into his torso, hips against his chest. The pressure must have been causing him pain, but he did not show it, his free hand unlacing her breeches in three deft jerks. Fetching threw her tunic off and Sluggard's mouth dove for the exposed flesh of her stomach. Embracing the short, twisted locks of his hair, Fetch kept his questing lips imprisoned, delighting in the shivers it solicited up her back. His arm released her just long enough for both hands to tug her breeches down. Her boots were still on, allowing her to be stripped only to the knees, but she was too engrossed to bother kicking her way free. Sluggard's hands grabbed her rump, strong fingers kneading the flesh, lifting the cheeks. They moved to her hip bones, pulling a bit more forward as his head went lower. His face pressed in, the angle awkward, but his tongue found its way. Fetch moaned as he worked her. The tangle around her calves prevented her legs from spreading further, limiting Sluggard's access, but it hardly mattered. A year's worth of pent-up frustration came shuddering out, guided by the nomad's tongue.

Sluggard pulled away when she was done. Fetching's knees went a bit weak and she eased down to straddle one of his legs, grinding a bit into the hard muscle of his thigh to reap the last few tingling pulses. Placing a hand on his chest, she pushed him back until he was propped by his elbows upon the bed. She giggled a bit when her skill at unlacing breeches proved less efficient than his, but soon she had him free. His cock was engorged to the point of heavy, but not yet rigid.

Fetch looked up at him with exaggerated reproach. "Shouldn't a whore be able to keep his thrum loaded at all times?"

Sluggard defended himself with three confident words. "Pain. Wine. Intimidation."

Fetching laughed, and stood up, making little stepping motions until she was out of her boots and breeches. Leaning down over Sluggard, she allowed her breasts to hang until they just touched him, sliding them down his chest and stomach. His cod jumped when it traveled between, jumped again when she took him in her mouth. That banished all impediments.

Releasing him, she crawled up his body. They both caught their breath when her hips lowered and he slid inside.

"You better not loose quick as I did," she warned in a whisper.

He grinned up at her. "No chance."

Fetching rode him, testing his bravado. Sluggard not only endured the long, slow strokes, he added to their efficacy, his hands guiding and caressing until, at last, pulling her down atop him. Holding her close by the nape of the neck and the small of the back, he thrust up into her with flawless speed until she again reached release. Rolling upon the bed, Fetch wound up on her back, Sluggard still firmly entrenched. Grabbing her behind the knees, he pushed until her thighs pressed into her breasts and her hips rose off the tangled bedding. He shifted both their entwined bodies effortlessly, until he was squatting upon the balls of his feet. He began to thrust once more, his legs drawing him out only to relax and send him plummeting back in, the depth of his invasion harrowing and exquisite. An intense, blissful pressure built. Fetch gave herself over to it, but then a familiar urge settled into her loins. She reached and made a clumsy attempt to ease Sluggard's exertions, hands fumbling across the iron-wrought muscles of his abdomen, but he pressed on.

Through her gasps and moans she managed a near-panicked entreaty. "Feels like I'm going to p—"

At that moment, Sluggard pulled himself out. Fetch felt his middle two fingers slide inside. Cupping his hand, Sluggard began making a rapid, forward pulling motion. Mouth agape, but unable to voice her bliss, Fetch felt a torrent escape, heard the flow sloshing in the nomad's palm. She went blind, eyes forced shut with a primal ecstasy, felt her legs spasm.

She regained senses to the sound of her own panting, punctuated by little moans. Her bedchamber ceiling was difficult to focus upon.

"What the fff—" She could hardly form words. "What . . . in fuck. Was that?"

Sluggard's pleased, only slightly breathless, voice answered from somewhere to the right.

"Have you never gushed before?"

Fetch could not stop smiling. "Oooooooh, fuuuuuuuck."

"Well . . . suffice to say *that* is the reason I am going to be a very rich whore."

They both laughed for a long while, and when Fetch recovered, coupled again. The candles burned out and she fell asleep, too sated to take up the worry over the morning.

She stirred when Sluggard's hand touched her face, growing annoyed when it lingered. Her eyes snapped open when the hand clamped over her mouth. A bulky shadow leaned over her, the narrow chill of a blade upon her throat.

"Hope you have some spirit left for me." Knob's hateful voice leaked into her ear.

TWENTY-FIVE

—

FETCH'S MIND RACED. She willed herself not to lash out, to fight, burying every instinct.

Knob had her head pushed deep into the bed. His hand smelled of hog, saddle leather, and soot. Both his grip and the knife were steady. He was calm, ready to kill, but not eager. Murder was on his mind, not yet in his hand, unless she forced it.

"Make a noise," came the threat, "fight me, and we open your plaything from throat to cod."

Keeping his hand upon her mouth, Knob turned her head, directed her gaze. In the starlight from the balcony, Fetch saw Sluggard, naked, held against the wall by a huge mongrel, a blade to his throat. His eyes gleamed, wide and furious and afraid.

The Orc Stains were inside Winsome!

How? Didn't matter. The question was how to survive.

Knob lifted his chin at the other thrice, soliciting the brute to stomp lightly on the floor. Five more hulking forms drifted into the room. They were equipped for a night raid, wearing only breeches, lest a gleam upon the metal studs of their brigands betray their skullduggery. To that same end, they were armed only with knives. Fetch did not hear them come up the stairs, so their feet must have been bare. Their flesh was smeared with soot, darkening their already ash-colored skin. Hells, they had climbed the walls, snuck past the sentries. The alarm would have been raised had they slit any throats, left gaps in the watch.

Outside, Winsome slept on, unaware of the vicious intent that had just skulked into Fetch's dreams.

The urge to fight intensified as the newcomers placed themselves at the corners of the bed, the fifth helping to secure Sluggard. A new impulse rose. Panic. It was harder to force down, but for Sluggard's life and her own, Fetch managed to remain still while her wrists and ankles were seized.

Now she could move only her eyes.

Her limbs were pinned, each held fast by an unyielding strength. Fucking thrice-bloods!

So, two at the wall, one on each limb, and Knob. Seven foes in her small chamber.

Fuck.

Slowly, the meaty palm peeled away from her lips, hovering close. Knob was perched on the bed to Fetch's right, between her and the balcony, his bald head and brutal shoulders etched in pale light.

Fetch risked a hissing warning. "Ride away, Knob. Take your boys and ride away."

A laugh responded, quiet and wet. "Oh, no. I swallowed your threat. I'm here now to see that you swallow mine."

Knob shifted, fumbling with his other hand. She could not see what he was doing, but could easily guess.

"I will swallow the entire fucking thing," Fetch vowed. "But it won't be attached to your body."

"Thought you understood?"

Cupping her chin roughly, Knob snatched her head around again. The Stain with the knife began to slice down Sluggard's chest while the other held him still, hand smothering his cries of pain. The thrice paused after cutting a hand's length. The wound was deep.

"Behave," Knob instructed, squeezing her face. He let go,

straightening. One knee upon the bed, he brandished his erection, fist entwining in her hair. "I feel teeth and he dies."

"Strange threat," Fetch replied, calm as stone. "You'll lose a cock. Taking nothing but a drifting gritter from me. Since you are determined to end up a eunuch. Go on. Give me the chance." She put laughter in her voice and opened her mouth wide.

Knob paused, but his response still held amusement. "You sorely tempt me to wager, girl. But I don't have to. Flip her."

Fetch waited for the chance to free herself, for a slackening in her captors' hold. It never came. They crossed her feet first, forcing her spine and pelvis to twist to their limit. Only then did they manipulate her arms, the mongrels at her wrists swapping which they held. Facedown now, Fetch felt the bed sink as Knob placed himself between her legs. He pawed at her buttocks, spreading them open, his thumb lingering as it brushed her anus.

"Mouth and ass," Fetch taunted, craning her head. "I always figured you were backy." She looked at the thrice holding her right arm. "You're welcome, Stain. He won't be buggering you tonight."

The mongrel struck, a downward backhand to the cheek. He was fast, his hand away from her wrist for only a moment.

It was all she needed.

Twisting her arm, she broke his one-handed grip just as his blow sent lights crackling in her skull.

"Fucking hold her!" Knob growled, his weight descending upon her back.

Fetch's free hand scrambled, but was immediately recaptured.

Knob's hot breath poured into her ear, sounding pleased. "I warned you. Gut him."

The sound of the door opening on the lower level froze the room.

"Chief!" A familiar voice called up the stairs just ahead of hurrying footfalls. "We got a fire at the—"

Knob lurched off the bed, moving for the door.

"MEAD! WARN THE HOOF!"

But Fetch's cry only brought him rushing into the room.

The drawn sword in Mead's hand caused the bedchamber to erupt, smoke in a hornet's nest. Knob was nearest, his large frame barreling at the smaller Bastard, causing him to slash out. The stroke was hurried, confused, half-blind. Knob jumped back, avoiding the cut, but the Stains at the foot of the bed reacted instinctually to their chief's peril, going to his aid.

Fetch found her legs free.

She tucked her knees up, gathered her legs beneath, planted her feet into the bed, and jumped backward. The distracted Stains holding her wrists were hauled off-balance, the one on her right letting go completely. The other stumbled but held firm, causing her to swing at the end of his grip, wrenching her shoulder. She tumbled to the floor, between the bed and the balcony opening. A foot smashed into her ribs, choking her lungs with emptiness and pain. The thrice, still holding her arm high, kicked her again. When the third kick came, she pushed off the floor with her free arm, trapping the oncoming leg with both of her own, wrapping it up. Twisting with every sinew, she dragged the thrice to the ground and stomped his fruits.

Finally, she was free.

With a jerk she snapped the knee of the howling thrice's pinned leg, snatched the dagger from his belt, rolled to a crouch, and sent it whirling across the room into the gut of Sluggard's blade-drawn captor. He crumpled, freeing Sluggard enough to grapple with the other.

The thrice who lost hold of Fetching came diving across the bed, tackling her and driving them both out onto the balcony. Fetch's head smacked the railing. This time there were no lights, just a blackness, threatening to engulf. The Stain's thick fingers were around her throat. Skull-cracked and befuddled, windpipe collapsing, Fetch felt her world darkening, shrinking to nothing but the face of the brute killing her. The same brute that had struck her, twice let her break loose. He was angry, senseless, lusting to end her with his bare hands.

Bare. Hands.

Weakening, groping, she searched. Found. Nothing to do but keep killing these fucks with their own knives. The angry face became confused, appalled, when the dagger blade plunged behind its ear. The throttling hands went slack and Fetch kicked the body away.

Wheezing, she looked into the room through a jumble of legs.

The pair of Stains who rushed Mead had pushed him back through the doorway, the narrow jamb preventing him from being surrounded, but neither could he win back into the room, his sword a hindrance in the close confines. One thrice fended him off, while the other pushed the door closed. Sluggard struggled, but was quickly overpowered, injured as he was. The thrice smashed its forehead into his face, dropped him with a pair of ruthless punches. The one gut-stabbed by Fetch's thrown dagger stumbled to his feet, cradling his leaking belly.

She tried to yell out, tried to stop the folly before any more died, but was trammeled with coughs. The sound drew Knob's attention.

Turning slowly, he towered above, taking a step.

Another.

Between them, on the floor next to the wall, was Fetch's sword belt. Following her bleary gaze, Knob grinned. A step forward, he would be upon her. A step left, he would reach her weapons. Fetch could hear Mead screaming her name, the sound of resounding steel as he tried to chop through the door.

"Walk away from this," Fetch managed, her voice ragged. "You got one dead, one dying, and one that will never ride again. I'll call that settled after this shit."

"You think these boys are all I brought? The rest of my hoof will soon be inside your walls, slut. You sure you want to settle the tally before knowing how many of your own are dead?"

Fetch went cold. From outside, she could hear the sounds of the village responding to the fire. The shouts were coming from the north end. Farthest from the gate. Her dismay must have shown upon her face, for Knob's grin broadened.

Fetch hardened her stare. "Stop dancing between me and the sword and make a fucking choice!"

Showing his teeth, Knob went for the weapons.

Fetch dove, confident she would be swifter, but one leg was snatched by the Stain with the broken knee. He could not hold her, but the stall was enough. Knob yanked the sword belt from the ground, tearing the tulwar from its scabbard. Fetch was belly-down at his feet, hand still outstretched over a vanished prize.

Knob gloated. "I wager you would eagerly take my cock now, rather than die. Rather than watch your boys die."

There was nothing for it. She was armed with only a knife, trapped in a room with four hale thrice-bloods, while outside her people were unknowingly under siege.

I'll make them stupid. You make them corpses.

Cissy's words.

Slowly, Fetch nodded.

Getting up on her hands and knees, she turned in place. She could feel Knob's eyes crawl across her unclad back.

"Toss the blade."

Fetch sent it sliding across the floor. Looking over her shoulder, she watched Knob hand the tulwar over to one of his mongrels.

Hating herself, hoping Sluggard would forgive her, in this world or in the hells, she made a choice.

"Mead! Fall back!"

Springing forward onto the balcony, she vaulted the railing. The quick drop sent a lurch through her stomach, but she landed well, rolling. Above, Knob rushed out onto the balcony, loading Fetch's stockbow.

She darted beneath the overhang, nearly colliding with Mead as he stumbled out the door of her solar. A quick glance showed two Stains rushing down the stairs after him.

Fetch and Mead ran for the hoof barracks, slamming the door behind and dropping the bar.

Inside, all the bunks were empty, the place turned out to fight the fire.

"My thrum's on the hook," Mead hissed. Fetch got the weapon and a full quiver before hurrying to Oats's chest. She snatched out a shirt and threw it on, the large garment nearly falling to her knees.

Culprit had left his sword belt behind, so Fetch claimed it, hoping she would get the chance to berate the new rider. Realizing finding boots was a fool-ass dream, she returned to the door, where Mead stood on guard, peering out the squint.

"They didn't pursue," he said. His stump was pressed to his side. Fetch cursed when she saw the blood. "Stuck me on the way out" was Mead's only response, not relinquishing his vigil. "What do you want to do?"

"Rally the hoof. Kill every thrice-blood within the walls that isn't Oats."

"Or Incus."

"Right."

"Sounds good."

"I need to know about that wound, Mead."

"It didn't take off a hand, so I've suffered worse."

"Mead . . ."

"Why do you think they didn't follow?"

Going over to the nearest bunk, Fetch tore a strip from a blanket and began bandaging Mead's side.

She answered his question while she worked. "I'm not raped and dead, so that fire was set too early. Knob had a plan, but it's gone sloppy. He's regrouping."

"Doesn't want to spread his boys too thin," Mead agreed, grunting as the bandage tightened.

Or Knob was taking his anger out on the mongrel she left behind. Fetch pushed the thought away.

"Don't reckon the Stains are second-guessing," Mead said, his tone snide. "Taking the chance to get away?"

There was no need to reply.

Knob was never going to abandon this raid. The Orc Stains had just embarked on something never before known in the Lots. They had just waged war on another mongrel hoof. There was no coming back from that, despite Fetch's offer of pardon.

Tonight, another of the half-orc hoofs would join the Rutters in ruin. Fetch had to make sure it was not the True Bastards.

"Where was the fire set?" she asked.

"One of the boarded-up houses," Mead told her. "Between the hog pens and the mason's shop."

Northwest side of the village. Across town from the well.

"That means we have at least one more Stain inside our walls. Shed Snake had the last gate watch?"

Mead nodded.

The brother leading the gate guard was not to leave for any reason. Fires were always suspected to be a diversion, so the slops on sentry duty were taught to hurry for the gate, leaving one in four to patrol the walls at double pace. That gave Snake a force of twelve slopheads. Knob would be hard-pressed to take it. He would also need more weapons than daggers, unless his thrice-blood pride made him arrogant enough to attempt it without swords and thrums. He didn't know Winsome, wouldn't know where they stored their arms . . .

"Fuck!"

"What?"

"They knew where I slept. No chance they searched all of Winsome looking for me without being spotted."

"They came right to you," Mead realized. "How?"

Fetch shook her head. "They likely know our watches. Know how we respond to a fire. They're not coming in through the gate. . . ."

"Then where?"

"Same as the rest, over the walls. Only other way. We need to move."

"Lead on."

Slipping out the door, Fetch moved swiftly along the wall of the bunkhouse, away from her solar, making sure to keep well out of sight of the balcony. They went around to the north side of the dormitory, winding their way behind the neighboring buildings, using them for cover before darting across the main thoroughfare.

They passed village men rushing to and from the well. Fetch ignored them. Reaching the house, they found it fully ablaze. Polecat and Oats were in the face of it, battling with buckets passed down the chain. Culprit came running up from behind with two sloshing pails, but he slowed when he saw Fetching.

"I don't think we can put it out, chief," he said.

"Drop those!" Fetch demanded. "Doesn't matter. TRUE BAS-TARDS!"

Her roar eclipsed that of the inferno.

Looking up, Polecat and Oats abandoned their efforts, running over, both sweating and squinting from the flames. Still, they noticed her appearance.

"The hells?" Polecat said.

"Weapons and mounts," Fetch ordered. "The Orc Stains are here to end us."

Oats growled and ran for the hog pens.

Polecat was bewildered. "The Stains? The fuck? Why?"

"No time!" Fetch barked. "Straddle your damn razor!"

Shaking off the confusion, Polecat nodded and ran after Oats. Fetch caught Culprit by the arm.

"Where is Hood?"

"He was running buckets. Thought he was right behind me."

"Go," Fetch said, removing the sword belt from her waist with one hand and throwing it at the new rider. "And take your fucking slicer this time!"

Fetch looked at Mead. "I know Hood. He smelled something. The Stains are about to make a move."

"I best saddle my hog."

"No. I need you up on the wall. Tell the sentries to watch for scalers. Get to the gate if you can, tell Snake what has happened."

Fetch was concerned about the hole in Mead's side. The bandage was already soaked through. She wanted him where he would be safest. He made for the nearest palisade stairs, not far from the house, while she headed for the stables.

Oats already had Ugfuck saddled and was working on Womb Broom. Polecat was seconds from finished with his hog. Culprit was only a little behind, nervous but keeping his head.

"We need to hurry," Fetch told her hoof, taking over tacking her hog. "There are at least seven Stains inside already, including their master. Two of them are wounded, likely still holed up in my solar. They may have Sluggard held there too." This drew a quick look from Polecat and a noticeable stillness from Oats. "Likely, he's dead, but keep an eye. The other Stains will be coming. It's possible they know all about how we work. Knob might make a move for the chandler's cellar."

"For our weapons stores?" Polecat said, climbing into the saddle. "Chief, there's nothing there. We took everything out and loaded it up for tomorrow."

Fetch had forgotten. The town was set to empty at dawn. The supplies, food and weapons, such as they were, were already on the wagons sitting near the gate. It was a piece of luck Fetch was willing to accept.

"We're going for the chandler's. If Knob doesn't know we stripped the weapons, we may be able to catch him there with his breeches around his ankles. Let's ride."

As they spurred out of the paddock, Polecat drew alongside.

"Chief. What the Stains are doing ain't right."

"I know, Cat. We will make them pay."

"No, listen. Sneaking around, setting fires, pilfering weapons. Sound like a bunch of thrice-bloods to you? They respect strength. Their own. This just doesn't . . . it ain't right."

Fetch slowed her hog. Polecat was right. Thrice-bloods were more orc than man. They were more savage, more bloodthirsty, this was known across the Lots. Were it not for Beryl, Oats would likely be little different, and he was still frightening when provoked. The Orc Stains did not fear the True Bastards. Knob did not fear *her*. Skulking into her bedchamber had been a need to punish her, to catch her unawares and make her feel helpless. She was not a threat, just something to be tamed. As for the rest of the hoof, they were lesser in the eyes of the Orc Stains, mere half-orcs, little better than frails. They would not avoid a direct fight, nor see a need to separate their enemy before striking.

The burning house raged, just ahead to the right.

"It's not a distraction," Fetch realized. "It's a fucking beacon."

One of the sentries began screaming. Sence. He was up on the palisade, just beyond the blaze, the intervening smoke and flickering heat turning him into a phantom. Another slophead came running, alerted by the call, as did Mead, both pounding along the wall walk from opposite directions. Still yelling, Sence cast his spear over the wall. The next instant, he reeled and fell to the walk, smote by something Fetch had not seen.

Giving Womb Broom a kick, pulling him to the right, she led the riders toward the wall.

Above, Mead reached Sence's side, looked over the palisade and, quickly raising his tulwar, began chopping between the stakes. The other sentry, Graviel, arrived. He pulled his arm back to cast his spear and was dropped. This time, Fetch saw the thrumbolt strike, taking the poor slop through the throat.

As she, Culprit, Polecat, and Oats skirted the edge of the burning building, a creaking groan sounded from the wall, loud enough to be heard over the holler of the flames. They were about to dismount, rush for the stairs when Mead looked down, eyes wide, and held his stump out to them in warning.

The wall lurched beneath him, timbers bending. A wide section of the stockade began to splay, the wood complaining. The planking coming apart beneath his feet, Mead fell back upon the sloping, creaking spars.

Polecat screamed his name.

Dazed and desperate, Mead tried to find his feet, but the beams at his back snapped in half, flinging splinters as large as hog tusks. Womb Broom squealed and reared. Fetch threw a warding arm across her face, shielding herself from the flying shards, but refused to look away, crying out with wordless, impotent grief as Mead pitched over the collapsing wall and toppled backward into the night.

The brutalized remains of the wall were dragged away, leaving a broken tooth in the mouth of Winsome's defenses. Through the ragged gap, revealed in the light from the house fire, were the Orc Stains. Afoot and arrayed in two lines, a dozen thrice-bloods still gripped the thick ropes they had used to rend the stockade in a terrifying display of raw power. Another four rushed between the rope lines, bearing a makeshift bridge.

"Bring them down!" Fetch yelled.

The Bastards let fly, but only one of the Stains fell. The remaining three planted the bridge on the far side of the ditch, heaved it forward to lean against the pile of fallen beams, creating a ramp. As soon as it was in place, the bearers scattered.

Hogs came charging out of the darkness.

Two surged across the ramp abreast, another three pair right behind. Though saddled, they bore no riders.

Culprit loosed at one of the lead hogs but failed to bring it down. The seasoned Bastards saved their bolts, knowing they could not stop a column of barbarians at full gallop. With no other choice, the riders scattered, allowing the eight swine to barrel through the gap. The scent of their masters in their snouts, the riderless hogs passed them by and ran into the heart of the town, a delivery of mounts and weapons for the raiders already inside.

"We are about to have mounted Stains riding up our asses!" Fetch called out.

"Gonna be some in our teeth soon too!" Oats declared.

Thrumbolts were already whistling through the gap in the wall, preventing the Bastards from taking up the defense, giving the Stains time to mount and gather for the charge.

"We don't have the numbers to hold that hole for long," Polecat said.

For the second hated time, Fetch gave the order to fall back.

Yanking Womb around, she led her boys in flight, away from the breach.

"Ride for the gate!"

If they could reach Shed Snake and the slop garrison, make a stand, maybe there was a chance.

Galloping down the center of town, they found Knob and four riders arrayed against them, charging. Thrumbolts were loosed from both sides. Fetch's shot spilled one thrice from his mount, a bolt in his chest. To her right, Polecat grunted but kept his seat. Culprit's hog squealed as it was struck. Trying to flee the pain, the barbarian lurched away, leaving a hole in the Bastards' line.

There was no time for another volley. Swords were drawn.

Her tulwar gone, Fetching drew a javelin from the saddle brace. Oats pulled ahead at the last moment, turning Ugfuck's bulk into the tip of the Bastards' spear. But the Stains' mounts were far from runts and they refused to break.

The barbarians met in a chorus of enraged squeals.

Oats sent his tulwar for Knob's head, but the chief turned the blow with his own blade. The mongrel on Oats's left sought retribution, but before his sword could descend Ugfuck jerked his head and plowed a tusk into the side of the other barbarian, sending it careening away. Seeing the opening, Fetching veered and thrust with her javelin. The Stains must not have had time to don their brigands. The javelin sank deep into the rider's exposed body, just beneath the rib. Snarling in pain, the thrice chopped the transfixing shaft in two.

And then Womb Broom galloped through the bloody press. Oats was ahead and pulled Ug around, though the gate was little more than a thrumshot away.

"We're not whole!" he declared.

Fetching turned in the saddle. Polecat was on foot, a thrumbolt in his thigh, his hog down and kicking, entrails spilled from a goring. Farther away, Culprit was still mounted, but slumped over his barbarian's neck. The injured animal had wandered near a house and come to a halt. The Orc Stains had ridden past, but were now turning for another charge. Behind them, the rest of their hoof appeared, a mass of blood-hungry mongrels astride snorting pigs.

"Forget her!" Fetch screamed, seeing Polecat begin stumbling toward his fallen sow. "She's done!"

Casting about, Polecat saw Culprit's hog and went back, as fast as his limp would allow. He leapt up behind, holding the younger brother in the saddle and taking control of his hog. Fetch and Oats both loosed bolts at the Orc Stains, trying to give Cat more time.

The answering bolts came in a swarm.

Fetch's arm was grazed by a barbed head, another sank into her saddle, and Ugfuck squealed and shied as he was struck in the face, his thick skull deflecting the shaft. Culprit's mount screamed again, a bolt sprouting from its flank just as Polecat was punched forward, hit in the back. But he kept Culprit and himself upright, pushing the hog through its pain to greater speed. When he reached Fetch and Oats, a thrumbolt piercing his shoulder blade, they all rode hard for the gate, where the garrison stood shouting encouragement. Bolts flew overhead as Shed Snake and the half dozen slops with stockbows pulled their ticklers. They launched two volleys at the Stains before Fetch and her riders reached the gate.

"They're scattering!" Shed Snake called down.

Turning, Fetch saw the Orc Stains' column split down the middle, taking cover behind the surrounding buildings.

Knob may not have feared a fight, but he was no fool. Rushing the gate, where foes on higher ground bristled with spears, was inviting the death of his hoof.

"How many?" Fetch asked Snake.

"Counted near twenty, chief."

"Twenty-two," Dacia amended. "At least."

Only two Stains lay unmoving in the thoroughfare, one Fetch had put down herself. Damn thrice-bloods were nearly as hard to kill as thicks. Of course, the same could be said for her own. Polecat had two bolts sticking out of him, but he still helped a pair of slopheads ease Culprit down from his hog. The young mongrel had taken a blow to the head, but was breathing, moaning.

"Get him up on the wall," Fetch ordered, "but give me his damn sword. You too, Polecat."

The hatchet-faced mongrel shook his head, slapped his saddle. "Aim to fulfill my creed."

Fetch did not argue. Not even a chief was bigger than the oath.

"Shed Snake, mount up."

Snake came down from the palisade and untied his hog from the hitching post near the gate.

Bolts began flying in from a few dismounted Stains leaning around corners to loose. A slophead on the palisade cried out and fell to the planks.

"Drop!" Fetch called out.

The garrison went to their bellies. Their vantage was useful, but it also made them easy targets.

Slinging his stockbow, Oats dismounted. "Cover my hide."

He hurried to the closest supply wagon, squatted, and took hold of the tongue. Taking his lead, Incus rushed to another. Fetch ordered a volley to keep the Stains tucked away while her thrice-bloods hauled the laden wagons across the mouth of the gate, giving the riders some protection.

The wooden frames drummed as they were struck.

Fetch looked at her riders. "Here is what we—"

"Chief!"

Up on the palisade, Touro was half-raised, pointing.

The Bastards looked out from the wagons.

Fetch's heart dropped into a queasy gut.

Knob and the Orc Stains led the orphans out into the open, thrums trained.

"Craven fucks!" Oats exclaimed.

Fetch had to grab his arm to keep him from spurring Ugfuck out from cover.

"Where are you, cunt?!" Knob shouted. "Let me see you!"

The look Fetch gave her hoof said all that needed saying.

Riding out from behind the wagon, hands empty, arms spread, Fetch began moving forward.

"Off the razor!" Knob commanded.

Fetch did as she was told. "Release the children."

"Once I have you."

"You have me," Fetch said, walking steadily. "Let them go."

Beyond Knob, his boys held Thistle. Her mouth was bloodied, but she was still struggling, screaming and pleading. There was no sign of Sweeps or the three infants, just the children who could walk.

That put a dread in Fetching she had never known. Her eyes shot to Thistle and the woman gave the barest shake of her head.

Fetch stopped halfway between the gate and the Stains.

"I'm here. Let them cross over to my hoof."

Knob ignored her, pitched his voice over her head. "Listen well, Bastards! I could kill every damn one of you. I *will* kill every damn one of you, if you force it! But I just want this slattern here. The runts and their minders are yours, so long as you stay put. Forget this hussy, choose a proper leader, become worthy of being called a hoof again. Do anything else, and the vultures will break their fast on everyone in this village come dawn!"

The Stains shoved the weeping children forward, but most of them were too afraid to move.

"Go on, now," Fetch told them. "Go climb the mountain. Go to Oats."

She turned and gestured. He could not have heard her, but she knew him well. Oats was already standing in the open, a harbor of safety for the foundlings.

That got a few of the older ones going, taking the hands of their quailing fellows. Once the children were past Fetching, the Stains released Thistle. She hurried after the orphans, weaving a bit. She mouthed something to Fetch. *Beryl?* Once she and the foundlings were all behind the wagon, Fetch walked the rest of the way.

The Orc Stains ringed her with their hogs. Knob shouted a final warning at the Bastards to stay put as his boys led Fetch away.

The houses were dark and silent, but she could sense the frightened eyes of the villagers watching the procession from hiding.

Knob rode up beside her, gazed down.

"You are not going to honor your word," Fetch said, keeping her eyes ahead.

There was triumph in the thrice's reply. "I am. I am going to bring you outside the walls and fuck you bloody. Then I will give you to my boys. All that they do will be in sight of your hoof. The acts they commit, your bewitched brethren will not be able to endure. They will come for you, I have no doubt. And then it will be they who break the agreement."

They were nearing the abandoned north end. The burning house had spread its destruction to the mason's hall, the breach in the wall hidden by the growing flames.

Fetch halted, turned to look up at Knob.

"Your boys may end up having their way with me, but not you. You're about to die."

Knob laughed. "Should I get down from my hog? Would that make it simpler for you to kill me?"

"I have no need to kill you myself, Knob. I'm master of a hoof. I can simply give an order and you die."

Knob's smile became a grimace. "You are no——"

"Hood!"

A thrumbolt came hissing in from above, sinking to the fletching between Knob's neck and shoulder, angled perfectly to find his heart.

The chief of the Orc Stains keeled from the saddle.

No one, not even Fetching, saw where the shot came from. She had trusted to faith that the pallid killer was creeping about nearby, waiting for a chance.

They won't see me. Neither will you.

Spitting curses, the Orc Stains trained their stockbows on the surrounding rooftops, sweeping, searching, but Hoodwink had already melted away from whatever perch he used to slay their leader.

Freeing the tulwar from Knob's corpse, Fetching tried to mount his shying hog. Some barbarians would suffer an unfamiliar rider. Others would try to kill any who dared.

Knob's hog was a killer.

As the animal twisted to seek vengeance, Fetch scrambled away and darted at the Stains to the rear. One had his stockbow leveled at her, about to loose. A bolt whistled into his eye.

This time Hoodwink allowed himself to be seen, giving the Stains another target. He was up on the roof of the house hemming them to the right, staying long enough for them to pull their ticklers. By the time the bolts shattered the tiles, he was gone.

Only one Stain remained focused on Fetching. Snarling, the thrice drew his blade, but his wrath was stilled by a sound he did not recognize.

Fetch did.

It was the laughter of dogs.

TWENTY-SIX

THE PACK PADDED AROUND the burning homes. Their measured pace was not born from caution but from relish. They were inside. And voicing their amusement.

The Orc Stains turned at the queer laughter, looking puzzled as the hyenas gathered. A score of the beasts materialized from beyond the flames, born in the darkness, revealed in the scorching light. Their squat muzzles grinned at the end of those thick necks, those hunched backs.

The laughter had snared Fetch's legs. Horror got them moving again.

She bolted, diving between a gap in the Stains' stamping hogs, winning free of the circle.

Behind her, the pack whooped and the thrice-bloods cursed, more annoyed than alarmed. Bowstrings thrummed. The curses gave way to wordless exclamations, swiftly followed by the squeals of savaged hogs and the disbelieving screams of their riders.

Fetch kept running. Did not look back.

Any moment, she expected to be dragged down by a slavering

maw, but she kept her legs pumping. When she reached the lower end of the village, still alive, she lifted her voice at the houses.

"Out! Get out! To the gate! The gate!"

A door opened a crack, the hint of a frightened face beyond.

"You have to flee!" Fetch screamed. "Death is here! Out! Bring your families, leave everything! To the gate!"

A man emerged from a house up the way, ushering his wife and child. Those three frightened forms brought the rest from hiding in a tide.

"Go!" Fetch encouraged, waving the folk. "The hoof is at the gate! Go!"

Hoodwink emerged from an alley and came to her side. His stockbow was loaded, aimed back the way Fetching had come. A hog appeared, spooked and bloody, eyes rolling white. There was no rider. Seeing Fetch and Hood, it turned and trotted between two buildings, fearing all it saw.

"Let's get to the gate," Fetching said.

Together, they caught up with the villagers and stayed at the rear of the group, watching for the pack.

The Bastards saw them coming. Shed Snake rode forward, the relief on his face quickly banished when told about the dogs.

"Open the gate!" Fetch commanded. "We need to get our people away from here."

"Never make it on foot," Hood said.

Fetch ran to one of the wagons and began throwing the supplies out, precious foodstuffs cast to the dirt. She waved a woman and her daughter over, picked the little girl up, and placed her in the bed.

The True Bastards, sworn brothers and slopheads, jumped to follow her example. The food and weapons were dumped, replaced with the young and old. While they were helping the people climb into the beds, Thistle hurried over, grabbing Fetch's arm with such force, her nails drew blood.

"We can't leave," she said, her voice tremulous. "Oats isn't back."

Fetch wrangled Thistle's clawing hands and looked around. She spied Ugfuck, but Oats was nowhere to be seen. "Where is he?"

"We hid the babes," the woman exclaimed, stricken beyond the point of tears. "You can't leave. We hid them! Before the thrice-bloods kicked the door in, we managed to hide them. Xhreka was the only one small enough . . ."

"Small enough for where?" Fetching pressed.

"The rain barrel! In the rear garden. There was no time. It was half full. They were smashing in almost before we could place the cover. Sweeps tried to stall them. They hit her! Fetch . . . she was so still, but her eyes were still open. Oh, hells!"

"Thistle—"

"I told Oats! He went. To get them. We can't leave!"

"We will get them, Thistle, but you have to get in the wagon."

Thistle shook her head, protests forming only as a humming moan.

"Thistle, look at me! We. Will. Get. Them."

The woman calmed enough for her voice to return. "Please."

Fetch took hold of her face, steadying the frantic nods, and helped her up into the wagon.

Shed Snake came to Fetch's side. "The wainwright fled without his team, so one wagon will have to stay. And most of the hogs are still in the pens. We don't have enough mounts for the slops. How are we going to protect—"

"There is no protection from these things!" Fetch hissed. "All we can do is run."

She barked orders at the slopheads and they began hitching the animals. While they worked, Fetch gathered the hoof, save for Culprit, who was still unconscious.

"Head for Batayat Hill," she told them. "It's close enough that you might make it."

Polecat was pale from blood loss. "And what are you about to do?"

"Find Oats and the babes. Mead and Sluggard too."

"You're not going alone," Shed Snake declared.

"She's not," Hoodwink said. "My hog is in the pen. I will not leave him."

The pale mongrel's dead stare left no room for argument.

Fetch swept what was left of her hoof with a pointed stare. "Batayat Hill. We will meet you. Live in the saddle."

The response came in quiet unison. "Die on the hog."

"Go."

The gate was thrown open and the True Bastards took the people of Winsome out into the night.

Fetch and Hoodwink exchanged a small nod.

"First to the orphanage," she said.

"Save that for last," Hood intoned. "The babes are either safe with Oats or dead. If we are to find Mead and Sluggard, and retrieve the hogs, we should not be burdened with infants. They will get us killed. If we die, they die."

It was likely the most Fetch had ever heard Hoodwink say at one time, and each word held the cold, pitiless reasoning that only he could conjure.

But he wasn't wrong.

"My solar, then."

"Best use the wall."

There were no stairs built near the gate, a design of Mead's to make it harder for an enemy to assault from within. Going to the ladders, Fetch and Hood climbed to the palisade, heading east along the walk until the wall curved northward. It was not the swiftest path to Fetch's solar, but it was safer from the dogs. Hoodwink led, stockbow pressed to his shoulder, she a few paces behind, tulwar drawn.

Below them, the remaining Orc Stains were scattered throughout Winsome, fighting to survive. Fetch and Hood saw one rider making a dash for the gate, but the surging forms of three hyenas ran his hog down. Farther on, another pair of Stains crept on foot, moving from shadow to shadow between the buildings. Both were bleeding from bite wounds and only one still retained a loaded stockbow.

Hood shot that one first, felling the thrice before he noticed they were above.

The other ran, ducking around a house, but a dog's chortle sounded and the Stain cried out. Both sounds were cut short, replaced by the wet gnashing of powerful jaws tearing flesh. Fetch hissed at Hood and they moved swiftly on.

Soon, they came to the back of the grovers' dormitory, a large building within a stone's throw of the wall. The foreman's house that Fetch had claimed was just beyond, its second story sticking up above the lower sprawl of the workers' quarters. There was nothing living in sight, though the body of a Stain lay facedown upon its own trailing guts. Fetch motioned for Hood to cover her and lowered herself over the edge of the walkway, hung for a moment, and dropped down. Staying beneath the palisade, she listened. There were no sounds, but that was far from reassuring. She sprinted for the rear of the dormitory, placed her back against the mudbrick, and looked to Hood. He signaled she was clear.

Without a sword belt, she was forced to hold the tulwar in her teeth to make the climb, the heavy blade straining her jaw. Thankfully, the building was squat, the roof flat, so a spring brought her hands to the edge. From there, she pulled herself up.

Hoodwink followed and soon they both crouched atop the dormitory, staying low as they moved for the far end, where the rear of Fetch's solar was close enough to touch. Another jump and a haul of the arms brought them atop the angled tiles. They moved to the peak and down the other side. The thrust of the balcony was below.

Fetch dropped down, noiseless, on her bare feet. Her guts soured.

Sluggard sat slumped against the wall, chin on his chest, head glistening. The Orc Stains had scalped him. Coming around the bed, the bed they had so recently shared, Fetch stepped in a sticky pool. There was no way to avoid the blood. It blanketed the floorboards.

Fetch tried to curse, but only managed a choked sound.

Sluggard's hair was not the only thing the Stains had cut from his body. But the gelding wasn't the worst of it.

He was still breathing.

Fetch knelt by his side. She reached for him, but her hands only hung uncertainly, moving for his face, withdrawing, his hand, pulling away. Guilt forbade her to touch him. Yet he must have known she was there, for his eyes opened, the lids fluttering with delirium. His hand snapped up, grabbed her wrist, breaking the barrier. His voice was weak, almost as weak as his grip.

"Sh-should never . . . have . . . come here."

Fetch did not know if he meant her or himself. Did not know where upon the path his regret was aimed. Ul-wundulas. Winsome. Her bed. He could have meant any of them. Or all. He should have stayed away from them all.

Sluggard's fingers slipped from her arm, his gory head lolling back against the wall. He was barely conscious, mouth moving feebly with airy ravings.

Hoodwink's voice drifted over her shoulder. "I can make it quick."

Fetch's eyes closed. She felt sickened as she stood. Without looking she reached back to Hoodwink. He placed his stockbow in her hands and went back to the balcony.

She aimed from the hip, straight at Sluggard's heart.

Her finger tensed on the tickler.

Hoodwink gave a sharp hiss.

Turning, she joined him at the balcony opening, followed his pointing finger and saw movement across town, near the orphanage. Oats and Xhreka, both carrying swaddled bundles.

Quickly, Fetch stepped from the shadows of the bedchamber and waved once when Oats's head turned to look. He began leading the halfling their way.

"Cover them," Fetch said, handing Hoodwink his weapon.

Fetch retrieved her sword belt. The kataras were still in their sheaths. She retrieved her tulwar from the floor and slid it back into the empty scabbard. Wiping her feet on the bedclothes, she found her breeches, brigand, and boots, and was dressed by the time Oats and Xhreka came into the room. The halfling was soaked to the chest, but the babe in her arms was wrapped in a dry blanket, as were the two Oats bore.

"Sweeps?" Fetch asked, knowing the answer before Oats shook his head.

He gazed at Sluggard, his expression grim.

Fetch took the baby from Xhreka. "Anything you can do for him?"

The halfling's single eye narrowed and she went to inspect the gritter, cursing under her breath when she looked between his legs.

"We can press hot iron. May kill him, but he's dead anyway if we don't. It's the only thing I know."

Oats paled. "Hells."

"Have it done by the time Hood and I return with the hogs," Fetch said. She looked at Oats. "Barricade the door below."

The infant in her arms was asleep but fitful, exhausted from the night's travails. She placed it on the bed.

"I sent the hoof to Batayat," she told Oats. "If we don't return, that's where you should try to go."

Oats placed his own pair of babes next to the other and unslung his stockbow. He held it out. "At least take this."

Fetch waved it away. "You'll need it. I'll get one."

"We need to go," Hoodwink said.

They left the way they came, over the roofs. When they reached the end of the dormitory, intending to again use the palisade, they saw something that made them pause.

A lone dog was stalking up the nearest stairs. It gained the walk and loped away toward the gate, Hood's thrum tracking it until it was gone from sight.

They exchanged a look, but did not speak as they pressed on.

The fire glowed in the north end of town.

The hog pens came into view below. Bodies of Orc Stain riders and hogs lay scattered across the ground in front of the fencing, all dragged down in an attempt to escape the walls out the hole they made. Other than the fresh kills, there was no sign of the dogs, but the feral pigs in the sequester yard were awash in panic. In the main pen, the doors to the stable were closed and intact. Rushing across the walk, Fetch and Hood jumped to its roof. Listening, they heard movement beneath, and fretting grunts.

Hoodwink nearly smiled with relief and went to climb down.

Fetch caught his shoulder. "They may be like Little Orphan Girl."

Unblinking, Hood considered this for a moment.

"Stay here."

It wasn't a command. It was a rider risking his life for his chief.

Without further hesitation, he went to the edge of the stable roof and lowered himself down. Fetch heard him open the doors. Several tense moments passed before a hiss sounded from below. Making her way down, Fetch found Hoodwink in one of the stalls, saddling his barbarian.

"It's him," the pale mongrel said with quiet certainty.

There were five other hogs within, including Mead's and Slug-gard's. Working quickly, Fetch and Hood saddled all the barbarians, rigging guide ropes to those that would not be ridden. For her own mount, Fetch chose Dumb Door's former hog, Three Tusks, so named because he possessed both swine-yankers, but only one lower tusk.

They rode out, each leading a pair of barbarians, stopping only for Fetch to retrieve a stockbow and a depleted quiver from the fallen Orc Stains. Reaching the breach, they guided the hogs over the debris and across the Orc Stains' ramp. On the far side, Fetching dismounted. Most of the ruined timber had fallen into the ditch, a choking mass of splintered stakes.

Signaling for Hood to stay put, she slid down the dusty embankment. A body was entangled in the pile. Though broken and bloodied, Fetch knew it wasn't Mead. The corpse had two hands. She picked her way over, having to climb a bit to reach the mongrel's head. Dull, unblinking eyes stared through her.

It was Sence.

A voice sounded from below, digging up through the pile.

Fetch scurried down, bending, trying to see between the haphazard spars. At last, she spotted him, pinned beneath a large section of what was once the walkway.

"Mead. Hold on."

She whistled for Hoodwink and together they were able to work their way through the timber to free their trapped brother. Mead was alert but weak, and looked more drawn and cadaverous than Hood. The fall had caused several cuts to his face, but none were serious. It was the stab wound, left untended while he lay in the ditch, that had leeched his strength. He was muttering something as they hauled him out. Only when they got him up on level ground could Fetch lean down and make it out.

"The . . . pack. Hyenas . . . inside."

"We know, Mead. We are all getting out of here." She looked across to Hoodwink. "He can't ride. Let's get him up in front of you. You'll have to hold him in the saddle. Get him to Batayat."

Inside the walls, they heard the cackle of dogs.

"Going alone is foolish," Hood told her, but he stood, picking Mead up.

"Oats and I will manage," she responded, helping them mount. "Now get out of here."

She squeezed Mead's arm just before Hoodwink kicked his hog into a trot.

Mounting up, Fetching rode back through the breach.

She rode southward, ears straining, keeping to the alleys when possible. No dogs were to be seen and Fetch feared she knew why. The sound of squalling infants reached her ears before the solar was in sight. She guided the hogs to the north side of the cooper's shop, peering around the building across the thoroughfare.

Eight hyenas were gathered beneath the balcony of her solar, laughing and hopping, the crying infants exciting their movements. One kept lurching back on its hind feet to scrabble at the door, giggling.

It was unlikely the dogs were getting in, but how was Fetch going to get her people out?

Dismounting, she untied the lead line from her saddle and quickly hobbled the other two hogs, loose enough that they could slip the rope if threatened. She just needed them to stay put long enough for her to tell Oats where they were hidden. Astride Three Tusks once more, she unslung her stockbow, loaded a bolt, and kicked him into a gallop. She loosed as soon as they rounded the corner of the building, taking a dog in the flank. The pack startled, lurching to face the oncoming hog. Reloading, Fetch shot another, but the beast was on its feet by the time Three Tusks smashed into the midst of the dogs. The hog gored one and trampled another. Fetch's tulwar was in her hand and she slashed downward on either side as they charged through.

"Hogs behind the cooper's!" she yelled, and spurred Three Tusks onward.

Whoops went up from behind.

Snatching a glance, she saw all eight beasts in pursuit.

She grinned. "Come on, you laughing bitches!"

Ripping her stockbow around, she loaded, turned in the saddle, and sent a bolt into the lead dog, spilling it to the ground.

Fetch knew better than to think the demon was dead, but she needed to keep their attention.

Pulling hard on Three Tusks's left swine-yanker, she guided him down an alley between the rows of Winsome's small homes. The pack followed, the encroaching buildings preventing them from fanning out and flanking her hog. Winsome had never been overly large, and the alley's end was soon ahead, the wall just beyond. Surging into the open, Fetch again pulled left, skirting the inside of the eastern wall. She was leading the pack back to the northern edge of town, giving Oats as much time and distance as possible.

But the pack was gaining.

Movement above drew her eye up to the palisade.

Another dog, barreling down the walkway, keeping pace.

Damn. They hadn't all gone to the solar. How many more were out there waiting to ambush Oats and the others?

Fetch began screaming, hollering with all her breath, cursing the dogs, baiting every blood-hungry one of them that might be lurking.

The beast upon the wall pounced. Fetch swung her stockbow up and loosed. The bolt caught the dog in the chest, the force of the shot arresting its deadly leap.

A formidable weight smote her blindside, knocking her from the saddle. Landing hard, she struggled against bristling hair and slavering, snapping jaws. Rolling, she threw the beast off, stood, ran. Three Tusks was well trained and had not bolted when his rider spilled. He waited ahead, fighting his instinct to flee with sidling steps and punching squeals. The pack was at Fetch's heels when she swung into the saddle.

Three Tusks needed no encouragement. Trotters drumming, he was off again, kicking dust into the open maws of the hyenas.

Fetch pulled her stockbow around on its sling, went to reload, and found one of the prods bent. Cursing, she tore the weapon free and cast it at the dogs.

The hog pens came into view, murky from smoke. The fire had continued to spread, turning the abandoned homes into an inferno.

Fire.

Fetch felt a savage glee. She knew where to lead the pack. The Kiln ruin. She'd run the beasts up the pile, burn them all. Herself, too, if she had to.

As they surged toward the breach, a hulking form stepped into their path, backed by the flames.

Ruin.

He could burn too.

Fetch rode straight for him, screaming and freeing her lasso.

The orc's hands were flexing to meet the charge. At the last moment, Fetch forced Three Tusks to a hard left. Flinging the rope out, she snared Ruin around the neck. Jerked off his feet, he struck the ground as Fetch spurred the hog to greater speed.

"Strong enough to halt a barbarian, you thick cunt?!"

Gripping the saddle with her legs, arm extended behind, Fetch dragged the great orc down the main thoroughfare toward the gate. Ruin tried to get his feet under him, but Fetch worked the rope, giving slack before yanking anew, denying all purchase. The tension tore at her shoulder, the rope sawed into her hand, but Fetch endured the pain and kept her captive on his back. Three Tusks bore them through the gate at a gallop. Fetch urged him off the track, into the rough country, shouting abuses at Ruin as he collided with jutting rocks. The hog wouldn't be able to haul the orc's weight at this pace for long, but they needn't go far.

The pack was in pursuit, but their snarls only goaded Three Tusks to devour the solitary mile. The hump of the Kiln grew from the dark plain, welcoming their arrival.

Hooves struck the edge of the debris and sparked up the sloped scree. Fetch jumped from the saddle before the rubble fully thwarted their speed and swatted Three Tusks to keep going. As soon as her boots touched the broken stone, Ruin was on his feet. Fetch released the lasso and fled up the pile.

"Come on, you fuck! COME ON!"

She heard his vengeful snarl, the slap of bare feet on hard stone as he pursued. Reaching the summit, Fetch bounded across the slag. Ruin was gaining. Another moment and he would catch her. She spun around just in time to dance away from a grasping hand. Ducking, she drew her tulwar and slashed in one motion. The blade took him across the thigh, its curved edge scraping as if on stone. Fetch stayed low, inviting the downward blow, then rolled away when Ruin took the bait. The dread orc's hand hammered the stone.

Nothing.

The pack arrived, slinking over the rubble, spreading out.

Fetch put her back to a heap of blasted rocks. She was done waiting. Flipping her sword around, she took it in both hands and plunged. A tulwar was no pickaxe, and the point blunted as it struck the rocks, sinking barely a finger's length into the scree. It was enough.

Fetch smiled as the pierced stone hissed.

Ruin rushed in as she leapt to the side. A jet of emerald flame belched forth, but the orc's reflexes were as unnatural as the rest of him. He halted, recoiling from the heat. The hyenas whimpered, dancing back as their master watched the fire's upward flight with a hateful grimace. Fetch plunged her sword again, mining for death. The ground rumbled as the baleful substance beneath roused to the disturbance.

The whining dogs fled.

Ruin remained, undaunted, eyeing Fetch as he stalked around the fire. Steaming fissures heralded the arrival of more gouts. A flaming tongue licked upward an arm's length to Ruin's left. The fire did not touch him, but its heat still burned. He winced, baring his teeth and snarling. In pain.

"See?" Fetch taunted. "This shit can kill anything."

Now she just needed to keep him from following the wisdom of his cursed dogs.

"Stay where the fuck you are!" Fetching cried, rushing him.

Leaping, she sent a reaping cut at his eyes. Ruin caught the blade, snapped it with a flick of his wrist. Releasing the fragment, the orc tried to seize her. Ducking the swiping arms, she rolled, came up at his flank, and hammered his kidney with her fist, nearly broke her wrist. He spun around, backhand leading. Fetch snapped out of the way, felt the weight of his hand punish the air a finger's width from her face. She got under his arm and pummeled his cods, cutting her knuckles on the bone piercings. Two quick, brutal strikes and she was out, rolling again. The Al-Unan fire belched from the ground she had just vacated. Shielding his face with his forearms, Ruin reeled. Fetch darted behind and kicked the back of the orc's knee with all her might. She rammed him with a shoulder, tried to force him into the fire, but the monster only stumbled. Launching a knee into his lower spine, Fetch hooked her arm around his throat, locked her wrist with the other hand, and began to pull back, using his chin as leverage, keeping him off-balance. Ruin thrashed, slung her about, but Fetch held fast and would not be dislodged.

All around, geysers of jade pillared the surface of the pile, their livid fury devouring the shadows, melting the rock, thinning the air. Fetch welcomed the end. Of Ruin. Of this danger to her people. Of the burden of being chief. It would all perish in the embrace of a green hell.

Ruin pawed at her arms. Refusing to let go, she licked his face, whispering orcish in his ear with a fierce joy.

"You taste weak."

The orc crouched and leapt. There was a lurching heartbeat as he carried Fetch into the cool air above the flames. Whistling wind. Hurtling ground. They didn't quite clear the pile. Ruin landed in the ragged edges of the fire, the impact breaking Fetch's hold. Her face smashed into the back of his skull. Black spots exploded with light as she bounced off his back, tumbling down the remainder of the slope. Forcing her eyes open through the dull pain of a busted nose, she found the flames had not touched her.

Ruin had not been so fortunate.

He staggered from the rubble, swatting at the green blazes dancing upon his massive form, his movements becoming more frantic as the sorcerous fire spread to his hands. When the fire would not yield, he dropped to a knee, dug into the ground, tried to smother the flames in the earth, but it was no use. The Al-Unan fire would not die.

Ruin's face wrinkled with confusion, pain. He did not cry out, did not panic. He looked up from the smoking dust, his gaze finding Fetch, eyes burning with greater violence than the flames eating his flesh. The orc stood, hands leaving the scorched earth still aflame, and took a step toward Fetch.

Hells, her plan was now his. He was going to take her with him.

Fetch went to rise, to flee, but froze before she reached her feet, rooted by the slavering dogs cutting off her escape.

Ruin's lips curled into something that might have been a smile, might have been a grimace. A few more strides and he would be upon her. Fetch had to make a choice. The burning orc or the dogs.

Spitting into the dirt, she ran at Ruin.

And the world bellowed before she reached him.

Blinded by sudden agony, Fetch did not remember falling. She writhed in the dust, horrible pressure building behind her eyes. She began to scream, a sound to sunder mountains.

But it wasn't her voice. She had reached the bottom of her lungs, yet the cry persisted, grew. She tried to rise, but the surrounding roar had weight, kept her down. Balling up, she clapped her hands over her ears. The assault did not cease. The dread cry bored into her bones, shook her sickened innards until she feared they would come spewing from her mouth, be shat out in a runny mass. She boiled within a cauldron of thundering rage, wishing to die, so the tumult would end.

It did end, swift as it had come.

Trembling, ears filled with an endless shrill pealing, Fetch opened eyes murky with tears.

She did not see the orc, or the pack, just a small figure approaching from the darkened plain, holding a hand over its face.

Zirko?

Fetch could not hear her own voice, was not sure she said the name aloud. She crawled to her feet and as she straightened, her addled head punished the effort by snatching consciousness away.

TWENTY-SEVEN

—

SUN. BRIGHT AND SPEARING.

Motion. Rough and revolting.

Sounds . . . sounds?

Fetch tried to speak. Unpleasant vibrations swam through her head. Nothing more. A hand touched her brow, callused and familiar. More vibrations, deep and distant. Fighting to focus, she followed the arm attached to the hand.

Oats.

He was turned, leaning to touch, to comfort, sitting upon a wooden bench, the glare of the sun attempting to devour his bulk. The hand came away and Oats turned to become a broad back. Next to him sat Xhreka, sharing the bench.

A sudden jostle sent javelins into Fetch's skull, forcing her eyes closed once more. When she opened them again, she found Sluggard lying beside her. His head was wrapped in a stained bandage and swaying with the movement of the wagon. Save for the fever sweat sheening his skin and the sporadic twitches of his brow, he looked dead.

Something kept tapping Fetch's head, gentle and irregular. Craning her neck, she found a mongrel babe, kicked free from its blanket, face bunched and mouth agape. Though it looked to be screaming enough to wake the dead, all Fetch heard were the trimmings of echo. Two other, calmer children lay next to the first, all resting in the wagon bed beneath the seat.

Reaching, Fetch's hand found the edge of the sideboard and she pulled, wincing with every bit of upward progress. She managed to sit up, but went too far. Head hanging between her knees, she fought the need to vomit. And failed.

Hooking her chin over the sideboard, she yielded the contents of her roiling guts.

The wagon halted.

Oats's face appeared. After the gags subsided, he wiped her lips with a kerchief. His mouth moved and the deep vibrations returned.

Can't fucking hear you.

Fetch felt her jaw moving, grinding into the sideboard, so she must have spoken.

Fuck.

Oats replied with unintelligible rumbling, accompanied by strong hands embracing her face. He asked her something, worry etched into his dust-powdered face. Having no notion of what he said, Fetch shook her head, the gesture a broad answer. No, she could not hear. No, she was not well. No, she wasn't going to retch again.

After a reluctant pause, Oats withdrew. The wagon rocked and sagged as he climbed back aboard, began moving once more. Fetch hung over the side for a long while.

Sluggard grew fitful as the wheels rolled and bumped across Ulwundulas. A blanket covered him below the waist, but his feverish stirrings threatened to cast it aside. Fearing to behold Knob's butchery, Fetch made sure the blanket stayed in place.

By the time Batayat Hill came into view, her stomach had calmed.

Batayat was a great formation of weathered rock that stretched for miles, accented with fallen boulders and tough shrubs. The place was replete with sinkholes and small caves, making it one of the most painstaking places to patrol on the Bastards' lot. Often, it became a place for raiding orcs to hole up against the hoof.

Fetch could only hope there were no thicks lurking among the rocks now.

They found the tracks of the other wagons. Unable to traverse the unforgiving inclines, they stood unhitched and abandoned in the shadow of the formation. Oats took up his stockbow and approached. Fetch tried to follow, but when she lowered herself over the side-board, her legs gave out.

Oats rushed back, no doubt at Xhreka's call, and helped Fetch sit up, propping her against one of the wheels. He said something that might have been admonishing before going away to scout once again. The sun had crawled deeply into the bosom of the western sky before he returned with help.

Shed Snake and Touro took Fetch's arms across their shoulders, helping her to stand, walk, though her toes dragged more than not. The rocks defeated any efforts she could make on her own behalf, forcing the mongrels to hook their hands behind her knees and carry her up. Oats bore Sluggard across his shoulders. Xhreka had a babe in her arms. The other two infants were carried by Thistle and Lopo. Dacia led the unhitched hogs, the ground too treacherous for them to act as pack animals. The ragged group had to stop several times as they ascended, and it was full dark before they reached the rough encampment.

It was nothing but a flat expanse upon the wide-reaching summit, screened by time-carved pillars of segmented rock. Winsome's villagers hunkered amidst the boulders before feeble fires. Fetch and Sluggard were taken to a patch of hard ground and placed beside Mead and Polecat. Fetching tried to protest, and might have managed some words, but her body betrayed all attempts to stand. She could only lie in that row of the injured and watch as the tatters of her hoof tried to stitch itself together without her help. With no strength to do more than give listless stares, she saw Oats speak with Shed Snake and Culprit, revived from his head wound, but still walking unsteadily. Later, Hoodwink appeared, clearly giving a report of the surrounding area. He glanced Fetch's way once, when Oats said something and gestured at his own ear.

The chief is deaf. Spread the word. Another ass-fucking in a long line of travails forming behind the hoof's bent-over backside.

Polecat awoke not long after Fetch arrived, sitting up when he saw her. Someone had removed the bolts from his leg and shoulder. He spoke, hatchet face frowning when she did not respond. They had all learned to recognize certain hand signs from Dumb Door, but being unable to hear was not among them. It wasn't a complicated thing to communicate, but Fetch could not bring herself to do it, using the infirmity to ignore Cat's insistent solicitations until Touro came over and explained. Polecat's brow furrowed further when the slophead went away. Fetch could feel his eyes on her for a long while after.

Mead lay between them, looking worse than Sluggard, if that were possible. He awoke once, hand questing feebly for hers. Fetch latched on to his fingers.

Stay with me.

A shadow fell over them. Incus. She lowered herself down and sat with Fetching. Nothing more. She just sat, sharing the soundless world.

There was no food, but pitiful sips of water were brought to all the injured. Fetch refused hers, directing Touro to give her ration to Mead. He complied, but moments after he went away, Oats trudged over. Squatting, face bordering on furious, he thrust a skin at her face. He said a single word. Even in the weak firelight, the shape formed by his lips was obvious.

Drink.

Fetch took half a mouthful and gave the skin back.

She stayed awake as long as possible, holding Mead's hand, placing her other on Sluggard's chest, fearing that neither would live to see dawn. So, she kept her eyes open and her touch firm, hoping to anchor them through the night.

Hogshit.

They anchored her. She feared to sleep, to let darkness in where silence already reigned. Filling her eyes with the stars, her hands with the touch of skin, kept that divestment of all sense at bay. But though her pain dwindled and her queasiness fled, the exhaustion remained, gnawing at the wispy tendrils of resolve. She battled, but at some unknown moment, was defeated.

Sun. Pale and tepid.

Motion. Only that in her hungering stomach.

Sound. Coughing. Weeping. Voices. All were distorted, as if wriggling through wet hay, but they were there.

Sitting up, tilting her head, working her jaw, Fetch found her left ear mostly clear, the right still muffled. She checked Mead and Sluggard.

Still alive. Both still alive.

Polecat was absent.

Incus was not.

"You can hear?"

"I can," Fetch replied, and nearly wept with relief.

The thrice gave a satisfied nod and lumbered to her feet, offering a hand down. Fetch took it.

Standing too swiftly, she nearly lost balance, but refused to let a spinning skull be her master. Incus's strong arm helped for the first few steps. After that, Fetch risked it alone, employing clenched eyelids and a few deep breaths. The rest came on instinct. The camp grew hushed. For a moment, Fetch thought her hearing had once again fled. Then she saw the stares. Villagers and slopheads, most milling and indolent, ceased their mumbling words to look with a mummer's show of emotion. Surprise. Relief. Resentment. Hatred. She saw it all, though the faces seemed to pitch and sway.

"Summon the hoof!" she told Touro, speaking louder than intended. A babe began to cry, startled by the outburst. Fetch guided her treacherous vision to the sound. The orphanage was now just a crude gaggle amidst a camp of crude gaggles. Thistle shepherded the children into a tighter cluster of haunted eyes set in filthy faces. But not all the short forms were children.

Fetch stalked over, weaving a bit, no doubt appearing a drunken hag to the young ones. She looked down at Xhreka.

"You come with me."

The halfling detached from the orphans without a word.

Fetch turned to lead her away, finding Polecat standing in the center of the camp, balanced on a rude crutch.

"Chief?"

"Where are the others?"

Cat released a small breath of relief. "Hunting."

"When they are all returned, we meet."

"Sure, chief."

Leaving Cat standing there, Fetch continued on, Xhreka trailing. She took the flattest route away from the bordering stone fingers, seeking a place free from other eyes and ears. Everywhere was rock and prickly shrubs. Fetch walked until the thrust of a butte blocked the path, the stone at her feet dipping down to meet its base. Not trusting she could walk down without falling, she found a likely boulder at the edge and sat.

Xhreka stood a few paces away, regarding her with that one bright eye.

"It was you," Fetch said. "The hellish noise that burst Little Orphan Girl. You. And again with the orc."

The halfling remained still.

"I feel a need to thank you," Fetch continued, "but also a strong desire to pick you up and throw you off this fucking rock. I took you in, knowing you would be of use. But you hid just how useful. What else are you hiding?"

Xhreka folded her arms.

"You are hiding from Zirko, I know that much," Fetch said. A tiny bit of doubt darkened the lone eye. "I'm not a fucking fool, Xhreka. I know what you are, why Strava wants you back."

"You know nothing of me, mongrel-girl."

Fetch stood. "Va. Gara. Attukhan."

The halfling's eye went wide.

"I don't speak the Unyar tongue," Fetch admitted, "but I damn well know what that means. Been hearing it ever since the mongrel I love went away. Heard it a great deal when I was last in Strava. The Unyars I stayed with were old, thought I was asleep, but coffin-dodgers can't whisper for shit. Can't hear themselves. I know something about that now, thanks to you. I'm not sure how, but the Unyars know I've lain with their precious hero, Va Gara Attukhan. Maybe they think I'm about to push Belico-reborn out my cunt. Doesn't matter. What does? I not only fucked the Arm of Attukhan, I know how he got the damn name. You bear some ancient holy relic, like him. Don't deny it, because I know what that power feels like, and I can damn well reckon it's what you used to twice destroy what plagued my hoof."

"I didn't—"

"You did."

"I didn't destroy the fucking orc!" The halfling's arms never un-crossed, but she did take a step forward. "If I had, you would not be alive now. So thank me three times. Or save the gratitude and just stop asking me questions."

"I can't do that. You are the only weapon I have to fight against the destruction of my hoof."

"Your hoof is already destroyed, girl."

It was Fetch who stepped forward now. "Not until every Bastard is dead."

"Well, I'm no Bastard. Nothing I owe you, any of you."

"Show her, Xhreka," a deep voice implored.

So intent on glaring at each other, neither Fetch nor Xhreka no-ticed Oats's approach. He stood a few paces beyond the halfling, walking the rest of the way when she turned to look.

"Please," he continued, kneeling so he could look at her squarely.

Xhreka eyed him for a long moment, her brown hand coming up to touch his bearded cheek. She took a breath and turned to face Fetching. Slowly, the halfling removed the eye patch. Beneath, Fetch was surprised to see a closed lid, a bit swollen, but otherwise un-marred. There was movement beneath the thin skin, the same as when someone dreamed and their eye rolled beneath the lid. The eye opened and Fetch recoiled.

A tongue, pink and moist, slithered forth, slow and searching. Curving up, it ran along Xhreka's upper eyelid, through the lashes, as if they held drops of wine that needed to be licked away. Putting the meat of her palm over the horrible appendage, Xhreka's face grew pained, turned away. Replacing the patch, she kept her head downcast.

"You're keen, girl," Xhreka said. "It is as you say. I bear something Zirko wants, something I found as a devout pilgrim long ago. Many of us leave Strava, search and scrape for a lifetime, never unearth a damn thing." The halfling gave a bitter bark and finally looked up, gestured at the eye patch, the motion hateful for what it concealed. "But I found this. Being a vessel demands sacrifice. I loved talking, food, the taste of a man's salt, wasn't about to tear out my own tongue, so I gave up an eye. Belief will make you capable of such things. Truth will make you wish you had never believed at all."

"Truth?" Fetching asked, becoming more disturbed and unsure of the reason.

Xhreka laughed, a hopeless sound. "It's not some arm bone of a warrior I got, girl. If the Unyars celebrated me like they do your hard-cock, then Strava would ring with Du Khaloi Belico."

Fetch only knew one of those words, but that one made her spine crawl. "Belico?"

"The Voice of Belico," Xhreka pronounced, her tone mocking, almost giddy. "Zirko claims to speak for the Master Slave, but I possess his actual honey lapper. The word of a god in my head, and I don't mean that poetical."

Fetch looked at Oats, still on his haunches. "You knew about this?"

"Not all of it," he replied. "I knew she would not return to Strava. Told me that in the Pit. Didn't suspect her for one like Jackal, though. Not until she saved you, drove that pillar of an orc off."

"Drove off?" Fetch didn't like the look on the thrice's face. "Surely he's dead."

"Told you. He's not," Xhreka said.

"The Al-Unan fire—"

The halfling cut her off. "The breath of a god blows out all candles."

"You should have let him fucking burn!" Fetch snapped. "There was no reason to save me."

"Didn't do it for you," Xhreka said. She hooked a thumb at Oats. "Did it for him. Elsewise, he was set to rush in and try to be some hero. Get himself roasted along with you, the ox."

Oats was unapologetic. "I was about to come for you, but Xhreka kept me back and unleashed that . . . well, voice, I guess. She told me after."

Fetch dug deep for some gratitude. It was there, buried beneath heaps of dismay that Ruin yet lived. She managed an appreciative nod.

"Why do you fear Strava?" she asked Xhreka. "They damn near worship Jackal. If that really is a piece of Belico in your skull, wouldn't they make you high priestess or some other hogshit?"

Xhreka sneered. "Likely. But it's not about what the Unyars would do, it's what Zirko would do. And Belico. Gods aren't that much different from us. They don't much like being enslaved. As you've heard, Belico is rather fucking angry. Strava would not stand long if he ever got a chance to make his displeasure known. Zirko may be able to subdue him, but I don't aim to find out. However it goes, I won't survive, of that I am damn certain. Better to live, I say. Better to let my folk and the Unyars live, happy in their belief."

Fetch did not want to go swimming deeper in matters of gods and priests. Religion was damn dangerous and the hoofs had no need of it. She understood enough now to know why Xhreka would keep secrets. She really only needed one more question answered.

"Could you kill the orc? Given another chance?"

"There ain't gonna be another chance," Xhreka replied. "I risked Zirko finding me twice now for you bunch. Don't think a few score miles prevents him from hearing the god. I was all set to run the first time, when that damn hog went blood-mad. Kept suspecting to see Unyar riders on the horizon. No chance they're not on the way now. Ain't about to give them another echo to follow. I'll tell you this. That thick was strong. Few in this world with the grit to stay on their feet and flee when Belico hollers at them. I held the Master Slave back, much as I could, for your sake, but even if I hadn't . . ."

"You wager that orc would still have survived?" Oats asked, disturbed.

Xhreka only shrugged. "Doesn't matter. 'Cause Belico's staying hushed. At least until I can get a few leagues between me and here." She looked hard at Oats. "You swore you would never give me over, Idris."

"I did."

His answer was directed at Fetch.

"I have no interest in handing you to Zirko," she assured Xhreka. "Oats will keep his word, so long as it does not endanger the hoof. You have my thanks for the risks you've taken."

"That mean you're not going to throw me off this hill?" Xhreka asked, sounding unconcerned.

"Not if Belico is going to have something to say about it," Fetch replied. "Stay with us as long as you wish. But know that if you go, you go alone."

"Very well."

Fetch waved for Oats to stand. "I need to speak with the hoof."

THE TRUE BASTARDS GATHERED AROUND their wounded. Fetch commanded the slopheads to the meet, breaking code and tradition, but they had more than earned a chance to hear what was said. Mead was awake, but his breathing was shallow and rasping. Fetch sat down next to him, the hoof arranged around, sworn brothers kneeling or squatting, the slops standing behind.

"So what now?" Culprit asked, breaking the silence.

To this, at least, Fetch had an answer. "The closest settlement is Thricehold. The Orc Stains are no more. Knob brought his entire hoof to wipe us out and got bit by the viper he put in our beds. Fuck him and fuck his hoof in all the hells. What was theirs is now ours."

Shed Snake scratched at his scarred arm. "Won't their hold have a garrison?"

"Hardly," Polecat said. "The Stains only accept thrice-bloods. Not many of those around, so keeping a crop of hopefuls is damn near impossible."

Shed Snake remained dubious. "So who is guarding their fortress?"

"Slaves."

All heads turned to Hood, his spare voice making the hoof more uncomfortable than normal.

"That's just nomad tongue-waggle," Polecat declared, but even he did not look convinced.

The half-orc hoofs were raised from bondage. Since male mongrels were sterile, it was not an inherited legacy, so much as adopted. The founders were slaves, chained and scourged by Hispartha. Therefore, though the Lot Lands contained hardship and cruelty in every mote of wind-flung dust, the keeping of slaves was forbidden. Hood was right, the Orc Stains were said to flout the restriction. But Polecat was not wrong, such knowledge was only ever borne on the lips of free-riders, whom the Stains never welcomed and openly scorned.

"If it's true," Fetch told her hoof, "then Thricehold will just be easier to take. With their masters dead, any slaves should be grateful. Why spill blood when you can have freedom? But we have to go. Our people need safe walls and full stores. Thricehold will have both."

The gathering began to break up, the sworn brothers rising, but a trembling hand rose from the ground.

"No," Mead rasped. Fetch was sitting near his head and barely heard, but the denial was there.

Polecat squatted back down, took the hand in both of his. "What did you say, brother?"

"I . . . vote no."

Tradition took hold. Without needing a command, the slopheads walked away while the Bastards came back together.

"What's your objection, Mead?" Fetch asked, hand still caressing his forehead.

"Thricehold. Not safe. The orc . . . the pack, they will follow. Need to go where they can't."

"Where?" Shed Snake asked, kneeling opposite Polecat and placing a hand on Mead's arm.

"Dog . . . Fall."

Looks were exchanged by the brethren, some questioning if their wounded comrade was in his right mind.

Fetch knew he was lucid. This was not the first time he put forth the idea. "The Tines may not welcome us, Mead. They might just as easily kill us."

"Warbler *is* already among them," Polecat said.

"At their invitation," Fetch reminded him.

Mead's throat was rattling with every breath. "They will accept you. If not . . . you die. No different than anywhere else. No fortress can protect the hoof from the Ruin Made Flesh. The Tines can, if they choose."

"Rustskins do have some potent ways, chief," Polecat urged. "Can get our boy back on his feet."

Mead pulled weakly at Cat's hands. "Won't help."

"Hogshit," Polecat declared. "They fixed you up once, they will again."

"I've got . . . moments, not miles."

Polecat grimaced and Snake let out a pained grunt.

Fetch leaned in, whispered. "You stay the fuck with us. Hear me? We need you."

Mead's lips moved, tongue clicking, each word a fight. "*Mi'hawa. Thiospa. Aschúte. Onáphit.*"

"You know my elvish is shit. Why you have to stay." He was drifting, eyes fluttering, trying to roll back. "Dammit, Mead!"

"You'll . . . learn," he hissed. Swallowing, he drew in a breath, managed to raise his voice. "Now . . . put m-me on . . . my hog."

Polecat shot a look at Fetch, shook his head rapidly, face contorting.

Shed Snake slapped furiously at his burned arm. "No, brother! You got me through this. Remember? Time to get you through. Open your damn eyes!"

But he was swiftly fading.

Hoodwink was the first to move.

Stooping behind Mead's shoulders, he slowly lifted. Gritting her teeth against the grief, accepting the task, Fetch helped, steadying her fallen rider's head. Oats took his feet, while Polecat and Snake shouldered their brother's back. Culprit ran to where the barbarians were hobbled, cut out Mead's mount and brought it over, holding it steady.

Jaws bulging against the falling tears, the True Bastards lifted Mead onto the animal's back, surrounded him, and held him up while he fulfilled his oath.

TWENTY-EIGHT

A PAIR OF SLOPHEADS LED Isabet to the door, made her knock, though it was the entrance to her own solar. There was no answer. She tried the latch, found it open, and pushed. A fire was lit in the lower room. Zirko stood before it, stoking the flames. Turning, he smiled, lifted the poker. It glowed, searing white. Marrow held Sluggard firmly down upon the Grey Bastards' voting table, coffin-shaped and bristling with embedded axes. Sluggard screamed, his cock erect, as Zirko approached with the poker.

Isabet went past, fled the sizzle as she went up the stairs.

The door to her bedchamber would not budge, forcing her to knock once again. The door swung open, revealing Grocer. The sinewy old frailing waved her inside, sour-faced. He turned, began walking through the musty stacks of the storehouse, his tangle of ropy locks falling beyond his bony backside. Isabet had a difficult time keeping up. Grocer turned a corner, vanished. She hurried past the barrels and crates, the coils of rope, hooks of tacking leather. She made the corner, but the old quartermaster was gone.

Knowing what she had to do, Isabet retrieved a saddle from the shelves. The girth strap and left stirrup leather needed to be replaced, and Grocer would not be satisfied until she cleaned and polished the entire saddle. Throwing her first chore of the day up on her shoulder, Isabet made her way to the back of the storehouse, where the light was best. She heard exuberant grunts and happy little moans as she neared the workbench, finding Thistle bent over it, heavy breasts dangling. Isabet was glad to see she was no longer so gaunt. As the woman moaned, rocking forward on the workbench, Knob thrust into her from behind. He was sweating greatly, droplets forming on his bald scalp, running to his nose and falling to splash upon Thistle's back.

Isabet tried to tell them to go elsewhere, so she could complete her work, but the words refused to come.

Milk was leaking from Thistle's breasts, sliding down the bench and darkening the floorboards. Noticing, she rose and reached back, slapping at Knob's stomach with annoyance until he halted his vigorous exertions. Thistle stood and strode away, full hips and thighs quivering a bit as she passed Isabet.

Knob gestured for her to approach.

Shaking her head, Isabet turned to go, but the thrice darted and caught her arm. She dropped the saddle. Knob pushed her against the sturdy shelving laden with rot-eaten brigands. His left hand was on one side of her face, forcing her to look at him.

"You sure you want this?" he asked with a voice not his own. It was dull-sounding, languid and cruel.

Isabet nodded defiantly.

Knob fondled her breasts, hooked a hand down behind the crotch of her breeches and tore them open.

"Join my hoof, girl, and this will be your life."

That voice, that dry, deep, creak.

"I'll have you ride patrols. Fight the thicks. Everything you want. But my word is law. And you will never change that. Whatever errand, whatever service I command, you *will* perform."

The voice was growing desperate, panting. It lusted to threaten, to punish, but the flesh would not conspire. Knob gnashed his teeth, growled, spit flying from between his grinding fangs. He cast a look down between his legs and Fetch followed his gaze.

The cock was tumid yet flaccid, hanging in a misshapen, discolored wad. Knob's hand came down to clasp the horrible thing, tried to work some life into it with fingers wrapped in linen.

Nothing.

The hand came away, slapped onto Isabet's jaw, forced her to look directly into eyes alive with rage, feverish with disease. The head that ensconced that glare was wrapped in the same stained linen as the hands, wispy, colorless hair escaping from the gaps. The sour, gagging odor of old sweat and fresh pus filled Isabet's nostrils.

The Claymaster gripped her jaw painfully, shook his hand to rattle her head against the wooden beams.

"This changes nothing," he said in that damn voice. "Cunnys like you have no place among the Bastards. Cunnys like you will only ever be good for two things. Fucking. And—"

"Fetching!"

Oats's voice snatched her from fitful slumber, his hand upon her shoulder.

Fetch sat up from the saddle pillowing her head and shoulders, ass and legs on bare earth.

"Time to move," Oats said.

"Right," Fetch replied, shaking off the sinister, stroking fingers of the dream.

The waking world provided little solace. Mead was still dead, buried under a hasty pile of stones atop Batayat. Fetch's people remained fearful and hungry on a forced march to forbidden territory, and she still had not recovered all the hearing in her right ear. Probably why Oats had a hard time rousing her from the damnably brief respite. That, and she was fuck-all tired, drained by defeat and dolor.

She rubbed at her head, startled for a moment by the strange smoothness at the sides before remembering. She'd had Xhreka shave her hair like Mead's, into the fashion of the Tines. The halfling was a deft hand and said nothing to make her feel foolish about the request. She'd undone every one of Fetch's mass of long braids, cut a forearm's length off, and properly shaved the scalp above her ears. At the time it had seemed a fitting tribute to her fallen rider, her friend, but now it only served as a physical, painful reminder of what had been lost.

It was two days since they left Batayat Hill, coming down out of the rocks, retrieving both wagons and striking north. Nyhapsáni and Palla—Mead's and Sluggard's hogs—served as draft animals for the hoof's wagon, with Polecat driving the team though he argued he was hale enough to ride. Fetch did not want to strain his injuries. His brigand had taken the brunt of the bolt that struck him in the shoulder blade, but the one that pierced his thigh had gone deep. It was closed and bandaged now, but time in the saddle would only serve to open it up. In the end, a stern command settled the matter. The wagon bed was reserved for Sluggard and the orphans. The rest of Winsome was on foot, strung out in a line behind the wainwright's wagon, drawn by mules and bearing the youngest of the town's children. The Bastards were all mounted, riding a screen around the sluggish procession with the help of Touro and Petro. Fetch had reclaimed Womb Broom, sparing her the need to ride a dead brother's hog.

Their progress was tortuously slow. The badlands were not kind, to the wagons or the walking. The heat was high, the ground pitted, rumpled with dry gulches, and festooned with rocky scrabbles.

Fetch had ordered a halt after they forded the River Lucia, and allowed the people to collapse along the northern bank. Those with the skill attempted to fish, catching enough to feed the children and a few more besides. Water from here to Dog Fall would be scarce if they continued on a direct course. They could strike west, stay with the Lucia until it met the Alhundra, then proceed north. Water would no longer be a concern, but such a route would add more than a week to their journey, and these people were not likely to increase the pace. Every day spent exposed in the Lots was a day that could bring the orc and his pack running up their heels.

And that was just the most likely threat.

A thick raiding party, centaur marauders, a band of deserters from the Hisparthan cavalry—hells, even loyal cavaleros—any one could spell the end of every life in the ragged caravan.

So, stay with the rivers and avoid dying of thirst, but increase the odds of being set upon, or move faster toward the Umber Mountains and risk the unforgiving badlands? The choice, like all in Ul-wundulas, was a hard one.

The hard truth was the last two years had culled the villagers of most of the weak and old. What remained were the hardy, the swift, the young, those who had endured the months of hunger better than their neighbors. Such a breed might survive a few dozen miles of dry, sun-scorched march. None would survive an attack by pitiless killers.

Still, when Oats woke her, Fetch had not settled on a course.

"Hood back?" she asked, receiving a head shake in reply.

"Not yet."

Fetch had sent him scouting to the north while the group rested through the night, the Bastards keeping watch in long shifts.

Dawn had come, but not their scout. Hood could easily track the caravan no matter which way it went, but Fetch chose to shorten his return.

"Let's get the people moving north," she told Oats. "Slow as they are, if Hood says we should stick to the banks, then we can strike westward without losing much ground, meet up with the river once it's bent. But we are on water rationing from here. Make sure everyone understands."

They had little in the way of containers, limiting what could be carried away from the river.

The people of Winsome stood in loose knots about the rough camp, most rooted by fear and indecision rather than confidence or loyalty. Among them, a man holding close to his wife and hip-high daughter imprisoned Fetch's attention.

She was not even certain of their names. It was their lives that concerned her.

"Let's move."

Without the wagons and the plodding people, the hoof could reach the mountains in less than three days, but they were shackled by their folk, forced to hold their hogs back and keep to the ponderous pace. It wore at the patience of barbarian and rider. Fetch had to keep yelling at Culprit when he strayed too far ahead. Once, she had to kick Womb forward and catch up, berating the young rider for leaving a hole in the screen.

Hoodwink returned by midmorning. His report was grave. No water for miles, certainly none the caravan would reach in the next day, possibly two.

It wasn't a surprise, but Fetch had hoped for a change in luck.

"We will push on," she decided. "If tomorrow yields the same, we will turn course and go the long way."

Night rides were common for the hoof, the eyesight of hogs and half-orcs keen in the dark. Frails, however, had no such benefit. Sundown brought an end to the march and the beginning of another long night, this one upon a tract of dusty plain devoid of shelter and the comforting reassurance of the river. The people began to doubt. Fetch could hear them, muttering in small groups, hushed voices ceasing when a Bastard drew near. She ignored it, trusting such fear was born in the dark and banished by morning.

During her watch, Fetch rode steadily around the tightly hunkered shadows, far enough out that the hoofbeats would not disturb. Shed Snake and Touro shared the watch, riding in staggered circuits. All was quiet, but Touro seemed distracted, nervous, his glances turning inward to the sleeping forms in the camp.

"What is it?" Fetch asked, stopping to press the slophead on their fourth pass.

"Nothing, chief," he replied, looking guilty and spooked. "Probably . . . it's nothing, I mean. Can't . . . uh, not sure I should say."

"You should."

Touro swallowed. "You may want to ride close to where Petro's bedded down. See if . . . it's something."

Not liking the slophead's manner, Fetch took the suggestion. Petro had placed his bedroll at the outer edge of the camp. When Fetch rode close, she discovered he was not alone. The movements beneath the blanket stopped as she approached, but there was no hiding the deed. Pausing briefly, Fetch turned her hog and left Petro to it. Who was she to deny her boys what few comforts remained? Whoever the slophead was bedding likely needed some too. They might regret the lack of sleep come the morning, but hells, there was little food, little water, little hope. Let them have this, at least.

Circling back to Touro, Fetch gave him a reassuring smile. "No need to worry."

The slop looked relieved. "Good. Just wanted to . . . I don't know. So long as you knew."

Fetch cocked a chin out toward the darkness. "You stay as vigilant that direction and all will be fine."

"Yes, chief."

When Oats relieved her, Fetch hobbled Womb Broom among the other hogs and trudged toward her patch of ground. But that hard piece of rest was not to be, for Xhreka stood waiting.

"The poor castrate's awake," the halfling stated. "Gave him some water. He asked for you."

Wearily, Fetch walked to the hoof's wagon, but fatigue was not all that slowed her steps.

Sluggard was propped up in the bed, his moonlit skin standing out starkly from the swallowing shadows. Only his eyes moved when she came to stand at the sideboard, rolling to look at her, watery with pain. Days of feverish stupor had left him looking wasted, cheeks and eye sockets sunken. His cracked lips were still bright with the water Xhreka had allowed.

"You . . . escaped?" he asked, voice brittle.

Fetch fought the flinch, searched for the right words, knowing none existed. "There was no choice. Had I remained, tried to reach you—"

"No." Sluggard's bandaged head shook, rocking against the edge of the wagon bench. "No, did you escape . . . harm?"

His meaning struck her in the guts with knuckles of iron. Hells, that was his worry? She nearly lied, nearly told him every one of Knob's boys had their way. It would have been an absolution, a false leveling of their measures of misery. But that would only ease her guilt, and do nothing for this poor mongrel.

"I am unhurt," she said.

Relief settled over Sluggard's face, momentarily replacing the agony, a balm born from needless gallantry. Civilized lands fostered strange ideals. Such would never survive in the Lots, but Fetch hoped this single bearer of such queer notions did not perish with them.

"Tomorrow will be difficult, Sluggard. Now that you are awake, the jostle of the wagon will not be easy to abide. But know that we are making for elf lands. They have skilled healers—"

A strange series of pumping breaths issued from the suffering gritter. It took a moment for Fetch to realize he was laughing, trying to control it in little gasps so as not to increase his pain.

"Point-ears can regrow my stones? Truly, they are a magical people. Think they will make me choose between my nut-basket and my hair? Because that will be a tough choice. I had wonderful hair." The laughter continued until the expulsions of mirth became the shamed exhalations of sobbing. "Perhaps you should leave me here. Give me a knife. I'll finish . . . finish what those thrice savages started."

Fetch stood there for a moment, frozen, watching the gritter weep.

Fuck that.

She reached over the sideboard, placed a hand on his face. The touch caused him to look up, ashamed. Damning all helplessness, she climbed carefully into the wagon, settled beside Sluggard, and coaxed his head into her arms. This morning she awoke from a horrid nightmare. Sluggard just awoke inside one. She held him as he surrendered to the pain, the loss. Those she could not begin to fathom, but she knew something of the fear he was feeling. Fear of what was to come in a life chosen yet far from designed.

There was a cost to existence among the hoofs, a price of blood and body, and rarely was there a chance to deny payment. It was wrested from you, snatched by greedy hands, gnashed by ravenous teeth, never sated. Ul-wundulas would demand more of Sluggard, would demand more of her, in the days to come. They would be forced to offer up more sacrifices in order to survive. There was a small, yet potent, power in that knowledge. Fetch was a rider because of it, was chief because of it, was alive because of it. The Lot

Lands shaped you, and often its molding hands were cruel. But any form that survived its touch was one better suited to endure its next caress, next crushing fist. It mattered not at all that you might not enjoy what you became. What mattered was that you lived. Sluggard would no longer be comely. Would no longer be a celebrated lover. He came to the Lots and now they had trapped him. But he was not ready for such unkind truths. For now, let him mourn for what was taken.

Fetch knew the importance of that too.

THE MORNING DAWNED HOT, reflecting the temperament of the villagers. A stubborn group of several dozen lingered around the wainwright's wagon when the order came to march. Glaucio was among them.

"Not certain we want to continue this way," the balding man said, hardening his voice, though the mettle did not quite adhere to his face.

"I *am* certain," Fetch replied, facing the dissenting group. She could feel the rest of the caravan watching, heard Oats's heavy footfalls approach and halt at her back. "Just a few days more and we will be safe."

Glaucio began to falter under the steel mask she wore, but the wainwright spoke up. He was an older, crook-nosed cuss from Anville, had seen a little of the world and much of Ul-wundulas, a rustic to the marrow.

"Elves don't suffer trespassers! Those rustskin savages will ride us down, lance us, and leave us for the vultures if we set foot on their land."

"We have permission, Guarin," Fetch lied. "The Tines will shelter you."

Glaucio again found his voice. "So would the castile. Be better for us there, among the cavaleros."

This drew grunts of support and agreement from the group.

Fetch looked to Glaucio. "What happened to fearing conscription? Not wanting your wives turned into barracks whores?" The small man could only cast his eyes to the dirt. Fetch pointed to the northwest, lifted her voice to the group. "The castile lies that way. Nearly a fortnight on foot. A long trek. And not a safe one. Now, let's have no more of this. We are wasting daylight."

Guarin spat her words back. "Not safe? Where were we safe? Not Winsome! We aren't safe now. Never will be so long as we are with you!"

The folk behind him were emboldened by his daring. Fetch could see heads nodding as the agreements became more than grunts.

"You're right," she said. "There's nowhere safe. But you, your children, are better off with the hoof than without it."

"That ain't so!"

Fetch turned at the sound of a woman's voice. She wasn't with the wainwright's group, but stood near the hoof's wagon. It was the tanner's widow.

Polecat was already up on the driver's bench. He stared down at his lover, a bit bewildered. "Estefania . . . what are you doing?"

The woman covered her fear with a frantic ferocity. "It's the hoof that's done this to us!"

"Fania!" Polecat barked. He didn't look angry so much as panicked.

Shit. Fetch realized, too late, what Cat must have confided.

He leaned down from the wagon bench, tried to pull her away, but the woman shrugged free and stepped out of his reach. Estefania's face was drawn, nearly skeletal, crazed eyes and flashing teeth looking overlarge as she thrust a finger at Fetching.

"The devil-dogs only come when she's near! That's why she's gambling our lives on the point-ears! Think they have some kind of sorcery that will save her!"

Polecat was cursing, rising from the wagon seat, trying to get down, to stop his bedwarmer's tirade, but was hindered by his wounded leg.

"Sit still, Cat," Fetch said, raising a calm hand. The hatchet-faced mongrel stilled, but did not sit.

Fetch looked away from the widow, swept the dissenters as she spoke.

"There is not a danger a hoof weathers that is not shared by its folk. That's the way of the Lots. You know that. Betrayer Moons, orc raids, famine, drought. We can't survive them without you, you die without us. These dogs are no different. This is a fucking terrible foe we are trying to outrun and Dog Fall is our only chance. I can't make you believe that. I also can't let you throw your lives away. The hoof is going north. You are all coming with us and that's the end of it."

But Guarin wasn't done. "I never swore no oath to the Bastards. Don't have to hold to some fucking code. I can go where I like."

Temper threatening to slip its tether, Fetch took a deep breath. "Go your way, then. I hope you make it."

"We have your leave, then?" Estefania asked, a triumphant, timorous smile playing across her face. She walked a few paces to approach a mounted slophead, sitting his hog close by. Purposefully close.

Petro.

Fetch cursed herself for a fucking fool. And cursed the widow for being a conniving cunt. Touro had warned her, told her to check. If she had just thrown back the blanket, looked to see who was beneath, she could have prevented this.

"Petro," Fetch warned, "don't."

The slophead blanched, lips tight with apprehension, but Estefania swung herself up behind him, hands slipping around to clasp his middle. That possessive touch steeled Petro.

"He's not sworn," the woman gloated over his shoulder. "Nothing in hoof code prevents a hopeful from leaving."

"So long as he knows he better never come back," Oats growled.

"Why would he?" Estefania spat back. "There are other hoofs, none as cursed. They should all abandon you."

"Hells damn you, woman," Polecat breathed.

Estefania looked at him, at last, and Fetch was surprised to see true regret. "I'd have asked you to come, Cat, if I thought you would ever leave." She stretched up in the saddle, looked at the ogling villagers. "You should all join us. There is nothing for you here."

Fetch ignored the reactions of the frails. Her eyes were on the other slopheads. Most were looking back at her, a few on Petro, some seemed tempted, all were afraid.

"Make your choice," she told them. "There will be no vengeance taken on those that leave. But know, only your lives are yours to take. All else belongs to the hoof. Any that try to ride out on hog-back will be shot down."

The sounds of locking stockbows clicked at her back as the True Bastards loaded. Keeping her own hands empty, Fetching slowly approached Petro. The now tremulous slop watched her come, sweat shining on his upper lip.

"She wouldn't," Estefania hissed in his ear.

Neglecting to look at her, Fetch stopped beside the hog and delivered her own whispered words to Petro. "Dismount and get gone. Your choice is made." She saw his hand tighten on the hog's mane. "I hope you try it. The bolt that kills you will be mine."

Looking sick, Petro swung a leg over the hog's head and hopped down. Unslinging the thrum across his back and unbuckling his sword belt, he let the weapons fall to the dirt.

Fetch reached up, grabbed the tanner's widow by the arm and hauled her off the barbarian's back. The woman cursed and struggled, but Fetch leaned close to her ear.

"Keep it up and I will give you to Polecat. He's lost two lots. Two women. Got shit for luck, that mongrel. Reckon he's ready for a reckoning."

Estefania stilled. Fetch thrust her roughly at Petro. The slophead recoiled as if a scorpion had been tossed at him.

Fetch pointed northwest. "Go."

They moved off, backward at first, fearing bolts in the back. After a few steps, they spun and hurried away.

"Any that are going to go with them, go now," Fetch called out, keeping her gaze on the retreating pair who started this. She heard the villagers begin to move.

"This team is mine," Guarin said, climbing aboard his wagon. "I'm taking it. Shoot me for it and be damned."

Fetch let him go. Guarin goaded his mules west, many more following in their dust. Families went entire. Two more slopheads, Uidal and Bastião, had dropped their weapons and joined the crowd.

Fetch watched the backs, counted. Of the one hundred twenty-two people under the hoof's protection, only forty-one decided they were safer staying with the hoof. Glaucio found the stones to look her in the eye as he went by.

"I hope you make it," Fetch told him.

And meant it.

TWENTY-NINE

THE UMBER MOUNTAINS had ever been a mute warning in the Lot Lands. They were a distant threat, a clenched and readied fist.

"Always makes me think of that old tale with the snake-hair lady," Oats said, when the brown peaks emerged from the diffused light of the horizon.

Fetch, Shed Snake, and Culprit all hummed or nodded in agreement.

"The fuck you on about?" Polecat asked.

Hoodwink, too, lifted what should have been an eyebrow, but on the hairless mongrel was nothing but a ridge of linen-colored skin. The cowl that contributed to his namesake was pulled up against the beating sun, protecting his fair flesh.

From atop Ugfuck, Oats looked from one querying brother to the other. "You two don't know that story? From ancient Al-Unan, right, Fetch?"

Her answer was a shrug.

Undaunted, Oats explained to Hood and Polecat. "She was this demon-goddess on an island, worse-looking than Ugfuck—"

"See," Shed Snake put in, "a *legend*."

"Don't listen," Oats told his hog with a comforting rub before returning to the story. "She had tusks and a goat's hide, scales. And snakes instead of hair. If you looked at her too long, you turned to salt. Killed a fucking heap of warriors that way if they came too close. That's what I always think about, when I see the Umbers. Look at them too long, get too close . . ."

"Would you, then?" Polecat needled. "'Cause we haven't eaten properly in months and the mound of salted meat you'd make would be a fucking feast."

That drew a round of low laughter, the first heard in a long while.

The sworn brethren had ridden ahead when what was left of the caravan neared the Tine border, leaving the wagon in the care of the slops. Polecat had insisted on coming, and Fetch allowed him, feeling the need for all the Bastards to ride together. They were taking a risk, coming here. If they were to die for their trespass, better to die as a hoof. The slops had orders to wait until the following morning. If the Bastards were not back by then, they were to risk taking the orphans and remaining families within sight of the castile.

"What was the name of that she-monster?" Fetch asked, grinning a bit at the memory of those nightly stories in the orphanage.

"The *gargós*," Culprit replied fondly.

Shed Snake nodded. "That's right. And it *was* Al-Unan, the island of Kisthedon. Mead told me that part. Always knew every damn detail. He didn't even come up with us in the orphanage, but he knew that story, more of it than I'd ever heard. Swear he must have invented some of it just to seem smarter."

The mention of their fallen brother brought a ripple of sorrow over the hoof, but there were fond smiles in the silence.

"Well," Oats huffed, "should we see how close we can get before we die?"

In response, Fetch kicked Womb Broom forward.

The southern border of Tine land was marked by nothing more than a thin tributary of the Guadal-kabir. The waters meandered through Ul-wundulas, often vanishing underground, eventually swelling to the mighty expanse that flowed past Kalbarca, many miles to the west.

As the Bastard barbarians trotted through the stream, hardly more than a rivulet, Fetch was struck by the weight of defying such an ephemeral barrier. She half expected to be struck down the moment Womb's hooves touched the opposite side. As one, the Bastards drew their hogs to a stop, waiting. They were trespassers from this moment onward.

The warm winds played in their hair, the manes of the hogs. Hoodwink's cowl crushed and filled in turns, and Oats's beard became a pennant at the end of his chin.

None of them had ever set foot here.

"Go slow," Fetch said. "Thrums slung."

With that she led the True Bastards forward across a flat, heat-baked plain so akin to much of Ul-wundulas, yet pregnant with an elusive unfamiliarity. The scattered boulders, the swaths of garrigue, all seen and traversed across countless patrols in identical surrounds, but Fetch felt as if she were a stranger.

Every mongrel kept watch for rustskin scouts, but found nothing. It was said that if you ever saw a Tine warrior, it was the work of heat-sickness. Hard to imagine anything sneaking unnoticed in the nearly flat expanse, save perhaps a dun-hued serpent. That impression changed when they reached the foothills.

As the scrub grew thicker, proper trees began to encroach. Oaks of cork and holm gated the rising land. Slowly, warily, the hoof moved deeper into the embrace of the wooded hills. Shadow and slope took turns dismissing the sun.

Now in the shade, Hoodwink pulled his cowl away, dead eyes coming alive with a hunter's vigilance. The tilt of his head showed he heard something.

Crashing movement to the left jerked the hoof's attention to the hemming brush. A trio of roe deer burst forth and away. More than one hand went to the stirrup of a thrum, but Fetch hissed, held out her arms, stopping her brothers from unslinging their weapons. Tempting as the meat was, she could not risk the ire of the Tines by poaching their game.

"Breathe easy," Fetch reminded her brothers. She caught Oats's eye and saw a mote of doubt forming. Flicking her chin, she directed him to keep an eye on Culprit, distracting the thrice from his own misgivings. The younger rider was moon-eyed and twitchy, clearly spooked. Oats reached over and touched Culprit's wrist, stopping the hand that was drifting to his tulwar. With a sheepish sigh, Culprit returned the hand to his hog's mane and gave a nod of assurance.

Ahead, they could see the hills were conquered by high crags, poplar groves yielding to rock faces. They were about to leave the wooded confines of the foothills and enter a canyon. Fetch held up three fingers, quickly reduced them to two, and pointed forward. The hoof went from riding abreast to a triple column, two riders deep. Fetch, Oats, and Polecat were in the lead, with Culprit, Hood, and Shed Snake following.

"I don't love this," Polecat muttered low in his throat, glancing up at the natural walls creeping higher, eating away more and more of the sky.

They rode into the defile.

A low trilling groaned through the canyon. It was not the sound of bird or beast, but a hollow undulation, swelling and receding in haunting rhythms.

"The fuck is that?" Shed Snake complained.

"Talking," Hoodwink answered.

Polecat threw a look back. "Talking?"

"It's the Tines," Fetch agreed. She had never heard the queer sound before, but Hood was right, the elves were creating it somehow, using it to speak to one another. The canyon was a natural channel, carrying the quavering hum in a living current.

Answering roars followed, the rock walls imbued with the vibrations.

Just when it seemed the sounds would die, they revitalized, clawing up from a dying echo to again fill the canyon with a grinding din. The hogs were shying at the noise, their squeals of aggravation drowned out. Fetch had to kick Womb hard to get the pig moving, and her hoof was having equal difficulty.

Oats leaned in, nearly yelling in her ear in order to be heard. "Think they are warning us off?"

Fetch could only shake her head. She didn't know. Didn't care.

They had come this far. Forward was the only choice. If the Tines wanted them gone, they were going to have to tell her in plain speech or bald threat.

Committed, she led the Bastards on.

The canyon widened some, accommodating a sizable pool fed from a waterfall rolling over the western crag. To the right of the falls, the defile narrowed once more. Movement drew the hoof's attention up to the ridge.

There, between the falls and the canyon mouth, a lone elf stood, arms whirling in furiously graceful patterns, spinning an object in each hand, too fast to see, producing the sawing groans.

Fetch signaled the hoof to halt near the edge of the pool. Slowly, she held her hands up at the ends of wide-flung arms. Her brothers did the same. The elf's feverish gesticulations went on, unabated. The noise from the implements in his hands was growing. Fetch could feel it burrowing into her chest, making her heart flutter. The hogs were bucking now, almost berserk. The canyon began to spin, the damn sound ass-fucking Fetch's balance. Reeling, she saw one of her riders fumbling to load his thrum, couldn't tell who. Didn't matter. She yelled a command to stop, but her voice was useless in the rattling canyon.

Fetch dove, straight from the saddle, doing little more than falling on the culprit.

Hells dammit. Culprit.

She wrapped her arms around him, dragging them both to the ground. They were destined for it anyway, dizzy as they were. Polecat had already collapsed, eyes crossed and clenching. Another rider tumbled to the earth. Hood? Snake? Fetch could not see details, her sight storm-tossed upon a sea of tears. Beneath her, Culprit began to convulse. His limbs tightened, muscles stiffening to entrap the bones. Rigid, he shook violently. Fetch tried to restrain him, but had little strength. Her limbs felt grossly heavy. Nearby, Polecat was also afflicted, frothy spittle blossoming from between his locked jaws.

Fuck all. They were dying. The Tines were killing them. She had been wrong, led them to this. Sought shelter from sorcery and were now to be slain by the same foul, unknowable shit.

Attempting to make sense of sky and earth, she pushed upward, was smote by a twisting hog, flung back down. Barbarians would not readily trample their riders, but they were in pain, confused. Balling up, Fetch weathered their flight, was kicked once in the hip, trod on, but not enough to cause much harm. When the hogs were gone, she unrolled, stood on shaky legs.

One of the others was also on his feet.

Oats, based on the size. He was rocking, a towering tree buffeted by a gale, fighting to remain aloft. He brought something up to his shoulder, aimed at the ridge. He would have one chance, their one chance. But was it a chance to save their lives, or end them?

Fetch stumbled forward, fell before she reached Oats. His leg was in reach. She snatched his ankle. Pulled. The brute should not have been so easy to budge, but the discordant assault had undermined his roots. The thrice fell with that one little tug, succumbing.

The noise reached a murderous pitch. All sense was enslaved. Fetch was cocooned in mayhem. She heard pain, felt sound, tasted light. Her violated perceptions nearly dragged her under. The void was there, the smell of it eager to consume. But Fetch floated along its surface, knowing to recoil would cause it to strike. Adrift, she waited. The noise faded, fled. Taste returned to her mouth, welcomed with the acrid flavor of bile. Moist grit was beneath her cheek, her clenched fingernails. The sound of splashing water asserted itself. Opening her eyes, Fetch saw the surface of the pool, wobbling with the falls and her own distorted vision.

Revolving her skyward eyeball, she spied the elf on the ridge. He stood, finally motionless, watching, for a long while. At last, he stepped to the froth of the falls and hopped over the edge of the crag. The height was enough to injure, even kill, but there was no hesitance in the leap. Water burst upward when the elf landed, knees bending slightly at the impact. He strode across the pool, the water reaching his mid-thigh at its deepest. Fetch watched him approach through an eye narrowed to a slit.

He wore nothing but leggings and a clout, both made from deer leather. His skin was the nut-brown of all Tines, incarnadined by the sun. His shoulders were broad, topping a powerful, hairless torso that cut down sharply to a narrow waist. Upon his head, long black hair was worn in the traditional plumage, shaved along the sides of the scalp, revealing ears gently pointed. Black paint covered half his face, from the nose up. The instruments in his hands proved to be a pair of lacquered clubs, flat along the grip, angling sharply at the wider head, where a smooth sphere of polished rock was affixed. Whispers of pale light mingled in the air around these stones and, as Fetch watched, coalesced into the spheres, shining within the center only to fade away.

Fetch closed her eye fully as the elf stepped out of the pool, drawing near. He stood there, dripping, for a time. She did not hear his footsteps when he moved again, but felt his shadow momentarily block the sun. Carefully peeking, she saw no sign of him, sensed he had walked over her. Fetch cocked her eye at Oats. He was still breathing. The elf would not have failed to notice that, but there were no sounds of his clubs striking helpless skulls.

The Bastards were alive. And the Tine wanted them that way.

Fetch thanked every god she had ever heard of and did not believe in. Her gut had been right, Mead had been right. There was a chance.

Slowly, she turned her addled head.

The elf's back was turned. He had walked through the fallen group of half-orcs and now simply stood. A moment of stillness before a flick of his left wrist, deftly spinning the club in a single rotation, releasing a trembling, airy note that fled through the defile.

A signal.

Fetch was close enough to see a series of delicate holes carved along the length of the weapon. She might have laughed if the act did not threaten a spell of vomiting. One fucking rustskin and a pair of fluted clubs, the downfall of the True Bastards. Beneath the weight of every hell, the Claymaster was laughing. But fuck him eternally, for she had been right. Now it was time to prove it.

Fetch pushed up, every sinew rebelling against the attempt.

The elf turned.

Keen, angled eyes regarded her above prominent cheekbones. He made no move as she reached her knees and held up shaking, splayed hands. She wanted to put one foot forward, have something to spring from in case she had this wrong, but resisted the impulse.

Hoping Mead was smiling on her, she spoke.

"*K . . . kao'lem.*"

Friend.

The Tine bared his teeth in a silent snarl.

"*Kao'lem,*" Fetch repeated. "*Mi . . . mi'hawa thiospa ascút . . . onáphit.*"

My tribe desires safety.

The snarl twisted to a sneer. Either she said something wrong or her very request was worthy of scorn.

The Tine hissed something. Fetch missed most of it, but she heard "blood" and "woman." The words mattered little. The elf's tone dripped with disgust.

"Three of my people here now," Fetch pressed on in elvish. "Old ones and a child. We need help."

Movement at the mouth of the defile beyond the elf drew Fetch's attention. A party of riders. Four more Tine warriors astride harrow stags approached the pool, fanning out, war lances lowered. Their mounts moved noiselessly, antlers shimmering with that same eerie pale light Fetch had seen imbued in the stones of the lookout's clubs.

One of the riders stared down at Fetch, his face a blank mask behind white war paint streaked with vertical black lines, save those that ran from beneath his eyes, which were red. His black hair was shot through with silver. "This one still stands."

Fetch mined the meaning of every word out of her aching mind. She also understood they were not addressed to her, despite the direction of the speaker's gaze.

"She is the *lya'ʒáta,*" the first warrior responded. There was one of those hate-filled words again.

The rider did look at him now. "And do you fear her, N'keesos?"

"No."

"Show this courage."

The Tine warrior dropped his clubs, a soft, mournful note issuing from each as they fell. Fetch tensed as the elf took two purposeful strides toward her. She wanted to get off her knees, to show these savages that she did not fear them either, to choke the disdain from this cocksure spy-hawk who defeated her brothers. All of this she wanted to do. All of this, she sensed, they wanted her to do. The Tine halted before her, eyes and lips turned down in revulsion. Quickly, his left hand rose. Fetch thought he was about to strike her, prepared for the blow, but the elf merely placed his palm forcefully across her brow, left it there for a moment before pushing away, causing her to rock back slightly.

The warrior, named N'keesos, shot a defiant stare at the older rider who'd challenged him, receiving a grim nod. Stepping away from Fetch, he went to the edge of the pool. She had to turn her head to watch him, unwilling to allow him to leave her sight. Reaching under his clout, N'keesos loosed his cock, directed it at the hand he had touched her with and pissed across the palm. When his flow ceased, he wrung the hand and squatted to rinse it in the water.

Rage filled Fetch's skull with fire. This is what they thought of her, these haughty tribals? Their indignation turned her stomach, put a torch to her caution.

Fetching stood.

The lead rider glowered. "You will remain here."

Without waiting for an answer or any sign of comprehension, he turned his stag, leading his fellow riders to the defile. In moments, they were gone. N'keesos retrieved his clubs and approached the wall of the gorge. His legs bunched and he leapt, reaching the top of the cliff in a single, incomprehensible bound. Once more upon his perch, he squatted. And watched.

Fetch cast a squinting, rueful look in his direction before getting to her feet and examining her fallen brothers. They were all unconscious, sprawled where they landed. It was a disturbing display of vulnerability Fetch would never have been able to imagine. She did not think she had ever seen Hoodwink with his eyes closed before. The rare times she had entered the bunkhouse, she had always found him risen, as if he heard her coming and refused to be seen sleeping. Picking her way through the tumble, she did her best to make the mongrels comfortable, arranging limbs, rolling some onto their backs. Oats had half fallen in the pool, and dragging him out of the water proved to be the toughest task. Fetch may not have been rendered senseless, but she could still feel the effects of those damn clubs in her weakened limbs.

Once her boys were seen to, she studied the churned hoofprints of the barbarians, found they fled to the defile the hoof had used to enter the gap. She walked to the mouth, hoping to catch a glimpse of their mounts, but a sawing note from above warned her against searching further.

So, she was to wait.

Skirting the pool, Fetch made her way to the waterfall and drank, catching the cold, pounding cascade in scooped hands. With nothing else to do, she returned to the others and sat down among them, making sure they all continued to take breaths.

The sun did not need to sink far past noon to abandon the gorge. A thin veil of shadow settled upon every rock and scrubby bush. The surface of the pool became darksome and uninviting. And still Fetch waited, watched from above by the Tine spy-hawk.

At last, there was movement in the defile the elves had used. Something heavy approached over the rocks, pushed through the brush.

A massive hog emerged, larger than Ugfuck, one that Fetch knew well.

Big Pox.

The sight of that lumbering swine still conjured feelings of revulsion. He had once served the Claymaster, pulled his chariot, but it wasn't the loathsome former chief of the Grey Bastards the hog now bore.

It was Beryl.

The half-orc matron had changed little. Like all of them, she was thinner, and she wore deerskins in place of linen and roughspun. Her face was dismayed at the sight of the prone Bastards as she kicked

Big Pox forward. Fetch stood to greet her, but was expectedly ignored. Beryl dismounted and went to her knees beside Oats, worry for her son in every motion.

"He's alive," Fetch told her.

It was Beryl's turn to cast a withering look up at the Tine warrior.

"Is your prowess proved?" she yelled upward, her elvish better than Fetch's.

The elf remained completely still.

"Fucking brave-sworn," Beryl muttered, returning to the coarseness of Hisparthan. She finally looked at Fetching. "Why are you here, Isabet?"

Rankled at the disappointment in those words, the blatant condescension, Fetch hardened her jaw. "I need to see Warbler. You can hear all when I tell him. Unless he's dead."

That last was a gnawing fear, but Fetch cast it as a barb of petty vengeance.

Gently, Beryl lifted Oats's head and rested it in her lap, stroked his brow. "He's not dead."

"Then why have you come and not him?"

"Riding is difficult for him now."

They traded no more words and even fewer looks. There never was much affection between them. Any that existed vanished on the day Beryl discovered Jackal and her son were secretly helping Fetch train to be a rider. She had actually attempted to forbid Oats to continue, as if he were still a child under her roof instead of a sworn brother with his own hoof name, hog, and Bastard tattoos. Even worse, it worked. Oats had pulled away for nearly a week after his mother's admonishment. Jackal and Fetch carried on without him, undeterred, and said nothing when the thrice sulked back to help once more. Beryl forgave him that defiance, forgave Jackal, who had always been a second son, but her indulgence never extended to Fetching.

Eventually, the True Bastards began to stir. Hoodwink was the first to fully rouse, Oats the last. The mongrels were so fuddled, none had the strength to make a jest at the sight of Oats pillowed on his mother's legs. When the big thrice did open his eyes, saw the face above, he reached up with one huge arm and pulled it down until it touched his own.

Fetch had remained standing since Beryl's arrival. Hoodwink got to his feet and joined her, making an effort to keep his steps steady.

"The hogs?" he asked.

It was Beryl who answered. "The Tines will round them up."

Polecat groaned, still flat on his ass, and pinched the bridge of his nose. "Why did the fucking cunts attack if they meant to allow us entry?"

Beryl scoffed. "It's their way. Show you that you pose no threat here."

"Give me back my hog and half a chance to load my thrum and we will see about that," Polecat said.

"Put a cock in that," Fetch ordered. "They are showing us they are strong. We need them to be, because we aren't, else we would not have come. Beryl, we have others waiting at the border. One is grievously wounded. All are hungry."

"Riders have already gone out," Beryl replied, reluctantly allowing Oats to sit up. "They knew you were coming since before you crossed into their lot."

"The slops and little ones going to get the same welcome?" Oats asked, rubbing the back of his skull.

Beryl looked at Fetch. "Depends on how stupid your slops are."

Fetch ignored that and addressed the hoof. "Find your balance, boys. Time to move."

Oats helped Beryl remount Big Pox and they all followed the hog away from the pool.

The gorge narrowed once more, but soon forked, another winding spur branching off the first, which appeared to climb uphill as it continued. To the relief of every shaky leg, Beryl took the more level path. Sparsely wooded dells and sunbathed saddle gaps pocketed the run of the canyon, but the cliff walls never retreated for long. Movement drew the eye of every half-orc as they proceeded through one particularly wide stretch of canyon.

Within the rock on both sides, elves moved inside what would have been cave mouths, except the openings were perfectly triangular and arranged in tiered rows. The highest of these neared the top of the crags, a dizzying height. The lowest were still two heights of a man from the ground, with no ropes or ladders to be found. Fetch might have wondered how the elves reached these grottos if she had not witnessed the Tine warrior's preternatural leaps. Yet, even as she made this conclusion, she spied squat huts with timber frames and earthen roofs among the wooded verges of the canyon. Many of these domiciles were flanked by gardens or nestled beside small yet flourishing groves. Dark-haired Tines, mostly women and children, but some menfolk, labored among the cultivation, bearing baskets of harvested fruit or cutting fresh rows in the soil. Fetch knew fuck-all about farming, but she knew Ul-wundulas, and the rich, dark earth the elves tended should not have existed here, especially this high in the Umbers.

None of the elves so much as looked up when the half-orcs passed through.

They traveled on, passing through a second inhabited canyon, almost identical to the first, before Beryl led them down another spur. This defile swiftly became a punishing downgrade, and was so narrow that Big Pox could not turn around if the need arose. The path was an ankle-busting trench of treacherous stones. As they made their way down, the trench grew damp, growing into a weak trickle as a mountain spring emerged from beneath the rock. Soon, the footing upon the loose stones was further challenged by their slick surfaces. The descending trail widened near the bottom, opening up into another gap enclosed by heavy shelves of grey rock face. The spring sought the low ground, pooling in the gap, making the air humid, and feeding a dense cluster of elms and poplar, blackthorns and myrtles.

Beryl took them into the shade of the trees, guiding Pox through the scrub, though the path was well worn and discernible. The depth of the ravine and the closeness of the trees permitted little of the sun, lending the gap a gloomy appearance. A lone hut stood near the northern end, away from the boggy ground of the mountain pool and backed by the striated cliffs.

A half-orc child loitered in front of the hut, rushing over on compact, pumping legs when he caught sight of the hog and its rider, but trundled to an unsteady halt once he noticed the hoof coming up behind. Beryl dismounted and went to him, drawing him close to her side with one hand.

Wily had grown since last Fetch saw him. Mongrel children tended to be large, especially thrice-bloods. Not yet four and he already reached Beryl's waist. From half behind her leg, he peered at the Bastards, chin slightly lowered. His entire left arm was wrapped in some kind of dark, glistening bandage. At the boy's neck, beneath the flaps of a deer-skin tunic, a few pale pustules stood out against his ash-grey skin.

Oats took a step forward and knelt. "There's my little bear. Remember me?"

It took a moment, but recognition dawned on Wily's face, just ahead of a smile. Oats clapped his huge hands together and held them out, the gesture calling the child out from hiding. Wily rushed into Oats's arms, his unwrapped hand instantly seizing the laughing brute's beard. Oats noisily pretended to chew on the boy before launching into a series of mock hog grunts. Wily, tickled by the burrowing whiskers and vibrating animal sounds, surrendered to a rolling belly laugh that brought smiles to every witness.

Those smiles faded when Warbler limped from the hut.

The grizzled old thrice-blood's back was still straight, only Oats overtopped him in height. His permanently sun-squinted eyes remained sharp, his mane of hair still thick and white. But his left leg was swollen to nearly three times the size of his right, the deerskin breeks cut off on that side to accommodate the hideous limb wrapped in the same shiny compress as Wily's arm.

Fetch could not speak for the others, but it wasn't Warbler's appearance that caused the momentary joy to wilt upon her face. It was the tidings she bore, the words she would have to speak to this mongrel who had helped win the Lots, found the hoofs, this mongrel who had been a fleeting mentor and a lifelong hero.

"Chief," Warbler said in his deep, resonant growl, dipping his chin in respect.

Fetch's resolve nearly crumbled hearing that title given her by the one who might have held it, in another time, had the Claymaster's madness not deprived him the chance. She couldn't help but wonder if the news she must now deliver might have been avoided with the old thrice leading the hoof.

"Winsome has fallen, War-boar."

THIRTY

THE SLOPHEADS AND VILLAGERS were brought down just before dusk, escorted by a single Tine scout. The wagons, of course, were not with them. Neither was Sluggard.

"Tines took him," Xhreka explained. "Figured it best to let them."

Fetch nodded in acknowledgment, allowing the weary halfling to seek what comfort she could. The marshy little valley contained only the one hut, leaving all but the orphans to sleep rough. Beryl would not hear of the foundlings spending the night outdoors and squeezed her recovered charges into the tight confines of the rectangular domicile. The Winsome children were not so fortunate, but they had their parents, water, food, and the surrounding safety of the gorge walls. After the past days, it was a welcome paradise for all.

The Bastards were busy rigging a pen for the hogs, building fires, and helping the frails find spots to bed down.

Fetching stood a stone's throw from the hut and the same distance farther removed from where Warbler spoke to the Tine. It wasn't the same elf who'd disabled the Bastards. This one bore more weapons; a bow in his hand, a quiver and knife at his side, and a pair of hatchets, crossed at his lower back. The conversation was brief and the elf soon turned to make his way to the trail and the long climb out of the depression.

Warbler hobbled back to Fetch.

"They are seeing to the nomad," he reported, "and will do what they can for him."

Fetch could not help but be dubious. "Will they?"

"They will," Warbler grunted. "Come, let's sit. Got to get off this fucking leg."

Fetch called for Oats.

Warbler led them around the back of the hut, where a stump stood for chopping firewood, and eased himself down, sighing in aggravation and keeping his bad leg straight. Fetch got a closer look at the dark bandages. They were made from fish skins. Likely that would not be the most curious thing she would see while in Dog Fall.

"You in much pain?" she asked.

Warbler waved the concern away. "Pfh! That's why I'm here, isn't it? Sit down, chief. You look near collapse."

He wasn't wrong. Fetch found a sizable log in the pile, turned it on its end, and rested her ass, though she had to keep her legs engaged to hold the balance. Oats remained standing at her side.

Warbler chuckled darkly. "I'd offer you some wine, but the elves don't make any. At least, none they've shared. If you had told me a year ago that I could go this long without a drop, I would not have believed it. Of course . . . there is much you have told me that is damn hard to believe."

There was sympathy in the old thrice's voice, but the judgment was there too.

"Hardest to imagine the Orc Stains turning on us like that," he went on, anger beginning to replace all other tones. "Fuck them eternal for that."

"They paid for it," Oats said.

"So did we," Fetch added softly.

Warbler frowned. "Still not certain I understand exactly why they did it."

"Knob tried to poach Oats. Refused to acknowledge me as a master of a hoof. I strongly reminded him that neither was his to take from me. He held a grudge."

Warbler glared at phantoms near the dirt for a long time before looking up and breathing hard. "What now?"

"That's what I need you to tell me, War-boar. I took a gamble coming here. Now that we're here and alive, what can we expect?"

Warbler raised his eyebrows in thought. "I told the hoof before I left that we understood less about Tine ways than we thought. This long living with them, I can tell you for certain I was right. I can also tell you I understand less now than the day we first arrived. I figured it would take time, but the longer we stay, the more we are left alone."

"They're neglecting you?"

"Yes and no. If there is a task to be done, they do it." Warbler hooked a thumb at the hut. "They built this. Helped us start a garden. Brought clothes, baskets, pots. Few months in, Beryl took ill. They came with a tea, poultices. That's how I know they will tend your injured nomad. Wouldn't be surprised if they showed up in the morning and started building huts for the rest of you. If there is something to be done, they will do it. Beyond that, the lot of them might as well be ghosts.

"We hear them up there sometimes, laughter and singing echoing through the passes. Never actually *seen* them in merriment, mind. And never invited to join. We are down here, they are up there. Clear to me, that's how they want it."

Fetch huffed with a resignation long past bitter. Half-orcs. Ever the outcasts.

She glanced at Warbler's leg. "Seems they have at least held up their promise to move the plague from Wily to you."

"That's another thing entirely, my girl."

"Tell us."

It was clear he did not want to, but he gathered his thoughts with another deep breath and obeyed, the words coming carefully.

"Figured it would suck hogshit, whatever they had to do. Didn't figure it would take so damn long. Fucking thing is alive. It . . . resists. Feared it might never leave the boy. When it did . . . the pain was . . ." Warbler shook his hoary head. "It's no wonder he went mad."

Fetch and Oats shared a look. They did not have to ask who he meant.

"When I woke up, days later, I thought, 'At least the lad is free of it.' Of course, he wasn't. Not entirely. And that's the way it's been. They keep trying, the Tines. Come get us every once in a while and take us up to a lodge they have built. The look on Wily's face when he sees them now . . ."

Warbler's voice choked.

"It's torture for all of us, even the elves. The chants they perform, the violent movements that I reckon you would call dancing until you saw it, it's all causing them pain. But for that little boy it has to be . . . hells he has my respect! Toughest mongrel I have ever known and he's not fucking four."

The tears were falling down the old thrice's craggy face, unashamed now that they were free.

"I took my time killing that twisted frail sorcerer that made this evil shit in the mines. I cut his cods off, fucked his ass with a knife, every savage cruelty I could invent in the moment. Wasn't near enough. If I had him living, right here in front of us now, I could not conjure agonies fitting to make him pay for what he birthed and Wily has now inherited."

Oats turned away, paced farther from the hut. Perhaps he was trying to spare Warbler the indignity of witnessing his grief. Or he did not want to expose his own.

"There's another wizard that needs killing before that score is settled," Fetch remarked.

Warbler wiped at his face. "Any word from Jackal?"

Fetch shook her head.

Warbler grew very still.

"What is it?" Fetch prodded.

The old mongrel's answer was grave. "We may wish him alive before the end. Crafty, I mean."

This brought Oats back around. "The fuck you on about?"

"This," Warbler replied, gesturing at his corrupted leg. "The elves can't get a proper grip on it. Like trying to ride a wild barbarian that's been shaved and greased. This plague refuses to stay put. I was blind a few months back. Leg was hale, but my eyes were closed by the pustules. Throat, too. I could tell from Beryl's voice I was a horror to look upon." Warbler gave a rough laugh. "Figures I'd get my woman back after long years only to be so hideous and sick she can barely stand the sight of me."

"Self-pity doesn't wear well on you, Warbler," Fetch said.

Oats huffed. "And Mother's got more grit than that."

"You're right. Both of you. So I will stick to unshakable truths. The plague likes to fuck around. Who knows what is going to happen the next time they come for us. What it will choose to do. I am not young. That ain't self-pity, but cold fact. And Wily? He is too damn young. Neither of us can do this much more. The point-ears give us the intervals to keep us sane, probably to keep themselves sane. But it's a wearisome war that the plague is winning."

"The Tines will succeed," Fetch assured, nearly grimacing at the empty words.

Warbler responded with a weary exhale. "I once knew a nomad that could tie a knot only he could loose, damn thing was that intricate. This Crafty? He did the same fucking trick. Vengeance is one thing, my girl. But if we want this weapon out of that boy, we better start wishing upon our plucked pubic hairs that Jaco brings the swaddlehead back alive."

Fetch stood, allowing the makeshift stool to topple. She went to the same spot Oats had, boots scattering the carpet of wood chips. Her back to the hut, she paused, stared into the trees at the cliffs a bowshot through the trunks, nothing but a black wall in the fading light.

"It's been over a year, War-boar. It's past time we faced the idea that he is not coming back."

It was Oats who responded. "You're giving up on him?"

Fetch turned. "I'm giving up on plans that require waiting for him. There are so many things that could have happened since he left . . . it's fucking useless to think on them."

Warbler's face hardened even as his eyes filled with affection. "I'm going to say something. May sound cruel."

"Go on."

"What choice do you have? The Bastards don't have much left. Our home is destroyed, our lot abandoned, our folk mostly fled. What remains of the hoof has just joined the oldest fart in their ranks in exile. We don't know how long the Tines will allow us to remain here. The reason they took us was the fucking plague. They know it's the only thing the thicks fear. But if they keep failing to get it under control, I sorely doubt our welcome will outlive their loss of patience."

"They are using us, we are using them," Fetch agreed.

"And we ain't all that useful," Warbler pointed out.

"So you are putting forth that we have no choice but to wait, but that we are running out of time to wait? That's some deeply shit counsel, War-boar."

"It's some deeply shit circumstances, chief."

The savory smells of Beryl's cooking drifted behind the hunt on the wings of woodsmoke, dispelling the bleak discourse.

"She'll pull up every crop we got to feed them little ones." Warbler chuckled.

"And throw every curse in her head at me for putting them in danger."

Warbler did not bother trying to refute that. Oats put a hand on her shoulder.

"All of this can keep until morning," Warbler said, at last. "Making any choices right now, after the last days' strife, would be beyond foolish. The two of you get some rest."

Fetch flinched at his mawkishness. "And it will all be better in the sunlight?"

"Or it will be far fucking worse," the old thrice growled, "but at least you will have slept."

Leaving Warbler on his stump, they walked back around to the front of the hut. Fetch considered checking on the orphans, but Beryl would have them well in hand. Plus, the matron's withering looks were more than she could swallow at the moment.

Sending Oats on, she made a quick circuit of the camps her boys fashioned. Dry, flat ground was in short supply, so the traditional separations had taken hold. The Winsome refugees clustered around their fires, the slops another, and the sworn brothers their own, closest to the trailhead. The rope corral for the hogs was close by, the barbarians snuffling through what remained of the figs they were given.

The Bastards were supping on the same fruit with only slightly less gusto than the beasts. Hoodwink was standing, the rest sitting on their saddles or lounging with their backs against trees. As she entered their midst, Shed Snake wordlessly offered up a whole fig. She took it, slumping down beside him, drawing her knife. There was some barley bread, as well, and dried fish.

The True Bastards chewed and none said a word.

Fetch had not realized how exhausted she was, but sitting shattered that ignorance, left her endurance in pieces. She lay back.

No solar. She was walled only by her surrounding brethren.

No bed. The hard ground was her mattress, and a saddle pillowed her head.

No feverish visions from foul potions. Only the natural, inexplicable cast of the dice that brought dreams or nightmares or nothing.

Fetch sighed and allowed the night song of the canyon to lull her.

Sleep.

A reward.

SHE AWOKE TO LAUGHTER in the sunlight.

The children were playing, dodging around trees as they chased one another, the rules seeming to change with every delighted giggle. It looked like all the orphans, plus most of the Winsome kids. The game had spilled right into the sleeping Bastards.

Fetch had not commanded a watch. The elves would either protect them, or not. For one night, at least, the hoof abandoned caution and left their fate in the wind. The result was sound sleep on hard ground, the oblivion of prolonged exhaustion. It took a pack of whooping children skipping over their snoring heads and out-stretched legs to rouse them.

Oats shook off the torpor almost immediately, gave an exaggerated bellow, and jumped up, giving chase to the blissfully surprised children, instantly transforming the game into a flight from the hunched monster with outstretched arms.

"Fool-ass," Fetch breathed with a grin, propping herself up on her elbows to watch Oats lumber after his squealing prey.

Across from her, Polecat sat up wearing a bleary but amused squint. "Must be nice."

"What?" Shed Snake asked, still on his back.

"To have already forgotten," Cat replied.

"In their waking hours, perhaps," Hoodwink said, standing fluidly. "But many wept in the night."

Polecat wrinkled his hatchet face. "Thanks, Hood. That adds cheer to my morning."

Culprit laughed, leaned, farted into his hand, and made a tossing gesture at Cat. "Add that to your cheer."

Polecat only gave a slow, resigned shake of the head, while Shed Snake rolled away from the offending odor with a disgusted noise of complaint.

Oats returned, wearing a huge smile. "That'll teach them."

"To do that every morning now?" Fetch said. "Yes. Well done."

Oats was unapologetic. "I can think of worse ways to be woke."

"I can think of better," Polecat said, moving a splayed hand up and down above his crotch.

Fetch got to her feet, stretched, and retrieved her weapons from her tack.

Movement in the brush drew all attention. Wily was half-hidden among the bracken, timid and curious.

"Looking for the others?" Culprit asked, his voice going all high and foolish and endearing. "They went that way."

Wily looked set to flee the opposite way, but Oats snatched him up before he got the chance.

"Let's go find them others," the thrice said, and charged off with his now-beaming passenger.

Fetch went in the direction of the hut.

Hoodwink settled into step beside her.

"Something on your mind?" she asked.

"Our boundaries here," Hood replied. "Are we prisoners?"

Fetch stopped, turned to look at the sallow killer. "There are two things I want to have this morning, Hood. Patience and a piss. Please don't thwart either one."

Hoodwink dipped his chin and did not follow when she walked on.

Warbler was sitting out front of the hut, mending a small pile of the orphans' shoes.

"Soil pit?" Fetch inquired.

The old thrice pointed to his left. "Near the eastern edge. Going to need a bigger one with this many new folk."

Fetch nodded. "I'll put the slops on it."

She walked in the indicated direction, picking her way through the trees and around the worst of the blackthorn thickets. The mountain stream was nothing but puddles connected by the odd runnel this far into the bowl. She should have figured the soil pit would be farthest from the fresh water flow, but even as small as the valley was, she could have wandered for a good while in the dense growth of the interior before finding the place. Soon, however, the smell served as a guide. A lashed framework had been erected to help folk take their ease.

Fetch was laughably grateful for the rough luxury that would spare her from squatting.

On the way back, she took a different path, cutting more through the valley's center, wanting to get a better idea of the land. She could still hear the echoes of the children's play, as well as birdsong and the clicking hums of insects.

A shadowy mass caught her eye through the elms. Approaching, she found the remains of another elf hut. The earthen roof had fallen in, one of the stone walls collapsed, the others crumbling. Despite its decrepit state it was obviously larger than the one occupied by Warbler, Beryl, and Wily. A shape darted from the shadows of the sagging entrance, startling Fetch. Her hand went for her tulwar on instinct, but froze on empty air.

"Bwah!" the little girl called out, face full of fierce glee. It was the farrier's daughter.

"Ollal," Fetch breathed, aiming for amused but hitting annoyed. "What are you doing?"

It was a fool-ass question. Fetch knew what the child was doing, even if she did not understand how to fit herself into the pursuit as easily as Oats.

Quickly realizing this particular quarry was no sport, Ollal scampered off in search of someone without a spear rammed up their ass.

Leaving the crumbling hut behind, Fetch followed the sound of gurgling water. The ground began to dip, the foliage giving way to scrabble. Emerging from the thickets, she discovered a shaded basin, the stream running in from the northwest, tumbling over a slope of rocks in a series of small falls on the opposite side from where she stood. About halfway down the slope, perched on a stable rock and leaning into the largest falls to scrub some linen, was Beryl.

A basket of clothes sat on a neighboring stone, waiting to be cleaned. The sodden victims that had already fallen to the matron's industry were laid out all around. Fetching stopped short, wondering if she could withdraw without being noticed.

"Toss me another, if you would," Beryl called out without ever having looked in her direction.

Fuck. No chance, then.

Fetch walked around the edge of the basin until she was above the basket, and made her way down the slope. Squatting on the jumble of rocks, she took up a tunic and flicked it over to Beryl. A soaking garment was tossed back.

"Lay that out anywhere you can."

Fetch climbed a bit back up and slapped the breeches across the curve of a boulder. "I best get back to the hoof."

"You can't spare a moment and help me?" Beryl asked, not looking up and continuing to scrub. "This too low a task for a hoof chief? Or are you just trying to get clear of me?"

"Yes. To both."

The back of Beryl's head shook as she wrung water from the tunic.

Fetch took another step upward. Beryl's voice stopped her.

"You think I'm cross with you."

It wasn't a question.

"You think I am cross," Beryl repeated, "because you think you know my mind. You didn't know it when you lived under my care, Isa. And you don't know it now. Thistle told me all that happened. If I didn't know that woman the way I do, trust her the way I do, I'd say she was mad. Dogs that don't die. Mongrel hoofs killing each other. But she is not mad. And I do trust her. After all I've seen in this life, do you know the toughest part of her story to believe? That through all that, not one of those children died."

Beryl gave the tunic a final twist and craned around to look up.

"They are *all* alive. Every last one I left behind and more besides. You must think me a monstrous cunt if you believe I would be cross with you over that."

Fetch was shaken by the gratitude in Beryl's voice, turned it aside as she would a sword stroke. "Didn't do it alone. It was the boys that got them away from danger. The Bastards and the slops."

Beryl returned to her chore. "Well, they will forever blame themselves for those they didn't save. Salik . . . Shed Snake, he apologized to me about Sweeps. The look in his face . . . worse than the news. Almost."

Fetch threw a short whistle and, when Beryl looked up, held an open hand up for the tunic. Beryl threw it. Fetch laid it out, returned to the basket and tossed her the last soiled garment. Only now did she realize the small size of all the clothes.

"These are all the orphans'," she said aloud, grinning at the thought of a wild herd of naked children running rampant through the brush.

"There is a pond at the south end of the valley fed by the stream,"

Beryl told her. "Thistle and that halfling woman rounded the wee ones up for a swim. They sorely needed to bathe."

"I just saw the farrier's girl," Fetch said.

"She'll find them," Beryl replied, unconcerned. "And her parents can wash her damn clothes. I got enough here."

"There was another hut too. Fallen in. Didn't look that old."

"Used to be for the elf girls. The ones Jackal and Warbler freed from the Sludge Man. They were already living down here when we arrived. None of them were of the Tine tribe, so they were kept separate until . . ."

Fetch frowned, not liking the turn in Beryl's voice. "Until what?"

"Until they tired of torturing Ignacio and finally killed him."

The pockmarked cavalero captain was not a man that often entered Fetch's mind. He had once commanded the commoner cavalry at the castile and was considered an ally of the Grey Bastards. In the end, he had been little more than the Claymaster's dog. A dog that was also running his own scheme bringing captive elf women to the Sludge Man. His last delivery had indeed been liberated, but not before enduring hells-knew-what-all while at the mercy of the bog trotter. It was also Ignacio who held Beryl and Wily captive during Crafty's ploy to transfer the plague from the Claymaster to Oats, threatening their safety to coerce the thrice to cooperate. The wizard's plan had been upset, but as always, Crafty had a fallback position in little Wily. Ignacio had fled, spooked when the plague came to claim the boy, but Jackal had set the Tines on his trail.

"None of us believed he would get far," Fetch said.

Beryl cleared her throat. "And he didn't. The Tines gave him over to the girls as some kind of ritual retribution. A man of his low cunning, I was sure he would murder them all and attempt escape. But he was already cowed, broken. I don't know what the Tines did to him before bringing him down here, but the women he once captured had more to fear from a horsefly. They treated him like a slave at first, then like a maligned pet. By the end, he was nothing but a cringing, mewling shell, simple-minded and beaten more than fed. We never allowed Wily to go close to that hut for fear of what he might see.

"And then, one day, they were gone. Warbler reckons they joined the tribe, but I have never seen any of them in the gorges above. Wherever they went, they left Ignacio's body behind, wasted and filthy just outside the door. I had Warbler put a thrumbolt in him before throwing his ass in a shallow hole. I hope one day you do the same to those that did for Cissy."

Fetch could see the spite in the face of fresh pain. Thistle, Sweeps, and Cissy had been Beryl's trusted hands for years, more like daughters than Fetch had ever been. Now, two were dead. It was a bitter draft to swallow.

Leaving the clothes to dry, they went together to the pond and found the children were not alone at their play in the water. Oats, Culprit, and Touro were all waist-deep in the pond, each with a foundling perched on their shoulders. The flailing children were trying to unseat one another, their conniving mounts waging their own war to upset the balance of their adversaries. An alliance quickly formed against Oats, but the thrice may as well have been a castle tower for all the chance the others had at toppling him. Cheering spectators had gathered at the edges of the pond. Most of the slopheads and Winsome villagers were encouraging their favorites, and Fetch could hear bets being placed, though there was nothing to wager. The other children swam around the borders of the melee, some in their own games, others trying to affect the outcome of the combat with incessant splashes.

Thistle and Xhreka sat at the water's edge, each holding a foundling babe. One of the Winsome men held the third. Sitting close beside his former nurse, Wily watched the contest with rapt attention.

"He can't get his bandages wet," Beryl said, though it was more a voiced regret than an explanation.

Fetch nodded in sympathy. The plague was not catching unless unleashed by its bearer, but that knowledge was difficult to impart to children, often not enough to curtail the fear in the fully grown. Wily had begun to be shunned by the other orphans before he ever left Winsome as the pustules became difficult to hide. That exclusion may have taken root again. Fetch hoped the recent horrors endured by the foundlings had toughened them against baseless fears conjured by unsightly buboes on a playmate. For this game, at least, his sequester was imposed by his caregivers.

There was only one other child not swimming.

Ollal had indeed found her way to the pond, but her mother was having a difficult time getting her to bathe. The beleaguered woman had managed to get the little girl's smock off, but appeared to have met resistance shortly after.

Fetch kicked her boots off while removing her brigand.

"Hells damn, Isa," Beryl griped. "Are you unable to resist a challenge?"

"Reckon not," Fetch responded, dropping her breeches. "Besides, I need a damn bath too." Hurrying over to the struggle between mother and daughter, stooping on the move, she plucked the little girl up. Ollal was installed on Fetch's shoulders before she could react, her mother issuing a surprised, amused sound.

"All right, you," Fetch told her rider, wading into the pond, "this game is called Bucking Centaurs, and I was really good at your age. All you need to do is knock those boys down."

The game was actually called Fucking Horse-cocks and Fetch used to play on dry, hard ground, but Ollal did not need to know either fact.

"What if they knock me down?" came the uncertain reply.

"Then you get soaked. So, if you don't want to bathe, you will have to fight to stay dirty."

Culprit was the first to see them coming, his eyes going slightly wide with disbelief.

"Uh . . . chief is joining the fight."

Before the others could quite wrap their minds around that, Fetch was upon them. The mongrel boys atop the Bastards were not trammeled by hesitance, and urged their mounts at the fresh opponents. Fetch could feel Ollal recoiling from their eagerness to fight.

"Push back!" she encouraged, and sent a foot questing forward beneath the water in search of Touro's. Finding it, she hooked his ankle and jerked with her leg. The slophead yelped as he fell, spilling his rider backward with a heaving splash.

"Chief fights dirty!" Culprit exclaimed with appreciation.

Oats began to back away. "You don't have *half* a notion."

Ollal was giggling now, hands and arms darting forward at Culprit's boy.

"I ain't going to roll over just 'cause you're my chief," Culprit said with a cocky grin.

"Good," Fetch replied. "I'll know my vote wasn't an error."

Culprit was sure on his feet, his rider more aggressive. Ollal's inexpert shoves were easily fended off. Knowing his boy had the advantage, Culprit pressed in, even had enough gall to reach for Fetch's thigh beneath the water to try to pull her leg out. She slipped his grasp, retreated a step before immediately wading forward again.

"Culprit." She pulled her shirt down by the hem, forcing the soaked linen to press tight. "Still think it'd be like your mother?"

His eyes dropped, mesmerized by the flesh showing through. One step and a hard shove brought the distracted mongrel down. He and his rider came up spluttering, both laughing.

Fetch turned on Oats. "Just you and me now."

"Tits won't work on me, little sister."

"I was beating you at this game before I had them."

The half-orc boy drummed on Oats's head. "Let's at them!"

The thrice grinned and surged forward, sending a tidal splash ahead of his advance with one great, sweeping arm.

Fetch danced back, shook the water from her face with a jerk of her head. She crab-crawled to the right, forcing Oats to pivot, breaking his momentum. Slapping at the water she threw her own splashes, the sound masking her voice. Quickly, she spoke to Ollal. And told her the plan.

Together they waded toward their foes. The boy upon Oats's shoulders was bigger than Ollal, made more so by his perch atop the looming thrice. The girl would be hard-pressed to reach him, much less knock him down. What she could reach was Oats's beard.

Ollal seized the dripping mop as soon as they all came to grips, just as Fetch had instructed. Oats grunted in surprise and tried to pull away, but the girl's bunched fists held firm. Ignorant of his horse's plight, the mongrel boy was pushing feverishly at Ollal and would have unseated her a dozen times over were it not for her tether of whiskers. Fetch could hear the guffaws from the shore even over the churning water and Oats's bellows of discomfort. He tried to barrel Fetch over, but she retreated. He tried to knock her off her feet, but she sidestepped his blows, deflected his hands.

"Damn clinging fruit monkey!" Oats complained.

Fetch gave a full smile. "Buck your rider, Big Bastard, and she turns loose."

Oats endured for another moment before uttering an "Aw, hells," and tossing his shoulders back, dumping his rider. The boy let loose a squeak of shock and fell with a satisfying splash.

Ollal's hands immediately left his beard and thrust into the air, renewing the cheers from the crowd.

When the laughter and whistles abated, Oats grinned at Fetching.

"I'm still standing, so I want another bout," he said.

"What do you think, Ollal?" Fetch asked.

"Yes!"

"Looks like you get your chance."

"Just let me get a fresh rider."

Smile widening, Oats turned and charged to the shore. Seeing him coming, Xhreka stood in alarm.

"Oh no! Don't you even think it!"

But Oats did not grab the halfling. He picked up Wily, set him on the saddle of his corded shoulders, and headed back out to the center of the pond.

"Idris, dammit!" Beryl yelled. "He has to keep those wrappings dry!"

"Don't worry," Oats replied with slow confidence. "He ain't gonna get wet."

As he approached, the thrice removed the soaked kerchief from his head and tied it around his lower face, hiding his beard. Fetch did not need to see the wink he gave to know his plan. Wily could not get wet. And Ollal still needed a bath. Raising her eyebrows, Fetch agreed to be a conspirator. They closed the distance, making a show of battling for their riders. They could not allow it to go too long or the splashing alone would do for Wily's bandages and then Beryl would skin them alive. Ollal was older by a few years, but no human girl had much of a chance against even a toddling thrice-blood. Without the assistance of her horse, she was quickly pushed backward, though Fetch made sure she did not fall too hard.

Ollal came up smiling.

"Well fought!" Fetch told her, offering a hand to help her float.

Wily was beaming atop Oats, basking in the praise from the shore and from the surrounding paddling children.

"We will get him next time," Fetch said.

"Right now!" Ollal exclaimed.

Oats was already taking Wily back to where Beryl and Thistle waited, both giving the thrice intense stares. His mother wanted to thrash him. Thistle wanted to fuck him.

Fetch gave the girl an accepting shrug. "Looks like that will have to wait."

Ollal's disappointment lasted all of a heartbeat. One of the foundling girls swam up and splashed her in the face, and the two of them were off in a furor of screeches and disturbed water.

Smiling, Fetch used the moment of peace to scrub her face.

"Chief?"

It was Culprit's voice, sounding very uncertain. Looking up, she found him wading a few strides away, closer to the shore, and pointing.

A Tine stood at the edge of the lake, a large fallow deer slung across his shoulders, the bow he had likely used to kill it in his hand. All were beginning to notice him, and the raucousness dwindled. Those on the shore closest to the elf drew back a bit, but he took no notice. He remained still, waiting, looking directly at Fetching.

With nothing else for it, she waded to the shore and climbed from the water to approach the elf. He looked to be the same scout who'd led her people down into the valley. He regarded her placidly, eyes never leaving her face.

Fetch wasn't certain what the Tine views were on nudity, still she did not feel much like a chief standing before this imperious point-ear wearing nothing but a dripping shirt. That is, until Oats and Culprit came up to flank her in nothing but tattoos. Well . . . Oats had his kerchief back on his head.

The elf was unaffected by the swinging cods and peeking minge.

"For you," he said in his tongue.

Fetch assumed he meant the deer, though he made no indication.

"We thank you," she replied in halting elvish.

There was a long silence. None moved.

Fetch risked stepping forward, reaching for the deer. The Tine leaned to accommodate the handoff. Oats sprang to help and Fetch allowed him to shoulder the kill.

That done, the elf again gave that stone gaze.

"The gelded one will live. A few days more, we will bring him to you."

Fetch allowed the relief to show on her face, hoping that bespoke further gratitude.

The Tine pointed at her. "Tomorrow we will come for you. Alone." He turned on his heel and began to walk away.

Fetch made to follow. "Wait—"

As soon as she moved, the elf whirled, arm extended. His bow was drawn, a steady arrow aimed at Fetch's eye. She heard Oats curse, the sound of the deer dropping to the ground. Fetch held her hands up, both to stop her brothers from action and to show the elf no intention of threat.

"A question," she said slowly. "Where will I go?"

She stared at the arrowhead, down the shaft to the hand, and finally to the eye. None wavered.

"To see if you may stay," the elf said.

Fetch nodded and took a step back, but the elf remained taut as his bowstring.

"Tell the white one to step from the trees. I hear him there. Smell his ugly weapon."

Fetch frowned, mind racing to decipher the words. "Hood?"

Movement to her left birthed Hoodwink from the brush, loaded stockbow in his hands. Hells, she had not seen him near the pond, had not known he was there.

With a liquid motion, the elf lowered his bow, relaxed the string. Turning once more, he departed.

Behind, Culprit let loose a breath. "Fucking hells."

Fetch found Oats wearing a concerned frown. She gave him a nod.

Hoodwink glided over and joined them, dead eyes still fixed on the spot where the elf melted into the trees.

"Well," Fetch told him, "I've had my piss. And you have your answer."

"And your patience?" the cadaverous mongrel hissed.

Fetch gave him a genuine smile. "We got meat, we're not wandering the badlands, and I ain't dying until at least tomorrow. At the moment, Hood, my patience is as bottomless as I am."

Oats and Culprit laughed as she slapped Hood on the arm and trudged back into the pond.

"Dacia! You and Incus, into the water and grab a girl! Time for the women to have a match!"

THIRTY-ONE

FETCH GATHERED THE TRUE BASTARDS before first light.

"I'm going up to speak with the Tines," she began simply. "We came for protection. Seems we've got that. But whether it continues . . . well, that's what will be decided. Either way, we need some answers."

There were nods of agreement.

"Mead always said my elvish was so bad it would start a war," she continued, drawing out a few chuckles. "So, there is a strong chance I will give offense. That happens, and I don't come back, do not ride out of this pit with cods stiff for a reckoning. Hear me? *Do. Not.* I am going up alone as they said, and whatever happens will be on my head. You will not insist on coming with me, you will not attempt to shadow me. Hoodwink, you see where I am looking right now? If this does not work, you vote a new chief. My suggestion is Oats. Or anyone other than Polecat." That drew more laughter. "Whoever it is needs to find a better way and succeed where I failed. Understood?"

Only Warbler and Culprit nodded.

Fetch glowered. "I need to hear I will be obeyed."

There were morose noises of assent, though two still remained quiet.

"Hood?"

"You go alone," he agreed after a slight pause. "No revenge."

Fetch looked hard at the last tight-lipped holdout.

Oats was scowling. "Heard and obeyed, chief."

"When do you think they'll be here?" Shed Snake asked.

Fetch looked to the head of the steep trail.

"Right damn now."

A pair of Tines came down into the gorge on foot with no light to guide their steps. Neither was the scout who brought the deer—and the summons—the day before, though they were identically armed. She went to meet them with no weapons save for the kataras, hoping the foreign blades would be viewed as less a threat than the familiar stockbow and tulwar. The elves made no move to take them from her, merely gestured for her to precede them in the climb out.

Well-fed rest had done Fetching good, making the trek up the trail a welcome exertion. Dawn broke along the way, the sky cloudless, the day building to hot. Eagles hunted in the blue expanse, circling the folded canyons of the Umbers that spread out before Fetching as she and the Tines progressed higher.

Reaching the top of the trail, they walked in the cool umbra of the surrounding scarps all morning. Fetch trudged along between her escorts. She was a stranger to these mountains, but her memory said they should have passed through the inhabited canyons with their walls of triangular caves long ago. Yet the cliff sides remained bare rock and there was sign of neither cultivation nor people. It was said that the canyons of Dog Fall were a riddle for which only the Tines knew the answer. Traversing its depths now, Fetch reckoned that was no child's tale. The trails the elves took became wild and elusive, often branching.

They were ascending now, their path nothing but a sunbaked track of dust pinched by steep banks of loose rock. Ahead, a wide bluff cut the sky in half. Forced to single-file, the elves put Fetch in the center of the line as they made the climb.

"Hope you got your wrinkled rustskin elders tucked away up

there," Fetch muttered in Hisparthan as she strode up the punishing grade.

Her lead guide was not slowed, and pulled ahead. Fetch was still a stone's throw from the top when the nimble Tine completed the ascent and stepped from sight.

"Must have had an overdue shit coming."

Fetch made the jest in Hisparthan, but she still turned to smirk at the elf behind.

And found the path empty.

The nape of Fetch's neck tingled. "Aw, hells . . ."

She dove to the side just as an arrow shattered where she'd been standing. The rocks hemming the path made for poor cover. Even belly-down, Fetch remained exposed to the ridgeline, and the next arrow sent a burning line of pain across her upper left arm as it grazed the flesh. She could not stay here. The face of the bluff was less than two dozen strides away. All uphill. Retreating down the path would leave her in range and vulnerable for far longer. Up, then. Her ambushers would have difficulty hitting her once she was directly beneath—and sheltered by—their rocky perch. If they wished to kill her, she would make them work for it.

Fetch darted forward, springing back to the path after two bounding strides. Arrows clacked and clattered all around, hissing by her ears. She felt the splinters from the snapping shafts sting through her breeches. She raced through a withering storm, knowing each step tempted an arrow in the heart, but fury kept her legs surging.

Diving for the bluff, she collided with the face, bashing hip and shoulder. Teeth gritted, she regained her balance, ran on, tight against the cliff. Voices came from above, shouts between the archers, directing one another, informing on her path. They were on the move, but so was she. The bluff was upon her left, a growing precipice to her right. Ahead was a fucking mystery.

An elf dropped from above, nearly landing atop her. He straightened, bow drawn and trained. Fetch did not slow. The elf loosed without hesitation, but Fetch was close enough to swat the arrow aside before it left the string. Drawing a katara with her other hand, she chopped across the lower curve of the bow, cleaving it in two.

The Tine warrior jumped back, producing a hatchet. Fetch pressed the attack, launching a knee into his midriff, folding him up and exposing the back of his skull to her hammering elbow. She barely heard the other elf land behind her. Barely was enough. Spinning, she found this warrior farther removed than his cohort, taking aim. Fetch ducked, snatched the hatchet from the fallen elf's hand, and flung it at the newcomer. He deflected the whirling ax with an impressive bowshot. But Fetch had rushed him as soon as the ax left her hand, eating the distance as he drew and nocked another arrow. They were damn fast, these point-ears, and the string sliced the air before Fetch was within reach. She twisted on the run and felt the arrowhead clip the muscle between her neck and shoulder as it flew past. Grunting against the biting pain she leapt at the Tine, flinging her shoulders back and leading with both feet. Her boots smote the elf's chest and they both fell hard upon their shoulder blades. Bunching her knees swiftly, Fetch thrust her legs forward, back arching, and sprang to her feet.

The elf performed the same flip and they were again facing each other.

Katara poised, Fetch sent rapid, snakelike strikes at the Tine's face to keep him off-balance. He danced back, an antler-handle knife appearing in his hand. Fetch kept coming and the blades scraped as he parried her thrusts.

Knife fights were delicate, perilous affairs that rewarded the patient. And Fetch had no time. The flights of arrows from the ridge were too numerous to be the work of only two elves. More would be coming, unless they'd gone for help. Either way, every moment Fetch spent fucking around with this one was a moment closer to him receiving aid.

One way to end a knife fight was not to fight.

Fetch sent a great, sweeping cut at the elf's gut. He jumped back, as she'd hoped. Using the newly forged distance, Fetching spun around and ran, keeping her ears open. If she heard pursuing feet, the ruse had failed.

There was a sharp clatter—an antler-handled knife falling to the stones. Smiling, she turned sharply and jumped toward the face of the scarp. Seeing her flee, the elf had gone for the easy kill, dropping his knife to quickly load the bow that remained in his other hand. He was fast on the draw, but was caught off guard by her sudden change of direction. Fetch planted a foot onto the rock and vaulted off and away, twisting as she came down. The Tine spun, trying to bring his bow around in time. He nearly managed. The arrow sped beneath Fetch's arm, the fletching hissing across her ribs. Punching downward, she sent the fist-blade sliding through the Tine's forearm. He didn't cry out the way most would, merely gave a clipped grunt. Landing, Fetch used her momentum to drag him to the ground and provided a balm for the pain by knocking him senseless with a boot heel.

Upon the trail, the dark line of the bluff's shadow sprouted a silhouette. Allowing the katara to drop from her grip, Fetch rolled, grabbing the elf's bow. An arrow bashed into the dirt she vacated. Upon her back now, looking up, she saw a Tine scout upon the ridge, another arrow already leaving his quiver. Rolling back, Fetch liberated an arrow from her defeated foe, nocked, held the bow crossways across her stomach, lifted it, and loosed.

The Tine cried out, the shaft slapping up into his armpit. He fell back, vanishing behind the lip of the ridge. It wasn't an immediately fatal shot, but he was likely to bleed to death. Nothing for it now.

Fetch pilfered the fallen elf's quiver, picked up the katara, sheathed it, and moved on.

An ambush. A fucking ambush! The Tines had given of their land, their food, all so they could try to murder her? A pang of dread for the hoof passed through Fetching, but reason would not allow it to take root. If the Tines wanted them all dead, they could have slaughtered them upon arrival. This was about her. Her alone. The offensive creature that dared live with their blood mixing with that of the orcs.

Hurrying along, she found the bluff broken by the threshold of a defile and entered. Unseen birds chirped within the sparse mountain trees. Otherwise, all was still. Fetch advanced with an arrow nocked, watchful and tense. The defile widened, becoming a cradle sheltered and watched over by the protective skirts of distant peaks. She walked through cultivated land. Small, pristine runs of persimmon trees bordered her path. Beyond, a dun wall of wheat, swaying languidly with the breeze. Any moment, she expected another attack, to see three-score Tine warriors emerge from the wheat, bows trained.

Who she met was the warrior from the falls.

N'keesos.

He stood between the trees, lacquered clubs spread low at his sides, blocking Fetch's way. The stones within the clubs were angry with that pale-blue light.

Fetching raised her bow, drew the string to her ear. "I don't want to—"

One of the clubs snapped upward, unleashing a sawing sound that buffeted the branches as it screamed between them. Fetch was struck by the reverberating wave, nearly lifted off her feet. The bow was torn from her grip. She gnashed rattled teeth, dug numbing toes into the dirt, and slid back a handspan but remained standing. The clubs were whirling now, producing a steady siege of sound. It kept coming, but so did Fetching.

She burrowed through the voice of the clubs, even as it burrowed into her bones, her guts. The pressure from the elf's song threatened her with blackness, but she took another step. Another.

The clubs continued to release their sorcerous din, but its force could no longer contain her. Fetch broke through the wave, the release of tension sending her bursting forward. N'keesos snatched the clubs to stillness and leapt back, away from her bull rush, legs carrying him unnaturally far at great speed. His retreat birthed new rage in Fetching.

Bellowing, she jumped.

And slammed into the elf midair.

Air whipping at them, they grappled. The ground landed the first telling blow, breaking them apart. Fetch crashed and tumbled through a field of grain, a rolling, grunting thresher. Coming to a stop, she made it to one knee before the elf came charging through the stalks. He'd lost one club in the fall, the remaining coming down at the end of his arm, screaming shrilly as it hurtled for Fetch's skull. She rolled forward, tangled the warrior's legs with her own, twisted at the abdomen, and flung him down. Springing to her feet, she went for the kataras. An impact to the ribs sent her flying sideways before she could draw the blades. Wheat scratched her face as she careened through the field, burst through the edge. N'keesos had risen and struck so swiftly, the pain from the club did not announce itself until she slid to a stop on the ground. She saw him shoot up from among the wheat, rising high and descending in an arc.

Fetch hopped back as he landed, bare feet indenting the earth. She waded in, dodging the swinging club, caught the wrist of the wielding hand, went to put a knee into his guts, and found herself being thrown.

Fucker was fast. Strong. It wasn't just the clubs.

Twisting, Fetch managed to land in a crouch and used the position to pounce, catching N'keesos around the waist, spearing him off his feet. She landed atop him and rammed her head up beneath his jaw. Scrambling to sit upon his chest, she pinned his throat with a knee, used the opposite foot to keep his weapon arm stamped down. His other arm swung up to hit her, but she caught it with both her own, twisted the elbow to the edge of breaking. The elf made no sound against the pain, but his determined face became stricken. She had him now, this potent warrior who took down her hoof, this arrogant point-ear that had pissed on his hand after touching her. Fetch grinned.

"Do I sully you, Tine?" she taunted, using her own tongue. "Do I dishonor you? Do I . . . let you live?"

N'keesos's face was puffy from the pressure upon his throat, yet he wheezed out a reply. Said something in elvish.

Another pair of warriors appeared, one striding boldly from the wheat, the other landing from some unseen vantage in the rocks. Both bore the same glowing weapons as the elf at her mercy. Angled eyes stared at her, watchful. Stern faces regarded her, contempt writ in stone.

She hated them as much. More.

There was no help in Dog Fall. Only the judgment of this imperious tribe. She opened her mouth to speak, to curse, to tell the Tines that the Bastards were leaving these damnable gorges, but the words were throttled by wrath. There was a crunching sound, followed by a stifled outcry of pain. Fetch let N'keesos's shattered arm slip from her grasp and stood.

She filled her hands with the kataras.

The newcomers charged, angling from opposing sides.

Fetch dashed to meet the one near the wheat field, was dimly aware of being struck in the back by cutting vibration. She shrugged it off, legs devouring the distance. The warrior was before her now, swinging both clubs. Fetch caught them on her blades. The energy from the clubs shrieked and warbled as they connected. With a sweep of her arms, Fetch turned the clubs aside, spun, and cut a kick across the Tine's face.

Knowing the other would be upon her, she whirled, leading with a reaping cut. The Tine bent backward, slid beneath the blow on his knees, and chopped across the side of Fetch's knee with one club. The leg buckled, forcing her down, level with her assailant. She tackled him, ramming the arm guard of one katara into his neck. Briefly, she was atop him, pressing down on his windpipe, but his clubs struck from both sides into her ribs. She reeled with the pain, giving the elf room to bring his legs up and kick her off, his preternatural strength sending her flying.

Flipping in the air, she brought her feet over and around, landing upright at the verge of the persimmon grove. The elves were all standing once again, including N'keesos, broken arm dangling.

Spite scratched into Fetch's mouth at the sight of their persistence. She didn't wait for them, leaping back into their midst, going for the weak one first. Even crippled, he was fast, parrying her slashes with his remaining club, weaving a perfect defense. His hale brothers came to his defense with the song of their clubs.

Three foes. Five weapons between them, each emitting unbalancing waves of sound with every swing, discharging bone-jarring power when the blows fell true. Fetch found herself inside a storm, assailed from all sides, yet she howled a fury of her own. A katara took one elf across the hip in a backhand sweep, her other blade half severing the screaming weapon of another. A club resounded across her cheek, snapping her head to the side, another pummeled her stomach. Either blow should have been the end for her, but Fetch found only anger where pain normally dwelt.

A cut across the chest sent one Tine reeling. The other two scattered, gaining some distance. As one, the trio began spinning their weapons, weaving the patterns. Caught between the warriors, Fetch was quickly encased in the roar.

"You want to kill me?!" she yelled into the agonizing gale. "What are you waiting for? FUCKING KILL ME!"

Screaming in defiance, Fetch tore from the invisible cocoon, rushing the Tine still in possession of both his clubs. The warrior twisted away from her first cut, sent a club barreling for her face in response. Ducking, Fetch tuck-rolled, came up on the elf's flank, and took his legs out from under him with a scything stroke. Cut deeply, he wriggled upon the ground.

The remaining uninjured Tine fell from the sky, bringing his club down with the force of his descent. Fetch crossed her blades and caught the stone embedded in the head, arresting the blow. Fetch saw fracture lines appear on the glowing surface of the orb. N'keesos was rushing in from the side. Snarling, Fetch dropped one of her kataras and seized the club's stone. The elf tried to pull his weapon free, but she held firm. And squeezed. Creaking a final complaint, the stone burst in Fetch's hand just as N'keesos arrived. A blinding flash. An explosive final note as the club's song gave a death cry. A spine-whipping jerk of weightlessness as Fetch was blasted off her feet.

She lay fuddled for a moment, ears ringing. Getting to her feet, she crushed the splotches in her eyes with hard blinks until her vision returned. She and the elves had all been tossed more than a bowshot.

Fetch was the only one standing.

Two of the Tines were motionless upon the ground. N'keesos was attempting to rise. Fetch's anger gave way to a grudging respect. There was no time to see if he would succeed. The voices of Tine windtalk sawed through the air. Mounted warriors appeared at the far end of the valley. Even across the distance, Fetch could see the red tears on the war paint of the lead rider. She ran back the way she'd come, snatching up her fallen katara on the way. The Tines' harrow stags moved silently, but she did not need her ears to know they pursued. A flung lance imbedded in the ground by her feet just as she reached the cleft, fleeing the defile.

Breaking out once more onto the precipice trail she heard shouts coming from the right, forcing her left. The hunters were closing in. Their calls came from behind and the ridge above. There would be scouts on foot tracking her from the high places, guiding the stag riders. If there were warriors ahead, she'd be forced to fight. For now, she would run.

A descending trail spurred off the precipice. Fetch hesitated. Shouts and arrows from above made up her mind for her. She took off down the path, fleeing the face of the bluff and the reach of the archers. Her new path ran straight and steep. Fetch courted a fall, a broken neck, as she sped down. At last the trail began to wind, continuing to drop farther into the embrace of the canyons. Fern and boulder began to insert themselves, tried to impede her flight, but she continued with her headlong dash. The dust at her feet darkened as the shadows deepened. The path turned to mud and then became the trickle of a narrow streambed. Fetch's boots slapped the shallow flow. And still she could hear the chasing Tines.

At last, she broke free into a small hollow. The light drizzled in, timid and weak. Though the sun feared to trespass, its heat did not. Ahead, a cave mouth sat in the cliff face, sticky with shadows. The stream fed into it, a meager drink for the gaping black. The entrance steamed.

Otherwise, the hollow was a dead end.

Without a choice, Fetch hurried within the dank mouth, its throat receding into darkness. Without a source of light, Fetch accompanied the rivulet deeper down the gullet. Soon the sun from the hollow was lost to distance and a nearly imperceptible decline. Fetch paused while the keen visions of her mixed bloodlines coaxed scant details from the black, enough to pick her way along with a hand on the rough, clammy wall. The echo of the muggy air told her the cave remained as large as the mouth, perhaps it had even grown. She could feel the trapped void above. Sound wandered, realized it was imprisoned, gave up, and died.

There was a smell too. Faint. Lingering at the edge of her nostrils, teasing at the shallow beginnings of every inhale. It was an unpleasant, delicate odor. Not the fetor of spoiled meat nor the eye-watering offensiveness of fresh excrement. It was the slippery funk of linens in an old person's bedchamber. When Fetch's steps at last brought her back to light, to sight, it was not a bedchamber she had entered but a vast cavern.

The floor was an uneven hazard of strewn stone and eroded shelves. Fetch stood upon a low point, a rough, natural gutter wedged between the shallow slope that brought her here and a steeper climb of flat-topped boulders ending in the distant cave wall. A triangular opening, akin to those in the Tine canyons, was cut into the rock face. Shaped with skill and care, the perfect edges were embossed, puckering from the shadow-draped stone. This carven threshold was imbued with pale light, so subtle it took Fetch a moment to realize it was the reason she could see. Within the triangle, however, blackness reigned entire.

The wall housing the luminescent opening was not the only perceptible limit of the cave. A sliver of the roof could be seen just above the pointed apex of the triangle. She sensed walls to the left and right, perhaps a stone's throw into the black.

With no other discernible path, Fetching resolved to climb up, inspect the glowing portal. Few of the shelves were higher than her waist. The ascent would be little more than a scramble. She studied the approach for a route that would most easily reach the wide ledge just beneath the bottom of the opening.

She took a single step and stopped.

A face appeared within the triangle, emerging slowly from the impenetrable black as if breaking the surface of ink. It was a woman's face, possessing the angular features of a Tine, though her skin was pale and shone with the same light as the stone in which she was framed. The face continued to glide forward, revealing an ensconcing headdress of feathers, icy blue, argent green.

Tilting, the face regarded Fetching from above, frigid and pitiless.

Fetch opened her mouth, preparing to speak, but the words died dry on her tongue as the face pushed farther from the shadows, supported upon the sinuous trunk of a great serpent.

THIRTY-TWO

—

UNBLINKING EYES WATCHED FETCHING as the thing eased downward, pale belly gliding audibly over the lip of the opening. Swaying and slithering, it descended. Distance had played Fetch for a fool and she now saw the true size of this horror. The face was large as a wagon wheel, the slit, golden eyes large as Fetch's fist. On it came, white scales glistening as the snake body flowed down the ledges.

Fetch snatched the kataras free, took a single step backward, fear sending a cold message down her spine from head to gut.

Run and you die.

The elf maid's face, plumed and hooded with feathers, was a merciless grave mask, devoid even of a predator's aggressive hunger. Its gaze skinned Fetching, rendered her naked and cold, extinguishing all fires of resolve, scattering her grit upon winds of hopelessness. The face hovered closer, level with hers, body still sloughing down the steps. Fetch could have spit and struck it between the eyes. So horribly near, the resemblance to an elf was made a mockery, leaving little but the monster. It drifted about her, seeming to both ignore and scrutinize her insignificance. As the neck and head came around to the side, rising all the while, the body continued to slink down-ward, heavy coils reaching the cave floor where Fetching stood.

Hells, it was surrounding her.

The snake-bitch's head whipped down, body constricting closer with violent tension. It was close enough to kiss now. Unnerved and sweating, trying not to tremble, Fetch stood firm. The nostrils of the thin nose tightened, smelling. The eye-slits narrowed, the sinister gold surrounding them filling with malevolence.

Shit.

The jaw hinged open, showing translucent teeth. Two curved fangs extended from puffy flesh at the roof of the mouth, long as tulwar blades. A true serpent would have hissed, but this abomina-tion remained as silent as a corpse's dreams.

Fetch broke that silence.

"You know . . . for a cunt, you look an awful lot like a cock."

She dove to the side, felt the rush of wind as the monster struck. Plunging one katara into the scaly flesh, Fetch made to vault over a coil to flee the living enclosure. But the trunk launched away as the snake moved, flinging Fetch to the side just as her feet left the ground. She tumbled, shoulder bashed by the stone floor, lost hold of the left katara. The head was coming again in a flat charge, crossing over its own body.

Too damn fast!

Fetch lurched out of the way, barely managing to avoid the fangs. Thrusting her free hand out, she snatched at the feathers, got a hold, and was immediately flung off as the snake recoiled. The edges of the flat boulders welcomed her with pain when she hit. Standing, she found herself halfway between the floor and the opening. The snake had risen up, holding its body vertical atop a tight base of coils, watching her, waiting for her to move so it could plunge and end her life.

Fetch made a promise. To cut that obscene head off and witness the writhing corpse toss blood about the cave in its death throes.

The snake-demon mouthed another mute hiss when Fetching raised the fist-blade. The beast lunged, a lightning bolt with scales.

Fetch leapt in response, legs surging with all her strength. They impacted with such speed, neither had the chance to strike. The woman's head rammed into Fetch's torso and she clung, her charge reversed. The ledge clapped into her back. Stone cracked. The snake rose, but Fetch held tight to its plumage with her unarmed hand and rode into the air. Dangling, she hacked at its neck, drew milky blood, but the stroke was far from deep, dulled by the snake's flailing. Returning to the ground, it ran swiftly along, trying to shake her off. She bounced and scraped along the rocks, refused to let go, but the feathers in her hand tore free. The snake looped around, once again attempting to encircle her. Fetch sliced the white scales, forcing the creature to flee her reach, climbing the steps. Bounding up the ledges, Fetching pursued. The creature coiled tight at the top, head pulled back against the bunched body.

It lashed out as she closed, but Fetch backhanded the darting mouth with the katara. Again it attacked and again she swung to rebuff the fangs, but the snake had feinted, a bluff-strike that recoiled halfway to its mark. It had wanted her to swing, leave herself open, and now bit in earnest. Fetch only just managed to interpose her arm, shielding her face.

The fangs overshot, missed her flesh. Fetch grunted against the impact as the mouth clamped down, tried to wrench her arm free, but the jaws held fast, trapping her weapon. Desperate, she went for the bitch's eyes with her bare hand, but the monster opened its mouth—freeing Fetch—and bulled forward, knocking her over. Crushed beneath the creature's weight, she tumbled down the ledges, blinded by pain and scaly flesh. The snake rolled, spiraling along its length, wrapping her up. She found herself upright, fully entwined, arms pinned, bones and lungs compressed as the coils constricted. The woman's face was suspended above, slack and uncaring once more, drifting ever so slightly to the side as she tightened her hold.

The edges of Fetch's vision blurred, invaded by a glistering halo born from the banishment of breath. Still, she saw the mouth open, saw the neck go still, gathering for the kill.

"*N'AI!*"

The constriction slackened. Fetch drew air in an agonizing, ecstatic rush. The face was no longer looking at her but over her, beyond. As the coils relaxed, Fetch revolved in their embrace, enough to crane her neck and look at what now held the monster's attention.

An elf woman appeared from darkness, coming down the slope, hands held up imploringly.

Starling.

"*N'ai! N'ai! Nagan'ai, Akis'naqam!*"

Pleading eyes locked on the snake, she spoke in elvish, too quickly and impassioned to understand. Hands lowering, she removed her garments, revealing a body heavy with child. Exposed, she knelt before the serpent, continued to entreat it, gestured with raw emotion at her swollen belly. Wits returning, Fetch was able to discern some of Starling's words.

"*Nagan'ai.* Help her! She is not *asily'a kaga arkhu.* You know this! I beg—*nagan'ai* as you once did."

The face appeared fascinated by its supplicant. It did not listen; it weighed.

Starling grew silent, hands clasped and raised. Her face was suffused with humility and respect, but there was the spark of challenge too, a courage that had no place on a battlefield and was therefore more potent. Fetch had only seen it a few times in life, mostly on the faces of Beryl and Thistle.

The snake turned back to Fetching, seemed to consider . . .

. . . and uncoiled.

Fetch's breath returned as the snake's retreating body spun her slowly in place, lowering her to the ground. The monster slithered up the rocky shelves and crawled back into the triangular cave.

Weakened and sore, Fetch remained slumped on the stones watching the last length of its tail vanish into the black. She shuddered.

Starling stood nearby, dressing. Her clothes were travel-stained. And of Unyar design.

"It *was* you at Strava," Fetch declared.

There was no response. The elf woman merely stared.

"Fuck." Fetch attempted elvish. "I saw you. Thought you were a . . . untrue sight."

Starling took a pair of steps and leaned over her, placed a hand beneath her chin. She opened her own mouth, the way a mother does when she wants a child to ape her. Worried the snake creature had poisoned her in some way, Fetch complied.

Starling spit full into her mouth.

Shocked and revolted, Fetch tried to recoil, but was too weak to do much more than wiggle. Starling forced her mouth closed, made an exaggerated show of swallowing.

Frowning, Fetch did as instructed.

Starling released her, walked a few steps away, and hunkered down into a squat.

Fetch made a noise and spit to the side. "The fuck?"

"You are rid of a brute's tongue," Starling replied.

Fetch had no notion what that meant, but at least the elf was responding.

"What in all the hells was that thing?"

"Akis'naqam is a protector of my people. The last left to us."

"I'd say you have plenty of warriors up to the task," Fetch scoffed.

"Even the bravest of them cannot triumph over the orc filth."

Fetch gave a bitter laugh. "Orc filth. Comforting to know that your people loathe me as much as the thicks."

"You misunderstand."

"Not as much as you think, point-ear! Your fucking tribe herded me down here. That N'keesos had some pride, tried to kill me himself. But I'm no fool! When he failed, the others harried me into this damn cave. Rustskins aren't known for missing their mark or letting their quarry escape."

Starling's face grew regretful. "Ghost Last Sung conspired to deliver you here, yes. His brave-sworn arrived ahead of your true guides. This was not the will of the Sitting Young."

Fetch let her face fall into her hands. "Oh, *now* I understand completely."

"You mock."

Fetch could only spill a second humorless laugh into her palms.

"Why did you come to Dog Fall?" Starling asked.

"My hoof needed help," Fetch said, raising her head. "We were driven from our lands by a . . ."—she readied herself to fail at the name, found it came easy—*"Asily'a kaga arkhu—"*

She stopped, puzzled and taken off guard. In trying to recall the words, not only did she remember them, she spoke them effortlessly. It struck her now—all this time she had been speaking to Starling in elvish and had trouble neither conversing nor understanding.

Fetch opened her mouth slightly, raised a hand to her lips.

You are rid of a brute's tongue.

"The hells did you do to me?" Fetch whispered in Hisparthan to make sure she still could.

"It will last so long as I am near," Starling answered in the Tine tongue. "There is much to say that will be difficult to understand. Your crude elvish was a hindrance."

"Fucking sorcery," Fetch griped.

"It is why you came here."

"To learn how to fight it! How to slay this giant thick that commands nigh-unkillable devil-beasts. But I see now I was right to avoid coming here."

"Help was not given?" The question was heavy with reproach.

"If exiling us to a gully and forbidding us from leaving is the Tine notion of helpful. Far as trying to kill me, I'd say that's a long ride in the other direction."

Starling looked at her archly. "Ghost Last Sung and his warriors defied our council. It was unwise. Fear led them to folly."

"Ghost Last Sung. That the rider with the red streaks beneath his eyes? He didn't exactly shit his buckskins when he saw me."

"The way of our warriors demands they confront their fears rather than allow them to flourish."

Fetch again thought of the way N'keesos—the name now came to her mind as Blood Crow—touched her at the falls.

"Why do they fear me?"

"Ruin Made Flesh," Starling intoned.

"He won't follow us here," Fetch insisted, though she spoke with more conviction than she truly possessed. "And if he does, your people have the strength to fight him. We don't! There was no other choice."

"It is not him they fear. It is you."

Fetch made a coaxing gesture with her hand. "We need to shovel this hogshit faster, elf girl. I'm only idling here because I just survived being squeezed by a feathered serpent with an old whore's face and my legs feel like two limp cods. And I don't know what is waiting when I leave this cave, so I'm content to laze for a moment or two. But I need to get back to my hoof before they do something fool-ass, so you need to start explaining."

Starling nodded, just once. "Likely you care nothing for the long, death-filled conflict between my people and the orcs. We have lost most of that past ourselves. It is enough to say that the ancient elves lived in a great forest basin for time unknowable. What magic we have left is from that time, mostly relics we no longer understand how to wield. If the tales we hear as children are true, our ancestors worked wonders and lived in great prosperity. The orcs destroyed that."

There was a pause and when next the she-elf spoke, her words came in a measured recitation.

"From somewhere in the steaming jungles of Dhar'gest they came, fathered in rage, with no wish or reason to be more than what they were. Bringers of slaughter and sowers of woe. They built nothing, crafted nothing, made no music. Animals feared and shunned them."

"Sounds like thicks to me," Fetch said.

"Such is the oldest record we have of them. They came down into the vast basin of our forebears and brought war. But the magic of the elves was strong, as were their weapons. They repelled the invaders and might have rid the earth of them, in time, but the orcs had unknowingly planted the downfall of the basin in the wombs of the women they raped. As the humans do now, some of those victims survived the violation and birthed their half-breed babes. They could not have known, but these offspring would become the doom of their world. That lush basin is now the Deluged Sea because for the first time since their creation, the orcs found a way to become stronger."

Stronger. Fetching felt a great sense of unease hearing that word. *Uq'huul.* Strongest. The orcs called their sorcerers *uq'huul.*

"They knew nothing of magic until mixing their blood with ours," Starling continued. "They would have remained ignorant, for they cared naught for the half-breeds they sired, but those half-breeds were all possessed of the same violent, blood-hungry nature as their fathers. They matured among the elves, but could be taught nothing of love. Using the magic in their veins they proved themselves to the orcs, became their fiercest leaders and deadliest champions. None remained true to those that nurtured them. They were Ruin Made Flesh."

Fetch leaned forward. "Are you telling me this orc that's made a hell of my hoof's life, that took a god's voice to drive him off, *he's* a damn half-elf?"

Starling nodded.

"Then . . . I'm not."

"You carry the blood of my people. That is certain."

"But you told snake-bitch—"

"Akis'naqam. Please, respect."

"You told her I wasn't one of these Ruin fuckers. I sure as shit don't look like the brute that's hunting us. And . . . I don't have his power."

She'd hesitated at the last, remembering her fight with N'keesos. The leap she'd made to reach him, the inability of the song-clubs to stop her.

"You are different," Starling said. "Your mother undertook great risk and trials in an attempt to change what you would become."

"How do you know that?" Fetch asked.

Starling's hands drifted to her stomach. "I share much with her."

It was known across the Lots, elves did not suffer bearing an orc's seed, their women killing themselves should they fall victim to rape. After pulling her out of the Old Maiden, Fetch, Jackal, and Oats had kept a watchful eye on Starling, in case she attempted suicide, though Fetch had advocated they let her do it and have done. At the moment, she was feeling very grateful Jackal had won that argument. How Starling again came to be carrying an orc's get was something even Fetch's blunt nature refused to ask. She settled for the next nagging question.

"Why did you save me?"

"I believe that you are not tainted by the curse of the Ruin Made Flesh. Thankfully, Akis'naqam agreed. It was she that spared you. I only asked."

"Reckon the ones that forced me down here didn't think that was likely."

"No. Even before the forest basin flooded, our ancestors saw the danger of our half-breeds and took steps to prevent their existence. They made pacts with ancient and powerful beings to help combat their evil."

Fetch tried not to look at the opening to the snake creature's lair. "Like feeding mongrel children to monsters."

"My people find the killing of children abhorrent. It is the duty of the despoiled mother to sacrifice herself before the babe comes."

"To a fucking serpent-woman?"

"Akis'naqam is the only one left to us. Only she has survived the long years since the flood. The seed of the orc is strong, impossible to rid once it has quickened. This is true for humans and elves, but for us the mother's death is not enough. We learned long ago that the polluted mixture born of elf and orc blood is frightfully resilient, a formless atrocity that survives beyond death."

Fetch's guts rolled over. "Wait. You mean . . . ?" She knew only the Hisparthan word. "Sludge."

"My people call it the Filth. Akis'naqam is one of the few beings with the power to destroy it."

"But I was living with that shit inside me! It was fucking killing me, not granting me any magical hoodoo."

"The power of all Ruin Made Flesh comes from the Filth. Yet it is not separate from them as it was from you. They are born with it suffusing their bodies, as much a part of them as their blood, muscles, and bone. Their flesh is hardened by it, their limbs strengthened by it. A Ruin and the Filth are one, as all elven half-breeds have been since the birth of the first."

"But not me," Fetch said.

"No. Your mother delved into the arcane teachings of the past, unearthed lore believed lost to find a way to rid you of the Filth before you entered the world."

"So . . . I wasn't born with it. It wormed its way into me from the Sludge Man."

"Yes. The Filth nesting in the Old Maiden Marsh were the remnants of the Ruin Made Flesh killed there during the Incursion. It was my people that fought there, slew the half-bloods at great cost. But we could not risk Akis'naqam in open war and so could not fully destroy the Filth. The Ruins were slain and their bodies left to rot, becoming what you name sludge, which found a host in a human boy and used him as a vessel."

"Corigari." Fetch spat the Sludge Man's true name. Memory brought bile to her next words. "And you're the one that sent him after me."

Starling was unaffected by the accusation. "To save myself and the life inside me. And to destroy him. That demon went eagerly to his doom. It was a trap, Fetching, but not for you. I knew what you were. Something that had never existed before. A half-blood free from the curse of the Filth."

Fetch grunted. "Yet this Last Singing Ghost and his boys don't believe that, so they tossed me down here to be food for the queen of all serpents. But here you come, ask her for mercy, and all's fucking well?" Fetch could not help but laugh, shake her head. "The fuck, Starling? Last I saw you, you were a wide-eyed, loon-brained slip of an outcast elf girl clinging to Jackal's saddle horn. Now you're entreating snake-demons on my behalf?"

"That is amusing?"

Face resting once again in her hands, Fetch chuckled noiselessly. "Oh hells. Yes!" Starling was smiling when Fetch looked up. It was a thin, uncertain thing, but it was there. "What?"

The elf woman looked away, the upturn of her mouth faltering, but not fading completely. More silence.

"Why did the warriors allow you down here?" Fetch pressed. "Why would a group of men with weapons let a pregnant woman interfere?"

The smile faded. The look Fetching received held bald sorrow. "Because I am honored. And feared."

Fetch wanted to laugh again, but kept it at bay this time. "Are you the fucking Tine chief?"

"No."

"Then what?"

"As you said. An outcast." The elf woman's hands came up and cradled the bulge of her belly.

Damning all couth, Fetch asked the question. "Starling? What happened to your first child?"

Thankfully, the elf did not take offense. She merely looked long at Fetching, as if judging whether she could be trusted. At last, she answered. "The life within me is the same one I carried when I left your fortress. I sought, and found, ways to delay its coming, keeping it safe until I am prepared."

"Ways? You mean Zirko. That's why you were at Strava. He was helping you."

Starling let her silence answer.

"You want your baby to be like me, not a Ruin."

"That is my hope. I returned to Dog Fall to place myself before Akis'naqam to be judged. I am grateful she has chosen to spare me, as she has you."

"So . . . you were down here to help me due to nothing but fucking chance?"

A small, sad smile pulled at Starling's mouth. "If that is how you choose to see it. However, my people view such a confluence as much more. As do I."

Fetch blew out a hard breath. "I don't mean to sound ungrateful."

"I take no offense."

There was a silent span.

"You said she spared me before. Akis'naqam."

"When your mother first came here, nearing her time. She had done all she could to keep you from becoming Ruin Made Flesh and placed herself before Akis'naqam for judgment. She was given her life, and so you were given yours. Yet still the council decided your mother could not remain with her people. She was forced to leave before giving birth."

"Shit," Fetch hissed. "Is that what will happen to you?"

Starling stood, sorrow in her very movement. "It is time to answer that question. For both of us."

THIRTY-THREE

STARLING LED THEM BACK to the sunlight. Steps from the cave mouth, she paused long enough to whisper a warning.

"Say nothing. *Do* nothing."

Out in the hollow, a score of mounted Tines waited with a dozen warriors on foot. They stood watch around the entrance, stags and elves shifting as Starling and Fetch walked toward their bulwark of war lances and bows.

Ghost Last Sung was among them, his face grim beneath the war paint.

"You live."

A blunt statement, neither relieved nor distressed. Fetch now caught the slightest inflection in his elvish, revealing he referred to both her and Starling.

"Akis'naqam deemed it so," Starling answered. "I go now to bring this news to the Sitting Young. Will you dishonor their wishes again, Ghost Last Sung, by preventing me? Will you further dishonor yourself?"

The warrior's gaze remained stern, but he lowered his lance. "No."

As Starling began walking forward, the riders guided their stags to allow her passage, eyes and weapons dipping. They seemed shamed by their own caution. *Respected and feared*. Starling wasn't wrong about her people's attitude toward her, that much was clear.

Fetching fell into step behind, but paused when she drew even with N'keesos standing among his band, broken arm in a sling. Licking the length of her fingers she pressed them into his forehead. His eyes went wide and wrathful, but he did nothing.

"Should have done it yourself, Blood Crow," she told him with the sincerity her now-fluent elvish made possible. Removing her hand, she pointed where she'd touched. "Get someone to piss on that for you. Clean it off."

Starling looked back with a small, reproachful frown. The other Tines glowered at Fetching. She kept a smile on her face and walked on. Together, she and Starling left the warriors and the cave behind, though Fetch was certain they would be shadowed.

They climbed out of the hollow, traversed the gorges. The walk was long. Dusk flushed the sky. By the time they reached a wide stretch of level canyon, the air was alive with the competing songs of night bugs.

The flicker of firelight drew Fetch's eye as they proceeded through. Within the rock on both sides, shadows moved within the triangular caves, some coming to the brink of the openings to look down upon their approach. Starling took a path leading to the canyon wall where the caverns were cut, a massive stone beehive looming above the tree line. Looking up, Fetch had a vision of each opening birthing a woman-headed snake and could not prevent the shiver that made merry down her spine.

A much larger cave, identically shaped, stood at ground level. It was here that Fetch and Starling went. Twenty warriors stood guard with spears and hide shields, but Starling announced herself and entered the cool shelter of the rock without being challenged. Starlight shone ahead as well as behind, bright at the end of the peaked passage. Fetch expected to emerge within another valley, but the passage led to a chamber, a hollow pyramid. The slanting walls were smooth, the pale light entering through the apex, lancing down from on high and diffusing to fill the space.

Fifteen Tine children sat in a semicircle within, each upon a patterned blanket. There were girls as well as boys, the youngest perhaps six years of age, the oldest at the threshold of adulthood. Behind each stood an adult elf, always the opposing gender. Like the children, their ages varied. Some looked to be from the warrior stock, others were white-haired ancients.

It was one of the children who first spoke, an older girl. Her voice, though youthful, had no trouble filling the chamber.

"You come again before us, Woeful Starling. Many here thought to be free of you, at last. Yet even the most wary can see the Selfless Devourer has spared you. Akis'naqam is wise, but she does not rule the Seamless Memory. Do not presume your continued existence in life grants you a place here."

It should have been ridiculous, being spoken to with such authority by a child, but the girl's manner was assured, calm, yet undeniable. The manner of a strong leader.

Starling bowed with earnest deference. "Nothing is presumed."

"The *lya'ʒáta* emerges also," said another girl, half the age of the first.

There was that word again, only now Fetch heard its meaning clearly.

The aberration.

Nothing further came from the girl. It was the blunt observation of a child. Fetch's scalp began to itch as her irritation grew.

"She was brought to judgment by the slyness of Ghost Last Sung," Starling said. "Though he tried to force her death, he became the hand which wove her life to mine."

One of the boys lifted his hand from his knee and the woman standing behind him leaned down to receive a whispered question. Her answer was given with the same subtlety before she straightened.

"She is the greater aberration now," the boy proclaimed. "Freed from the Filth in the womb, possessed by it in recent days, and now spared by Akis'naqam a second time. I say this should not be ignored."

"It *cannot* be ignored," the first girl added, "but do we agree with Woeful Starling that it portends well, or side with our ancestors and brand it an unacceptable threat?"

The eldest boy smote his leg with an open palm. "It is a threat. We would be wise to cast the aberration back to the Devourer and forbid any to intercede."

"You need not," Starling put in. "If you wish Fetching dead, you do not require Akis'naqam. The Devourer has fulfilled her oath and made her choice. This is no Ruin Made Flesh that stands before you. She is, as the humans say, a half-orc. They name the obvious blood, the source of the other half means little to them. They brand the threat with their words. Yet, I would ask this council see her—and name her—differently. See that half the blood being judged is ours. Name the woman you could execute as half-elf before making your choice. Akis'naqam has returned to slumber. She will not rouse herself for a threat that can be ended with lance or arrow. It is the Sitting Young of the Seamless Memory that will have to command, and witness, this death."

A younger boy, blind by the look of his colorless eyes, added his voice. "We need not call for her blood. Neither must we accept her among us. Exile from our lands is wisest."

Starling was quick to counter. "Exile is the same as death. Fetching is not Ruin Made Flesh, yet one does hunt her. Without our protection, she and her tribe cannot hope to survive."

The council was silent for a time.

"We will consider," the first girl pronounced, and signaled the warriors.

Fetch and Starling were led from the chamber. Outside, they were taken to a place a little removed from the cave mouth and commanded to wait. Standing there in the night, surrounded by armed Tines, Fetching ventured a question.

"What was that?"

Starling was taking in the night, infuriatingly at ease. "My people are governed by the most promising of our children. We believe the fate of the tribe should rest with those that will inherit its future. The adults behind them act as mentors, but can only offer counsel if directly asked by the child they support. No matter what advice the elders give, the decisions rest with the Sitting Young."

"Great," Fetch whispered. "Tell the men here to go ahead and put a good point on their spears." Silence. "What will you do if they don't allow you to stay?"

For the first time Starling's calm was rippled by surprise. It was a small thing, more curiosity than shock, but it drew the she-elf's eye. "The Sitting Young debate the wisdom of your execution and you worry over my fate?"

Fetch didn't respond. What could she say? That she had no intention of going to her death without a fight? Unless . . . she was given promise that her hoof and its people could shelter safely in these canyons. Was that even true? She didn't know. The thought of being condemned to die was merely that, a thought. She'd known the sludge was killing her, *would* kill her. But that was a notion of the future, never truly drawing closer despite the evidence of her failing strength. Death itself remained distant, dwarfed on the horizon by the biting and clawing of each waking hour. What had Oats called it? The daily struggle. He'd given it thought. Fetch never had. Survival was instinct. It was akin to hunger or breathing. They happened without thought or permission. Sometimes, they were a challenge. Fetch had been on the verge of starving, of her lungs failing, but she did not dwell on them as looming axes that would inevitably fall. Their descent could be halted, their blades blunted. Anything, everything, could cause pain. Ul-wundulas was a land of pain. It had hurt Fetching every day that she could remember. But it could only kill her once.

And hadn't yet.

Her thoughts were scattered by the arrival of Ghost Last Sung. Down from his stag, he presented himself before the guards and was admitted into the cave.

"Your child council about to judge him too?" Fetch asked.

"They will hear what he has to say," Starling replied. And that was all.

They spent the rest of the wait in silence. Ghost Last Sung

emerged, pausing outside the cave entrance. He looked at Starling for a long moment, face betraying no emotion, yet his stillness—and hers—were heavy with regret. Averting his gaze, the older warrior continued on, shoulders held strong. Starling watched him go and Fetch was struck by the undeniable change in the she-elf. This wasn't the withdrawn, frightened waif pulled from the Old Maiden. She had been lost then, the trials of the marsh numbing her to the world. This Starling, though reserved, had shed that sense of hopelessness. She was focused, vibrant even, the way a wildflower upon the parched plain was vibrant. She was rooted, quietly thriving. This Starling was easy to respect. And trust.

There was a long span after Ghost Last Sung's departure. At last, the guards summoned Starling and Fetch back to the Sitting Young.

The same girl spoke for the council.

"Woeful Starling, we accept you are returned. You have suffered much in pursuit of ancient mysteries. Time and powers beyond our reasoning have shown that pursuit will not be ended. We would be unwise to cast you out as was done in the past."

"You humble me with your kindness and forethought," Starling replied, and Fetch heard the slightest quaver in her voice. "However, with respect, I cannot remain. My task is incomplete."

"Then we will not hinder you. Know that Ghost Last Sung was offered a path to restore his honor. He refused and must be banished. He renounced his brave-sworn to spare them punishment. Only his son will follow him into exile."

Starling bowed her head in acceptance. "This brings grief to my heart."

"It brings grief to all the Seamless Memory. The loss of Ghost Last Sung and Blood Crow is a great one."

The eldest boy now spoke, turning his attention to Fetch. "As for the aberra—the half-elf, you and your tribe may continue to dwell here."

It took Fetch a moment to realize what had been said. "My people can stay?"

The eldest girl dipped her chin. "Yes."

"What of the Ruin Made Flesh?"

"Should it dare come here, the Selfless Devourer will destroy it."

"You have my thanks," Fetch replied, her words borne on a flood of relief. They were led from the chamber as swiftly as they arrived.

"Come," Starling said. "I will return you to your people."

As they walked, Fetching could not keep the grin from her face. "You should know, I start getting ornery with folk that save my hide more than twice."

Starling gave no response.

"That's my fool-ass way of expressing gratitude." Still nothing. "Starling? They said you could stay. Why would you leave?"

"I cannot linger. I came to put myself before Akis'naqam as I must, but for the salvation of my child, I must go."

"Won't you both be safer here?"

Starling did not answer until they reached the top of the trail that led down into the swampy valley that was the Bastards' new refuge. Here she turned. They were alone now, well away from the fires and huts and caves of the Tines. The glow of the night sky was trapped in the she-elf's eyes.

"You thank me for saving your life. In many ways I have ended it. I do not believe the Ruin Made Flesh will be foolish enough to come here. He will not risk facing Akis'naqam. Here, you are safe from him. And so, you can never leave."

"He's a tough son of a thick," Fetch agreed. "But we won't hide from him forever. When the Bastards are ready, we will return to the Lots."

"Perhaps. If you wish them to have a chance, you will not ride with them."

Fetch's jaw clenched. "This is another of those times, Starling. You got something to say, say it."

"It will bring you pain."

"I'll manage."

"The Ruin Made Flesh is drawn to you. Not to your land or your tribe. You. I believe you know this, though you have feared to speak it aloud."

Fetch went cold, her jaw tightening further. "Do you . . . know why?"

"Yes." Starling's voice was soft, contrite. "You and the Ruin Made Flesh are *ta'thami'atha*."

The meaning blossomed within Fetch's mind. She began to quiver, the pale light from the dark sky ice upon her flesh. She laughed, fighting the building, painful shivers.

"He didn't touch me," she hissed through clenched teeth. "Kicked me. Strangled me. Beat me near to death. But he didn't touch me. A fucking thick that's not a raping cunt." She laughed again, enjoying the effortless way the Tine words for "fucking" and "cunt" entered her mind and danced off her tongue. "Who would have thought, you rustskins are as nasty as us half-orcs."

The she-elf looked down at her mournfully. "You again mock."

"I do! It's a damned jest. It must be!"

"No. No, I am afraid not."

"So say it."

"Why must I? You know. You understand."

"Because I can't!"

Starling gathered her breath. "*Ta'thami'atha* . . ."

The barbed blade of that word's meaning stabbed Fetch once more.

Womb-joined.

"It is what my people call siblings that are twin-born. The mysteries your mother uncovered prevented you from being cursed, but they did not prevent the creation of the thing she feared. That all elves fear."

Fetching gagged on a scream as Starling finished.

"The Ruin Made Flesh is your brother."

THIRTY-FOUR

HALF-ORCS WERE NEVER TWINS. NEVER. Orc seed did not share the womb.

The thought burned a circle in Fetch's brain as she descended the brutal trail into the swampy valley. Starling followed, close and silent. Down in the hollow, the closeness of the trees permitted little of the moon. They had not taken a pair of steps from the trailhead when they were challenged from the darkness by a familiar voice.

"It's me, Cat," Fetch answered.

Polecat walked from behind a cluster of dense hawthorn, stockbow held at his waist.

"Chief? Thank all the hells. We were set to come looking for you at dawn."

"What did I say about that?"

"Not to," Polecat confessed, "but—"

Fetch walked by him without slowing.

"What happened up there?" Polecat asked.

"A heap," Fetch replied.

"Should I gather the boys?"

"No, let them sleep. Keep your watch."

"Who is that with you?"

Fetch did not break stride. "What, Cat? You no longer recognize women you wanted to fuck once they're pregnant?"

Polecat called after them, sounding hopeful. "Does she want to fuck?"

Fetch led Starling through the dark toward the hut. Big Pox grunted and stirred in his pen as she passed, her fury intruding on the beast's dreams. Fetch gestured for Starling to wait and crept inside. Stepping carefully over and around the sleeping orphans, she went to the bed shared by Warbler and Beryl, Wily tucked in between them. Beryl's eyes were open before Fetch reached her side, shining faintly in the scant light.

"Outside," Fetch whispered, and left without waiting for a response.

Beryl emerged from the hut a few moments after Fetching. Seeing Starling, her face wrinkled with puzzlement before relaxing with recognition.

"That's—"

"Yes. Pay her no mind for now. Tell me about my birth."

Warbler appeared in the doorway, a Tine blanket draped over his bare torso. Beryl grew still, stubborn.

"Why? You never wanted to know before."

"Just tell me."

"Fetch?" Warbler's deep, hushed voice rumbled. He limped away from the hut. "What is this?" His craggy features took in the three women.

"Avram," Beryl addressed him without taking her eyes off Fetch. "Go get Idris."

The old thrice took a step.

"Stay put, Warbler," Fetch said. "If I wanted Oats here, I would have brought him. I got a Tine woman none of us have seen in near two years telling me that the thick preying on the Bastards is my fucking twin. I got no reason or inclination to be patient right now. So tell me what I want to fucking know."

Beryl took two steps and slapped her. It was a hard blow, jerked Fetch's head to the side. She tasted salt as her teeth cut the inside of her mouth. She whirled back with a snarl, ready to strike the older woman, but was stopped by Beryl's face, steel tempered in fury.

"You're not a chief here, Isabet. Not in this moment! There isn't any Fetching or Oats or Warbler in this moment because I say there is no hoof. *I* say! This is family and when it is family I give the commands. I did not expect to ever have to talk about this, but if I must, then I am damn well going to do it the way I want it done." Blazing eyes moved to Warbler. "Go get our son."

It was not a choice of words Fetch had ever heard Beryl use. Warbler was briefly taken aback too, but he recovered quickly and hobbled off without so much as a glance at Fetching. Beryl went around behind the hut. Fetch followed, unhurried, Starling her shadow.

Beryl stood by the woodpile, back turned. She did not speak or move until Warbler came thumping up with Oats in tow. The younger thrice looked near panicked, but his bearded face relaxed after seeing both his chief and his mother were well. Warbler approached Beryl, touched her briefly on the shoulder, and sat upon the wood-splitting stump. Oats drifted to Fetch's side, eyes clinging uncertainly to Starling as he moved.

Unlike Fetch, he knew better than to voice any questions.

Beryl began slowly, talking to the night. "She was calm, your mother. Never seen a laboring woman so calm. Didn't speak a word of Hisparthan, but not much needs to be said when a baby's coming." She turned now, gaze eschewing all but Fetch. "I don't know what you want to hear, Isa. After nearly thirty years I don't have many details left. It was the easiest birth I had ever tended . . . until it wasn't. You came out and I was surprised she wanted to hold you. I was afraid she might harm you until . . . I saw her smile."

Fetch's teeth were clamped on the cut inside her mouth, the pain fortifying. She had not expected this would be difficult to hear.

Beryl saw the struggle, acknowledged it by continuing. "You were in her arms, safe. I was watching close, still not trusting. And a good thing, because I was able to grab you quick when her fit started.

I thought it was her expelling the womb sack, that's often a killer. I helped it out, knew the bleeding would be the end for her. But the sack in my hands was heavy. And moving. Your mother was dead before I had the thing cut open. Never saw she gave birth to an orc."

Oats made an involuntary noise, choked it back. Fetch felt him looking at her as his mother went on.

"Hells, it was the first thick infant I had ever seen, but there was no mistaking it. The two of you looked nothing alike. That happens with humans, sometimes, even with twins, but this was different. You weren't much different from any other mongrel, but . . . he was bigger, darker, even than a thrice-blood."

He. Fetch felt sick. It was true.

"An elf woman birthed one half-breed and one full-blood." Beryl shook her head. "Never heard of anything like that, but I didn't know anything about point-ears, really."

"They were both half-elf," Starling said, her accent thick when speaking Hisparthan. "He was corrupted by the Filth. She was not."

Beryl gave her that look that could drive a nail. "I don't know about that either. Just what I saw."

"How is he still alive?" Fetching asked, trying not to shake.

Beryl squinted, perplexed and angry. "You ever killed a babe, Isabet? Of any kind? Answer me!"

"No."

"Neither have I. Seen enough die on their own for that." She took a long, fluttering breath. "I buried the Tine woman myself, hid the boy. An old frail named Branca was still alive then; it was her orphanage before mine. Her hearing was nearly gone and little could wake her, so it wasn't difficult. But Warbler rode in, so I had to wait for him to go back out on patrol before I could leave."

"Leave?" Oats asked, confusion boiling over his tongue.

Fetch voiced the answer. "You took him to Dhar'gest."

The thought was near impossible to fathom. Few went south to the Gut, crossed the Deluged Sea and into the dark lands of the orcs. Few, hells, none! But a woman with a baby? It defied all reason, challenged everything Fetch thought she understood.

Beryl lifted her chin defiantly, as if she still suspected to be punished. "I took a hog. Rode west and south until I reached the Fangs' lot. They helped me get across the Gut. Saw what I was doing as . . . I don't know, sacred? Saving an orc child. They almost took him in, but the vote didn't pass. I guess even the Fangs of Our Fathers aren't mad enough to try and raise a thick. Dhar'gest was the only place he had a chance of surviving, with his own kind."

"How?" Fetch said, hearing the awe in her voice. "How did you make it back?"

Beryl's lips parted to answer, but a pall settled across her face, caused her to falter. Eyes bright and brimming she went to Warbler, placed a hand on him, and faced away to hide the tears. The grizzled mongrel's hand covered hers.

"I went and got her," he said, gruff voice cracking. He looked haunted as he began to talk. "She'd been gone for days when I returned. It was another two before the Claymaster allowed me to go searching. Might have caught her, otherwise. I tracked her, but the Fangs had already helped her cross by the time I reached their lands. Had them shave my head, left Border Lord in their keeping, and swam the Gut. Covered my Bastard tattoos with mud when I made land. Never been so glad to be a thrice-blood. Still, I had to keep my distance from any thicks I saw. Slow-going, not sure how long, but I finally found her . . . among them."

Warbler's eyes went blank, stared at the ground, drowning in the memory. He blinked, dislodging tears. "More days just watching, waiting for my chance, wanting to die, to kill, every time one of them . . . hurt her. Used up all the luck I would ever have in this life, sneaking in there . . . but I got her out."

He wept freely now, silent and unashamed.

Beryl turned, composed, kept her hands upon Warbler's shoulders and took up the story once more.

"We made it home," she said. "The Claymaster was furious, wanted to oust me for the theft, but he saw reason when I told him what the Bastards would gain if he waited half a year." Her eyes went to Oats, adoring and afraid. He looked back, finally understanding why he was standing there.

Beryl gave a small, almost apologetic, shrug. "Best to tell all of it, all at once, if I had to at all."

"I wasn't ever going to ask, Mother," Oats said, an old, inner promise given voice.

"I know." Beryl's eyes shifted to Fetching and hardened. "Satisfied, chief?"

Fetch was numb, but she gave an answer. "Are you? That babe you saved is a devil now. He's the reason we're hiding in this hole."

Oats did not hinder his grunt of surprise this time. "The huge orc that nearly killed you? *That's* your brother?"

"No," Fetch snapped at him. "Don't call him that. I got brothers. And he is not one of them."

Clutching each other, Beryl and Warbler stared. The older half-orcs were wide-eyed, worn out. Warbler looked regretful, but Beryl was incensed. She came out from behind him and strode toward Starling.

"How did you know about this, point-ear?"

Starling remained untroubled in the face of aggression. She studied Beryl, her patience seeming to feed as her confronter's unraveled. At last, the elf woman took a breath.

"The mother you aided, her path is now mine. I have walked it since leaving the marsh, though it took me time to understand its mysteries. What she intended to do, I must do. Where she partially succeeded, I must fully."

Oats was visibly troubled. "What the hells does that mean?"

"Fetching's mother divested her of the Filth, but it would not be fully denied. A Ruin Made Flesh was still created." Starling looked at Fetch. "That it did not consume you in the womb is a testament to the potency of the magic your mother invoked. I believe this is why Akis'naqam spared her, despite the continued presence of the Filth. To destroy her would be to destroy you, something that had never existed before."

"How does that help me stand against him?"

Starling grew hesitant. "I do not understand."

"The Filth didn't kill me in the womb. It didn't turn me into a loon-brained puppet like the Sludge Man. Ruin hesitated to kill me the first time. This magic has kept me alive. Reckon it can also be used to kill him."

"That will be . . . difficult."

"Killing orcs always is."

"This is no mere orc."

"I am very fucking aware."

"Yet you fail to see your very nature. You are *lya'ʒáta*. My people are not wrong to name you an aberration, but they are wrong in their scorn. The Filth cannot corrupt you, for it was never meant to be part of you. Your very being is a victory against its evil. You are pure."

"Fuck purity! There must be more. Some chanty elf hoodoo involving spit and blood and hells-knows-what-all that is going to give me some way to fight him."

The look Starling gave her was pitying. "No."

Fetch raised an arm, pointed upward. "What about when I was fighting N'keesos and the others? There was . . . something. For a moment, I had the same strength, speed."

"You carry elven blood," Starling said. "The weapons of our ancestors are difficult to wield and require much training, yet they offer gifts to those that carry them. Na'hak Ee'eyo Lya and his brave-sworn fought you as they would a Ruin Made Flesh, using the *kurheul* to harm. It is possible the song from their clubs granted you power as well as pain, but . . ."

"But?"

"My people will never concede to offer you instruction in such weapons, nor would they part with them. Without them, you have no hope of harming the Ruin Made Flesh. Without Akis'naqam you have no hope of killing the Filth within him. Yet here both can protect you, so long as you remain. Should you leave, he will continue to hunt you. He is drawn to you, though I doubt he knows why. His confusion and curiosity will not restrain him forever."

"It already ain't," Oats rumbled. "Fetch, I saw him at Winsome. You couldn't have—"

"I could have burned him to fucking ash, Oats! The Filth too!

Yes, I'd be dead, but the hoof would be free of him. Estefania was right. Hells, Polecat—who told her—was right. The dogs, Ruin, they only wanted me."

"Hogshit," Oats said. "Have you forgotten Slivers? The riders from the Tusked Tide? The Stains? This damn thick is doing what thicks do. He's killing mongrels. You sharing a mother don't mean you caused this. Far as I can see, the only thing it's done is kept him from killing you, which is a stroke of luck we should be grateful for."

Warbler stood, took a limping step. "He's right. Hate to throw your own words in your face, Isabet, but self-pity doesn't wear well on you. I been in this gorge longer than I expected. Might be you are too." The old thrice cocked an eye at Starling. "Where I disagree is the notion that this Ruin can't be killed. Hispartha made this plague that I'm carrying for one purpose. To kill thicks. Their sorcerers too. And it does the job well, none know that better than me. We might need to dig deep for some patience, but once the Tines help me master this shit, we will ride out together and, chief, I swear to you I will show this orc what a ruin the plague makes of flesh. His."

Fetch allowed Warbler the bluff, chose not to remind him that he'd confessed he did not think the elves capable of fully ridding Wily of the sorcerous sickness. Perhaps, in the moment, he'd found fresh hope. She wouldn't rob him of it.

"We came here to regroup, Fetch," Oats said, knowing her silences better than anyone. "Give it some time. Dog Fall ain't the end of the Bastards."

"I know." But it might be the end for her.

"You need food and sleep," Beryl said, placing a hand lightly upon her elbow. It was a touch Fetch had often seen her give Oats and Jackal, but not one often received. She met the older woman's eyes, held them.

"I'm . . . sorry," Fetch told her.

Beryl gave her arm a gentle squeeze and let go.

"I, too, must rest," Starling said. "With your permission, I will pass the night here. My presence among my people causes them discomfort."

"Of course," Fetch replied. "Can you find a place?"

"Yes."

Fetch reached out and stopped the she-elf as she turned. "Thank you."

Slipping gently from the grip, Starling made her way around the hut.

"Can you explain that now?" Oats asked. "That's not a face I ever expected to see again."

"She's . . ."—Fetch struggled with an answer—"doing everything she can to survive. You were right, War-boar. We know shit about these people."

"We know they've saved our hides more than once."

"Yes, but not all agree with being charitable. One of them had his warriors try to kill me. Would have too, but for Starling. The Tine chiefs didn't take kindly to it, but only the leader was punished, this Na'hak Ee'eyo Lya. Ghost Last Sung. His boys are still around and may be holding a grudge. Something our boys need to know in the days coming. We have to stay vigilant."

"Na'hak?" Warbler said, looking perturbed. "Older? War paint looks like he's weeping blood?"

Fetch nodded. "You know him?"

"Don't *know* any of them. But I've seen him before. We all have, though Hood and I were the only ones that rode with him. He led the Tines that charged the orc *ul'usuun*."

"The day the Kiln fell?" Oats asked. "Hells. Means he saved our rumps."

Warbler grunted in agreement. "More than that, it was Starling that convinced him to do it. I watched her talk to him, could tell they were familiar."

"Her father, maybe?" Oats offered.

"Hard to say, these rustskins all look ali—"

"*Avram*," Beryl warned.

Warbler shrank a little. "Point I'm aiming for is, Na'hak rode to war to help us on Starling's behalf. Now she's still our ally, but he's not? Something powerful strange there."

"Know what's stranger?" Oats asked, running a hand along his jaw and pulling at his beard. "They put on these performances in Hispartha where the Claymaster's a hero." The withering looks he received left the big mongrel confounded. "What? It's true! Slug-gard told me."

Fetching, Warbler, and Beryl all groaned, spoke at the same time. "Shut up, Oats."

THIRTY-FIVE

—

THE TINES MADE GOOD on their word.

Sluggard arrived in the gorge two days later, under his own power, with no escort. He looked thinner, a bit pale and drawn, but was much improved from the last time Fetch saw him.

"Took me as far as the descent," he told the hoof a little breathlessly, sitting on a rock in front of Warbler's hut. "They just pointed down. I reckon they knew there was nowhere else I could go."

The top of his head was covered in the same fuliginous fish skin worn by Wily and Warbler, but where theirs were wrappings, Sluggard's was a single piece fitted over the surface of his ruined scalp, close as his own flesh.

Seeing their eyes keep drifting, the nomad gave a grin. "They made it clear I was not to remove it. Hoping I sprout hair like theirs."

Polecat cleared his throat. "They do anything for . . . uh . . . your . . ."

"They did," Sluggard said with good nature. "Gave me a pair of ox balls. Used their magic to do it. I fill hog troughs with spend now."

"Fuck yes!" Culprit said, nodding with fierce approval.

Shed Snake slapped the back of his skull. "He's jesting, fool-ass."

The Bastards heckled their youngest rider for a moment before Polecat looked eagerly at Sluggard. "What did you see up there? Any rustskin girls with feathers in their hair and swaying hips?"

"Not that came my way," Sluggard replied. "I was mostly lost in fever dreams. The bitter stuff they poured down my throat made them rather vivid, though nothing so pleasing as swaying hips. After that, my view was limited to the roof of a hut. There were . . . charms? Fetishes? Hanging ornaments of polished stone."

Warbler grunted in understanding. "That's a medicine lodge. Same as they take me and the boy."

"Glad to know I wasn't in a chicken coop," Sluggard said, drawing chuckles. "They permitted me out yesterday to see if I could walk. A grey-haired man helped me, and there was always a warrior close by. Once they saw I was able . . . well, here I am."

"We are glad to have you back," Fetch told him. "Rest and eat."

"There's little else to do," Culprit told the nomad with a laugh.

He was right. And that was the problem.

The slops had made short work of expanding the soil pit and were now tasked with restoring the abandoned hut. The larger domicile would greatly improve the comfort of the exiles. The Winsome folk were surprised when Fetch told them the remaining hut would be for their use once complete, no doubt believing she would take the dwelling for the hoof. But she did not want her boys getting comfortable. This was not permanent. A hoof was meant to ride. Their place was in the badlands, spitting in the eye of every danger drawn to, and conjured by, Ul-wundulas. Fetch needed to get them back to that bone-deep purpose. With or without her.

"True Bastards, open your ears."

Taking that for a signal, Sluggard stood to take his leave. Fetch put a hand on his shoulder.

"Your place is here. If you want it."

Reluctance flooded the gritter's face. The others were looking on. Fetch cursed herself, regretting foisting such a decision on him now.

"Think on it," she added, coming to both their rescue. Nodding, the nomad walked away.

Shaking off the misstep, she regarded her brethren.

"Clearly, we're getting stronger. Healing. That's good and was sorely needed, but our slops need to be trained. That's still our duty."

Shed Snake raked at his arm. "Gonna be tricky, chief. We got no room to run hogs down here, so riding drills are impossible. Stockbow drills will waste bolts we can't replace. Without a proper forge, sword work will eventually wear our tulwars into pry bars. What can we do?"

"Anything else," Fetch told them all. "*Everything* else. Drill hand signals until they know them cold. Hand-fighting. Knife-fighting. Run hog formations on foot. Get damn creative."

There were determined nods of agreement.

"Whether we stay another day or another year, we are leaving Dog Fall a hoof. I won't have it any other way. Warbler, Hood, get us all thinking and acting like nomads. We can't allow our tack and harness, or our stockbows to go to shit. Be diligent about upkeep. Watch the hogs closely too. They get lazy or feisty when they're not run, so find ways to work them. Go."

The boys jumped to it.

Fetch went to find Starling.

The she-elf had remained aloof since coming down into the valley. She slept apart, ate apart, and her whereabouts were often unknown. Yesterday, she had remained perfectly elusive. The rest of the hoof thought nothing of it. Those who had known her from the Kiln recalled her taciturn manner.

Fetch found her sitting on a tall pile of tumbled stones at the western wall of the gorge where the trees did not grow. The morning light slanted down, bathing the rocks with warmth and the elf's face with serenity.

"Well, you've allowed yourself to be found," Fetch called up. "Keep thinking you've left."

She was taken aback when Starling shushed her. It was a slow, gentle sound, the kind used to soothe. But it was still a fucking shush.

Fetch opened her mouth to rebel, hesitated, closed it, opened it again. Without lowering her face from the sky, Starling patted the rocks beside her in invitation. Feeling oddly foolish, Fetch glanced around for prying onlookers before ascending the pile. The flat perch was small and there was no way to sit without pressing ribs with the elf. Settling down, uncomfortable with their closeness, Fetch waited, drawing her knees up and crossing her arms atop them. The warmth was truly pleasant, however, massaging away a chill Fetch had not known she possessed until it began to dissipate. She grew drowsy.

"Forgive my reticence," Starling said, just as Fetch was beginning to doze. "Truly, I had not expected my people to permit me to linger. Returning. Being . . . home, it is intoxicating. Ul-wundulas had all but banished the notion of safety."

Fetch raised her mouth out of the crook of her elbow enough to speak. "So why banish yourself?"

"I must. The salvation of my child demands I not linger long."

"How . . . how do you know it will be different for you? Different than it was for my . . . mother?"

Starling looked at her now. "Because some sorrows are too great to be repeated."

Fetch opened her mouth to argue with that. And was shushed again.

THE LIGHT IN THE CANYON was failing when Fetch led the slopheads to the pond to wash. All moved a bit stiffly, sore and filthy from repeated tumbles from the saddle. It was a tedious drill, sitting the back of a motionless hog and purposefully flinging oneself off. It was far from close to the real thing, little more than trying to force memory into the body and hope that when the hog was actually running, the enemy was actually screaming, and death actually hunting, a life would be spared. All because she ordered these hopefuls to take a hundred falls. Besides, it prevented the hogs forgetting the weight of saddle and rider.

Fetch was trying to keep the barbarians from being spoiled. Hells, she was trying to keep her entire hoof from being softened, but it was hard not to see even the most forsaken of Dog Fall's gorges as a paradise after the slowly devouring hell of Winsome. Scrubbed clean, sitting on the rocky shore of the pond after a day of work, knowing a meal drew closer with the sinking sun, Fetching could not inure herself completely to the seductive contentment that gripped Starling.

Most of the slops were lounging on the opposite bank, a few already sleeping. The Bastards were half a turn along the edge of the pond, the distance they had given their chief to bathe born out of an awkward mixture of respect for her position and a powerful need to avoid getting a stiff cod. Fetch had donned her shirt and breeches a while ago, but the separation lingered, waiting for her to break it. She sat, finding no desire to stand and traverse the gap.

Dacia did it for her.

At first, Fetching thought the woman was just leaving the company of the slopheads, but she walked the circuit of the shoreline and approached without hesitance. No more than a stride distant, she produced a razor.

Fetch's hand darted for one of the kataras in the belt splayed on the rocks beside her.

"Peace, woman! Damn," Dacia said, grinding to a halt and holding up her hands. She was more perturbed than alarmed. "Any trying to kill you are going to need more than a cock's length of sharp steel to do it."

Fetching relaxed, moved her hand back to her lap. "Reckon I'm less certain about my vulnerabilities."

"Well, I've only a mind to cut hair, not throats," Dacia said, still galled. "That head of yours is getting prickly. You want to keep the elf coif, it needs seeing to."

Fetching rubbed a hand along the side of her bristly scalp. "I dunno. Not sure why I did it in the first place. Seems a fool-ass thing to do now."

"You wanted to honor your rider. Nothing foolish there. Keep something of him around. He'd have liked it."

Fetch felt her lips tighten. Mead would have loved it.

"You want me to see to it or not?" Dacia goaded.

"Yes," Fetch told her. "Please."

Mouth curling down with curt approval, Dacia came and squatted beside her.

Fetching eyed the small razor in her hand as it came up. "Cock's length of steel?"

"You've clearly never fucked a frail," Dacia grunted, and pushed Fetch's head into a tilt. The blade scraped, smooth and straight.

"You've done this before," Fetch said.

"I've sheared more sheep than you can fathom," Dacia replied. "Gelded them too. Shaved a man's face a time or two."

"Geld any of them?"

The razor scraped. The woman did not answer. Finishing one side, she stood, took a step, and squatted again to begin work on the other.

"He'd have liked this place too," Dacia said, her breath brushing the skin along with the blade. "Being in elf country."

Fetch focused on remaining still. "Who? You mean Mead?"

"Hard for me to think of him as anything but Fadrique, but yes."

"He told you his birth name?" Fetch was surprised.

Dacia made a careless noise in her throat. "Only name he had when I knew him."

Fetch craned away from the razor a bit too quickly. The blade nicked her scalp and Dacia cursed.

"Hells, you! Hold still! You want to be as scarred as me?"

"You knew Mead?" Fetch demanded, glaring.

"Half a lifetime ago," Dacia said. Licking her thumb, she daubed at Fetch's head, pressing the tiny point of pain. "I'll finish when that quits leaking."

With an accusatory look, Dacia settled down next to Fetching.

"We worked the same lord's land in Hispartha," she explained. "I had a dozen years on him or more. Was already letting the handsomer field hands get their fingers sticky in my quif before he was old enough to reap a swath of wheat. No reason for him to remember me. Plus, I didn't have these yet." Dacia swirled her hand in the air in front of her scarred face. "My hair liked to have turned white when I saw him at Winsome. He'd grown up, filled out, lost a hand, but it was him . . . that little mongrel boy in love with the elves. Fadrique. Couldn't believe it. But I took it as a sign."

"A sign?"

"That I was doing the right thing, seeking the Bastards."

Fetch smiled a little. "Because he'd left to do the same."

"Fuck no. That boy had left to join the damn elves. Here! In Dog Fall!"

Fetch peered dubiously at that.

"Sure as shit!" Dacia proclaimed, holding up a hand in a mock oath. "One of our harvesters was a rustskin. Kind sort. Tireless. Loved to tell stories, elven legends and whatnot. Tell them to anyone who'd listen. About how his people had once lived, about the orcs coming and destroying their lands, how only a few elves kept to the ancient traditions and were the proudest, strongest, wisest of all point-ears. He was right backy with love over these savage sorts, saying that the elves had forgotten how to live, that civilization had made them traitors to their traditions. On and on!"

Dacia made a wet noise that managed to convey both amusement and disgust. She picked up a rock and flicked it into the pond.

"After a few years, none of us cared to listen anymore. Except little Fadrique. He ate it up and asked for more. They'd work side by side all day, that old elf's tongue never ceasing to wag and the mongrel boy's ears never tiring to hear. Legends turned to lessons and soon all the words that passed between them were in elf-speech. That boy was sharp as a bailiff's whip and twice as quick."

"Sure was," Fetch said.

"You ain't gonna cry if I keep talking, are you?" Dacia asked, looking worried. And not for Fetch's sake.

"Fuck you."

Dacia gave a satisfied nod and a relieved breath. "So, just when Fadrique started to get hair on his balls, he up and left. Damn head was shaved into that plume and all. He was bound to find the elves that kept to the old ways, down in Ul-wundulas, he said. Tried to get the old elf to go with him, but turned out that one was all bluster. Too tamed by Hispartha, I reckon. Or just a coward liked to hear himself speak. I dunno, he didn't live but a year or so after his disciple took off. We figured Fadrique for dead too. The Lots had a solid enough reputation for swallowing the lives of hard men, to say nothing of a moon-eyed mongrel boy looking to join the Tines. Never heard of a more fool-ass notion. Reckon he found out quick that it was, but he still found his place because there he was, astride a hog, sworn brother to a hoof, as at home in the Lots as any. And still with that damn Tine plume! Being honest, it didn't look so foolish now. It looked . . . I dunno, *right*."

"Earned," Fetch said softly.

"That's it. Earned."

Fetch had known little of Mead's life prior to the hoof. She doubted if even Shed Snake knew everything, despite their closeness as slopheads and after. Mead never spoke of where he came from. His thoughts were always firmly fixed ahead.

"You ever tell him?" Fetch asked. "That you'd known him?"

"Nope. Have to admit, it gave me some small joy to have a secret. Be something that keen mongrel didn't figure out. Now, though . . . I wish I had said something. Would have loved to see his face when I told him I'd left like he did on a fool-ass notion."

"To find the woman chief?" Fetch threw her own rock into the water. "Far more than fool-ass."

"Hells." Dacia barked a harsh laugh. "Wasn't even certain it was true. Stories from the Lots are rife in Hispartha. Hard to sort the wheat from the chaff. But somehow, hearing that, I could no longer stay. Life on that damn land was never one of ease. And it could often be one of nostril-deep misery. Never much worried about orcs or centaurs, but . . . we had our monsters. Worse in ways, because no one wants to fight them. You do and you pay for it. And not with death, but daily, over and again. It's life they punish you with on a lord's demesne. Fadrique heard those old elf tales and he couldn't stay anymore. Thought he was mad. And then I didn't think about him at all. But one night, I hear about the mongrel woman that became master of a hoof. Next morning, my mind left that farm. The day after, my feet. Just couldn't stay. Not anymore."

"Fortunate for you the tale was true, I reckon."

"Fortunate for me I met Incus on the way south!" Dacia exclaimed. "I would never have made it through the Smelteds without her. Ran off from her masters too. And for the same reason as me. When we reached the Lots, we learned from some free-riders that you weren't no fable. They told us to make for the brothel nearest the castile, that riders from your hoof would come through one day or another. So we waited. Incus had some coin from her winnings, so Rhecia let us a room."

Fetch tried not to ask, but curiosity forced the question out all the same. "And Ahlamra?"

"Ahlamra was already there," Dacia replied, trying to sound careless, but some tension had entered her voice, the set of her shoulders. "Like you, I figured her for a whore. But no. Just another drawn by the idea of . . ."

She trailed off, fiddled with the razor.

"Me," Fetch finished.

"Reckon so," Dacia said, her jaw working in an aggravated grind as she continued to stare at the razor. "Didn't know her well enough to say what she'd conjured you to be. Something of worth, to come far as she did. But you didn't see any in her, so what does it matter?"

Fetch let that be the final word. She'd gambled on Ahlamra's worth. Time would see if she'd made the right wager. Time, but possibly not Fetch herself. If she never left this valley, she'd have to tell the next chief what she'd done. Until then, she'd hold quiet.

After a moment, Dacia bottled her discontent and squinted at Fetch's head. "No more blood. Let's finish this job and see if we can avoid making a further pig's ear of it."

Fetch complied, bending her neck and remaining motionless while the razor made its final swipes.

"There," Dacia pronounced. "You look a proper elf now."

"Thank you," Fetch said, feeling the smoothness.

Dacia stood, considered something.

"How did he get that name?" she asked. "Mead?"

Fetch looked up. "I'll tell you the reason for his hoof name the day you get yours."

"I'll hold you to that."

"I don't doubt it."

The gorge hummed with the now-familiar sawing noise of a Tine war club. Fetch jerked her head skyward. The sound grew in intensity, the sharp waves of its song overlapped by answering clubs.

"The hells?" Dacia said.

Starling appeared through the brush.

Fetch jumped to her feet, threw the elf a questioning look.

"Intruder," she said. "Within Dog Fall."

Shit.

Fetch shouted across the pond. "Weapons!"

Most of the hoof—brethren and slops—were already on their feet, roused by the noise. Dacia ran to shake Incus awake.

"Slops!" Fetch called out. "Gather our folk. Get everyone to the main hut. Stay together. Go! Bastards, with me!"

She took off running for the hog enclosure.

"What we got, chief?" Polecat asked, hoisting his saddle. The alarms continued, rallying and insistent. "Rustskins sound spooked."

Fetch snatched up her own tack and threw it over Womb Broom's back. Starling came up on the other side of the hog. Her normally placid face was frozen in a twist of dismay. She'd said Ruin would not risk coming here. Her error had left her stunned.

Fetch cinched the girth strap tight. "Is it him?"

"None could trespass this far," Starling replied.

"Get back to the hut."

"No. You will need me to read the warning songs."

Fetch gave an accepting shrug. The Bastards were mounting, awaiting instruction.

"We found any other path into this gorge?" Fetch asked.

"No," Shed Snake replied. He pointed at the nearby trailhead. "Anything not a bird that wants in will have to come down that."

"What about those dogs?" she pressed. "Can we wager our lives they can't manage another way?" There was a pause. "Shit. Hood, get moving. Check every damn cranny."

He rode off into the thicket.

"The rest of us are staying right here," Fetch ordered. "Feather anything that comes down that trail." She swung up onto the saddle and loaded her stockbow.

They took a position set back from the defile with clear sights. They would get maybe two volleys before being forced to charge. The Tine alarms kept sounding, but they seemed to be moving, the patterns fluctuating. Starling stood at Fetch's knee, focused intently on the reverberating notes.

"The warriors are searching," she related after a time. "The intruder eludes them."

Stockbows trained, the Bastards kept guard. Fetch considered sending a runner to Warbler's hut, cursed herself for not telling the slops to send a report. She turned to tell Culprit to go, but her command was swallowed by a thunderous roar. It filled the gorge, stirred the air. It was different from the song of the Tine weapons, though no less familiar.

It was the wrathful Voice of Belico.

Fetch met Oats's eye.

"Xhreka," he said, and tugged Ugfuck around.

"Stay here!" Fetch told the others. "Watch for dogs!" She kicked Womb to follow.

The gorge howled from its core, as if a storm had fallen from the sky and landed among the trees. As their hogs surged through scrub and around swollen logs, charging for the source, Fetch was relieved it was not leading them toward the hut but into the marshy center of the hollow. Choking bracken, mud, and thorns impeded their way until they were forced to dismount, leave their hogs, and continue on foot. Oats crashed through the underbrush, ducking branches, jumping boulders, using his bulk to clear a path when nimbleness failed. Fetch stayed on his ass.

The sound ceased, as swiftly as it came.

They halted for a moment, looking at each other, panting. Xhreka had repelled the orc once before. They could only hope she had again. The alternative to the cessation of Belico's rage did not bear thinking upon. They kept going. This deep in, the gorge was veiled with gloom. Without the voice to follow, Fetch worried they were doing little but running about in a blind, desperate search. But Oats must have known the halfling's habits, for he led them to a clearing veined with the shallow rivulets of a broken stream. A basket laid there, the snails spilled from it already making their sedate escape. From there the trail was easy to follow. Trees were bent and leaning, some uprooted, the sodden turf replete with fallen branches. The results of a god's breath.

They found her not far from the worst of the havoc in a flooded dell. The halfling was on her knees, waist-deep in the stagnant water, chin touching her chest. Sliding down a stony embankment thick with moss, Oats reached the bottom of the dell, stomped through the pond, and came to Xhreka's side. Fetch stayed at the water's edge, stockbow sweeping the surrounds.

"She's alive!" Oats announced.

Fetch sloshed into the pond, still vigilant. The halfling was barely coherent, mumbling something and swaying as if drunk. Oats had the back of her neck cradled in one great hand, steadying her.

"Xhreka! Where did he go?"

She pointed. Her hand wavered and wandered, encompassing half the surrounding thicket before steadying. Looking, they discerned a rough corridor of crushed scrub and snapped limbs leading away from the pond's far end.

"Get her out of here," Fetch said, moving toward the place Xhreka had clearly flung the orc.

"You're not fighting that thing alone."

"What choice is there? Maybe I can stall him until the Tines arrive. Get going."

Unhappy, Oats stood, scooping the halfling up.

Fetch entered the tunnel of punished foliage. If Ruin was injured, perhaps she could finish him. See if he could shrug off a bolt through the eye. She came to the end, found an empty depression of blackthorn. He had fallen here, but was already gone, on the move.

"Shit!"

She whirled, doubled back to the pond.

Across the way, Oats was ascending the embankment, leaving the dell. A dark shape was coming across the top, moving quickly, preparing to converge on the thrice when he crested the rise. He did not see it.

"OATS!"

He turned at her call, saw her gesture, and immediately reversed his course, sliding more than running, Xhreka held protectively to his chest. The shadow pursued.

Fetch pressed the stockbow into her shoulder and loosed. The charging figure lurched and fell, tumbled down the embankment with a bolt through the thigh. Oats had reached the bottom, turned to look at the fallen form, too small to be Ruin.

"It ain't no orc!" he called across the pond. "Some damn swaddlehe—"

The figure jumped up, darted at the thrice. Oats went for his sword, but was hampered by the dazed halfling. Cursing, Fetch sprinted to help, boots crashing through the pond. Oats's tulwar was half drawn from its scabbard when his black-clad opponent flung an arm forward, arcing an azure powder at his head.

Fetch had seen that blue shit before. Crafty threw it in her face at the Kiln when she came to kill him. It had done nothing but briefly sting her eyes.

Oats dropped as if struck in the forehead by a mallet.

His attacker was dressed in the garb of the east, a head scarf covering the face. A powerful frame moved fluidly beneath the dark, loose garments, bending to seize Xhreka, now toppled beside Oats.

But Fetch was upon him, yelling in a fury, ripping her tulwar free and slicing in one motion. Her foe ducked, rolled, and sprang up at her flank. Her sword arm was seized, twisted. She moved with the pressure, crouched swiftly, and slipped the grip. Straightening, she launched a shoulder, knocked the masked figure back, and slashed again. Steel rang on steel, her tulwar parried by the figure's own swiftly drawn, curved blade, wider and heavier than hers. Fetch had seen similar swords on the hips of the Zahracenes.

Xhreka had said Zirko would come for her. It seemed the conniving priest had named his price for warning the swaddleheads of the Betrayer Moon and turned them into his errand boys.

Fetch sent cuts whipping at the man, keeping him on the defensive. He turned or avoided the strokes with skill, wielding the larger blade with the speed of a true swordsman. Only, he wasn't just a swordsman. Fetch remembered the powder, the thrumbolt that did not even hinder, and kept wary for further sorcery.

As they fought around the edge of the pool, shouts could be heard in the distance, coming closer. Oats's name and cries of "chief" became distinguishable. The hoof was looking for them.

"Down here!" Fetch called out, sending another reaping cut at the Zahracene. He swayed from the steel, snapped back in, catching her cross-cut with his scimitar. Within a heartbeat, he was on the attack. A cut came for her head, but it proved to be a feint, the blade twisting away to chop at her leg. Side-stepping to avoid a severed limb, Fetch was forced into the pond. It hardly reached her knees, but it was enough to slow her down. The Zahracene's hand went into his robe, flicked out again, and tossed something small that plopped and sank beside Fetch's leg. The water erupted. Fetch was picked up by the force, thrown backward. Her spine slapped the water. She went under for a moment, came up sputtering, sword still in hand.

The Zahracene went sprinting back toward Xhreka. Up on the lip of the dell, three familiar figures appeared, stockbows in hand.

Fetch pointed to the running man with her tulwar. "Bring him down!"

Culprit was the first to loose, but he hurried and his bolt went wide. Polecat was on the edge facing the Zahracene, and let fly. Without breaking stride, the swaddlehead cut the bolt out of the air. He was four strides from the halfling when Shed Snake's bolt took him in the back, just above the hip. The force spun him around, tripped him up. He fell within reach of Xhreka, and Fetch was no longer surprised to see him begin to stand. She plowed through the pond, knees cutting the water. The Bastards above were reloading their thrums.

Oats came to just as the Zahracene rose to a knee. The thrice growled and pounced from the ground, spear-tackling the man. Pinning him, Oats rained down punches from fist and elbow, but he was still stupefied from the powder and the blows were clumsy.

Polecat was shouting for him to get clear. Culprit was scrambling down to help.

"Stay back!" Fetch commanded, knowing the young rider lacked the skill to take this opponent. She was a few strides away when the Zahracene grabbed the hand holding him to the ground and wrenched it, upsetting Oats's balance. The thrice fell forward, his last punch pounding nothing but mud as his captive rolled out from beneath him.

Culprit rushed in, heedless of Fetch's yelled protests, swinging his tulwar. The Zahracene caught his wrist, hammered his guts with a knee, grabbed his stockbow harness, and threw him to the ground, breaking the strap. He threw the thrum at Polecat, sending it spinning into the mongrel's own trained weapon. Grunting, Cat stumbled back, his bolt loosed into the air. Oats was up and grabbed the man from behind just as Fetch reached them. He kicked out, booted her back into the water. Struggling to stand once more, she saw Oats's massive arms wrapped about the smaller combatant, but his hold was yielding. Emitting a guttural sound of exertion, Oats windmilled his captor, hurled him over Fetch's head. He landed in the center of the pond.

On his feet.

He started forward and Fetch readied her tulwar.

"Girl." Xhreka's voice from behind. "Get clear."

Knowing what was coming, Fetch dove to the side.

Belico howled his displeasure, turning the world into a shrieking gale. Raising up from the muck, squinting against the onslaught of debris, Fetch saw the halfling woman standing, feet planted, head thrust forward, the lids of her missing eye gaping to reveal a screaming mouth. The pond rippled out from the power pouring forth, blasted to a fine mist. Buffeted by water, wind, and the brutal tumult, the Zahracene braced himself, wet robes billowing and snapping. His left arm came up, shielded his face from the brunt of the maelstrom.

Fetch cursed when he managed a step forward.

She stood, not knowing how they were going to prevail if Xhreka failed. The halfling was flagging, already fallen back to her knees. The Zahracene continued his slow yet inexorable strides. The din was weakening, enough for Fetch's own voice to be heard.

"Get ready!" Bringing her thrum around, she reloaded.

Xhreka collapsed. Belico was silenced.

Stockbows were aimed, but as the Zahracene lowered his arm, no bolts were loosed. The head scarf had blown back and the face revealed beneath caused Fetch's fingers to freeze upon the tickler.

In the stunned silence, Oats was the one to say it.

"*Jackal?*"

THIRTY-SIX

JACKAL. HE WAS BACK.

And chaos arrived with him. Chaos within and without.

The Bastards were shouting.

"Jack? The fuck you doing, brother?!"

Oats. Demanding answers. Large form hovering between rushing to his friend and staying to protect Xhreka.

"Chief! What are we doing here!?"

Shed Snake.

"That ain't fucking him!" Polecat. "You all blind? Crafty's turned him. Oats, get your fucking thrum up!"

Movement behind, above. More shouts. These in elvish. The Tines had arrived, bringing more demands, more taut bowstrings. Fetch heard it all, felt the motion, the confused anger, the impending violence. The chaos without.

Within it was slower, torturously so. Her shoulder was still filled with the stockbow, her eyes still sighting along the bolt, pointing at that face, the one that should not be here.

He, too, was ignoring the upheaval he had conjured, looking only at her. Dripping water was all that moved upon him.

And Fetch saw it. He wasn't enthralled, no wizard's puppet. He was Jackal. The same cunning, the same daring, the same fool-ass choices. It was all written there in that bright, unwavering stare, the one that showed regret for being discovered, the one that asked her forgiveness.

For what, Jackal? Which trespass do you want pardoned? She wanted to shout, add her voice to the growing turmoil. There was no need. It was all there in her face for him to read.

Fetching lowered her thrum.

"True Bastards! Put them down!"

Turning to make sure she was obeyed, she found a dozen Tines along the lip of the dell, two with song clubs. Polecat and Shed Snake relinquished their aim. Nearby, Culprit was picking himself up, only now recovering his wind. Oats's stockbow was already pointed at the ground.

In the pond, Jackal's scimitar remained in his hand.

"Your hearing not recovered?" Fetch demanded. "I just told the members of my hoof to drop weapons."

Jackal opened his hand, allowed the water to claim his blade.

Half the Tines began to come down, converging on him while the rest covered their approach with bows.

"He is one of mine," Fetch told them in elvish. "This was a misunderstanding."

They paid her no heed. Jackal was surrounded, herded out of the water. He went calmly, though Fetch could see in the set of his shoulders that he was riled. She watched him go, and within moments returned to the comfort of his wonted absence. The Bastards were left alone in the dell casting dumbfounded looks at one another.

Polecat and Shed Snake plodded down, gathered around Fetch and Culprit. Oats was again kneeling beside Xhreka, eyes far away and burning.

"You good, chief?" Polecat asked.

She scowled at the off-putting concern. "Go dredge up Jackal's sword."

No one else spoke while Polecat searched about in the muck, muttering complaints.

They all looked up at the sound of footsteps, were surprised when they heralded Hoodwink at the top of the dell. He rarely allowed anyone to hear him coming, but that was not all that was off. He was paler, if that was possible. He joined the group right as Polecat waded back with the scimitar.

"You will never guess who we saw," the hatchet-faced mongrel chimed.

"Jackal," Hood replied.

"You saw him too?" Shed Snake asked.

"No. He smells the same. Caught his scent just before——" Hood-wink stopped short, wearing a pensive expression. Another rarity.

Polecat snapped his fingers. "He got you. Oh, fuck! He took you down!"

It was clear from Hood's careful stillness, Cat was right. Still, it was damn hard to fathom, for Hood more than any of them. Perhaps it wasn't the same Jackal.

Fetch found herself looking past the others, down at Oats, his thumb rubbing Xhreka's forehead. The halfling was alive, breathing regular, but out cold.

"Let's get her back to the hut," she said.

On the walk back, Fetch motioned Shed Snake away from the others.

"What made you come looking for us?"

"Starling. She kept . . . reading those sounds. Told us the intruder was already here, that the only thing coming down the trail was Tines, so we ran to help." They walked side by side for a moment, both quiet and pondering. Snake broke the silence, barely above a whisper. "Hells, chief. How did he do it? Sneaking into Dog Fall. Taking Hood down. I heard things about him back in the slops. Mead told us stories. Saw him around the Kiln, of course, like all of you. But damn. Was he always like that?"

"No." Fetch scrubbed at her bedraggled hair. "Yes. Somewhat. I don't know."

They put Xhreka in Beryl's bed. Wily climbed up next to her, held her hand. The other orphans kept coming in, the curiosity and concern of children mixing into a tide that Beryl had to keep chasing from the room. Fetch pulled Warbler aside, told him the news, and waved off the questions before they came.

"I don't know, War-boar. It was him, that's all I got for now."

She walked away from him, from everyone, went down to the bathing pond and cast stones into it until the ground surrounding her boots was picked to the mud.

Hells' cocks, she was relieved!

He was alive, he was back, at a time when the hoof sorely needed him. An experienced rider, a canny fighter, to say nothing of the powers Zirko foisted on him. His was the kind of strength they needed against Ruin. That was, if the Tines didn't burn him alive for invading their home on whatever foolish fuckery he snuck back to stir up!

Fetch stalked over to the biggest rock on the shore and heaved it over her head with a vengeance, finding relief in the massive splash. She stood watching, stewing, until every last ripple was chased away by the pond's placid surface.

Starling was now standing beside her.

"It wasn't Ruin," Fetch offered. Uselessly, it turned out.

"I know."

"It was Jackal." Fetch wasn't sure if Starling knew that too, but said it anyway. "He's here to bring Xhreka back to Strava. Certain as shit. Because fucking Zirko told him to. And they call me Fetch-ing!"

"He made a bargain."

Fetch snorted. It was that simple, wasn't it? The consequences, however, were not.

"What will happen to him? Because if your people don't want to lose their big snake, they may want to think twice about throwing him in her cave. Jackal has a way of . . . who the fuck am I telling, you know what he's like."

"Brave. Impulsive. Tireless."

"He's a fucking idiot."

"Akis'naqam's purpose is to consume the Filth. All else is beneath her notice."

"What, then?"

"He will be judged by the Sitting Young. As his leader, it is likely you will also be summoned."

"I got no notion what to tell them about him."

"The truth would be best."

Fetching's mouth soured. "There's over a year's truth about him I don't know."

"Then that is the truth you must speak. The Sitting Young will not allow my presence in this matter. You will need to be able to speak and understand. Open your mouth."

Fetch grimaced. "Not this again."

"No. Something more is required."

Liking the sound of that even less, Fetch parted her lips. Starling reached up and pressed her thumb down on one of Fetch's lower fangs until the flesh was pierced. Fetch suffered the flow of blood on her tongue and swallowed it down once Starling removed her hand.

Fetching coughed and groaned. "Hells, I hate magic!"

Starling was right about the summons. The Tines soon came down, demanded Fetch accompany them, along with Xhreka. The halfling woman was awake, but still very weak.

"Tell them she ain't hale enough," Oats growled from her bedside.

"We don't have a choice, Oats," Fetch told him, gentle as she could.

Xhreka sat up, wincing a bit. She swatted Oats's helping hands away. "I'm fine. Stop fussing over me." Her one eye revolved to the other side of the bed to glance at Beryl. "Though you get it honest."

Fetch made way for her as she moved out of the hut, less stable than she claimed, but hiding it well. The trek up the trail would not be easy on her. Oats must have thought the same, for he had every intention of coming along. The Tines had other designs.

"Only you," one of them said, pointing at Fetch and Xhreka.

Oats's elvish was limited at best, but he took the meaning and bristled. "Try and stop me."

The mood he was in, the thrice-blood was likely to stomp the entire escort, but Fetch stepped in, put a hand on his chest.

"What is this? Trying to be me and start a war?"

"I'm going," he claimed, sounding just as he did when they were children.

"Oats. I won't let anything happen to her. Hear me?"

Jaw working beneath his beard, Oats's gaze darted uncertainly from her to the halfling and back again. His breathing was quick and shallow.

Fetch blew a short whistle through her teeth to get his attention. "She'll be safe."

He nodded. "If you say so, chief."

She slapped him lightly on the cheek. "No. Fetch says so."

Oats exhaled, relieved and sheepish, backed up a step.

Xhreka shored up the reassurance. "See you in a small while, Idris."

They went with the elves. Soon as they were out of earshot, the halfling fell into step next to Fetching.

"Figure we were lying to him?"

"Oh, fuck yes."

The climb was difficult, but Xhreka would not suffer to be carried, so the going was slow. At last, they reached the cave of the Sitting Young.

Jackal stood in the center, unguarded, unbound. He did not appear injured, but that meant little. The Tines could have been torturing him since he left the dell and the restorative gifts of Attukhan would have erased the evidence. Still, Fetch did not believe that was their way. At least, not yet.

Their guides motioned for Fetch and Xhreka to join him before spreading out along the walls flanking the entranceway. As Fetch came up alongside Jackal, putting herself between him and Xhreka, she felt him look over, but kept her gaze fixed on the council before them.

The eldest girl was the first to speak, addressing Fetch.

"We wish to hear what you know of this one that intruded upon our lands."

"His name is Jackal," Fetching answered, heeding Starling's advice to respond with honesty, and inwardly thanking her for the fluency in the elf tongue. "He is a member of my tribe, but has been away on a task I set him."

"And?" This from a younger girl.

"And he should not have come here."

The blind boy cocked his head. "Why did he?"

"Did you ask him?"

"We did," the same boy replied. "But we want to hear what you believe."

Fetch took a breath, let it out slowly. "He is beholden to Zirko, high priest of Belico." She tilted her head to the side in Xhreka's direction. "Zirko wants her, so he snapped his fingers and my roving brethren here came running, wagging his tail."

"I came running when told my hoof was in danger!"

Jackal's words were passionate, directed at the council, but meant for Fetch. She should not have been surprised that he now understood and spoke elvish. More changes, more mysteries.

"Zirko said there was something hiding among my brethren," he went on, "something they may not know was there. It needed to be removed before it destroyed them. When I reached our lands . . . I thought it already had."

Fetch felt a moment of sympathy. But it was fleeting, chased away by the greater pain, the living knowledge of what really happened.

"Xhreka did not destroy our home," she told the Sitting Young. "She helped us survive the attack of those that did."

The eldest elf girl's face turned grave. "The Ruin Made Flesh."

"Him, yes," Fetching replied before glancing at Jackal, "and the Orc Stains." She looked away before he met her eye.

"The Orc Stains?" the smallest boy on the council asked.

"Another half-orc tribe," Fetch answered.

An older boy gestured at Jackal. "What was the task this one undertook for you?"

"To bring me the head of a Tyrkanian wizard that wronged our tribe."

"You did not know he was coming here to attempt this intrusion on our land?"

"No."

The first girl held up a hand and the elf man behind her leaned down. There was a hushed exchange. When it was over, the man straightened once more and the girl returned her attention to Fetch.

"Why does the Hero Father of Strava want this halfling?"

"You will have to ask her."

"I got the god he made inside my head," Xhreka announced without waiting. She spoke Hisparthan, though it was obvious she understood the Tines.

Over half the Sitting Young sought advice after that statement, some needing a translation. While waiting, Fetch could no longer resist. She looked at Jackal.

He turned immediately. He was angry at her for calling him Zirko's dog, confused by the answers about Winsome's fall, but those were only the freshest emotions, a few leaves newly fallen into a well. The deep waters beneath were uncertainty, regret, longing, and the same conflicted relief that had caused Fetch to throw stones into a pond. As he returned her gaze, the leaves were chased away and she saw a cautious joy pull at the corners of his lips. Fetch itched to punch him, ached to fuck him. One, then the other. Or one during the other. Repeatedly. Neither would likely be well received in this solemn chamber full of children.

They were both pulled back to the council by another youthful voice.

"We are not familiar with all the mysteries that the followers of Belico believe."

Xhreka's mouth twisted. "If I go into all that, you lot will be old enough to stand behind your replacements before I'm through. We will just say that I have no desire to go back to Strava and leave it there."

"The half-orc man claims you are dangerous," a girl said.

"Not if I am left alone."

A boy looked at Fetching. "Did you know what the halfling possessed?"

"Like you, I don't understand most of it. But yes, I knew she had power."

The eldest girl did not look pleased. "We cannot deny Akis'naqam's judgment nor our returned sister's wisdom and intercession on your behalf. However, you also brought this godling among us, without our knowledge or permission. You *willingly* brought a potent, destructive force into our lands. By his own admission, your wayward rider bears similar, dangerous blessings. His intrusion was due to your presence, or more correctly, the presence of the halfling under your protection. It is not our place to interfere in the affairs of outsider gods, but neither was it our wish to host a conflict between Belico's disciples." The girl looked at Jackal. "You will be taken immediately from our lands. Tell the Hero Father that he has earned the ire of the Seamless Memory. That he would send a servant creeping beyond our borders dishonors decades of peace between us. If he ever sends another, we will ride to Strava and bring war."

Tine warriors surrounded Jackal and began to lead him from the chamber.

"I need to speak with him," Fetch told the council, but was met with no answer. The guards did not hesitate and were soon gone, along with their charge. The firm words of the girl again filled the chamber.

"And you, chief of the True Bastards, your part in this has forced us to consider the wisdom of allowing your people to dwell here."

Fetching tensed as the Sitting Young delivered their judgment through the eldest girl.

"You will leave our lands, never to return."

"You can't mean . . . all of us?"

"All," said the girl.

Fetching swept the faces before her, careful not to look at the adults. "My brothers and I will leave. There will be no more threat to you from those that remain. They are only children, families, farmers and grovers and tradesmen. They are not a danger, I swear it."

"When you came to us we thought you to be the danger, Aberration. Now we see more perils were nested within those you brought here. This halfling was not one of your riders. Who else among your people will reveal themselves as capable of bringing woe to our tribe? We would be unwise to allow any to remain within our borders."

Fetch hit her knees, desperation pushing her words forth in an airy torrent. "Please. Do not do this. I will take my riders and the halfling woman and be gone. Only allow the rest to stay safe. Please!"

The faces of her judges were youthful, soft and smooth, but their eyes were cold and jagged as flint.

THIRTY-SEVEN

OLLAL CLUNG TO HER MOTHER as Fetching spoke, one fearful face amidst two score. Some tried to hide it with outrage, others disbelief, but all were afraid as they heard the news.

They could no longer stay. The Tines were demanding their withdrawal.

Beyond the shelter of the canyons, Ul-wundulas slavered, eager for them to once again place themselves upon its altar and expose their throats. The slops wore the most convincing masks, but Fetch saw through the set jaws and folded arms. Dog Fall was a strange and stifling home, but there was food and water, and the nights were free from the laughter of demons. There was no choice. They must leave. Both feeble statements issued from Fetch's mouth, her voice the filthy outreaching hands of a beggar.

She had called her folk together in front of the larger hut, the one the slops had worked so hard to restore. She now sent the same diligent young mongrels away to help the Bastards, already informed and making preparations. The survivors of Winsome remained, the parents' faces growing numb as the questions of their children drifted up to ears deaf to all but ill tidings. Fetch forced herself to look at Thistle. The fear stained her too, but the woman was quick to take it in hand, mold its wet uselessness into something resolute for the sake of the sixteen foundlings arranged around her skirts.

"Where will we go?"

It was Ollal's father, the former farrier, who spoke.

"Mongrel's Cradle," Fetch answered. "The Sons of Perdition will take you in."

She walked away before more voices could be found. There was no time for empty consoling. Moving across the canyon toward the other hut, Fetch squared her shoulders.

The worst was to come.

Beryl and Warbler were speaking heatedly when Fetch entered, her presence halting their raised voices. Wily was sitting on the hearth between them, his bandaged hands fiddling with an eagle feather.

"You have to make them reconsider!" Beryl declared, changing targets.

Fetch said nothing. It was a battle she had already fought with the Sitting Young.

Beryl charged around the table. "Then I will go up. Make these elves see reason!"

"Beryl," Warbler attempted, but she went headlong for the door.

Fetch blocked the way, keeping all aggression from her stance.

"Move, Isabet."

She didn't, stared at the place where the nearest table leg met the floor. If she looked up, Beryl would see the fear.

"The Tines will not be swayed," Fetch pronounced. "Not by you, not by me. Their choice is made."

"But the orphans," Beryl's anger was tinged with a plea. "They should stay! Why are they blamed for your failure?"

Again, Fetch kept silent. She needed to just say it, couldn't.

Frustrated, Beryl spun, paced a moment, launched her assault anew.

"All your lives, you and Jackal made each other worse! Why is it that the pair of you delight in such havoc? He wasn't here a heart-beat! And now this?" Beryl gestured at Warbler and Wily, to herself. "*We* are here because of you two. Had grown used to it. The soli-tude. Then you come and Wily had others to play with and now those children are being cast out into the badlands! They should be allowed to stay with him, with me. Dammit, go back and talk to the Tines. Thistle and the foundlings are not a danger to them. Make them understand!"

"If I go back up there . . . it won't help."

"Then why are you here, Isa?" Beryl demanded. "Just go. You kept them all alive once. Maybe you will have the fortune to manage that miracle again." She blew out a disgusted breath, shook her head dismissively, and turned away.

"Beryl," Fetch said, unable to avoid the moment any longer. "The Tines will not allow any but the bearers of the plague to re-main."

Beryl froze.

Nearby, Warbler blanched.

Slowly, Beryl turned. "What?"

"Wily and Warbler are the only ones the elves will allow to stay."

"With me." Beryl pointed hard at the floor of the hut. "They will allow them to stay *with* me."

Fetch's answer was a whisper. "No."

"I was here already," Beryl's voice was edged with panic. "That was the first agreement. Me and them! I've been here, I'll be here. You will go, everyone will go, but we will stay. Me and Wily and Avram, as it was!"

Fetch could only shake her head.

Beryl let out a cry of pure anguish, face contorted, hands twitch-ing, clutching at nothing. Wily looked up from his feather, the first notice he had taken of the others in the room. His face held surprise, incomprehension, the sight of Beryl's grief frightful and paralyzing. Fetch, too, found her body chained. She had never seen Beryl cry, not in a lifetime.

Warbler went to her, tried to contain her grief in his scarred hands. His touch only agitated her more and she tore away. She could not master the sobs, kept beating them back to cast condemning looks at Fetching only to have them return and conquer her face.

"They can't do this! You can't do this!" The protestations fell from warped lips, borne to the ground upon spittle thickly weighted with sorrow.

Warbler stepped for her again. "Beryl, we will go. We will all go. They can't keep us here. We will stay together." He managed to wrangle her into his arms. "All will be well. I swear it. All will be well. We'll go together."

She made a strangled noise and calmed, but it was not relief that brought the sudden, terrible stillness. She looked down at Wily. When her eyes returned to Warbler, her jaw quivered once more.

"No."

Warbler grimaced, took a breath to reply, but was silenced by Beryl's hand gently stroking his thick white hair, down his cheek. Her thumb rested at the sun-creased corner of his eye.

"No," she repeated. "You must stay. For him. Get the Claymaster's evil out of him. All of it."

"We can find another way," Warbler objected.

Beryl shook her head. "This is the way." Stretching up, she kissed him. When their lips parted, Warbler allowed her to slip from his embrace, his chin falling. Beryl knelt, pulled the still puzzled child to her, kisses and tears showering his scalp, cheeks, neck.

"Love my little boy," she whispered.

Watching their goodbye was an intrusion. Fetch wanted to look away. But it was also a punishment, so she accepted it, kept her gaze firm.

"Going to do wash, Mama?" Wily asked, his little voice slightly muffled in her arms.

"Yes," Beryl told him.

"Can I help?"

She nearly broke again. "You're going to stay here, play with Wubba."

Heeding the hidden instruction, Warbler sat down on the hearth, his swollen leg forgotten.

Shattering, Beryl let Wily go and fled the hut. Fetch moved aside to let her pass. Warbler was bravely focused on Wily, robbing him of his feather and swooping it around the boy's face, darting in to tickle him and coaxing giggles.

Fetch turned to go and was stopped by Warbler's gritty voice, roughened further by emotion. "Have her take Big Pox. No need for a hog here now."

Fetch nodded even though he was not looking at her. "I'm sorry, War-boar."

Warbler did not pause the game, deftly balancing his own sadness against the joy of the child that was now his alone to care for. "Just go, Isa."

Outside, Fetch rejoined the Bastards. Starling was among them. She would depart with the hoof, stay with them until they left Tine land, then go her own way. Fetch had argued against her leaving, encouraged her to stay within the safety of the gorges for as long as she was able. The she-elf had given her a firm denial.

Mounted now upon her hog, Fetch led her people out of the humid valley. Their Tine escort awaited them at the trailhead, no fewer than thirty stag riders, replete with war lances and full quivers. The Tines took them up and through the canyons. The day receded along with the mountains. Before dusk they emerged from the Umbers and found their wagon waiting beyond the foothills, loaded with supplies and watched over by a half dozen Tine scouts.

"Tell the Sitting Young they have our thanks for this," Fetch told the lead stag rider, but her courtesy went unacknowledged.

They rested a moment while Big Pox and Palla were hitched to the wagon, Beryl and Sluggard climbing onto the seat to drive the team, Xhreka between them. The goods prevented any from riding in the bed, but the presence of food was a welcome sight to walkers and riders. The Tines took them across the last long stretch of plain to the edge of their lands. It was full dark before they crossed the stream at the border. The elves waited for every last foot to be properly expelled before turning their stags back toward the mountains, visible in the distance as star-eclipsing swaths reaching into the night sky.

The lead rider lingered a moment.

"Do not return," he said in Hisparthan, his words meant for all. Then he, too, was gone.

Fetch gave the order to make camp. The villagers were weary, but there was water, and the border offered some protection by its very presence. Few ventured this close to Tine land. Yet the hoof and its people proved not to be the only loiterers in the dark.

Fetch was taking an inventory of the wagon with the aid of a torch when Hoodwink drifted into the light.

"What is it?" she asked, squinting into a sack of dried meat.

"Jackal."

"What about him?"

"He is here."

She dropped the sack. "Making another attempt on Xhreka?"

Hood gave a hint of a headshake. "No. This time he wanted me to see him."

Fetch jumped down from the wagon. "Show me."

They went beyond the western edge of the slowly forming camp, walked out into the barren plain, dirt shining silver with the moon. And there he was, sitting a hog less than a thrumshot away.

"Stay here," Fetch told Hoodwink.

Jackal dismounted as she drew near, still dressed in the garb of a desert frail. Mean Old Man, the black hog Warbler had gifted him when he left, snuffled when Jackal left his side.

They stopped an arm's length apart. There was a long silence.

"I thought she had destroyed Winsome, Fetch," Jackal said, at last.

"I had it solved."

Her words had been hissed through clenched teeth, barely heard by her own ears.

Jackal leaned in. "What?"

"I had it solved," she said, louder. "They were safe. They were all going to be safe. I had it solved!"

She drew a katara, snatched her arm back, eager and willing to punch the blade into Jackal's chest.

He did not move.

Neither did she. "Hells, if only I could hurt you, Jack. If only I knew you wouldn't mend."

"I know your looks, Fetch. You want to kill me. You think that doesn't hurt?"

"That your idea of asking pardon?" She felt her voice wanting to rise, got it under control. "Why didn't you come to me?"

"I didn't know you were alive until I saw you."

It was a lie and she smelled it. "Hogshit."

"It's not."

"Well, it's a fucking half-truth, then! Taking down Hood, hiding your face, fighting your own fucking hoof? You knew damn well what you were doing. You did not want us to know you were back, that much is plain. What I want to know is why."

Jackal looked at her. "There is no easy answer for that."

"Why?!"

"Because I haven't killed him yet!"

Fetch did not need to ask who he meant. She lowered the katara.

Jackal took a breath. "I was just going to have to leave again, soon as Zirko got what he wanted."

"I was right." Fetch scoffed from her throat. "He summoned you all the way back here just to be his hunting dog."

"I thought it was the Betrayer Moon," Jackal said. "But when I reached Strava—"

"Stop. Right now I need to know if your loyalty is to the waddlers or this hoof."

"I'm a Bastard. You know that."

"I don't know shit right now!" She pointed hard at his face with her weapon. "You've been gone a long time, Jackal. There's a heap of questions and ignorance between us that needs to get sorted. One of which we are going to solve right damn now. If I allow you into camp so you can speak with the hoof you claim loyalty to, are you going to keep peace with Xhreka? Because I can promise you the True Bastards will protect her. And that's to say nothing of Oats."

"Fetch . . . Oats will always protect what he thinks to be small and vulnerable. Same as when we were children. Remember the rats? He hasn't changed. Grocer had to make sure Oats was away from the Kiln every time a sow had a new litter because he always took to the runt. This halfling is no different in his mind. Another harmless pet he needs to keep safe. But she's not harmless. Is she?"

"No," Fetch admitted. "But so far she's only harmed our enemies and we need all the allies we can get. We got something after us, Jackal, that you know nothing about. Makes the Sludge Man look like a garden slug."

"An *uq'huul*."

"Zirko told you. Then you know something of it. But not nearly all."

"Tell me."

"Later. For now I need to trust that you will not do anything without my command, Zirko be fucked."

"You can trust me."

Fetching squinted at him, wanting to take his word. "Let's go talk to the boys."

She started to turn, but he didn't move. There was a small, distracted twist to his mouth.

"What?"

"Your hair. It's Tine-cut."

"Wasn't to honor them. For Mead. He's dead. Dumb Door too."

Jackal's face fell. He nodded in grim acceptance. "I tracked you from Winsome. Found the grave at Batayat. Moved enough stones to see who it was. Didn't know about Door. Good mongrels, both of them."

Fetch ignored his sympathy. "We should get back."

"Fetch. One thing more. I didn't do this because Zirko wanted it done. I agreed because he said my hoof was in danger. This Xhreka may not have destroyed Winsome, but that does not mean he isn't right about her."

Fetch set her jaw. "Jack, at the moment, you and I have put this hoof in more danger than anyone. Think about that. I'll vouch for the halfling."

"Like I did for Crafty? We've been deceived by powerful allies before."

"That was your mistake," Fetch said, turning toward camp. "Never mine."

Hoodwink was still waiting where she left him, a pale statue in the moonlight. With the sun down, he did not need his cowl and his white skin seemed to glow. His eyes were fixed on Jackal leading his hog a few strides behind.

"Sorry about before, Hood," Jackal offered when he got close.

"It won't happen twice."

The three of them walked into the heart of camp. The villagers hardly took notice of Jackal's presence, too preoccupied with building fires and stamping out sparks of worry. The slops gawked some at the returned Bastard until Fetch told Lopo to tend Mean Old Man and sent the rest to stand their watches. As the hog was led away, Polecat came up grinning, gave a clap on Jackal's shoulder, and offered him back his scimitar.

"Hope there are no hard feelings about urging the boys to shaft you. But you were acting fucking loon-brained, brother."

"None," Jackal assured him, taking the sword.

Shed Snake and Culprit gave only nods in greeting. To them, Jackal was little more than a name and a reputation. As slops they knew his previous hog, Hearth, better than they knew the rider.

Oats stood beside Xhreka, near where the orphans were gathered around a small cook fire being seen to by Beryl and Thistle. The thrice stared at Jackal for a long moment before striding over.

"You sorcelled me," he accused.

"You punched my face," Jackal returned.

Oats scrutinized him. "Yeah, you're still pretty."

Jackal mirrored the look. "Did you always have a beard?"

The laughter came. Next the rough, back-slapping grapple that settled into a genuine embrace.

Fetch's chest tightened with envy. She wished it were so simple for her to return to the old affections, the newer passions. Perhaps it would have been possible if she wasn't chief. But . . .

Sluggard stepped up to stand beside her, cocked his chin at the reunited friends.

"Who's that?"

"Jackal," Fetching answered, glancing over. "One of our own. Been gone awhile."

"He and Oats backy?"

That forced a laugh from Fetch. "Maybe you can finally convince them."

Seeing Beryl, Jackal took a step, intent on another reunion, but Oats put a big hand around his arm, stopping him.

"Now ain't the time, brother," he rumbled. "Need to give some space there."

Jackal did not push the matter.

The way he and Oats now stood together, to Fetch's heart it was as if no one had ever been gone. Though now she saw Jackal in better light, and began to notice the changes in him. Not simply his foreign garb and sword, but the differences writ in his face, the way he moved. They were small, as if the world had etched him a bit with each day away from the Lots, honing him into something that could fit into any land. The perfect wanderer. She'd no idea where he had gone, but in his form was inscribed the story of myriad distant soils, leagues uncountable, and many dangers survived. He claimed to remain a Bastard, but she feared he'd ridden too far to return.

Time to find out.

Fetch took a half step forward. "True Bastards, gather up! We got some snakes to kill." She motioned to a cluster of rocks a short distance away from the camp. The boys began ambling over.

"Did you mean what you said?" Sluggard asked as she turned to follow. "About having a place in the hoof?"

"I did," Fetch replied, uncertain if she was lying. "Let's get you back in the saddle. Then we can talk about putting you up for a vote."

Sluggard gave a satisfied grin and a small wave that was both a show of gratitude and an acknowledgment that he could not follow.

The boys had thrust torches into the surrounding dirt to light their talk by the time she joined them.

Fetch began by having Jackal explain his foray into Dog Fall. Oats wasn't pleased at the idea of Xhreka's presence putting the hoof in peril, but he merely scowled and kept his mouth shut while Jackal finished. The thrice's displeasure spread to the rest of the hoof when they heard Jackal had yet to kill Crafty. Shed Snake and Culprit may not have been sworn members during the wizard's treachery, but they had fled the fiery destruction of the Kiln and survived the fall of the Claymaster.

Polecat rubbed at his sharp nose. "So . . . if Crafty's still alive, what the fuck you been doing?"

"Chasing him," Jackal replied. "Across half the world it seemed at times. His trail was nearly cold when I left, but I reckoned he would want to flee the Lots entirely. That meant either Hispartha or the eastern coast. I took a chance that he wouldn't go north, figuring he didn't have many allies left in Hispartha after his plans failed. I got lucky in Urci. The harbormaster remembered seeing him, said he took a ship bound for the Stripped Islands."

"Are the women there truly always naked?" Polecat asked, brightening.

"The men, too, I heard," Jackal replied mildly. "But I couldn't say. I doubted Crafty would have allowed his destination known unless it was a false trail. I sailed directly for Kyrneolis, from there to Traedria, where the gamble paid off. I nearly had him a few times, but he knew the cities far better than I did and had friends within the guild families. He slipped me and fled to Majeth. From there it was a chase east. Once I reached Ul-Kadim, I ceased to be the hunter. Crafty vanished into the courts of Tyrkania and I had to begin hiding from the knives of the Black Womb."

Culprit's brow creased. "Black Womb?"

"A cabal of sorcerers that Crafty both serves and commands," Jackal said.

Culprit remained confused. "Cabal?"

"They're like Crafty's hoof," Shed Snake told the younger rider. "Ah."

Jackal folded his arms. "They also employ assassins, princes, merchants, pirates, prostitutes, anyone they can buy or manipulate. That is to say nothing of the demons they bind to their service."

"And they sent all that after you?" Oats asked.

"They did," Jackal replied simply.

Polecat issued a low whistle. "So . . . with all that, and what we saw you do in Dog Fall, you're, what, a wizard too now?"

Jackal put on his reassuring grin. "No. I found I had to learn a few of the wizard's tricks if I wanted to have a chance of surviving the rest of them." The stares he received made the grin widen, but its edges now contained quivers of apprehension. "Brothers, it's me. Same Jackal as ever."

It was obvious from the twitches, scratches, and throat clearings, he was the only one who believed those words.

Shed Snake's fingernails raked absently down his scarred arm. "If you can't take Xhreka now, and you haven't killed Crafty, that mean you'll be leaving again?"

Jackal hesitated.

"It's not his decision," Fetch said, drawing all eyes to her. "And the answer is no. Crafty can wait. Jackal, we need you here in the Lots. Without a home, we got nowhere for a bird from Strava to come. The Betrayer Moon could rise and we would be caught unawares. But you'll know, won't you? You'll be pulled back to Strava."

"Yes," Jackal said.

"Then that's all the warning we'll get. You stay until then."

"Yes, chief."

Fetch took a steadying breath. "Boys, we got our people to look out for. They have to reach the Cradle. Nothing else matters. Set yourselves to it. Come morning your only concern is leading our people safely south. I don't want you to think about anything else until you smell saltwater. We'll be passing through the Skull Sowers' and the Tide's lots. If they agree to take us in, all the good, but we won't count on it. Tomb isn't given to generosity and Boar Lip's likely all out of charity for us. Plan on having to go all the way to the coast. Bastards, you got them to Batayat, you got them to Dog Fall. I need you to be the best damn riders in the Lots just one more time."

"Hells-damn fucking right," Polecat said.

"Can I offer an alternative?"

The entire hoof was taken off guard by Jackal's mildly voiced question. Intrigued, Fetching nodded.

"We ride east," he said. "Make for Urci and take a ship from there, sail to Mongrel's Cradle. Use the coast to reach the coast. Urci is closer by land and over easier ground. We just have to pass through the Stains' lot. Even with the walking, it's less than a week."

Urci was little more than a fishing village resting almost square in the middle of Ul-wundulas' eastern shore. Like most of the coast, it belonged to the Crown, but like all of their lands here, it was all but neglected.

"How do you know there will be a ship there to take us?" Fetch asked.

"Because the one that brought me is anchored there, waiting for my return."

He knew the admission would cause her pain. He was right, but it helped that it hurt him to give it voice.

"What do you think, brethren?" Fetch asked. "Any of you mongrels get seasick?"

"Wouldn't know," Shed Snake said.

Culprit rubbed the shaved half of his head. "Can hogs get on a boat?"

"Not on all of them," Jackal replied with a smile. "But this vessel has enough room on deck and in the hold for us, our barbarians, and our folk."

"Listen to this mongrel," Polecat muttered, nudging Snake. "Captain Jackal the Backy Seafarer."

Fetch chewed on it. A ship was safer, though it had never occurred to her. Why would it? The hoofs rode. They weren't fucking seamen. Still, if Jackal could put them on the waves, then their folk could be delivered far more swiftly to the Sons of Perdition. An easy decision.

She looked at Jackal. "Are you certain the captain of this ship of yours will agree to take all our folk?"

"He's a good man," Jackal replied. "You'll see."

Another moment's consideration and Fetch nodded with approval. "Reckon we're sailing, then. Hood, I need you to ride out now, scout a path for tomorrow. Be back by morning."

The pale mongrel slid away.

"The rest of us will stand watches. Go."

The hoof began to break away, but two remained behind.

Oats tilted his kerchiefed head at Jackal. "You need to tell him, Fetch."

"I don't."

"Then I'll tell him."

"No, you won't."

"No, he won't," Jackal agreed. "And no, you don't. But I wish you would." ⚹

He'd lowered the head wrapping of his desert garb, exposing all of his troubled face. He waited, fixed her with those damn eyes, encouraging without demanding. She almost gave in.

"It can wait for the sun to come up," Fetch told him, and turned away.

She checked the camp, made certain the orphans weren't frightened, the Winsome folk were as comfortable as possible, the slops were steady. It was only when she'd finished those duties that she realized Starling was gone. Fetch didn't bother asking if any had seen her slip away. All she could do was choose a direction, stare into the night, and silently wish the elf all the fortune she would need. And more.

Fetch placed herself in the middle of the watch rotation, paired with Culprit and Gosse, ordering them to the flanks of the camp, nearer the river, while she took the center. She patrolled a crescent between them, far enough out to prevent Womb Broom's hoofbeats from disturbing the sleepers, but close enough to see the light of the fires. At the apex of every circuit she pulled her hog to a stop and scoured the night-shrouded badlands for signs of threat.

What she feared most was the end of her watch.

The Claymaster's inner torments had destroyed the Grey Bastards. His thirst for vengeance against Hispartha brought Crafty into their midst, drove him to make a pact with the orcs, tore his hoof apart from within. She would not make the same mistake. She would not seize the Bastards in a death grip and drag them down when her own demons came baying. She hated the Claymaster, but hells fuck him, she understood him now too. The fear of showing weakness, of losing the confidence of the hoof, of thinking their voiced opinions eroded her leadership. The same impulses had weighed on the Claymaster. Fetch only wished it were as simple as knowing what he would have done and taking the opposite path, but the foul mongrel's mistakes were not so simply sifted.

Neither were her own.

There might have been another way. She wished for it, battered her brains to find it, but her watch ended without finding one. She ordered Gosse and Culprit to their bedrolls, told them she would rouse their replacements.

It was Xhreka she woke.

They exchanged no words, not even in whispers, understanding passing between their shadowed faces the moment the halfling opened her eye. They'd said all they needed after leaving the Sitting Young. Together, they crept from the camp, stealing off to Womb Broom, left waiting behind the same boulders where the hoof met. They had just mounted when Jackal stepped around the rocks.

Fetch shook her head, loosed a soundless laugh. "Time was, only Hoodwink could have caught me sneaking."

"Time was," Jackal said. "That's why you sent him to scout." His gaze shifted to Xhreka, remained placid as he spoke. "You don't have to run. You have nothing to fear from me."

"Don't fear you at all, cheekbones," Xhreka said. "Don't trust you at all either."

"Then trust me." Oats appeared behind Jackal.

Xhreka loosed a weary breath. "Idris . . ."

"I know this mongrel, Xhreka," the thrice said. "Knew him long before he was the Arm of Eat-A-Quim. And I got his word. You're safe. No one here will take you back to Strava."

"I know. Because I won't be here." The halfling held up a hand, halting Oats's next protest. "I'm going, Idris."

"You can't do this, Fetch," Jackal put in.

"I have to."

"Your people need you here."

"They need me far from here. It's for their sake I am leaving."

"Don't mean the two of you have to go alone," Oats said, setting his jaw. "Just let me saddle Ug."

"And what of our people, Oats?" Fetch asked. "You trying to sell me that you'd leave them alone in the badlands? You'd leave Thistle and the orphans? Beryl?"

The thrice's bearded face fell.

Jackal came to his rescue. "Then I'll go. Oats and Xhreka stay with the hoof. Fetch, I'll go with you."

"You don't even know what's happening here, Jack."

"Then tell me," he said, his voice gaining some heat.

"Fucking hells, this orc . . . he's hunting me. He wants *me*. Anyone, everyone near me is in danger. Do you fucking see? I'm not taking Xhreka with me to protect her from you, Jackal. She's coming to protect me from *him*."

Jackal took a step closer. "I'll protect you."

"The hells you will," Fetching said.

"I understand you don't trust me. I even understand why." Both lies, but Fetch let them go unchallenged. "But from what I've heard of this *uq'huul*, I have the best chance of keeping you safe."

It wasn't a boast. Jackal made the claim without passion, a calm truth. Hells, she wanted to allow him. The thought was a comfort. A fierce, hateful joy filled Fetching at the thought of having Jackal by her side when she faced Ruin. If there was one mongrel in all the Lots who could stand against that dread thick it was him. Fetch wanted to accept the offer, almost as much as she wanted to spit it back in his face. As her instincts went to war, Jackal went on.

"Let me come with you. I can help."

His voice remained even, but his gaze held the stirrings of a plea.

Fetch's conflicted feelings slaughtered each other. Sick of the temptation that clung to his every word, she gritted her teeth and loosed a harsh, aggravated breath.

"Don't you see? I don't need you." She pointed beyond him, to the camp. "They do! If you believe you're the greatest protection I could have, then you damn well can be the greatest protection for them. You want to right a wrong, start there! Because that is where I need you, Jackal. It's what you wanted, remember? You wanted to lead a hoof. There it is. See if you can keep them alive. I promise it'll be a damn sight tougher than you ever imagined."

"I'm not the chief of the True Bastards. You are."

"And as chief, I am ordering you to do this. Stay with our hoof, prove you're still one of us, fix your mistake. Our folk were safe. You robbed them of that when you came back. Make it right! Lead them to the Sons' lot. Talk to Father. And don't hesitate to accept what he offers you."

Jackal's eyes narrowed. "What will he offer me?"

"The same thing I'm entrusting to you. A hoof."

Jackal took a deep breath, and for the first time his calm countenance cracked, revealing the old, jagged defiance. He wrestled with it, eyes smoldering, jaw bulging. Fetch had seen him fight his nature many times. It rarely lost. She steeled herself against the fight that was brewing.

"I will stay," he said, swallowing the rebellion. "I will see our folk to the Cradle. And when that is done, I am coming to find you. Fuck Father and his offers."

Xhreka clicked her tongue, craned around to look at Fetch. "He's no Hoodwink. But I'm starting to see it."

Fetch had to smile. "Me too."

Womb Broom snorted and shook his head as Oats approached.

"Shut it, pig," the big mongrel said. He leaned to embrace Fetch and Xhreka in turns. "See you both in a small while."

As he stepped away, Jackal was there. He reached out and Fetch allowed him to grasp the back of her neck. Their foreheads met.

"Stay alive," he whispered.

"Talking's a waste of your damn lips."

And he kissed her.

It was strange after so long, after so much misery. Strange and rejuvenating. She broke it off long before she wanted to, pushed him away.

Fetch turned her hog and left all she loved to the embrace of shadow.

THIRTY-EIGHT

—

THE RABBIT SIZZLED on the spit. Fetch gave a final turn and began to lift it away from the fire.

"Not yet."

It was the fourth time Xhreka had thwarted Fetch's impatience.

"It's going to be dry," she complained, resetting the spit.

"That's hunger speaking."

"Damn well is," Fetch muttered.

She had shot the rabbit near dawn while still in the saddle and on the move. Her stockbow was loaded with a broadhead, making a mess of the meat, but it was better than nothing. Besides, she didn't have any blunts or game points in her quiver. She'd chosen not to stop immediately; they needed to gain some more distance. So she kept her hog's ass facing the rising sun until it was well above the horizon. Now she squatted by the fire, willing the rabbit to cook faster.

"Enough," Fetch declared, taking up the spit once more. "We're eating."

She began portioning the game with her knife.

"Maybe if you'd taken a moment to take some proper meat before we rode off, you wouldn't be so itching to tear into this *undercooked* coney," the halfling said.

"Wasn't about to take any supplies from my people, Xhreka."

"Not the meat I meant, mongrel girl."

Fetching looked over the fire to find a single eye twinkling at her.

"Hells," she grunted through a mouthful. "Only permitted that kiss so he'd be forced to endure the pain of pregnant cods all night."

"If you say so."

"Oh, fuck my ass!" Fetching shot to her feet and pointed at the tiresome halfling with a rabbit leg. "If I'd known you were going to be a waist-high cunt about it, I'd have left the rabbit until it was charred."

Xhreka looked up, brow crinkled. "Aren't all cunts about waist-high?"

"So you're a jester now?"

"You'd rather I was angry, like you?"

"Angry is how I greet the days, waddler."

"Truly? Appears to me you greet them hungry." Xhreka took a slow, purposeful bite. "Perhaps I should finish this quicker. Before you snatch it from my hands with your teeth. Like a bitch."

Fetch felt a smile growing. "Why, you little . . ."

Xhreka put a hand to her ear, leaned forward a bit. "Little . . . what? You've used 'waddler.' That all you got?"

"Yes," Fetch said, shaking her head in defeat. "My quiver of half-ling insults is empty."

Xhreka went back to her food. "Shame. 'Little black shit' is my favorite."

Fetch resumed her squat.

The morning wind was mild, but they rested on the bald plain so the fire was bullied by every gust, smoking and sputtering. For long moments, the thumping gasps of the flames were broken only by the sounds of grease being sucked from bones and fingers.

"Why did you come with me, Xhreka?" Fetch muttered through a fresh mouthful. "I'm grateful, but . . . you could go your own way. No need to face this with me."

The small woman tossed a stripped bone into the fire. She picked some gristle from her teeth before answering. "Spent years running and hiding from my kin. Know well the turmoil of being hunted by a single-minded man that wields great power. Can't do much about that. At least, not without causing a mountain of destruction to fall on those that don't deserve it. No need for you to suffer the same if it can be helped, if *I* can help. Letting Belico off his chain, at last, giving us both a chance to unleash some of this wrath, I'll take it. Even if it's not pointed in Zirko's direction."

Fetch took a breath.

"And that's all I'm going to say on it," Xhreka told her, looking sharply over her meat.

Fetch held up a hand in acceptance. "Can you destroy him? Ruin?"

"Ever tried to hold a hot coal in your mouth? No, of course not, because that's a half-wit thing to do. But imagine you did. How long could you endure? Now imagine that instead of your mouth, it was your eye socket, and instead of a hot coal it was an earthquake. In your skull." The halfling's eye pierced Fetch. "Got no problem killing this orc for you. You been good to me. But I'll need everything I can muster to do it. I won't make you any promises."

"Understood."

"Now I got a question for you, hoof chief. Why are you here? Why are you not taking ship with that smolder-eyed mongrel who just spent a night walking tender on account of his desire for you? Ain't no orc can follow you across the Deluged to points east. There's a stretch more world than Ul-wundulas out there and your Jackal has seen a good portion. The pair of you could have left all this, never looked back."

"No, we couldn't."

"No. *You* couldn't."

"We both swore the same oath, Xhreka."

"Girl, if I were asked, I would say you're keeping that oath because you don't know nothing else. Same can't be said of your man."

The halfling was only echoing Fetch's own fears, but inner worry and voiced wisdom were a different breed of pain. "Reckon it's a good thing I didn't ask you, then."

Xhreka gave a little smile. "Reckon so."

"Besides, you're the same breed of fool." Fetch pointed west. "Strava is less than four days' ride that way. And yet here you are, daring Zirko to come find you. Last I heard, ships can still bear the weight of a halfling."

Xhreka grew intensely still, save for one finger giving her eye patch a single tap. "You have any notion how far away I was when I found this? You never heard the name of that land, Lot-born pup. It was the Master Slave that brought us back here after I liberated him from centuries of dark decay. And believe me, he pitches a tantrum to wake all the hells if I try to leave. *When* I try to leave. I'd be suffering the cold of Calmaris or the demon warlords of the Dragonfly Islands this very moment rather than hide in the worst holes in Ulwundulas if I could. But Belico won't allow it. So don't speak to something that reveals you for an ignorant."

It was Fetch's turn to employ a twinkling stare. "Who's angry now?"

"Belico's Cock!" Xhreka blew out an astounded breath. "Idris told me you like your petty reckonings."

"Guilty," Fetch admitted. "Came by them honest, coming up with him and Jack."

"I heard plenty enough of the stories to know that's true."

"Seems he kept no secrets. Shame you had to."

Xhreka sobered. "Well, I don't speak of it. But if I did . . . it'd have been a waste. Rather have heard him talk than till the muck of my life."

"You love him." It wasn't a question.

There was a pause, but the halfling was considering her words rather than stalling.

"I do," she said, at last. "But it's not like what you got with your man. And it ain't how I want that pale mongrel to just let me do whatever I'd like. With Idris . . ."

"What?" Fetch coaxed, curious.

"I've never seen someone so equipped to survive these lands. Big as a thick, near as strong. I've seen him fight. Seen him kill. Washed him when he was covered in the blood he spilled more times than is healthy to count. He's more orc than man; savagery is his birthright.

But he never reveled in it, never got drunk on the death or lusted for more. He would talk of you or Jackal. Both, most times. Tell me stories of your youth. Of raising Ugfuck from a runt. He would tell me of his mother. Here he was, slaying giants with his bare hands in a pit while hundreds of ravening men bellowed his glory. And after? He would speak to me of the joy of playing games with a simple-minded stableboy or a mongrel orphan riddled with plague sores. I've seen all manner of men in this life, but I'd never seen that. I don't even have a name for it. And every time I cleaned the gore from his face I was terrified whatever it was would be wiped away too. I love him because it never did. Because he never let it. I love him because he gives me hope that these badlands don't turn us all into beasts gnashing and clawing to survive."

"Reckon you hate me for putting him in that pit."

Xhreka dismissed that with a hum. "Maybe I would have. But that's the other thing about Idris. It's damn near impossible not to love what he does. Though Ugfuck tests that a bit."

Fetch smiled an agreement, allowed the wind and fire to argue for a span.

"Do you want to know the real reason I didn't drag Jackal into a shadowy spot and strip him to the skin?"

Xhreka's face lit with interest.

"Because right now, I can smell my own crotch."

Standing, Fetch put some distance between her nostrils and the offense that was between her legs as Xhreka burst into laughter.

"That's what swearing an oath to live in the saddle will get you," the halfling guffawed.

Fetch added her own laughter, shook her head ruefully.

Hobbled a few strides away, Womb Broom looked at their mirth and snorted with annoyance.

Soon, having cowed the fire, the wind's voice was all that remained.

Xhreka surveyed the badlands spread in every direction. She gave a sniff. "You certain this is where you want to be?"

Fetch nodded, rotating slowly in place. "I want to see him coming."

"And then?"

"Then it ends. No matter what, it ends."

And so they waited, watchful, the day tense and tedious as it drew on. Night fell and still Fetch stood watch, moon and stars providing enough for her vision. The heavens made their slow progress across the sky. Xhreka dozed. Fetch refused. But it was not Ruin that finally appeared on a horizon purpling with the coming dawn. Nor his dogs. Fetching roused Xhreka with a short, sharp whistle.

The halfling rose, her single eye narrowing. "Is that . . . ?"

"Yes," Fetch replied, raising her loaded thrum.

It was a harrow stag, and the elf upon its back was familiar.

N'keesos.

The young warrior's broken arm remained slung, causing him to ride with no weapon in hand. Still, Fetch took aim.

"That's far enough!"

She didn't know if he spoke Hisparthan, didn't care. A bolt in his mount's neck would be her translator if he didn't heed.

N'keesos pulled the stag to a halt, half turned the animal, and pointed back the way he'd come. His painted face was etched with the haunting glow of his stag's antlers.

"*Kakío Wa'supá.*"

Fetch no longer possessed the mystical gift of the Tine language, but she recognized the name of the elf that bestowed it to her.

Woeful Starling.

N'keesos spoke again.

"You get that?" Fetch asked Xhreka without taking her eyes, or her aim, from the stag.

"Not me, but Belico did. He's telling me the rustskin wants us to follow him. That his father has Starling."

"Shit."

"Doesn't have to be our problem," the halfling offered.

"She helped me. More than once. So, yes, it does."

By the time she and Xhreka were mounted, N'keesos was riding away. They followed him to the southwest. The ride was not long. Starling had been on foot. She hadn't made it far. And there had been nowhere to hide.

Ahead, the plain was interrupted only by folds of blanched dust and lonely, stubborn stands of scrub. Starling stood in the ghostly, parched vastness screaming at Ghost Last Sung. He sat his stag above her, silent and pitiless. Spying Fetch's approach, Starling tried to come to her, but Ghost Last Sung's war lance thrust out to block her path. Yet he could not hinder her cries.

"Leave here!" Starling entreated. "You must go!"

Once again in the she-elf's presence, the Tine tongue blossomed in Fetch's mind.

"Let her go," she told Ghost Last Sung, pulling Womb to a halt. The older elf was a javelin toss distant, his son half that distance off to the right. "Keep your eye on N'keesos," Fetch whispered to Xhreka sitting before her in the saddle.

"This hog twixt our legs won't take kindly to Belico shouting this close," the halfling muttered back. "Neither will that pregnant elf."

Fuck.

Fetch turned her stockbow on N'keesos, but kept her words trained on his father. "I won't play this game with you, elf. Release Starling. Let her walk to me. Or I will put this bolt through your son's eye."

Neither warrior reacted to the threat. Their faces were stone. Ghost Last Sung's response was ice.

"You cannot cause me further pain. You cannot harm Blood Crow more than he has suffered."

"A broken arm isn't death," Fetch replied.

"Death is better than shame," Ghost Last Sung declared. "Death is better than banishment and dishonor."

"You chose that path," Starling said.

"For you fear to walk upon it!" The older Tine's outburst caused his stag to shy, but he mastered the animal with no effort and returned his gaze to Fetching. "This aberration must not continue to curse my family."

Starling continued her pleas. "Ride away, Fetching!"

"I can't do that." Fetch signaled for Xhreka to dismount with a nudge, helped the halfling from the saddle before climbing down from the hog's back herself. No doubt Womb would bolt at the sound of Belico, but at least he wouldn't be harmed. Or harm them. That was one impediment gone. Now Fetch just needed to get Starling clear. Na'hak and N'keesos had left Dog Fall before Jackal arrived, leaving them unaware of Xhreka's power. They were only wary of Fetching, so she kept their attention fixed by walking forward, stockbow lowered.

"You told the Sitting Young our lives were woven," she said to Starling. "Can't believe that and ask me to abandon you. And I'm not in the habit of leaving a woman and her unborn child to be killed."

"That is no child," Ghost Last Sung said. "You understand nothing." Removing his lance from Starling's path he gazed down at her. "Do what you must."

Fetch had halved the distance between Womb Broom and the stag. She was close enough now to see the tears of Ghost Last Sung's war paint. Starling walked forward and met her the rest of the way.

"You must go," she hissed. "Now!"

"We're leaving together."

"No. That cannot be. Ride away! They will not hurt me. You must not stay! Please!"

Starling's face was desperate, nearing panic.

Ghost Last Sung eclipsed her words with his commanding voice. "End this!"

Starling spun to face him. "I will not!"

"You have been given another chance and still you refuse to cleanse our shame!"

The fury in the aging warrior's face caused Fetch to step in front of Starling. "The shame is yours, elf. You say I understand nothing, but I hear you speak of family. You think I can't see a father renouncing his daughter. The shame is yours."

Ghost Last Sung's eyes widened, the hard set of his jaw going slack.

"Daughter?" he said, his glare moving to Starling. "You have hidden the truth."

The accusation was edged, affronted.

Fetch felt Starling grasp her arm. "Ride away."

"She is no more daughter to me than you," Ghost Last Sung said.

The she-elf's grip tightened. "Do not listen."

"Woeful Starling lacks the courage, so I shall tell you."

"Keep silent, Na'hak!"

Ghost Last Sung was deaf to Starling. "The woman you think to save is—"

"Do not heed him, Fetching!"

Releasing her, Starling snatched a handful of dirt from the ground, spat into her palm, and cast the earth to the wind.

"—*m'hun nahi N'kees'elo da wiyela.*"

Ghost Last Sung's words no longer held meaning. Robbed of understanding, Fetch cast a look at Starling, but the elf would not meet her eyes, so she turned to Xhreka.

"The fuck did he say?"

The halfling stood bemused.

"Xhreka!"

"He . . . he said—"

She was cut off by Ghost Last Sung's deep tones speaking Hisparthan. "I say. Starling"—he pointed at Blood Crow with his lance—"N'keesos's mother. And"—the lance moved to Fetching—"yours."

When his halting words faded, the night was silent.

Fetch would have chased the quiet off with her laughter, but Starling's face strangled the mockery in her throat.

All desperation was gone. The she-elf's mouth was drawn tight, a bulwark against an outcry of pain. Her eyes were bright, wet, incensed, brows above knit close. She shook. A few hissed words were flung at Ghost Last Sung. The Tine tongue was once again a mystery, but the ire was evident. It was a curse. And an admission.

Fetch felt the madness the world had tried to plant over the last months begin to sprout as Starling's countenance added affirmation to the claim. The weight of pregnancy aside, she looked no older than Fetching. Hells, the rare times she smiled she appeared younger.

Seizing Starling by the shoulders, Fetch forced the elf to look at her. "She died. My mother died. She died! Beryl fucking buried her!"

Tears crawled down Starling's cheeks, slow as the erosion of her composure.

"And that body remains under the dust," she said, mouth thick with grief. "The one standing before you belonged to a poor daughter of my tribe taken by illness in Dog Fall."

Fetch's grip tightened, her hold all that kept her from falling as the world upended. "I don't . . . I don't understand."

Starling nearly succumbed to grief, the silent tears threatening to break her. She buried them in a hole of deep regret, covered them with a mound of defeat. Slowly, she reached up and ran a trembling thumb gently across Fetch's lips. When she spoke, the language of the Tines flowed from her tongue and it fell upon Fetch's ears as if she'd been born to it.

"I am Returned. A rare happening among my people, even at our height, but a mystery my tribe yet honors."

Fetch had heard the council call Starling such, but did not recognize they spoke a title of reverence. Honored. And feared.

"How?"

"I cannot say. In the beginning I could not discern the visions ever in my mind from the terror of the world before my eyes. There was life and memory of life, currents in the same stream, both cold and inescapable. I lived a forced reflection, my new steps tracing the path of the old. I wandered from the land of my tribe as before, but my journey was impeded for I was taken by cavaleros, sold, and imprisoned in a broken tower by the man Corigari. And there, again, I survived the violations of orcs."

Fetch felt ill at the thought of such suffering twice endured. And ill at the realizations born from the elf's recounting. The first time she'd seen this girl, she was filthy, lying unconscious upon the bog. Jackal and Crafty had saved her from the Sludge Man's hut, all three about to be food for a rokh when Fetch and Oats finally caught up. They'd all had to flee the Sludge Man. Starling awoke during the chase when Crafty had tried to pass her from his mount to . . . Fetch's.

"You've known," she said, fighting to look the elf in the eye. "You've known since that first day."

"I knew nothing," Starling replied, the denial a plea for absolution. "Nothing of speech, nothing of myself. Nothing of you. It was a birth and I was a babe."

"When then?" Fetch nearly screamed the question, uncertain why it mattered, but driven to know.

"It was not until Jackal bore me from the fortress and Warbler set me free that I began to sift the truth of my existence. Even then, I thought myself mad."

"But the Tines didn't," Fetch declared. "They obeyed when you asked them to ride to the Grey Bastards' aid. And again with the Sitting Young."

"The path of the Returned is one of redress. The Seamless Memory has long believed we live again to mend the grievous wrongs from before the grave. The family of the dead woman knew I was not her, though I wore her face and burial blanket. Yet it is not they who are honor-bound to aid the Returned, but the family from the life once lived." Starling raised her reddened eyes to Ghost Last Sung. "My husband. And our son."

Fetch found Blood Crow's face averted.

"Both were slow to accept," Starling said. "And so I wandered from Dog Fall alone, ignorant and near witless, guided by nothing but fate's hand."

"We searched for you," Ghost Last Sung said.

Blood Crow's head snapped up. "*I* searched."

His father shot him a look that sent his eyes back to the dirt. Looking upon the chastened warrior now, Fetch recalled Roundth's report of a lone Tine stag rider on the Grey Bastards' lot shortly after Starling came to the Kiln.

"I rode to war at your insistence," Ghost Last Sung told Starling. "I sent my brave-sworn against the orcs to save your aberration and her tribe. You claim I was slow to my duty when you continue to refuse yours. You have hidden and fled and schemed to avoid the path you must take."

"Tell me, my lost love," Starling replied. "Can you recount the reasons for your creation? Did you scheme prior to your birth? Awareness of life came to me a second time the same as it did the first, in a prolonged instant. I did not choose this. I do not know how it was done. And I do not know why."

Ghost Last Sung pointed at Fetching with a fury. "To mend the mistake of her! The orcs despoiled you with their Filth and you shamed us by fleeing Akis'naqam."

"For I sought a better way!" Starling declared. "I journeyed and suffered, alone, to find a way to prevent a Ruin Made Flesh and to live. I . . . thought I succeeded. The Selfless Devourer spared me when I finally placed myself before her. The Sitting Young judged I could remain if my blood kin would accept me. You refused, husband! You cast me out to deliver and die in the care of a half-orc tribe."

"A mistake," Ghost Last Sung said. "Yours. You are Returned to set it right. Cease running, my wayward wife. End this."

The older warrior's disdainful eyes drifted to Starling's belly.

Starling encircled her middle in protective arms. "I will not."

"What is it?" Fetch demanded.

"It is . . . you," Starling replied. "An echo of you. As with all in this second life, it runs in conjunction to the first. When I awoke in this body, a part of you returned to me. Both of you."

"Both?" Ghost Last Sung said, his stag shifting in response to his agitation. "Why do you speak such?"

Xhreka's taut voice answered. "You're about to find out."

Fetch followed the halfling's westward gaze. "Fuck."

A score of low, loping shadows sped across the plain. There was no sign of their master, but he wouldn't be far behind.

The dogs laughed.

And Starling cried out, staggering as she clutched her belly.

Fetch caught her as she crumpled. "What is—"

"Get. *Away.*" Starling told her, face contorted with pain. She shoved Fetch with enough strength to push her over into the dust.

"We only got moments, mongrel girl!" Xhreka warned.

Scrambling to her feet, Fetch shouted at Ghost Last Sung. "You need to get Starling out of here!"

If the elf heard he gave no sign. Shrieking a war cry he kicked his stag and charged the oncoming pack.

Fetch turned to his son. "N'keesos!"

The younger warrior's eyes snapped from Ghost Last Sung to Starling, torn between the father riding into the maws of the pack and the mother writhing in agony upon the dirt. Confused and troubled, he was trapped by indecision.

"Shit!" Fetch gnashed her teeth. "Xhreka, be ready!"

"With that point-ear in the wa—"

The halfling had turned her head to speak. She didn't see the dog coming.

Fetch did. Too late.

Too late to raise her stockbow. Too late to do anything but realize the others had been a distraction, to keep the attention away from this lone beast sent in to pounce on the most dangerous quarry from the flank.

The hyena slammed Xhreka to the ground, seized her arm in its jaws, and took off. The halfling was dragged, bouncing on the hard-packed earth, limp as a child's doll. Fetch snatched her stockbow up, sighted. Before she could pull the tickler, a wave of sound lashed the dog, bowled it over. Xhreka tumbled free. The dog was rolling back to its feet, but N'keesos rode his stag between the beast and its prey, a song-club in his good hand, guiding his mount with nothing but his legs. Swinging his weapon in downward arcs, he chased the devil off with whipping shrieks.

Fetch sprinted to Xhreka's side. Her head must have struck a rock. She was unconscious, hair sticky with blood. But she was breathing.

"My father," N'keesos said.

Fetch looked up. Nodded. "Go."

As his stag sped away to aid Ghost Last Sung, Fetch scanned the horizon for any more skulking dogs. And that's when she saw them.

The sun was rising upon the plain. Against its glare rode silhouettes Fetch would have known by the drumming of their hoofbeats alone.

Her True Bastards.

THIRTY-NINE

SHE DIDN'T KNOW HOW they were here. They weren't supposed to be. But she knew why. They'd come for her. Her heart should have soared, yet it felt nothing but dread for their lives. They could not save her. Not from this. She wasn't certain she could save them.

Turning, she saw Ghost Last Sung fighting amidst the pack. His harrow stag darted and bounded through the snapping press, antlers aglow as it dipped its great head to sweep dogs aside. The elf's war lance was never still, and the devils within its reach yelped as the keen blade speared their hides. None were slain.

N'keesos was upon them now, his club scattering the pack with its clamorous assault. The magic of that weapon had felled the Bastards, and Fetch felt a kindling hope as the hyenas were tossed and buffeted by its power. But there were too many. Forced to keep nearly twenty at bay, N'keesos could not focus the song on any one beast long enough. Yet neither could the dogs overwhelm the Tines. As if sensing the futility of bringing the elves down, the pack broke away.

And came for Fetching.

Seventeen dogs ran full-pelt, spread out and kicking dust. Fetch sighted, tracked one on the far edge, and loosed. The bolt struck its neck, dropping the beast. Fetching cursed as it twitched, rolled, and regained its feet, surging forward once more to rejoin its devilish brethren. She locked the string back, set a bolt, raised, loosed. Another dog fell. Didn't stay down. She was only stalling them, but it was all she could do. A chance for one more shot and then they would be upon her.

Lock. Set. Raise. Loose.

Her last bolt was joined by three others. Four dogs tumbled. Hooves thundered, shaking the ground as Mean Old Man and Ugfuck rushed past, Jackal and Oats upon their backs. With them was Hoodwink on his nameless barbarian. Her best, her deadliest. Behind them came Polecat and Shed Snake. Culprit. And Incus, riding Big Pox. They rode full into the jaws of the converging pack, hurling javelins, their hogs goring and sweeping with their tusks. One hyena shrieked as Oats thrust a javelin straight through its middle, pinning it to the earth. Hood had drawn his tulwar and sent reaping strokes in every direction.

Fetch stood and cast a look at Starling as she reloaded. The bulge of the elf's belly was thrust skyward atop an arching spine, cries of agony lifting higher.

"Starling! I need to know what's happening!"

The only response was a tortured scream.

Fetch put another bolt in a dog. None were staying down long. Na'hak and N'keesos rejoined the struggle. Together, hog and stag riders caused the pack to scatter. It was no victory. Only the dog Oats had impaled could not rise, though it kicked and hollered. Thrumbolts and javelins stuck out from every one of the beasts' bodies, yet none were slowed.

The Bastards knew better than to linger and rode back to where Fetch stood over the fallen Xhreka.

Oats jumped from Ugfuck before the lumbering pig had fully stopped and hit his knees beside the halfling. The rest remained ahog, forming a protective ring. Fetch saw bite wounds on Polecat's hog and Ugfuck, but otherwise the hoof was hale.

"Good to see you ignored my fucking orders, Jack," Fetch said.

"Not me," he replied, keeping one eye on the pack. "I told them what you wanted. These hard-nosed mongrels voted me down."

"Our place is here with you, chief," Shed Snake said.

"Where the fuck are our people?" she demanded.

"Safe in Thricehold," Shed Snake replied.

"*Thricehold?*"

Polecat grunted an affirmative. "Bit of a tale."

"I suppose there's also a tale as to why you brought a damn slop?" Fetch exclaimed, pointing at Incus.

Polecat clicked his tongue. "No. None of us wanted to tell her she couldn't come."

"You said if I ever held back again, I would be out," Incus said in her toneless voice.

"Not what I meant!"

The thrice's shaggy head tilted slightly. "Must have misheard."

Culprit laughed. "Oh, shit! I taught her that one!" He winced as Starling's wails reached a fresh height. "What's going on there, chief?"

"The fuck does it look like, half-wit?" Shed Snake said.

Fetch knew what it looked like. She still didn't know what it was. "We need to get her out of here."

"No time," Hoodwink said.

Fetch looked through the ring of barbarians. The pack was regrouping.

"These beasts are corrupted by Filth." Ghost Last Sung's grim face thrust blame at Fetching. "This fight cannot be won."

Jackal hummed appreciatively. "You said they were devils. I know a few ways to kill devils." He slid from the saddle. "You all get going. I'll handle this."

"On foot?" Polecat called out.

"Don't want my hog getting hurt," Jackal replied without turning.

"Is he . . . sauntering?" Shed Snake asked.

Polecat made a noise in his throat. "Fucking Jackal."

Fetch did not stop him—these creatures needed killing—neither did she get on her hog. She would not run from this. Nor would her brothers. They'd made that known.

Oats had Xhreka's head cradled in his huge hands.

"How is she?" Fetch asked.

All she received in response was a shake of the head.

Starling continued to suffer. Fetch ached to help her, but knew she would be rebuked.

"Any of you know anything about birthing . . . babies?"

"Piglets," Shed Snake offered.

"We all know how to do that," Culprit told him. "*Half-wit.*"

"Can't be much different," Snake countered.

"It is." Hoodwink slid from the saddle. The hoof watched, un-blinking, as the pale killer knelt before Starling. "I have her."

"I ain't even gonna ponder that one," Polecat muttered.

Out in the plain, Jackal stood, sword sheathed, thrum slung. The dark cloth of his desert robes stirred in the wind. The pack sur-rounded him, yowling but reluctant to attack. They padded about, sniffing and baring their teeth in turns.

"The hells are they doing?" Culprit asked, his voiced hushed. "They afraid?"

"No," Fetch said, guts turning frigid.

They were waiting.

Beyond raced the frightening bulk of Ruin.

"Bastards, stay here!" Fetch shouted. "Protect Xhreka! Protect Starling!" She didn't wait, she didn't mount. She ran, matching Ruin step for step. They reached opposing edges of the encircling pack at the same moment. The dogs allowed him to pass. Not her. Jumping and biting, they blocked her path as Ruin charged and Jackal darted to meet him, sword leaving its scabbard. Fetch itched to draw steel, to fight her way to Jackal's side, but the message in the low, warning growls of the hyenas was clear.

Do not interfere.

If she broke through, her brethren would follow. And die. She could only watch. And place her faith in the most brazen mongrel ever to ride the Lots.

Jackal ducked a blow that would have removed his head, danced back, sidestepped another of Ruin's terrifying fists, and cut across the orc's ribs with his Tyrkanian blade. He may as well have sliced a fortress wall. Ruin snatched at him, but Jackal twisted away, chopped down on the offending arm. This time, his blade bit. Fetch felt a tingle of triumph as dark blood spurted from the cut.

Hells, he can be hurt.

But Ruin gave no sign he felt any pain. He swiped with the dripping arm, no doubt could have felled a tree, but again, Jackal slipped from harm. Ruin was larger, stronger, faster, his reach greater, his savagery unmatched, and still his foe remained untouched. Jackal moved with a spare grace Fetch had never seen in him before. Ever a skilled fighter, he was now honed into something sharper, more precise. And yet, the old Bastard tricks were there too.

He sent a flurry of whirling cuts at the *uq'huul*'s face, and when Ruin shielded himself with his forearms, Jackal booted him brutally in the cods. It was a baiting strike. Ruin's massive arms made a sweeping grab. Jackal hopped back, forcing the brute to overextend. Spinning, Jackal put his entire body into a crosscut that smote the side of the thick's skull. The blade rebounded off the bone, battering Ruin's head. He stumbled, had to place a hand upon the ground to keep from falling. Jackal did not waste the opening. He rushed his staggered opponent, leapt, placed a boot on the brute's broad shoulder, and used it to vault above him. Jackal hung in the air, twisting as he reversed the grip on his sword. Stabbing downward as he fell, using all the strength of his arms and the force of his descent, he drove half the curved blade's length into the meat of Ruin's shoulder next to his neck. Forced to his knees, Ruin gagged, vomited blood. Jackal held fast to the sword, tried to twist the blade, plunge it deeper, but Ruin threw an arm back, grasping, forcing him to jump clear.

It was a wound that would have slain any orc. And yet, Ruin stood.

Inured to his dread vitality, Fetch did not feel any surprise. Not even when he reached up and began to slide the sword from his body. Jackal was not so benumbed. He had sensed victory. Seeing it flee left him standing momentarily rooted.

"Jack, get mov——!"

Ruin pulled the sword free, whirled, and flung. The blade flew straight as a spear, ripped into Jackal's chest, and punched him off his feet. He landed on his back in the dust. His legs kicked feebly for a moment, a constricted groan escaped his lips, and he shuddered to stillness.

Shock's icy hands twisted around Fetch's spine. A scream froze in her windpipe, yet Jackal's name still smote the air, borne on the stricken voice of Oats. Tears boiled in Fetch's eyes before they could fall. Fury filled her muscles, but her limbs refused to move.

Ruin gave an aggravated grunt and jerked his head. Cackling, the pack darted to her fallen lover, eclipsed him with their loathsome bodies, and began to feed.

Everything holding Fetch snapped.

Drawing the kataras, she rushed the roiling heap of dogs. The pack turned on her. She punched one through the eye as it lunged, driving the dagger's entire blade into its head. Powerful jaws closed around her calf, fangs driving through the leather of her boot to pierce flesh. She gnashed her teeth against the pain as the latched cur pulled her leg back until she lost balance and fell. Her vision shrank to a wall of hideous muzzles, leering teeth, round ears, and black eyes. She rose to a crouch, slashed out with her blades, but could not hope to hold them all at bay. Her wrist was seized by a sudden constriction and she was jerked backward, dragged out of the stinking mass. She ate dust for a short span and the pulling ceased. A lasso was about her wrist, slackening, Polecat at the other end, jumping from the saddle.

"Chief, we have to go!" he cried, hauling her to her feet.

Fetch shoved him. "Get off! Jackal!"

"You can't help him. He's fucking gone! Chief!"

She thrashed against his continued grapple.

"Chief, dammit, look! You want Jackal to be the last? Or the first?"

Polecat managed to swing her around. A stone's throw away, Oats was enraged. Culprit and Shed Snake had his arms, straining to keep him from rushing Ruin. They'd never have held him were it not for Incus grabbing him from behind. Still, Oats was crawling forward, screaming to snuff the sun.

"We have to ride! Now!" Polecat insisted.

None were impeding the Tines. Na'hak and N'keesos kicked their stags forward, loosing their war cries. The elder warrior led, the blade of his lance now sizzling with the same pale light held trapped within the stone of the son's raised club. Ghost Last Sung threw and the lance shrieked in flight. Ruin lurched as the weapon sank deep into his chest. The lance began to hum, the haft vibrating. Snarling, Ruin reached to remove it from his flesh, but the lance burst in a storm of eldritch light, sending him reeling. Ghost Last Sung peeled away as N'keesos charged through the hanging azure vapors left behind, song club whirling above his head. His stag lowered its head as it closed on the injured monster.

Ruin caught the antlers. A sickening crunch burst from the animal as he twisted its head fully around. Keeping hold of the twitching beast, Ruin spun in a circle, throwing N'keesos off and hurling the stag's corpse into Na'hak's animal. The elder Tine vanished beneath the fallen, kicking bodies of the stags. N'keesos had landed hard upon his injured arm, but was still struggling to rise, gasps of pain issuing from between his clenched teeth.

Slowly, Ruin approached him, intent on the kill.

Polecat tugged at Fetch's arm. "Chief!"

He was right.

She broke loose.

Enough.

She threw the kataras down.

No more would die for her.

She ran.

Straight at Ruin, snatching up Blood Crow's fallen club.

Fetch dove, shouldered one hated brother away from the other. Ruin turned just as she collided, hitting him with her entire body. She launched the club into his gut, felt the impact of the sound wave. Her strength surged. Punched across the jaw, she kept coming, power growing with every blow given or received. She could hear herself grunting, snarling, every breath a defiance of her foe's might, a war drum for her own. She pushed forward, digging at a mountain.

Ruin fought back, heedless as a rockslide. His fists were nearly the size of her head and they sought to shatter it. Fetch ducked, came up club swinging. The monstrous *uq'huul* caught the blows on his arms, swatted the club from her hand. A punch took her across the face, the next in the gut, doubling her over his massive fist. Bloody spittle flew from her lips and spattered up his arm. Retching on a throat full of bile, she waded back in, slipped what she could, weathered what she could not, but keeping herself from harm was an instinct burned away by the need to cause harm. She sprung back each time he struck her, a steel blade standing against a hill of solid iron. Weaving beneath a propelling arm, Fetch snatched the limb, yanked, sent Ruin stumbling forward, and brought her boot down on the side of his knee. Bones should have snapped, but the brute's leg only buckled. He flung an elbow, caught her ribs as she scrambled onto his back. He stood, tried to throw her off, but she clung to the bones in his flesh with her hands, her teeth. She got an arm around his throat, dug the fingers of her other hand into the sword wound Jackal inflicted. And still Ruin did not cry out.

He pried her arm from his throat, used it to swing her over his head, and chopped her body into the ground. Hard earth hammered Fetch's back. The pain was nothing next to the anger. She was lifted, dragged up by the arm to dangle before Ruin's vengeful stare. She punched him across the cheekbone with her free hand. He caught the second blow and bashed his forehead into her face.

Fetch couldn't see through the wet agony. Warm, sticky fluid dripped from her chin. Blood and spit and the stuff pummeled out of her stomach.

"CHIEF!"

She could hear her brothers—her real brothers—coming. She raised a trembling hand, stretched it out behind her, commanded them to hold. They wouldn't obey. They'd die, despite all her efforts.

Bastards.

Yelps went up from the dog pack, snatching Ruin's attention. Fetch craned to look through flooded eyes. The beasts had fallen, were writhing atop one another. A dark substance crawled over their flopping bodies. Fetch took it for sludge until her focus returned. It wasn't a fluid mass, but a swarm. The morning sun reflected green and purple upon the black shells of thousands of beetles. They surged into the dogs' mouths, sloughed into their ears, and where they went an oily smoke emerged. One by one the dogs began to succumb, giving a final twitch before going limp as the last of the insects vanished within their swiftly bloating corpses. Corpses that were shoved aside as Jackal crawled from beneath the mound.

His clothes were in tatters, his flesh shredded, both covered with blood. Deep bite wounds gaped across his body, exposing bone, one making a horror of his throat. The desert scarf had been torn from his head and his unbound hair hung heavy with gore. He climbed to his feet, sword still transfixing his body, and let the glinting shards of some crystal vessel fall from his fingers.

"I . . . told you . . . I knew how . . . to kill devils," he said, voice ravaged. He pointed at Ruin. "And you . . . you're not the only one who can do . . . this."

Jackal grimaced, grabbed hold of the sword and pulled it from his chest.

Ruin's face went slack.

Fetch gave him a triumphant grin. "*Va Gara Attukhan,* you fucker."

She drew her knees up, kicked out, and drove her feet into Ruin's chest, breaking his grip. Hitting the ground, she turned the tumble into a roll that put her back on her feet.

"Out of the way, mongrel girl!" a familiar voice cried.

Fetching jumped clear as the wrath of a god knocked Ruin over.

Belico's scream battered his body, causing his flesh to ripple, the bone piercings to burst.

"Die," Fetch hissed. "Die, fucking die!"

But Ruin climbed to his feet. And took a step, his mouth gaping in a howl that was devoured by the tumult. He planted a foot, another. Unstoppable, wroth, he strode toward Jackal.

Fetch was startled by Incus passing by, the kataras in her hands.

"Don't!" Fetch yelled, grabbing the thrice's prodigious arm, forcing her to turn and see her lips. "Incus. Belico's voice is more than sound. It's fury itself. You won't be immune to the pain."

"Hurt me less," came the reply. Incus held up the kataras. "Borrowing these."

Incus barreled forward, visibly slowing as she waded into the earth-rattling din. She cut Ruin off and rammed one katara into his chest, the other. He reeled backward. The thrice kept coming, punching with her bladed hands. Ruin's flesh parted beneath the might-driven knives, his torso awash with blood. He put a palm in the path of Incus's next strike, allowed the blade to stab through his hand, and wrenched the weapon out of her grip. Bulling forward, he tackled her to the ground. Incus twisted to avoid being pinned, hooked a leg behind Ruin's knee and rolled them both on their sides. They came up grappling. For all the thrice's great size, she was made normal by the hulking *uq'huul*. And yet, he could not throw her off. Incus had him seized around the middle, feet planted. Ruin brought his hands together into one fist, raised his arms to strike. Belico voiced his displeasure. Ruin stumbled as the ear-breaking sound increased.

Fetch cast a look back. Xhreka stood, pouring on the god's unfettered temper. The halfling was flagging, supported by Oats. Incus's back was to them, forcing her to take the brunt of the cacophonous assault. Corded arms straining, the thrice lifted Ruin and turned, shielding herself with his body. Though blood was running from her nose, Incus thrust a leg back to brace against the gale and held. Ruin's movements were sluggish in the hellish current. Reaching down he took hold of the thrice's hair, began forcing her head back. Her arms began to loosen. Either her hold would break or her neck.

Incus refused to let go.

It was Xhreka who succumbed. The halfling collapsed. Belico was silenced.

Ruin brought his conjoined fists down on Incus's back. She was hammered to the dirt and did not move. Stepping over her, he continued toward Jackal, standing unsteady among the dead pack, barely able to keep his sword raised.

Fetch turned to yell for her hog, but a horrendous squeal cut her off. Ugfuck was stamping, shaking his great head. He began to twist, movements growing aggressive as the squeals turned to screams. Oats left Xhreka and scrambled to get in his barbarian's face, snatching at his swine-yankers, but Ug refused to be calmed. Culprit, Shed Snake, and the other hogs were forced to flee the big pig's stamping, whirling form. Hood and Starling were in danger of being caught in Ugfuck's fit, but the pale mongrel either could not or would not move the prone, laboring elf. Hood's back was to Fetching, leaning between Starling's knees. He continued to attend his charge with uncanny calm, ignoring the growing calamity. Whatever was coming, was coming now.

Oats was yelling at Ugfuck, finally had hold of him, and was wrestling with the berserk animal. "Ug! Settle! What is wron—"

"Chief!" Culprit's warning was strident. His pointing frantic.

Fetch spun in time to see Polecat's hog charging. There was no time to get clear. The barbarian hit her full with its head and she went spinning legs-over-ass before she struck the ground. She heard Jackal shouting.

Raising her head, Fetch saw him try to come to her, but his legs would not carry him. He collapsed as Ruin reached him, looming above.

Fetch made to rise, but the *uq'huul* flung an arm in her direction and she was battered back into the dust beneath trampling hooves. Reaching down, Ruin lifted Jackal by the neck. His legs hung over the dirt. Polecat's hog had turned and was galloping for another pass. Fetch waited until the last instant and rolled out of the way.

Jackal struggled in Ruin's strangling grip.

The brute's voice was a hateful, grinding toll. "Where?"

His eyes alighted on Jackal's left forearm and he snatched it up in his free hand, brought it to his nose and sniffed.

"There!"

Groans pulsed from Jackal's entrapped throat as the *uq'huul* stretched his arm to the side and began to pull.

Horrified by what Ruin intended, Fetch got to her feet and was again dashed to the earth by the ensorcelled hog. Culprit and Shed Snake were trying to get lassos around Polecat's barbarian. Cat himself was down, dead or unconscious from his mount's sudden, crazed betrayal.

Jackal's agony rattled in the air. Fetch needed to get to him. She rose to her knees, but a sudden sense of disquiet seized her. She was struck again.

But not by the hog.

It was sludge. The living blackness knocked her back down. She felt the ink adhere to her flesh, its lathing touch familiar and frightening. It crawled to her face. Lurching backward, blind, she tried to tear it away, but it clung to her hands, sucked them in to aid in smothering her. It flowed into her nostrils, leaked between her sealed lips. She choked on its vileness, gagged as it lodged in her throat, began to drown as it flooded her lungs. The darkness slid away from her eyes as the last of the loathsome tar crawled into her nose. There was no air, yet she breathed as gently as an enwombed babe.

Visions burgeoned against her clenched eyelids.

Beryl, younger, with bloody hands.

Blackness began to descend over her desperate, moist face and Fetch knew, with awful impotence, that it was the inescapable pull of death. She screamed against its coming, a plea of rage. And still it claimed her.

Drums.

She heard the furious beating of drums, the guttural, brutal howls of the orc tongue. An aged thick hurt her beneath a hellish sun, pushed sharp curved bones through her flesh. The excruciation threatened to drown her mind in madness. But she did not scream. Pain was nothing. It was as empty as the surrounding sands.

Fetch shoved the agony aside, allowed the flooding power to take its place.

Her hands knew strength and hungered to crush. She broke bone, skulls. She broke free.

There was hunger and hunters. She quashed them both with blood. The desert yielded to her southward steps and her feet touched the grasslands. There, the pack came. Less foolish than the orcs, they did not hunt her. They gathered about her, she slept ensconced by their breathing beneath every phase of the moon. Her strength, shared, became theirs. The pack aged, cubs growing to mothers. The orcs still searched, still died. Farther south, into the steaming jungles. A place of monstrous life and quick death. Not for her, not for the pack. They survived. Ruled.

Until the call. The pull.

Back to the grasslands. The desert. The pack followed. And together they saw the great water, long forgotten from the time of pain and drums.

They crossed.

And Fetch knew Ul-wundulas.

The badlands, lush after the barren desert. She knew the rivers. The call, the pull, forced her onward. Orcs roamed here too. In her path, killing lesser of their kindred that sat astride tamed boars, plundering the food they hauled. Fetch knew the tattoos of the riders.

The Tusked Tide.

She set the pack upon the orcs, slaughtering them as they had slaughtered the others. The pack dragged the orcs away and feasted on their flesh. The source of the call drew close and Fetch saw Slivers, felt the disgust blossom at the sight of him. He was nearing the source, a place he was forbidden. Angered, she sent the pack . . .

Fetch shot up from the dirt, sucking air. The visions were tattered banners, blowing in front of the world before her eyes. Tendrils of memory tickled her spine, felt more than seen or heard. The revelations threatened to bury her.

Dizzy and disturbed, she beheld Ruin still tormenting Jackal.

No.

Fetch pushed herself out of the dust, stood.

". . . no."

Balance betrayed her after two steps and she spilled upon her face. She began to belly-crawl.

"No."

Fetch got her hands under her, her knees, made her way like a beast, gaining speed.

"Stop."

The toes of her boots found purchase.

"Enough!"

She found her legs.

"STOP!"

She spoke in orcish, a tongue he knew, but rarely used.

Ruin's rage was unquenched.

Fetch grabbed his arm.

"Please."

Ignoring her, he continued to pull. Fetch heard the knocking pop as Jackal's shoulder left its socket. She tried to pry Ruin's grip in vain.

"I didn't know!"

Jackal was thrashing as he hung. The skin at his shoulder was stretching, starting to rend. His sword lay beneath his convulsing feet. Fetch snatched it up and looked into Ruin's savage face.

"Don't make me," she pleaded.

He would not be swayed from vengeance.

Raising the scimitar over her head, Fetch gave a tormented cry and brought it down on the flesh she knew would part.

The Arm of Attukhan sundered with the fury of a thunderclap.

FORTY

"CHIEF..."

The word reached Fetch's ears through a swarm of swollen bees.

"Chief."

Wincing, she sat up, a firm hand helping.

"Chief, thank hells!" Culprit knelt beside her, mouth half open. "We don't know what to do. Savages won't let us near him."

Fetch looked around, the movement of her eyeballs igniting ropes of pain in her skull. She'd been moved. No, thrown. She and Ruin and Jackal. Tossed into the air, scattered. But Jack was beside her now, Oats kneeling opposite. The thrice's face was an uncomprehending mask. He would not look at her, only at the stump she'd made of Jackal's arm, severed just above the elbow. The wound was bound. The wrapped, stained bundle nearby could only be the rest of the limb.

"He's not dead," Culprit assured her.

Fetch's eyes told her that was a lie. A hand upon Jackal's chest proved Culprit spoke true. Jack was breathing. Barely, but he was alive.

And not the only one.

Incus lay to Fetch's other side, her great maned head stirring. Xhreka, too, though she was still out. Polecat sat nearby, looking dazed and stanching his split brow with a kerchief. Beyond, Shed Snake kept watch on the Bastards' hogs, all hobbled, all docile.

Across from Fetch, N'keesos knelt behind Starling, holding her despite his broken arm and obvious pain. Na'hak stood removed. The older elf was battered and cut. Hatchet in hand, his gaze was fixed on Ruin, a javelin's toss away.

The *uq'huul*'s great frame slumped in the center of his dead pack, head bowed. Only one hyena remained alive, slinking and whining at the borders of its bloated brethren, the haft of a snapped javelin protruding from its side. The animal was not the only feral thing that kept a vigil on Ruin. Sitting their hogs, the Fangs of Our Fathers formed a rough screen around him, almost two score mongrels festooned with bone fetishes and little else.

Kul'huun was at their center, speaking with Hoodwink.

"They arrived right after you . . . uh . . ." Culprit cleared his throat. "Right after you got possessed by the thing that came out of the elf's quim and hacked Jackal into two pieces."

Fetch placed a hand on the young mongrel's shoulder, used him to push up from the ground.

"I don't understand, chief," he said, rising beside her.

Fetch didn't answer, looked at Starling. She did.

The look on Starling's drawn face gave it away, a mixture of fresh guilt, old sorrow, and, despite her exhausted appearance, great relief. It was a look Fetch had seen Beryl wear many times, especially when she looked at Oats and Jackal, but a time or two she'd seen it directed at herself.

"Give me a moment," Fetch said to Culprit, and went to join Hoodwink with the Fangs.

"I cannot allow you to kill him," Kul'huun announced as soon as she drew near.

Fetch rubbed at her eyes. "If we could have done that, he'd be dead by now."

Kul'huun studied her a moment. "You know what he is."

"More than you do. But come, you can tell my boys. They might . . . have trouble trusting me."

The wariness in Hood's unrelenting stare proved it wasn't an unworthy concern.

Kul'huun dismounted, leaving his hoof to gather with the Bastards around their injured. Incus was upright now. Fetch motioned for Shed Snake to leave the hogs. Only Jackal and Xhreka had not awoken, though Oats was nearly as insensate. Fetch hoped the truth would bring him around. As for the other two . . .

"I began hunting the *uq'huul* as soon as I left Strava," Kul'huun began, abandoning orcish for Hisparthan. "He remained elusive for many days. When I found him, I was cautious. I tracked him from afar, watched him when there was a vantage. His movements were strange. He would travel south and west, intent. Yet he would grow agitated after a time and return the way he'd come. Always back."

"Back where?" Culprit asked.

"Our lot," Shed Snake replied.

Kul'huun gave a single nod. "He did not wish to remain, yet he could not leave. A caged animal with nothing barring him."

"Nothing you could see," Starling whispered, though her elvish words were lost to most.

Kul'huun only glanced her way before continuing. "I came to understand he was aware of me, yet he did nothing. He did not fear me. He paid me no mind, as a bear pays no mind to the fox. Orcs believe themselves stronger than we half-breeds, but they never refrain from killing. He did not set his dogs upon me." The Fangs chief looked at Fetching. "That made two this *uq'huul* had allowed to live. I did not understand this creature, so I rode back to my lot, commanded my brothers to take an orc alive. We hunted, found an *ulyud*, and killed all but one. This orc I questioned about the *uq'huul* that commands beasts. I have never seen an orc show fear. Until that day. It tried to mask its fear with spite, but I saw what it hid. We pulled the tale from the orc, along with its entrails."

Fetch watched her brothers as Kul'huun spoke. Her gaze kept returning to Oats, but he showed no sign he was even listening.

"It told of a child brought willingly to Dhar'gest by a mongrel witch that vanished from the slave pens not long after being taken. Had it been known what she left behind, the orc said, the babe would have been left in the desert to die. Ignorant, they gave the child to the care of their sorcerers, for he was one of them. Another *uq'huul*. He was raised by them, endured the trials of their tutelage, learning to draw out the magic in his veins. His power rivaled that of all his masters. They saw in him the champion that would lead them in a *Duulv M'har* to finally conquer Ul-wundulas. But, nearing maturity, he defied the *uq'huuls*. And slaughtered them."

"Wait." Polecat cringed against the sound of his own voice, pressed the kerchief back to his head. "Fucking all of them? How many were there?"

Kul'huun did not blink. "None now. The bloody-handed youth made himself the last. He fled the orcs after the killings and made the deepest reaches of the inner jungles his domain, suffering no trespass by any other than beasts, which he could bend to his will. Entire *ul'usuuns* were sent against him, hundreds of orcs led by strong *t'huruuks* with a mind to increase their standing among the hordes by killing the traitor *uq'huul*. None succeeded or survived. Now they leave him be, avoiding his lands. U'ruul Targha Bhal they name him."

Culprit's brow wrinkled in concentration. "Death's . . . Empty Belly?"

"Those are the Hisparthan words, but not the meaning," Kul'huun replied. "He is something the orcs do not understand, a thing with no appetite for slaughter, yet possessing a capacity for destruction without end. They seek to insult him, unable to admit it is also a name given in fear."

Shed Snake grunted. "They're calling him a coward, but they don't dare challenge him anymore."

Kul'huun dipped his shallow nod.

Polecat cocked a squinted eye at him. "And you Fangs are here to, what, worship him as some thick-slaying god?"

"We came to tell what we learned," Kul'huun replied, an edge to his patience. "And found your holdfast destroyed. There was evidence of the *uq'huul* and his pack, but also of the Orc Stains."

"Thrice-blooded fucks tried to end us," Polecat said. "Your new hero and his damn curs too."

"No. He was trying to help us. Help . . . me."

All eyes went to Fetching. Even Oats looked up and, though the anger was far from comforting, his face gave her the will to voice the hard truths.

"Ruin . . . U'ruul . . ." She broke off, frustrated. Fuck. All she now understood and she still didn't know what he called himself. All she had were names foisted upon him. Hateful, condemning names. "He was drawn here, to me. He didn't know why, tried to resist and couldn't. But he saved me from the cavaleros."

You taste weak.

"He was . . . curious. Thought perhaps I was another *uq'huul* coaxing him into a trap. But I was sick, dying. Not a threat. He tried to return to Dhar'gest." Fetch took a deep breath. "Had I not survived, he would have. By reaching Strava, getting rid of the sludge, I lived. So . . . he could not leave. And was drawn back. More than that, he was compelled to protect me. So he came again when the Stains attacked."

"Hogshit." Oats's growl possessed none of Kul'huun's patience. "Those dogs attacked you."

"They're still animals, Oats. And I attacked them."

"Because they were trying to get their jaws on me and Xhreka and three babes!"

Fetch shook her head. "Just you. Just the thrice-blood. Like the Stains."

"They didn't come for me," Incus said.

"You had already fled Winsome," Fetch told her. "You weren't near me."

Oats's face fell for a moment, but hardened again. "I know what I saw! He wasn't protecting you at the Kiln pile, Fetch. That monster wanted to kill you."

Fetch recalled that night with more than memory now. She could see Ruin stepping in front of her, relived the rage he inspired within her. She roped him, dragged him to the death trap of the Kiln. She recalled Ruin trying to strike her. Only, he'd been trying to grab her. He could have leapt clear at any time, left her to burn, but he didn't, not without carrying her out with him. And *he* had burned.

"I tried to kill him," Fetch said. "Nothing has been able to cause him pain since the orcs. The Al-Unan fire, that . . . changed things. I was now a threat, no longer a confusing curiosity. I was the source of what kept him from going home and had the power to harm him. So, he came to free himself. Today, he wanted me dead. He meant no harm before."

"No harm?" Oats was so incensed his voice had gone quiet. "Dumb Door's dead, Fetch. And that wasn't the Stains. That was *him*! He took hold of a hog with his hoodoo and killed one of us, well before the night you burned him."

The hoof stared at Fetch, awaiting an answer. It was a difficult one to give.

"That wasn't his doing. It was mine."

Her brothers shifted uneasily.

"The Filth that gives the *uq'huuls* their powers is hateful shit," Fetch told them. "Evil. It is why all of them, since the beginning, have served the orcs. They are driven to destroy. Not Ruin. He possesses the same magic, but it doesn't corrupt him. Somehow, he dominates it, and can even share it. The Filth is in the dogs, same as him, and they passed it to Little Orphan Girl when they nearly killed her. Without Ruin's influence the dogs would be driven mad by the Filth. He wasn't in control of Little Orphan Girl, so she succumbed."

"I don't see how that's your fault," Shed Snake said.

"The dogs attacked Slivers because of me. I told him if he ever returned to Winsome, I would kill him. Ruin felt that through our . . . I dunno, fucking bond. Like me, he wasn't aware of it. He didn't know why, but he felt rage and hatred for Slivers. So, he sent the pack after him. Slivers was killed and his hog corrupted because of me. Dumb Door is dead because of me."

Shed Snake's mouth twisted in disagreement. "You can't shoulder that, chief."

Polecat eyed the line of barbarians. "So . . . that mean Clusiana and Ugfuck are going to go mad?"

"No. He's freed them of the corruption."

"How do you know?" Polecat asked.

"How do I know any of this," Fetch replied. She looked to Starling.

Culprit snapped his fingers, beamed with pride at his own intuition. "The sludge baby!"

"I do not understand," Kul'huun said.

"The chief and that big, terrifying fuck are twins," Culprit replied. "Can't you tell?"

Fetch kept her eyes on Starling, wanting her own answers.

Oats forced her to wait.

"Why, Isa?" he demanded, a big hand and great concern still resting upon Jackal.

Fetch pointed to where Ruin still knelt among the swollen remains of his pack. "Look at him, Oats. What do you reckon you'd do if you were him and those dogs were the hoof? Your brothers. Jackal did that. For me. *I* did that. That rage you feel, we feel, for Dumb Door, for Mead and Sweeps, and all the rest, we gave it to him. Tell me you wouldn't have torn any of their killers limb from limb."

Oats set his jaw, trying to hold on to his anger, but the fire in his glare was cooling.

"I couldn't stop him," Fetch said. "All I could do was show him we were done trying to hurt him."

"Reckon that worked," Culprit said, blowing out a long breath as he stared at Ruin. He looked back at Fetch, a little worried. "Right?"

She didn't have an answer.

Starling did.

"He will come to understand," she said in accented Hisparthan. "I will help him. That is my path now."

"Better to just allow him to go back to Dhar'gest," Fetch said.

Starling shook her head. "He was compelled here for a purpose. Just as I am Returned for a purpose." She looked to Ghost Last Sung. At last, he met her eye and there was a long moment before Starling continued. "I feared it was as Na'hak said, that my purpose was to rid the earth of my children. Your birth was my death. I could not allow my rebirth to be yours. I feared what would happen if we three should meet, for this could only end the way it began, with us to-gether. In this I was right. Our convergence brought forth what I carried. I am thankful it proved not to be an instrument of your deaths."

"What was it, then?" Culprit asked. "Because I nearly shat my breeches when it came out. I swear even Hood blinked. Like once, but he did!"

If Hoodwink had blinked, he didn't now.

Starling gave her answer to Fetch. "It was him. Your *ta'thami'atha*. You had been born when death took me, the cord joining us cut, but he was still within. When I awoke in this body, a part of him Re-turned as well. I did not know this, but now I see. Though it was a shadow of him, it came to you, as he was drawn to you. He jour-neyed from Dhar'gest to find you, as I journeyed from death."

"But why?"

Starling grew visibly saddened. "I have hidden so much from you, I fear you will not trust me when I say . . . I do not know."

"It was to bring us the orcs' champion," Kul'huun said, eyes alight with flames of certainty. "He shunned them. Fought them. Now he will help us destroy them."

None added their voice to that belief.

"I think," Culprit said, rubbing at his head, "any mongrel *that* tough is going to do whatever the fuck he wants no matter what we say."

Shed Snake rolled his eyes. "If he could do whatever he wanted he wouldn't be here, fool-ass."

"Oh, right."

Polecat looked to Fetch. "What's the move, chief?"

"You're going to sit there until that head's no longer addled. We're riding out soon as Culprit and Snake get a skid made for Jack and Xhreka." The elected mongrels jumped to it. "I don't need you falling off your hog again, Cat, so stay put. You, too, Incus. Rest until I say."

"Wouldn't have gotten thrown if that sorcerous shit hadn't hexed my sow," Polecat groused. He grimaced at Oats. "How come you ain't hurt?"

"No magic in this world that can force Ug to turn on me," Oats replied.

Fetch went to him and placed a hand on his shoulder. "Reckon there has to be some boon for having to suffer looking at him."

"Damn right," Oats grunted, and clapped a hand over hers. The other never left Jackal.

THE SUN WAS HIGH BY the time the skid was built. Shed Snake and Culprit had been forced to range far for the wood. When they called to Fetch, letting her know it was completed, she had been crouching among the dead dogs for some time.

Ruin's eyes never raised.

He did not weep, he did not hold one of the fallen animals, nor touch them in any way. He merely, awfully, sat. There was no sign of the beetles Jackal had unleashed to slay the hyenas, but neither would the flies of Ul-wundulas, ever eager to descend, gather upon their bodies. Ruin's own wounds had already ceased to bleed. Fetch wondered if the rest of him would heal as swiftly, or at all.

She'd risked squatting within reach. He'd given her presence no notice. The Fangs had kept a watchful eye, so had her own riders, for differing reasons. Neither hoof understood. They could no longer hurt each other. Not any further. Not anymore.

So Fetch hunkered across from Ruin, took in the sight of him. This close, his sheer size, even in near complete stillness, was difficult to face without trepidation. The beating sun carved the slabs of muscle, wrought by savage survival, into a primal nightmare. The cruel, hooked piercings of bone that covered his flesh were hard to look upon. They'd been inflicted upon him by the orcs, and Fetch found herself wondering why he'd never removed them. The answer forced a rueful snort.

"Women are only good for two things," she muttered. "Fucking and fetching."

Her words had been in Hisparthan, meaningless to Ruin, yet the sound of her voice drew his attention. His chin lifted from his chest, his eyes were amber beneath the heavy brow, sagging with grief.

She spoke again, this time in elvish as well as Hisparthan, hoping two languages would make up for the lack of her words in orcish.

"Thank you." And. "I am sorry."

She stood, picked her way through the dogs.

Starling met her just beyond the cordon created by the Fangs of Our Fathers. She was a little unsteady on her feet, but like her monstrous son, the she-elf was frightfully resilient.

"You going to stay with him?" Fetch asked, glancing back at Ruin.

"Yes," Starling said. "I will honor him as Returned. It is the duty of his blood kin to help him find his path."

"Where will you go? I can't imagine Dog Fall will allow you back. Not with . . . him."

"Perhaps one day. For now, we shall remain with Kul'huun and his tribe. They have pledged to aid us. Their knowledge of the orcs is deep. My hope is that they will bridge the divide between the world my son knew and the one he now faces."

Fetch lowered her voice. "Be cautious. Kul'huun is a strong warrior and a good ally, but the Fangs are bent on Ruin being something he may not wish to become."

"Thank you for this warning. I will keep it close to mind."

Farther out upon the plain, Na'hak and N'keesos were holding a private, heated council.

Fetch lifted her chin, directed Starling's gaze. "And them? They staying with you?"

"Blood Crow, yes. He wishes to restore his honor."

"But not his father."

"No. The wounds in Ghost Last Sung's heart are too deep."

Fetch considered a moment before shaking her head. "It's not his heart, Starling. It's his eyes. He's too blinded by hatred to see the truth."

"What truth?"

"That you succeeded. Not partially, but fully. You brought no Ruin Made Flesh into this world. You did what you set out to do."

The she-elf looked at her with woeful, careworn eyes trapped within a face of beautiful youth. "You have grown wise, daughter."

The word caused no small amount of discomfort, but Fetch said nothing. Telling Starling not to call her that would be . . . cruel.

"Starling, I know that I'm also . . . blood kin. But I cannot go with you. I have—"

The warmth of a hand upon her face stopped her words. "You have your brothers. I have my sons. And they are not the same."

Starling's other hand came up and she cradled Fetch's face, held her eyes with her own. There was pride and hesitance in that stare, the one deepening as the other fled. Leaning in, Starling placed a lingering kiss upon her forehead. Her lips were trembling. When she withdrew, her hands remained a moment longer.

"When next you see Beryl," Starling said, "please deliver these words: I thank you for your past kindness. I thank you for the lives of my children. For suffering to save my son. And for surviving to raise my daughter. My *Ka'siqana*."

The meaning of that last elvish word came immediately to Fetch's mind.

Purest Lark.

It was an additional, aching heartbeat before she realized it would have been, in another life, her name.

FORTY-ONE

IT TOOK THE TRUE BASTARDS the remainder of the day and all the night to reach the Orc Stains' lot.

The entire ride Fetching feared Jackal would die, hoped Xhreka would wake. Neither did.

The rising sun caught them fording the River U'har at Guliat Wash. Fetch was long familiar with the border, but had never set foot on its eastern bank. Her boots were still damp from the crossing when the other riders appeared.

There were eleven of them, all on hogs. They came at an uneven trot, spread across the plain. The Bastards rode to meet them. As the distance dwindled, Fetch scanned the haphazard line, saw the prodigious size of the barbarians. The riders atop such weighty pigs were far too small to be thrice-bloods. Only one straddled a razor with any skill, and he appeared to have a bit more meat on him. They began to rein up a stone's throw from the Bastards, though most were within spitting distance by the time their large mounts agreed to halt. Fetch's eyes darted among these gaunt, inexpert riders. Her brothers had given her ample warning, but the appearance of these mongrels still gave Fetch pause. Every last one was bald and shabby.

None wore a brigand. Half had tulwars at their belts, the rest equipped with everything from rough-fashioned spears to wood-cutting axes. Fetch counted the slung straps of only four stockbows. They were stiff in the saddle, most unable to sit their hog without both hands gripping the barbarian's mane. Above every unhealthy gaze, the puckered scar of a brand adorned their foreheads; three ragged, vertical lines.

The Orc Stains' rumored slaves in the flesh.

And among them a familiar, though nearly unrecognizable, face.

Fetch dipped her chin. "Marrow."

"Chief," the nomad responded. His whiskers were thin and wispy, blanched of the flaxen hue that had once made them so conspicuous. The yellow had fled the hair to take up residence in the eyes. Above, his brand was pink, where those of his compatriots were pale.

"We've got wounded," Fetch said.

"Come. Thricehold is not far." Marrow motioned for the riders to move out. "Caltrop, you have point."

"Yes, chief," answered one of the scrawny mongrels.

The rest turned their hogs, most with obvious difficulty, and entered into a slipshod formation that was not likely to last a league. The Bastards resumed their protective positions around the skid pulled by Big Pox.

Fetch kicked Womb Broom forward and wove her way to Marrow's side. He continued to stare ahead.

"Thank you for taking my folk in," she told the side of his head.

Marrow was tense, uncomfortable. "There's no need for that. It is you who have our gratitude. You rid us of our captors, though you suffered much in the doing. I count it fortunate that my hoof came upon yours. Our lot is vast and our numbers few. These boys are still breaking in, but are diligent in patrolling the crossings."

Fetch's brothers told her about Marrow and the other slaves, but their encounter had been brief. The Bastards were eager to track her down and had not lingered after receiving assurances the Winsome folk would be looked after.

"What happened, Marrow? How did you come to be a prisoner?

You're seasoned enough to know free-riders weren't welcome by the Stains."

Beneath the pale whiskers, Marrow's jaw pulsed. "They took me almost within sight of Winsome."

Fetch let out a sigh. "Knob had his boys watching us."

The nomad did not respond. It hadn't been a question anyway.

"I'm sorry, Marrow."

He remained silent. It was no wonder he had come to lead this ragged bunch. In the absence of their masters they would have looked to the strongest and, haggard and haunted as he was, Marrow was still a brute compared to the rest. The former Skull Sower who'd once challenged Tomb finally had his hoof.

"What do you call yourselves?" Fetch asked.

"We are the Thrice Freed."

"Fitting."

"Yes. But it is not only our escape from the Orc Stains we honor." Marrow's detached stare brightened. "First, we were freed from the womb. Next, from our slavers. Death will free us the third time when we give our lives in defense of Ul-wundulas."

Marrow continued to face forward as he spoke, but even in profile, Fetch could see the wild glint in his eye, hear the resolve of a zealot in his proclamation. Fetch worried the nomad's time in chains had tarnished his mind with madness.

She rode close to him for the remainder of the journey.

THRICEHOLD WASN'T AN IMPRESSIVE FORTIFICATION. The mountain it was built upon, however, was. A massive chunk of limestone, it rose from the surrounding flats, an isolated island of towering rock, dominating the surrounds with its bulk.

As the conjoined hoofs neared the peak, Fetch noticed steaming pools nestled among the boulders, the air heavy with the moisture and smell of hot springs. Like the slaves, it was always rumored the Orc Stains' fortress sat atop a dormant volcano, but most took that as the useless wind of braggarts.

The riders approached from the southwest, but rode around to the mountain's northern slope to begin the ascent where a trail climbed through thickets of pine. It was a long, tedious trek and near noon when they reached the summit. The whitewashed walls of Thricehold were only half the height of the Kiln's when it stood, and possessed none of the artistry. The Claymaster had been a hateful, rotten fuck, but he knew how to construct a fortress. Whoever the founder of the Stains had been, he'd settled for a round barbican, two square towers, a curtain wall, and a central keep to defend the dozen-odd buildings that comprised the rest of the compound.

At the moment, Fetch cared nothing for the quality of the walls.

More bald mongrels stood along the battlements and a shout from Marrow set the portcullis creaking upward. They rode through the gate and reined up in the sizable yard.

A familiar voice called from the walls.

"Chief!"

Touro came down the stone steps two at a time, spear in hand, and rushed to greet her.

"Chief. The slops will be reliev—" Seeing Jackal, the young mongrel's mouth fell open. "Fucking . . . hells. Is he dead?"

"He will be if you stand around gaping!" Fetch exclaimed.

"I'll get Beryl!" Mouth still slack, Touro hurried off.

"Let's get him inside," Marrow said.

Beryl emerged from the keep as Oats was lifting Jackal from the skid. For the briefest of moments, she froze. The next instant saw her gesturing them inside.

"Idris!"

Oats carried Jackal up the steps and followed his mother into the keep. Leaving the hogs with the hoof, Fetch followed the thrice's broad back, hurrying through a gloomy central hall and down a wide corridor. Oats bore Jackal into one of the rooms off the corridor and laid him on a sizable bed.

"We need boiling water!" Beryl told the room. "Wine or vinegar. Needle. Gut string. A sharp knife. And any herbs in this place."

Touro, lingering in the passage, rushed off once more.

"You two," Beryl said to Fetch and Oats without looking up from unwrapping Jackal's stump, "we're going to need to sew this up. But first we have to make a flap. It's going to require more cutting. If you can't bear that, find me help that can."

"No," Fetch said. "We're not doing that."

Beryl's head snapped up. "Fetch! He's going to di—"

"No!" Fetch spun on Oats. "Go. Tend to Xhreka. The moment she's awake, I need her here."

Oats's uncertainty lasted only a moment. Nodding, he rushed from the room.

"Fetch," Beryl pleaded, "there's not time!"

"There is! I know Jackal. He never thinks overlong on anything. Any choice! He just makes it. So if he was going to die, he would have done it already. Now I need you to believe that too. Please! Just . . . believe it. And help me get him cleaned up."

The two of them got his boots off, stripped what remained of his clothing. Touro, Dacia, and Little Tel brought everything Beryl requested. And more.

The Bastards entered and loitered at the edges of the room until Fetch ordered them out, and then they only retreated to the corridor.

"We need to tend the rest of these," Beryl said, taking in all of Jackal's injuries.

Fetch helped wash him, helped clean and stitch the bite wounds, helped change the bedclothes while Incus lifted him. Only when there was nothing more to do but wait did she sink into a chair. It, like everything about the room, was large. The Stains had built with a mind to the comfort of thrice-bloods. When Incus left with Beryl, she'd been spared having to duck beneath the lintel. The bed was wide too, and the space next to Jackal tempted Fetch to lie down. She stayed in the chair, too rank, too filthy, too tired.

The last days caught up to her in a stampede of fatigue.

She stirred a few times. Once when Beryl entered the room to light candles, check Jackal's fever. Once when Culprit kicked the leg of the bed by accident and swore. Once when Thistle put a blanket over her. Exhaustion and the deep furs covering the chair tugged her back to slumber each time.

Sleep fled with the swiftness of a frightened hare when she awoke to find Marrow standing in the room with a loaded stockbow. Behind him, the door was closed and latched. Beneath the blanket, Fetch's hand slid to the handle of her katara, still sheathed along her thigh. She tried to draw it without the motion giving her away.

"You won't need that foreign knife," Marrow told her, not moving away from the door. She would never cover the distance before he shot her and they both knew it. "Rather my end come from a good thrum if you'll give me the choice." Holding the weapon one-handed at the foregrip, he offered it out.

Confused and unnerved, Fetch could only shake her head.

"I've come to give you the chance to kill me," Marrow said. "My hoof will not seek retribution, so long as you allow them to vote a new chief from among their own. You and the Bastards may remain here for as long as needed."

"Marrow . . . what? Why would I kill you?"

"Because I told Knob how to take Winsome."

The confession was bluntly made, but the shame of it covered the nomad's face. He had more to unburden, so Fetch waited.

"They waylaid me. Questioned me about your defenses, the watch patrols, asked where the hoof was housed, where . . . you slept. I told them."

Marrow's voice was quavering.

"They tortured you," Fetch said, trying to thrust sympathy in front of anger.

"No. They threatened Dead Bride. Threatened my hog! Said . . . they were going to blind her to start. Said I'd be eating her by the end. How could I . . . ?" His shame increased with the arrival of his tears. He cleared his throat, rallied. "Knob vowed I could straddle the razor and ride on if I told what he wanted. So I did. I told him all. He broke his word, made me a prisoner . . . and fed me my hog. I am the reason your hoof has suffered. Because I was too afraid to watch my sow die. Too afraid to die myself, I reckon. So . . ." He held up the stockbow once again.

Fetch took her hand off the knife. She studied Marrow, saw his need to absolve himself. The easy way. She took a long breath, let it out.

"You didn't cause this shit, Marrow. You just helped it along.

Doesn't mean what you did wasn't the path of a coward. It was. You feel a need to die for it, point that bolt beneath your chin and jerk the tickler. You want my forgiveness? Earn it."

The stockbow lowered. "Tell me how."

"Helping me and mine is a damn good beginning. Continuing to help through the shit that's coming, one way or another, will make an end."

"The Thrice Freed are yours."

"No, chief. They're yours. But I need *your* loyalty."

Marrow's jaw set, turned to stone. "You have it." After a moment, he filled the silence with a question. "Did you make Knob suffer?"

Fetch considered lying, thought better of it. "Thrumbolt through the heart. Quick."

Marrow's tongue rolled around within his tightly shut mouth, bulging the skin. "Pity. But a greater one had he not died at all."

He startled as the door thumped behind him, trying to open.

Oats's voice came through the wood. "Fetch! I got Xhreka!"

Shooting to her feet, Fetch opened the door. Oats came in, eyed Marrow with confusion as he slipped out. Xhreka and Beryl followed the thrice. The sight in the room froze the halfling at the jamb, but the half-orc matron pushed past and went straight to Jackal's bedside.

Fetch placed a hand on Xhreka's shoulder. "Help him."

Xhreka tore her eye off Jackal long enough to give Fetch an incredulous glare. "I've told you before, girl, I'm no healer."

Fetch leaned down and thrust a finger at Xhreka's eye patch. "*Help* him."

"Have you lost your mind . . . ?"

"Let's find out."

Reaching into her saddlebag, Fetch removed the bundle. Unveiling the severed arm, she carried it close to Xhreka. Beryl expelled a curse and Oats retreated a step when the hand began to spasm and clench. A wet, resonant whisper filled the room. Xhreka clapped a hand over her missing eye, recoiled from the severed limb.

"You don't know what you're doing!"

"I know you got Belico in there," Fetch said. She raised the jerking arm. "And I got Attukhan here. They were brothers in life, yes?"

"Near enough," Xhreka muttered, keeping her face averted.

"Closer than, I wager. You going to tell me your god won't help his warrior? Because he sounded eager just now."

The halfling remained motionless and silent.

Oats's deep, strained voice reached out to her. "Xhreka. Please."

The little woman straightened, faced them, but her hand stayed fixed.

"You never struck me as happy this one was pledged to Zirko," she told Fetch, pointing at Jackal. "You don't think the Master Slave will demand a price far greater than the Hero Father? 'Cause he will, girl. He will!"

Fetch heard the wisdom in those words. And ignored it. "Like Belico, I'm willing to do all that I can for the man that's bled for me."

She went to the bed and placed the arm flush with Jackal's stump. Stepping back, she made room for Xhreka.

The halfling approached with slow steps, removing her eye patch. "Whatever befalls is on your head, girl."

The whisper returned, sibilant and lustful. As Xhreka reached the bed, the lids of the missing eye parted and the tongue emerged, searching the air. It stretched toward Jackal, and the halfling gave a noise of discomfort, seemed to resist as her head was drawn downward. The tongue began to drip, tears of slaver running down Xhreka's face, falling upon Jackal. Across the bed, Beryl's face curdled. Xhreka's nose was nearly brushing the wound as the tongue licked along the ragged gap above Jackal's elbow. The flesh sizzled as it joined, reknit. When the upper curve was complete, Xhreka lifted the arm off the bed so the lapping tongue could complete its work. A thin, encircling strip of darkened flesh was all that remained. The tongue withdrew and Xhreka lowered the mended limb, replaced her eye patch with deliberate dignity, and moved toward the door.

Oats reached a grateful hand toward her.

"Leave me be!" Xhreka snapped, and left the room.

Oats made to follow but was stopped by Beryl.

"Idris. Leave her."

Breathing out hard, rubbing a hand down his face and beard, he did as told.

Fetch stared down at Jackal. She'd hoped for an immediate change, for the blessings she had long resented to take hold, but the dog bites remained angry, some leaking. Jackal still looked a cunt hair away from dying.

"You two get some rest," Fetch said. "I have this."

When they were gone, her eyes fell on a bucket filled with fresh water, a rag draped over its rim. She'd asked for it at one point, couldn't recall when. Sighing, Fetch removed her clothes. She scrubbed with the rags, cleansing her flesh, but her thoughts became as murky as the water in the bucket. Latching the door, she lay down beside Jackal, put her hand on his chest to feel its rise and fall.

Sleep did not return.

A need to be free from the chamber drove her from the bed and back into her clothes.

Oats was on a stool in the corridor. Hoodwink stood leaning against the opposite wall.

"I need some fucking fresh air," she told them.

Looking both directions, Fetch realized she did not remember from which way she had come when arriving. Seeing her hesitation, Oats stood up.

"I'll show you."

Fetch looked to Hood. "Stay with him for me?"

Hoodwink nodded.

Fetch followed Oats down the corridor, through the great hall, and out into the fortress yard. Members of the Thrice Freed walked the rampart, and that's where Oats took Fetch. The shave-pate mongrels did not challenge them, merely glanced when they reached the walk and continued to patrol. It was nearly dawn on the mountaintop and Fetch was struck by the vastness of the sky. This high, with the sun's light still preparing to invade the sky, the badlands were hardly visible. The stars were still entrenched upon a sloe field draining to blue.

Beneath, Thricehold was an ugly, inelegant necessity.

Fetch leaned on the edge of a merlon and inhaled deeply.

Oats aped her, bumped her elbow with his. "You need to swear to me, if Jackal . . . dies, you won't blame yourself."

"Why not? You will."

"I won't." He nudged her again, hard enough to make her fight for balance. "I'll blame you."

"That's what I meant, fool-ass."

Oats nodded, sniffed as he took in the sky. "I know. But me blaming you won't kill you, so you gotta swear."

She looked at him, lied. "I swear."

He gave a satisfied nod. "Good."

Oats was wrong, confusing her nature for his own. Jackal's death would bring guilt and pain that would never fade, but it wouldn't kill her. The knowledge made Fetch a little sick and she would never admit it to Oats. Still, the bitter fucking fact was she would keep striving. She knew that in her bones, wondered if it made her heartless. More than that, she wondered if death was the only end to the struggle. She tried to imagine the Lots without the hardship, the bloodshed, found she couldn't.

And that was the answer.

Oats was peering at her. "The hells is your mind whittling away at?"

Fetch blinked. Somehow, morning had come. "Shit."

"What?" Oats stood away from the merlon. "What have you been thinking about?"

"Corigari."

"Cori—? The fucking Sludge Man?"

Fetch nodded. "Kul'huun said Ruin was the last of the *uq'huuls*. That he killed the rest."

"Thought you said this was about the Sludge Man!"

"It is. He was trading for elven women, believed he could use them in some sacrifice to heal the Old Maiden. He was killing orcs too, thought both were needed. When he found out about me, a mongrel with elf and orc blood, he came for me. Thought I was the answer."

Oats leaned in, gave a flummoxed shrug.

"But he was nothing but a puppet, Oats! The sludge was driving him. The Filth. It was trying to make more *uq'huuls*. More Ruins! They must not have been able to communicate too well, or Corigari's madness got in the way or . . . fuck, it must have taken them years to herd his wriggling mind in the right direction. Like a damn hog trying to get its rider to sit backward in the saddle and settling for sideways."

"You can't know th—"

Fetch shushed him. "The orcs committed many of their strongest to the Incursion and they were all killed in the marsh, becoming sludge, which found a vessel and began clumsily trying to replenish the ranks because the *uq'huuls* still in Dhar'gest were killed by U'ruul Targha Bhal. My fucking twin! The orc the Fangs questioned said there were none left but him."

"Fetch, we can't trust some orc getting his guts torn out would speak earnest. Hells, it also said my mother was a witch that disappeared! To say fuck-all of Kul'huun and his bunch getting stiff cods when it comes to anything orcish. A thick could tell them all orcs fight with their nut baskets stuffed up their assholes and the Fangs would be shoving their hanging seed sacks between their cheeks the next day."

"What about Crafty?"

"Well . . . yes, I'm sure he'd be willing to do that too. Still fair certain the chubby fuck was backy."

Fetch clutched at the air in front of Oats's face. "No! Crafty made a bargain with the orcs. Promised the plague would not be used against them. And they came, Oats! Do you truly think the thicks would make a pact with a fat, foreign, half-breed wizard if their own sorcerers were still leading them? The *uq'huuls* would have killed him before he could get his jowly mouth open."

"Say you're right. I still don't see which horizon this crazed hog you're riding is heading for."

"This could be our one chance, Oats."

"Chance for what?"

"To—"

A voice from the yard cut her off. "Chief."

Hoodwink.

Fetch's breath caught. She stepped to the edge of the wall and looked down at the pale mongrel. "Jackal?"

"Awake."

Rushing into the room, Fetch found he was not only awake but sitting up, bare legs hanging over the bedside. Beryl was trying to keep him from rising and losing.

"At least allow me to put some breeches on," he complained.

"You got nothing I haven't seen before, and bigger," Beryl said. "You need to lie back!"

"Fetch, would you call her off?"

She forced herself not to go to him, crossed her arms. "You can listen to her or we can have Oats put you back in bed." Soon as the words left her mouth she got bumped by something big and heavy. Having no need for restraint, Oats barged right over to his friend and wrapped him in a crushing embrace.

Polecat's hatchet face leaned around the doorjamb. "Hhhmm. Oats is hugging Jackal. Annnnnd Jackal's naked. I'll tell the boys everything's normal, chief."

He slid from view.

"Had me hells damn worried, brother," Oats proclaimed, releasing his hold to stand with a sheepish expression.

"Me too," Fetch said, drawing Jackal's eye.

"Well, if you won't lie down, you will at least eat," Beryl said, going for the door. She paused and looked back with a dubious set to her mouth.

"What?" Oats asked.

Beryl peered at all of them. "Just . . . always makes me a little nervous to leave the three of you alone in a room together."

The door closed behind her.

Jackal hadn't removed his gaze from Fetch. "Did I dream you cutting my arm off?"

She could only shake her head.

"Well, you said you wanted to hurt me." His grin showed there was no ill feeling. "Just tell me that giant orc is dead."

Oats's cheeks blew out huge. "Alive. *And* Fetch's twin brother."

"The fuck?" Jackal was astounded.

"Sure as shit," Oats said. "That huge son of a thick? Her honest, blood-kin, same-orc-was-their-papa brother."

"You hadn't already told him?" Fetch asked.

Oats pointed a big, blaming finger. "He wouldn't let me!"

Jackal's slack jaw was aimed at Fetch. "It's true?"

"It's true," she replied, and added, "and Starling is our mother."

That got Jackal laughing, but after a moment of seeing her face, he stopped dead silent.

Raising her eyebrows, she slowly nodded. "Returned. From the dead. Into the body of another elf girl." She let it sink in. "You got any tales from afar that can beat that?"

"No . . ." Jackal stated, mouth still open.

Oats had a huge smile splitting his face, his eyes directed at Jackal's arm.

Jackal leaned away from the scrutiny. "What?"

"I was just thinking," Oats said, scratching at his beard. "Remember those lizards we used to catch when we were little? The ones that could shed their tail and it would grow back smaller and a different color?"

"Yes," Jackal droned.

"Well . . . I was wondering. If you lost a part—not the Arm of I Took a Cock—but *another* part . . . would that part grow back smaller and a different color?"

Oats burst out laughing at his own jest and nudged Jackal so hard he nearly toppled off the bed, which set him to laughing.

"Fool-asses," Fetch said, but by then their mirth had spread and she was joining them.

Oats caught his breath. "I'll go find you some breeches, Jack, and bring the food with me when I come back. I . . . might get lost. Still don't know my way around . . ."

"That would have been better if he'd resisted the wink," Jackal said when the thrice was gone.

Fetch slid the latch. She walked back to the bedside and his arms came up to receive her. Exhaling, she relaxed into him, buried her face against the side of his neck. They remained that way for a long time.

"Thank you," he said, at last.

She straightened, faced him. "Don't thank me. I don't know where my mistakes end and my good deeds begin. But that's being chief, I've learned." Fetch was getting her first good look at him, free from grime and the fear he would die. She traced the tattoos of Tyrkanian script and other strange sigils upon his chest. "These are new."

"An Uljuk mystic did them. Said they would help protect me from *afrite*."

"*Afrite?*"

"Devils made of fire and dust."

Fetch's finger followed the scrawl of ink down to his stomach. "Did they work?"

"Well, the *afrite* the Black Womb sent to kill me didn't succeed, so . . ." He gave a boyish shrug. "Reckon I might have some stories to rival yours, after all."

Fetch shook her head. "Don't even aim for that shot. I'll still best you."

"You haven't heard the story—"

She placed a finger on his lips. "Centaurs saved my life."

"Hogshit!"

"Not. Fed me, tracked my hog down, let me go."

Jackal performed a hard blink. "Helpful horse-cocks. Why did they do that?"

It was Fetch's turn to shrug. "You can ask them at Strava when Zirko summons you next Betrayer Moon." She shook her head, angry at herself. "Shit. Sorry. Thought I'd milked all the venom, but looks like the snake is still quick to strike."

"Fetch . . . I don't think I'll be at Strava." Jackal raised his left arm, continued to hold her with his right. "It's difficult to explain, but Zirko . . . he was always there, in the back of my mind. Not his voice, but . . . his awareness. That's gone. I don't feel it anymore. Reckon your cut severed more than my arm."

"And Attukhan's gifts?" Fetch asked, leaning back a bit to take in his injuries. The bites were much improved.

"They are returning," he said. "Slowly."

"Then Zirko's hold may return too."

"It may," he conceded, dropping the arm.

"Even if it doesn't . . . Xhreka warned us, Jack. Belico would not give aid for nothing. You may be bound to far more than Zirko now. And for that, I don't think you'll be thanking me."

"What was it you said about mistakes and good deeds? For now, how about we just be glad I'm alive."

Fetch grinned. "That all?"

Jackal started as her hand brushed along the inside of his thigh, just enough to bring his mouth to hers.

"We don't have long," she whispered when his lips moved to the spot just behind her ear and the familiar tingles put a smile on her face.

Jackal only hummed in agreement and continued his blissful gnaws down her neck.

She put encouraging hands in his hair.

Suddenly the door was hammered by obnoxious banging, the kind Oats had mastered when he wanted to startle them.

"Mop up, I'm coming in!"

"Just in time!" Jackal yelled back, vexed.

Fetch smacked his face affectionately and opened the door to admit Oats. He bore a tray in his hands and garments over his shoulder. Seeing Jackal, he closed and averted his eyes.

"Hells overburdened! How can you have a stiff cod? You were just eaten by dogs and fucking dismembered!"

Laughing, Fetch took the tray from him, freeing Oats to throw the clothes at Jackal.

"Cover your pride, you rutting mongrel!"

The tray was burdened with an entire roast fowl, two wheels of cheese, bread baked with raisins and cherries, a string of sausages, a basket of walnuts and figs. There was even a milk pudding. And there was wine. The first pouring solicited groans and entranced stares from Fetching and Jackal.

Oats filled his own cup. "Say one thing for the Stains, they kept a good larder. Marrow says their stores are filled to the crucks."

Any more words were forced to wait. You learned to eat quickly when you ate with Oats. The three of them sacked the tray, drained the wine jug. Halfway through the meal, however, Fetch was no longer tasting anything. She couldn't be seduced by this, by feasts and fucking and strong walls. She couldn't let the Bastards be seduced by this. This was what they conceived when their thoughts turned to notions of a hoof. This was what they knew from better days. Dog Fall had been a haven, but alien, untamed. Comfort there remained skittish as a hand-fed fox. But in this fortress of stone, bolstered by wooden furnishings and glutted with cherished, half-forgotten foods, the brethren's ease would swiftly return, along with old, futile habits.

Fetch looked at the fig in her hand, tossed it back to the platter.

Oats frowned. "Would you stop with the black, unblinking stares? Starting to look like Hood."

"I woke up to that," Jackal said, throwing back the last of his wine. "Please don't make me relive it."

Fetch would not let his smile reach her.

Oats leaned in. "Fetch. What the hells has got you bothered? You did it. Our folk, the foundlings, they're here. Safe. The boys are here. Jackal's back. We're together. Whole. None are trying to kill us. All that tried were beaten. Tomorrow may be different, but today's struggle? Chief, it's over."

Fetching stood. "No. It's not. We're not whole. Not yet. There's one more of our own still out there. One more enemy that still needs to be put down."

"Fetch," Jackal said. "Warbler is where he—"

"Not Warbler. Oats, gather the hoof. I need to call a vote."

THEY LEFT BEFORE NIGHTFALL. Ears filled with the thunder of hooves, teeth with flung grit, the True Bastards charged the rising sun. Their hogs, unhindered, dared the badlands to impede them. Scrub and boulder, ridge and rift, nothing slowed their eager, powerful forms.

With no wagon to pull, no people to guard, the barbarians were free to run, their riders basking in near-forgotten speed.

Fetch gave herself to the rhythm of the gallop, the wind in her face a deliverance from doubt. No longer were they fleeing. They were chasing a reckoning.

FORTY-TWO

—

THE CASTILE BROODED BENEATH the threat of rain.

Unlike Thricehold, where the mountain provided the greater defense, the last Hisparthan citadel in the Lots dominated the hill upon which it rested. The weight of its fortifications seemed to subdue the rocky rise; a man in full armor standing upon the back of a dusty, steadfast peasant.

Fetch watched the walls as her hoof moved across the expanse of badland toward the great stronghold. She could not see the guns, but knew they need not be visible to kill every one of the mongrels behind her. She'd ordered they approach in a single column, the hogs at a walk. Their formation, their pace, their slung stockbows, all were an obvious display. The hoof was well within the reach of the guns now. Fetch had cautioned her brethren against their fury. Every rider knew to scatter if the walls belched smoke and thunder. Incus was put at the rear with only Oats behind her, so she could see if the column broke. Fetch had drilled the maneuver along the way and after three days she was confident every rider could perform it without difficulty. She was less confident it would save them should the order be given to discharge the guns.

So, she watched the walls.

And exhaled when they reached the start of the trail leading to the gatehouse. The hoof maintained their column along the switch-backs. A quarter of the way up, the dark shapes hanging from the battlements became discernible as corpses. As the first to make the turns in the trail, Fetch could see the looks of all her riders as they caught sight of the dangling ornaments. They faced it with grim determination. Three turns more proved what Fetch suspected. The bodies were half-orcs. The heat and birds had been to work, but there was enough grey tattooed flesh remaining on the freshest corpses.

The gatehouse greeted them at the top, a castle of its own. The gates were closed, the portcullis lowered, and the helms of archers could be seen through the embrasures along the battlements above the high arch. Fetch pulled Womb Broom to a halt and half turned the hog, so the hoof could see a patient face. They were strung out down the sloping trail, which cut left a dozen strides from the gate.

"Ho, ho! If we've not been blessed with a visit. The chief-quim and her pack of ash-coloreds."

The hoof looked to the bartizan overhanging the left corner of the gatehouse. There, leaning out from the crenellations of the open-topped turret, was Cavalero Maneto. The bartizan was lower than the battlements, allowing them to see the man's smile within the dark mass of his beard, the black space of his missing tooth a gloating hole. Fetch had warned her brethren to keep their tempers, no matter what was said. None bristled, though she could feel the tension born from their restraint. They all waited for Bermudo's new hound to finish his yapping.

"Seems you've forgot you're a wanted mongrel, pretty cunny."

"Haven't forgotten," Fetch said, pitching her voice. "I just don't care a fuck. Besides, I ain't the most wanted one down here." She hooked a thumb behind her at Jackal. "Reckon this one's bounty is twice mine."

"At least," Jack said.

Maneto shifted to look at him. "Looks same as any other half-breed to me."

"Likely you're more familiar with my name. Fair wager Bermudo screams it out when he's milking his cod."

"You're Jackal, then."

"I am."

Dismissing that with a throaty, labored sniff, Maneto returned his attention to Fetch. "Looking to trade this one for your own clemency?"

Fetch didn't respond. The question had been a mocking one. Maneto spit, the gob falling on the snout of Culprit's hog a little farther down the trail.

"So what could it be, I wonder? Ah! Can't run the thicks off yer lot. Here to beg for Hispartha's gallant men of arms to see to it!"

This one had been for the benefit of the guards above the gatehouse, drawing rough laughter.

"The gallant men of Hispartha won't need to journey to our lot for a fight," Fetch replied. "We've just brought you one."

Maneto added his guffaw to the mirth of the men. "Come to lay siege, mongrel queen? 'Tis but seven I count sniffing the divine cleft of your arse. That won't do."

"Let us in. See if you're right."

"And admit a whole sty of shit-reeking pigs inside the gates? To say nothing of the hogs they're riding!" More laughter. "Nay, missy. I think you're where you need to be down there. Pity about these clouds. I do enjoy watching soot-skins sweat. But!" Maneto loosed an overwrought sigh and hung his shaggy head. "It would be a shame for the captain not to know his prize half-breed was at the gates, begging to be let in after so much time beating the scrub for him. Best we remedy that, eh?"

Fetch took a steadying breath as the cur of a cavalero ducked back out of sight. Womb Broom stamped beneath her, growing restless. Getting the hog in hand, Fetch twisted in the saddle.

"Steady now," she told the hoof.

"Chief!"

Shed Snake's warning gesture caused her to look up. She flinched as a large shape fell from the battlements above the gate. The snap of a chain made several of the hogs squeal, and Fetch was showered by something sticky and evil-smelling. She guided Womb back a few steps. A body swung directly above, the foot of its single leg just brushing the top of the gate's arch. Unlike the others, it wasn't stripped. And it wasn't a half-orc.

Bermudo.

Only the missing limb and the captain's cloak spoke to who the man had been in life. The corpse was bloated, slimy, and dripping with the juices of rot.

Maneto hopped atop the wall and sat down in the embrasure above the horrid remains. His feet kicked a little in the air.

"I know, your lordship," the cavalero said with a ponderous shake of the head. "I know you did not fancy being dragged up here. But look! The half-orc hussy brought you your greatest desire. No, not a new leg! The skulking mongrel what humiliated you time and again." Maneto feigned listening to the corpse, head bobbing. "You're right, sir, you're right. It was, yes, it *was* perfidious of me to neglect to tell the hoofmistress that you were hosting a dinner for the crows. I agree, I do, *I* most certainly should be, yes, yes, indeed, excoriated—fine word, lord—for such a lapse. The shame will follow me to the grave, lordship, that I have so dishonored myself while in yer service."

Fetch's mouth was sour.

"Fucking mad dog," Culprit growled from behind her. She hissed him quiet.

"Dog? Dog?" Maneto sounded earnestly injured, acting as if Fetch had been the one to speak. "Loyal and mindful, you mean. That is my nature, I suppose. Always willing to do as I'm commanded after the proper, harsh, repeated training. In that, yes, yes, ladyship! I am a dog. But do not mistake, like any good dog, I do yearn to play. Always eager to fuck. Always eager to . . . *fetch*. In that, I warrant, we are beasts of the same hide."

The angle was steep, but there was noticeable movement along the battlements where Maneto sat. Fetch could see little of the second tier set farther back above him save the merlons, but knew with cold certainty men were gathering up there as well. The inward-facing curves of the towers were replete with arrow slits, thin eyes hiding death within their blackness.

Maneto stood and balanced atop a merlon. Nimble for a big man with bandy legs, he began stepping over the embrasures, using the merlons to pace the battlements.

"Loyal. That's what I am. Takes a loyal man to hold a fortress when his captain dies. Takes a loyal man to send missives back home informing of his passing. The letter of deep regret I sent to Hispartha telling how the good captain at last succumbed to his injuries would have made your eyes wet with emotion. Perhaps yer quim too, if poetry stirs yer mongrel passions, eh? 'Course—with a mind to sparing the delicate feelings of the dainties at court—I didn't relate how noble Bermudo's injuries *worsened* when I kicked him for half a night as he crawled on his belly through the castle." Maneto paused, balanced on one leg, arms stuck out childishly. "Not certain where he thought he was going . . . his horse, maybe?"

Putting his foot down, Maneto sniffed again. He scratched idly at his crotch and slid the chain-mace from his belt. Working his wrist, he spun the weapon in lazy circles at his hip.

"This is the part where you cozen me. Express joy that a better man has command. A *common* man! No more blue bloods, just villains and mongrels. That's the throbbing cock of the Lots anyways, hey?!" Maneto mimicked milking his cod. "Thicks will choke on such grit! The captain's mouth was full of commands, so I invited the maggots to take their place. Losing a shank to the thicks didn't teach him. Still of a mind to fight, that one. Only he wasn't going to be riding glorious at the van, was he?" The mace quit spinning. "Sending us sure and certain, though. Cavaleros, aye, but those of low birth with too many debts o' blood and coin to run back north. Reckon if we have to die in these fucking lands, best do it behind solid walls. The Crown's content to allow us too. So long as my pretty missives deliver horseshit tales of our valiant efforts in its defense."

The knavery stopped for a moment. Ignoring the hoof, Maneto looked straight out over the badlands. When next the man spoke, he actually sounded regretful, betrayed.

"Ul-wundulas. Nothing but a child's crude trap. Something for the thicks to stub their toe on while the blue bloods hide the silver and bar the doors. You know it, well as I."

Fetch did know.

"You don't belong here," she agreed. "Time Hispartha understood that."

"Is it?" Maneto said, amused.

Fetch didn't answer. She twisted in the saddle, looked at her riders. Farthest down the trail, Oats and Ugfuck anchored them. Incus was in front of him, face hidden in the shadows of her hair. Shed Snake slung his half cape over his shoulder, freeing his scarred arm. Hood pulled his namesake back. Culprit was smirking. Polecat, too, eyes glinting. Just behind her, Jackal winked.

Slowly, Fetch got down from her hog, looked up at Maneto. "Yes. It is."

"Best straddle that leather, missy. Or you won't die by the words you mongrels so value."

The switchbacks would hamper any retreat. The volleys from the archers would cut down mongrel and hog. Perhaps a few would reach the plain. And then, the guns would finish them.

It was Fetch's turn to laugh. "You think we rode all the way up here just to ride away?"

"You rode up here to die. No mongrels are setting one ash-colored foot inside these walls, I promise you."

There was movement along the battlements, the garrison stirred by something happening within the walls. Fetch couldn't see it, couldn't hear it, but she knew well what it was.

"You broke that promise long ago, frail," she said, competing for Maneto's attention now. "You had two inside last night. Of course, Hood didn't stay long. Just slipped over for a span, find the one that's been living among you for weeks. I was happy to hear she hadn't been found out, but not surprised. She don't look like a half-breed, 'cause she ain't, really. Figured it'd be easy enough for her to get in, with all the supplies coming down from the kingdom."

Shouts of alarm were going up now, coming from the yard, enough to be heard through the bulk of the gatehouse.

It was done.

Ahlamra had let the slops and the Thrice Freed in through a postern gate.

"Your promise just got broken a hundred times!" Fetch called to Maneto. "Think we don't know about the Whore's Slit? Sancho's girls were sneaking in and out for years. Not much of a secret. Only trouble is having someone who knows you're coming and can open it for you."

Maneto got down from the merlon, began shouting orders, sending runners.

There weren't a hundred mongrels inside. There weren't half that. And they weren't coming in the Slit, but a sally port in the north wall. Maneto was diverting too many men in the wrong direction. Fetch would not give him time to realize his mistake.

"Maneto!" she hollered.

The fury in her voice forced the mad cavalero's face to reappear between the merlons.

Fetch grinned. "Told you I was going to add you to my tally."

The man's shock and ire melted away, replaced by that poisonous smile.

"See there?" he chuckled. "Beasts of the same hide."

His arms came up holding a stockbow. He loosed.

The bolt struck Fetch in the chest, punched through her brigand. And shattered against her flesh.

"No," she said. "Mine is a bit thicker, now."

She reached the battlements in a single leap. The second tier.

Landing among the stunned archers, she yanked the first man within reach over the wall. His scream distracted the men surrounding Maneto below; his body breaking on the rampart scattered them. The man to Fetch's left was still not certain how she was standing beside him. Snatching the stockbow from his hands, she flipped it around and feathered him through the gut. The archer behind had the empty weapon thrown into his face. His head snapped back, he dropped to the flags and did not move. Fetch's tulwar was in her hand now. There were men to both sides. She spun to the left and slashed. Her blade took the first man across the throat. His blood

fountained over the wall and she shoved him after it, advancing on
the next frail. This one managed to train his stockbow and loose.
The bolt took Fetch in the shoulder, sprung away. The disbelief in
the man's face vanished when Fetch chopped it in half. He, too, was
made a gift for the lower tier. The men behind him fled, panicked
feet bringing them to the door set in the side of the gatehouse tower.
They slammed it shut. Fetch turned around to find the men behind
had done the same.

Below, the archers on the lower battlement had recovered enough
from the rain of corpses to begin loosing bolts over the wall, but the
Bastards were answering with volleys of their own. Fetch heard the
squeal of hogs, the shouts of men and mongrels. She vaulted the battlement, dropped down, and started killing. This time, she allowed
none to escape. But Maneto was not among the slain.

A glance over the wall showed the hoof regrouping. With the
battlements cleared of defenders, only the towers remained, bolts
spitting from the arrow slits. Bolts stuck out of Jackal's shoulder and
chest, but he stayed ahog, shouting and drawing the attention of the
defenders. Hood and Incus rushed the gate and dismounted. She
placed her hands together and when he sprang upon them, bolstered
his jump to catch hold of Bermudo's foot. The slick corpse began to
come apart as Hood scrambled up. The body detached from the head
just as he reached the chain. He slapped hand over hand and swiftly
gained the wall.

Fetch nodded at him and sprinted for the right tower.

Time to open the gates.

The door burst beneath her boot, startling eight men inside the
circular guardroom. Neither she nor Hood hesitated. They set upon
the frails, swinging their tulwars. Fetch screamed, helms and breast-
plates parting easily as cloth beneath the curve of her blade. Hood
did not even seem to breathe as he darted through the room, opening
jugulars, lopping limbs. They were hindered by nothing but the effort of the butchery.

The door at the opposite side of the room was open. The spiral
stairs beyond led up as well as down. Fetch and Hood raced downward a turn and sundered another door to charge back into the tower.

The men here were more prepared and a thrusting halberd came to meet Fetching. She felt the spearhead punch her ribs, but she kept coming, knocking its wielder over. Ignoring the downed man, she cut down guards at the arrow slits before their stockbows could loose any more bolts at her unseen brethren. Hood dispatched the rest. There was no door in the arch before them, just two steps leading down into the winch room. A man knelt with a shield, another behind him training a stockbow. Fetch bulled down the steps, kept her face turned away as the bolt broke against her chest, and kicked the shield, launching its bearer into the crossbowman. His back broke against the ponderous mechanism behind, and a downward stroke of Fetch's tulwar finished his sprawled companion.

Men from the opposing guardroom rushed down the far steps. Hood sent a bolt flying past Fetch to take the first through his open, howling mouth. She arrested the charge of the second with a thrust through his middle, lifting and pushing him back up the stairs. Bolts thudded into the man's back as his companions loosed in a panic. Fetch let him fall along with her sword as Hood followed her in, feathering another man. He let his stockbow fall to the end of its strap, filled his hands with knives, and tossed one to Fetching. Slaying the remaining five men was close and bloody work. As the last frail gurgled to stillness, they returned to the winch room.

"Cover the doors," Fetch said.

Hood loaded his stockbow while she unlocked the winch and began spinning the handles. The chains groaned as the backside of the portcullis began to rise up through the floor. The great drum of the winch had wheels upon both sides and likely took four men to operate. Fetch revolved it with such speed, the chains shrieked. She locked the winch once the portcullis was raised.

"Hold here. Do not let them retake this room."

Hood nodded.

She left through the first guardroom, ran down the stairs, killed the four men coming up without breaking stride and went another turn. Though she'd never set foot within these towers, her visits to the castile had made her very familiar with the tunnel beneath the gatehouse. There was a large murder hole set within its ceiling. Sprinting through the interior of the barbican, she found the room housing the hatch. Maneto must not have suspected the hoof would ever breach the gates, for the room was free of guards. Fetch quickly hauled the hatch open and lowered herself down the shaft. The final drop was more than three times her height, but with a piece of Ruin now within her veins, there was no danger in the distance and she landed without harm. The dark tunnel was sealed by gates at both ends. Fetch rushed to the outer doors, tossed the beam away, and flung them wide.

"True Bastards!"

Incus, remounted on Big Pox, was the first to reach the shelter of the tunnel. She had Shed Snake up on the saddle in front of her, a bolt in his arm. Polecat rode in, followed by Culprit, both unhurt. Womb Broom and Hood's hog followed the other barbarians, urged along by Oats and Ugfuck. Jackal came last.

"Got more plumes than a goose, Jack!" Polecat taunted.

"Next time you can stand still and draw their aim," Jackal replied, gritting his teeth and grunting as he pulled the first of seven thrumbolts from his body.

Fetch pointed over their heads. "Cover that hole. Feather anyone leans over it. They'll be in a hurry to drop rocks on us now that we're in here."

She went to the wall of the tunnel where Incus had propped Shed Snake. There was a bolt just above his right hip as well as the one through his scarred arm.

"Got the worst fucking luck, chief," he muttered as she knelt in front of him.

She pawed his face. "Alive, aren't you?"

"Ready to murder some frails too. They killed my hog."

The sound of thrums drew their attention as Culprit, Oats, and Polecat loosed through the murder hole.

Polecat sent screams up along with his bolts. "We're coming for you, frails. Hear? WE'RE FUCKING COMING!"

Fetch went to Incus, gestured at Snake. "I'm going to need you to stay with him. Don't know that there'll be anywhere safe once we go through these gates, but if you see a place, get there. He's your ears. You're his legs."

"Yes, chief."

Jackal snapped off the head of a bolt stuck through the meat of his forearm and pulled the shaft out. "Castile yard has room for at least three score cavaleros mounted and ready to charge, soon as we break through the gates."

It wasn't a warning, wasn't a profession of doubt. He was simply figuring how many they each had to kill.

Polecat showed his teeth. "Frails on foals."

"How are we going to break through?" Culprit asked, eyeing the huge doors.

"Fair certain the chief's got that," Oats said.

He directed the hoof to pull their barbarians to either side of the tunnel.

Fetch turned to look at her Bastards.

"The only way forward is through," she told them. "The only way to survive is to kill. Live in the saddle."

"DIE ON THE HOG!"

Fetching charged the doors, flung her shoulder at the crack between. The iron-banded wood buckled and the beam on the other side snapped. Heaving with both hands, she threw the gates wide as the hoof charged, splitting to pass her. Fetch jumped into the saddle while Womb Broom was on the run.

There were no cavaleros arrayed against them. What men and horses they saw were running about in a panic. Smoke darkened the air, thickest beyond the roof of the barracks. That could only mean . . .

"The stables are on fire!" Culprit called.

Fetch smiled. Her slops and the Thrice Freed had managed far more than she ever expected. They were told to cause what mayhem they could, keep the garrison scattered. She never thought they would attempt to reach so deep into the center of the castile.

Her joy died when she saw Oats's dismay.

"Muro . . ."

He kicked Ugfuck into a gallop.

The Bastards sped through the bailey after him. A group of men-at-arms tried to stand against them, halberds leveled, but a volley dropped the front rank, causing the rest to flee in the face of the on-rushing hogs. Oats and Ugfuck ran most of them down; the hoof saw to the remainder.

Several burning horses screamed as they galloped past. The overcast sky mated with the smoke to turn the surrounding bailey into a pit of gloom. Reaching the stables they found grooms and un-armed cavaleros slinging water, running buckets. All abandoned their efforts and scurried away into the jumble of buildings crowding the bailey as soon as they caught sight of Oats, furiously shouting Muro's name.

Jumping off Ugfuck, the panic-stricken thrice rushed headlong into the growing blaze.

"Oats! Dammit!" Fetch shouted. It didn't stop him. Nothing could.

Jackal made to dismount, but a roar went up in the yard, voiced by a block of men-at-arms moving on their position, spears thrust-ing forth from their shield wall.

"Need to tusker that to break it!" Polecat said.

More shouts, these coming from above, growing closer. Through the drifting smoke, Fetch caught glimpses of the western wall. The fire had broken the back of the cavaleros, but the men remaining in the gatehouse towers were coming out to defend the bailey. Fetch wanted to go in after Oats, drag him out of the burning stables if she must, but if the archers surrounded their position . . .

"Cat!"

"I know," he replied. "We got to bristle-brush the walk."

"Jack."

"I'll buy you time."

Spurring Mean Old Man, he charged the spearmen.

Fetch directed Polecat to the western wall. "You take that side."

"And me?" Culprit asked.

"Afraid this takes a *Grey* Bastard," Fetch told him.

She made directly for the walls, Cat going the opposite way. Bolts began to streak down. Fetch could see the men drifting out of the gatehouse, the boldest running ahead of their comrades along the rampart. Fetch spurred Womb across the bailey, using the store-houses and workshops to help shield them. The wall was ahead. Fetch pulled her hog to the right and skirted the stones until they reached the steps leading up to the rampart. The barbarian hardly slowed as he surged up them. Womb Broom was a sizable pig, but the walls of the castile were wider than the Kiln's. The Claymaster had trained the Grey Bastards to run their hogs along the rampart as a means of clearing them of any would-be besiegers. They'd never had need to actually do it. Seeing the dread on the archers' faces as Womb began charging down the walk, Fetch had to give the vile old chief credit.

The first man took a bolt in the throat. Fetch let her thrum fall to its tether and drew her tulwar as her hog jumped the jutting end of a gun carriage. There was little need for the sword. The barbarian cut a swath along the wall. Men began leaping from the rampart to escape his reddened tusks and trampling hooves, some made so foolish by desperation they jumped over the outward-facing side. Across the castle yard, Polecat went plowing down the western walk. The gatehouse would prevent them from meeting, but the frails who managed to run back inside wouldn't be eager to come out again.

There was one last stumbling archer before her. Fetch had to slow Womb before they ran headlong into the tower, so this fortunate wretch would live . . . long enough to stagger backward out of the door with his guts spilling out. Hoodwink emerged after him, blood standing out brightly against his white skin.

Fetch reined up. "You whole?"

Hood's hairless brows lowered, as if the question were confusing. "Yes."

Swinging Womb around, Fetch looked to the yard. Jackal and Mean Old Man had broken through the spearmen's line. The hog was twisting, tossing men as Jackal's sword went to work, coring out the center of the infantry. One mounted mongrel against three score men and still he broke them. They fled. Right into Marrow and his

Thrice Freed, all on foot, eager to prove themselves warriors. Culprit sat his hog near the burning stables, watchful for Oats. He had not emerged. Movement upon the tower behind drew Fetch's focus. The shapes of men, laboring with something heavy, moving it. The wind stirred the smoke, offering her a cruel glimpse of the gun now facing the bailey, the crew angling it down.

"OATS!!!"

The gun's shout devoured her own.

The burning roof of the stable blasted apart, throwing flaming debris. Fetch barely heard the other boom before a chunk of the tower shattered over her head. Womb squealed and spooked, sidling away as rubble smote the rampart. Fetch wrestled the hog, got him under control. The door to the tower was obstructed by fallen stones.

"Hood?!" Fetch called out.

The pale mongrel appeared in the blackness above the blockage, unhurt.

"Get to Polecat. Silence those fucking things!"

Hood vanished into the gatehouse.

Looking down the wall, Fetch saw the wind carrying a gun's breath away atop the nearest tower. The mouth of the weapon was pointed in her direction, men working quickly on the reload.

Snarling, she spurred her hog. The men spied her coming, began to shout at one another. Womb's hooves drummed the rampart. The gun began to tilt. Fetch hopped up into a crouch, balls of her feet pressed into the saddle. She jumped for the tower at full gallop, cleared its battlements, and cut the head off the man lowering the match cord in flight. Landing, she spun and faced the other four. Seeing she stood between them and the stairs, they struck their knees, pled for their lives. Fetch took a step, smashed one man's skull against the gun, slashed the throats of two more with one stroke. The last man made a run for it. Fetch windmilled her dripping tulwar into his back.

Raised voices and the stomps of armored men sent her to look down into the bailey. Two dozen cavaleros were making their way deeper into the yard on foot. They had arranged themselves into a block of shields and lances to defend against a mounted charge. Even Jackal would have difficulty cracking their armored formation, and the Thrice Freed would be crushed.

Fetch took hold of the gun. The wooden carriage squealed against the flagstones as she dragged the weapon to the edge of the tower. She tilted the barrel down, took up the match cord, and touched it to the small hole at the rear. The gun bucked, thundered, spewed smoke, and pieces of screaming men went flying. The block of cavaleros was reduced to lucky men fleeing, crippled men crawling, dying men wailing, and the silent, shattered dead.

A livid, savage noise burst from Fetch at the sight. Part laugh and part scream, she spat it down at the smoking pile of dismembered frails with almost as much force as the cannonball. Upon the opposing tower, she could make out Hoodwink and Polecat killing the gun crew who'd destroyed the stable. That left only the towers attached to the keep.

At the rear of the citadel, where the hill was highest, the imposing structure waited. She could see no one atop the towers, the guns there standing mute and unmanned. The roof of the keep, however, hosted a solitary figure. Fetch left her stockbow slung. Retrieving her sword, she hopped down to the wall and made her way along the walk toward the keep. The tower door stood open. None opposed her. She went up the stairs, circled the turret, and crossed to the massive roof of the keep.

Maneto waited at the rearmost battlement. His back was turned, the shrouded sky spread out around him as he gazed north. His chain-mace hung from his hand, the heavy, flanged steel head resting on the stones. He spoke without turning.

"You half-breeds have an enviable talent for killing. All mine fled or dead in the time it takes to have a good shit."

"You brought this, frail," Fetch said moving forward. "You all did."

"Nay, Chief Quim. *We* brought this. And together we'll bring what neither of us could do alone."

Maneto turned. His other hand was close to his chest, clutching the calm form of a messenger bird.

Fetch stopped.

" 'Castile fallen to mongrels. Garrison put to the sword.' " Maneto grinned, flicking the small tube attached to the bird's foot. "Not my most eloquent, but as the poets say, breviloquence is the life's blood of truth. They will come now. Aye, they will come. Not for my pleas, not for yours, not for the invading thicks, no. They'll come for honor. Blue bloods hate when their lessers rebel. All are beneath them o'course, but none so much as you rutting soot-skins. They'll come just so the peasants won't grow ideas along with milord's crop." Maneto half turned and extended his arm out over the parapet. "Wonder how many of you they'll leave alive to bring back north in cages?"

Fetch returned the smile. "Send it."

The victorious gleam died in the man's eyes. "It's why you came. Blessed Magritta, you want a war."

"Send it."

Maneto's hand opened.

Dropping her sword, Fetch pulled her thrum around, loaded, shouldered the weapon. The small shape of the bird was dwindling against the blanket of cloud. Fetch jerked the tickler. And brought the bird down. She did want Hispartha to know what she'd done here.

Just not yet.

Maneto had fled. She caught a glimpse of him disappearing through one of the towers. Fetch pursued.

The cavalero made it as far as the great hall. Fetch found him there, sprawled on the floor, Dacia bashing his head in with his own chain-mace. The scarred mongrel turned, blood-spattered and breathing heavy.

She held up the mace. "Spent my whole life threshing grain with something like this. Fool-ass should have known better than to come at me with it."

Fetch gave Maneto no more thought. "You find Ahlamra?"

"Come see."

Keeping the chain-mace, Dacia led her out into the bailey. Dozens of men were lined up on their knees. Most looked to be castle servants, but there were some cavaleros and men-at-arms. They were watched over by Incus, Culprit, and Jackal, all still ahog with loaded stockbows. Bekir and Lopo, on foot, held thrums on the surrendered frails as well. Shed Snake was sitting nearby with his own weapon, Touro standing beside him. Gosse stood with Ahlamra, the swords in their hands bloodied.

But it was the sight of Oats that gave Fetch's breath back. Covered in soot he walked over, carrying the clinging form of Muro. The simpleminded boy was crying against the thrice's neck.

"It was him," Oats said, still shaken. "Muro set the stable fire. Heard that loon cavalero say the Bastards were riding for the gates . . . and was going to kill us all. He set the fire to save us."

Fetch placed a hand on her friend's arm, the other on the boy's head.

Marrow and his Thrice Freed strode around the corner of the granary, fewer than they'd been, but more than they were.

"Castle's yours, chief," Marrow said.

Fetch swallowed.

The True Bastards had voted to attack the castile. But it was a Tyrkanian prostitute, a few brave slops, a gaggle of former slaves, and a maligned child's long-cherished memory of the thrice who'd once played with him that had allowed them to take it.

FORTY-THREE

—

IT TOOK THE BETTER PART of a fortnight for the other hoofmasters to arrive. From atop the gatehouse Fetch watched them ride up the trail. They were accompanied by Zirko and a sizable troupe of Unyars. The gates stood open, the portcullis raised. Fetch went down to the bailey and met her guests.

One of the castle grooms came to take Zirko's mule, but was run off by a glare from an Unyar tribesman.

"You'll have to see to your own mounts," Fetch told the mongrel chiefs. "The frails can't handle hogs."

Pulp Ear scowled, but Notch found it amusing.

The Shards' chief swung down from the saddle, adjusted his crimson sash, and pointed. "Stables are this way, if I recall."

"Not anymore," Fetch said. "We're using the parade yard. I had the carpenters get a shelter up that will serve for now."

Notch took in the castle servants going about their tasks in the yard and smirked. "Won them over quick."

"Wasn't too difficult. I'm not the previous steward." Maneto's inconstant temperament had left more than a few scars on the castile's residents. "But they don't trust us. Just doing what they know, hoping being useful will keep them alive. We're still figuring out which of them *we* can trust, so I'd caution against eating or drinking anything they serve you."

Fetch led the way to the parade yard and waited while the chiefs put their hogs in the three-sided shelter.

At last, she gestured toward the keep. "Now that we're all here."

"All here?" Pulp Ear complained. "Where's Knob and the Fang?"

"Kul'huun has already arrived. Knob is dead."

"Dead?" Boar Lip was more curious than alarmed. "The bird I received telling me to make haste for Strava came from Thricehold."

"As did mine," Father said.

"Come" was all the answer Fetch gave, and began walking to the keep.

She'd chosen the captain's audience chamber for the meet. Bermudo had kept the room sparsely appointed, always preferring people stand in his presence, the castellan said, but there were chairs placed before his table now. Kul'huun stood in front of one, Marrow sat in another. Tomb halted when he saw him. His large, pale frame stilled, his expression darkening beneath the brim of his hat.

"What does this one do here?"

"Marrow is chief of the Thrice Freed," Fetch said, going to lean against the front edge of the captain's table.

Notch chuckled as he dropped into a chair, legs splayed. "The fucking what?"

"The Thrice Freed," Marrow answered. "We are the mongrels once held in bondage by the Orc Stains, now a hoof. We hold their fortress, their lot, and claim them as ours."

"*You* sent the birds from Thricehold," Father said, a glower growing on his craggy face.

Zirko moved to the stool provided for his small size. "And one to me to escort you all here."

"The Thrice Freed owe a debt to the True Bastards for destroying the Orc Stains," Marrow replied. "Our loyalty is pledged to their chief."

Notch cocked an eye at Marrow. "Reckon you could have just said 'yes.'"

Incensed, Father turned to Fetching. "You destroyed another hoof?"

"Knob attacked us in the night," she replied, refusing to match his anger. "He destroyed the Orc Stains with his pride."

"If he kept slaves, he fucking deserved to die," Boar Lip declared, studying Marrow as he sat.

Pulp Ear followed once Kul'huun also took a chair. Grudgingly, Father eased himself down, joints popping.

Only one chief remained standing.

"Tomb," Fetch said. "Marrow is no longer some rider that issued challenge to lead the Skull Sowers. Accept it, so we can get to matters."

"Very well," Tomb tolled. He still did not sit.

"Why are we here, girl?" Father grumbled.

"We are here, old man, to do what you wanted. To make Ulwundulas strong." Fetch turned to Kul'huun, addressed him in orcish. "How many orcs have your riders seen in Fang lands since last spring?"

"Few."

"You rode all the way to Strava from the Cradle," Fetch said to Father. "How many thicks?"

The old mongrel shook his white head. "None."

"Pulp Ear, what about the Brotherhood?"

The hideous mongrel made a wet noise in his throat. "What is this? You summon us with a dead chief's birds, bring us to the castle you foolishly took, and now you're playing the general! No! We've seen nothing. Not that it should concern you. You, woman, have far bigger troubles with the Crown wanting to throw your guts in a fire while you look on!"

"They do and I promise you'll be right there next to me."

Pulp Ear shot to his feet. "Don't threaten me, cunt!"

"Threaten?" Fetch blinked. "Your bashed ears must not have heard. I said promise. And it's not mine, it's Hispartha's."

Zirko cleared his throat. "Hispartha will come to know which hoofs assaulted the castile. I doubt any but the Bastards and these . . . Thrice Freed will be made to answer for it."

"Tell that to the rotting nomads we cut down from the walls," Fetch pointed out.

Notch snorted and bobbed his head appreciatively.

"Clever jibes change nothing," Pulp Ear said, still standing. "Hispartha is coming for you. They won't kill us all. They need the mongrel hoofs."

Fetch moved around behind the table and put a hand on the back of the captain's chair.

"The mongrel hoofs," she mused. "Bermudo told me the mongrel hoofs were nothing but watchdogs, that our time was ending. He was wrong. Our time isn't ending. It's over. Father knows it." The old chief looked grim as all eyes shifted to him. "I know it. I suspect some of you know it too. Hispartha is marshaling, a little quicker now because the half-breeds must feel the king's justice, but make no mistake, they were always coming. Giving the Rutters' lot to the Zahracenes, strengthening the defenses here at the castile, resettling Kalbarca. You ignored it. All of you. You can ignore this too. Stand back and be entertained by the bloody display the Crown makes of the rebellious Bastards. Pulp Ear thinks they'll be content with my head. What then? They turn around and go home? What do you think will happen to my lot and Thricehold? They'll take that land back, and if you try to stop them, you'll be on the executioner's wheel beside me."

"Then we let the frails settle," Boar Lip declared. "We allow them to share the burden of fighting the thicks. They will remember why they need us when we show Hispartha that none stand against the orcs as we can, when we show them that we live by our creed."

Father sighed. "And we will. We'll fight because we'll have to. Because the frails will send us to the heaviest fighting. I saw it before. They'll squeeze every drop of blood we have in favor of their own. We will, every one of us, die on the hog before it's over. We'll prove nothing to Hispartha save what they already believe. That we are here to throw our lives away for them."

"That's a more glorious end than you're like to get, Father," Fetch said. "You're musing on an Incursion that may never come."

"Explain," Tomb said.

It was Kul'huun who answered. "The orcs do not have the strength or leadership they once did. Their strongest are no more. And something they fear now dwells in Ul-wundulas."

Father looked disturbed rather than heartened. "What?"

"A weapon created by the Tines," Fetch put in. She wasn't about to shit in this bath by explaining Ruin. "For now it's in the Fangs' care, close to the Gut. Once word of that reaches Dhar'gest, the thicks won't be eager to make the crossing. Which means we have a chance."

Boar Lip leaned forward, his huge teeth leading. "What chance is that?"

"To take Ul-wundulas. To have a land of our own."

She expected Pulp Ear's temper to unravel again, but he simply stared at her, uncomprehending. It was Tomb who filled the silence with a single pronouncement.

"Impossible."

"I don't think so," Fetch said. "But even if it is, I'd rather die trying than allow Hispartha to rid the Lots of us one hoof at a time."

Pulp Ear found his voice again. "You're mad!"

"Perhaps. But I ain't blind."

The swaybacked mongrel pointed a finger at her. "This slattern is trying to do to all of us what she did to the Bastards. Seduce us into doing her bidding. She's trying to save herself and using us to do it."

"Maybe she is." Notch gave a languid shrug. "But I'll say this. If Kul'huun says the orcs aren't coming, that's good enough for me. Should be good enough for the rest of you. And the Bastard's right. We ignored Kalbarca, the hunting of the nomads. All of it. Don't see how we can ignore her taking the castile."

"We don't," Pulp Ear declared. "We'd be best served by delivering her and her hoof into the Crown's hands."

Notch laughed. "Her hoof? You *are* fucking blind."

Pulp Ear scowled at the amused Shards chief. "Meaning?"

"He means the castile is all but deserted," Fetch said. "The Bastards aren't here. If Hispartha wants a head they will have to settle with mine. And it won't come off easy."

Marrow stood. "Know that I will not stand by if any of you attempt to make Fetching a bargaining piece. Draw steel against her, and mine will be bared against you."

"I add my warning to his," Kul'huun told the chiefs. "Though it protects you more than she."

Pulp Ear's ire faded under the fiery stares and calm voices of the liberated slave and the half-clad savage. He returned to his chair. Beside him, Boar Lip's frown deepened, though whether it was anger over the threats or at Pulp Ear's bluster, Fetch could not tell. Father was equally grave. Zirko sat in detached contemplation while Notch's relaxed posture was belied by his active eyes.

Tomb stood behind the others, as silent and stony as his name.

Fetch took a breath, swallowed her own emotions. "I lost a rider to the Stains, a good one. He told me once that the core of a hoof was just one thing. Mongrels on hogs. He was right. And . . . it's no longer enough. Training hopefuls to ride patrol, hunt *ulyud*, taking the best and the strongest, putting a brigand on them and welcoming them into our small fold, it's not enough for what we must now do. And that's fight a war against Hispartha. You think I started it by taking the castile? No. This wasn't close to first blood. They drew that a long time ago. And they were going to keep bleeding us until we were too weak to fight back. Keep ignoring that and your lands are just undug graveyards."

"That's what the Lots are," Tomb said. "The Skull Sowers have always accepted this."

"Not me," Fetch said. "I don't accept anything for the sake of how it's always been."

"And how do you expect to change it?" Boar Lip asked.

"By destroying the Lots for the sake of Ul-wundulas. By taking this forsaken land and making it *our* kingdom."

"Looking to be a queen, are you?" Notch asked, grinning.

"I don't want a crown on my head. I just want the weight of Hispartha's off our backs."

Pulp Ear's sour expression went rancid. "What makes you think you can fight them?"

"Alone? I can't. With all of us—"

"Impossible." Tomb echoed himself.

THE TRUE BASTARDS 567

"Have to agree," Notch said. "Even without the orcs coming. Our smaller numbers will serve us well in the beginning. We can avoid battle, harry their supplies. Winter's nearing, so the passes through the Umbers and the Smelteds will be difficult. But once they're open again . . ." He clicked his tongue. "We don't have the strength for pitched battle."

"Then we must be stronger by winter's end," Fetch said.

"Words!" Pulp Ear declared. "You've offered nothing but words. *Stronger.* We've already lost the Orc Stains. We're no stronger today than last Betrayer and we won't be stronger in a moon's turn, if we're alive at all."

"If you think only of the hoofs, you're right," Fetch said. "If you ignore the Traedrian mercenaries, you're right."

Notch cocked his head as if he misheard. "What Traedrian mercenaries?"

"The ones we'll hire," Fetch replied.

There was a silence as the chiefs absorbed her words.

"Hire?" Boar Lip grunted. "With what? Ul-wundulas has never been a land of riches."

Fetch came around the table. "There'll be coin aplenty. The Pit of Homage has enough to choke even the greediest sell sword."

Pulp Ear scoffed. "The Pit? The cutthroats in those hills will never let you take any of that shine."

"I have a pair of thrice-bloods who will be very persuasive. The Big Bastard is revered among those cutthroats and more than a few will have heard of the Anvil's Bride. They'll get the coin for the mercenaries, and spread it among the bandits as well. Those men won't need much coaxing to go raiding into Hispartha, give the kingdom something else to send troops against. There may even be a few with cods enough to come south and help take Kalbarca, though I'm mostly counting on Zirko's halflings in the tunnels beneath for that task. Far as the hoofs, your own numbers will be bolstered by the free-riders. Hoodwink is already out rounding them up. The canniest will have eluded the cavaleros. More mongrels will be coming down from Hispartha, as well, once I send a gritter and a runaway harvester back north. They know what it is to be a half-breed in civilization and each now has a taste of life in the Lots. Mad as it sounds, they assure me there are others like them who would rather die free down here than live working a lord's fields or entertaining blue bloods in a carnavale up there."

Notch gave a cough. "You've already planned this war."

Fetch nodded.

Pulp Ear gestured at Notch. "And you've just told Hispartha everything! This one used to scout for the Crown."

"Let them know!" Fetch exclaimed. "Let them fear! Any one of you could betray this information. Pulp Ear, you wanted to turn me over just a moment ago. And that's why we're weak. That's why we don't have a chance. The Bastards don't. The Thrice Freed don't. Nor the Fangs of Our Fathers. Put all together, the mongrel hoofs don't have a hope of victory. And we never will with our traditions. We need seasoned, hardened, blooded hog riders, yes, but we also need help, allies, and we are going to have to seek them out. We stay divided, we die. Fast or slow. But we stand together, we may be able to forge the Lots into something new. Something that can resist Hispartha, Dhar'gest, and anyone else that tries to put us under their heel. We join together now and our hoof, our *one* hoof, will grow. And all of Hispartha's gilded armies will be ground to dust beneath a thunder of cloven feet.

"We have a better chance if you're all with me, but even if you're all against me, it changes nothing. I am fighting this war! The True Bastards are fighting this war! You're here to tell me if we're the only hoof with the courage to make Ul-wundulas more than a land of castoffs."

"No," Marrow said without hesitation. "You're not. The Thrice Freed are with you."

Kul'huun stood, rapped his knuckles on his chest. "The Fangs of Our Fathers will live in this battle."

Father hung his hoary head, took a deep breath. When he looked up, he was smiling.

"Those Traedrians are going to need a port. Mongrel's Cradle will be open to them. The Sons of Perdition will serve, chief."

Notch sucked his teeth. He threw up a hand. "Hells, Shards will fight anyone. Might as well fight everyone."

Boar Lip glanced at his fellow chiefs, considering. "Very well. The Tusked Tide will add their strength."

"As will the Cauldron Brotherhood," Pulp Ear said. The doubtful stares he received made him add, "We're no damn cowards."

"Tomb?" Notch prodded. "Silence ain't an answer."

Tomb's thick white arms crossed. He was silent for a moment. At last, his choice rumbled forth. "If we're all going to die, the Skull Sowers will be there to help bury us."

The mongrels were decided. The halfling remained quiet.

Zirko was deep in thought. His hands rested on his knees. He did not look to any, was not affected by the swell of half-breed furor. Fetch recognized the burden, the weight of a people's lives upon their leader. Zirko took a small breath and gave a single, deciding nod as if agreeing with whatever his mind's voice had just told him. The halfling rose from his stool.

"No."

The chamber grew tense.

Zirko looked only at Fetching. "No. I cannot commit to such a war. Strava was here long before the mongrel hoofs. With the good-will and protection of Great Belico, it shall still be here when this conflict you foment ends. We survived the Great Orc Incursion. I dare hope we will survive this. I will not command the Unyars—who have served my people and my god so faithfully—to die against a foe they need not fight. We bear Hispartha no grudge, nor will I court their wrath." The priest swept the room with his limpid gaze, dwarfed in stature by all, but equal in his authority. "I will not stand against you, hoofmasters, so long as you do not bring harm to those under Belico's protection. That is all I can pledge."

Fetch felt the doubt begin to poison the room. The Unyars were the largest fighting force in Ul-wundulas. Losing them would be a grave turn, more so if it caused others to falter. She looked down at the little priest.

"You will do this."

"I cannot."

His calm detachment made Fetch smile. "I need to remind my fellow chiefs of something Knob said, the day you showed us the Zahracenes, Hero Father. Much as it makes me gag to say it, he was right, laying the blame of the Rutters' destruction on you. We have one less hoof because of you, Zirko. You withheld warning of the Betrayer Moon and they never recovered from the damage the centaurs did. You punished them because they refused to bleed for you. You expect the mongrel hoofs to help protect Strava, but withhold your help from us."

"I have aided the hoofs many times in the past," Zirko said. "Yours most recently, Fetching of the True Bastards."

"Would you have?" Fetch wondered. "If the Arm of Attukhan didn't reside in one of our riders, would you have helped the Bastards?"

"It seems your mind is already made on the answer. It serves nothing for me to give mine. As to Attukhan's vessel, I would say he is evidence enough of my assistance."

"In the end, it's still to your gain, Zirko. You don't do anything that won't benefit your people."

"It seems it is now I that must remind you of help given that benefited me not. Of an evil purged without any mention of recompense."

"You saved my life," Fetch agreed. "At the insistence of another you aided. Starling came to you, Zirko. She needed protection and you gave it, but don't think I haven't reasoned why. You knew what she carried. Perhaps not precisely, but you knew there was a great power within her womb. And you wanted it. Don't think that I— that *she*—didn't see the bend of your mind. I don't know how you intended to use it, but you had a design, priest."

"What are you speaking of?" Father asked, his voice wary.

None answered.

Zirko gave Fetch a pitying look. "I will not help you fight Hispartha."

Fetch took a step, leaned over the halfling. "You will or I swear to you, Zirko, it won't be the orcs or the centaurs or the frails that bring destruction to Strava."

The halfling lost his placidity. The whites of his eyes flared within his dark face. Half her height, in simple linen robes and sandals, the priest radiated menace as the room seemed to shrink around him. The chiefs rose from their chairs. Even Tomb took a step back.

"I sense that same power in you, Fetching, chief of the True Bastards. Beware it does not make you overconfident. You imperil yourself threatening my people."

"I'm not threatening you," Fetch responded. "Xhreka is."

The room, and the priest, returned to mundanity. He attempted to restore his calm mask, but it was cracked at the edges of his tight mouth, at the corners of his worried eyes.

"I don't know much about gods," Fetching told him, backing off. "I do know Belico is angry. I've heard his wrath. Unlike his worshippers at Strava, I've heard his true voice. I wonder how he'd sound speaking to you, the man that keeps him the Master Slave. Xhreka seems to think he would destroy you. And Strava."

"She cannot," Zirko whispered. "She must not."

"So stop her." Fetch felt the venom in her words. "Send Jackal to take the tongue of Belico from her."

Zirko's face betrayed the slightest twitch.

"You can't, can you? He's free of you. Attukhan is no longer yours to command."

"You did this?"

"*I* did this! I am doing all of this so my people will endure, same as yours. I need your help. I asked for it. Now I demand it! Only I know where Xhreka is, Zirko. She does not wish to confront you. To do so would destroy the Unyars and the halflings. She doesn't want that. I don't want that. Question is . . . do you?"

The halfling's gaze dipped for a moment. When it returned to her, the bright eyes were once again calm. "No."

"Will you join us?"

Zirko exhaled. "Yes."

Fetch hadn't wanted to do it this way. In forcing an ally today, she'd made an enemy for tomorrow. But there was no choice. That battle would have to be fought after the war was done.

A war the chiefs of Ul-wundulas sat down to plan.

The next morning, they all returned to their own lands and the tasks set before them. Fetch tried to think of some words for Kul'huun to take back for Starling, but could conjure nothing but feeble hopes for her well-being. The elf was right. The Bastards were her true kin, and Marrow bore orders to Thricehold for them to return to the castile.

Zirko, too, carried a summons.

FOUR DAYS LATER, THE ZAHRACENES arrived.

Two hundred horsemen waited just outside the reach of the guns.

Fetch rode out of the castile alone and down to the plain.

Tarif Abu Nusar met her halfway on a strong stallion draped in armor. The man, too, was covered in a coat of scales, a scimitar at his hip. Unlike his men, he wore no helmet, only a green headscarf.

"Chief Fetching," he said, greeting her with a crisp dip of his head.

"Tarif. I'm afraid I don't have tea."

"Tea is for guests. Not enemies."

"Are we enemies?"

"I spoke truthfully when I said I would oppose you if you made an enemy of Hispartha."

Fetch looked beyond at the horsemen. "You intend to retake the castile."

"For now I am here because I was invited to talk. So first, I intend to listen."

"You won't need to storm the castile," Fetch told him. "However this goes. I don't have the means to defend it. Which is the reason I asked you here. Because what I intend, Tarif, is to give the castile to the Zahracenes."

Tarif peered at her. "My people have fought many wars, chieftain. We do not fall easily to traps."

"No trap. I can give myself over to your men. You can ride into the castile, look for yourself. There are none waiting in ambush. You have my word."

Tarif considered but a moment. "Your word will suffice. Your offer will not. You cannot give what is not yours."

"You just said you've fought in wars. Reckon you know it's mine because I took it. The castile is the most formidable stronghold left in the Lots, and you have the men to fill it. Eight hundred horsemen that can strike from the protection of these walls is a force these lands haven't known in many years."

"Why would you do this?" Tarif asked.

"To make Ul-wundulas stronger. Because Hispartha won't."

Tarif waved a fly away from his face. "Tell me, chieftain of the True Bastards, why you would ask me to dishonor myself by betraying those that gave my people a new home."

"Because they betrayed you before you ever set foot on this soil," Fetch replied. "Because they gave you nothing. The land you have now was empty. It used to be the land of the Rutters, but the badlands did what the badlands do and made them a memory. But that lot didn't belong to them any more than it belongs to the Zahracenes. It's not your home. You're tenants, vassals of Hispartha. They'll use you up and when all your people are in the dust, they'll forget you."

"So you say."

Fetch gritted her teeth. She wasn't getting through.

"Tarif, when we met, your pride bruised at being named a Tyrkanian. It's an insult to be mistaken for those that took your homeland. What do you think you are to Hispartha? Do you think they know the difference? Do you think they care? The half-orcs that have lived here for decades will tell you. No. You're a swaddlehead and a sand-eater. Just another mongrel chained to your patch of ground, expected to bark and bite when given command. Don't remain loyal to a cruel master just because he hasn't kicked you yet."

"You speak of our meeting. I recall you did not trust me for fear my people had another master. The half-orc wizard. Is he not still your enemy as well as Hispartha?"

"Yes."

"Then why trust we Zahracenes in your coming war?"

"Because I failed to keep one good, proud warrior away from his schemes once. I want your help in this fight, but I also want to save you from whatever Crafty has in mind."

"Know that I respect your intentions. My answer remains the same." Tarif drew his scimitar. "You are alone, so we shall keep this between us. My men will honor the outcome of our combat."

"Tarif—"

"If you slay me, they will not harm you and they will return to our land. The castle will remain yours. It will be the burden of the new *shaykh* to decide the Zahracenes' course should Hispartha bid them return."

"Dammit, hear me! This isn't a fight you can win."

Heedless, the man turned his horse, put some distance between them.

Fetch gnashed her teeth as Tarif faced her once more, a thrum-shot away. He raised his blade. Fetch still hadn't pulled her tulwar when he spurred his stallion forward.

"Fuck!"

She ripped her slicer free.

The Zahracenes began shouting, cheering their leader. No, not cheering. Warning. Their calls caused Tarif to rein up. His men were pointing, drawing their own blades. Fetch looked. Another rider was coming across the plain from the east, barbarian at a gallop. Straight for the two hundred Zahracenes. Alone.

The distance was great, but Fetch didn't need details to know who it was.

"Jackal! Stop!"

He was supposed to be leading the Bastards back from Thrice-hold, must have also acted as scout. The Zahracenes were between her and Jackal, and their formation was now wheeling to converge. Tarif's horse raced to join them.

Fetch kicked Womb Broom forward, but she had no hope of reaching them in time.

Worse, Oats wasn't far behind. Heart in her throat, Fetch rode hard for the yelling mass of cavalry, dreading the moment the men's voices were joined by ringing steel and the screams of horses.

The Zahracenes' war cries were strange. No. Familiar. They were . . . laughing.

The horsemen had halted their steeds, and parted as Fetch came up.

Jackal and Tarif were both down from their mounts, embracing and speaking in a tongue she did not know, smiles on their faces. As she got down from her own hog, bewildered, the closest Zahracenes erupted in fresh laughter over something Jackal said to their leader. As he glimpsed her coming forward, Tarif's face fell and he spoke to Jackal in hushed tones. Clapping him on the shoulder, Jack shook his head, responded. He gestured for Fetch to join them, as Oats rode up from the other side, a wary frown on his bearded face.

"Chief, this is Tarif Abu Nusar," Jackal said.

"I know who the fuck he is," Fetch told him, covering the last few steps. "How do you?"

"We fought together," Jackal replied.

"That is a modest answer," Tarif said, still smiling. "He saved my life and those of many of my men. This is the one I told you of, chief Fetching. It was he that told us of these lands and suggested we might dwell here."

Fetch thrust a finger at Jackal. "Him? He's no fucking wizard."

Tarif gave her a dubious squint. "He stood against a pair of *afrite*, suffering wounds that should have slain him countless times, and prevailed. Such demons do not die at the hands of regular men."

"I said the wizard was fat!" Fetch declared.

Jackal's mouth twisted. "Fat?"

"No," Tarif raised an eyebrow. "You did not. You said he was a large ass. This means he is humorous, yes?"

"*Lard*-ass!"

Tarif's other eyebrow came up in realization. "Ah."

"Fair mistake," Oats said, chuckling as he reached down from the saddle and seized Jackal's butt. "Damn thing is fairly meaty!"

Jackal swatted at his hand. "The fuck off!"

"Why didn't you tell me?" Fetch demanded, screaming into his face.

"I only knew his name, Isa! Not that of his people. Not until just now. We found ourselves on the same side of a battle against the

Black Womb. When it was done, it wasn't safe to linger, but I could tell they were nomads and were damn fine fighters in the saddle, so I suggested he come to the Lots."

Fetch took a deep breath, backed away. And punched Jackal in the face.

The Zahracenes burst into fresh laughter as he fell to the dust, Tarif loudest of all.

"He said you didn't mention us!" Fetch yelled down at him. "You didn't have time for that?"

"I knew he'd have to petition Hispartha to come here!" Jackal said from the ground, wiping the blood from his busted mouth. "My name would only have caused him trouble. And I didn't know he'd come."

"I told you!"

"You didn't!"

". . . yes!"

"Are you certain?"

Fetch's hands clawed at her hair. "No! Fuck!"

Oats was laughing so hard he couldn't breathe.

Tarif offered a hand down to Jackal, helped him stand. "No harm. The strands of Fate cannot be severed. All is as it should be." His face turned serious once more as he regarded Fetching. "Jackal is not my enemy. I see now, neither is he yours. And I owe him my life, a debt greater than any due Hispartha."

"You owe him that twice if he just stopped you from fighting the chief," Oats said, wiping his eyes.

"The Zahracenes are your allies in any fight," Tarif proclaimed. "If you require us."

"We do," Fetch told him.

"Then let us see our castle."

FETCH HAD AHLAMRA SHOW Tarif the castile. The woman knew the fortress as well as the man's native tongue. When the inspection was complete, he left half his men behind and rode out with the rest to begin preparing the Zahracenes to move. Fetch sent Ahlamra with him to act as envoy.

"He'll likely fear he's made the wrong choice in these first days," Fetch told Ahlamra as she saddled a horse for her. "Help keep him steadfast. But . . . try to prevent his wife cutting his throat. Or yours."

The beautiful frailing gave a patient smile. "That will not be a danger. The key to a man like Tarif Abu Nusar *is* his wife. She will keep him steadfast, and so it is her I must win to your cause."

Tightening the girth strap, Fetch snorted. "You were around him for an afternoon. You can't already know that."

"Tell me, chief, when you raise your stockbow, how long does it take for you to know your aim will be true?"

"A heartbeat," Fetch conceded.

Ahlamra allowed herself a smug look.

The wagon full of orphans was just trundling under the gate when the Zahracenes departed. Upon the bench, Sluggard drove the team of barbarians, Thistle beside him. The rest of the Bastards rode behind. Oats approached to help Thistle down, Muro nearly attached to his leg.

"See that they're fed and settled," Fetch told him.

Jackal came up and stood beside her. "Went down to my old chambers."

Fetch smiled. He meant the dungeons.

"Less crowded than before we left for Thricehold," he said.

The thought put a bad taste in Fetch's mouth. "The men that were obvious trouble I had Hood quietly take care of. The rest, we will have to see. Hoping a few will help us understand how to properly use these guns."

"I might be some use there," Jackal said. "Saw a few used in Tyrkania."

"Good."

"I could have a look, as well," Sluggard told them over his shoulder as he continued to unhitch the wagon team. Finishing, he turned the hogs over to a waiting Bekir and approached. "Some of the carnavales I rode with used black powder in small amounts. One even had a fake cannon."

"You two are on it, then," Fetch said.

Sluggard looked at Jackal. "Say we head up and have a look in a small while? I need to wash the dust from my throat."

"Wine and incendiaries." Jackal chuckled. "Can hardly wait."

"Well, I meant water, but if you want to make it interesting."

"Let's . . . start clearheaded, see how it goes."

"Very well. Chief." Sluggard nodded at Fetch, clapped Jackal on the shoulder, and ambled off.

"Careful, Jack," she said when the gritter was out of earshot. "Between him and Tarif, Oats could get jealous."

He waved that off. "Oats is like the rest of us. Had his share of whores. Besides, any man gets jealous of one that's lost what Sluggard has . . . he'd be a damn petty son-of-a-thick."

Fetch returned the smile he gave. She'd hated Jackal being gone, but liked what the world had done to him.

AS THE SUN ROSE the next morning, Fetch climbed to the roof of the keep. She looked north, right eye squinted against the glare. She'd always hated the dawn, for the same temptation was always there. The call to quit, feeding on all the struggles of her life. She hated herself for it, the desire to embrace such weakness. Hated herself almost as much as she hated the Claymaster, and Maneto, and Knob, and every other cunt who made her doubt her earned place in these badlands. Another of those days was beginning.

Fetch looked at the stone of the merlon in front of her. Thrusting her arm forward, she punched through the block. Mortar and rubble fell away when she removed her fist. She watched the wind blow the dust from her knuckles, carry it away. Every foe could be as easily broken now. Yet the sunrise still heralded the same old desires. The call to abandon this life verged on irresistible.

The road behind was strewn with pain, doubt, cruelty—every step a defiance. And it had brought Fetch to power, such that she need never again fear another living thing. But what of her people?

Shielding them, fighting for them, it was a monstrous task. She could break their enemies, but the shards of so many battles could still destroy all she loved, leave her kneeling in a pile of their corpses. This strength did nothing to lighten the burden of so many lives. The road ahead was terrifying, yet she could not share her dread with those she must lead.

Not with them.

Fetch went to the dovecote housed atop the keep and threw the doors wide. The birds took flight in a flurry, two dozen or more. All went north, all bore the same message. Fetch had written it so many times, she knew it by heart.

You name us mongrels. You name us soot-skins. You name us ash-coloreds. You name us in hatred. What will you name us, when you learn to fear us?

Fetch gazed at the sky as her challenge flew to Hispartha. She whispered at the new day.

"Let's find out."

ACKNOWLEDGMENTS

This book took more than two years to complete. In that time, the list of people who supported me has lengthened while my memory has . . . not. Apologies to those who deserve a mention and do not see it here. Feel free to send me a "What the hell, bro?" message.

First, I need to offer heaps of gratitude to my undyingly patient editor, Julian Pavia. He stuck with me through what can only be described as a bout (or two) of "draft madness." All the classic doubts and fears of a sequel hit hard, but I never received any judgment or guilt trips, despite the headaches of adjusted launch dates. Julian, thanks for all the understanding and for helping me bring the best version of this story to the readers.

Also, great appreciation to the rest of the stellar folk at Crown: Angeline, Kathleen, Stacey, Lance, and everyone else who I may not know. I'm still awed to have so many dedicated professionals working on behalf of hog-riding half-orcs.

Across the pond at Orbit UK, thank you Anna, James, Nazia, Emily, and crew! You guys have turned your corner of the world into one hell of a dedicated hoof with your infectious enthusiasm for this series.

Thank you to Julie Wilson at PRH Audio for bringing in Harry Nangle and Will Damron to produce the audiobook of *The Grey Bastards*. Y'all did a kick-ass job!

I am blessed to have Josiah Bancroft as a sympathetic ear. Like my great influence, Robert E. Howard, I have a writer friend who understands what this journey is like (good and bad). Though, to be frank, my pen pal is way cooler than Lovecraft.

Those of you sporting *Grey Bastards* shirts, huge props for the extra (and visible!) support. Those mongrel-worthy designs were done by the talented Ian Leino, and I am very fortunate to have his talents unleashed on this brand.

Much respect to my late grandfather, Charles Arthur French Jr. (Graddy to me). Thanks for deepening my understanding of the deaf and showing me the nearly superhuman possibilities of lipreading.

I am indebted to the brilliantly profane writing of Jesse Bullington for providing the name of Fetch's hog.

I also purloined from Mike "Everest" Evans (at his request) when adding Dark Hog to the Lots' canon. Cheers, mate!

The Grey Bastards was lucky to have some incredible cheerleaders among the bookstores, most notably Victoria at Mysterious Galaxy and Beth at Powell's. Thank you for recommending the book to anyone who didn't run away at the initial premise . . . and for tackling a few of those who did.

Jim Hodgson, I can't wait to see you again on the next season of *Outlander*. I miss your musk.

Appreciation to Dr. Aleron Kong and Dr. Davis Ashura for confirming my instincts on surviving castration.

It's also fashionable these days to tip the hat to Dyrk Ashton. Perhaps because he's the most genuinely kind person in the writing world. Or a nefarious villain. Kinda depends on who you ask. But he's always been a staunch ally of mine, so we'll go with the him being genuine and nice thingy.

Vas, long before Live in the Saddle, we had another salute. My friend, as always, Above Ground!

Mark Lawrence, the tithe of my soul is coming by courier.

Rob, thanks for accepting who I am, for always checking in, and for keeping me afloat.

The amount of daily support I receive from my family is staggering. Mom, this book was served and informed by you providing a lifelong example of resilience, compassion, perseverance, and grace. You are at your best when those you love are at their worst, which is a blessing and a burden that you carry like no other. Dad, I may not always seek your help, but I know I can and that when I do, you'll give your all and more. Wyatt, you're too young to read this book, but here's one word just for you: POO. You are the treasure of my life. Liza, perhaps the best expression of gratitude I can give you is: this one is finally behind us. Thanks for digging in and staying sane, even when I wasn't. Love you all.

This year I finally got to meet my agent, Cameron McClure, in person. This was after she slogged it out in the trenches with me during the writing of this book, especially the last months when things got rough. Cameron, you're the best agent in the business because you're so much more than that. You're a collaborator, a confidant, an adviser, a mentor, and an incredible friend. You're incapable of bullshitting and don't suffer it in me. There's only one hoof name worthy of you. Thanks for riding with me, Chief.

And, finally, to all the readers, this dream would evaporate without you. I'm forever grateful to each and every one of you.

Stay in the saddle, mongrels!
Jonathan